The
SECRET
OF MORE

Also by Tejaswini Apte-Rahm

These Circuses That Sweep Through the Landscape: Stories

The
SECRET
OF MORE

A Novel

TEJASWINI APTE-RAHM

ALEPH

ALEPH BOOK COMPANY
An independent publishing firm
promoted by *Rupa Publications India*

First published in India in 2022
by Aleph Book Company
7/16 Ansari Road, Daryaganj
New Delhi 110 002

Cover photograph: Kenrick Mills/Unsplash and
Rossendale 2016 (Old Bombay)

ISBN: 978-93-91047-75-7

1 3 5 7 9 10 8 6 4 2

Printed in India

To my father, Arvind Apte

Contents

PROLOGUE

There was the sound of surf pounding on the black rocks. There was the spray of salt water under the hardy coconut trees clustered by the shoreline. The stretch of light brown sand was strewn with washed-up pebbles and seashells. Further inland, a broad, leafy road ran along the length of the seashore, lined with bungalows and mansions, their roofs, terraces, and gables visible among the foliage. One mansion stood out amongst these, for it was built on a small natural hillock that looked out to sea. The tree-filled grounds of this mansion habitually attracted flocks of bright green parakeets. Often the young parakeets were easy prey for the kites that roamed the sky, the majestic span of their brown wings dipping and soaring with the wind. Now, high up above the grey-green sea, a kite gave a single lazy flap of its wings, and then turned its hooked beak towards the mansion in a soundless ferocious dive. There was a green flutter of small wings just outside the bedroom window, and then silence.

In the bedroom stood Tatya, his back towards the window and the dusk. In front of him was a giant four-poster bed with its expansive mattress, twice the size a married couple needed. The wooden cupboards and cabinets at the other end of the room appeared far away to him, hazy. He was struck, for the first time, by the absurdly enormous proportions of the room. He looked down at the floor, covered in mangoes. A carpet of mangoes. And crates of mangoes stood stacked up by one wall too. Their sweet, drowsy scent filled the room, the fragrance ripening and expanding in the warm air, so that it seemed as if the room might burst at the seams. It was all for his wife. Tomorrow was the thirteenth day since her death. In the morning there would be rituals, priests, and a crowd of family members and close friends. His mind had fixated on the thirteenth-day meal, when it was customary to prepare a sweet dish that was a favourite of the person who had died. It had to be aamras, it was imperative that everyone ate their fill of it. What would he have done had she gone not in the summer but in the monsoon or winter? Neither his lakhs of rupees, nor all the will in the world could have produced this fragrant carpet of hapus and pairi mangoes.

His sense of self had remained the same over the decades—till the day she died. His body had aged, his responsibilities had changed, but he had still felt a sense of youth, a sense of sameness, as if she were keeping time at bay, like a resolute boulder blocking it from flowing by. But now that she was gone, that terrible reservoir of time had turned into a torrent, crashing by him, and within a period of twelve days, all their decades together had drained into the sea. Now all that was left was this mansion, these mangoes, and a flutter of wings at the window behind him.

In the darkening room, as the evening breeze from the open window brushed against his bent neck, the shape of the mangoes reminded him of a pattern on a sari she often wore in the early years of their marriage. She would place an oil lamp on the threshold of the small door that connected their two meagre rooms. One lamp placed in this position, she would say, could light up both rooms, for oil was scarce. The glow of the lamp illuminated the golden thread woven into the mango-shaped pattern on her green sari. And then another memory, from many years later—her laughing face in the moonlight, on the terrace, as she vigorously turned the handle of the ice cream machine, surrounded by eager smiles, handing out bowls of kesar ice cream topped with chunks of mango to the children.

And then came that unspeakable thought again, the one that made him feel like he was being strangled: her body had wasted away, infected with tuberculosis, but her mind had been active. Which was why, in her last days on earth, she had betrayed him.

Part I

CHAPTER I

1899

In the summer of 1899 in Bombay, a young man of about seventeen was walking with his older brother through the crowded lanes of Kalbadevi leading to the Mulji Jetha Market. Both were in white cotton dhotis, sadras, and narrow black caps. The older brother, Dattatrey, carried a small leather case strapped shut with a buckle while the younger man, Tatya, clutched a simple cloth bag bulging with three sets of clothes brought from Dhangadh. Mulji Jetha Market was the largest cloth trading market on the continent and Dattatrey meant to leave his young brother here in the care of Haridas Zaveri, a cloth seller. In Dattatrey's bag was a letter of introduction written by the diwan of the small state of Dhangadh, certifying that Shri Dattatrey Abhyankar was the personal tutor of the Rajesaheb's children. Neither brother knew what Mulji Jetha Market was like, but simply walked in the direction they had been pointed to. Everyone around them appeared to be selling things and hurrying somewhere. Pairs of handcart pullers barged through the narrow streets, one pushing, the other pulling and shouting at people to get out of the way. A small-time fruit vendor wiping his sweaty face with the end of his turban sat by the roadside with a basketful of purple figs, while a man nearby conducted a brisk trade selling peanuts by the seer. Another sold coconut water, wielding a terrifying scythe, while the watermelon seller next to him held his own with a footlong knife that he used to slice open the fruit to display their blood-red insides. Horses neighed, trams tooted, shoulders shoved a dozen other shoulders, and the heat beat down on Tatya's ears, which were left uncovered by his narrow cap. The coconut seller called out to the brothers, but Dattatrey pushed forward despite the heat and their parched mouths. Tatya should have been feeling nervous. He was about to be left in strange surroundings, in a place that had more people and noise than he had ever witnessed. But instead he felt a rush of energy, and all he wanted to do at that very moment was to start sprinting, to pound over the ground faster than he ever had in his life. Why should he feel that way, here in this throng? And sprint where? So, of course, he continued walking by his brother's side, as the sweat dripped into his eyes, making all the colours around him shimmer bright.

A sudden turn to the right and they were confronted by a modest cream-coloured stone arch with a red swastik painted at the top. Here, finally, was Mulji Jetha Market. The brothers inhaled deeply and stepped through the arch into a cool, covered arcade, suddenly quiet after the din of the street outside. Underfoot was bare, brown soil. A long row of small shops stretched ahead of them. Every shop consisted of a clean white mattress on a platform; each platform extended further behind into a single small room, which was often just a nook, and on each mattress sat two or three men. To the right, another row of identical shops, and to the left the same. They had entered a grid, lanes and lanes of shops laid out in a neat maze, and they had to ask the way to shop number seventy-three. 'Haridas Zaveri,' said a placid old man on a white mattress, 'is in the sixth lane of Chandra Chowk.'

'Do you mean to say that the market has chowks of its own?' asked Dattatrey.

'Of course,' said the man, rolling a paan around his red-stained mouth, 'there are so many lanes here, they all have numbers and the crossroads have names. Go on, he's in there, he'll be back from the mill by now.' The man scratched his unshaven chin and yawned.

'It doesn't appear much like a market,' said Tatya in a low voice, as they walked on over the rough brown pathways. 'Nobody seems to be selling anything.' Dattatrey nodded. He was beginning to appear a little unsure of himself, Tatya thought. 'Dada,' he whispered, leaning a bit closer to him, 'don't worry. If this place isn't what we thought it would be, something else will work out. But it is certain that I am staying in Bombay.'

'Don't be a fool,' said Dada. 'If this Haridas Zaveri does not work out we will go back to Dhangadh and try something else.'

Having travelled a day and a night to get this far, Tatya disagreed utterly, but nodded. He would not disobey Dada, of course. But he would find a way to make his point later.

The reason they had reached this unpromising juncture in their thoughts and conversation was that after the bustle and energy of the vendors on the street outside, this famed market of textiles exuded an air of peace and tranquillity, as if nobody had anything much to do. The deeper they went into the market, the dimmer the light. Rows upon rows of pristine white mattresses and no goods in sight; huddles of men talking in low voices was about all the activity that was going on here.

After several false turns in that neat yet confounding grid of shops, they eventually found Chandra Chowk and its sixth lane. And finally, they stood in front of shop number seventy-three. Haridas Zaveri sat on the inevitable white mattress, leaning against a large white bolster with his legs stretched out in front of him, doing nothing at all. He wore a loose mulmul kurta and a white dhoti. On a peg behind him hung a beige cap. The wooden shutters of his shop were painted a pale pistachio green, the paint beginning to flake off in a genteel sort of way, and Tatya at once liked the smiling, middle-aged man in the midst of this serenely coloured shop.

Ten minutes later the brothers were sitting on the mattress with Zaveri, the diwan's letter of recommendation had been read and laid aside, and a young boy of about ten was trotting away, having delivered three cups of tea to shop seventy-three.

'What is one-fourth of seventeen,' Zaveri asked in between sips of tea. 'And twenty-four times thirteen? What about two and a half multiplied by nine?'

Tatya answered fluently. 'Four and one quarter. Three hundred and twelve. Twenty-two and a half.'

'Actually,' said Zaveri to Dattatrey, who looked on anxiously, 'I don't need an accountant. I don't need help with my bookkeeping. But if you want to learn to do business, you will be useless without a head for numbers. I think this boy can learn bookkeeping too, he has an instinct for calculations. You can play with numbers, eh?' he asked, looking at Tatya, but it wasn't really a question. Zaveri was smiling, and his tummy jiggled as though he were laughing, but he gazed at Tatya with a shrewd sort of look in his eyes. Tatya nodded, though 'playing' with numbers was a new concept for him. He looked down at his cup of tea and considered how the extensive chart of mathematical tables he studied every evening before reciting his Ram Raksha—didki, paoki, nimki, and all the rest—could be brought into what Zaveri called 'play'. He was beginning to see, as he sat there, things he hadn't noticed so far. He was starting to observe that the market was more than just white mattresses and cubby-hole rooms. It was more than the wooden chests and coats hung on pegs, and more than the men with their outstretched legs and their cups of tea and the dollops of paan they held in their mouths. For at the back of Zaveri's shop stood two stolid steel almirahs, hiding some silent treasure inside; and tucked in even further back was a little stairway that ran a level up, the sort a crafty, cautious creature might use to squirrel away its booty. And below the stairs, in a nook, sat an accountant—a gumastha—on a square pillow, bent over a low wooden desk, making notations into columns of numbers in an old book bound in red cloth. Presiding over it all was a framed picture of Lakshmi on the wall, smeared with the red and yellow of daily devotion; and a curl of sandalwood smoke wafted up from a glowing incense stick in a silver lotus-shaped holder.

As Zaveri and Dada talked about the details of his apprenticeship—so many rupees a week, directions to a Brahmin chawl for a room to live in, and so on—Tatya looked at the shop opposite Zaveri's, and an almost identical shop met his eyes. He looked over to the rows of shops on the right and to the left and he felt as if something were falling into place. The understanding came upon him with a startling suddenness: that Zaveri's shop, with its locked almirahs and cross-legged gumastha and inkwells and columns of numbers and hidden staircase and the smiling, incense-wreathed Lakshmi was replicated a hundredfold in this market. That the men were not sitting idle in their groups of twos and threes, but were *talking*, exchanging chits of paper, consulting the newspapers, and that the groups were fluid. When someone got up and walked away, the group was joined a while later by one or two other men. That, most intriguingly, all those hidden staircases led to a mezzanine floor, enclosed by a front of stonework and grills and wooden shutters, that ran along the top of the market. Now he noticed the quiet buzz of conversation around him, and he was reminded of bees talking about honey.

CHAPTER 2

Zaveri, picking up the diwan's letter again, said, 'So you are from Dhangadh. That is why you speak Gujarati so fluently. I know Diwan saheb well, my son was his brother's student many years ago. How long have you taught Rajesaheb's children?'

'For two years,' said Dada. 'It is normal, of course, that the princes are educated at home. But Rajesaheb is a forward-thinking ruler, and in fact he had considered whether to send his children to our school, which, after all, is his school, as it is funded by the palace. Since I am the principal of the school, I assured Rajesaheb that his children would be well looked after. But in the end, it was decided that I would go to the palace every morning to tutor the children. It was mainly a question of time. The princes also need to spend part of their day doing other things like horse riding and archery. The princesses learn music and horse riding. And perhaps it was felt that mixing with other children....' Here Dada stopped discreetly and let the sentence trail off.

'That is all how it should be,' nodded Zaveri, 'and yet times are changing. The Rajesaheb of Mukhilanagar set up a household in Poona so that his daughters could attend school there. They went to school every morning in style, in a buggy drawn by a white Afghani horse, accompanied by four soldiers on horseback. One of the soldiers would carry their school books for them. But once the princesses were inside the school, they were treated just like the other girls—that was the condition laid down by the English headmistress. I have heard this from my brother.'

'Yes,' said Dada, 'though perhaps it is easier for an English mistress to say so.'

Zaveri responded by putting a piece of supari in his mouth.

He looked at Tatya. 'You know this market is dominated by Gujaratis,' he said. 'It is rare indeed to have a Marathi man working here. Why are you putting this boy to work instead of educating him? After all, you are a learned man yourself.'

'Unfortunately, there have been too many gaps in his education,' said Dada. 'Before I became principal at Rajesaheb's school, I was posted to

Palsana, then Pattan. Then I was sent to Dwarka for a while. My brother has had to change four schools in six years and...I think he is fed up with it. Who knows how long I will stay in Dhangadh. I felt it is better for him to learn a trade now, rather than pursue a mediocre education.'

Zaveri nodded. 'You are a man of good sense,' he said, 'though it is unusual to hear a Marathi man talking of trade. And it is lucky that your brother is fluent in Gujarati, or he would have no chance in this market. Well, there is no reason why he cannot try his luck here.'

'Zaveri saheb,' said Dada, 'there is a question I would like to ask you. I am very grateful that you will take Tatya on as an apprentice in your cloth business. But we have been wondering—where is the cloth? None of the shops here appear to have any.'

Tatya's ears pricked up at this. This question had been troubling him too.

Zaveri raised his eyebrows and smiled. 'Diwan saheb has told you that I sell cloth,' he said, 'and that is true. But I see that you have arrived in Bombay without an understanding of what exactly I do. Let me tell you something. I am not a shopkeeper and number seventy-three is not a shop. It is a pedhi. And I? I am a selling agent. Tatya, if you want to buy a piece of cloth, where do you go?'

'There are some cloth shops in the market on Mehtaji Road in Dhangadh,' said Tatya.

'Good, correct,' said Zaveri. 'But where do those shopkeepers get their stock of cloth from?'

'From the mill that makes the cloth,' said Tatya promptly.

'Wrong,' said Zaveri. 'Think. If the mills started distributing cloth to every small-time shopkeeper in India, they would have no time left to run the mills. Remember, the mills only produce the cloth. And once the cloth has left the mills, it is sold through selling agents like me, entering a vast system of distribution. Think of a tree with branches and twigs and leaves covering the country like a giant canopy. The mills are the tree trunk. And we selling agents are the branches and leaves. The life of the tree, the sap that runs through it, is the cloth. Longcloth, sateen, madapollam, cambric— that is what we agents deal in. Bales and bales of it. For us, in Mulji Jetha Market, that tree is kalpavruksh, the tree of life. Through those branches we move our cloth out to all parts of the country.'

'But where are the bales?' asked Tatya, though he didn't know what exactly a bale was.

'In the warehouses nearby,' said Zaveri. 'Nobody keeps stocks of cloth in this market. Here I only keep the samples I need to show my customers. And my customers are the wholesalers who supply shopkeepers.'

Tatya looked around curiously as if he expected to see a sign leading to the warehouses.

Zaveri laughed and patted Tatya on the back. 'Come back in the morning and I will explain everything to you.' To Dada he said, 'The boy seems keen to learn.'

In the days that followed, it became evident that Tatya and Dada had arrived at the Mulji Jetha Market on a slow day and at a sleepy hour. The muted buzzing of bees that Tatya had heard on that first day was replaced by a whirling bustle, the trundle of handcarts, loud discussions over samples, trips to the warehouses, and shouted greetings to the harried guards who walked around the warehouses with thick sticks, beating to death any rats they encountered. Cats were let loose to roam over the bales of cloth to catch mice, and monkeys were a menace at the market, for they darted down from the trees to steal peanuts and overturn urns of water. They stole shoes too, which people slipped off their feet before entering the pedhis. Tatya was mystified as to why they would steal shoes till he realized that they were simply making mischief, grabbing shoes and even caps, and leaving them dangling on nearby trees from where they had to be retrieved by the tea boys who kept long bamboo poles for the purpose.

Every morning Tatya arrived at the pedhi and waited for Haridas Zaveri. Often Zaveri did not arrive till eleven o'clock, having visited one or the other of the mills he sold cloth for. Meanwhile Tatya set about tidying the pedhi, changing the sheet that covered the mattress, dusting the tops of the almirahs and wooden chest, wiping the frame in which stood Lakshmi, and replacing the burned-out incense stick with a new one in the lotus-shaped holder, ready for Zaveri's puja. The pedhi had always been well kept, but now when Zaveri arrived every morning he found it spick and span—Tatya's earnest eye for detail made all the difference. The sheets were pulled down taut. The spots of ink around the inkwell on the desk were wiped clean. The account books were stacked in two symmetrical piles. Tatya fashioned a small floor-standing shelf out of a wooden crate discarded by one of the fruit sellers nearby, so that slippers could be kept neatly on it instead of being scattered haphazardly on the floor next to the pedhi. When Zaveri arrived, Tatya made sure that the tea boy brought him a hot cup within five minutes. Barring that first day when Zaveri had offered him and Dada welcoming cups of tea, he made sure he never drank tea in Zaveri's presence. In time, he began accompanying Zaveri to the mills in the morning.

Over the first few weeks, Tatya grew less bewildered and more confident about his new life. Every day he learnt some new information about the market or about the business. He learnt that the gumastha, Govardhanji Zaveri, was about fifty years old, and a distant relation of Haridas Zaveri. Govardhanji rarely sat at the desk downstairs and was usually in the room on the mezzanine floor, climbing up the narrow steps at the back of the pedhi every morning. One corner of this small, dim room was Govardhanji's fiefdom. In that corner he had created a sort of fortified room within a room. He sat on a small rectangular mattress with a bolster to lean back on. On his left was a small safe, its front decorated with an orange haldi-kunku swastik. On his right was a low bookshelf, on which lay carefully arranged papers and account books. In front of him was his low desk. He was a mild-mannered man till he settled himself cross-legged at his seat, nested amidst desk, shelf, and safe. He would then commence a short, muttered prayer over his books of accounts, following which he would not look up from them till lunch time. Tatya learnt soon enough not to disturb him. He crept in and out quietly when Haridas Zaveri sent him upstairs to retrieve cloth samples. For once Govardhanji's work began, the affable half-smile on his rotund face disappeared, to be replaced by a closed expression that reminded Tatya of an unblinking pigeon counting its hoard of seeds. Govardhanji kept a meticulous account of the wholesale traders that were due to make payments to Haridas Zaveri. If the payment did not arrive on the correct date, he would make the appropriate notation in his books with a look of contempt on his face, shaking his head as if there were a tremor at the top of his spine.

Every day traders came to meet Haridas Zaveri and, as they all gathered in a group on the mattress, Tatya sat by and listened to snatches of their conversation.

'Chunnilal was complaining about the quality of the long cloth, too many defects, I had to refund him for part of the bale.'

'The next lot will be better. Chand Mills has just gotten rid of the new supervisor who made a mess of things. There were too many complaints.'

'Demand for voile is slow, why don't you tell your Saheb that it is not moving? What is the point of keeping such huge stocks of it?'

'I think that Diamond Mills is not revealing their true costs of production. How can I judge what kind of discounts to give if they do not tell me their costs?'

Tatya understood very little but tried to follow the thread of conversation till it started making some sense.

He soon learnt the names and peculiarities of the various traders. There was Jamnalalji who catered to semi-wholesalers around Belgaon and Hubli, and never made a single notation on paper but miraculously remembered all quantities and prices discussed. There was the dignified Vallabhdas Shah, in his spotless white dhoti, who had known Haridas Zaveri for thirty years and used to have his own selling agency but was reduced to working as a small-time wholesaler after heavy losses. There was the pot-bellied Nattubhai who rarely spoke more than a few words because his mouthful of paan never seemed to end. Other regulars were the brothers Manoharlal Mehta and Chandulal Mehta, who had their own wholesale pedhi at the other end of Mulji Jetha Market. There were other traders too, who appeared intermittently to buy cloth from Zaveri as well as from other selling agents in the market.

In Tatya's first week he learnt that Haridas Zaveri was the selling agent for three different mills. He also learnt that the mills delivered cloth to their selling agents, such as Zaveri, in bales, which were enormous bundles of securely packed cloth. Zaveri's job was to sell the bales of cloth to wholesalers, on behalf of the mill. And he had a habit of quizzing Tatya to test whether his new apprentice understood the nuts and bolts of the matter.

'So, Tatya, remind me, what exactly happens to the bales of cloth after the mill has delivered it to our warehouses?' It was the hour after lunch, when Zaveri had a habit of pretending to have forgotten everything except for the pleasure of the small mounds of ground supari he palmed into his mouth every now and then.

'We store them till the wholesaler is ready to pick them up. He needs to pay us within seven days of taking the bales,' said Tatya.

'Correct. And who are our most trusted wholesalers?

'Jamnalalji, Vallabhdasji, and Nattubhai, because they pay on time.'

'You have forgotten about Manoharlal Mehta and Chandulal Mehta?'

'No, Seth, I did not forget. But last month they did not pay within seven days. They took nine days to pay.'

'Hmm. Of course, I have known them for a long time. Personal relations count for a lot in business, remember that.'

'Govardhanji said that this is the fourth time since Diwali that they have not paid on time.'

Zaveri looked thoughtfully at Tatya and nodded. 'Let's move on,' he said, 'I have also suddenly forgotten what a wholesaler does. Let us say that our wholesaler Jamnalalji wants forty bales of long cloth from Diamond Mills by a particular date. What do we have to do?'

Tatya smiled, sure of himself. He knew this too. 'We have to make sure that Diamond Mills delivers forty bales to us in time, so that we can hand them over to Jamnalalji.'

'And what does Jamnalalji do with the bales?'

'He takes the bales to his own warehouse and opens them up. In each bale the cloth is folded in separate bundles of ten or twenty metres. He sells the bundles to his network of ten semi-wholesalers in Belgaon and Hubli who, in turn, supply shopkeepers. And the shopkeepers display and sell the cloth in their shops.'

'Very good,' said Zaveri, 'that sounds like a good system. But I have not understood two things. First of all, how do I get any money out of all this?'

'Jamnalalji pays us, and then we have to give the money to the mill.'

'Yes,' said Zaveri, 'and, remember, I have to pay the mill whether or not any of the wholesalers have paid me. And then I get my commission from the mill, which is why I am able to give you a wad of rupee notes every month to sit here and remind me of these things.'

Govardhanji, who happened to be sitting at the desk downstairs this afternoon, gave a small grunt without looking up. Zaveri acknowledged it with a humorous sideways glance in his direction.

'Now, the second thing that I have not understood is this—how do you know that Jamnalalji has ten semi-wholesalers? It is news to me, because for years he has been selling to a network of fifteen. How do you know it, and what difference does it make to you?' Zaveri looked closely at Tatya.

'I know it,' said Tatya, 'because a guard at the warehouses told me that Jamnalalji has recently used less warehouse space than usual. And because I did not want to rely on rumours, I simply asked Jamnalalji how many semi-wholesalers he currently supplies. And I need to know it because if his network has reduced, that means he is going to buy less cloth from us. So perhaps we need to look for another buyer to make up the shortfall.'

At this, Govardhanji did what he had never been known to do—he

Tejaswini Apte-Rahm

stopped writing in the middle of a column, raised his eyes from his book of accounts, and looked at Tatya. And Zaveri too looked at the new boy from Dhangadh, a strange smile on his lips.

Wherever Zaveri went, Tatya would follow. He learnt about twill weaves and satin weaves, and the tactile distinctions between cambric and long cloth; he learnt to appreciate the robust nature of drill and understood the nuances of soft finishes as he let muslins and sateens slip through his fingers. He went with Zaveri to the warehouses to oversee delivery of the stock to the wholesalers. He noted that the bales from Chand Mills were enormous bundles of two thousand metres of long cloth, while Suraj Mills packed its superfine cloth in bales of a thousand metres each. The stock was moved urgently, quickly, under the eye of the wholesaler making the purchase, and loaded into horse carts and bullock carts. Sometimes a smaller load was pushed by workers on handcarts. Tatya helped with the loading and the supervising, and if a load was especially heavy, helped to push the handcarts himself.

It was exhilarating to see that the deal-making at the pedhi, the cloth samples that sat quietly on the mezzanine floor, and the scratching sound of Govardhanji's reed pen on paper, all translated into this great movement of goods. Tatya felt that he stood at the starting point of a great chain reaction, where the cloth began its journey, moving through the hands of the selling agents, wholesalers, and semi-wholesalers, and finally landing in shops where shopkeepers would display it in a medley of textures and colours, to be turned into blouses and curtains, school uniforms and sofa covers.

Amid the shouted instructions and turning of wheels, as the bales of cloth trundled out from the darkness of the warehouse into the golden sunshine, Tatya felt that without Zaveri and himself to deliver those bales from the mills into that precisely plotted progression, without Zaveri and himself to launch the thousands of metres of muslin and sateen, cambric and long cloth on to this great journey, the country would, quite literally, be stranded without any cloth. And though Tatya knew that this was a wild stretch of imagination—and that Zaveri was a fairly small-time selling agent and he himself only his apprentice—he felt that the essence of what he imagined was true.

CHAPTER 3

1901

Tatya sat down to write a letter to Dada at four-thirty in the morning. It was two years since he had moved to Bombay, and he was now nineteen. At this early hour in Khatryachi Chawl, there was a hint of blush in the dark sky and the breeze was cool. He could hear a murmur run through the chawl, a hushed gathering of noises as people began waking to make the most of this cool hour before the morning sun began raining down daggers of heat. It was a particularly scalding summer. Tatya sat on an upturned wooden crate in the open balcony outside his room on the first floor. Above him was a clothesline on which hung his sadra and dhoti, which he had washed and wrung dry that morning behind the chawl while bathing. His small room, with its narrow rectangle of kitchen space at the back, was at one end of the balcony which ran past eight other rooms on the first floor of the chawl. The wooden railing of the balcony was punctuated with slim wooden pillars on which people had hung calendars, or cotton panchas, or bunches of bananas. There was a second floor above with similar rooms, while the ground floor had been rented by small businesses such as Vishnu Gokhale's chakki, where Gokhale ground wheat and millet all day; advocate Dattopant Apte's small office with his desk and chair; and Nagesh Godse's cycle repair shop. It was a small, compact chawl, newly built on a quiet street, unlike Tatya's former residence, the old Damulji's Chawl further inside Girgaon, which was a large, unkempt three-storey structure, with only a narrow, congested courtyard separating it from the neighbouring chawl.

Nana, the boy he shared his room with, was still asleep. Chin resting on his hand, Tatya took a moment to cast his gaze on the black sky dissolving into day. What should he write? Dada was still in Dhangadh, now firmly established in his role of school principal and tutor at the palace. It seemed that his days of being posted to different schools around Gujarat were at an end. Tatya was glad for his brother's sake, and also because he liked the small, prosperous town of Dhangadh. He looked forward to visiting Dada there sometime soon. Not too soon, of course. It would be an unnecessary expense. He liked being in Bombay, and was in no mood to be anywhere else at present. His chawl was a pleasant place, and Nana had turned into a good friend, someone to laugh with, eat meals with. He had learnt a good deal during his two years with Zaveri. But though he had developed an affection towards his mentor, he doubted whether he could learn much more from him. It was time to move on. He wondered, for the hundredth time, whether he might be able to start his own business somehow. But how? How did one create a business out of nothing? And where would he get the money to do so? These questions buzzed round and round in his head, but with no solution in sight. Was he simply to settle down in Zaveri's employ, doing the same thing month after month, getting by with the occasional pay rise?

He heard Nana stirring and sighed. Better get on with his letter. As usual, he wrote in English, for Dada had insisted that he keep up the practice.

My dear Dada,

I am writing to inform you that as per your suggestion I have moved to Khatryachi Chawl. It is pleasant indeed to be near the Leles, and, unlike in Damulji's Chawl, there are no problems of congestion and irregular water supply. Nana, who I used to share my room with there, has joined me, for now we are used to each other. His only condition is that he bring with him his cousin, one Balwant Ponkshe, so that we may all share the cost of our room here. I felt this was a good idea and would lessen the burden of the rent, though it is already reasonable enough. His cousin will arrive from Nagpur in a few days.

You wanted some additional reassurance regarding Khatryachi Chawl in your last letter—there is no cause for concern since there are only Brahmin families living here and it is clean and well kept. The chawl has been built only recently and the landlord, though I have never seen him, must be a respectable man, for his rent collector is of a most polite variety (I must add here that Damulji's Chawl was lacking in this regard). I do not remember any boyhood meetings with Lele mavshi, but she never tires of reminding me that she was by our mother's side when I was born. She is an affectionate soul and laments the fact that I had been living in Damulji's Chawl nearby for so many months, unbeknownst to her. She has asked me to let you know that she is in good health. Her husband has chosen to live in their village rather than in Bombay, for reasons that are unclear to me.

I did not wish to pry into this delicate family matter, but she seems in perfectly good spirits about it. You asked about her sons—you are right, Jagannath Lele works as a clerk in Britannia Powder Works, a company manufacturing talcum powder. He lives with Lele mavshi, along with his wife and two children. Her other son, Ram Lele, is a cashier in Bank of Bombay, and lives in a nearby chawl. He may take a room upstairs and come to live here with his wife. As instructed by you, I spoke to Jagannath Lele—he suggested that I complete my matriculation with monetary help from the Brahman Sabha, which is a charitable institution for Brahmins in Girgaon, and then he could perhaps get me a job as clerk in Britannia Powder Works. However, I have no wish to move at present from my occupation at the market. It is true that cotton scarcity due to the famine has slowed down business. The market is quieter these days. But Haridas Zaveri is a good man and I am learning a great deal from him. I hope to start my own small business soon, but more of this in my next letter, for I do not wish to make plans in haste before I have thought things through.

Before Tatya had finished his letter, he heard Nana stretch and plod out of the room behind him, on the way to the toilet.

'Better hurry,' said Tatya, 'or you'll need to wait your turn downstairs.'

'How long have you been up?' said Nana, tousling his hair with both hands as if to wake his brain up.

'Few ever lived to a great age and fewer still ever became distinguished, who were not in the habit of early rising,' quoted Tatya in English, grinning, as he folded up his letter.

'Another one of your gems. From your brother I suppose?' Nana understood just enough English to follow Tatya's occasional lapses into the language.

'Of course. Not his own, though. John Todd.'

'I hope he's also told you that it's not true. My father and uncles have spent their entire lives waking up early to chant prayers at the temple, at the sun, at the river, but not a distinguished man among them.'

'There is still hope for you, my dear Nana,' said Tatya, 'You've worked at the silver shop for four years now. You could think of starting your own business soon.'

Nana merely grunted and headed downstairs, calling over his shoulder,

'Leave that to the Marwaris, my friend.'

Tatya went inside and started boiling water for tea on the small kerosene stove at the back of the room. Soon he and Nana were sitting on the floor of the balcony, drinking sweet tea and eating day-old polis, occasionally dipping pieces of the bread into their cups. By the time Tatya nipped down to buy a couple of bananas for Nana and himself, the street had come alive with scores of people in the sunshine, and there was a rising rumble of noise and clamour. Mill workers were setting off for the day, carrying their lunch in small cloth bundles. Hawkers walked by with baskets on their heads or slung over bamboo poles on their shoulders, shouting their wares, each with his or her own peculiar call. A fruit seller walked by with a basket of mangoes and a nasal shout of 'badami-badami-badami', while another hawked sweet and salty neera. The man selling turmeric from Rajapur rapped his ring rhythmically on his pot like a musician, the sound mingling with the strident bird-like call that Tatya heard without fail every morning. For days he had not been able to identify where it came from and was eventually surprised to find that the sound was made by a frail young woman who carried a platter of chilli and lime pickles on her shoulder. There was the distant sound of trams and the ringing of cycle bells, and two small boys led a group of grunting and snuffling buffaloes to graze in the open space behind the chawl.

The shops downstairs started to open their shutters. Nagesh Godse began tinkering with an upside-down bicycle, occasionally spinning its wheel to test it, while Gokhale's wife gossiped loudly with her regular customers as they brought her bags of wheat to grind. Lele mavshi bustled in and out of her room next door, talking to the two boys who sat eating bananas and sipping tea.

'Arre, Tatya, Nana, I don't have enough pohe today, otherwise I would have made some for you to have with your tea.'

'Don't worry, Mavshi, we are just leaving now, we have eaten enough.'

'And your evening meal? Going to Mameenchi Khanaval again? Do you know I could have done something like that, the old woman must be making good money. This Jagannath got upset when I told him so. I said, I am not saying that you do not provide for me. Have I ever said you don't provide for me? Do I not have the good fortune to have two sons, with fairly good wives? Now when I say fairly good wives, I mean that there are a few things which you would expect them to know, but for some reason they do not. So I have to teach them. It is God's wish that they learn everything very slowly.' She disappeared inside again.

Nana and Tatya looked at each other, drained their cups, and got up before Lele mavshi returned to launch on a new subject.

'Seven o'clock at Mameenchi Khanaval?' Nana trotted off in the direction of the tram with his cloth bag under his arm without waiting for an answer.

Tatya nodded as he lit up a bidi and walked away in the opposite direction. 'If I finish in time,' he said to no one in particular, for Nana had gone.

'So, Tatya, off to work?' Nagesh Godse called out from his shop. Tatya raised a hand in friendly acknowledgement as he walked by. 'I can get hold of a second-hand bicycle for you at a good price so that you save your tram money.'

'Who has the money for a bicycle? Anyway, I walk. I save my tram money for bidis.'

Godse laughed and waved him on his way.

Tatya was walking in the wrong direction today. Haridas Zaveri was not expected to arrive till late in the morning, and Tatya wanted to take some time to think before heading to the market. Khatryachi Chawl was not far from Chowpatty and he was soon at the waterfront, the soft sand seeping into his slippers. A few paces away was a pile of timber next to a shed thatched with dried coconut tree fronds. A pair of bullocks hitched to a cart stood by, waggling their ears peaceably as two men loaded logs of wood on to the cart. Far to the right, across the water, where Malabar Hill rose up, were the faint outlines of beautiful houses and gardens on the waterfront. Tatya gazed absently at them for a moment. They belonged to rich people and to Englishmen, and held no relevance for him. He found a large black rock to sit on and stared out to sea.

He liked the way the waves approached him all the way from the horizon, tried to follow the journey of a single far-off wave as it came rushing forward with a shushing sound, ending its song in small trickles and splashes and sucking noises as it retreated from the shore. Nearby, a couple of fishing boats lay at a slant on the wet sand, their masts creaking in the breeze. More fishing boats appeared on the horizon as small dark silhouettes, like coconut shells bobbing on glittering sunshine.

A vision appeared before him—a small fleet of sailboats—not sturdy enough to go into the high seas, but plying the waters for riverine and coastal trade from Rajapur, down the Arjuna River towards Jaitapur, and further up and down the Konkan coast: his father's boats, carrying small cargos of cashews and rice, jackfruit and mango, and miscellaneous provisions. He could hardly match the shadowy memory of his father—a quiet, broken figure—with the proud man he must have once been, striding about among the fishermen who sailed his boats, loading goods and shouting out instructions as they prepared to navigate the river through dense groves of coconut trees, till the river spilled into the Arabian Sea.

He had a clear memory of a sudden storm one dark afternoon when the wind screamed over the land like a crazed giant, and his mother looked in superstitious fear at the flickering lamps in their small house. But then everything else that followed had blurred in his mind and all he could remember was a sense of rising panic—the banging at their door late that night, the wailing of the widows whose husbands were lost at sea on his father's boats, the pale, stricken face of his father, and the final hurried flight into the night as they left their life behind and fled towards Baroda to take shelter with his mother's relatives. Tatya couldn't remember any details for he was only a child of five. But Dada had been fifteen years old and he told Tatya of the creeping realization that the creditors could not be paid, and that their father seemed to collapse overnight, that the only way for him to flee his guilt at the deaths of the fishermen was to escape with his family into the night. He had run away like a fugitive. Run away! Tatya could not bear to think that his father had been unable to face that sudden turn of fate. Within a year of arriving in Baroda, his father was dead. They said it was typhus but Tatya could not rid himself of the notion that he had simply given up the fight to live. He was ashamed at having run away, Dada told Tatya many years later, but it was too late to retrace his steps. In any case, their father had nothing to offer to the fishermen's families. The creditors had probably taken over the remaining sailboats and their house.

Tatya felt a need to complete something his father had begun, a desire to finish a circle that his father had begun drawing and left half-finished. That circle had started by the sea, and so it was fitting, perhaps, that it was once again by the sea that Tatya hoped to revive his fortunes. It occurred to him that it was also the sea that had carried within it his family's misfortune. But he tried to put that thought out of his mind. While his father had run away from life, Tatya wanted to run towards it.

He wanted to find problems and solve them. He felt as if he were looking for something, some puzzle, some secret that dodged him. The secret of doing more, being more. Frustratingly, it eluded his imagination; he could not conceive of the end point in concrete terms, but rather as vague possibilities of indefinite shape. It would be easy for him to become a salaried clerk in a Bombay company and sit at a desk under a fan, instead of loading bales of cloth on to handcarts with sweat streaming down his back. But if he ended up at a desk with a pen in his hand, there he would remain all his life, like Jagannath Lele at the Britannia Powder Company was bound to do. Had there been no storm that afternoon in Rajapur, surely his father would have expanded his fleet of boats. Had it been me, thought Tatya, looking at the far away boats bobbing on the sparkling water, I wouldn't have been content to let my boats serve out their days hugging the coast. What is the point, he thought, of living by the sea if you don't set your boats sailing as fast and as far as they can go? What is the point of the sea staring back into my face if I don't try to match the relentless energy of its tides? I would have wanted to send more boats, bigger boats, into the high seas, to trade in faraway lands. Where those distant shores might have been, or what he would have traded, was but a fanciful notion, a fiction. And in any case, it was irrelevant, for he had no boats. What he had was knowledge. He had gathered it painstakingly over two years. In his mind he had constructed, just like in Haridas Zaveri's shop, a slim back staircase that ran up to a little mezzanine floor, and this was where he stored his accumulated knowledge. His body felt cool and fresh as if he had splashed cold seawater on his skin. The slippery jewels that glinted on the ocean's surface made him restless, as if they held within them an unnamed challenge. He had learnt a great deal since he had started working for Haridas Zaveri. The question was, what was he going to do with that knowledge?

Into his mind came the image of the warehouses. And in a certain warehouse, a dark corner where the goods had not been moved for weeks. Bales stamped with the smudged but unmistakable shape of a star. He stood and began walking down Sandhurst Road towards the market. Before heading to Pedhi Number 73 there was something else he had to do.

CHAPTER 4

No sooner had Tatya arrived at the pedhi, than he was surprised to see Haridas Zaveri striding towards him in heated discussion with a man. The man wore a dhoti and black cap, and carried a file of papers under his arm, and was evidently in a hurry to get away from Zaveri. By the time Zaveri reached the pedhi, the man had made himself scarce.

'What is the matter, Seth?' asked Tatya.

'That scoundrel Popatlal has sent his man to say that he cannot pay me for another week. He has taken fifty bales of manjarpaat and I have to pay the mill from my own pocket in the meantime. He gives me a headache every time he takes cloth from me.' Zaveri leaned against a bolster and mopped his face with a handkerchief. Tatya bent over the earthenware water pot and picked up the ladle to fill a glass of water for him. He glanced at Zaveri. Zaveri looked unusually morose.

'Seth, can I say something?' said Tatya, handing him the water, his heart beating fast.

Zaveri grunted.

He had been waiting for this moment. He must speak. But then his courage failed him. Foolishly, he found himself talking about Popatlal instead. 'Why do you indulge that Popatlal? He has never agreed to a single long-term contract. His payment is always three or four days late. He is not even one of your regular dealers. He shows up now and then, and nobody knows where he disappears in between.'

'There is no such thing as a regular dealer, boy. Whoever can pay the money gets the goods.' Zaveri grumpily drained his water and handed the glass back to Tatya.

'But he pays the money as per his convenience,' said Tatya. 'Why not supply only to those who are reliable?'

'I usually get a better price from him,' said Zaveri, his voice brusque. 'When he pays, he pays in full. Meanwhile, I have to suffer.'

Tatya did not understand why suffering needed to come into it, but he did not dwell on it. He had overstepped the mark with his impulsive words about Popatlal. It was foolish of him, for he needed to tell Zaveri something.

He hesitated, gathering the courage to do so. He feared he was going to speak above his station and that Zaveri would not approve. But he needed to move fast, because the information must be acted upon without delay.

'Did you collect the samples from Chand Mills yesterday?' asked Zaveri, frowning.

Tatya nodded.

'Let's see them.'

Tatya climbed up to the mezzanine floor. It was smoky with sandalwood incense. Govardhanji was muttering over his books with a glowing incense stick in his hand. Tatya picked up the bundle of sample cloth and hurried down again. Zaveri opened up the packet and began examining the contents. 'Longcloth,' he complained, looking at Tatya as if it were Tatya's fault. 'They were supposed to send me cambric samples. And their costing is...'

But Zaveri's thoughts on Chand Mill's costing remained unknown to Tatya, for Jamnalalji, the dealer who never wrote anything down, arrived at the pedhi waving a rumpled copy of the *Mumbai Samachar*. 'Read this,' said Jamnalalji. 'It says here that cotton supply is not likely to improve anytime soon.' He slipped off his shoes and climbed into the pedhi, hitching his dhoti between his thighs before settling on the mattress.

'Nothing to be done, Jamnalalji, it's all down to the famine. Cotton supplies are low.'

'But we have a contract, Haridas bhai, you are supposed to supply me with ninety bales of drill over three months, and after two months I have only half the goods.'

'Jamnalalji, it is out of my hands,' said Zaveri testily. 'Cloth production has slowed down. So many mills have simply halted production. If the mills do not have enough cotton, how are they supposed to produce cloth? And if they don't give me cloth, how am I supposed to supply you? I am lucky I still have my pedhi. There are others in the market who are selling up and leaving.'

'I am in trouble, Haridas bhai. I have borrowed money and I can't repay it till I manage to sell some bales. But I am not getting any supply from you.' Jamnalalji sat kneading his large hands, looking worriedly at Zaveri.

'Just opposite my pedhi there is Shyamlalji. Old man. Been here thirty years. Says he's had enough, wants to sell up and go back to Navsari,' said Zaveri. 'Arre, stay, Jamnalalji, have some tea, we will work something out.'

But Jamnalalji heaved a sigh of impatience and left. Zaveri sighed too and shook his head.

Now was the moment. Tatya cleared his throat. 'Seth, can I say something?'

Zaveri frowned at him.

'There is a stock of drill in the warehouse. It hasn't moved for days. I told the owner you would buy it.'

Zaveri blinked his eyes as if waking up from a nap, and then his expression changed to one of consternation.

'What? You said I would buy it? Why? Who does it belong to?'

Heart thumping wildly, Tatya managed to get the words out, one sentence tumbling over the next. 'I have been seeing this large stock in the warehouse for days. I wondered what it was, and why it wasn't moving. It is at the back of the warehouse in one corner. On one of the bales I saw the stamp of a star—the stamp of Manekchand Mills. So I knew that it must be either drill or cambric, because it is a small mill and they don't make anything else.'

Zaveri was now looking intently at Tatya. 'Go on,' he said.

Tatya swallowed hard and continued. 'I knew that Lalubhai, in the second lane of the market, is the selling agent of Manekchand Mills, so I asked his assistant about it yesterday. He confirmed that it is drill, but he didn't know why it was not moving. I knew that Jamnalalji needs drill, so this morning I went to Lalubhai's pedhi. I thought he might cuff my ear if I dared to speak to him. But when I saw that he was sitting and quietly reading a letter, I picked up the courage to speak to him. I said, we need an urgent supply of drill, and I noticed your stock has not moved for many days. He looked up from his letter and said, "where are you from?" I said I am from Haridas Zaveri's pedhi. I said I am certain that Zaveri seth would want it.'

'How many bales?'

'Fifty bales.'

'And why hasn't the stock moved? Is it defective?' Zaveri said, his eyes fixed on Tatya's face.

'No, Seth, Lalubhai had promised the goods to his sister's husband, so he held it for him for more than a month, even paid the money to the mill on his behalf. But just this morning, I think about five minutes before I approached him, he received a letter saying that his sister's husband is ill with tuberculosis. So I said we would take the lot.'

A large smile broke out on Zaveri's face. 'You are a fool,' he said, 'for doing all that without a word to me. And a greater fool for not telling me as soon as I arrived.' He pushed the samples to one side and got up with surprising alacrity. As he walked rapidly, almost jogged, towards Lalubhai's pedhi, his words came out accompanied by his panting breath. 'If Lalubhai has already sold it to someone else I will give you the cuff on your ears you deserve. With the cotton scarcity, this is gold. Gold. I know Manekchand Mill's quality. They make good drill. Highly likely that there will be no defects. Especially since he was holding it. For. His. Relative.'

Here Zaveri's breath ran out and Tatya, who had been keeping up with quick footsteps, took the opportunity to say, 'Seth, there is one problem: he said that in the same stock there are also ten bales of cambric. We have to take that as well.'

Zaveri trotted on without a pause, and said, 'My dear boy, I am buying fifty bales of drill from Lalubhai. If he wants to sell the cambric you will have to buy it yourself.'

'What?' Tatya stopped in his tracks. 'Seth, I don't have the money for it!'

'For the last few months, you have been cooking my ears with stories of how you want to start your own business,' panted Zaveri, as he jogged on past surprised stares. 'Well, here is your chance. I will extend you credit for the ten bales of cambric. Sell them and the profit is yours.'

And as Zaveri descended upon Lalubhai with smiles and commiserations and fixed the deal on the spot, Tatya realized with a thrill that he was the owner of ten bales of cambric. And just like that, it appeared that Zaveri had turned him into a businessman.

'You want to be a player?' said Zaveri, as they hurried back to Pedhi Number 73. 'You have five days' credit from me. Sell the cambric in five days, or I'll write to your brother to say you owe me money.' He clapped Tatya on the back with a smile, but there was no levity in his expression. 'You have a real chance, boy. It was foolish of you to promise Lalubhai that I would buy his stock. If I hadn't been able to, my name would have turned to mud. In this market, a man's word is gold. Now go find Jamnalalji and tell him he will get his supply today as long as he pays me by tomorrow. I've overpaid for the drill and he needs to make good.'

Exactly five days later, as Haridas Zaveri took out his post-lunch tin of supari, Tatya handed him a bundle of notes wrapped in a piece of cloth. 'The cambric is sold,' he said quietly.

Zaveri took the bundle from Tatya in silence and counted the money. He looked up. 'Who did you sell it to?'

'Kailashnath Karsandas in Mahavir Galli. He's a young man. His father passed away recently, leaving him the pedhi.'

Zaveri nodded. 'I know the name. But I heard he is not doing too well. Not enough experience. And your profit?'

Tatya remained silent and shook his head.

Zaveri looked surprised. He raised his eyebrows at Tatya and looked shrewdly at him. 'After all that I taught you?' And he waited, for he knew that there was more.

'Kailashnath has a small wholesale pedhi. He needs a business partner to prop it up. I agreed to put the profits of the cambric into the business and also paid him some more from my savings. I am a four-anna partner now—I own a quarter of the business. But I told him that I will not leave your service for at least another month. Till you find a replacement for me.'

Zaveri motioned to Tatya to sit down next to him, and patting Tatya on the back, said, 'Shabash.'

Unexpectedly, Tatya felt like weeping. 'I will always be grateful to you, Seth, for allowing me to work for you, for teaching me so much, and...'

'And I,' said Zaveri, 'thank you for reminding me of what it is to be young. To be alive to the possibilities around you. As a man gets older he forgets. He fails to recall why he started working in the first place. To earn money, to be sure. To fill his belly. But also to find his place in the world. I am going to give you some advice. You Marathi people have a certain pride. You would rather break than bend. But you, Tatya—you are adaptable. Your brother is a learned man, a school principal, but despite that you have carried bundles of cloth on your back for me. This is your greatest strength. You may become a great man one day. Or you may not. Either way, don't take good fortune for granted. Otherwise this city will grind you into the dust. If, one day, you find that you are able to buy your own horse carriage, or even an automobile—don't. Buy your own horse carriage only when you have the capacity to buy three of them. And even then, don't lose the habit of walking. You must always be willing to carry those bundles of cloth on your back.'

Since Tatya was still saving his tram money to buy bidis, he thought Zaveri was being overly enthusiastic, talking about carriages and motor cars. But he nodded, because he was touched by Zaveri's sincere affection. He felt that his head had stopped buzzing, as if the bees that lived there were resting on a blossom, preparing to suck its nectar. It was only a matter of time before they grew restless again. He knew that owning a quarter of a small business couldn't possibly be his final aim, but for now he was satisfied. He couldn't wait to get started.

'Now,' continued Zaveri, 'I am going to point out something to you that should be obvious. You see Murari Bhanushali there?' Zaveri indicated a spot about twenty feet away with a discreet flick of his eyes.

Tatya knew Murari, of course. Murari Bhanushali was a short, fair man with a perpetual smile on his face. He seemed to know everybody in the market. He wore a light, crumpled kurta-pyjama that hung loosely over his portly belly. He was in and out of the market at odd times of the day and seemed to spend all his time accepting cups of tea from various traders. He often came to Zaveri's pedhi, perching himself on the mattress with his legs dangling off the side, and sat there like a smiling sack of sugar till someone offered him a cup of tea or a paan. Tatya never had the time to pay much attention to Murari. Only occasionally had he seen him conversing with Zaveri, and sometimes wondered what they found to talk about.

'Why do you think I tolerate the fellow?' said Zaveri.

'I heard someone say that he was in your pedhi when you acquired the Chand Mills selling agency, and you think he is your lucky charm,' said Tatya. It was in fact his new business partner, Kailashnath, who had told him this many months ago, when they first became acquainted.

'Do you think I am a superstitious donkey?' said Zaveri, calmly.

'No, Seth. No, no.'

'What do you think Murari does all day? He goes about scrounging for free cups of tea. Everywhere people give him tea. Most people think he is a soft-headed fool. It is true that he is childlike in many ways. But those who know better—like me—are careful not to say too much in his presence. Why? Because he listens.' Here Zaveri dropped his voice, as if someone might hear. 'He talks to me sometimes. And it always helps to know what is going on in the market.'

After this, in his last month at Zaveri's pedhi, Tatya kept a watch out for Murari Bhanushali. Sometimes Murari wore a faded pink kurta, sometimes a pale yellow one. It was easy to spot his lumbering, childish walk from a distance, especially when silhouetted against the golden sunlight that streamed in at the edges of the market at a certain time of the day. Tatya began striking up conversations with him and was astonished at Murari's knowledge. When Murari spoke, his voice was soft and songlike, as if a child were speaking, giving the impression of a feather brushing over one's ears. But the information he imparted was anything but childlike. The very morning after Tatya had announced his intention to leave Zaveri's employment, Murari appeared at the pedhi and informed Tatya that the accountant who was currently in the employ of Tatya's new partner was a useless fellow. He spoke as if he were imparting a lovely and harmless secret to Tatya, smiling all the while. He often laughed dismissively at the end of his sentences, as if inviting the listener to please ignore a foolish man's fancies. At other times he told Tatya about the old days. 'You have come to Bombay at a good time,' he would say, in his smiling, whispery voice. 'Did you know that just twenty years ago there were only forty textile mills in Bombay? Now there are one hundred and forty mills, spinning yarn and weaving cloth, day in and day out. And I'll tell you a secret. They might as well be spinning gold. Yes. But you know that already, boy, don't you? Oh yes.' And here Murari looked closely into Tatya's watchful, dark brown eyes and let out a tinkle of laughter.

Early in the morning and late at night Tatya looked into the account books of his new business—he tried to inject some order into the delivery system, convinced his new partner that it would benefit them to buy cloth from Zaveri, got rid of the accountant who had been fiddling negligible amounts but which, in Tatya's eyes, was unforgivable cheating, and installed in his place a serious fellow who was Govardhanji's nephew. Tatya was working eighteen-hour days.

But he still found time to sit with Murari Bhanushali in the quieter hours of the humid afternoons, when Murari told him stories about the plague that, only five years ago, had swept through the city and through its hundreds of thousands of souls like a fanged snake after helpless rats, when thousands died terrible deaths, and those who could, ran for their lives; how the city had emptied out, and how there was open bidding for labour on street corners. And he told Tatya even older stories from half a century ago when Bombay's first locomotive train left from Bori Bunder, and the people, overcome by fear at the demonic forces that moved carriages without horses or bullocks, broke coconuts and prayed to that unearthly force to propitiate it, even as a celebratory band played in all its pomp in one of the flag-festooned carriages.

CHAPTER 5

Tatya trusted Kailashnath Karsandas implicitly. He would never have entered into a partnership with him had his gut instinct not told him that Kailashnath was incapable of being dishonest. But now, working daily at close quarters with him, his partner appeared to be an uncertain and nervous man. The lack of confidence, which Tatya had at first assumed was due to the sudden loss of his father, turned out to be an innate characteristic of Kailashnath. Tatya discovered, to his frustration, that Kailashnath regularly did the rounds of his innumerable uncles and cousins for advice, and every few weeks put forward the various conflicting opinions he had heard from them. It turned out that his relations were in the dry fruits business and owned a couple of well-known shops in another part of the city. They convinced Kailashnath that he would be better off converting his wholesale business into a retail shop and running it along the same lines as their own dry fruits retail shops.

'Think of it, Tatya,' said Kailashnath one day. 'We could convert this pedhi into a shop. As it is, we are located at the edge of Mulji Jetha Market. We have people walking up and down the street in front of our pedhi all day long. They would see our goods and buy from us. Why not construct a few shelves, put up an attractive board, and decorate the shop with lights? We can display all kinds of silks and cottons for people to buy. Then all we have to do is sit behind the counter and sell.'

'But Kailashnath, there is more to running a shop than sitting behind the counter and selling,' said Tatya in exasperation. 'What exactly that might entail I have no idea, because I know nothing about the retail business. With our expertise we can make a lot more money moving large stocks of cloth. And we are in Mulji Jetha Market, the biggest wholesale cloth market in the country. Your father did well for many years. People know the Karsandas name as wholesalers. Why do you want to let go of our position as well-known wholesalers?'

'Yes, yes, you are right,' said Kailashnath nervously. 'But don't you think such a shop would look attractive? My aunt said we can even sell bangles and saris.'

Tatya looked at him in consternation and Kailashnath piped down. A few months later he proposed a semi-wholesale shop, and weeks after that he wondered whether they would be better off as selling agents for a mill instead, like Zaveri.

'Kailashnath,' said Tatya patiently, 'trust me. Trust your instincts. It is not an easy task to get a selling agency for a mill. Let us build on what we already have.'

And so Tatya would calm Kailashnath for another few months. Meanwhile he worked hard at establishing the business. Often he felt that despite being the junior partner in the business, with only a quarter share in it, he carried the responsibilities of a sole owner. But there was no doubt that Kailashnath's contacts among semi-wholesalers, who bought their stock, were invaluable. Old man Karsandas's name still generated an enormous amount of goodwill in the market, and Kailashnath was good at keeping their customers happy with sweet words while Tatya worked behind the scenes to ensure that deliveries and payments happened on time. Unfortunately Kailashnath made no move to expand his circle of regular customers. He was content to carry on with the same semi-wholesalers who had bought cloth from his father, content to carry on with the same terms of business. Tatya began to realize that it was not only the accountant who had been fiddling with the figures; some of their buyers, taking advantage of Kailashnath's mild-mannered nature, began delaying payments. It was left to Tatya to insist that his partner pursue the matter, which Kailashnath did with some amount of reluctance. Despite all this, somehow—Tatya himself did not know how—at the end of a year and a half, it appeared to Tatya that perhaps the business was approaching some kind of an even keel. The old problems remained, but he had become used to dealing with them. He worked hard at balancing the books. He felt he was successfully absorbing the strain of managing Kailashnath's nervous swings of temperament.

And he walked endlessly. The city seemed to demand that he keep moving, the pavement beneath his slippers moving of its own accord, making him put one foot in front of the other, in an unceasing motion. When he wasn't working with Kailashnath at the pedhi, he would meet the selling agents of various mills to strike deals to buy their cloth. He waited anxiously at the warehouses as the mill deliveries came in, tracking down the selling agents to get the stock he had booked, of jaconets and long cloth, muslins and sateens.

He went to the wharf at Arthur Bunder to see the majestic amounts of cotton being unloaded from the boats for the mills, not because he needed to, but because he felt a burning curiosity to see the origins of the cloth that passed through his hands—the grainy dirty cotton that came straight from the fields and would be sent for cleaning and ginning. He went to the Cotton Green at Colaba to look at the walls of cotton bales, tall as houses, creating a maze through which he wandered.

He went to the docks to see the unloading of coal and fish, grains and wood, absorbing the thrumming energy of the deal-making and the nimble movement of goods. He walked through noisy markets selling precious stones and Amritsari shawls, dried fruit imported from the deserts of Muscat, and body oils to make you strong—things he could only dream of possessing. There were flower extracts and clay pots, dealers of walnut wood, and displays of sweets that looked like princely treasure chests filled with lime-green, marigold, and honey-coloured jewels covered in beaten silver; there were fifty different kinds of mangoes in hues of saffron, capturing the air with their heady, juicy smells of sweetness. Once he even saw a real prince driving along the seashore, down the wide, metalled Queen's Road in a magnificent open carriage. The carriage was drawn by four black horses, golden plumes on their heads and festooned with a royal crest of roaring lions, flanked by cantering soldiers. The opulence remained in Tatya's mind as no more than a dream of crests and flags and the soft golden velvet that the prince reclined on—a kind of brittle, fleeting beauty. He wanted to hold the scene in his palm, like a fragile and slippery-skinned bubble, rainbow-hued in the sunshine; a whole other city lay within, simultaneously real and a phantasm, a mirage.

In the wake of this dazzling vision and the receding sound of hooves, Tatya walked down Queen's Road, with the sea shining blue on his right, and a salty breeze rustling the fronds of the coconut trees on his left. A train track lay between the road and the sea, and he perched on it on his haunches, resting for a while, looking at the white-peaked waves, wondering what it would be like to look inside a grand carriage. There was no possibility of doing so, of course; but then someone told him of a workshop in Byculla that made fancy vehicles, where he went one day and saw, to his amazement, the half-built interior of a carriage inlaid with small mirrors that shimmered in the shifting light, and another where tasselled red velvet cushions concealed panels of polished wood which were actually miniature drawers to store handkerchiefs and cigar cases. The workshop sold

Tejaswini Apte-Rahm

these carriages for thousands of rupees.

And when he returned home via the clock tower with the sound of its bells ringing 'God Save the Queen' and 'Blue Bells of Scotland' and other tunes that he had no name for, and saw the grime of Girgaon, the open sewers between the poorer chawls and the jostling men, women, and children waiting around a tap for a meagre trickle of water, he was filled with a kind of frenzy in his heart. He started feeling a weight on his chest, as if time were running out, as if the city of Bombay was running away from him, the island floating away on the sea, and as if he must run too. His mornings, afternoons, and evenings began merging into a single seething movement, and when he rolled out his thin mattress and fell on it at night, sleep came quickly like a carpet of darkness unrolling over his eyes. But often, before passing into sleep, when he tried to recall what he had done that day—dodged a horse-drawn tram on his way to work, signed chit after chit to account for the day's transactions, tramped for miles to three different warehouses in the hot sun on a single afternoon to track down a missing delivery of cloth, counted bundles of rustling notes and let the heaviness of coins slip through his fingers—he could never remember whether it had all happened on the same day, or in the previous week, or whether parts of it had existed only in his dreams. As he slipped into darkness he could see Murari's eyes looking at him knowingly, and heard Murari's tinkling laugh in his ear.

CHAPTER 6

1903

When he woke one morning it was with the sun beating down directly on his face, creating an aching prickle behind his eyes. The room was empty and quiet. Nana and his cousin Ponkshe had gone to their village for a few days. The door to the communal balcony was still shut. He had pulled it close the previous night. He found that in his sleep he had rolled off his mattress and lay on the cool hard floor by the open window. Here the sun's rays had found him. Surely it was late, for the sun was beating down straight into the room. He tried to move—at least he thought he was trying to move—but it was only a faint effort on his part. He felt an overwhelming sleepiness and, turning his face away from the sun, closed his eyes again. The noises of the street—an indeterminate cloud of human voices and cycle bells and children's games—seemed far away. He wondered where Lele mavshi was, and why she hadn't popped in to wake him. He wondered, too, why he had slept so long, and why it didn't seem to bother him. He heard the bawling of a child and a brief ripple of feminine chatter smothering the sobs till the sound trailed off into a muffled whimpering and gurgling. His eyes opened, and then closed again. The inside of his eyelids looked yellow—the sun seeping in—dotted with dark shapes like pinheads doing a slow swirling dance. Then a cloudiness, as if evening might have fallen, with blue-grey clouds floating across his closed eyelids. He appeared to be waking again, though he didn't really feel like he had been asleep. How long had he slept?

Through his eyelashes, as if peering through some kind of thick grass that was obscuring his vision, the open window came into view. It was now black night. And there was a deep thudding sound that might have been his heart. He felt alarmed at the thrum in his chest, and, with his head pounding, he sat up and listened hard. The sudden movement made the room spin slowly. Drums beating in the distance, advancing closer, accompanied by a growing roar. Was it a riot? His disorientation turned into terror. He forced himself on to his feet, wrestled with the chain on his door, only to discover he had never locked it, hauled the door open, and emerged stumbling on to the balcony. All at once the drumming magnified, accompanied by harsh shouts and yells, and the whoops of children who capered about on the street. Dozens of people milled about in the darkness. A few faint lamps flickered inside windows and shops, illuminating the insides of cube-like rooms. Tatya's chest pounded and his tongue felt dry and heavy as he leaned over the balcony railing, his eyes darting along the street. Through the darkness emerged a fearsome group of men. They leaped forward bare chested, in skirts of grass, wielding massive, coiled whips. Hanging from their necks were small drums which they beat with thin long sticks. Their beards were thick and black, and their dark foreheads plastered with red vermillion. They stopped stock-still in the crowd, directly below the balcony. One of the men suddenly flashed a glance up at Tatya, who recoiled as if the man had thrust the whites of his eyes into Tatya's own face, but then the man looked away and swept his eyes over the crowd. The sudden halting of the rhythm created a moment of eerie calm, during which one man uncoiled his whip—a thick, reptilian creature of preternatural length—and began whipping himself as the drums rose to a crescendo, as if the rhythm were running up a hill, and the crowd erupted in cries of fear and applause. There was a frenzied jangling too, for the men all danced and on each one's ankles was a golden mass of bells.

It was only the Kadaklakshmi.

Tatya was irritated by his foolish fears. It was just a group of three men after all, creating all that commotion. He turned away in revulsion at the sight of men flagellating themselves for money. But, in morbid fascination, he could not help turning his head—how heavy his head was!—to look down on to the street once more, at the whip coiling around the man's body. Crack. Crack. Crack. He was a giant of a man, but he must feel it now. Surely he must. Tatya's forehead felt hot, and something inside his temples began to splinter. Crack. Crack. Now the burly man withdrew and an old wiry man—how frail he seemed with his hair all grey—took to the centre of the circle, his belled feet skittering across the ground with unexpected grace as he uncoiled his own whip. It was as thick as a muscular arm. Tatya clutched at the railing, unable to look and unable to look away, and as the old man let the whip slam on to his old, frail skin, sweat drenched Tatya's body and his vision blurred. A searing pain pierced his left leg as he heard the crack, but he couldn't be sure whether it was the sound of the whip or the sound of his own head crashing down on the floor. He lay on his stomach, ear to the ground, looking down the length of the balcony through hot, bleary eyes—how far away its end was! And each wooden slat a rough and uneven terrain measuring a mile! Not a soul was on his floor—they must all have gone down to look at the Kadaklakshmi. The absurd thought came to him that this was how the balcony must appear to an ant.

And just before his eyes closed, from some deep primal part of his brain, the part that alerts animals to danger, floated up a memory. The heat of an afternoon outside the Suraj Mills warehouse—and a water tank—a small one, dark and dank. He was tired, he had walked for hours that day, and of course he only meant to splash the water on his face, to feel its fingers spreading on his scalp like a cold crown, and no, of course he hadn't meant to let some of the cool water trickle down his parched throat. But he had been thirsty, so thirsty....

The next sound that Tatya heard was Lele mavshi's lament.

'He's waking up! He's waking up! What evil spirits entered me that I did not come to wake you up that morning! It was so quiet and so late, I thought you had left for work already. I did not think you were still in your room burning up with fever. Oh, Ahilya's son, how will I face your mother when I meet her after I die?'

He felt something damp being removed from his forehead. Then he realized that Lele mavshi's rough fingers were brushing against his skin and gently laying a wet, cool strip of cloth on his forehead.

His eyes flickered open and he saw Nana hovering in the background.

'Nana? You're back?' he said, barely whispering, surprised to see Nana's robust face looking down at him.

'Of course. I came back yesterday,' said Nana briskly, though his eyes appeared anxious. 'Can't I go home to my village without you dying?'

'Shut your mouth or I'll cut off your black tongue!' Lele mavshi said, frowning.

Tatya managed a weak smile. It was good to have Nana back. 'How long have I been lying here?'

'Two days!' said Lele mavshi, wiping her wet palms on the end of her sari. 'We found you burning up with fever, lying outside in the balcony. My head started spinning when I saw you there, I thought I was going to faint and join you on the floor. Jagannath ran for the vaid, and the vaid said you have naroo.'

'Also called Guinea worm,' called a voice from somewhere in the room. Her son, Jagannath, was there too, it seemed.

'You need to have it pulled it out,' said Nana, 'now that you're conscious.'

'Why hasn't it been pulled out already?' asked Tatya confused. And then came the burning pain in his left leg once again. It was in his calf. He tried to move his leg, but several pairs of hands pressed down on his thigh to prevent him from doing so. 'What's the matter?' he said, alarmed, and wondered how many people were in the room with him. He became aware then, that his leg was hanging off the side of a cot and was immersed in a bucket of water. He struggled to sit up.

'Lie down,' said Lele mavshi, a hand on his shoulder.

'Aai, let him sit up and eat some rice,' said Jagannath. Tatya saw Jagannath's wife hovering in the doorway stirring a small bowl.

Nana helped him sit up and lean back. The cot, borrowed from Chinmay Phadke upstairs, had been pulled into a corner of the room, with the wall providing a comfortable backrest.

'Arre, somebody explain to him what naroo is,' said someone.

'What's that?'

'Call the vaid, only he can explain.'

Now that he was awake, there was a sudden flurry of activity and a growing clamour inside and outside the room. Several children were hanging on to the door frame and peering in. Nagesh Godse, lanky and slouching, had left his cycle shop and stood with his arms crossed over his chest, as if waiting for someone to tell him what to do. Gokhale's plump wife bustled in with heavy footsteps, her daughter-in-law in tow, to confer with Lele mavshi. Judging by the voices and shuffling feet outside, there were several more people in the balcony. Jagannath sat cross-legged in a corner on a neat square of cloth, giving the appearance of having sat there in this precise manner for days, with no intention of moving any time soon.

'What needs to be done, exactly?' That was Dattopant Apte's reasonable, lawyerly voice, cutting through the increasing hum of chatter. He was standing in the middle of the room, looking down at Tatya with his hands clasped behind his back, a tall figure in a black coat and clean white dhoti, apparently on his way out somewhere.

'And why is my leg in a bucket of water?' said Tatya, his face twisting in pain.

Soon the vaid, known as Vaidyabua, arrived and explained that there was a worm in Tatya's leg, and that it would only come out if surrounded by water. Hence the bucket. Just a day after Tatya awoke, the wound broke and the worm became visible to Vaidyabua, who began teasing it out, winding it round a twig.

'Just pull it out, pull, pull!' That was Nana, as if enthusiastically cheering at a kabaddi game. Vaidyabua pierced him with an icy glare.

'Listen to me, all of you,' he said sternly, glancing around the small crowd that had gathered to watch. 'If this worm is pulled too hard it will break in two. If it breaks in two, and one part remains inside the leg, the leg will be poisoned. I do not want anyone trying to pull this out. I will come and do it myself every day. It needs to come out alive.'

Tatya listened wearily. He was in pain, and he had a horrible feeling that this was not going to be easy.

'What do you mean every day?' said Nana in astonishment. 'Aren't you removing it now?'

'No,' said Vaidyabua, 'only a small bit will come out every day.'

'How long is the cursed thing?' asked Lele mavshi.

'Hopefully not more than about a foot long. It should be out in a week.'

'But how did it get in there?'

'Dirty water. Don't drink dirty water.' He looked sharply at Tatya, and Tatya nodded, feeling defeated and miserable. He had never experienced such pain in his life. He was lucky—the worm was out within four days. But the fever did not leave him for six weeks; it slipped in and out of him, sending him into a delirium with his skin burning up on his flesh, and at other times dropping him into a still pond of glass, when he lay with cold eyes turned up to the ceiling, and the world around him—including his own life—appeared to be crystal-like and sharp-edged and fragile.

CHAPTER 7

Dada arrived with his wife, Anandi vahini, within two days of hearing of his illness, and Tatya had never been happier to see his brother and vahini. They stepped over the threshold of his room, anxiously clutching their small bags and three-year-old son Mandar. They had left their two older daughters with Vahini's sister and rushed to Bombay.

Tatya was overcome with contentment as he saw the domesticity that Anandi vahini quickly established in his small room. At night she and Mandar slept next door in Lele mavshi's room, leaving Dada to occupy Tatya's room along with Nana and Ponkshe. But in the day, with his roommates away at work, she took charge of the small room with the kerosene stove at the back and turned it into a kitchen. The stove that had only ever been used to produce tea and, at a pinch, a poor bit of boiled rice, now turned out soothing meals of varan-bhaat, khichadi, and bowls of tomato saar, and, as Tatya grew stronger, layered polis with ghee brushed on to every soft fold, served hot with brinjal bhaaji and spiced slices of potato.

Zaveri came to see him one day. He seemed to bring with him a nimble breeze that blew through the room, carrying within it all the bustle and vigour of the market. The deal-making, the trundling carts of cloth, the calculation of profits, the splatter of ink as reed pens scratched out columns of numbers, the sheer elation of it all—it is all going on without me, thought Tatya. A dark weight settled in his gut, and he felt exhausted, cast aside, as if the market—and the city itself—had chewed him up and spat him out. He thought of Kailashnath, nervous and scattered as usual, trying to manage the business and the bookkeeping on his own, no doubt running to his uncles for advice. Tatya wanted nothing more, in his enfeebled state, than to return to Dhangadh with Dada and Vahini.

'Seth,' Tatya said, looking up at Zaveri with weak eyes, 'it is time for me to go back. I cannot carry on any longer. I've tried my best. I can never repay you for all you have done for me. But let me go home now. At least for a while.'

'Under no circumstances,' said Haridas Zaveri, perched on a low stool next to Tatya's cot. 'That is your fever talking, not you. You must not leave

Bombay. I won't allow it.'

But Zaveri had brought bad news. Kailashnath had decided to sell his share of the business. And Tatya, after the initial shock of hearing this, knew at once that as owner of only a quarter of the business, it would be madness to work with the new owners, people he knew nothing about. It was simply another portent that his time at the market was up.

'I trusted Kailashnath,' he told Zaveri, 'but I am not willing to put my money in the hands of strangers. Please tell the new owners to buy out my share too. Don't you see that this is a sign that it is best for me to go back to Dhangadh?'

'Listen to me, Tatya,' said Zaveri. 'There will always be setbacks in business. It is the nature of business.'

'Maybe I am not cut out for it,' said Tatya, feeling weary as his head lay heavy on his pillow. So much uncertainty after so much hard work. After years of sheer doggedness he had finally taken a leap forward, only to fall off a cliff and lie broken on this cot, within the four walls of this cramped room. He could hardly bear to think of strangers taking over the wholesale pedhi he had toiled in day and night.

Zaveri leaned over his plump stomach and spoke close to Tatya's ear, as if they were at the market and one of their competitors might hear. 'Shyamlalji is moving out,' he said in a low, raspy voice. 'There is opportunity even in famine. He is an old man with no sons and can't hold out much longer. Rent the pedhi from him. In time you may be able to buy it. Forget about wholesale and retail, forget about Kailashnath, forget about business partners. I trained you to be a selling agent. I will help you get a selling agency at a mill. You can be your own boss. Be your own man.'

Tatya shook his head and stared up at the ceiling. He looked at the open door, a blazing rectangle of sunlight that hurt his eyes. He felt he would never have the strength to pass through that sheet of light. And if he did, he would not have the strength to come back to this bare room after Dada and Vahini had gone.

Zaveri spoke some more and Tatya coughed a dry cough and wished Zaveri would leave him alone. He wanted to sleep. He wanted to get back to work at the market. He wanted to catch a train back to Dhangadh with Dada. He wanted to look at the monkeys and laugh at the shoes hanging from the green branches around the market. He wanted to feel his hands on his own bales of cloth and know he was the owner. He didn't want to leave the smell of the sea behind. He had boats that still needed to be launched. Not actual boats of course, but something like it. Something that still needed to set sail, but he just couldn't put his finger on it. He felt confused as the fever started rising in his head again. And then the tenacious Zaveri spoke some more and finally Tatya nodded his head, and said yes, Seth, yes, and closed his eyes, feeling happy and weak.

It was barely a week later that he felt he really might be able to get back to the market. It was now almost two months since he had fallen unconscious in the balcony of Khatryachi Chawl.

'No, you can't go back to work. Not for another ten days,' said Vahini, frowning so that the large red circle of kunku on her dark forehead turned into a crumpled oval. 'At least.'

Zaveri had arranged with old Shyamlalji that Tatya would rent his pedhi at Chandra Chowk. A relieved Dada agreed without hesitation to help with Tatya's expenses till he found a firmer footing. ('"A man is fit for neither business nor pleasure,"' quoted Dada, encouragingly, '"who either cannot, or does not, command and direct his attention to the present object and, in some degree, banish for that time, all other objects from his thoughts"— Lord Chesterfield's letters to his son—both form and content are admirable, Tatya. I have set the princes to studying them.' Later when Dada returned to Dhangadh he left Tatya a copy of *The Pickwick Papers*.)

Now whenever Tatya lay awake on his bed he thought of his new pedhi, just a few steps away from Zaveri's. He felt rested and clear-headed, as if the fever had scrubbed his brain clean. He ran through a list of mills in his mind, thinking about which he would approach first for a selling agency. There was New Islam Mills. He had heard they were going to start drill production. Perhaps they had not settled on a selling agent as yet. Chand Mills was likely to break up their sale territories and get more agents, in which case Zaveri would be sure to put in a word for him. And, of course, there was Imperial Mills, the prize catch, but there were too many experienced agents angling for it. He doubted his chances there. He sat up, irked at his confinement, as he heard the shouts and whoops of children on their way home from school. It was late afternoon. Three-year-old Mandar was probably being spoilt by Lele mavshi next door. Vahini was in the back room, chopping onions, judging by the crisp slicing sounds of her knife. In another minute he heard the sizzle of oil as the onions went into the pan. He waited for her to appear with whatever she was preparing. His appetite had returned.

She soon emerged and handed him a plate. He looked with pleasure at the yellow mound of pohe covered in peanuts, coriander, and grated coconut. 'Vah,' he said, in satisfaction. 'Is there any lime pickle?'

'Of course,' she said, gesturing to his plate with her chin. 'I think it got covered with the coconut. Do you think I'd give you pohe without lime pickle?'

Dada entered with a letter in his hand, and she hurried inside, but not before Tatya saw a quick glance exchanged between them. In a trice she was out again with a glass of water and a plate of pohe for Dada. He motioned for her to place it on the window sill. Then she sat down on her haunches, in her usual purple nauvari sari, looking expectant.

'What's going on?' said Tatya, his spoon poised mid-air.

Dada sat on a chair next to his bed, looking pleased. 'Tatya,' he said, 'I've arranged your marriage. The next auspicious day is Akshay Tritiya. The girl's family has agreed to the date.' Dada waved the letter at him and grinned.

'When is Akshay Tritiya?' asked Tatya, sitting up.

'Next month,' said Vahini. 'Enough of this kind of living with Nana and Ponkshe. The girl is good, from an educated family near Solapur.'

'Her brother is an engineer. Just completed his studies and already has a job in the railways,' said Dada.

'Only one thing bothers me about her. Apart from that everything is fine,' said Vahini.

'What is bothering you?' asked Tatya, blinking at this sudden spurt of information. It made sense, of course, he was twenty-one, but so far the idea of marriage hadn't occurred to him.

'She's a bit too old,' said Vahini, a discontented expression on her face.

Dada nodded but then shook his head reassuringly at Tatya. 'It's all right, the main thing is that she's from a good family. And Ranga mama has written that she looks healthy.'

'Ranga mama?' said Tatya, puzzled. Ranga mama was their mother's cousin.

'He is the one who has arranged the match,' said Dada. 'The girl's family lives in a village called Shervi, not far from Ranga mama's village. He says the girl is educated too, she knows how to read.'

'Reading is all very well,' said Vahini. 'Who needs a girl who can read, that is hardly going to help her run her household. As for her advanced age—well everyone has their own destiny, who can say when a good match will come along. At least it means that she has had more time to learn from her mother.'

'How old is she?' said Tatya.

'Twelve,' said Dada, 'Nothing to worry about. It might turn out to be a good thing in fact. She can come here sooner.'

Vahini seemed satisfied despite her misgivings about the girl's age. 'We'll take her home to Dhangadh,' she said, 'I'll train her properly.'

Tatya nodded.

The following week, he went back to work.

In the days that followed, though his feet tramped to mills and warehouses and his eyes pored over columns of numbers in ledgers, now and then he found himself looking back on Dada's unexpected announcement and wondering at his own equanimity. His new pedhi, festooned with a string of saffron marigolds, opened auspiciously with a Lakshmi puja with Dada, Zaveri, Govardhanji, and Murari in attendance along with a dozen other well-wishers and acquaintances from the market. But even during the preparations for opening the new pedhi, he wondered at his lack of imagination in the matter of his marriage. He had launched imaginary boats in his mind, constructed honeycombs of knowledge and nectar in his brain, but had not been able to fathom a bride here, in Khatryachi Chawl, within the four bare walls that had so far served as no more than a room to lay down his head. What was he to do with her, he wondered, when she arrived. He thought back to himself at the age of twelve, sitting cross-legged on the loose brown earth under the banyan tree of the school in Palsana, rocking back and forth, fiddling with the strings of the sacred thread around his chest, reciting the tables with twelve other boys as the master strolled about rapping the dreaded cane against the side of his thigh to keep the rhythm. He had a habit, while sitting there, of scraping together small stones and clumps of soil from the ground around him and with each repetition he furtively picked one and put it on a growing pile. It was a game, like building a mud fort, without which the morning melted into a confounding muddle of repetitions. He tried to relate this image of himself with the bride that was to arrive. He had been a child then and she was a child now. What on earth was he to do with her?

CHAPTER 8

There was no reason for Dada and Vahini to return to Dhangadh. They would all travel to Shervi for the wedding from Bombay itself. Theirs was a small contingent, for it was a long journey. Lele mavshi would come with them from Bombay. Chhabi tai and Rama tai would come with their husbands and children from Baroda. He hadn't seen his Baroda cousins in years but remembered them as inseparable and voluble sisters. They had been married into the same family to two brothers and lived together, talking all the while, no doubt. Then there was Ranga mama, who had arranged the match, along with his family.

When Tatya first saw his mother-in-law in Shervi he realized, with a jolt, that she was a widow. Dressed in red garb, she was a small, slightly bent figure, the end of her sari wound tight around her head to hide her shaved scalp. She blessed Tatya when he bent down to her feet to do namaskar to her, but did not say a word to him. Mai, as she was known to all, was absent from all the wedding ceremonies that took place over five days, for even the shadow of a widow was considered inauspicious on such occasions. But now and then Tatya would catch a glimpse of her within the wada, where she lived with her daughter, looking out of an open window or peeping out from behind a pillar, her pale grey eyes—like smooth grey pebbles—staring at him. Of course, as soon as he caught her eye she would quickly look away, but it disconcerted him. Dada and Vahini did not seem to notice this, and he did not say anything to them for they would have surely disapproved.

Vahini spoke to Tatya briefly about Mai in a hushed voice. The wada in Shervi was not Mai's husband's home, but her father's home. After being widowed, she had been brought back to Shervi by her father-in-law who said that he could not guarantee her protection. Tatya immediately understood what Vahini was telling him. Widows were shunned, but he knew that they were often taken advantage of by men who shamelessly used them for their own desires. So Mai had been returned to her father's wada with a young son clutching her hand and an unborn child in her belly.

'I heard that it broke her father's heart,' whispered Vahini to Tatya. 'He had watched his only daughter setting out for her husband's village in her wedding finery. And he could not bear it when he saw her return home with a bare forehead, the kunku wiped off, walking into her childhood home with her head shaved and dressed in a widow's red sari. It was a great shock for him. He died soon afterwards. Since then Narayan bhau has looked after her. It seems he is very fond of his sister.'

Narayan Bhatt was Mai's brother, and was several years older than her. As the head of the family, it was he who had accepted Ranga mama's marriage proposal—Ranga mama was known to him through a common acquaintance. Narayan bhau was an only son and presided over the small, crumbling wada that was his ancestral property. The wada was a one-storey, square-shaped building, built around an inner courtyard with several bedrooms running all around the upper floor. The lower floor had larger communal rooms that opened into the well-swept courtyard. There was an annex at the back, built much later than the ancient wada, to provide more rooms. Dada informed Tatya that the farmland that came with the wada had long since dwindled away, being divided and sub-divided among male members of the family. Only a few small fruit orchards remained with Narayan bhau, who spent much of his time in the town of Solapur as a legal clerk. He was a genial man with an enormous moustache and a thin circlet of gold pierced into each earlobe. He received Dada warmly and was clearly pleased that his niece was to be married into the family of a school principal.

Tatya had expected quite a large wedding contingent in Shervi, compared to the small party that accompanied him. But there were not more than about twenty people living in Narayan bhau's wada. Narayan bhau was a widower, and had only two sons who lived in the wada with their wives and children. A couple of cousins also lived there with their families. And of course there was Mai's son, Raghu, a smiling young man who worked for the railways and whom Tatya immediately liked.

The wedding was held in the small Ganpati temple in Shervi flanked by an onion field and a millet field. The Ganpati here was known far and wide—though Tatya had never heard of it—for having been found in a well more than a hundred years ago. Somebody put a bucket down the well and up came the idol serenely cradled at the bottom of the bucket, holding a modak in one hand.

'Ever since then the well has had the sweetest water you ever tasted,' said Ranga mama, 'because of the modak.' Dada listened appreciatively and later related it to Vahini.

'They are preparing all the wedding meals using the water from that well,' he said, as she joined her palms in gratification. 'This is truly auspicious,' she told Tatya. Indeed, the idol was a work of fine craftsmanship. It appeared to be made of gold. As the wedding ceremonies and pujas commenced, the Ganpati disappeared under a mound of red and pink petals and orange garlands, though the tip of his trunk could be seen, as if he had swatted away a few of the flowers to be able to breathe. There were five days of rituals, including one where the bride had to press her feet into a platter of flour. The priest was an ancient—so old, thought Tatya, that surely he must have been present when the Ganpati emerged from the well. His chest was marked with dabs of sandalwood paste and his forehead streaked across with white vibhuti and the only parts of his body that had escaped the overall withering down to skin and bones were his pale green eyes, the small black pupils sharp and alive. He looked carefully at the footprint made by the bride and declared, 'This girl has Lakshmi in her feet.' He raised his head to look at the rapt audience around him.

'Vah,' said someone in awe. Everyone listened intently.

'Lakshmi,' repeated the priest, thoughtfully, gazing at Tatya. 'She will bring prosperity with her when she crosses the threshold of her husband's home. But she must not be named Lakshmi. What are you going to name her?'

Tatya looked quickly at Dada. As far as he knew, none of them had given a thought as to what to name the girl. He saw Narayan bhau and Raghu, gratified in the extreme by the priest's words, now looking with interest at Dada and Vahini.

'We hadn't really thought about it,' said Dada, apologetically, 'what with the wedding preparations and the travel and so on....'

'Her name is Yamuna, isn't it?' said Lele mavshi, 'Why not another sacred river? Call her Ganga.'

The bride sat motionless on her low wooden paat by the ceremonial fire, looking down at the floor. Tatya had barely dared to glance at her so far, though he was seated on a paat just next to her. From the corner of his eye all he could make out now was a small, plump figure draped in green and gold. The wedding had been a rather confused blur for him so far. Now and then he tried to tell himself that this girl would soon be his wife, but it seemed so unreal a proposition that he had decided not to dwell on it for the time being.

'Not Ganga,' said Anandi vahini, 'that was my name before marriage.'

'What does that matter?' said Lele mavshi.

Vahini looked unconvinced.

'Call her Parvati,' said Ranga mama, 'just like Parvati, the girl will be the mother of a son as intelligent as Ganpati. We are in his temple, after all.'

This seemed a good idea to everyone, and the dozens of people who had crowded around the fire began nodding and murmuring. But then Chhabi tai and Rama tai, the Baroda cousins, who had been hurriedly conferring with each other, piped up.

'Why are all of you thinking so much? Isn't Tatya's real name Govind?' said Chhabi tai.

'So his bride should be Radha, of course,' said Rama tai triumphantly. 'They will make a fine pair.'

A ripple of approving laughter ran through the crowd. Dada smiled in appreciation, and even the green-eyed priest smiled. Tatya felt his face grow hot and looked steadfastly at the ground, but that was that, and when the time came for it, somebody urged him to remove from his finger the new ring which Dada had gifted him, and the priest held forward a shallow platter filled with uncooked rice. Using the thin gold ring he furrowed through the pure white grains and wrote his bride's new name in the rice.

By the time Tatya and Yamuna, now Radha, had done the rounds of various houses in the village to seek the blessings of elders, returning with gifts of coconuts and khuns—cloth pieces used to make sari blouses—Tatya was chafing to get back to the pedhi. There was the question of what to do with Radha. Of course, she was to go to Dhangadh with Dada and Vahini till she came of age—but should they go to Bombay first? Tatya was of the opinion that it was pointless for everyone to go back to Bombay for just a few days; Dada, Vahini, and Radha should leave for Dhangadh directly from Shervi. But the question had been solved by the priest who had declared that the new bride had Lakshmi in her feet. Vahini was now determined that the goddess of prosperity should cross Tatya's threshold as soon as possible.

Narayan bhau had arranged a rather grand send-off for his niece. On the morning of their departure from Shervi, a bullock cart stood ready, harnessed to two white bullocks, their horns painted red. The bullocks were draped with thick embroidered cloths bordered with bright pink and yellow tassels. Extravagant loops and strings of silver bells tinkled around their necks as the animals shifted restlessly on their hooves. The air was sharp and fresh at that early hour of the morning, a moist leafiness on the trees. Tatya saw Mai wiping her eyes with the end of her red sari, though her face was expressionless and there was only the hint of a crease between her brows. Tatya looked at Radha. The child's face was as unyielding as her mother's, but there were dark smudges under her eyes—as if she had lain awake all night—and her hands trembled as an aunt placed a tightly packed cloth bundle in her hands.

As the bullock cart began to trundle forward, towards the train station, Vahini put a reassuring hand on Radha's arm. Radha now looked stricken, and a single tear fell on to the back of her hand as she gazed down, spine curved as if defeated. In a moment she appeared to rouse herself, as if she had forgotten something, and sat up straight, looking at her family gathered in front of the wada; her eyes searched for, and fixed on, the diminishing figure of her mother, clearly visible as a red smudge amid brown earth and green foliage.

'Take heart, child,' said Dada, gently. Nobody said any more.

Tatya looked at her with pity, this girl being taken away from her mother by strangers. He hoped she would not remain despondent for long. He exchanged a glance with Vahini who raised her hand slightly in reassurance, as if to say 'she'll soon be all right'. Tatya now had an opportunity to look at Radha. In the whirl of the wedding, there had not been a single moment when he could look into her face and gain a clear impression of her features. Her oiled black hair was combed back severely over her scalp into a khopa, a tight bun. Her eyes were large and serious. Thick, dark eyebrows that gave the appearance of pressing down heavily over her eyelids. She was short with rather childish, chubby cheeks. There was a slight horizontal dent on the bridge of her nose, no doubt the remnant of some accident. It made her small nose appear creased and disproportionate to her face, as if it were still growing and unfolding into shape. A large, bright circle of red kunku marked her forehead—too large, in Tatya's opinion, for such a small face. Her wrists and forearms were covered in green glass bangles, and two gold bangles that had belonged to Tatya's own mother. Around her neck was a thin gold chandrahaar that was a gift from Narayan bhau, and a simple mangalsutra of black beads. A large nose ring strung with small pearls and beads of gold all but obscured her mouth. Her skin was the colour of dark, milky tea. Obviously, a fair-skinned beauty would not have remained unmarried till the age of twelve.

What pleased Tatya the most was the air of stoicism about her. He was relieved that she did not start sobbing as they climbed into the bullock cart, or when they boarded the train, or when the engine started its slow chug-chug and she leaned out of the window to wave to her brother Raghu who had hurried to the train station in advance with two men to stow the luggage in their compartment.

He realized that he had been looking for some sign of weakness on her part, for he was anxious about how she would adapt to life in Bombay. It would not be long till she returned to Bombay from Dhangadh, since she was already twelve. A few months at the most, was Vahini's estimation. Khatryachi Chawl was clean, of course, and it was on a relatively quiet street but for all that, how could communal bathing and cleansing facilities used by twenty Brahmin families be compared to those of the quiet ancestral home in Shervi? How would the grime and clamour of Bombay compare to the tang of the rich wet soil at the wada, where early mornings were filled with the birdsong of bulbuls, the backyard carpeted with delicate white and orange parijat blossoms, and the vegetable patches lush with young dill and vines of plump green tondli? All this Tatya had noted with pleasure while at the wada, for though he could not see his bride, he felt he could perhaps get a measure of her character by observing minutely the house in which she had grown up. But now it was the same idyllic backyard and flowering trees which troubled him, for Khatryachi Chawl was a far cry from the wada in Shervi. He felt he must ascertain the girl's feelings about going to Bombay. But he had not said a word to her so far. He had barely heard her voice, for even when she recited an ukhana—something about the reflection of the full moon at Poornima—while putting a morsel of food in his mouth at the wedding lunch, her voice had been drowned out by the chatter of women around them. Nobody, in fact, heard her, and she was urged to repeat it, till a couple of old aunts took pity on her, and assured everyone that they had clearly heard Yami say her husband's name, woven into the ukhana.

He spent much of the journey pondering over what to say to her. His only opportunity would come if Dada, Lele mavshi, and Vahini all simultaneously left their seats. This possibility seemed more and more remote as the train approached Bombay and began filling up with an increasing throng of people. But a brief delay at a stop provided the opportunity for them to stretch their legs on the platform and let little Mandar run about for a while. Tatya found himself alone with his wife in the compartment. The other passengers barely glanced at them. He knew that Radha had never been to Bombay, but he started with the only opening gambit he could think of.

'Have you ever been to Bombay?'

From the corner of his eye he saw a sudden movement of her head, as if he had startled her. Then she silently shook her head. He could tell that she was looking at the floor. He took care not to look at her directly. He looked instead at the platform where a water seller carrying two pitchers was crying out, 'Hindu water! Mussulman water! Hindu water!'

'Do you think you will like it?' he said. For several seconds she remained motionless. Perhaps she hadn't heard him? Too late, for Vahini and Lele mavshi returned.

'Not long now,' said Lele mavshi, sitting down heavily. She opened a tin and put a handful of crisp shankarpalya into Tatya's hand. Radha did not want any. Neither did Tatya. He held them in his palm till they got clammy and soft, and eventually put the sweet diamond shapes into his mouth just to get rid of them.

By the time they arrived at Khatryachi Chawl late at night, three days after getting married, she had still not said a word to him.

Tejaswini Apte-Rahm

CHAPTER 9

There was not much that could be done within the confines of Khatryachi Chawl, in terms of a varaat. They certainly could not afford a proper bridal procession, and in any case, thought Tatya, they had already brought the bride home, so he did not see the need for any further ceremony. But Anandi vahini and Lele mavshi had other ideas, wanting to make an occasion of it.

'Otherwise,' reasoned Vahini, 'we will have done nothing in your own home, in Khatryachi Chawl itself. Surely that can't be auspicious.' So Lele mavshi took upon herself the mantle of the mother of the bride, and kept Radha in her room that first night. The next morning, the groom's varaat, made up of Nana, Ponkshe, Lele mavshi's sons, and of course Dada and Vahini, walked the few steps from Tatya's room to Lele mavshi's room to 'fetch' the bride home. Gokhale bai and her daughter-in-law tried their best to make it as festive a walk as possible by creating an elaborate pattern of white and red rangoli from Tatya's doorstep to Lele mavshi's room. Jagannath Lele had looped strings of marigold along the balcony railing for the entire length of the corridor. When Radha accompanied the varaat back to Tatya's room, a small urn of uncooked rice stood ready for her on his threshold. As she entered, she knocked it over gently with her right foot, and the rice spilled into the room. Vahini had never looked happier, thought Tatya, smiling—for the girl with Lakshmi in her feet had arrived, and spilled her riches into Tatya's life.

The following day the new bride departed with Dada and Vahini, and Tatya returned to work after accompanying them on the tram to the train station. He took a box of sweets with him to the market, and distributed the small yellow pedhas to his acquaintances. Back at the market, back to his pedhi, his wedding seemed a dreamlike interlude in his ordinary life. He had been away for no more than ten days, and the strange anticipation he had experienced in his chest had faded away. Once more he ate his meals at Mameenchi Khanaval, paying three annas for a plate of rice, bhaaji, and aamti, and an extra coin if he indulged in a sweet preparation now and then; once more he shot the breeze with Nana and Ponkshe by the gymnasium that stood behind the chawl, and listened to Murari's whispers in the hot, still afternoons at the market. After a few days, it was as if he had never been away. Occasionally, he thought of the girl. Her image floated into his mind now and then, but she was still an abstraction. He wondered what changes would occur in his life when she returned to Bombay, but there his imagination fell short. Now that he was back at the market, he could, in fact, think of little else besides how to build up his business at his new pedhi. He could not put a foot wrong now, could not afford another failure.

Zaveri was as good as his word. He arranged for Tatya to meet the manager of Chand Mills, an Englishman called Matthew Wales, and vouched for Tatya's character. Tatya amazed Zaveri by speaking to Wales in fluent English. 'High-class English,' Zaveri enthused as they left, though he had not understood most of it, 'Swept that Wales off his feet!' And the very next week Tatya had word that he was now a selling agent—not of Chand Mills, since they already had all the selling agents they needed—but of a newer concern, managed by the same company: a small mill called Rose Mills. Wales wanted Tatya to sell the long cloth produced by Rose Mills.

'It's a start,' said Zaveri, beaming, 'a very good start. It is time for you to hire a gumastha, eh?'

'Not yet, Seth,' said Tatya, 'I can do my own accounting for now. It is only one mill after all.' And he stayed late into the night, working his books, his own pile of chopdis covered in red cloth. He knew from Govardhanji the importance of regular and neat entries; payments from wholesalers to Tatya, payments from Tatya to Rose Mills, and, most importantly, his profits in the form of commissions that Rose Mills paid him.

Soon, one mill turned into two. Within a few months, cotton started coming into the city in larger quantities again, candies and bales moving from fields in Mehsana and Surat, Bharuch and Khandesh, to the docks and warehouses and mills. The mills turned a corner. One afternoon, Murari brought news that Noor Begum Mills had recently reopened after a fire had destroyed part of it two years ago.

'Go meet the owner,' said Murari. 'He also happens to be the landlord of Mastani Chawl, a stone's throw from your Khatryachi Chawl. Get a selling agency from him. His name is Karim Shahpurwala.'

'What about his old selling agents?' asked Tatya, 'Who were they?'

Murari laughed his tinkling laugh, like a descending scale of chiming bells, rubbing his potbelly in relish. He took a slurping sip from his cup of sweet tea, taking his time. Clearly, he had a punchline he was waiting to deliver. He then leaned closer to Tatya to whisper in his ear, though a noisy handcart was trundling past them at that moment, and nobody could possibly have overheard him.

'His primary selling agent,' whispered Murari, 'was the very man in whose pedhi you sit.' He then sat back to take a happy look at the effect his words had caused.

'Old Shyamlalji?' said Tatya disbelievingly.

'Yes!' Murari almost shouted, slapping his thigh and shaking with laughter. A few heads turned towards them from the neighbouring pedhis.

'How unfortunate...' began Tatya, a wondering look on his face. Murari stopped laughing and looked at him. But Tatya was lost in thought for a moment, thinking about old Shyamlalji in his billowing mulmul dhoti, his beige cap bordered with fading gold thread, the careful shuffling walk as he approached his pedhi and touched his head to the goddess Lakshmi's feet. By the time Tatya had returned from his illness Shyamlalji had gone, having agreed to rent out his pedhi to Tatya, had given up too soon, ended his life's work at the market just before the cotton started flowing again, just before Noor Begum Mills opened again. Tatya felt his heart miss a beat—or perhaps it had beat twice instead of once—for the thought of making a small, profound mistake like that jarred something inside him. Step carefully, tread carefully, he told himself. He looked around his small pedhi, as if to make sure it was real, and especially at the carved idol of Ganpati that he had installed on top of a small steel almirah. Ganpati looked back at him calmly, interested only in eating the modak in his palm once the market had emptied out for the night. Tatya felt fear and inexplicable guilt—inexplicable, for he had done nothing wrong—at having stepped into Shyamlalji's place so easily. Too easily. Surely he would be called to account for it. A sudden superstition descended on him, a suspicion of his good fortune. Only weeks ago he had found himself in a pit of despair. And now, far from packing up and going back to Dhangadh, here he was, sitting on a starched white sheet, in the old trader's pedhi. Would the ground slip away from under his feet again? It seemed wrong—an ill omen—that he should benefit from Shyamlalji's loss.

'It has nothing to do with you,' said Murari, staring hard at Tatya, as if deciphering some inscrutable alphabet on Tatya's forehead. 'The old man gave up too soon. But that was his decision. He left at low tide, because he saw the debris of the sea floor all around him. And even after a lifetime of experience he forgot something important.'

'What?' said Tatya, uneasily.

'That the low tide is simply the sea breathing in, breathing deeply. But even the sea cannot hold its breath for long. The time soon comes when it must exhale. And when it exhales is when the high tide comes crashing in, bringing with it the wealth of the seven oceans to kiss the shores of Bombay. And this time—this time—it just so happens that you, dear Tatya, are here to take a ride on one of its salty waves.'

Tatya said no more. The following day he went to Wadala to meet Karim Shahpurwala. He waited outside Noor Begum Mills from eight in the morning till eleven, when a small landau, drawn by a pair of sturdy brown horses, rolled in through the mill gates. He had struck up a conversation with the gatemen by then, who let him through at once. His modest manner and neat appearance gained him an entry to see Karim Shahpurwala right away, to whom he introduced himself as a selling agent of Rose Mills, new occupant of old Shyamlalji's pedhi, protégé of Haridas Zaveri of Mulji Jetha Market, erstwhile partner in a small wholesale business, and resident of Khatryachi Chawl, and assured him that any reference he chose to follow up would show him to be an honest and efficient sales agent. Shahpurwala, a slight, elderly man in a long white sherwani, loose white pyjamas, and black shoes, sat on the edge of his chair as if about to get up and leave. He wore a round black Bohra cap, its border embroidered with gold thread, and rested both hands on top of a polished black walking cane. He listened with a troubled expression on his grey bearded face, as if listening to Tatya was a terrible strain on his health. Tatya soldiered on, nevertheless. He found out later that Shahpurwala looked troubled at all hours, the effect, perhaps, of having had to close his mill for two years. But before Tatya left an hour later, Shahpurwala's face had relaxed somewhat, and Tatya had been promised a selling agency of Noor Begum Mills on a trial basis once the mill commenced full operations the following month. He would be selling small stocks of drill as a start.

'Meanwhile,' said Karim Shahpurwala, carefully, 'I will have a word with Haridas Zaveri. I know something of him. It is a pity about Shyamlalji's departure. On the other hand....'

He trailed off. Tatya waited, the tick-tick of a large, grim wall clock filling the still air. He was about to take his leave when he realized that

Shahpurwala was going to speak again.

'On the other hand,' continued Shahpurwala, in a soft tremor, 'it is good to have young blood.'

Back at the market, Tatya went to see Zaveri the same afternoon.

'Does Karim Shahpurwala have any sons, Seth?' asked Tatya.

'I suppose so,' said Zaveri, 'why?'

'He's frail,' said Tatya. 'Noor Begum Mills may yet hold up, despite the fire, but will its owner?'

'Shahpurwala has looked exactly the same for the last twenty years,' chuckled Zaveri. 'He is like a cactus. Drinks his fill when it rains and then outlives all the healthy plants through famine and sun. Don't you worry about him.'

'He's going to contact you,' Tatya said, 'about my selling agency. On a trial basis for now. Drill. Maybe muslin too, soon.'

Zaveri clapped him on the back. 'Well done,' he said.

Six months later Tatya's trial period with Noor Begum Mills had successfully translated into a full-fledged selling agency for drill, muslin, and sateen. Far from showing any sign of frailty, Karim Shahpurwala proved to be a canny investor, pumping capital into his mill, re-opening it with the latest spinning and weaving machinery imported from England, and producing high quality textiles that Tatya had no trouble selling to the wholesalers who were gathering in increasing numbers at his pedhi every afternoon. Tatya hired a young gumastha, Kishan Mehta, and took great pleasure in seeing that he set himself up on the mezzanine floor in an almost identical fashion to old Govardhanji. Govardhanji came over one day to inspect the new arrival, and looked critically at the arrangement of chopdis, the small floor desk, and the safe, and peered at Kishan Mehta through his round, wire-framed glasses. He had evidently taken it as his duty to ensure that the former protégé of Haridas Zaveri was in good hands.

'Who taught you?' he asked bluntly.

'Vasant Agarkar, accountant at Bank of Bombay,' said Kishan Mehta in deferential tones. 'My tutor for many years, after which he took me as a trainee at the bank.' He was a young man with a formal expression that looked as if it was going to break into a smile at any moment. Govardhanji was clearly not impressed by this trait.

'Why did you leave the bank?' he asked, his eyes narrowed.

'They did not need any permanent employees at that time.'

While Kishan Mehta was undergoing this inquisition, Tatya suddenly felt for the letter in his pocket. He had forgotten about it after stuffing it into his coat that morning on his way out. He left Kishan Mehta and Govardhanji on the small mezzanine floor and made his way down to the front of the pedhi, sat leaning against a bolster, and tore open the envelope.

Tejaswini Apte-Rahm

CHAPTER 10

1904

It had been months since the wedding, and there appeared to be no prospect of Radha joining Tatya in Bombay. The letter was a brief note from Dada informing him as delicately as possible that her thirteenth birthday had come and gone, and that Vahini was taking all precautions to ensure that she could commence life as a householder as soon as possible. This consisted of rubbing heated mustard oil on the soles of her feet thrice a day, feeding her sugared sesame balls as well as black peppercorns fried in ghee, burning twigs of neem and lime for inhalation, and other remedies involving gourd juice and crushed lotus seeds of which Dada did not have the details. The only thing to do now was to wait. Apart from that, he said, the girl was spending her afternoons learning to cut cloth and stitch, and had demonstrated that she was already quite accomplished at preparing dry foods such as sago papdya, metkoot made of ground dals and spices, and bhazani flour.

Two months later, the monsoon arrived with a ferocity that was unusual even for hardened Bombay souls, and the ground floor of Khatryachi Chawl stood marooned in knee-deep water for three days. The filth of the toilet behind the chawl flowed over and swirled about in this new urban lake. Pelted by rain, the tin roof of the chawl shuddered and rattled violently for weeks as if pummelled by the hooves of horses thundering into battle. Everything was cloaked in a humid blanket of damp. Within days mould bloomed in every crack in the walls, every crevice in the doors and staircase bannisters. The pages of Tatya's copy of *The Pickwick Papers* wilted like flower petals and, shortly afterwards, succumbed to a creeping speckle of black dots. There were reports that a group of young Marwari boys, newly arrived from the deserts of Marwar, had been so dazzled by the water pelting down from the dark grey heavens into the heaving expanse of the Arabian sea, that they had rushed joyfully into the spectacular crashing arcs of water on the beach and been swept away. A few days later came a further report that only one among them had returned, with a tale of seeing a fearsome sea creature, part-fish, part-lizard, which had unleashed a noose upon the group to drag them out to sea and drown them. 'The bearer of Varun, god of the sea,' said Lele mavshi touching her earlobes with the tips of her fingers in fearful reverence. Her hushed voice was all but drowned out by the uproar of rain on the windows. And there was no way of ascertaining either tale.

By some miracle the postal service was still functioning, for a damp, bedraggled letter arrived from Dada, stating that Vahini had insisted on sending Radha home to Shervi. If she did not come of age within six months, they would have to look for a new bride for Tatya.

'Let us not be hasty,' replied Tatya by return post, writing rapidly in the rain-darkened afternoon, 'for we have already gone to the expense of a marriage, not to mention the time I must be absent from the pedhi, to accomplish yet another. In any case it would not be possible for her to come to Bombay under the present circumstances for the monsoon is particularly dangerous this year and there is talk of typhoid appearing in some chawls of Girgaon.'

It was not clear to Tatya whether this missive reached Dada, for two weeks later he received a postcard from Dhangadh that made no mention of his letter; instead, Dada informed him that Radha's mother had taken her on a pilgrimage to the temple of one Jambul Mata, a goddess who lived in a sacred forest in the northern regions near Nandurbar. Dada had evidently scrawled the few lines quickly, perhaps to catch the next post, but had managed to convey within those few lines that Mai, Radha's mother, was dealing with the matter with 'the utmost seriousness'. Tatya felt ill-tempered at this note. There was no need for this distasteful, frantic behaviour, this scrambling across the country to some temple in the wilderness. Who was this Jambul Mata, and why did she demand that a thirteen-year-old girl toil for days over difficult terrain to gain her blessings? He thought of the small, plump, downcast figure of the child he had last seen almost a year ago, wrapped in her green and gold sari, and he thought of the single tear that had fallen on the back of her dark brown hand as they drove away from her home in the decorated bullock cart. A feeling of heaviness settled on his chest, and pity for the girl. For Radha. He had slowly started thinking of her as Radha, not simply as 'the girl'. He hoped that no one had been cruel enough to tell her that she was in danger of being replaced by another wife, some healthy ten-year-old perhaps. But then he thought of his mother-in-law, she of the pebble-grey eyes, and felt certain that she was a woman who would hold back no information from her daughter, however ruthless it might be. He pitied them both, mother and daughter. He felt weary at the panic that must have enveloped the old wada in Shervi. The frantic pujas, the rites, the preparation of special foods. Who would have thought that Radha was not healthy enough to begin life with him as a wife? But did a lack of that time of month in fact indicate a lack of good health? Tatya had no idea. He must trust Vahini's judgement in the matter. There was nothing to be done but wait for further news or instructions from Dada. But he felt a profound reluctance, a deep dislike, at the idea of shunning his bride.

In the weeks and months that Tatya waited for Radha to return to Bombay, he had begun to see more and more of Balwant Ponkshe, who had left his job at a grain merchant's, and appeared to be spending most of his time at the Hanuman Vyayamshala, the gymnasium behind Khatryachi Chawl. It was understood that as soon as it was time for Radha to come to Bombay, Ponkshe and Nana would move into other rooms, but as there appeared to be no prospect of this for the time being, their search for alternative accommodation had been laid to rest for now. They often met at Mameenchi Khanaval where they sat arrayed on the floor with a dozen other men eating Mami's usual fare of dal, rice, and vegetables.

'Why did you leave the grain merchant?' asked Tatya, puzzled, as he ate rapidly. There was a particularly good lime pickle at the khanaval that day and he wondered whether he could ask for another spoonful of it.

'Balwant can't sit still for more than ten minutes at a time,' said Nana, in his usual placid manner, sipping a bowl of buttermilk. 'That's why he left his father's farm to start dancing around Bombay.'

'You would too, if you had to share the farm with five brothers,' said Ponkshe. He was a short, compact man with a thick neck. There was something curiously like a tree trunk about him. Tatya felt that if three men picked him up and held him horizontally, Ponkshe could well be used as a battering ram to break down a door and be none the worse for it.

'So now he's doing something at the Hanuman Vyayamshala,' continued Nana. 'By the way what exactly is it that you do there?'

'And is the salary as good as your granary job?' asked Tatya.

'Not as good,' said Ponkshe, 'but not bad. Gajanan Raut, the owner, needs help getting new customers. I'm going around some of the chawls talking to the men, telling them to come learn the lathi. Better than heaving sacks of grain for that bania.'

'Want to try the lathi, Tatya?' said Nana, grinning. 'Tighten your dhoti and give it a shot.'

'The perfect occupation for a selling agent of cloth,' said Tatya.

'Believe me, one good man with a lathi can fend off fifty attackers,' said Ponkshe enthusiastically. 'Come for a free lesson.'

'I don't see myself being attacked by fifty people anytime soon. By the way, Nana, feel free to come and hide among my bales of drill and long cloth in the warehouse in case fifty men ever start chasing you. Mami, some more of that excellent lime pickle and I'll be a happy man.'

'You work all the time,' said Ponkshe, shaking his head, as Tatya received an extra dollop of pickle. 'Now that I am out and about, free from that wretched grain shop, I see how much is going on that I missed before.'

'I have no time for loafing about Ponkshe,' said Tatya. 'And loafing costs money. A cup of tea here, a tram ride there. Forget it.'

'Look at this handbill,' said Ponkshe to Nana, ignoring Tatya.

Nana looked at it and passed it on to Tatya. It was a small square of cheap paper with the words 'Patwardhan's Shambharik Kharolika' on it.

'What's this?' said Nana, 'Who is this Patwardhan?'

'Magic lantern,' read Tatya and looked up. 'It looks like some kind of drama with special lights. On Sunday they are doing the story of Ram Vanvaas.'

'How much are the tickets?' said Nana.

'It says one anna for a seat in front.'

'So we can sit at the back.'

'Let's see,' said Tatya, dubiously.

Ponkshe grinned and punched Tatya's arm playfully. 'Yes, you shall see. You shall see this drama, whatever it is, with us on Sunday. Stop saying no to everything.' And for good measure, he also gave each of them a handbill for the Hanuman Vyayamshala which showed the outline of a lithe man vigorously wielding a lathi.

Two days later, on Sunday evening, Tatya, Nana, and Ponkshe stood among a small group of people outside a tent, under a hand-painted sign that said 'Patwardhan's Shambarik Kharolika'. The tent had been set up behind the ice-factory in Girgaon, and a bullock cart plodded past, loaded with blocks of ice covered in sack cloth, leaving a trail of dripping water in its wake. A couple of small boys jogged along behind it, laughing and squealing as they reached out and felt the cold ice with their fingers. The thick flap at the front of the tent was lifted, and everyone crowded in. A rectangular box-like enclosure, made of thin black cloth, tall enough and wide enough for four men to stand in, stood at the back of the tent. Long wooden benches were arranged to face a large white rectangle of stiff canvas that hung down from the ceiling.

'What's this?' said Nana, 'Where's the stage?'

'This is not that kind of show,' said a man who was moving down their bench collecting half-annas in a brass bowl. 'Wait and see. This is the story of Ram's exile but you've never seen it done this way.'

It was true. They had never seen anything like it.

How did those paintings move? They were works of art, lovingly rendered down to the minutest detail. What a strange illusion it was, sitting in the darkness watching the glorious adventures of Ram playing out on the canvas in front of them. Invisible musicians played the harmonium and tabla and sang praises of Ram and Sita. Intricate showers of petals fell about the couple as they moved through a leafy landscape of forests and bowers to return to the golden spires and domes of their capital Ayodhya. How did the figures glide about and how did the pink and white petals fall with such abandon? And Raavan was a daunting sight with each of his ten heads appearing and reappearing one after another, his mouth gaping wide with rage, and then the final spurt of blood that ended it all. Tatya was entranced by the spectacle.

They walked back to Khatryachi Chawl in the late evening, passing young boys with long poles lighting the gas lamps along the street. Tatya felt as if he had been transported into the sacred world of Ram and his long years in the forest. The final crescendo of music and the majesty of Ram ascending his throne and miraculously raising his hand to bless them all, flanked by Sita and Laxman, had made Tatya, Nana, and Ponkshe, along with a tent full of people, join their palms together in reverence. And yet they had not been in a temple. They were in a tent, next to an ice-factory, and someone at the back of the tent was making the paintings move in a mysterious feat of light and shadow. He must go back and see how it worked.

'Let's go back next week and see the show again,' he suggested to Nana and Ponkshe, who immediately seconded his idea. They too had been held in thrall by the show and were loudly debating as to how exactly the pictures moved.

The next Sunday, however, neither Nana nor Ponkshe was able to go with Tatya, and he sat by himself on a bench in the tent. This time he took care to find a place not in the centre of the crowd but at the far right of the tent. From here he could observe the black curtained enclosure at the back, the canvas screen, as well as the audience. He saw, also, that there was a square of thick cloth on the floor next to the screen, on which were arranged a harmonium and tabla. As the tent flap closed, and darkness fell, there was a brief scuffling sound as the musicians settled down to their instruments. Then they began playing a bhajan about the devotion of Hanuman. Tatya looked back at the enigmatic kiosk made of black cloth and saw that a man was opening the front of the kiosk to reveal a box-like contraption with a glassy eye pointed at the screen. So that was the machine that threw pictures on to the canvas. This time, as Sita wept under the Ashoka tree, he noticed a scratch in the paint at the hem of her sari; he noticed a chipped feather on a peacock's gorgeously painted tail of blue and green and gold; under the melodious blanket of the singer's voice soaring through the tent, he heard a soft clacking sound emerging from the glassy-eyed contraption every time the pictures on the screen moved. As the tabla player began a cascade of joyous drum rolls to mark the ascendance of Ram to the throne, an ecstatic viewer broke a coconut in front of the screen to mark the triumph of good over evil.

And Tatya heard the soft but distinct clink of a stream of coins being poured from a brass bowl into a cloth bag.

CHAPTER 11

After the show, as the audience stepped out of the tent, chattering and stopping to buy peanuts and chikki from roadside vendors, Tatya hung back. He saw now that the black cloth had been drawn apart and the machine was clearly visible.

'Namaskar,' he said politely to a morose-looking man next to the machine. The man held a rag in his hand and was polishing and dusting the contraption. 'My name is Govind Abhyankar. May I have a look at your machine?'

'Certainly,' said the man, cheering up, as if welcoming the distraction. 'Just don't touch it.' He watched as Tatya peered at the machine with his hands clasped politely behind his back.

'It's just a box,' said Tatya, puzzled, 'with this glass eye coming out of it. How does it hold all those enormous paintings? And how do you make them move?'

The man pointed to a sturdy table next to him. On it were piled neat stacks of small glass windows framed with wood. 'There are your enormous paintings,' he chuckled. 'All I have to do is insert the picture frames into the machine. The light from these kerosene lamps shines through and throws an enlarged image of the paintings on to the screen.'

He looked at Tatya as if evaluating whether to indulge a stranger, and then seeing Tatya's intense look of concentration, he placed one of the wooden frames in his hands.

'Hold it carefully,' he said.

Tatya looked down at a scene of Sita sitting under a tree and Hanuman peering down at her through the branches above. The white colour of her garments was luminous in the midst of the emerald-green foliage, each gem-like leaf and brown twig painted in painstaking detail. 'Beautiful,' said Tatya, appreciatively. 'Do you paint these yourself?'

'Not me, I'm just a servant. But the master's whole family is trained to paint these scenes. Now look at how we make the figures move.' He showed Tatya another glass frame which was completely blank but for the figure of Hanuman kneeling on the ground, with some leafy branches above him.

'Put the second frame on top of the first one and see what happens,' said the man.

Tatya did so, and all at once the original scene changed. Hanuman appeared to have jumped down from the tree and was kneeling at Sita's feet, while the branches above had closed to show only green leaves.

'Incredible,' said Tatya, astonished. 'So you make the images appear to move by simply sliding one frame on top of another?'

'Like magic, isn't it?' grinned the man, enjoying the look on Tatya's face. 'That's why it's called the magic lantern. Now get going before the master sees me talking instead of working.' And, still smiling, he resumed his polishing and dusting.

Nana and Ponkshe listened with interest as Tatya relayed this information to them.

'But what's the point of having a black curtain around that machine?' asked Nana.

'It's just to make people forget that the pictures they are looking at are coming from a machine. It feels more magical if they don't know how exactly it's happening,' said Tatya. The servant polishing the magic lantern hadn't actually told him this, but he felt instinctively that this must be the reason.

'Let's go back to see another show,' Nana suggested. 'This time I'll make sure to be there.'

'Well, I've seen it twice and that's enough for me. The second time wasn't as interesting as the first. And it doesn't seem so exciting once you've seen how it works.' But as Tatya spoke, he was very aware that even on his second viewing he had been carried away by the spectacle. It gave him a vague feeling of discomfort, as if he had been made to feel and see things that weren't quite real.

'Forget the magic lantern,' said Ponkshe. 'I have a better idea. Jhakaas Mandali are putting on a show at seven tomorrow evening.'

'What kind of show?' asked Nana.

'Lavani,' said Ponkshe, winking at him. 'What say you, Tatya?'

'I told you before, I have neither time nor money to waste,' said Tatya, uncomfortably.

'If you can go to a magic lantern show, why not a lavani show?' said Ponkshe.

'It's not the same, Ponkshe,' said Tatya. 'Anyway I won't be going back to see the magic lantern again. Better to be a puppeteer than a puppet who gets carried away with a bit of music and light. The show is just an illusion.'

'The women of the lavani are no illusion, I can tell you that,' laughed Ponkshe, and Tatya glanced at him with distaste. Ponkshe was changing, slowly but surely. Away from the restrictions of his old job, he had become brash and now there was something uncouth about his words. Nana looked away, embarrassed.

Tatya suddenly wished that he could be rid of Ponkshe from his room. The sooner Radha arrived, the sooner that would happen. He hoped he would not have to wait much longer. He would be sorry to lose Nana's company, though.

He spent the next six months fearful of receiving a letter from Dada informing him that a new bride had been found for him. He was afraid that Vahini would get impatient and not even wait for the promised six months to pass.

Meanwhile his selling agency began finding a firmer footing. He spent his mornings at Rose Mills or Noor Begum Mills, and his afternoons at the pedhi meeting with the wholesale dealers who bought cloth from him. He had received a few complaints from dealers who said that the cloth from Rose Mills was not up to the mark. The only solution had been to offer them a discount; on another occasion an irritable dealer insisted on returning the bales and refused to make a payment. It had all been a headache and had cut into his profits.

He gained an appointment with Matthew Wales and took a tram to Fort, to the offices of Imperial Industries. Imperial Industries was the renowned managing agency that ran Rose Mills, Chand Mills, Imperial Mills, and several other concerns including roadworks and shipping. Matthew Wales, who had assigned Tatya the selling agency, was a young man from Lancashire and had arrived in India just a few years ago. He was in charge of getting the new Rose Mills up and running. Having arrived early, Tatya waited outside his office. He had barely settled into his chair when the door opened and Wales appeared. He was a tall, broad man, just a few years older than Tatya himself, and yet looked rather boyish with his brown hair cut like a schoolboy's. Wales was politely—and with great ceremony—ushering out another English gentleman who was short and stout, dressed in an immaculate navy-blue suit. The gold chain of a pocket watch hung on his lapel, and his full head of white hair made two precise waves on the top of his head. Tatya wondered where he had seen him before. He would not presume to ask Matthew Wales, of course. But Wales remarked on it himself.

'That was Sir Francis Wheeler, one of the managing directors of Imperial Industries,' said Wales, taking Tatya into his office. 'He takes a direct interest in the running of Imperial Mills and much of the shipping business.'

Of course—that was where Tatya had seen him. He had been to the Imperial Mills once on an errand for Zaveri, and had seen Sir Francis, with his distinct wavy white hair, in a sleek grey car that glittered in the sunshine and slid smoothly through the gates. 'That car is called a Bentley, you didn't know that did you,' one of the gatekeepers had announced with a swagger to everyone and no one in particular, as he let Tatya in along with several other people. 'Fine car, eh?'

Tatya longed to be a selling agent of Imperial Mills. But it was such a venerable old mill that it was a closed fortress for a relative newcomer like himself. He decided to focus on the task at hand.

'Mr Wales, I want my business to be known as the selling agency where it is easy to do business,' began Tatya, sitting down in Wales' spacious, high-ceilinged office, 'and where buyers never have to check the cloth because it is consistently of high quality. But there have been some problems lately, particularly with the dyeing of the cloth.' And Tatya told him all about the defective bales that he had sold at a discount. 'Surely Rose Mills also would like to be perceived as the mill that supplies only top quality cloth.'

Sitting behind his enormous claw-footed desk, Wales looked surprised at this little speech. Tatya was aware that he was equating his own reputation with that of Rose Mills, rather presumptuously, but he had to let Wales know that he was dead serious about getting good quality cloth for his customers. 'It is a seller's market, Mr Wales,' he continued, 'I don't need to tell you that. Everything you produce is sold, one way or another. But the sooner the quality of Rose Mills' cloth is established in the market, the better it will be for your business. And mine, naturally. My aim is to sell large volumes of Rose Mills cloth at premium prices. But I can only do that if the quality is consistent and competitive.'

'I am aware that we are going through some teething problems,' said Wales, nodding, 'and there have been a few unfortunate changes of personnel even at this early stage in the mill's functioning. Since you mention recurring problems with dyeing I will, of course, look into it.'

'If I may,' said Tatya, 'I would like to be more closely involved in checking the quality of the cloth. If I could regularly visit the holding department,

I would be able to immediately pinpoint any problems.'

'By all means,' said Wales shrugging, 'check the quality of the cloth at the mill itself. It would be beneficial to both of us.'

So it was that Tatya began a close and daily interaction with Rose Mills, to check that he received the promised quantities of cloth without any defects. Rose Mills bore all the marks of the pomp associated with Imperial Industries. Mounted above the entrance was a giant stone medallion carved with a rose. The modern red brick structure caught the sunlight and emitted a rosy glow, while inside, its cavernous spaces were filled with row upon row of looms tended by an army of workers, the women in thin cotton saris and the men in loose sadra-pyjamas. He spent most mornings in the holding department where the finished cloth came for packing. Here he kept a sharp eye on the quality of the bleaching and dyeing. It then gave him immense pleasure to see the cloth passing through the folding machines with the operator cutting the cloth into the required lengths. Neat bundles of ten or twenty metres, all passed on to the inky fingers of the workers who squatted on the floor and used a manual screen and ink to stamp the cloth with the Rose Mills icon. With an efficient clack-clack sound, the red outline of a large rose appeared on one bundle after another. It was satisfying beyond measure to slap his palm down on a bale of cloth and know that he was going to pass on good, sturdy quality to his buyers.

In fact, he thought, the only way to get a grip on the whole thing was to familiarize himself with how the cloth was produced from start to finish. He began going to the mills earlier and earlier, so that he could observe their functioning as a whole.

At Noor Begum Mills, which spun its own yarn, he saw cleaned, ginned cotton arriving at the mill in giant bundles bound with iron hoops. He learnt to distinguish between the superior cotton that would be combed and pampered for shirt material, and lower quality cotton destined for rougher use. He watched the shuttles on the clattering looms as they shot back and forth to create the weft of the cloth, while the warp went up and down, up and down, in different patterns, as if it were a pen writing a cacophonous and splendid poem. Towering over it all were chimneys that dwarfed the mills, the humans, and the land itself.

And Tatya began to think of the mills not simply as the place where he procured cloth, or a structure in which were arrayed innumerable machines and vats and spindles—nor simply as an assemblage of departments and foremen and schedules—but as a thing of exhilaration. As certain as the sun that rose at dawn, so it was certain that if you inserted cotton from a sun-baked field in Surat into the clattering, grinding system of a mill in Bombay, it would come out at the other end as thousand-yard bales of cloth. It was a strange thing of beauty, this system that was as implacable as a set of mathematical equations.

Long after he made his way out of the mills to head to his pedhi, the rhythm of warp and weft pulsed in his eardrums like a compelling drum beat.

CHAPTER 12

1905

It was still dark when Yamuna stirred in her bed and heard the faintest timorous sounds of the morning. Unnameable, nothing more than a pre-dawn cool that brushed against fronds and leaves. And then all was hushed again. She opened her eyes, looked at her palms and murmured a mantra. *Karaagre vaste Lakshmi, karmadhye Saraswati; Karmule tu Govind, prabhate kardarshanam*—Lakshmi is in my fingertips, in my palms lives Saraswati, Govind resides in the heel of my palm, I pray to them all this morning. It was important that her gaze fell first on the pure and the divine in the morning. She rubbed her palms over her face and then sat up. Her room was on the upper floor of the small, silent wada. She peeped out of the latticed window. Usually when she woke the sun blessed the top of the mango tree with a drizzle of light which soon spilt its golden liquid on to the cowshed nearby. But this morning all was dark. She lay down again and stared at the ceiling. But this did not feel right either. She stepped out of her room, looked down into the central courtyard around which all the rooms were arranged, and listened carefully. Mai was not up yet. Nobody else in the wada seemed to be awake either.

Tucked away in rooms adjoining the wada at the back were Krishna kaka and his family, relations from Chakhan who had settled permanently in the village. They were asleep too. Yamuna quietly made her way down the narrow staircase, ornately carved but the wood tired and faded. Most of the rooms in the wada were empty, crumbling.

This morning Yamuna's mind felt like a damp blanket, as if she hadn't fully woken from a long, puzzling dream. She stepped down into the courtyard and the square structure of the wada rose above her on all four sides, foreboding in the darkness, the open doorways of its empty rooms like blank eye sockets staring down at her. She felt a tingling at the back of her neck. Was it possible that it was still the middle of the night? Had she simply risen, feeling wide awake, because of what happened yesterday? No way of telling what time it was—all was dark and quiet. She tucked in her padar at her waist as she stood there, indecisive. Then she stepped towards the entrance and pulled aside the ancient chain that hung across the large double doors. Its heavy links slipped through her fingers like a live thing and crashed to the floor. There was no response from within the wada to this thunderous sound. Once outside, she heard a muted clang, perhaps the bell that hung around the neck of their neighbour's bull. Then there was silence again, as if the bull had simply shifted in its sleep. She walked round to the side of the wada towards a large earthen pot. She dipped a smaller pot in. A bubbling, gulping sound as it filled up with water. She picked up a long stick lying nearby. Then she began making her way through a small thicket of coconut trees to the forested area beyond. All the way there she banged the stick on the ground to warn away snakes. At the edge of the forest, she stopped where the mud was damp and clean, gathered a handful, and went further in. Then she squatted down for her morning routine and, more importantly at the moment, to check for blood. But it was too dark to see much. She would have to check again later. She was far too early. She washed herself with the water, rubbed the mud on her hands and feet to clean them, and then washed off the mud.

As she trudged back to the wada a faint glimmer from the sky lit her path through the tangle of trees. So faint and silvery, it might as well have been moonlight. But it was light nevertheless, and she ceased banging her stick on the ground for she could see now. She could check once more here. Once again she squatted down to look. No blood. Her clothes were clean.

And now the weight of last night came slithering down on her again. Last night she could bury Mai's words under her blanket, push them down into her pillow with her weary head. But those words had escaped from that bed now. They had risen with her, flapped their wings behind her back and set themselves free into the darkness of the wada; and they had followed her here, slowly drawing their strength from the approaching morning. It was not yet dawn. There was still time, and the words still felt newborn, their eyelids were still glued shut. But she knew that with the morning's first light they would open their pebble-grey eyes and harden in the rising heat of the sun. It was still quite dark, though. Almost as dark as last night when Mai appeared by her bed. She had not slept in Mai's room since she returned from Dhangadh—Mai said she must not get used to sleeping with her mother again, because she would soon go to Bombay. She must get used to sleeping away from Mai. And so she was alone in her room and Mai was

Tejaswini Apte-Rahm

alone in hers. It may yet prove to be a pointless discipline, she thought, since.... Well, that was the point of it all. The point of Mai's shadowed face, the point of coming to Yamuna when the oil lamp in the room was on the verge of dimming and dying. In the darkness there was a crinkling of paper. Yamuna stared, frightened, at the shape of her mother drawing closer to her bed, at the silhouette of her smooth skull wound tight under her thin padar. Her fearless mother had chosen to keep her face in the shadows. She could not bear her daughter to see her face when she said: they have started looking for a second wife. You will always be the first wife. You will be taken care of. They will send us money. But you cannot go and live with him. *You cannot go.* Mai rested her palm on Yamuna's small forehead, lightly at first, and then firmly, pushing the back of Yamuna's head into the pillow, willing her to bury herself in sleep, sending the spoken words into dreams that spiralled away into the night. Yamuna fell asleep.

But now the sun had risen, and shown her everything: how it was, and how it would be. The dull yellow colour of the wada, its neat bright yard with a fragrant corner swathed in the morning star-fall of the parijat tree, and the rows of methi and small cucumbers which Yamuna had planted; and how she had cried to leave it all behind, and how sad it was that she would live among all these things forevermore.

CHAPTER 13

As Yamuna walked back towards the faded yellow walls of the wada, absently breaking off a twig from a low branch of a kadu-limb tree, she felt Mai's eyes on her. Sure enough, as she lifted her gaze to the first floor, Mai was standing there, immobile at her carved wooden window, watching her. Her red sari covered her head and arms so completely that she looked like an old red cloth doll with a face stitched on. By the time Yamuna reached the heavy double-doors of the wada, Mai had descended the stairs and stood at the doors, waiting. This morning her eyes were as cold and stone-grey as ever, but her mouth had a gentle, weary smile on it. Come child, she said, as she turned to go in, there is warm milk for you. Yamuna nodded, and returned a tentative smile. Quickly she chewed one end of the twig till it softened into a fibrous mass, rubbed her teeth with it till they felt clean and fresh, and washed her mouth with water just outside the yard. Then she poured a tumbler of water on her feet and followed her mother inside.

The day must be lived like any other day. Before bathing Yamuna swept the yard, but did not feel like singing any bhupalya today, the way she usually did. She wrapped her padar around her face so that the dust would not fly into her nose, but it was no good, there had been a wind in the night and the ground was covered in bits of earth and leaf litter that flew up around her as she swept. She fetched a pitcher of water and sprinkled it across the yard to settle the dust. After that she got on better and soon all the leaves and twigs and pebbles were swept to one side.

'Eh Jhumpya,' she shouted. 'Bring me the mud and dung.'

Without waiting for Jhumpya to appear, Yamuna started walking with brisk steps to the cattle shed. She could hear the sounds of the wada waking and stirring. Behind the wada, a wheel creaked as Lata tai, her cousin's wife, drew water from the well. From within came the scraping sound of the inner courtyard being swept, and the morning clatter of pots in the kitchen. The air was still cool and the light was temperate and mellow, for the sun hadn't warmed up yet. The smooth, milky cry of a peacock flew through the air, joining the growing chirruping and cawing tumbling forth from trees and across yellow fields. Soon she was back in the yard along with Jhumpya, a bucket of cow dung in her hands, while he carried a bucket of mud. Jhumpya was the boy who looked after their cattle—they didn't have too many, just two cows, two buffaloes, and a bull. He was an obliging fellow, helping with all sorts of odd jobs around the wada. He was a bit older than Yamuna, but short and undergrown. Mai fed him buffalo milk every day, but it appeared to make no difference to his height. He was, however, very strong.

'Shall I mix it up?' asked Jhumpya.

'No, I'll do it,' said Yamuna. 'It won't take long.'

'It won't take you any time at all,' observed Jhumpya. 'I got good yellow mud from the forest yesterday, you won't find too many stones or anything in it.'

'Where from? Next to the tamarind grove up the hill?'

'Beyond that,' he said. 'Closer to the stream near Dinkar rao's land. I made three trips yesterday, we have plenty now.'

Yamuna dumped half the dung into the mud, quickly removing any small stones and twigs. Then she poured in water, kneading it in till she got a thick pasty mixture. Jhumpya settled down on the ground waiting for her to finish.

'This is good dung,' he said. 'Our cows are always at home, you see, they don't eat any old rubbish. Not like that Sambhaji's cows. He lets them roam anywhere they like, eating all kinds of things, and then complains that they give neither good dung nor good milk. But why should I go blabbing to him, he'll just give me a cuff on the ear. Has he ever taken advice from anyone in his life?'

Yamuna only half-listened to Jhumpya, letting the words wash over her, soothing her by not letting her think too much about other things. As soon as she had finished preparing the mixture, Jhumpya picked up the bucket with the remaining dung and trotted away to milk the cows. The cows and buffaloes were stirring now and Yamuna could hear a lowing in the cattle shed and the restless rustle of hay. Now and then the clang of a cow bell rang out clear and bright. She began spreading the mud and dung paste over the yard, moving quickly on her haunches.

'I'll give you a hand,' said a voice, and Gopi tai, Krishna kaka's daughter, appeared, tucking in one end of her padar at her waist. She was married and lived five hours away by bullock cart and visited about twice a year. Yamuna was glad of the help, but also glad that she had blended the mud and dung before Gopi tai arrived. Gopi tai always made the mixture too liquid, which meant the floor took forever to dry. Gopi tai settled on her haunches and got to work, but not before a look passed between them. Yamuna stared miserably at the floor. It was pity she saw in Gopi tai's eyes. Had the news reached her already? Or was she imagining it?

Gopi tai was in the habit of wearing a large red kunku on her forehead. It always reminded Yamuna of the blazing sun. Not today, though. Today she simply noticed how blood-red it was. And so it went on through the day, Yamuna going about her chores in the wada, in the backyard, in the courtyard, noticing all the reds that reminded her of blood. Perhaps it is not too late, she thought, they can't possibly have found a new bride already. This is simply a letter informing Mai of their *intention* to find a new bride. Perhaps my blood will still come before they find one. This thought soothed her for an hour or so, it allowed her to eat her late morning meal of bhakri and aubergine bhaaji without her stomach churning. But then another question began haunting her. When had that letter really arrived? Perhaps it had arrived several days ago—a month ago, even!—and perhaps Mai had kept it to herself, hoping that everything would turn out all right and that she wouldn't need to tell Yamuna about it. *Perhaps Mai decided to tell me now because she has already received the next letter informing her that a new bride has been found.* Yamuna did not dare to ask her mother, of course. And once again, the cycle of worry and despair spun through her head, and she went through the day noticing the reds everywhere, the mocking blood-reds. The delicate hibiscus she plucked for her daily worship, her offering to Ganpati. The chillies spread out to dry in the yard, crackling red in the sun. The ripe tomatoes, hiding under tiny green leaves that crouched low on the ground. The red paint decorating the horns of their majestic white bull. The pretty pomegranate she picked in their little grove of fruit trees, slicing the fruit open to reveal its dripping insides, each seed a juicy bloody jewel.

It was only in the early afternoon, when Mai lay down for a nap, and the still landscape of onion fields and millet fields simmered under the mid-day sun; when nothing moved save for the thick lines of large black ants skittering up and down the waxy green banana trees under Mai's latticed window; when Yamuna settled down to mend a tear in her choli, chequered by the diamond-shaped sunlight that streamed in; when the needle pricked her finger, drawing a bright bead of blood—it was only then that the tears pricked her eyelids and she could not stop them from streaming down her cheeks.

A stifled sob was all that was needed to wake Mai, who opened her eyes, blinking and squinting at a beam of light that fell across the grey stone floor. In another moment, she had crossed the room and her arm was around Yamuna.

'Cry all you want,' she said. 'Sometimes it is our destiny to cry. Let all the tears fall and get them out of the way once and for all.'

'What was it all for,' sobbed Yamuna. 'Our journey to the forest temple of Jambul Mata. And all those months I spent in Dhangadh with Vahini and Dadasaheb. They treated me so well, Mai. They are such good people. Vahini taught me so much. Why are they doing this to me now?'

'Nobody is doing anything to you,' said Mai. 'This is the way of the world.' Her arm around Yamuna's shoulders tightened. 'I lay awake at night, thinking,' she continued. 'They—including your husband, I think—are not keen on choosing a new bride. They simply feel that they have no other choice left. So I do not intend to give up yet. We will ask for six more months. I will speak to Narayan bhau today. He will write to them.'

Yamuna's tears stopped, and she wiped her face dry with the end of her padar, with a small feeling of hope. It was Mai's fear last night that had frightened her so. Seeing the usual determination on Mai's face made her feel very much better.

'Do you think they will agree?' she asked.

Her mother looked at her for a moment, and then said, 'It does not matter what I think. It matters what they think. We will wait for their reply.'

Yamuna stared at her mother, her eyes swollen and red. Mai looked at her daughter's tear-streaked face. 'Meanwhile,' said Mai, 'we have much to do.'

And so, with the fear of six months hanging over her head, Yamuna embarked on every fast and ritual that the months threw at her, every form of self-purification and atonement for past sins that Mai could think of. She fasted for nine days for Ram Navmi, eating one frugal meal of bananas and milk a day; on the ninth day, she rocked the cradle with a silken baby Ram in it; put sunthavda on her tongue, savoured the sweet spiciness of the ginger–sugar preparation, and showered the silken baby with petals and grains of rice at noon, the time of the divine birth. If only, if only, my blood arrives, she prayed, I might have a son like you, divine Ram. At Gangaotsav, there was no river nearby to wash away her sins, so for ten pale dawns she stood ankle-deep in a pond fed by a stream, pouring water on her head, chanting 'Har Har Gange Bhagirathi', accompanied by the wet plopping sounds of frogs. To the stream she offered flowers, a ripe mango, wheat, and rice, closing her eyes and praying for the holiness of the Ganga to wash away all ten sins. The small trickle of water, like a thin, watery twig, flowed past her and pooled at the foot of a low, smooth stone dabbed with yellow and red—a devi at the edge of the pond. At Vat Savitri she ground a nugget of sandalwood into paste and used it to trace out on a wall, with her finger, the outlines of a banyan tree, and the figures of Satyavan, his wife Savitri who brought him back to life, and Yamraj the lord of death. She fasted and worshipped these images for three days. Bless my husband with a long life, bless me with a long married life, she prayed. During the divine month of Ashaad, she observed the Kokila Vrat, fasting and worshipping Parvati, praying for a healthy body so that she might bear a son. She broke her fast only when she had heard the sweet sound of the kokila bird and, rushing outside, glimpsed a flash of its black feathers before it flapped away. She joined her hands in prayer at the sight, for Parvati had existed as a melodious kokila for ten thousand years. She launched the holy months of Chaturmas by fasting all day and eating only in the evening, abstaining from onion and aubergine and garlic and radishes and various kinds of beans and a host of other ingredients. When Shraavan began, the cool, wet month of rains, she observed Shraavani Somvar, worshipping Shiva every Monday for a month by offering him bel leaves. The other women fasted on this day too, but Yamuna was already in the midst of a four-month fast for Chaturmas. On Janmashthami, yet another fast, and she once again rocked the cradle, praying for blood, praying for a child, and gazed down at the infant Krishna who had taken the place of Ram in the cradle; she once again showered the baby with flowers and grains of rice, and shared the ginger–sugar sunthavda with the other women.

She had fasted before, of course, as did all the women and girls in the wada, but never had she done it for months at a stretch, never with such single-minded devotion, never had she so willed the gods to protect her. Never had she been so terrified that if every prayer, fast, and ritual did not attain an impossible perfection, the gods would never notice her miniscule existence among the vastness of the fields and villages that tumbled away into the distance and the chorus of millions of prayers sent up into the sky.

CHAPTER 14

After a rain-soaked night came the festival of Pola. At midnight, gusts of wind bore down on the landscape, driving in front of them a single massive sheet of water that beat down for hours, bending every plant, tree, and blade of grass into shivering, hunchbacked shadows. But the morning of Pola emerged washed and clean, all the greens of fields and fruit orchards glorious in honey-coloured sunlight.

It had been months since Yamuna had felt so cheerful. She loved Pola, the festival of celebrating and worshipping the family's bull. She adored the rituals around her uncle Narayan mama's bull, helping to decorate him as majestically as possible, after he had been drenched in water and scrubbed to a pure white.

'Do you remember, Mai, the two small clay bulls Narayan mama gave me when I was small? How I loved them!' Yamuna and Mai were sitting on the floor of the kitchen making alu vadis. Mai was slicing rolls of steamed, spiced alu leaves into thin spirals, and passing them to Yamuna to fry.

Mai nodded, smiling. 'I remember very well.' She turned to Lata tai and Manda tai, Narayan mama's daughters-in-law, who sat next to them. Both were heavily pregnant and busy rolling out puran polis. 'Yami even wanted to wash them and scrub them just like real bulls. I had to convince her that if she immersed them in the pond, they would break. How she cried when I stopped her from washing them!'

'I had clay bulls too,' said Manda tai, stopping to rest a moment, sweat glistening on her plump face. 'I painted them red with kunku and made yellow haldi spots on them.'

'Oh, that's what I did!' said Yamuna in delight. 'And I tied a marigold on to the back of each one to pretend that....'

Jhumpya interrupted from the window. 'Mai saheb, where are the garlands?' he called.

This year Yamuna, Lata tai, and Manda tai had made several garlands of red and yellow tassels to tie around the bull's neck. Mai, meanwhile, had stitched together pieces of old saris, several embroidered in gold thread, resulting in a large colourful rectangle to drape over the bull's broad back.

75

'Go on, quick,' said Mai to Yamuna. 'It looks like they are almost ready to leave. I'll carry on with the alu vadis.'

Yamuna carried the garlands and patchwork cloth to the yard in front of the cattle shed where the bull stood obediently. Jhumpya, looking proud and important, was in the midst of tying bunches of marigolds to the horns of the bull. The horns were so tall that he stood on his toes to tie them, and Narayan mama remarked, 'Shall I lift you, Jhumpya, so that you can reach them?' and everyone standing around, including Yamuna, burst out laughing, though it was not a particularly funny joke. All the men were there, only her brother Raghu was missing, for he was away at work. Narayan mama's sons, Anant bhau and Purshottam bhau, were there, and so were Krishna kaka and Shridhar kaka. Krishna kaka's son, Viju, was jogging towards the cattle shed, carrying a sheaf of banana leaves. Ahu kaku and Shanti kaku, the wives of Krishna kaka and Shridhar kaka, stood by, having just completed an elaborate pink and white rangoli. Several small children capered about, giddy with the festive air about them, making Yamuna feel rather old. But she was all smiles today, and felt proud and gratified when Narayan mama said 'vah!', looking thoroughly pleased as the tasselled garlands and patchwork cloth added a sudden splash of colour to the animal. Manda tai, as the older of the two daughters-in-law, waddled out of the house and bent down to wash the hooves of the bull, and worshipped him with lit camphor and incense sticks and flowers, applying haldi and kunku on his beautiful broad white forehead. From nearby rose a cacophony of drums, and it was clear to everyone that the dhol tasha had started. The procession of bulls was underway.

'Chala, chala,' said Narayan mama. 'It is time. Jhumpya, get going.' And off they went, Jhumpya leading the bull with Narayan mama, following the exciting sounds of the dhol tasha. Further down the path, they joined other brightly decorated bulls being led by their owners. From afar came the sound of someone breaking into a bhajan about Lord Mahadev.

Watching the menfolk and children go down the path, Yamuna felt light-headed. Every few days, the strain of fasting made the daytime hours a struggle, and some days she longed for the evening to come so that she could eat her fill. She took the puja platter from Manda tai and they both headed back to the kitchen, the house now quiet. Yamuna was subdued, she no longer felt the happy excitement of just a few minutes ago. Her spirits had soared that morning, only to come crashing down. It must be the lack of food, the stillness after the animation, perhaps she needed to drink some water. She did not know the reason. In any case there was no time to think now, for she must participate in the increasing clatter of the kitchen where the women prepared the meal, as well as the naivedya of puran poli and alu vadis that must be fed to the bull on his return. Yamuna cut onions, plucked methi from the backyard, peeled potatoes, and stuffed karanjis with jaggery-sweetened coconut because Mai had decided that they needed to make another sweet in addition to the puran poli. By the time the bull returned home to the accompaniment of a single tasha player, who Narayan mama had roped in to play for them, Yamuna was drenched in perspiration. Mai glanced at her once or twice, puzzled, but there was too much to do to stop and talk about anything. Yamuna hoped it was not a fever, though it certainly felt like it. She would get a quick drink of water in the kitchen before going outdoors again. All the women had deserted the kitchen now for the return of the bull, carrying the naivedya with them, and she stood leaning against the window, peering out, as the drumming grew louder and louder. Mai stood outside, watching from a distance, for she could not, of course, allow her shadow to fall on the ceremony.

Her head aching, Yamuna took another sip of water. As it trickled down her throat, she felt another trickling sensation, this time on her thighs, and the next thing she saw was Mai gazing at her through the open window, watching her intently.

'What is it?' Mai said, tersely.

'Mai,' said Yamuna, her voice shaking, 'should it feel sticky?'

'Yes,' said Mai, stepping forward and clutching at the windowsill, her eyes wide and shining with tears. 'Yes, go and check.'

'Then I do not need to check,' said Yamuna, breaking into a sob.

And Mai joined her palms in prayer, raising them to her forehead. Then she pulled herself together and rushed into the kitchen to hustle Yamuna out of it, for Yamuna was now a polluting presence. Under no circumstances must she go into the kitchen, or near any cooked food or source of water, or near the gods. Yamuna knew this already, of course, for all the women of the house observed these rules of purity and pollution once a month. And yet, it was a minor shock to her to be pushed out of the kitchen and into the small shed behind the wada, in a small barren clearing, shielded from the house by a few shrubs. Here she must stay for three days, letting no man see her. The room was completely bare, save for a frayed mat rolled up in a corner of the room. Mai shut the door, enclosing Yamuna inside. In a short while she returned with an old sheet, washed but stained with past traces of blood, and a pile of old rags. When Mai opened the door, Yamuna was still standing in the middle of the bare room, in exactly the same position, with a dazed look on her face.

Mai studied her a moment, and then said, 'Sit down, you foolish girl.'

'Your fasting and prayers have borne fruit,' she said, as Yamuna cautiously settled down on the ground, unused to the alien sensation between her legs. 'God has been kind to us. I have decided that there is no need for you to fast anymore. Any sin you commit by breaking your fast, I take upon my head. You are weak from fasting and you will become weaker with the loss of blood because you are not used to it.'

Yamuna nodded, relieved that she would not have to go hungry till the evening. Absurdly, her first thought was for the alu vadis and puran polis, last glimpsed hot and fresh in the kitchen. In the distance she could hear the sounds of the tasha, joyously beating out its rhythms. It all seemed so far away now, as if she had seen the procession go off not this morning but weeks ago.

'You need your strength for the journey to Bombay,' continued Mai, 'for it is imperative that you lie with your husband within sixteen days.'

Yamuna nodded again. That seemed far off in the distance too. As far in the distance as the sounds of the tasha and the stomping of their bull. She wondered whether Mai would tell her anything about the part where she would lie with her husband. It was a mystery to her. She dared not ask, of course. Perhaps Lata tai or Manda tai might enlighten her. But she would not dare ask them either.

Mai put the rags into Yamuna's hands. 'Put that where you are bleeding and sit still. Sleep if you want.'

Yamuna took the wad of cloths gingerly, and looked at them. They had been cut from old cotton saris. Mai glanced at her and said, 'Do you know why there is no pillow or mattress for you to sleep on?'

'No,' said Yamuna, looking around her. It had not occurred to her that her bed would be a hard one tonight.

'It is because a pillow and a mattress cannot be purified by washing. You will, of course, wash out the mat and the sheet at the end of the three days,' said Mai, briskly. 'Either I am a fool for not teaching you this earlier, or you are a fool for not observing what all the women in the house do every month.'

For days now, indeed for months, Mai, known for her brusque tongue, had been kinder in her speech, at least towards Yamuna. As if she wanted to cocoon her daughter in gentle words, to soften the pitiless workings of fate. But there was no need for that now, and Yamuna, recognizing this, smiled broadly at Mai.

'Has anything entered your head or not?' said Mai, crossly.

'Don't worry about me, Mai,' said Yamuna, still smiling, 'there is plenty for me to learn, and I will learn it all.'

'You had better,' said Mai.

It was as if another festival had broken out in the wada, completely overshadowing the gaiety of Pola. Except that Yamuna did not witness any of it, save for the smiling faces of Lata tai, Manda tai, and Mai peeping in at her with joy and relief on their faces. Even Shanti kaku and Ahu kaku, normally sour-faced, found it in themselves to look in on her.

'Great preparations are afoot,' announced Lata tai, teasingly, 'for you will soon be going to your husband. I hear that your Narayan mama is going to send a telegram to Bombay.'

Yamuna sat leaning against the wall, feeling the uncomfortable damp spread beneath her. The wad of rags between her legs was no match for the wetness, but she had no chance of changing the rags or even going to relieve herself till nightfall, since it was forbidden for any man to see her, even accidentally, for three days.

'Lata tai, wait,' said Yamuna, shifting awkwardly. 'Is it always so uncomfortable?' Lata tai paused a moment, and nodded, a sympathetic look on her face.

'Yes,' she said, 'except when you are with child. Then there is no blood for at least nine months.'

Yamuna's eyes widened. 'Really? I didn't know that!'

'Haven't you noticed?' said Lata tai, in an admonishing tone, 'Manda tai and I have not used this room in months.'

'Oh,' said Yamuna, 'how foolish of me. I did not realize.'

'Better look about you, my girl,' said Lata tai. 'You're going to your husband's home. You can't live with your head in the clouds and expect to be treated the same way as you are here, in your Narayan mama's house.' She laid on the floor a pannier of toor dal for Yamuna to pick over and clean and hurried away.

Mai prepared a different sweet dish for her on all three days, sent with Shanti kaku, Shridhar kaka's wife, who, by the third day, appeared to have had enough of the fuss. She put down the plate of shira mixed with soft pieces of banana and sliced soaked almonds, muttering something inaudible about extravagance and almonds. Yamuna decided to avoid ruffling her feathers any further, and simply pushed forward her plate and bowl from her morning meal. As per custom, she turned them over so that they were face down. Shanti kaku sprinkled some water on them as purification before picking them up and, unable to stop herself from speaking, said, 'Do you think anybody made this kind of fuss over me when I started my monthly time? I was in my mother-in-law's house. She pushed me into a stinking room and left me there for three days with only one meal a day and one tambya of water that had to last me till the next meal.' And she added, with relish, 'Don't expect this outside of your Narayan mama's house, my girl.'

'Kaku, all these sweets are only because it is my first time,' said Yamuna. 'Mai said so.'

'Your Mai can say whatever comes into her head,' said Shanti kaku, resentfully, 'it's her brother's house after all.'

Yamuna said no more. Let her say what she likes, she thought, annoyed, knowing full well that Shanti kaku would not dare to say anything of the sort to Mai's face.

She was also annoyed, and rather apprehensive, at the various warnings from people about life with her husband. She thought back to her months with Vahini and Dadasaheb, which were hard work but perfectly peaceable apart from a few scoldings received from Vahini about mistakes she made in the kitchen. Vahini had schooled her well in their family's way of doing things, and Yamuna was fairly confident of remembering most of the things Vahini had drilled into her. But any misgivings melted into nothing at the sheer joy and relief she felt at having escaped a life lived in the twilight, neither married nor widowed, neither bound nor free.

A couple of stray pups gambolled about outside her window on the first evening, till their mother, a lame creature with a torn ear, led them some distance away where Yamuna could hear their squeals and whimpers in the approaching darkness. Late at night, overcome with fatigue, having cried streams of tears, without knowing why she was crying, she fell into a deep slumber.

The next morning, under cover of the pre-dawn darkness, when she headed off to relieve herself, and wash and change her blood-soaked rags, her head was as light as a single petal of a bougainvillea flower; it had been stuffed with coal before, which had gone up in smoke. By afternoon, she was itching for a bath, but she wasn't allowed one for three days. The sweaty stench that surrounded her and the physical discomfort dampened her spirits. The exhilaration of the first day had sent birds from her chest soaring forth in flight, and now she waited, expectant, feeling rather empty, for them to return.

On the second morning, she peeped out to look at the children playing in the backyard. She could see the five-year-old twin sons of Manda tai and the nine-year-old daughter of Ahu kaku who had already recieved a proposal and would be married the following Diwali. She shouted angrily at the older children for letting Lata tai's year-old baby crawl towards a goat that had strayed into the yard and made funny faces at the children to make them laugh when they pranced up to her door to wave at her. As her three days of seclusion passed, one long day at a time, myriad weights tied to her neck, ankles, and shoulders, floated off into the air. Anxieties she did not even know existed loosened their hold on her hair and her chest, seemingly by the hour. And so it went on, one weight after another dissolving into nothing.

When, on the fourth morning, she was finally allowed to bathe, she felt nothing but elation. Her skin came alive as the cold water washed away sweat and blood, and she emerged fresh and glowing. After another two days, there was the garbhdaan ceremony. During Yamuna's seclusion Mai had spread the word among their immediate neighbours, and five or six women from the neighbouring households arrived on the morning of the sixth day, wearing smiles and bearing small gifts of rice and coconut and grains.

Once again, Mai had to stay away from this auspicious ceremony, while Ahu kaku and Shanti kaku, the eldest married women in the house, took the lead. In a small, enclosed courtyard by the kitchen, Lata tai had laid out a low wooden paat and drawn a simple but colourful pattern of red and white rangoli around it. As Yamuna sat on the paat, she caught a glimpse of her mother peeping into the courtyard from the kitchen. Their eyes met and Yamuna gave her a small smile before Mai disappeared. Yamuna knew that Mai had returned to the smoky stove, busily continuing the preparations for lunch. She felt unexpected tears in her throat, for she was overwhelmed at the thought—not a new thought, but a miserable one nonetheless—that she could never share the happiest, most auspicious occasions of her life with her mother. And she sent a prayer up to the gods in the sky—*do not let me become a widow, let me die before my husband.* She blinked away the tears in her eyes as Lata tai appeared with a bowl of coconut oil and a fragrant utne made of turmeric, chickpea flour, sandalwood, and khus, mixed with warm milk to make a paste. Then the women crowded around her, all taking turns to rub the oil and utne on to Yamuna's body, applying shikakai to her hair, pouring tambyas of warm water on her, and patting her dry. Finally, they dressed her in a new sari.

All the while, the women talked and gossiped in low voices amongst themselves, asking her a question now and then, such as when she would leave for Bombay, and whether she had already been bathed in her marital home.

'Yes,' nodded Yamuna, 'Vahini bathed me once in Dhangadh.'

'What did she say, did she say anything?' asked a stooped, wrinkled woman, her faded green eyes squinting at Yamuna.

'No, nothing,' said Yamuna.

'What could she say, Ajji,' replied Manda tai, vigorously rubbing utne on Yamuna's back. 'You can see for yourself—our Yamuna's skin is flawless, everything is perfectly fine.'

'That's all very well,' said the old woman known simply as Ajji in the village, 'but when my mother-in-law bathed me to check for defects, she threatened to tell everybody that I had boils on my back if I wasn't obedient. Those boils existed only in her mind. But I was scared as a mouse afterwards and always did everything she told me to do. Who wants the shame of people talking about you like that?'

Her daughter-in-law, a grey-haired grandmother herself, said sympathetically, 'What could you have done anyway, you were only nine years old.'

'Nine?' said Ajji, indignantly. 'In my family all girls were married by seven, none of these new customs of waiting till the girl is nine and ten.'

'Poor Yami has waited long enough,' sighed Gangu mavshi, their neighbour. 'Lord Mahadev has saved her.' Overwhelmed, Gangu mavshi wiped her eyes with the end of her padar and repeated, 'Mahadev saved you, dear child.'

Yamuna looked fondly at her. 'Don't cry, dear Mavshi,' she said, and looking around at the other women, was touched to see that many of them had wet eyes. She looked down again, thinking how narrow their individual roads were, and how small missteps of fate could push them all on to a dark path of no return.

Still, by the end of her bath she felt radiant and special, and she settled down to a short puja conducted by the village priest. Then the women blessed her, circling her face with a tabak, a small platter on which were arrayed a niranjan with a lit flame, a whole supari, grains of rice, and a small vial of haldi-kunku which they applied to her forehead.

And then it was all over.

The months of waiting, the terror, the fasting, the weeping, the seclusion, the stink of the bloodied rags, the bathing, and the ceremonies. It was over. Even the all-encompassing feeling of relief had faded. All that remained to be done was for the gathered women to enjoy a delicious meal of sweet, creamy shrikhand and hot puris that had been prepared under Mai's supervision. It really was the very last thing. For the next morning, Yamuna's brother, Raghu, arrived to take her to Bombay.

But she was Yamuna no longer. Now she would be Radha.

CHAPTER 15

There he was at the train station. He had come to receive them. She remembered brown eyes but not much else, for she had never looked at him directly. It had been more than a year since she had seen him. There was a small bird in her heart, and it kept fluttering its wings so that she could not help but smile. No more the sadness of leaving home. Happy, laughing Raghu would not stay the night, he refused to stay a moment more than necessary in her marital home at this glad, auspicious time. It was her time now, the time for her married life to begin, no time at all for her girlhood to intrude in the form of her brother or any talk of her old home. In any case, he must get back to work, Raghu told her husband, and there was a late night train he could catch. There her husband sat, across from her in the tram, smiling at Raghu, as they rumbled through wide roads full of noise and sunshine. Would she ever know the names of these roads, of all these grand buildings, would she ever know about the outlandish ways of those people she had heard of—the Parsis and the Pathans? She had heard of odd women who wore saris back-to-front, and as she thought this, she caught a glimpse of a light-skinned woman in a long black robe, and a man with a black beehive beard, and another with a red hat that looked like a plump handful of dough on his head, and there, just across the road, was a giant swaggering along in a red turban that sprouted from his head like a stalk of sugarcane, which made him appear even taller than he was. She would be frightened of encountering someone like him, she thought in delight, and then she spotted a man with curious slanting eyes in a maroon and white robe with sleeves that yawned down to his knees, all this strangeness steaming in the bright sunlight through which she squinted as if through hot liquid glass; and, her buoyancy undiminished, thought, no, I couldn't possibly manage it, it is too much to know about or learn about, I simply want to learn the names of all the people in Khatryachi Chawl, and where to buy vegetables, and what time my husband would like to eat, and what he would like me to do for him.

As they left the environs of the train station, the strangeness started to fall away for they were no longer amidst wide thoroughfares and grand buildings that looked like carved stone palaces. The roads became smaller, narrower, dirtier, more clamorous, and yet more comforting for now she saw people like herself, women in nauvari saris with baskets on their heads, bare-chested Brahmins entering a temple, little girls wearing parkar-polkas with half-moons on their foreheads, small white-capped boys herding along goats and buffaloes, rapping the hind quarters of the animals with short switches.

It took two months for the limes in her first pickle to absorb the sugar, salt, and chilli through their bitter skins and turn into sticky delight. It took only a few days for the nervousness to fall away so that she and her husband could lie together without him making some excuse to hurry out and return only after she was asleep. She did not know whether he was nervous or being considerate. Perhaps both. He seemed taller and broader now. The way you don't get the full measure of a tree's height till you stand right next to it, she thought. The months rolled by in a delightful manner, though she was continually overcome with bashfulness in front of her husband. She became rather anxious as Diwali approached, not only because she wanted desperately for her first Diwali preparations to be flawless, but also because she knew she must prepare her husband for an oil bath. She was ready with the fragrant oils at three o'clock in the morning, waiting for her husband to rise at four and sit on the low wooden paat around which she had drawn a simple rangoli pattern of flowers. And she pretended to be brisk and business-like as she rubbed a deep red hibiscus oil on his chest and back and arms, then a dark green amla oil on his head, and finally dipped her fingers into the mirror-like bowl of coconut oil—all the colours gleaming like liquefied jewels in the flickering light of the oil lamp. The granular utne, which she had pounded to a paste the previous night, fell off his skin in little drips and drops as she smeared it over his body. He watched her with his serious brown eyes, and an amused smile on his lips, which flustered her so much that she was rather relieved when it was over and he stood up to go to the bathing area behind the chawl.

One day she found herself at the centre of a minor hubbub in Khatryachi Chawl, for the postman had brought her a parcel. A parcel! For a woman! A newly married woman! How can it be, asked the chawl; and Lele mavshi, into whose hands it finally fell after every woman in the chawl had examined it, eyed it suspiciously.

'You will not open it, of course,' she told Radha, a look of disapproval in her eyes.

'Of course not, Mavshi,' said Radha. 'Please keep it with you and give it to him in the evening.'

And so it seemed as if the entire chawl waited for her husband to return from work. He arrived at the end of the day in his sweat-stained sadra and dhoti, removing his narrow cap from his head as he climbed up the steps. Radha had barely handed him a cup of water when Lele mavshi appeared with the infamous parcel in her hands, a little square thing tied with string, oil-stained now from the fingers it had passed through. Radha could not think what it might be, or who from, for out of modesty she had barely touched it herself, barely glanced at it, lest Lele mavshi think her too forward. She hurried inside to start making tea but kept one ear on the conversation outside.

'Ah, it is good to see you relax after your long day at work,' Lele mavshi began. There is more to come, of course, thought Radha.

'Come, Mavshi, sit down,' said Tatya. He had settled down cross-legged on the wooden paat Radha had set out for him, with a small mat laid on the floor for his tea. This was where he sat every evening for an hour or so, reading a newspaper or chatting with any of the neighbours who might wander in, sometimes smoking a couple of bidis. Their room was mostly bare, save for a low wooden cupboard which was a recent addition, and which Radha found a great convenience for storing Tatya's clothes. Her own things were in a small trunk under the window. Sometimes she used the trunk to sit on and clean grains in the sunlight, since the back of their room and the kitchen were dark and cramped. At night they rolled out a thin mattress to sleep on. During the day the mattress stood like a lumpy, cotton-filled sentinel by the open door. Like everyone's door in the chawl, their door perpetually stood wide open through the day.

'Oh no, I have no time to sit,' said Lele mavshi, settling on her haunches. 'I have come to give you this. This came for you in the post today. But it has your wife's name on it. What could it be?'

Radha peeped out and saw Tatya open the parcel with a puzzled expression on his face. A small envelope fell out, and two small books.

'It is from my mother-in-law,' he said, baffled.

'Oh, you are blessed with a fine mother-in-law,' said Lele mavshi, her eyes on the two books. 'Keeping well, I hope?'

'That is something I can't tell you, Mavshi,' said Tatya, looking at the envelope and making no move to open it. 'This letter is not addressed to me, it's addressed to your daughter-in-law who is busy making tea inside.'

Lele mavshi's voice dropped to a hurried whisper, but Radha could hear every word nonetheless. 'Do you mean to say you are not going to read the letter first?'

'There's no need. I'll read it later.'

'And these books? What is the meaning of this? Are they for you or for her?' Still the same hurried whisper.

'Must be for her, I suppose, since the parcel has her name on it.' Radha detected a slightly strained quality in her husband's voice and her heart started pounding, a tremor in her fingers as she lifted the steaming pot of tea off the stove. He does not approve, she thought, in a panic. She tried hard to remember whether Vahini had ever said anything about receiving letters, but she was quite sure that Vahini had never mentioned anything of the sort, and now she was not sure whether Mai should have written to her.

She took another quick peek around the door frame and saw Lele mavshi getting up to leave. 'Well, do as you think right,' said Lele mavshi, reluctantly, still in a low voice, but she appeared rather relieved. Radha couldn't tell whether she looked relieved because she had gotten the parcel off her hands, or because she sensed that Tatya too disapproved of the whole business.

She waited till she saw Lele mavshi's plump figure pass by their open window and go towards her own room. Then she emerged with the tea and a plate of pohe, the lime pickle and curd arranged exactly the way Vahini had taught her, and set both down in front of Tatya. He said nothing to her, so she went back into the kitchen and waited, nervously fidgeting with some onion peels. In a few minutes she heard the clatter of the spoon on the empty plate and peered into the room again. He had finished eating and was quietly sipping his tea, looking through the two thin books. He glanced up at her, and she emerged from the kitchen. He held the envelope out to her.

She made no move to take it. 'Will you read out the letter to me?' she asked, timidly.

'Certainly,' he said, and proceeded to open the envelope. Radha was relieved that it turned out to be just a short, bland note, informing her that all was well at home, that Ahu kaku's daughter was expecting her third child, that Raghu had received a salary raise, and blessing both husband and wife. Her mother could have simply addressed the letter to Tatya and saved her all this anxiety.

'Sit down,' said Tatya, after folding up the letter and putting it back in its envelope. But she remained standing, she never sat in his presence. 'Did you read often at home?'

'Sometimes,' she said. 'Mainly religious books. Mai likes to read the Bhagwat Puran so I got into the habit of it too.'

'That's a good habit,' said Tatya, 'I am sure you know more about it than I do.'

'No, oh no, that can't be,' she said disbelieving. Then, taking courage from Tatya's mild expression, she continued, 'May I ask you a question? Are you angry that Mai sent me these books?'

'It's very unusual, I must say,' he said, frowning. 'Why did she send you these?'

'But are you...are you angry?' said Radha, ignoring her husband's question in her anxiety.

'I have no objection to you reading,' he said, looking at her, 'as long as it does not interfere with your housework. It would not be appropriate for you to sit and read here on your own. If you have finished your own work you must go and see whether Lele mavshi needs your help with anything.'

'Yes, of course,' said Radha, 'I do that already.'

'Well, then, these books seem all right to me, they appear to be instructional poems. I have no objection to you reading these at all.'

Tatya handed the books to Radha, who felt rather shamefaced at all the bother she had caused. 'I will be back in a while for dinner,' he said. He started to leave but then stopped and turned as if something had occurred to him. 'I never asked you,' he said. 'Did you go to school?'

'Only for a few years. When I was about nine, Mai said that it was time to stop, otherwise...' Radha halted her words in their tracks. She had been about to repeat Mai's words that she would not be able to get a husband if she were educated further and bit her tongue in embarrassment.

'Otherwise, what?' said Tatya, puzzled.

'Only that—it was time to stop,' said Radha, looking down.

He smiled, his brow clearing of the creases that had appeared while he appraised the books. She felt reassured and heaved a sigh of relief as he stepped out into the balcony. The chawl had become increasingly noisy with the return of children and men at the end of the day.

Eagerly, Radha glanced at the slim books, for they were a little piece of home, the covers only recently touched by Mai herself. One book was about the importance of one's ancestors. The other was about how a young bride ought to behave in her husband's home. She knew some of these verses already. She had not known that they were part of a longer work. How wonderful to read the verses in the form of a book, she thought, slowly sitting down and opening one at random. But what could have possessed Mai to suddenly send her these, she thought, in some exasperation. Mai had been used to getting her own way in her brother's house. Narayan mama was very indulgent towards his only sister. His wife had died a few years after Mai arrived back at the wada, and so Mai had taken over the running of the household. Radha knew that there were some who whispered that the widow had brought bad luck with her, causing her sister-in-law's illness and death. But such vile whispers only made Narayan mama all the more determined that Mai should have her way in the household. It was not difficult, for she had a way of cowing anyone with a stare of her cold grey eyes. Nor did Mai see why she ought to be neither seen nor heard simply because she was a widow. Only once had Radha seen Mai weeping uncontrollably, on the night that Narayan mama's wife died. She said things to Radha that night that she never spoke of again.

As she wept, she had held the small girl close to her—Radha in utter distress and in tears at feeling her mother's body shaking with great gasping sobs and suppressed whimpers. It had frightened Radha because it made her mother sound like a child, and because it all reverberated through her own small frame, for her mother held her tight. When her sobs subsided Mai began to speak in a small, quavering voice, and once the words left her mouth they would not stop. She did not stop speaking till she had told her small daughter everything, even though Radha then barely understood how big the world was and how enormous her mother's thoughts. Yet she understood much of what Mai said that night. And she remembered almost all of it, so that whenever she thought back on Mai's words, she felt she understood a bit more. How fortunate my brother's wife was to have died a married woman, Mai had wept, for she will never have to bear becoming a widow and losing the dignity of a married woman, the dignity of a human being. And Mai recounted her terror at being left a widow in a house full of brothers-in-law who looked at her with veiled eyes after her husband died, so that she did not know what they were thinking; of her pleading with her mother-in-law to spare her hair. Of course it was impossible for her to keep her hair, she knew that even as she pleaded, lying face down on the floor as if her mother-in-law were a fearsome goddess who might pardon her the full weight of the arid life that lay before her. She knew full well that nothing good was possible anymore, and yet it was a shock when her husband's youngest brother grabbed a fistful of her hair, yanked her to her feet and delivered a ringing blow to the side of her head. Shameless woman, he had screamed at her, and what terrified her more than anything else was the calculating look in his eyes that believed that she indeed had no shame, and that he might profit from it. And so the barber came, and the other widows in the house watched as he touched her scalp with his cold razor and she felt the prickling sensation of her hair falling away in clumps, leaving her feeling naked and ashamed, so that at that moment she wanted nothing more than to cover her baldness with her padar.

'Your mama's wife was fortunate, child,' said Mai that night, her voice dry and whispering. She had gone into a sort of trance now, staring at the dark room without seeing it. 'Make sure you die before your husband, make sure of it. Till then, till that day, be aware of everything around you. Especially people.'

'People, Mai?' said Radha, fearfully.

'Yes,' said Mai, calmer now, and she looked at her daughter. 'A woman must be like a snake, a nagin. She must be aware of everything around her. She must slither forward quickly.'

And Mai had insisted without fail that Radha should read, not only the holy puranas but also the newspaper whenever one happened to fall into their hands. She made Radha write to her big brother, Raghu, for he lived in town where he studied and later found a job. To the consternation of Ahu kaku and Shanti kaku, she made Radha sit with Narayan mama in the evenings, when, after listening to her recite the Ram Raksha, he formulated sums for his clever niece to work out in her head. The newspaper bored Radha, and she enjoyed the sums only as long as they were not too complicated, but she liked reading the stories in the puranas, and she loved writing to her brother. And so why should it surprise her that Mai had gotten it into her head to send her two books of poems?

And yet, while everyone back at the wada was used to Mai's idiosyncrasies, which would not have passed muster in most households, Radha's husband was certainly not used to them, much less the folk of Khatryachi Chawl.

Radha remained alone with the books for just a few minutes, for Lele

Tejaswini Apte-Rahm

mavshi and her daughter-in-law, Kashi, were hovering outside, and shortly after Tatya left they arrived to have a good look at the books and exclaim over them. Kashi, in particular, kept raising her eyes to look at Radha in wonderment, so amazed was she that Radha had received books in the post. They were soon joined by Lele mavshi's other daughter-in-law, Pami, and they all flipped through the pages, talking all the while, till Lele mavshi shooed them out, saying that Radha had better get on with her cooking. Lele mavshi was rather gratified now, having found that the two books were instructional poems on good behaviour.

'My dear Radha,' she said, fondly, 'why don't you read out some of these verses to us tomorrow morning, when all the menfolk are away, when we can all sit peacefully for a while? I have some stitching to do while these girls clean the rice and vegetables. That will be a fine time for us to listen to your poems.'

'With pleasure, Mavshi,' said Radha, gladly. After that day, many of the women in the chawl came to Radha if they wanted a letter or a newspaper article read out, and she was much in demand to recite a few of the instructional verses whenever the women gathered to chat or to roll out hundreds of papads for each other, and once, even at a wedding when the women had recited their ukhanas and were in the mood for something different. She was known as Radha-who-receives-books-in-the-post for a long time afterwards, though Mai never did such a whimsical thing again.

Now, as Radha settled down on the floor to chop and fry for the evening meal, she thought of the verse on the page which had fallen open in the few moments before Lele mavshi came in. She knew those words, she had memorized them as a child. Her eyes filled with tears, for sometimes she missed her mother. The anxious events of the day now reminded her of how far away her mother was, and how Mai must miss her too, and the tears fell as she repeated the verse in her mind:

The invitation has arrived, it is time for the young bride to leave for her new home,
The mother adorns her child with ornaments, and tells her gently to look after them well,
The young bride's forehead is bright with red vermillion, her sari cradles the auspicious coconut.
May your future be bright like your forehead today, whispers the mother,

Do not let your heart grieve even a little, child,
Do not be sad, you must leave now,
Look, I tell you, I will bring you home soon for Sankranti,
Wipe your eyes, child, do not sadden your heart even a little.

Tejaswini Apte-Rahm

CHAPTER 16

1906

Tatya now entered a period of great prosperity. Nothing could go wrong, and nothing did go wrong. He felt as if a shimmering scene of plenty was unspooling past him as he walked on, and all he had to do was reach out and take from the sparkling panorama what he willed. A star here, a moonbeam there, a skein of water flecked with gold dust—they were all his for the taking. The yellow warmth of the sun in the rains, the icy cold of the moon in summer; he seemed to conjure these up as he went along. His life was drenched in golden light, and the very leaves on the trees quivered jewel-green. The ancient priest who had presided over their marriage was proved right—Lakshmi, the goddess of prosperity, had indeed entered his home in the guise of Radha.

From the day of her return to Khatryachi Chawl, Radha had not disappointed him. She was still short of height, she was still no beauty, but she was a child no longer. He found everything about her pleasing. Her dark eyes looked at him as if she would rather be here with him than anywhere else. She had a friendly nature and blended in seamlessly with the women of the chawl. She was trusting of everyone; he felt a trusting nature such as hers would never do in the wider world. As it was, she remained at Khatryachi Chawl most of the time, only venturing out occasionally when the other women asked her to accompany them to the temple, or for a special occasion like a haldi-kunku in a nearby chawl. Always with his permission, of course. She did not speak much, but whatever she said was spoken with disarming frankness, the frankness a trait inherited, no doubt, from her mother. There was something so peaceable in Radha's dark eyes and wide forehead, and such a wonderful discipline in her habits, that she had turned Tatya's small, two-room dwelling into a home, a place of restfulness.

A far cry from the scrappy way he had lived there with Nana and Ponkshe, and yet, in those days, he had not imagined there could be another, better way of living. The kitchen was still dark and cramped, and yet whatever sunlight did filter in now showed the gleam of scrubbed, shining utensils.

She had economized to a startling degree, without compromising on his comfort. To save oil, she would use a single oil lamp to light up both the front room and kitchen, placing the lamp on the threshold between the two rooms so that it lit up both areas. In the summer she suggested that they eat only mangoes, for they were cheap and delicious, and that they cut out other fruits and vegetables entirely—it was only for a month or two, she reasoned, and why not make the most of their favourite fruit? He had agreed wholeheartedly. For weeks they ate their fill of mangoes cut into slices, mangoes squeezed into aamras to be eaten with hot polis, mango flesh kneaded and softened in the skin with their fingers, and its glorious, juicy pulp sucked straight out of its skin after biting off the bitter stem. He had never seen her do this, of course, for she always ate after him, separately.

He marvelled, sometimes, at how cloistered Radha's world of chawl and kitchen was from the life he lived. Of course, it could be no other way; he had never yet seen a respectable woman set foot in either mill or market. And yet it was strange, he felt, that she would never see his pedhi, the precious place where he had placed his bee-buzzing soul and spun out their good fortune, hour by hour, day by day, so that slowly, the need to count their annas, the need for fierce economizing, had begun to dwindle.

Tatya was now the sole selling agent of Rose Mills cloth. Every piece of cloth that left the Rose Mills compound passed through Tatya's hands, and was sold by him to wholesale dealers, earning him a handsome commission. Rose Mills had expanded, it no longer produced only long cloth and cambric, but voile and canvas as well. There was even talk of setting up a separate silk weaving unit. Sir Francis Wheeler, he of the immaculate suit and sleek Bentley, who took a personal interest in the great Imperial Mills, had unaccountably started taking an interest in Rose Mills, small though it was compared to the sprawling interests of Imperial Industries. Apparently, according to a stray remark by Matthew Wales, Imperial Mills was such an old and established business that it did not need much looking into anymore. Sir Francis had therefore cast about for a new concern to turn his attention to, apart from handling the mighty shipping business of Imperial Industries, and had landed on Rose Mills as the place to build up.

Tatya had never seen Sir Francis appear at Rose Mills himself, but heard from Matthew Wales about the huge new injection of money into the business. The mill would now expand into spinning its own yarn. New spinning machinery was imported from England to start a vast new spinning department. In fact, Rose Mills started making so much yarn that not all of it could be woven in-house into cloth. So a yarn selling agent was duly appointed to sell Rose Mills branded yarn, and Rose Mills came to be known as the spanking new mill of Imperial Industries that was poised to be a player in the yarn and textile markets.

Tatya had built up a good working relationship with Matthew Wales, who was impressed by Tatya's persistence in going to Rose Mills every single day to check on the quality of the cloth produced. He was equally impressed by Tatya's quick turnover of sales and his reliable payments. Slowly, Tatya became a keen participant in discussing with Wales and the sizing master the costs of producing and selling various kinds of cloth. So canny was Tatya's knowledge of the market that he usually had the last word on what to produce and how much. It was unprecedented for a mere selling agent to be so intimately involved in the functioning of a mill, and Tatya knew this. He was aware that he was carving out an entirely novel role for himself. And so he was cautious, taking care not to step on anyone's toes. Tatya's head for numbers, Matthew Wales' easy talent at management, and the sizing master's technical skill—the combination was unstoppable. Rose Mills was fast turning into one of the successes of Imperial Industries.

As for Tatya, it seemed to Khatryachi Chawl and the denizens of Mulji Jetha Market, that as fast as Rose Mills spun its cotton into yarn, so Vaman seth spun cloth into gold. For he was no longer simply Tatya or even Govindji. Murari had started calling him Vaman seth as a joke, but the name stuck. Now they called him Vaman, the diminutive dwarf who conquered all three worlds in three celestial strides. He was not quite there yet, thought Tatya, amused, not quite master of the three worlds. But the joke made him pause, ponder, and then go back to work.

As much as Tatya respected his mentor, Zaveri, it began dawning on him why Zaveri's business remained stagnant, while his own was growing faster than he could have dreamt of. For one thing, Zaveri sold his cloth to the highest bidder of the day, rather than only to trusted dealers, creating headaches for himself like the notorious Popatlal who never paid on time. And, most fatally, Zaveri was content. He was satisfied with what he had, and felt no urge to do more than he had ever done. Tatya watched his old mentor, took his advice from time to time, but determined never to be content.

Not that he needed reminding, for there was a pit in his stomach that thrummed with hunger and excitement. Like a cavernous honeycomb, filled with bees that were constantly putting their heads together to hatch new and impossible schemes. Sometimes they would tell him their schemes, at other times they would keep it a secret. Secrets, he knew, that would soon ooze out of them, honey coloured and sweet, like the puzzle of numbers, and the shape of thoughts in other people's minds, and the secret of more.

Now that Tatya had become known as the only person who could sell Rose Mills cloth, he decided that it was time for an overhaul of his system of selling to wholesale dealers. In consultation with Kishan Mehta, his gumastha, he weeded out the dealers who did not pay on time, or whose orders were irregular, and looked with satisfaction at the select list of fifteen dealers he was left with. Kanjibhai Parekh, Pareshbhai Patel, Tansukhrai Bhatia, and the rest, all men with whom he had good, courteous relations, and who, most importantly, were reliable.

'Do you mean to say that you will turn away our other customers? Even those who want to place a large order?' Mehta said to him in surprise. They were poring over the accounts late one evening and Tatya had just told his gumastha about his new plan.

Tatya thought for a while and then said, 'At the moment demand for cloth is greater than the supply. So selling cloth is not a challenge. And Rose Mills produces cloth of consistently high quality. How can I, as a selling agent, use this to my advantage?'

Mehta looked mystified. 'How can you do more than sell whatever cloth the mill produces?' he said.

'There is always a way to do more,' said Tatya. 'Stop thinking of the mill for a moment and think of the pedhi. First of all, there will come a time when supply finally catches up with demand. At that point of time, I should not have to chase after wholesale dealers to buy my cloth. They should come willingly to me. How do you think I can ensure that?'

'But they will always come willingly to you, Seth,' said Mehta. 'They know that it is easy to do business with you.'

'They will not always come willingly to me,' said Tatya, 'unless I set that process in motion now.'

'What are you going to do?' said Mehta, smiling. He was always game for a new idea, and Tatya liked this quality in his gumastha.

'I am going to create a demand not only for Rose Mills cloth, but a demand for doing business with me. I want to create a sense that it is not possible to simply turn up here and get hold of high-quality Rose Mills cloth. You have to be part of an exclusive group of wholesalers to get it.'

Mehta's jaw dropped open at the audacity of this idea. A golden circle of fifteen dealers, that would be vetted and expanded carefully over time. It would become a matter of prestige to do business with Govind seth and acquire Rose Mills cloth.

'You do know that nobody in the market has ever tried creating an exclusive list of buyers?' said Mehta, frowning.

Tatya leaned back on his bolster and smiled comfortably, gazing at his gumastha with steady eyes.

'What about Noor Begum Mills,' Mehta said, after a moment. 'Will you operate a similar system for their cloth too?'

'No,' admitted Tatya, 'for the simple reason that I am not their only selling agent—it is impossible to create an exclusive circle of dealers when I myself am not the sole agent.'

'I am surprised that old Karim Shahpurwala has not given you the entire selling agency,' said Mehta, looking puzzled.

'I'm not surprised,' said Tatya. 'The only other selling agent of Noor Begum Mills, apart from me, is his son-in-law. So you see, there is no chance of my becoming his sole agent. I am lucky he hasn't given my selling agency to his son-in-law too.'

'I doubt he would do that,' said Mehta, shrewdly.

Tatya raised his eyebrows. 'Why?'

'He will keep his son-in-law on his toes by using your sales as a point of comparison,' said Mehta, with a grin.

Tatya laughed but had to admit Mehta was right. Karim Shahpurwala could be counted on to do exactly that.

Not content with his new role at Rose Mills and his innovations at the pedhi, Tatya travelled to Calcutta. The partition of Bengal the previous year, as well as a trade quarrel between Calcutta merchants and English manufacturers had led to a boycott of Manchester cloth and other British goods there. Demand for cloth made in India, and its price, had suddenly increased.

'Now is the time for me to get my foot in the door and build good personal relations with traders in Calcutta,' Tatya told Kishan Mehta, 'so that even once the boycott ends, we will be able to continue selling cloth there.'

Mehta listened carefully to what he needed to do while Tatya was in

Calcutta. In addition to the situation in Bengal, a swadeshi movement had simultaneously been sparked off in Bombay and Poona, urged on by Tilak, with political gatherings throwing British cloth into bonfires, further increasing the demand for Indian cloth. Rose Mills and Noor Begum Mills, not to mention dozens of other mills, were already dispatching hundreds of extra bales of cloth to Bengal by sea and by train. Meanwhile they could barely keep up with the new demand for Indian cloth in the Bombay Presidency. Mehta would have much to do while Tatya was away—in addition to the accounting, he would have to handle the deliveries of large quantities of cloth. But Tatya was confident that Kishan Mehta would hold the fort at the pedhi while he was travelling.

And he returned from Calcutta with a formidable list of personal contacts and friends, dealers won over by his charm, by his wide-ranging knowledge of cloth, and by the fact that he had made the effort to travel to Calcutta and understand first-hand the requirements of the Bengali market.

His tales about his travels made Radha's eyes widen in disbelief. He told her of the fine muslin woven in the regions of Dhaka, where they separated tiny cotton fibres using the miniscule, pointed teeth of the local boal fish; where they teased the fibres into a cloud of gossamer down, and covered it with the skin of the kuchia fish to keep it clean before spinning it into yarn and weaving it into cloth.

'They use the skin of a dead fish to keep something clean?' said Radha, in wonder. 'Someone has been pulling your leg.'

'It's true,' Tatya protested, and, of course, she had to believe him. 'What if I tell you that there is a kind of muslin so delicate that it is woven underwater?'

She gazed at him, a half-smile lingering on her lips, enthralled by the idea and wanting to believe it.

'Don't believe everything you hear,' he smiled, 'for it is just a legend. The finest muslin is woven when the air is wet and moist, especially during the monsoon. Why do you think that is so?'

'I don't know,' she said, puzzled.

'It is so that the wetness in the air makes the cotton filaments stretch. The weaving is often done early in the morning on a boat on the water, to take advantage of the moist air, which is why a story grew that it was woven underwater.'

She smiled, her forehead creasing a little as she tried to imagine a fabric

Tejaswini Apte-Rahm

so fragile and elusive that it would feel like mist wrapped around her body.

'And now I will tell you my last story of the night,' Tatya said, for it was late. He was lying on his back on their mattress while Radha sat beside him, looking down at him. Her face was aglow in shifting shadows of russet and orange as the flame of the flickering oil lamp played on her skin. He put out the flame and pulled her to him.

'What is your last story?' she said, softly.

And he wrapped his arms around her and whispered in her ear, telling her of a legendary muslin worn by a Mughal princess that was so sheer, so like a translucent pearl, so delicate, that the princess appeared to be naked. And she felt her face grow hot and was glad it was dark and that she needed to make no reply. For it was an entirely improper story, and yet, in the darkness, it made her breath catch in her throat and her heart pound in the most bewitching way.

CHAPTER 17

1911

A sea-soaked fistful of sand at Chowpatty twinkled with millions of stars in the dazzling sunshine—was it silver dust or the remains of ancient seashells? Who could tell? But the owner of the small hand that clutched the sand looked up at Tatya and exclaimed, 'Diamonds!'

Tatya looked at the swirl of sand on his son's open palm. 'I will take these home for Aai,' the boy declared and Tatya scooped up three-year-old Ganesh, laughing. His older boy, five-year-old Sharad, was squatting down by the shoreline, poking at the delicate eddies of water with a twig. It was a holiday and Dada strolled nearby, drinking in the sea breeze, enjoying being amongst the gay crowd of people on the beach. A rather miserable-looking bear danced nearby with its owner rattling coins in a tin. A small thin girl in a knotted blouse walked with eight small pots balanced on her head and arms, and her mother began adding more to the tower. They were nomadic folk, wearing large amulets and nose rings.

Dada and Vahini had arrived a few days ago from Dhangadh on the occasion of the new king's coronation. The coronation itself had happened in London months earlier, in June, but there would be a grand durbar in Delhi in about two weeks' time to proclaim the king's role as the new Emperor of India. The royal couple would arrive in Bombay the next day, on Saturday, en route to Delhi. Dada's son, eleven-year-old Mandar, had recently had his thread ceremony in Dhangadh and, as part of his continuing education, Dada wanted him to see the pomp of the royal celebrations in Bombay. On this Friday evening, a day before the king's arrival, a sense of celebration already filled the city, and Chowpatty was more crowded than usual.

'It is ironic, is it not, that the man who succeeded the longest living queen ever, the Maharani Victoria...how long did she reign, re?' Dada called out to Mandar, who was busy collecting seashells. His two older sisters were already married. It was Mandar who bore the brunt of being the school principal's only son.

He stood up quickly and said, 'Sixty-three years, Baba.'

Tatya looked at Dada playfully. 'Must you test the boy continuously through the day?'

Dada, however, was in full flow, and Mandar, apparently well trained to keep one ear alert for questions his father might fire at him, looked relaxed. He was thoroughly enjoying his first look at the sea.

'It is ironic, indeed,' resumed Dada, 'that Edward VII, who succeeded the longest reigning queen, the Maharani Victoria, lived a mere ten years after ascending to the throne. One had gotten used to the idea of a British monarch with an air of immortality. And yet, here we are, a new king already. Who is the new king, re?'

Mandar stood up again, to respectfully address his father. 'King George V, Baba.'

Dada waited, eyebrows raised, and Mandar realized that he was expected to continue, to tack something on to his answer and show that he knew more. A pause ensued, Mandar's fingers fidgeting with a seashell as he stood digging one toe into the sand. 'King George V,' he continued, finally, 'by the Grace of God, King of the United Kingdom of Great Britain and Ireland and of the British Dominions beyond the Seas, Defender of the Faith, and Emperor of India.'

'Good,' said Dada, frowning. 'Hopefully it will be of some use bringing you to Bombay.'

Tatya cleared his throat. 'Dada, surely you are not teaching him to unthinkingly bow down to the British?'

'Certainly not,' said Dada. 'But the boy must know the correct form of referring to the king. I am teaching him everything that I taught the princes. The princes of course have to know how to conduct themselves when the British Resident visits the Rajesaheb. And they cannot appear ignorant of basic information about the monarch.'

'How often does the British Resident visit Rajesaheb?' asked Tatya, curiously.

'Not often,' said Dada. 'Once every six months or year. Rajesaheb always throws a lavish welcome for him. Last year he took him on a shikar with three elephants and twenty horses. The year before that, there was a tea party. Rajesaheb had ordered that the two-hundred-piece silver tea set be brought out and polished for the occasion. I saw the servants sitting and polishing the pieces five mornings in a row. You should have seen the sparkle at the end of it!'

Tatya smiled, thinking of the splendour of the Rajesaheb's court. He had only heard about it from his brother and longed to see it with his own eyes. 'That must have been a sight,' he said. 'Is Rajesaheb invited to the imperial durbar in Delhi?'

'Invited? My dear Tatya, he is commanded to attend. As are all the princely rulers. They all have to go and pay their respects to King George.'

Tatya nodded. 'Of course. I should have known. And what do you think of that?'

'Of what?' said Dada, looking at him.

'What do you think of Rajesaheb being commanded to do anything?'

'We are at a juncture in history when it is inevitable,' said Dada. 'What more can one say about it?'

'A lot more, judging by the articles in the press,' said Tatya.

'Look here, Tatya,' said Dada. 'You are the selling agent for a British-run mill. It is not wise for you to get mixed up in any of this talk. Don't throw away what you have earned. The British will not stay for ever. When the time comes, they will leave. When the time comes, Rajesaheb will not have to welcome the British Resident with sandwiches and elephants. But remember this—nothing happens before its time.'

Tatya could not imagine such a time. He could not imagine Rose Mills being run without Matthew Wales and Sir Francis Wheeler. Nor could he imagine the British leaving India altogether. It was idle talk for the likes of him and Dada.

Sharad chose this moment to sit down in the wet sand, just in time for the arrival of a thick wave which lapped up and encircled him in a pond of water before swirling away again. He cried out in delight, pointing at the deep hole he had dug. 'My well! My well is full of water!'

Tatya slapped his forehead in dismay. 'You rascal, look at your clothes!'

Sharad stood up, a mess of sand and water dripping from his clothes, his white cap askew on his head. Dada and Mandar burst out laughing and little Ganesh clapped his hands in delight. Tatya struggled between scolding his son and suppressing a smile. A charming grin was spreading over Sharad's face—like sunlight flooding the sea with sparkles, thought Tatya with a twinge in his heart. It is too much, he thought, my good fortune is too much.

The more money he made, the more anxious he grew—not because he was worried about losing it—but because he feared he would somehow be called to account for it. He had never heard of anyone being as lucky as he was. And yet, he wanted more. Could it be right, wanting more, when he already had more than he could ever have imagined? And when such thoughts came to him, at unexpected moments, he grew overwhelmed with anxiety for his sons, and his voice seemed to catch in his throat as if it were wrapped in dry parchment. What was it that would be taken away from him? He felt that a storm might be gathering in the distance, just over the horizon, so that he could not see it but could feel a sense of something pending. Something pending that was yet to play out. On some days he thought that the thing that waited for him over the horizon was no more than a cool breeze. On such days he felt loose-limbed, free, as if he wanted to run a mile, and after a mile keep pounding the street with his feet, without looking back. On other days, he felt that he might be in the path of a baleful wind blowing his way, or in the orbit of an ill-starred moon that would cause the tide to turn. And then he feared for everything. He feared that when the sea inhaled again, it would take something away from him. Something that he had not earned, something that the wind had simply dropped into his lap on its way elsewhere.

CHAPTER 18

The next morning they headed towards Apollo Bunder with the crowds to try and catch a glimpse of the new king. 'Baba, let us go as early as possible,' Mandar had begged his father, 'otherwise we will miss everything!' Dada needed no convincing. Determined to make the most of the occasion for which he had especially come from Dhangadh, he had thoroughly scanned the newspapers for information about the day's programme.

Radha handed a cloth bundle to Tatya as he readied to leave. 'I have packed some poli-bhaaji,' she said, 'and some sweet snacks. Who knows how long you will have to wait there.' Armed with these supplies and two screw-top tambyas of water, Tatya, Dada, and the two boys, Sharad and Mandar, headed out. At the last moment it was decided that three-year-old Ganesh would be left behind with Radha, for his eyes were pale and his forehead was hot.

Judging by the horse-mounted police that were clip-clopping up and down Sandhurst Road, just near their chawl, it was all but certain that the royal procession would come down that way at some point during the day. Early that morning there was a curious anticipation in the neighbourhood, as if the air had stilled and was waiting. But soon the children began dancing about as if it were the start of a festival. Some people started setting off fireworks saved up from Diwali. The previous day, Tatya had proudly taken Dada to see the decorative arch put up by wealthy cotton merchants at one end of Sandhurst Road, in honour of the royal procession—an arch almost forty feet high, made up entirely of cotton bales and loose cotton, its value rumoured to be twelve thousand pounds. The king's route would surely pass that way. Other neighbourhoods had also put up their own welcoming decorations, here an arch erected by Maratha chiefs, there a pair of grand pillars put up by the Goans, while Bhendi Bazaar was enthusiastically swathed in a canopy of green silk held aloft by minarets.

Khatryachi Chawl seemed filled with experts that day on what exactly the king and queen were going to do. News was exchanged thick and fast, some of it improbable, such as Nagesh Godse's claim that jalebis and ladoos were going to be distributed to the general populace as the king drove past;

some more believable, such as Dattopant Apte's information that the king was sailing in with an entourage of ten ships. In the event that the procession did come down Sandhurst Road, Lele mavshi would lead a group of the chawl's women there, since it was less than a minute away on foot. Radha could hardly believe that she might lay her eyes on the king and queen of England and she, along with all the other women, spent the morning in a state of nervous excitement, exchanging opinions on what the queen might look like. Radha had been in great demand among the women to read out reports about the royal visit that had started appearing in the newspapers in recent weeks.

'We shall have to set you up as a school mistress,' Tatya teased her in the days prior to the royal arrival. 'I hear you have been educating the other women about the royal schedule. The date their highnesses set out from England, the time they will arrive in Bombay. I suppose you know all about the arrangements for the durbar in Delhi too. Tell me, how many cannons have been prepared to fire a salute to His Majesty the King?'

'Me, a school mistress!' scoffed Radha, half-smiling, half-annoyed. 'To simply read out what someone else has written, what is so great about that? My mother forced me to read the newspaper whenever Narayan mama brought it to the wada, that is why I know how to read it.'

'Well, then we must call it Mai's achievement, not yours,' said Tatya, laughing.

At such times, when Radha wasn't busy with the boys, or in the kitchen, or neck-deep in communal activities with the other women of the chawl, the rare, quiet moments when she sat quietly stitching or mending while the boys played outside, he talked to her. He wondered aloud who his sons would grow up to look like. 'I hope they grow up to look like Dada,' he would say. 'Dada was a fine-looking man ten years ago. His neck stoops a bit now, though it should not, at this age.'

'At least let one son look like me,' Radha would say in mock exasperation. 'What do you say, Lele mavshi,' she would call out, appealing to Lele mavshi, who often sat outside in the common balcony.

He told her of his plans for the boys, for he dreamt, now, of taking Sharad and Ganesh with him through the buzzing lanes of Mulji Jetha Market, and to see the steaming chimneys of Rose Mills, and the high arched gateway and massive squat buildings of Noor Begum Mills. He had proudly changed the small nameplate above his pedhi so that it now read

Govind Abhyankar & Sons. When he took Sharad and Ganesh with him to the pedhi for the Lakshmi puja at Diwali, he watched with an absurd fondness and pride as the other traders and cloth merchants pressed small gifts of a sweet pedha or a one paisa coin into their chubby little grasping fingers. I will train Sharad to be a fine cloth trader, he would tell Radha, he is a clever boy, good with numbers. He can get a good education, complete his schooling in an English medium school. Ganesh can start off as an apprentice with one of the other traders, perhaps Champak bhai, who is a yarn selling agent. We will expand our business, see if we can get a bigger pedhi. Sharad can look after the cloth selling agency, Ganesh can be a yarn selling agent. Perhaps one day they can open their own small textile mill. I will have the capital by then to set them up well.

Wait a bit, Radha would say, smiling, your mind is running faster than a train. Ganesh is barely three years old, Sharad only five.

But I must plan, everything must be planned from an early age, Tatya would say restlessly, as if he could not wait for the boys to grow up, could not wait for the long dreary years of school to be over, could not wait to introduce them to his world of ledgers and chopdis and cloth and textures and the clacking of looms and spindles, and the vast, vast movements of cloth and wealth. They were now in their mother's world, Radha's world of chawl and kitchen and tugging at her sari padar when they were hungry. It was no place for his boys, he would think, their place was out there, in the buzzing city where business chuntered on relentlessly, where there was no time to stop; the city of bees and honey.

That morning, though, the day of the king's arrival, there was no time to sit with Radha, or with anyone else for that matter, for all was abuzz with talk of the royal procession.

'Aai, will the king be sitting or standing when he drives past us on Sandhurst Road?' asked Ganesh, as Tatya and Dada made ready to leave for Apollo Bunder.

'He will be sitting, of course, probably in a splendid carriage of gold,' said Radha, soothingly, for the boy was upset at not being able to go with Mandar and Sharad.

'Oh,' said Ganesh, downcast. 'I wish he would stand.'

'Why?' asked Radha, surprised.

'So that we might be able to see his tail.'

'His what?' exploded Dada, and Tatya, on the verge of stepping out of the room, looked at his son in consternation.

'Lala and Tapu and the other boys say that all Europeans have a small tail.' Ganesh held out a finger to demonstrate the exact length of the tail.

'You fool, even if he had a small tail it would be hidden inside his clothes,' began Mandar in contempt, and received a slap on the back of his head from his father.

'Can't you teach him to stop talking nonsense?' said Tatya irritably to Radha.

Radha and Vahini waited till both men had stepped out, and then dissolved into laughter.

For days, thousands of people had been arriving in Bombay by train and by road from the interiors of the Bombay Presidency and from beyond, to witness the spectacle of the king's arrival in India. Tatya, Dada, and the boys had left not a moment too soon, for entire families were already jostling for space on the roads leading to Apollo Bunder, and Tatya despaired of being able to get within reach of the jetty. Dada, of course, knew nothing of Bombay, so Tatya led the small party. It was difficult to tell who was more animated, Dada or Mandar, thought Tatya, as he tried to make his way through the throng. He had to admit he was excited himself, though since he worked regularly with Matthew Wales, the novelty of gazing at an array of Europeans was far more piquant for Dada and Mandar than it was for him. He found that the best way to move ahead was to slowly, but persistently, nudge his way through the crowds that lined the streets, and the families that had hunkered down to wait out the day, come rain or storm. Everyone had come with a bundle of food, just like Tatya.

'Is this a good place to stop?' asked Dada, looking in admiration at the wide, gaily festooned road that led to the seafront. They now had a glimpse of the grand brick-coloured dome of the new Taj Mahal Hotel which had opened a few years ago. 'We'll get a good view from here as they go past.'

'No, we are too far off here,' said Tatya, craning his neck. 'Let's go further ahead where we can get a view of the ship as it comes into Apollo Bunder.'

'But how will we get any closer?' said Dada in despair. The crowd had now massed into a wall of humans, murmuring with anticipation in the cool air of the morning. Every time a pair of soldiers trotted by on their horses, sitting upright and fierce in black boots, scarlet cummerbunds, and emerald green turbans, a cheer went up and children clamoured to be lifted on to their fathers' shoulders.

By eight o'clock that morning Tatya, Dada, Mandar, and Sharad had miraculously manoeuvred themselves to a spot where they could not only see the open waters of the Arabian Sea, but also a graceful domed pavilion of pure-white, garlanded in flowers and flanked by gold-topped minarets, perched on the edge of the pier. It appeared to be a sort of gateway from the water on to the land. A pathway of dazzling white sand, with a long red carpet at its centre, ran inland from the gateway, lined with white columns decorated with gilt lions. The pathway ended in a small but majestic shamiana. The shamiana, adorned with all manner of fluttering banners emblazoned with coats of arms, was topped by a canopy of royal blue embellished with the imperial crown. In the shamiana were two thrones covered in gold cloth, awaiting the royal presence. The shamiana itself was dwarfed by a huge semi-circular amphitheatre of white and gold, open to the sky, adjacent to the Taj Mahal Hotel, with seats and steps of pale green cloth that rose in dozens of tiers to face the sea. The seats were filled with smartly dressed British men and women, as well as a few Indian dignitaries. The Royal Navy guards were out in full force in blue and white, swords and bayonets at the ready, and there was a regimental band in scarlet and yellow, their brass instruments glinting under the blue morning sky.

'Look at this,' said Dada, in awe. 'Last time you brought me to Apollo Bunder, none of this was here. They've put up all these pillars and everything. Looks like the king will enter through that gateway.'

'It's all temporary, bhau,' said a short man in a brown coat and dhoti, who was in the process of edging his way forward even further. 'This white gateway is only for today. It will be taken down soon.'

'Did you work on the construction?' asked Tatya, curiously.

'A little space, a little space,' the man said in apologetic tones, and disappeared as he squeezed his way through the restive crowd. Tatya barely had time to marvel at the fact that all these elaborate structures were just temporary, for there was the thunderous noise of three guns going off and a cry went up. Someone shouted, 'The ship! The king's ship is here!' and others took up the cry and repeated it so that the news was likely relayed from Apollo Bunder to Queen's Road in a matter of seconds. Everyone craned their necks in the direction of the water. Several stately warships were moored by the jetty, festooned with gay, fluttering pennants, all decorated with the blue, white, and red of the British flag. But no ship could be seen approaching the shore, though Tatya, Dada, and the boys squinted hard at the horizon.

'Nothing,' said Dada, finally, still gazing at the open sea. 'They are not here yet.'

'So why did they set off the guns?' asked Mandar, but he was drowned out by a huge cheer, and Sharad, who was perched on Tatya's shoulders, yelled and pointed at a distant smudge of smoke that could as well have been a low hanging wisp of cloud. It was no cloud, though, and what was rapidly approaching the shores of Bombay was the HMS *Medina*, escorted by four enormous cruisers which followed in its trail in perfect formation. It was another hour and a half till the *Medina* appeared to halt its progress and drop anchor, and all the warships gave a thunderous salute of gunfire to signal that the royal journey had been completed. The king was now in India. Another great cheer erupted, and someone in the crowd started playing a dholak, accompanied by clapping and hooting, while by the waterfront the regimental band struck up a jaunty melody on shining trumpets and trombones, accompanied by the smart rapping of drums. Several small launches began busily swarming their way from the shore towards the ship. Now the crowds milled around in a general atmosphere of anticipation and gaiety, during which time Tatya opened the bundle of cloth full of poli-bhaaji, chiwda, ladoo, and chakli, to share the food between the four of them. As the sun rose blazing over the water, they found the shade of a tree under which to have a nap, undeterred by the teeming crowds. They were determined not to go home till they had spotted the king himself. It was hours later that a small dark blue launch detached itself from the HMS *Medina* and made its way across the waves to the white pavilion. Through the gateway of the pavilion, to a deafening roar from the crowd and a fanfare of trumpets, stepped King George in a white naval uniform, and Queen Mary in a long white dress, ribbons and bijoux fastened to one shoulder, and wearing a large hat decorated with an abundance of flowers.

Sharad and Mandar were both hopping up and down in excitement, and Tatya and Dada took turns to hoist the boys up for a better view.

'Baba, do you think the king likes it here?' asked Sharad.

'Why wouldn't he like it,' said Mandar, 'look how beautiful it is, with the flowers and the band and the golden thrones.'

'Everything must seem so strange to him,' said Sharad in delight. 'Does he know about aamras? Has he ever tried eating potato bhaaji? He should watch us play kabaddi and lagori so that he can teach our games to the boys in England!'

Tatya and Dada laughed heartily at the small boy's prattle. 'A fine idea, wanting to feed the king of England potato bhaaji!' said Tatya, playfully twisting Sharad's ear with his fingers.

'But it's the king's first time here, so he must learn everything!' protested Sharad.

'It's not his first time here, my boy,' said Dada.

'What?' exclaimed Mandar. 'But you said that this was the first time that a British monarch would set foot in India!'

'Indeed, it is the first time,' said Dada. 'Amazing though it may seem, despite ruling us for one hundred and fifty years, no British monarch has so far found it necessary to visit India. But in fact the king visited India a few years ago when he was the Prince of Wales....'

'...And he still hasn't tried any potato bhaaji,' finished Sharad, solemnly, sending them all into peals of laughter. Tatya laughed till tears came to his eyes. Later he always recalled that when he saw King George V walking down the red carpet to his throne, it was through eyes filled with tears of laughter, as if viewing the scene through a shimmering mirror. And how it had struck him that the small domed gateway with its minarets at water's edge, built for the king, was like a toy Taj Mahal, as white and delicate as paper, and how it was dwarfed by the newer Taj Mahal, Tata's hotel, which gazed down on it in majestic grey stone with its lofty cupolas the colour of brick and rose.

And later the king and queen sat in an open landau pulled by six horses, accompanied by eight carriages of officials, innumerable columns of mounted soldiers, regimental squadrons and a marching band, the whole mass of red and blue and silver, and flags and horses, trotting slowly down a road lined with slender white columns, golden domes, and an infinity of people.

CHAPTER 19

Typhoid is a fever that starts with deception. It is a black spider extending its crooked legs, feeling its sly way out of a dirty corner. Just a cough. Just some tiredness. Sharad was constantly afflicted by coughs, nobody knew why. Perhaps it was the dust motes in the air. Perhaps because he liked to splash in puddles on the road. Perhaps because he liked to wet his head under a tap and run out into the hot sun to feel the cold water trickling down his cheeks and drying in cool patches around his ears. He would cough for a few days, a dry, irritating cough that made its way into his mouth at three in the afternoon and disappeared by six in the evening. Who could tell why? Nobody paid any attention to it. He never stopped playing with the other boys in the dusty patch of ground behind the chawl, from where Radha could hear their shouts and the pounding of their bare feet on the hard-baked soil, while she cooked in the small back room. When Ganesh began a dry cough, nobody remarked on it either. Just like his big brother, laughed the boys. Look, Sharad, your shadow is coughing! For three-year-old Ganesh followed Sharad everywhere, like a shadow, and he chortled now, pleased with his cough, proud to be like his big brother. Ganesh had been left behind on the day of the royal arrival because his forehead was warm and his eyes were pale and his dry cough seemed more pronounced.

But, after all, it was just a cough. And the next day, just some sweating, because it was hot those days, humid. A bit of pain in his stomach because Radha had made some sweet chirote and he had probably eaten too many, though he said he hadn't, because he hadn't been hungry. Then the fright, when a baby on the upper floor caught a fever, and the same night Ganesh's forehead grew hotter too. Cool wet strips of cloth on his forehead. The fever rising with the sun in the morning, and Tatya hurrying to fetch the vaid.

Later, Tatya could not recall the day-to-day details of those weeks because it felt, now, as if he had been moving under a sun so hot that it burned everything around him, the air so thick and humid that he could not see anything but the shapes and the faces directly in front of him. He remembered Ganesh lying limp on the mattress. The wails of the Phadkes upstairs when their baby died of the fever—it was not surprising, for it was barely a few weeks old. But Ganesh—with his bright eyes and sturdy limbs, more robust than his elder brother, full of laughter and life—that was the surprise, the riddle, which even the vaid could not solve and for which there was no answer. Two weeks of fever that crept and scuttled over and under his smooth childish skin, erupting in a starburst of red spots on his chest. Ganesh lay motionless for three days. And then he died. Just like that, thought Tatya, just like that. One moment there was life in him—the next moment it had vanished. There was a second—a pinprick in time—which marked a disappearance, a dissolving. On this side of that second, his chest rose and fell, for a last breath; on the other side of that same second, his body was still.

In the neighbouring Kashinath Chawl, four children died of typhoid fever that month and in Vitthal Wadi near the vegetable market, twelve people died, including seven children. Khatryachi Chawl was considered to have gotten off lightly. Tatya was alone when the health inspector came, for he had sent Radha away—Radha, who had cried so hard, hugging a sobbing Sharad so tightly to her chest that Tatya had to pull the boy away so that he could breathe. He had sent her and Sharad—and the baby she carried in her belly—to her mother in Shervi, to the clean air and fresh well water of the village, to recover among the pomegranate and guava trees of the wada. Away from the dirty damp of Bombay's air, away from the vile disease that wandered through its crowds.

A trio of health officials visited Khatryachi Chawl and other chawls nearby to inspect the water pipes and the drains, and one of the officials, a British man, wrote copious notes in his book. Two weeks later, on a Sunday, a young English lady appeared at the chawl, wanting to talk to the women. Nobody knew whether she had anything to do with the official and his book. She came speaking 'Hindustani' as she called it, but no Marathi, so the women of the chawl, squatting in the balcony of the first floor, simply stared at her warily as she spoke, understanding nothing.

Tatya sat in his room that day, leaning against the wall, exhausted in mind and in body for it was only a month since Ganesh had died. He eavesdropped in a desultory way on the lady's voice outside in the balcony, the curious inflections and lilt she brought to a language he only half-understood himself. It filled him with fear, this half-understood prattle, fear that they—they who were in charge of sewers and notebooks—could not be trusted even to send someone who spoke the language of the chawl.

Though they can certainly be trusted, he thought, to put on grand spectacles with ships sailing in from the horizon, and they can fly flags and pennants and erect fake gold-topped minarets, and entertain everyone with their marching bands.

Less than two months had passed since that day of parades and kings and queens at the jetty when the city and its sparkling sea were enclosed in a golden sphere of light. It seemed a lifetime ago now, it resided in a foreign corner of his life: that morning which had become as worthless as a bauble that had rolled out of sight into a dusty corner. Tears came to his eyes when he thought of that day. They had all been happy together, he and Dada and Sharad and Mandar.

He thought of money. He must make more of it, for he did not wish to live in the chawl anymore. It was a jolt, this thought, for the happiest moments of his life had been lived in Khatryachi Chawl, among its friendly faces.

They must move to a better place, more ventilated, more spacious, with better water, for he and Radha would have more children, at least two more sons, and they would need the space for them. An apartment block, perhaps. But he could not afford it yet. Could barely imagine living in one. He was sure Radha would hate it. He had seen apartments a few times—no communal balconies where you could pop in and out of friendly open doors. There would be no Lele mavshi to shout through the walls to Radha when she needed a bit of extra sugar, no mass rolling out of papads and papdya to the sound of the women's rhythmic songs. These were the things that Radha loved, he knew. But there would be running water in the apartment, no need for crowding around the communal tap in the mornings, no running down to the outhouse to use the lavatory. No need for Radha to erect a makeshift curtained corner in their small room and retreat behind it when it was her time of month, when the room felt heavy and odorous for three days while he cooked tasteless hurried meals of dal and rice in the kitchen for them all. There would be space for a separate room for her. Perhaps they could get a woman to help with the cooking.

But he could not afford to move yet. He could not afford to sink his substantial savings into an apartment, for he needed it as capital for his business. He needed it as a safety buffer, and to keep his business growing. And now, suddenly, he needed to make more money. What had seemed like a growing abundance just a few months ago had turned, overnight, into not enough. *Not enough*—the thought made his insides curl with a strange fear. He felt as if he had been twiddling his thumbs, had lost sight of the ships he still needed to launch, been swept up in the happiness of his wife and his sons, had not thought sufficiently about what to do next. He had slipped—he had become content—he was no better than Nana in his contentment. He felt a moment of shame at this thought about his friend. And in the same moment he felt a weary sort of resentment towards him—for Nana lived a quiet, modest life with his wife and three sons, still an employee of the same silver shop, still perfectly content with his lot—and Tatya envied him his peace of mind, his patience with the world as it was, without the hunger to progress, to move ahead, to make more money, to know more and be more.

When Radha returned to Bombay after four months, it was only with Sharad, for the baby boy born in the wada in Shervi had died within a few hours. And almost three years later, there were still only the three of them—Tatya, Radha, and Sharad—in their room in Khatryachi Chawl, the room which Tatya had resolved to leave but saw no way of doing. And now, in 1914, there were whispers of war, and a sliver of panic was creeping through the markets.

CHAPTER 20

1914

A circle of five men sat in Tatya's pedhi late one evening. Occasionally someone said something in a low voice, but for the most part they sat in silence. Tatya leaned against a large white bolster, lost in thought, staring at the closed wooden shutters of the pedhi opposite. Zaveri, who had huffed his way up the two steps of the pedhi ten minutes earlier—his knees were bad these days—shared the wide bolster with Tatya, and leaned back with his legs stretched out, massaging his right knee. His eyes were closed, as if in meditation. The other three men were Tatya's most trusted cloth dealers—Kanjibhai Parekh, Pareshbhai Patel, and Tansukhrai Bhatia. All three were wholesale merchants who regularly bought large quantities of cloth from Tatya.

A steady August rain drummed on the roof. Tatya leaned over to look out of his pedhi and peered to the left, down the long row of quiet pedhis, towards the entrance of the market. A dark rivulet of water was making its way down towards him, all the way from the entrance. Outside he could see the rain, darkling streaks of ink. Moths fluttered around the yellow lamps that hung down from the arcade ceiling at intervals. The sky rumbled and a moth fell against the glass of the oil lamp placed in the midst of the men. It struggled for a while, its wings beginning to fragment, and Tatya watched it absently, to see whether it would escape. He looked away for a moment, and when he checked on the moth again, it had disappeared. The pristine white sheet on which they sat was scattered with small black insects that had tumbled down through the heavy, humid air to die.

Kanjibhai Parekh was a lean, wiry man of forty-five with a bony face. He sat cross-legged and upright, scanning a newspaper with a frown. He was the only one who had not removed the black cap from his head. Pareshbhai, a good-looking man with light eyes and a rotund face, looked at the world through small round glasses. Zaveri had once said he looked like a bespectacled full moon, and Tatya forevermore thought of Pareshbhai as a young, good-humoured moon. He wasn't in good humour today, though, and sat as glum and taciturn as the rest.

Tansukhrai Bhatia, a small man with a pencil-thin moustache, and with something of a squirrel about his black, beady eyes, now spoke.

'The British are saying the war will be over by their Christmas festival. That's just four months away. Let's say they are wrong, for argument's sake. Let's say it will go on for a bit longer. But the question is, how much longer? And how long will this war-time slump in prices last?' Tansukhrai's family had been in business for three generations and he knew the workings of Mulji Jetha Market like the back of his hand. Tatya had the distinct impression that this man knew the exact contents of every warehouse in the vicinity. He would not have been surprised had Tansukhrai casually and accurately stated the annual income of every member of this gathering.

'But that, dear man, is precisely what nobody knows,' said Zaveri, opening his eyes. 'How long are the bankers going to wait before they get jittery and start calling in their loans? When war breaks out everybody wants to be sure that their money is safe in their own pockets.'

Tatya looked at Zaveri. 'Seth, that time is already upon us. Look at Pareshbhai. His bankers gave him a loan to set up new warehouses in Surat. The whole market knows that Pareshbhai has never defaulted on a loan in his life. He pays in full and with interest. But they are pressuring him for an early repayment.'

Zaveri looked in alarm at Pareshbhai who nodded. 'It will be all right—I think,' muttered Pareshbhai, and then fell silent again, frowning. He looked angry. Tatya wondered whether he should have kept his mouth shut about Pareshbhai's predicament.

Kanjibhai Parekh looked up from his newspaper and began folding up the thin pages, which were limp with humidity. It was getting too dark to read. 'Vaman seth,' he said, looking at Tatya, 'there is a feeling of dread in the market. Prices of cloth and yarn, and even raw cotton, are falling so fast that nobody knows when they will hit rock bottom. But keep in mind that these are panic prices. They have nothing to do with supply and demand. The prices are behaving as if there is a glut of cloth in the market—which there isn't. Cloth production is the same as before. So let us not panic and lose our heads. This state of affairs cannot last.'

Tatya's gumastha, Kishan Mehta, sat cross-legged at a low writing table at the back of the pedhi, ostensibly writing by the light of a small floor lamp. But the pen in his hand hovered above the page more often than it made contact with it. Twice he had dabbed away spots of ink which had dripped on to his page, obscuring the figures there, and now he gloomily gave up the pretence at writing. He sprinkled fine grey sand over his page to blot the wet ink, put the reed pen back in its holder and replaced the cap on his bottle of ink. He listened intently to the conversation.

'But how long can we hold up against such low prices?' said Tatya, sitting up restlessly in his worry. 'The answer, surely, is....'

Zaveri raised his eyebrows. 'The answer is?'

'The answer,' said Tatya, 'is not to rely solely on cloth.'

The other men looked at him in surprise. Tatya himself looked startled by what he had said. He had scarcely been conscious of the words that came out of his mouth. Now that they were out, though, he realized that he had been gripped by the idea for days.

'Let us speak now, as businessmen,' he said, warming up as he spoke. 'We have all made our money in cloth, and Mulji Jetha Market is like the goddess Lakshmi for us. But I did not come to Bombay to become a cloth merchant. I came to Bombay to make money. There is a saying in English—it sounds a bit odd in Gujarati, but I will say it anyway—don't put all your eggs in one basket.'

'Eggs?' said Zaveri, puzzled. 'What does a Brahmin want with eggs?'

'Seth,' said Pareshbhai, 'diversification of risk.'

'Oh, I see. Speak in normal language, can't you,' said Zaveri to Tatya.

It turned out that Tansukhrai Bhatia was the only one among them, apart from Tatya, who had the liquidity to diversify his business—and had the appetite for risk—at this point of time. Indeed, Tansukhrai seemed to thrive on uncertainty, and was the least fazed of Tatya's circle by the war hanging over their heads, and the record slump in cloth prices. He went with Tatya to have a look at a small factory that melted and recycled scrap iron and steel near the docks, which Tatya had found out was up for sale.

'The war has just started,' Tatya said to Tansukhrai. 'There will surely be high demand for iron and steel during the war. Even if the war lasts only a few months, we will make decent profits because this factory is going at a good price.'

'Neither of us knows anything about iron and steel,' said Tansukhrai, but his small black eyes glittered with interest, and his moustache twitched. He can smell a large store of nuts, thought Tatya, suppressing a smile despite the serious nature of their conversation. If this venture did not pay off,

Tatya's hard-earned savings would quite literally go up in the smoke of the factory. Yet, there was nothing for it but to take a risk now. He did not want to remain stuck relying on cloth sales in the midst of this slump, and he needed a way to increase his profits.

'The foreman is known to me,' said Tatya. 'He eats in the same khanaval in Girgaon I used to eat at in the old days. I see him now and then. He told me the owner has become jittery because of the war and wants to sell the factory since it is rather old and run down. But the foreman reckons that with a bit of extra cash the factory has a few more years of life in it.'

'What's in it for him?' said Tansukhrai, a slow smile spreading on his face, as if he already knew the answer.

'An annual bonus linked to profits,' said Tatya with a grin. 'And, of course, he gets to keep his job. Some other owner might bring in his own man for the job. He's a trustworthy fellow. And in any case my gumastha, Kishan Mehta, will keep the accounts.'

'This foreman of yours will have to be very smart indeed if he manages to fool Kishan bhai,' said Tansukhrai with a laugh. 'All right. Let's do it.'

As it was, none of the traders in Mulji Jetha Market need have worried. Far from cloth prices continuing to slump, as the war progressed in Europe, they began rising with astonishing rapidity. Cloth shipments from Europe began to decrease as the transport system was diverted towards the war effort, and as British mills began intensive war work to supply material to the armed forces. Imported textiles became scarce, and the price of cloth made in India ballooned and floated upwards, untethered.

'God Save the King, God Save the King,' chortled Zaveri in delight as business boomed. It was one of the few phrases in English he knew, and these days he scattered the words through his day as liberally as if he were showering flowers on the goddess Lakshmi. Every trader in the sprawling maze of Mulji Jetha Market developed a passion for newspapers, poring over the *Mumbai Samachar* every day, anxiously tracking the progress of the war and of commodity prices. In the run up to war came news of Tilak's return from his prison in Mandalay, at which Girgaon, a delighted Tatya wrote to Dada, had erupted in a blaze of festivity. Then there was the arrival of their fellow Gujarati (Tatya considered himself something of an honorary Gujarati of Mulji Jetha Market by this time), Mohandas Gandhi, the lawyer who had decided to return to India from South Africa during the war. Murari was in his element, walking up and down the lanes of Mulji Jetha Market in his rose and pistachio-coloured sadras, full of whisperings about politics and prices, and ships diverted for war purposes, and consignments of cotton from Surat and Khandesh. The good humour returned to Pareshbhai's moon-face, while Kanjibhai Parekh took it all in his stride and pretended that the price slump had never bothered him at all.

Tatya too could not believe his luck. It was the first time he had witnessed such a boom in the textile business. Indeed, there were just a handful of old traders in the market now who had been witness to first-hand accounts, or had vague childhood memories of their own, of the only other comparable boom of fifty years ago, when the American Civil War had stopped the supply of American cotton to Lancashire's mills. That was when miraculous fortunes were made among cotton traders in India, for Lancashire had to look to Indian cotton to keep its mills running, making the demand and prices for cotton shoot up.

'And fortunes were lost too,' smiled Murari, in his low tinkling whisper to Tatya one evening, 'when the war in America ended. Those who had invested everything in cotton at the height of the boom were ruined. They were left in the dust. All that beautiful money—gone! All those palaces they started building for themselves—gone! Left half-built! Only the crows remained, building their nests in the ruins! There was a time when cotton prices were so high that people were ripping open their mattresses to sell the cotton inside.'

'What? Really, Murari, that is hard to believe,' said Tatya. He was enjoying Murari's stories. He couldn't tell whether to believe all his tales or not, but this evening, after a day of brisk business, when deliveries from the mills had arrived on time and payments from his trusted circle of merchants had poured in, he was ready to sit back and enjoy a steaming cup of tea with some sweet biscuits on the side with Murari, as he waited for Kishan Mehta to finish the last of his accounting for the day.

'Oh yes, their own mattresses that they slept on,' nodded Murari, enjoying himself just as much as Tatya. 'Now that should have been a warning sign. When people are willing to sell the thing on which they lay their heads at night...well, it could not go on forever. Of course, there is always opportunity in war. But if you let it turn your head...well, let it be. I am speaking to the wrong person, am I not?'

'What do you mean?' said Tatya.

'I mean, I don't need to tell you, of all people, not to let these booming times turn your head,' said Murari, slyly. 'You get cloth from the mills and you sell it to your dealers, eh?'

'Yes, of course,' said Tatya, puzzled. 'How else should it be?'

'Well, you know what they are saying about some of the cloth dealers around here. Even some of the mills are doing it. Money is pouring in, yes. But there is still bigger money to be made. You know it very well. Have you never considered it?' Murari smiled mischievously over the rim of his teacup and took a small bite of a sweet biscuit. But there was something dead serious in his eyes, and Tatya felt that Murari was on the brink of saying something, making him some offer. For the first time ever, Tatya wished that Murari would stop talking. He did not want to hear what Murari was about to say.

'Are you suggesting that I indulge in hoarding cloth?' said Tatya quietly.

'You would not be the only one,' said Murari, still with a sweet smile on his face. He could have been offering sweetmeats to a child. 'I know someone who can arrange it for you. Keep your stocks well out of sight, while you wait for the highest bidder.'

Tatya stared at him.

'I only say this as a piece of information,' said Murari, his smile widening further, his eyes soft and pleading as if pained at the thought that Tatya might possibly misunderstand him. 'I think you would never consider such a thing, would you? But, after all, information is king in the market. And that is all I bring to you. Information. Knowledge.' And here he made as if to join his palms together, in deference to the divine nature of knowledge, but his teacup was in the way.

Tatya did not want to say anything that would damage his relations with Murari. He had come to respect his store of knowledge, had even formed an affection for him. But disappointment welled in him now. Could a war change people so much? Or had Murari always been an opportunist? Perhaps that was how he survived, by holding on to a loose web of morals that could be twisted as needed. Avoiding Murari's eyes, he took a quick, last gulp of tea, aware that Murari was watching him.

'You're right, Murari,' he said briskly, gathering up his things. 'You know me too well. As you know, I work with an exclusive circle of dealers. Trustworthy men. Like them, I would never hoard cloth to drive up prices. Nor do my mills hoard cloth—neither Rose Mills, nor Noor Begum Mills.'

'*Your* mills?' said Murari, still watching him.

'Yes, my mills,' said Tatya, an unfamiliar anger rising up his neck and face, till his head was filled with heat. He knew very well what was going on in the market, but he had not expected Murari to make him a dishonourable proposal. He spoke harshly. 'They make what I tell them to make. Their fortunes are my fortunes. So, yes, my mills.'

Kishan Mehta, sitting at the back of the pedhi, was looking open-mouthed at Tatya, his pen suspended in mid-air.

Tatya looked at Murari with a steady gaze. 'I would never cheat my mills by hoarding their cloth and skimming the profits off higher prices. And the mills would never hoard cloth to raise prices either. That's because the management of Rose Mills and Noor Begum Mills is made up of honourable men. And I have every intention of leading an honourable life too.'

Tatya took a deep breath to try and calm himself. His fingers were trembling as he put on his red pagdi. Murari looked nonplussed and just a little shamefaced as Tatya stepped down from the pedhi. Tatya forced himself to nod cordially at Murari before walking out of the market. Nobody had ever suggested to him before that he cheat, and the very idea made him feel unclean, as if his reputation for integrity must be low indeed, for anyone to suggest that he indulge in underhand practices.

Kishan Mehta, still open-mouthed, turned his gaze to Murari who sat there, teacup in hand. Murari looked defiantly back at him. 'He likes to keep his hands clean,' said Murari. 'Yes. But the money clinking through that account book of yours? It is not only because of the war. All that extra money is thanks to the hoarders. The mills and agents who hoard cloth have driven up prices for everybody. *Everybody* benefits because of them.'

Murari heaved himself up and straightened his clothes. Then he grinned at Mehta. 'You may think your hands are clean. But…but…but…! Don't forget the grime under your fingernails,' he said. He began laughing softly, his gaze thoughtful and benign once again, his belly jiggling under his rose-coloured sadra. Mehta heard his tinkling laughter floating back towards the pedhi as he strolled away.

CHAPTER 21

1916

'I hope the money reaches you in time for Vahini's pilgrimage to Pandharpur,' wrote Tatya to Dada. 'I have sent a larger sum than the usual monthly amount, not only for Vahini's journey but also since Sakhu is coming to stay with you.' Sakhu was Dada's eldest daughter. She would be visiting Dhangadh for a wedding along with her in-laws, which would surely create a good deal of expense for Dada.

Tatya was tired after a long day at work, but he wanted to get the letter done. Radha had unrolled a mattress for Sharad, and the boy was sleepily getting ready for bed. Tatya sat at a small wooden table by the window, writing by the light of a lamp hanging from a nail on the wall. It was quiet, save for muted voices floating up from the road where a few people from the chawl had gathered under the tamarind tree for a last chat before bed. Over time people had laid out small piles of bricks under the tree to serve as makeshift seats, and the shady tree now regularly attracted groups of women during the day, and clusters of men in the evening. He could hear the creak of a branch and a sudden rustle of leaves as someone began poking a stick into the tree to knock a tamarind pod or two to the ground. A rare cool breeze wafted in through the open window, lightly lifting the corners of the papers under Tatya's palm.

'Meanwhile business is doing exceptionally well,' he continued writing. 'Not much cloth is coming in from abroad, because of the war. The mills can hardly keep up with the demand. Ordinary long cloth used to sell at six or seven annas for a pound. It is now almost three rupees a pound. Even coarse yarn has gone from four annas to a rupee.'

He paused for a moment to consider how to proceed. With difficulty he forced himself to write the next lines. 'You had asked me to keep you informed about Radha's health—she is well and in her fifth month. She has decided, this time, to remain in Bombay for the delivery since there are better doctors available here, should any complications arise. Of course, I have told her that her mother may come here for the delivery if she wishes.'

Here Tatya stopped writing, laid down his pen, and closed his eyes. He couldn't bear to write any more. He felt that simply to write that she was well, to acknowledge the success, so far, of her pregnancy, was to invite the evil eye. Radha was with child after five long years, after suffering a miscarriage in the interim. Through the day Tatya found himself silently praying to the idol of Ganpati in his pedhi, that his child might live. Another son who would once again be Sharad's shadow, bring the old smile back to Sharad's face. For Sharad, though he played with the other boys as before, had never been the same after his brother's death. Children heal quickly, thought Tatya, they forget easily, but this boy is different. Ganesh's disappearance from their lives appeared to have gouged something out of Sharad. Perhaps it was the shock of seeing his brother's lifeless body, perhaps the fear of seeing his parents helpless with grief, or perhaps he had been jolted by his sudden removal from Bombay to Shervi for months. Tatya could not tell. The boy's eyes retained a smudge of black shadow under them, acquired during those months of sadness and upheaval, giving him a wan, thin look even as he laughed and chattered with his friends. He was now ten years old, and a quiet fellow, given to dreamy spells which he snapped out of when Radha spoke to him sharply. A new addition to the family, a smiling, gurgling baby brother, would be a wonderful thing for the boy—for all of them.

Tatya looked down again at his letter. He couldn't just end it there. He hadn't written to Dada for several days, and didn't want to end his letter on an abrupt note. Nor did he want to elaborate on Radha's pregnancy, for he felt it was a fragile thing; on some days he could hardly bear to look at her, as if she might break under his gaze. Though of late her cheeks had acquired a healthy glow; her eyes were bright and she looked healthier and happier than she had in a long time.

But his old superstitions kept resurfacing, and he felt a foreboding—had he been too fortunate, too fast? Ganesh's death had felt as if he were paying his dues to some cosmic scales of balance, as if his prosperity had been somehow balanced out by that calamity. Surely there must be yet another reckoning for his astonishing success in business. But what about all the other traders in the market? They too were prospering, everyone was making money these days. Was he expecting the sky to fall down on their heads too? He was being a fool. He stretched his stiff neck from side to side. He got up, walked a few steps away and then sat down again. What was the matter with him? He must finish this letter and send it by the morning post. He needed to find something else to say. He picked up his pen.

'It may interest you to know that I have been to the cinematograph, or what is known as the bioscope. I have had neither the time nor the inclination to do so in the past, and in any case I did not see how these cinematographs from America would hold any interest for me. But Nana and Ponkshe told me that one made in India was showing at the Coronation Theatre. It made a great deal of money two or three years ago, and it is still popular so they keep on showing it from time to time. I was pleased to hear that it was titled *Raja Harishchandra*, so I went along. The bioscope is a remarkable invention indeed. It was as if the king and queen had come to life to play out their story of sacrifice. I enjoyed it very much. Ponkshe informed me that when it was first shown, it was introduced to the audience by a troupe of dancing girls. To think that the noble story of Raja Harishchandra was offered to people with such a display. You will be glad to know, however, that that form of cheap entertainment is no longer required to lure people to see the bioscope. I am told that some other similar shows have been made since then, showing stories of our Hindu gods. Incidentally, Ponkshe has been doing well, and is now part owner of the gymnasium behind our chawl.'

Someone rapped smartly on the open door of the room. Tatya looked up, startled, to see the dark outline of Ponkshe standing in the doorway, as if on cue. Catching sight of Sharad settling down to sleep, Ponkshe ducked back into the dim light of the open balcony and peered in at Tatya through the window instead. Grinning, he gestured for Tatya to come out, and then disappeared.

Radha looked up at the noise and raised her eyebrows at Tatya.

'Ponkshe,' said Tatya, in a low voice. 'God knows what he's doing here at this hour.'

Radha smiled at him, amused as usual at Ponkshe's unorthodox ways. Then she sighed and laid down her heavy body on her mattress.

'I'll be back in a while,' he said, and she nodded, eyes closed. Tatya watched her for a moment and then stepped out. He knew that she found Ponkshe's presence entertaining. She had become fond of him, ready as he always was to crack a joke or regale her with amusing anecdotes. Tatya wasn't sure, though, that she would be quite as fond of him if she knew of some of his activities. He knew that Ponkshe frequented the lavani theatres, and suspected that he had struck up some kind of an arrangement with a woman there. He felt quite sure that Ponkshe would never marry. Fortunately, he hardly ever came to the chawl despite its proximity to the gymnasium. Tatya preferred it that way. He liked Ponkshe, but all the same it was best not to encourage his presence near his family. He certainly did not want Sharad to overhear any of his cruder jokes, though of course Ponkshe did not dare to speak that way in front of Radha.

Tatya found Ponkshe under the tamarind tree. With him was a man Tatya did not recognize. The group of people who had been sitting under the tree earlier had disappeared, and the last bit of indigo was fading from the sky, dissolving into darkness. A small herd of buffaloes ambled past, snuffling. There were the muted sounds of trams and the tinkling of bicycles from Sandhurst Road nearby.

'Tatya, this is Chandu Barve,' said Ponkshe, with a friendly hand on the man's shoulder.

'Namaskar,' Barve said politely, joining his palms.

Tatya did the same, and looked enquiringly at Ponkshe.

'Let's sit,' said Ponkshe, and without waiting for the others, he settled himself on one of the brick seats. 'I've been thinking, Tatya, and making some enquiries. About the bioscope we went to see.'

Tatya nodded, wondering what was coming.

'You're a businessman, aren't you. And so am I, now, in my own small way, but you're the real businessman among us. You've made money in cloth. And you own that iron and steel factory—how is that doing, by the way?' asked Ponkshe, as the others sat down too.

'It's doing well,' said Tatya, with satisfaction. 'There is plenty of old iron available around the docks—we are also doing some shipbreaking work and melting down the iron. Demand is high because of the war, of course.'

Ponkshe looked at him thoughtfully. 'It is as I told you,' he said to the man called Barve.

Barve was a nondescript-looking fellow of about thirty. He wore a narrow black cap, a black coat, a white dhoti, and could have merged without difficulty into any ordinary crowd on the street. He had a thin black moustache and close-cropped hair just visible under his cap. He maintained a very polite expression on his face throughout, as if aware that his welcome was uncertain.

'What are you talking about?' said Tatya, at a loss.

'I mean, you are not afraid of investing your money in different things. You have a cloth business. Now, suddenly, you have an iron and steel business,' said Ponkshe.

'I don't know anything about iron and steel,' said Tatya, pointedly, as if to put things in perspective. 'The foreman is running it, for all practical purposes.'

'But it's your money that's keeping it running,' said Ponkshe.

'Of course. Tansukhrai Bhatia and I are in it together. And he has found a relative of his who used to work in a shipbreaking business. Tansukhrai talks to him for advice sometimes.'

'So it's not necessary that you know all about a business before investing in it, is it?'

'I suppose not,' said Tatya, 'as long as you are sure of the returns and have trusted advisers to guide you.'

'Well, I have a new business proposition for you,' said Ponkshe, smiling, putting his hand on Barve's shoulder again. 'The cinematograph! What do you think, Tatya?'

'I think you have gone mad,' said Tatya, calmly. 'You go to see one cinematograph and you think you know all about it, do you? And what does your friend here have to do with this?'

'Barve knows how to work a camera. And he has worked in the theatre. The cinematograph is a good business to get into, Tatya. That show we went to see—*Raja Harishchandra*—do you know how much money it has made in just two or three years? Thousands of rupees! After that the same man made another mythological film called *Mohini Bhasmasur*—people thronged to see it. It's a sure thing. Better to jump into the business now, I say, for it may be a temporary craze. Make some money on it, and get out.'

Tatya sighed, the tiredness of the day seeping into his head. He did not want this ridiculous discussion about Ponkshe's flight of fancy. Perhaps another day he might have laughed about it, but at the moment he didn't have the energy.

'My dear Ponkshe,' said Tatya, 'have some sense. I am a selling agent of cloth. I happen to be making some money from an iron and steel factory, probably just for the duration of the war, however long it lasts. What makes you think I want to have anything to do with theatres and all that nonsense?'

'Not theatre, Saheb,' said Barve, hesitantly joining in. 'The cinematograph is different. We use a camera to....'

'It's all the same to me,' said Tatya, shortly. 'Actors dressing up in costumes and dancing about on the stage. I want nothing to do with it.'

'Saheb, we can make a beautiful bioscope about our Lord Ganpati,' said Barve, joining his palms in reverence as he uttered the words.

'I appreciate your coming to see me, Barve,' said Tatya, as politely as he could, getting up. 'But I am really not interested.'

Barve stood up too, his palms still joined in a namaskar, to take his leave. He looked disappointed. Tatya beckoned Ponkshe to walk with him to the chawl staircase.

'You really are the limit, Ponkshe,' he said, annoyed. 'What possessed you to think that I would want to get involved with your song and dance people? You realize I have a young son, do you think I want him to get involved with these theatre folk? Where did you meet this Barve, anyway?'

Ponkshe did not look in the least apologetic. 'He came to the lavani theatre looking for actors for his cinematograph. But he doesn't have the money for it. Look, I'll come and talk to you tomorrow. Explain it all to you.'

'I don't need an explanation,' said Tatya, wearily. 'Let's just drop it.'

'You don't understand, Tatya,' said Ponkshe. 'Barve isn't a song and dance fellow, as you call it. He's a technician.'

'A technician?' said Tatya, puzzled. 'What do you mean?'

'I'll tell you tomorrow. You look like you need some sleep. But listen, Tatya, Barve is serious about making a bioscope on the story of Ganpati. And there is something more to it—it's not just about making money.'

Tatya had no idea what Ponkshe was talking about, but wanting to be rid of him for now, said, 'See you tomorrow then.'

Ponkshe waved jovially as he walked back to Barve, who still stood under the tamarind tree.

'Or some other day if you don't have time tomorrow,' Tatya added, for good measure.

But Tatya was not destined for sleep that night. Radha mumbled and moaned in her sleep, and when he sat up on the mattress and put a hand on her forehead to calm her, he was horrified to find that her skin was hot under his palm. He did not dare wake her up, even to get her some water to drink, but sat there looking at her in dread for what seemed like hours. Finally she settled into a deep sleep, her hot forehead cooled with a drizzle of perspiration. He could not bear the thought of losing this child too. It seemed as if this box-like room of theirs was suddenly marooned in a night filled with superstition and shadows and malign forces. He recited the Ram Raksha in his mind to calm himself. It was almost morning when he lay his head on his pillow. He could hear life stirring in the darkness outside, the first chirrups of sparrows and the rustle of the tamarind and neem trees stirring in the first cool morning breezes. He must have fallen asleep, briefly, for the next thing he heard was the sound of Radha quietly making tea in the kitchen. He sat up, feeling as if the cotton from his pillow had seeped into his head, leaving him unable to think clearly. It was still very early. Sharad was asleep. He looked at Radha anxiously.

'What happened at night? You were moaning and troubled in your sleep. Do you have a fever?'

'No, no, I am fine,' said Radha, but her eyes were bright, as if there was a flame burning in them. Or was it a reflection of the first ethereal lights of dawn?

Tatya looked at her closely, and then made up his mind to tell Lele mavshi to keep an eye on Radha that day. He stared at the floor, unwilling to ask Radha anything further. Perhaps she was all right. It had been a warm night, after all.

Radha observed him with concern. 'There is no need to worry,' she said. 'You will be the one falling ill if you worry so much.'

Tatya nodded, glum. His night-time fears were receding. Radha really did look all right this morning. He wished he had slept better himself. He felt bleary and unfocused. He headed out to bathe, to pour tambyas of cold water over himself.

'What did Ponkshe want last night?' asked Radha, when he returned. Tatya looked at her standing there, a rounded figure in a mustard-yellow sari, her wrists covered in green glass bangles and her hair pulled back into a neat, severe khopa.

'One of his absurd ideas,' said Tatya. 'He brought a fellow with him who wanted money to make a bioscope about the story of Ganpati. He thinks I will make a good profit on it.'

'The story of Ganpati?' repeated Radha in wonder, joining her palms in reverence. She fidgeted with her dark green bangles, a sound like a cascade of cold, glassy water. Then she said, softly, 'It was Ganesh's favourite story.'

Tatya nodded, not looking at her.

'Perhaps it is a sign,' she said.

'A sign of what?' said Tatya, his heart beginning to beat strangely.

'I don't know. It feels like a sign. From god.'

Tatya gazed at her, and then said, 'I refused him. Because it is a foolish idea for me to get involved in something like that.'

'How can we say no to Lord Ganpati?' she said, joining her palms again, a worried crease on her forehead, a hopeful light in her eyes.

'I am not saying no to Ganpati. I've said no to that fellow who wants to make a bioscope,' said Tatya, frowning.

Radha said nothing more. But Tatya could not stop thinking about her words. A sign...could it truly be a sign from god? The idea soothed his mind, calmed his head, which had been churning with a peculiar heat, as if his fears were getting in the way of thinking clearly. Last night he had been weary, tired. Now, in the fresh light of morning he unexpectedly felt that the idea might be worth exploring. And what had Ponkshe said—he had said it was not simply about making money, but something else too. He must find out what Ponkshe meant.

Ponkshe, true to his word, turned up at Tatya's pedhi that afternoon. He looked around appreciatively at the pristine white mattress and bolsters, the steel almirah, the stack of cloth samples, and the silver platter laid out with betel nut, paan, and sugar crystals for visitors. He engaged in a bit of small talk with Kishan Mehta, who, at the end of a ten minute chat, was all smiles and chuckling to himself as he returned to the columns of numbers in his ledger.

'Made a new friend, I see,' said Tatya, looking up from his newspaper as Ponkshe finally settled down next to him with a charming smile.

'I'm a friend of the world, Tatya,' said Ponkshe, comfortably. 'Now speaking of friends, I have to tell you that Barve isn't exactly a friend. I don't know him too well. But he seems a sincere fellow.'

'And you met him at the lavani theatre,' said Tatya.

'He has nothing to do with the lavani troupes,' said Ponkshe, ignoring the note of disapproval in Tatya's voice. 'He came to find out whether any of the dancers wanted to act in his bioscope. He needs women to play Parvati and her maid servants.'

'But why does he want women? After all, men take on the roles of female characters on stage,' said Tatya, puzzled.

'He says that the cinematograph is different. That it will look much better if women play the female parts.'

'What did the dancers say?'

'They said no. Not a single one of them was willing. They said it was beneath them to do any such thing. Barve will probably have to make do with male actors.'

Tatya was taken aback. 'But, Ponkshe, if even the women of the lavani troupes think it is beneath them to work in a bioscope, why do you want me to get mixed up in this?'

'It is a temporary problem, Tatya,' said Ponkshe. 'The bioscope is new to them, and so they feel it is beneath them. Think about it. There is nothing about the cinematograph that is any better or worse than being on the stage. The only difference is that instead of acting on a stage, you act in front of a camera.'

'What you say makes sense,' said Tatya, thoughtfully. In fact, he was relieved that the lavani women would not be involved in the venture. He had no desire to come into contact with them. Now that he and Ponkshe were discussing the idea rationally, he was prepared to give it his full consideration. 'What does it matter whether an actor performs on a stage or in front of a camera? And *Raja Harishchandra* was a fine, clean story with no actresses in it. What could be wrong about bioscopes showing the stories of our gods and goddesses?'

'Exactly,' said Ponkshe, looking pleased. 'Now about Barve—he used to work with a man who made short films. People have been making short films about topical events for a while now, filming King George's durbar in Delhi, Janmashtami celebrations, and so on. Did you hear about that South Indian mathematician who got a degree in England many years ago? Somebody even made a short film about his return to India.'

'Really?' said Tatya, impressed. He had not considered the possibility that the cinematograph could be a way of educating people about current events.

'Haven't you seen the newsreels brought out by the British?' said Ponkshe, impatiently.

'No,' said Tatya, 'where would I have seen such a thing?'

'They show them along with the American bioscopes,' said Ponkshe.

'So you go to American bioscope shows?' said Tatya.

'I go everywhere and do everything,' said Ponkshe, grinning. 'Which means that I am much better informed than you about what is going on in the city. I suggest you go and see one of these American bioscopes.'

Tatya ignored the suggestion. 'What were you saying about the short films on current events?'

'Barve has worked as assistant to a man called Kulkarni, who made a few short films. Now Barve wants to make a longer film, something like *Raja Harishchandra*. He has managed to arrange for a camera from Kulkarni, but he needs money to make the film.'

Tatya thought for a while. 'How much money does he need?'

'He needs ten thousand rupees. He reckons you will make a good profit on that—at least double the amount. And he plans to show it at the time of the next festival of Ganesh Chaturthi. Just think, Tatya. People go into ecstasies during the worship at Ganpati pandals in their neighbourhoods. Now imagine people coming to see your bioscope on the lord Ganpati—what could be more like devout community worship than hundreds of people flocking to see his story on film?'

Into Tatya's mind floated the scenes in Girgaon at Ganesh Chaturthi— community courtyards packed with people raising their voices in devotional song, bells clanging, and fragrant smoke rising, streets surging with Ganpati after Ganpati being escorted towards the sea for immersion, the flare of lamps, the intonation of mantras, the thrill of the divine among them. And what if all those people, in their devotion, came to see a bioscope about Ganpati? Not only could it make a very large amount of money, but it would also be a personal act of devotion to offer such a bioscope to the public. So that's what Ponkshe had meant when he said it wasn't just about the money! A slow excitement began welling up in Tatya's chest. This was what made him feel alive, this feeling of kicking balls in several directions at once, and running after them with all his might. The worry that had been nagging him about Radha and her pregnancy was pushed aside and he felt his spirits lift.

He smiled at Ponkshe, and nodded. Ponkshe grinned back at him. 'I'll bring Barve to see you again,' he said. 'He says it will take him only about six months to make the bioscope.'

It was three months later that Tatya wrote to Barve in Poona, where he was making the bioscope, to enquire about progress. Barve replied with a vague letter, to say that it would be ready very soon though he could not give a specific date. 'This is a project that brings together art and the spiritual,' he wrote, 'both of which work through the divine illusion of maya. Rest assured that we are proceeding with the blessings of Lord Ganpati.' Tatya clicked his tongue in annoyance at this language. He felt impatient with Barve's roundabout way of expressing himself. He walked over to the gymnasium the next morning to show the letter to Ponkshe. Ponkshe was standing by the wrestling pit, watching the young wrestlers commence their day by constructing a Shivling of the soft red earth in the pit. One of the young men, his bare torso already glistening with sweat, lit an incense stick and began the morning worship of the Shivling.

'Look at this,' said Tatya, showing Ponkshe the letter. 'Why can't this friend of yours communicate clearly?'

Ponkshe read a few lines and then laughed. 'As long as he makes the bioscope, who cares how he talks or writes?'

Tatya was about to say something to the effect that people should give straight answers to straight questions, but was interrupted by a cry from the road. A moment later, as if dropped from the sky by a yellow sun beam, he saw Nagesh Godse's lanky form pounding towards them from the direction of the chawl. His clothes were oily and black as if he had jumped up in the midst of repairing a bicycle. Tatya's mouth went dry.

'It's Radha vahini,' panted Nagesh Godse. 'She's....'

Tatya did not wait for him to finish. He raced back to the chawl, bounded up the flight of stairs to the first floor and found his way blocked by about a dozen women in the corridor, their voices buzzing with questions, concerns, and loud commiserations.

And above all came a horrible guttural voice, a groaning, and then a sudden scream.

'Lele mavshi,' he shouted, pushing his way through.

He heard Lele mavshi's voice inside, indistinct and muffled, and his terror grew. Why was she not coming out to him? Should he call Vaidyabua? What should he do? He realized that he did not have a clue as to what was to be done in the circumstances, for Radha had gone to Shervi for all three of her previous deliveries, and in any case she had never had a baby earlier than it was due. Kashi, Lele mavshi's daughter-in-law, hurried out to Tatya, her face pale.

'Please don't go in now,' she said. 'The pains started very suddenly, and the baby is coming. With God's grace, it will go well.'

She turned to hurry back inside, but Tatya stopped her and said, 'But why now? Why in the eighth month? What does it mean?'

She managed a weak smile and said, 'It simply means that the baby is ready to come out.'

It was evening by the time Tatya stepped into his home, a weak tingling in his legs, to look at his newborn. There was an uncanny hush as Lele mavshi called him in. Kashi stood unmoving as Pami quietly fussed with some cloth, folding it into wads. Chinmay Phadke's elderly mother, who by good fortune was visiting him in Bombay, had helped a great deal. She sat on the floor by the window. He had heard in the intervening hours that she often helped the midwife in her village. None of the women would meet his eyes. And why were they all mute? With fear in his heart he looked at Radha lying on the mattress—a far-off part of his mind noticed that his eyes searched first for her, not for the new baby—and when he saw her wan, perspiring face blinking up at him, he exhaled. He hadn't even been aware that he'd been holding his breath. She was all right. Of course she was all right. He had heard her voice through it all, hadn't he? And now he looked at the baby, lying in the crook of Radha's arm, a wrinkled little doll of flesh and bone. The eyes were closed in two puffy slits, and the baby was in deep sleep, a picture of peace and fragility. His realized his eyes were wet.

'He is the most beautiful baby I have ever seen,' he said, kneeling down to lean over his wife and child.

'Not a he,' whispered Radha. Her eyes were dark and afraid, as if she were forcing herself to look into his eyes. Her cheeks were stained with tears, dried streaks. 'I'm sorry. We have a daughter.' And Tatya understood the silence in the room. He felt a silence in his heart too. In his mind a slow shattering of the world he had built up, stone by stone. He had plans. He needed two sons to see his plans through. His business was meant to be Govind Abhyankar & Sons. And yet, and yet it was impossible that Radha should apologize for bringing forth a child as delicate and wondrous as this one. And so he shook his head at her, and smiled.

'I never saw a more perfect child,' he whispered. He knew then, that till his dying day he would cherish Radha's smile of relief and delight.

Days of thin, reedy wailing, nights that smelled of milk, and an abundance of soft cotton squares stitched for the baby, arranged in clean piles or washed and hung out to dry, turned their home into a kind of soft nest. And in the midst of it all, the new baby, like a newly-hatched bird, barely moving in its fragile beauty. Tatya lost his heart to his baby daughter.

But a week later, Chinmay Phadke's mother informed them that there was a reason why the child was so quiet and still and delicate.

'Look at her left arm,' said the old woman, in low, authoritative tones. 'She is not moving it at all. Look how she waves her other arm about, clenches her fist. Now look at her left leg. She does not kick it about like her right leg. It just lies still.'

'What does it mean?' asked Tatya, a catch in his voice.

Chinmay Phadke's mother was a brusque woman, unsentimental about the mundane business of childbirth. But she paused now, looked Tatya square in the face, and spoke softly.

'It means that her left arm and her left leg do not work,' she said. 'Your child will live. But one arm and one leg will not work.'

Tatya stared at her, and tried to shut out, with all his might, the gulping sobs of Radha who sat curled in the corner of the room.

Tejaswini Apte-Rahm

CHAPTER 22

1916

She was a thin, pathetic looking thing. When wrapped in Radha's sari padar, she could have been mistaken for a doll. She lay as still and placid as a teaspoon of water, barely moving. It was an ordinary day at the chawl. Sharad had gone to school, there was the clanging of pots from the kitchen next door, the usual shouts of vendors of peanuts and guavas and bananas floated up from the street. The walls of their room were freshly painted a light blue, against which was offset the wooden furniture, a small writing table, the low cupboard, two chairs, all shiny and newly polished in their excitement and anticipation of the new baby. When Sharad and Ganesh had been born, they had made do with a small borrowed cradle. But now there was enough money and more for comforts of all kinds, and so there was a new wooden cradle with a dark ebony-black frame in which were arranged, like a colourful nest for eggs, soft blankets and sheets embroidered by Radha in the last weeks of her pregnancy when she had sat still and dreamt with a small smile on her face, only her fingers busy with little silver needles and threads.

The new addition to their room in the chawl was Mai, who had arrived from Shervi early that morning. She had missed the delivery, for the baby had come a full month earlier than expected. But she was here now, to inspect the misery of her daughter giving birth to a girl. Except that her daughter did not seem miserable in the least. Mai sat on the floor by the wall and Radha noticed that her mother refused the comfort of leaning back on the bolster arranged behind her. She stared at Radha who sat on the floor too, rocking the cradle, rhythmically pulling on the rope attached to it.

'There was no real reason for me to come, I suppose,' said Mai. She did not explain herself, but she didn't need to. She had pointedly not bothered to look at the new baby, had shown not the slightest curiosity to peer over the rim of the new cradle to look into her granddaughter's face. 'Still, you insisted, so I came. At least you are looking well.'

Radha felt that Mai's stone-grey eyes were berating her for her unseemly display of contentment. 'I am happy you came, Mai,' said Radha.

'By God's grace, you may yet be blessed with a son,' said Mai, sighing. She held the end of her red sari and pulled it tighter around her head, firmly tucking the cloth behind her ears. 'Well, now that I am here I can help you get on with a few things while you look after the child. I have brought some mango pickle with me and some of our dried red chillies. I will pound them for you while I am here. I noticed you have a bag of raw salt lying there, I can help you clean it. You need to drink milk. It will make you strong again. I have heard that the gawlis here are crooks and that they add water to the milk. Are you sure you are getting undiluted milk?' Mai got up and went over to a cloth bundle she had brought with her, which was still lying next to the door. Tatya had deposited it there and stepped out to let his wife and mother-in-law talk undisturbed. Mai began to undo the large knot at the top of the bundle. A small golden stain had appeared on one side, and she clicked her tongue.

'Looks like some oil has leaked out of the pickle jar,' she muttered. She was clearly getting ready to bustle about Radha's home. And she still refused to come near the cradle.

'Mai,' said Radha, softly, looking at her mother. 'Don't you want to see your granddaughter?'

Mai nodded, but continued fiddling with the bundle till she managed to prise open the knot with her thin brown fingers. Finally the cloth bundle lay open, revealing a large jar with an orange streak of oil running down its side. Then she heaved up her bony frame with a groan, and walked over to the cradle with mincing steps. She peered in, at the baby lying amid embroidered flowers and spirals and starbursts.

'I see you've been embroidering,' she said. Then she nodded, gazing at the baby and continued, 'Yes, all right. Of course, all babies are the same, eh?'

Radha felt a tightness in her throat, but she could delay the news no longer. 'This baby is not the same as all the others,' she said, her voice wavering. The room darkened, and she realized that Tatya had appeared at the door, blocking out the light. He stood there, waiting, as if aware that a thing of import was unfolding in the room.

'What do you mean?' said Mai, frowning into the cradle. 'What's wrong with her?'

In a small voice, not daring to meet her mother's eyes, Radha said, 'There is something wrong with her left arm and leg. They don't move.'

And tears filled her eyes, her brave front dissolving in an instant. She wiped the tears rolling down her cheeks.

For a moment, Mai was stunned into silence. 'What are you saying, Yamuna?' she exclaimed, frightened. She reached into the cradle and began unwrapping the thin cotton cloth that cocooned the baby.

'Don't! Don't wake her!' cried Radha, in distress, jumping to her feet, but it was too late. The baby began wailing as the warm covers were ripped off, and began to flail about on her back. Mai bent down to look at her movements, noted the sickening stillness of half her body, and then abruptly picked up the baby and walked over to the window, oblivious to her son-in-law standing nearby. By the light of the sun that filtered in, she gazed into the baby's face as if she might find a clue to this turn of events there.

'She'll be all right,' said Radha, taking her child back from her mother, and cradling her and hushing her. 'With the proper care....'

'Care?' said Mai, with incredulity. She walked to the empty cradle and gripped it, as if she needed to do something with her hands. 'What care can you give her?'

'The doctor said that we should massage her regularly and see if it helps,' said Tatya, speaking up.

'Help to do what?' said Mai.

'Blood circulation, perhaps...' Tatya said, hesitating.

'There is a special oil...' added Radha. She exchanged a look with Tatya, and knew that they both sounded as weak as they felt.

'She might still walk,' said Tatya, 'There are similar cases. She might be able to walk a bit. Maybe with a limp.' Mai looked at the child, which now lay quiet and somnolent in Radha's arms. Then she shook her head as if her daughter and son-in-law had taken leave of their senses.

'We will look after her,' said Radha, 'we will make sure we do everything we can to strengthen her arm and leg.'

'But why? Why look after her?' said Mai, in a temper, her voice suddenly harsh. 'What is the meaning of looking after such a child?'

Radha stared at her, shocked. 'She is my....'

'Yes, she is your child. But what is the point, really? Leave her fate to god. There is no need to look after her, no need to give her any special treatment. God made her the way she is, and he will look after her if he wishes to.'

'Do you mean to say we should abandon her? I will do no such thing!'

said Tatya, losing his temper too, and forgetting to speak in the tone of respect he normally used with his mother-in-law.

'I do not suggest that you leave her out for the crows,' replied Mai, her anger unabated, 'but there is no need to look after her either. Feed her if you must, and forget about her. Don't waste your time. Yamuna must not slave over this child. She must conserve her strength to produce another son.' Mai, too, had forgotten her usual reticence with her son-in-law and stood erect, looking straight into his eyes, and gripping her red sari tight around her thin, bony shoulders.

Radha stood stock-still, frightened, clutching her baby.

For a moment they all stood motionless, Tatya and Mai glaring at each other. Then Tatya shook his head, his gaze fixed on Mai's grey eyes, and spoke in a low, calm voice. 'She is my child. My precious child. I will not abandon her to her fate. I will protect her. You will see.'

Mai nodded almost imperceptibly. 'You may protect her now,' she said. 'Protect her if you wish. Go buy your special oils and consult your doctors. You have the money to do it. But for how long will you protect her? A girl is a burden at the best of times. And a girl whose body only half works? She will be a chain around your neck. Around both your necks.' With an arm outstretched, Mai pointed at both Tatya and Radha, as if foretelling the doom that awaited them.

'Who is going to marry her?' continued Mai, her hands trembling as she tucked the end of her sari evermore tightly at her waist. 'She will remain unmarried and be a burden first for you, and then for her brother. If you do find somebody willing to marry her, it will be someone far beneath you. Good luck finding a groom for a cripple. And how do you think she will be treated at her marital home? Like dirt. So what exactly are you saving her for? For a life of misery? Misery for you and misery for her.'

Radha swallowed deep gulps of air into her throat, but could not stop the tears from pouring down her face. She looked down and noticed that the embroidered cotton wrapped around the baby had wet splotches on it. She could see her baby's skin through it, delicate, wet skin, clinging to the wet cloth. The hum of voices next door had stopped. They must be listening, she thought, miserably. All right, then, let them listen. Let Lele mavshi and all of them know what my mother is like. But she would guard this baby with her life, even though she knew that everything Mai said would probably come true. But till those bad things happened—whatever

Tejaswini Apte-Rahm

the bad things were—she would let only good things happen to her child. She looked at Tatya. His face was grim and set, like a stone. Say something, she pleaded, silently. Say something, anything. But he didn't. And finally when a voice spoke, it was her own.

'Her life will not be a misery,' she said, and was taken aback at how loud her own voice was, how it rang out in that small room. 'I will make sure of it.'

She had never dared to speak with such confidence in front of Mai, and certainly not in front of her husband. They both looked at her now, in surprise, as if remembering her presence in the room.

She saw, to her astonishment, that her unexpected words appeared to have doused the temper in Mai's eyes. And Tatya was looking at her with the beginnings of a small smile on his lips.

Mai looked at both of them with pity, and shook her head as if giving up the fight. 'It's your decision,' she said. 'Just remember, child,' she continued, in softer tones, addressing Radha, 'that I know what misery the life of a woman can be.'

At these words, Tatya looked away, discomfited. Then he said, 'Sit down, Mai, it is almost time to eat. Rest now.'

Mai continued looking at Radha for another moment. Radha returned her gaze with a small nod, an acquiescence on this point; she and Mai shared knowledge that no man would ever know, the knowledge of how narrow their path was as women. The daughter she held in her arms had already wandered off that path, begun life with a fateful misstep. For no fault of her own, thought Radha. But the things that mattered—her mother's fate as a red widow, her own narrowly missed fate of a twilit life—how often were they really one's own fault anyway?

'I will leave tomorrow,' said Mai, bending down to lift the jar of pickle.

'Please stay, Mai,' said Radha.

Mai shook her head, stubborn. 'There is no need for me to stay now. You must manage things yourself.'

'Won't you at least stay for the naming ceremony?' said Tatya, gently.

Mai hesitated.

'Just a few days,' said Radha.

'I don't know what name you will find for a child like her,' muttered Mai, and then said, 'What are you going to call her?'

Radha opened her mouth to say that they hadn't yet decided, when Tatya spoke.

'Durga,' he said, firmly. 'She will be called Durga. The invincible. She won't need me or her mother or anyone else. She will meet her fate with a weapon in every one of her eight arms.'

CHAPTER 23

1917

For months Tatya heard nothing from Chandu Barve. The festival of Ganesh Chaturthi, for which the bioscope should have been ready and shown in Girgaon, came and went. Tatya gritted his teeth and thought of the ten thousand rupees he had invested in Barve. Throngs of people strolled along the streets around Khatryachi Chawl, buying colourful clothes and festive sweets at makeshift stalls, people who should have been spending their money on seeing Chandu Barve's bioscope. Instead, the Coronation Theatre on the corner of Sandhurst Road, which Tatya thought would have been the ideal place to show Barve's film, was running some American film about sailors and pirates. The bioscope, promised Barve now in a letter, would be ready well before the following Ganesh Chaturthi, saying that this would give them plenty of time to publicize it and pull in large crowds.

Barve would fall silent for weeks on end. Then like a bolt from the blue, a letter would arrive with an excuse for the delay. The lead actor had malaria. Barve's sister was getting married; he needed to organize the wedding. The monsoon had put a stop to the filming for two months because the film could only be shot outdoors. He blames everything and everyone but himself, thought Tatya in disgust. But there was nothing to be done now. Tatya could only wait.

Meanwhile, the price of cloth, and the fortunes of the traders at the market, fattened like a man fed to bursting, and Tatya felt that now, surely now, this engorged creature would explode. But it didn't. It ripened in the heat of the faraway war. The cloth coming in from the mills of Lancashire, and the city called Manchester, dwindled away, soaked up by the war, unable to cross the water for lack of ships. And the only cloth that mattered, now, was that made right here in India.

Tatya hired a couple of extra hands at the pedhi to deal with the sheer volume of textile that was passing through the looms and through his warehouses. Matthew Wales was perpetually harried because what he really wanted was new machinery from England to conjure up more cloth, and he wanted, in a moment of desperate fantasy, the government to lay new rail lines, buy new locomotives, which could transport even more cotton to Bombay. But the war prevailed, of course. The British had no money, no materials for such fancies. It was all spent on the war, in the hope that fewer Englishmen would die.

Ponkshe dropped in at the pedhi one day with a message for Tatya. Tatya was looking over Kishan Mehta's accounts with great satisfaction; the profits were unbelievable.

'What's this message you have for me?' said Tatya to Ponkshe. Ponkshe had put on weight, Tatya noticed, but it wasn't the idle weight of prosperity. He had become more muscular, more like a tree trunk than ever. It was all that time spent at the gymnasium.

'From Chandu Barve,' said Ponkshe, leaning against a bolster and helping himself to some sugar crystals from the tray laid out for visitors.

'What does he say?' said Tatya, sitting up.

'Well, the message is not exactly from him. Someone who knows him arrived from Poona this morning at my chawl. Says Barve's bioscope is ready and he is planning to bring it to Bombay in the next few days. I expect you'll get a letter from him.'

'It's about time,' said Tatya, in exasperation.

It was ten days later that Tatya sat down to watch the bioscope that Chandu Barve had brought from Poona. It was late at night at the modest Sharada Theatre in Girgaon, which was no more than a large, sturdy tent. Tatya had hired it, agreeing to wait till after the theatre's last evening show, to watch Chandu Barve's bioscope. The projector came to life, throwing black and white moving pictures on to a thick white canvas stretched taut. In the midst of the flickering rectangle stood actors, gesticulating extravagantly, dressed in saris but oddly masculine. Behind them, a crude painted backdrop of a palace. The actors stood on a low platform, like a stage.

Ganpati appeared on the scene, with an elephantine head of absurd proportions, the monstrous head dwarfing the body of the actor who was wearing it. He was mostly immobile, as if moving might cause him to stumble and topple over. Shiva emerged from a clump of bushes with a black rope around his neck which was, presumably, meant to be a snake. Tatya could barely make out what story the sorry ensemble of actors was trying to convey. It was all made worse by the fact that freakish dark splotches appeared periodically around the edges of the frame, obscuring the images as they flickered in a patchwork of light and shadow, as if someone were blinking their eyes rapidly at the sun.

After about twenty minutes, a slapping, flapping sound from the projector. The film reel had run out. Tatya sat still in his chair for a moment, as if waiting for the next reel to be loaded, hoping, and at the same time dreading, that there was more than this miserable twenty minutes. Then he turned to Barve.

'Is that it?' he said, quietly. He felt a rising heat in his neck and face.

'Yes, Saheb,' said Barve, smiling apologetically, 'For now.'

The theatre tent had fallen dark and quiet. The man running the projector lit an oil lamp and sat back into the darkness outside the dim glow, as if waiting to be dismissed.

'What is the meaning of this...this...mess?' said Tatya, incredulous.

'Saheb, making a bioscope is a new technology in our country,' said Barve, with that infuriating smile on his face. 'We ran into many problems. I have worked very hard, Saheb, but the developing was faulty and the printing of the film leaves much to be desired. To tell you the truth, the man who did the developing was a wastrel. I told him that Abhyankar saheb in Bombay has set his heart on serving the lord Ganpati, and you have let him down. I resolved to immediately come here, and lay the result of our humble efforts before you. If you so desire, we can try and try again. With god on our side anything is possible.'

Tatya could hardly believe his ears. The man appeared to want more money from him.

'Barve,' said Tatya, in as calm a voice as he could muster, 'what has become of my ten thousand rupees?' He was determined not to lose his temper—not yet—there must be a way to resolve this, he thought, though for the life of him he could not see what the solution might be. He could not stop a slow fury beginning to surge through him.

'Saheb, the ten thousand rupees—the actors needed to be paid, and the hire of the camera, and all the costs....'

'You mean the costs of making that ridiculous elephant head? The costs of hiring men to wear saris and look like clowns?' It was no good, he could not keep his temper, and his voice rose and shook with anger.

'As Saheb knows, women do not wish to act in the bioscope,' began Barve, defensively, but Tatya cut him off.

'I am well aware of that,' he said, his voice scathing, 'but I also know that there are actors who are more than capable of looking like women. Have you ever heard of Bal Gandharva? He is more feminine than a real woman. Have you ever seen the other talented actors who work on stage dressed as women? Do you take me for a fool?'

Barve said nothing. Tatya could barely see the expression on his face, but he ranted on.

'You told me that you needed sunlight to make the bioscope—so why that ludicrous platform with the painted backdrop? All you have done is put actors on an outdoor stage. Why would people come to see something like that? They might as well go to the theatre! Where are the hills and rivers that I saw in *Raja Harishchandra*, the action across forests and grand palaces, the sunshine, the wind in the trees, the costumes? I have seen what the bioscope is capable of achieving. And you dare to bring me this mess after one whole year!'

As Tatya shouted, Barve shrank into the shadows.

The loud scraping of a chair near the entrance brought Tatya's words to a halt. The tent flap opened for a moment and someone slipped out. Someone had been sitting at the back of the tent the whole time. Who cares who it was, thought Tatya, bitterly, whoever it was has seen me for the fool that I am. He gave Barve a last scornful glance, and then strode out of the tent himself.

Tatya set off for home at a furious pace, through the dark streets and the hot humid air, stepping over men sleeping on the footpath, dodging cyclists and murky puddles. His mind turned from Barve in revulsion—the man was no more than a charlatan. The loss of his money he thought of for no more than a few moments. Enormous as it was, it would not make a dent in his fortunes. Money lost could be earned again. But he had lost something more valuable, he had lost his self-respect, and he loathed himself for it. He was angrier than he had ever been in his life, and it was all turned on himself. After almost fifteen years as a businessman he had been a shameful dupe. He would give Ponkshe an earful. This was his fault, with his big talk about replicating the community worship of Ganpati in the bioscope theatre. And Radha's fault. How can we refuse the lord Ganpati, she had said, joining her hands in prayer, the foolish woman. This was what came of listening to women in matters of business. But by the time the dimly lit outlines of Khatryachi Chawl came into view, he had admitted to himself that he was being unfair to her. And to Ponkshe too, infuriating as he seemed to Tatya just then. Ponkshe had made it clear that he personally knew nothing of Barve. He was only the messenger of a business proposition. The final decision had been Tatya's alone. It was his heart that had beat strangely, insistently, at the thought of crowds of worshippers thronging to see his bioscope. He was the one who had been swayed by the memory of his son, who had loved listening to the story of Ganpati. A bioscope about Ganpati for his namesake, Ganesh. An offering to the gods. How neat it had seemed, how satisfying, like tying together two fraying ends of a rope that fluttered in a desolate wind, knotting them together to still them, to still his own grief. He had ended up serving neither Ganpati nor the memory of his son, he thought, bitterly.

He made his way to the tap behind the dark chawl to wash his feet, and cursed just as the cool water splashed over him. He truly was a fool, no better than a goat that blindly heads home on instinct.

Khatryachi Chawl was no longer home, had not been for the last two months.

He turned back the way he had come and trudged to the new apartment in Jamshedji Mansion on Sandhurst Road, a few minutes away. His wet feet squelched in his slippers and he left streaks of water all down the road like a wading bird walking awkwardly on dry land.

Part II

CHAPTER 24

1951

He remembered now. He had been having tea. A cup of tea with Marie biscuits. He had been dipping one Marie biscuit after another into the hot, steaming circle of milky-brown. A moment too long and it would be a soggy mess, crumbling and turning into wasted dregs at the bottom of the cup. But held just the right number of seconds, he could produce a delicious crescent-shaped morsel of moist sweetness. It required a delightful concentration soaked in anticipation. And so it was that he had ignored the odd humming in his ears, a tightness in his chest. The first signal that something was dreadfully wrong was the fact that he was staring at the biscuit disintegrating before his eyes, even as he held it in the tea, and couldn't do a blessed thing about it. His arm wouldn't move. A sudden clatter—the cup, the biscuit, the saucer, everything fell down—and he felt himself tilting sideways, slowly, through an eternity, as if time had slowed down, as if it were trying to save him and catch him in its arms. And who knew, perhaps time had indeed succeeded in slowing down, for there had apparently been enough time for Sadaa to dash out from the kitchen and hold him in his strong arms before he hit the ground. He had heard something in the interim—what was it? It was a rhythmic thudding, like a pestle striking a mortar in the heart; but it was in fact the sound of Sadaa's feet on the floor, pounding towards him.

It was no use trying to remember any more. It had all been rather vague, an interlude filled with panicked voices and car doors slamming and the clackety-clack of the phone dial as god-knows-how-many people were informed. He lay supine, meanwhile, having somehow been transported to the living room sofa, and from thence to his bed. An unknown doctor's face bobbing about above him, full of forced joviality, and a stethoscope around his neck. The heaving sighs of the blood pressure instrument. The roar of cars outside the bungalow, and then a continuous blur of blue sky as they sped to Bombay with him lying on the back seat. Hours and hours of blue sky, the drooping green tops of sugarcane stands falling behind them, and then the vast bare branches of gulmohar trees hung with long brown seed pods as they passed through Poona, the peaks of arid brown hills, the whole plateau baking and steaming in the sun, the twists and careful drops as they descended the ghats, and then, finally, the smell of the sea and the frenzied hooting of Bombay as they plunged into the city.

It turned out later that four cars full of people had made a six-hour dash from Bombay to Gulwadi to escort him back to Bombay.

'Have you people gone crazy?' he said weakly when he heard this.

No, they had not gone crazy, he thought, even as he said it, for how else could it have unfolded?

But, for the sake of form, and to put the family at ease, he continued, 'Were you planning to transfer me from one car to the next on the journey home?' And so he got the sheepish smiles that he wanted, the relieved titter that erupted in his bedroom. He was home, he was in charge again, and everything would be fine: this was what he wanted to convey to all those loving faces, those beautiful grandchildren, and most especially to his daughter, Durga.

He slept. Around him, the large bungalow in its tree-filled grounds, buffeted by the sea-breeze and the cries of circling kites, dozed too. He dreamt—or perhaps he overheard—the voice of the doctor speaking in low tones. 'It was a minor stroke.' He said it to Durga, Nandu, Bhaskar, Sharad, and Shalu. 'A minor one,' the doctor repeated, not sounding terribly convinced, Tatya thought. The air felt heavy and humid, as if filled with tears. Don't cry, he wanted to tell Durga, don't cry, my child, and he opened his eyes. He realized, then, that it was his own face that was wet.

CHAPTER 25

1951

'How old was I when we moved into Jamshedji Mansion?' asked Durga.

Tatya screwed up his eyes to think. The skin around his eyes felt dry, as if his eyelids were made of fragile paper. These days he could sense the faintest of lights even when his eyes were shut.

Durga sat next to him as he lay in bed, recovering.

'You were very small,' he said. 'But I can't remember exactly how old you were. I remember when you started crawling—how amazed we were! Somehow you supported yourself on your paralysed arm, using the elbow to prop yourself up. You dragged your left leg behind you, and soon we noticed that you were even using that leg to push yourself forward slightly. You managed. It became clear that your arm and leg were not completely useless. I thanked god every day for it.'

Lying on his back, he looked straight up at the ceiling as he talked. It seemed like yesterday that he had stood in the freshly painted rooms of the apartment in Jamshedji Mansion, watching his daughter crawling crookedly, oblivious to everything but a red rubber ball rolling away from her, determined to catch it. Big dark eyes in a face as round as a besan ladoo. He had never seen a more beautiful baby. The remembrance of that long-ago joy put a smile on his lips. He gingerly brought his hand out from under his layer of blankets and patted Durga's arm. She was thirty-five years old now, a mother herself. When she laid a palm on his forehead, her hand felt cool and soothing. How glad he was to have her here with him. She was only visiting, of course, and would have to go home sooner or later. He didn't want to think about her leaving just yet.

'Actually, I do remember now,' he said. 'You were about a year old when we moved into Jamshedji Mansion. Which means Sharad would have been eleven or twelve. That was the year Mandar came to live with us too. A strapping boy of eighteen he was. It must have been around the end of 1917. And the following year, in 1918, the war ended, thank God. The fool was talking of enlisting in the armed forces and going to fight for the British.'

'Who?' said Durga, taken aback.

'Mandar,' said Tatya.

'I didn't know that. Mandar bhau, a soldier at eighteen! He would have been...I mean....'

'Yes,' said Tatya. 'I knocked some sense into him. Dada was powerless. He said, "Tatya, you are the only one who can bring him into line." So Dada packed him off to us in Bombay, and I packed him off to Elphinstone College.'

He sighed. Then he said, 'Help me sit up, will you?' Propped up by some cushions, he squinted out of the window at the sea, as if trying to peer into the past. The sea was a choppy green today. Some small shapes bobbed and cartwheeled far out in the water. Possibly a large bunch of coconuts that had been washed out to sea. He imagined the coconuts tumbling on to a different strip of coastline, and turning into trees.

'I often wondered how it would have been for your mother,' he said, 'moving out of the chawl and into Jamshedji Mansion, I mean. It was a huge change for her. But you know how she was. Acted as if she had lived in an apartment every day of her life. As if nothing much was the matter. But I knew she was sad at leaving our old friends behind at the chawl. They were nearby, of course, and we saw them often. But it was not the same anymore.'

'She used to talk about it sometimes,' said Durga. 'How sad she was to leave the chawl. And Lele mavshi.'

Tatya chuckled, thinking of Lele mavshi and her eternal chatter. 'Lele mavshi had decided that she was to play the role of your mother's mother-in-law,' he said. 'Your mother loved Lele mavshi very much. You should have seen how she looked after her in her last days. She did more than Lele mavshi's own daughters-in law, Pami and Kashi.'

'I know,' said Durga.

'Tell me,' said Tatya, looking at Durga, 'tell me how it was for her when we moved from Khatryachi Chawl to Jamshedji Mansion.'

'I can only tell you what she told me years later, of course,' said Durga. 'For the first few weeks Aai was constantly walking over to Khatryachi Chawl to see Lele mavshi and Kashi tai and Pami tai. As soon as Sharad left for school, she would tuck me under her arm and head to the chawl. After living there for so many years with its chatter and friendly faces popping in and out of her home, the apartment in Jamshedji Mansion felt lonely and quiet.'

Tatya closed his eyes, and listened.

CHAPTER 26

1917

For the first few weeks, Radha was constantly trotting down to Khatryachi Chawl to see Lele mavshi and Kashi and Pami. As soon as Sharad left for school, she would tuck Durga under her arm and walk down the three flights of stairs at Jamshedji Mansion, taking with her some sweetmeats or freshly prepared savoury snacks, and invariably returning home with something tasty from Lele mavshi's kitchen. After living for years in their homely little room and cramped kitchen at Khatryachi Chawl, constantly hearing Lele mavshi's voice from next door, the clatter of pots, the pattering feet of children and the whirring and clanking from Nagesh Godse's cycle repair shop downstairs, Jamshedji Mansion felt lonesome and quiet. She missed the friendly faces of the women who had popped in and out of her home all day.

The apartment had five large rooms, two bathrooms, and a kitchen. Everything seemed outsized and cold and empty. She would never be able to fill it with enough things to make it appear as if anyone actually lived there. Her chest of clothes, the little chair and writing table, the low wooden cupboard in which she arranged her husband's clothes, the rolled-up mattresses—all these things had formed a familiar and reassuring circle of possessions around them at Khatryachi Chawl, but now appeared threadbare and sparse, oddly diminished in these large, freshly painted rooms. Like children's clothes, outgrown. She felt as if her family had arrived at Jamshedji Mansion with their old, small life in tow, only to find that their lives now needed to expand to fill their new home.

Their old things looked especially shabby in the evenings, in the glare of the electric lights, the brightness accentuating the empty corners of the apartment.

'Look,' said Tatya, 'you just flick the switch up and you get light. Flick it down again, and it goes off. Try it.'

She tried the switch reluctantly. 'It's not really necessary, is it,' she said. 'It's too bright, in fact. We can manage with our oil lamps as usual.'

'But the electric lights are much better,' said Tatya, impatiently. 'For one thing, you don't need to waste time cleaning the lamps every day. And no matter how long you leave these lights on, it will never get hot or smoky.' He smiled. 'You'll get used to it.'

For a few days, she had stubbornly continued using the old oil lamps, sticking to her routine of cleaning them before the day turned dark, filling them with kerosene. Just a year ago, Tatya had bought two new lamps imported from Europe, each with a clear glass globe that Radha liked to keep clean and sparkling. He had told her they were fifty-candlepower lamps, which meant that each lamp gave as much light as fifty candles. They didn't really need two in their small chawl dwelling, and usually used just one, and it lit up their room in a delightful way. She kept both well filled with Russian Baku oil, which was delivered home in a large tin. Now, though, even both fifty-candlepower lamps together seemed dim and inadequate in the large rooms of Jamshedji Mansion, and she soon gave in to the new electric lights.

Of course, she could not spend hours at her old chawl anymore, for she had work to do at home. But whether it was for half an hour or ten minutes, she made sure she walked over to the chawl once or twice every day, and was invariably welcomed by Lele mavshi as if Radha were her own daughter. It was almost like leaving home a second time, thought Radha, feeling rather melancholic.

But the melancholy lasted no more than a month or so. New furniture began to arrive, ordered by Tatya. The old mattresses were no longer needed, for they now had a large four poster bed of polished black wood, cut in simple, elegant lines. One day the living room filled up with the arrival of a set of three plump armchairs and a sofa. A compact bookcase was installed in the same room, and Radha was surprised to find that their old wooden writing table and chair seemed right at home next to it, under a large leafy window. She moved Tatya's clothes into a tall new wardrobe in the bedroom, while her own clothes occupied the smaller, older one. In the spacious kitchen arrived large, floor-standing brass containers for storing grains and legumes: Ambemohar rice, bought only after it had been ripened in storage for six months till fragrant; wheat waiting to be milled into flour; and her stock of legumes and beans like moog, matki, and pavte, which the family loved to eat all year round, but which mainly came in handy in the hot summers when good vegetables were harder to come by. She moved these large brass containers into the storeroom adjoining the kitchen, and made sure that the wheat was liberally mixed with neem leaves to keep insects away.

Soon the shelves and cupboards in the kitchen were arrayed with polished brass tins filled with everything needed for daily use—toor dal and sago, pearl millet flour to make hearty bhakri flatbreads in the winter, and flour of sorghum to make lighter bhakris in the summer. There were jars of jaggery and sugar, the lids tied down with a cloth to prevent ants getting in, tins of oil and ghee, china jars filled with chilli pickle, mango pickle, and an especially large quantity of lime pickle. No more did she have to scrabble for space in the tiny, dim kitchen of the chawl, moving ten containers out of the way before she could get to the one she needed. She hadn't noticed how little space she had made do with, till they moved to Jamshedji Mansion. Now there was ample space to store papads and peanuts, milk and yoghurt and creamy balls of white butter, everything in its appointed place and within easy reach.

One day a pair of sparrows circled the high kitchen ceiling, oblivious to Radha furiously flapping a cloth at them from far below. Sharad doubled over with laughter till he cried, and Radha, vexed, decided that while large, open windows were wonderful in the living room and bedrooms, they were decidedly not so in the kitchen. Clearly the sparrows had been enticed by a platter of cleaned coriander seeds lying near the window. So she had a carpenter put up nets on the kitchen windows.

She discovered that above their third-floor apartment was an expansive open terrace. Its smooth stone floor blazed with heat in the afternoons, and cooled rapidly in the evening as sea breezes washed over it. Here she sun-dried red chillies and tamarind. She could see all the way to the Hanging Gardens from up there, just about making out the tumble of crimson bougainvillea that draped the slopes of the hill. Later, as she tied a cloth around her nose, and oiled her hands to start pounding the chillies into powder, she would hear the rumble of the tram along Sandhurst Road, punctuated by the clacking sounds from a typing institute across the road. Most of the students were earnest young men, but Radha looked in fascination—and some amount of disapproval—at the few women who attended in neat saris, draped in the odd back-to-front Parsi style, along with a couple of exceptionally fair young women who appeared to be Anglo-Indian. Below the typing institute was an eatery called Kelkar Bhojanalay, a fierce new competitor to Mameenchi Khanaval around the corner that Tatya had frequented in the old days.

Radha marvelled at how she had previously failed to see the busy, alien energy of Sandhurst Road, despite Khatryachi Chawl being a mere street away. Her world at Khatryachi Chawl had revolved around her interactions with the other women—they had all been the building blocks of each other's lives. Their ideas, their food, their children were all as familiar to her as if they had been members of the same family. They were all Brahmins, after all. But here, in Jamshedji Mansion, everything was turned on its head. On the first floor of the building lived, to her amazement, a Chinese dentist. He ran his clinic in a front room, and lived with his family in the rooms at the back. Radha shuddered at the thought of ever having to consult him. She would rather die than let a strange man peer into her mouth. And yet, when she ran into him a few times on the stairs, he was a most genial and decent man, even joining his palms and saying namaskar to her. His wife, a small Chinese woman who wore a sari, and sometimes a long skirt with a long-sleeved blouse, always nodded and smiled too, though she did not attempt to start an acquaintance with Radha.

And there was Mrs Kanhere on the second floor, a real revelation. She had completed her schooling up to matriculation and had even considered going to college, when her parents intervened and arranged her marriage to Dr Kanhere.

'He is not a real doctor,' explained Mrs Kanhere to Radha one day, 'not the kind that treats sick people. He is a doctor of physics, and teaches at Wilson College.' She had invited Radha to drop in for tea that morning, and now she placed a small plate of something fried and hot in front of her. Golden-yellow balls studded with green chillies and coriander. They smelled delicious. Radha looked appreciatively at the plate, wondering what the preparation was. Chickpea flour perhaps, mixed with something. Or some kind of spicy bhaji.

'You should not have gone to the trouble,' she said, smiling at her new neighbour and taking a piece.

'I had to welcome you in my own small way to Jamshedji Mansion,' replied Mrs Kanhere, leaning back on the sofa. Radha sat perched on the edge of her seat, not used to sitting on chairs. At home she always sat comfortably on the floor. 'I hope you will like it here. The previous people in your apartment were a Parsi family. I hear they have built a house in Poona now. They've started a new business there, something to do with horses.'

Radha didn't know what to say. She knew nothing about horses. 'This is really very good,' she said, finally, taking another bite. 'What is it?'

Mrs Kanhere looked at Radha in surprise. 'Have you never had it before? It's batata vada. It's easy to make, with potatoes. I'll send some hot fresh ones for your children this afternoon.'

'Oh no, please don't bother, but I'd love to learn how to make them,' said Radha, sure that Sharad would gobble them down.

'I'm guessing that you cook only traditional Brahmin food at home,' said Mrs Kanhere.

'Naturally,' said Radha, slightly puzzled at the question. She would certainly learn to make these batata vadas, but they would only ever be an occasional novelty in her household. In fact, even her brief visit to Mrs Kanhere was a novelty, not often repeated. For in the following days the Kanheres' large family returned home from a pilgrimage to Kashi, and Mrs Kanhere was constantly busy with her sons who would soon matriculate, and assorted cousins and in-laws who appeared to be perpetually camped out at her place. Though Radha liked her neighbour, she felt rather out of place among her family, for their conversation was peppered with English, a language Radha had never felt the need to learn, and references to outings and picnics and some kind of sewing circle near Churchgate that Mrs Kanhere was a part of. To Radha's astonishment, she even had two English women visit her at home once, the wives of her husband's English colleagues at Wilson College. The Kanheres' lives extended far beyond Jamshedji Mansion and Girgaon and seemed to embrace the entire city of Bombay in a way that Radha found unsettling. She retreated back to her third-floor apartment, to Sharad and Durga and Tatya, and the new addition to their household, the cook, Uma bai, and wondered how Mrs Kanhere dared to go out and do all the things she did.

Uma bai was entirely Mrs Kanhere's doing.

Mrs Kanhere had unexpectedly rung the doorbell one day. Radha, unused to doorbells, always left the apartment door wide open, just like in the chawl. She felt rather suffocated knowing that she was shutting herself up in their 'maze of rooms' as she called it, to Tatya's amusement. So she jumped when she heard the sharp ring of the doorbell, and was horrified to see Mrs Kanhere standing outside the door like a stranger.

'Please, tai, you mustn't stand outside like that,' she said, hurrying forward and ushering her in. 'We are neighbours, are we not? You must come in whenever you want. You'll usually find me in the kitchen.'

Mrs Kanhere looked startled at this open invitation, but said, 'Listen, my dear, I know that you are constantly busy. Don't you want someone to help you? What if you have guests to feed?'

'Actually we are looking for a cook,' said Radha, 'because soon there will be more of us in the house. My nephew Mandar is coming to stay with us from Dhangadh.' As she said this, she couldn't help but smile broadly. She was very much looking forward to his arrival.

'I'm glad,' said Mrs Kanhere, looking pleased. 'He will be good company for you. A house is not a home till you fill it with people, is it?'

'Yes, absolutely,' said Radha, her neighbour's words a sudden revelation. Here she was, filling her apartment with new furniture and constantly running back and forth to Khatryachi Chawl, when what she really needed was to fill her home with people.

'Well then, I have a Brahmin woman downstairs, sent to me by one of my friends. It seems she is a good, honest woman. She needs work and a home, poor thing.'

'Doesn't she have a home of her own?' said Radha in surprise.

Mrs Kanhere shook her head. 'She was widowed as a young girl, before she had any children. Her husband's family disowned her many years ago. Since then she has worked as a cook, most recently with a family that moved away to Madras. Would you like to meet her?'

Uma bai's fate was sealed as soon as she stepped over Radha's threshold.

She was a laal bai—a red widow. And she reminded Radha very much of her own mother. Unlike Mai, who wore saris of a deep red colour, Uma bai wore a faded red. But her way of wrapping her padar tightly around her bare scalp, and tucking the end firmly at her waist, was exactly like Mai's. The same exactness of language; the same use of concise sentences; like Mai, she never spoke more than was strictly necessary.

But she had none of Mai's imperiousness, none of Mai's harshness of tongue. Narayan mama had given Mai a free hand in his home, ignored the superstitious whisperings about how ill luck and widows were knotted together. But Uma bai was like a leaf blown about by the wind. A frail, thin thing, slightly stooped, though she could not have been much older than Tatya. She owned two saris—one of which she wore. The other one she brought in a small cloth bag, along with a religious pothi which she read every morning. She had no other possessions. She was ill nourished, for she had spent the last two months living quietly with a relative, eating as little as possible so as to not cause a nuisance to the family, while she looked for work. She had a hesitant manner of speaking, as if she expected someone to interrupt her. Radha learnt to remain completely quiet when Uma bai spoke, for the slightest sound which could be construed as a hint that Radha wanted to say something meant that Uma bai immediately ceased to speak, sometimes mid-word. But for all her frail look and hesitant voice, when it came to work, there was a quiet confidence about her. She charged through the morning, felling chores one after the other, so that within weeks Radha wondered how she had ever managed without her.

Radha was pleased to see that Uma bai was fastidious about observing sohle, the rituals of purification, that she herself adhered to. Only after bathing and wearing clean saris which they themselves had washed did Radha and Uma bai enter the kitchen. Nobody else, unless they too were in sohle, could touch them till they had finished cooking, or enter the kitchen. Apart from her cooking skills, Uma bai was a stickler for domestic order. She made tooth powder using almond husk and charcoal powder for the adults, and also kept a neat bundle of babool twigs at the ready for Sharad to chew on first thing in the morning. She ground shikakai bean pods for Radha to wash her hair with. Every morning she massaged one-year-old Durga with warm coconut oil, gently trying to massage life into her left limbs. She was particular in the extreme about keeping the pots and pans sparkling. After using the iron tava, she poured buttermilk into it to prevent rusting. The outside of the cooking utensils must be coated with ash before cooking, she said, so that they did not blacken and were easy to clean. In her opinion, Monkey Brand soap or, for that matter, any store-bought soap was a useless innovation. Far better, she said, to use wood ash or coconut fibre or tamarind. She had an innate suspicion of milkmen too, and was convinced that one day the gawli would fool her into accepting milk mixed with water.

She said, in her usual mild-mannered way, 'Bai, can you tell me how you test the milk to check that it is unadulterated?'

'Don't worry,' said Radha, wiping the mortar and pestle so that she could start crushing peanuts. 'In all these years I have never faced the problem of milk being mixed with water.' She had just finished roasting the peanuts, and they were still warm. A delicious, slightly charred smell pervaded the kitchen. She put a few handfuls aside on a small platter for Sharad to munch on later.

'But all these years at the chawl you had a different gawli supplying your milk, did you not?'

'Yes,' conceded Radha, 'but still….'

Uma bai shook her head. 'Do you dip your finger into the milk? To check it?'

'Of course,' said Radha, beginning to pound the peanuts, 'and the milk is always thick and white on my finger. So, you see, there is nothing to worry about.'

'But that is not a good test. You only dip your finger into the top layer of milk which has all the cream in it. That is why it seems thick to you. The milk which has been mixed with water will be underneath.'

Radha looked up, astonished at the assumption that their milk was adulterated.

'The best test,' continued Uma bai, 'is to mix the milk by pouring it from one pot into another. Then you take some milk and splash a drop on the ground, or on the wall. If it does not spread, it is good milk. If it spreads in a watery puddle, well then you know the milkman is a scoundrel. Shall I say something, Bai? All milkmen are scoundrels.'

In the face of this firmly held belief, Radha gave up the argument. Within a few days it emerged that the milkman, too, had resigned himself to Uma bai's dogged testing of the milk every morning. He had initially been rather sulky, but soon became quite cheerful again, because Uma bai carried out her testing in the most charming way, smiling gently as if it were an unfortunate, but necessary game that the pair of them were being forced to play at the crack of dawn every day.

'The day I stop checking it,' said Uma bai, 'is the day he will start mixing water in the milk.'

Radha stood by the door as Tatya ate his dinner, sitting cross-legged on a wooden paat. He had finished his dal and rice, and started on the vaal usal, flat yellow beans heaped on his plate. There was methi bhaaji too, the dark tangle of greens studded with hidden green chillies, to be eaten with hot polis smeared in ghee, which Uma bai was busy rolling out in the kitchen. Twelve-year-old Sharad sat next to him. Radha and Uma bai would eat later.

'Aai, can I have some jaggery with my poli?' Sharad asked, with a sideways glance at his father.

'Of course,' said Radha, smiling, and she put a big sticky brown dollop on his plate. He attacked it with his poli, and began wolfing it down.

Tatya looked at him in amusement. 'If your mother gave you nothing but jaggery all day, you'd be happy. You need to eat more vegetables. Look at your skinny arms.'

'Here, have some butter,' said Radha, dropping a ball of creamy white butter on Sharad's poli. 'That should fatten you up.'

'Look at the spoilt son,' teased Tatya, 'His mother feeds him sweets and butter all day. But to no effect. We'll have to send him to Ponkshe's gymnasium to build him up.'

'Do you want to turn your only son into a wrestler?' said Radha, rising to the bait. 'He's just a child, you wait and see how he turns out.'

Sharad grinned and continued eating. He never had much to say in front of his father. From the other room Durga wailed in her sleep, but then settled down again into slumber.

'Vah,' said Tatya with relish as he finished up the last of the beans and the cucumber-peanut salad. 'There was something different about the usal today.'

'Uma bai made it,' said Radha, in satisfaction. 'I'll ask her how she prepared it.'

'I'll have rice now,' he said, leaning back against the wall in contentment.

'Have another poli first,' urged Radha, 'Have it with the beans since you liked them so much.' She always thought that Tatya ate too fast, as if he were rushing to go somewhere, even though it was the end of the day.

Tatya shook his head. So she hurried inside and brought out a platter of steaming rice, which she spooned on to his empty plate. Tatya liked to clean everything off his plate, even the salt and pickles, before he started on his final course of curd and rice. He emptied a small bowl of curd on to the rice and mixed it well with his fingers. Meanwhile Sharad wanted his rice mixed with buttermilk.

Radha waited for the right time to say what had been on her mind all day. She cleared the dinner things while Tatya and Sharad went to wash their hands. Sharad immediately changed into his night clothes and settled down in his bedroom with a school book to do some last recitations in preparation for the next day.

'Don't you think Sharad is a bit too much on his own?' said Tatya, glancing towards the open door of Sharad's room. He was sitting at the desk by the open window in the living room, and had begun looking through some letters. In the still, humid night air the room filled with the sweet, heavy fragrance of the raat rani tree below their window.

'It will be good for him to have Mandar here,' said Radha.

Tatya nodded. 'And good for you too,' he said looking at her.

Radha lowered her eyes modestly so that they were not looking directly at each other. 'I'm fine as I am,' she said, quietly.

'But you miss your friends at Khatryachi Chawl,' he said, 'and you refuse to make friends with the Chinese dentist's wife.'

She smiled at the joke, and looked up to see him observing her with merry eyes.

'A likely thing,' she said. 'Next you'll want me to invite her home.'

Tatya looked amused, but his smile faded somewhat. 'Times are changing,' he said. 'You see the difference in our lives simply by moving one street up on to Sandhurst Road. We must learn to relax our customs a little. I don't suggest that you start gallivanting around the city like Mrs Kanhere. But....'

'But what?' said Radha, taken aback.

'Never mind,' said Tatya, 'Did you want to tell me something?'

'Yes,' said Radha, rather confused at Tatya's words. 'I wanted to ask your permission for something. This flat feels so large and empty. I am very happy that Mandar is coming to stay with us. Please ask Dadasaheb and Vahini to come with him and stay a few days too.'

'Of course,' said Tatya, surprised. 'I should have thought of it myself.

I will write to Dada at once. Is that all you wanted to ask me? You hardly need my permission for that.'

'There was something else,' said Radha, hesitant. She was so unused to asking Tatya for anything, that she felt awkward and embarrassed. 'I am always running to Khatryachi Chawl to see Lele mavshi and Kashi and Pami and everyone else. I would like to fill our own home with people too. All this new furniture—and still the rooms look big and empty to me. Do you think I can have a haldi-kunku here? And invite all the women I know?'

'Without a doubt,' said Tatya, at once. 'In fact, it is an excellent idea. Have it when Vahini comes with Dada and Mandar. And why don't you invite the wife of Haridas Zaveri? He is my old friend and mentor after all. And the wife of Tansukhrai.'

'They are not Brahmins like us, are they?' said Radha, bemused. 'How can we have them eat in our house?'

'I mix with people who are not Brahmins all day,' said Tatya, looking keenly at her. 'It is the nature of business. And you see that no harm has come to us by doing so.'

'What are you asking me to do?' said Radha, troubled. 'Are we to have people of other castes coming into our home?'

'Not unless you would like it,' said Tatya. 'I don't want to force anything on you.'

Radha stared at the floor. This was what came of moving to strange apartment blocks. Everything was being turned on its head. Then her face cleared, and she looked up in relief, smiling. 'We'll have the haldi-kunku on the terrace. That way they need not enter the apartment.'

Tatya, who was gazing at her, gave a small nod and looked away.

CHAPTER 28

1951

He had brooded a week, ten days, a month, who knew how long? He could not remember how long after Barve's disastrous bioscope screening he had alternated between self-loathing and a trembling fury. But even today, after more than three decades, the sting of that night was easy to recall. And uppermost in his mind had loomed the question of how he would explain it to his elder brother. There was no necessity to tell Dada, of course, but he could not have kept it a secret from him. He had no intention of informing Radha of more than the bare facts. He did not expect her to know or understand more than that. But his brother was another matter. Tatya recalled writing a tortuous letter to Dada about it. He had tried to add a self-deprecating, humorous slant to it at first. He remembered crushing that letter in his palms and throwing it away. There was nothing humorous about losing ten thousand rupees to a charlatan, bearable though the amount was, given the wealth he was accumulating. Even as he wrote the words he found himself play-acting, affecting to be the rich young fop to whom money came easily, and who could afford to play with a few thousand rupees on a whim. 'After all, there is more where that came from,' he found himself writing, in an attempt at light-heartedness, and then, nauseated, had slammed it into the waste paper bin next to his desk. He remembered trying another tack, writing something like 'losses are a part of business, but it is another matter altogether to be an easy dupe.' But he had been too ashamed to call himself an easy dupe, though that was exactly what he had been.

What sort of letter he did eventually write to Dada, he simply could not recall, which was most curious, considering that he remembered well the convoluted lines he had written and rewritten and binned. Nor could he remember what Dada's response had been. Perhaps it lay among the assorted pile of postcards from Dada that he had preserved. His eyes turned to the small, white painted cabinet in his room, next to the wardrobe. So well did he know the contents of that cabinet, it was as if he could see straight through the wood, his eyes alighting on a dusty, brown leather folder, thick with Dada's missives. It had been an age since he had looked at them. Dada liked to write postcards in those days, quick, concise lines scrawled in black ink. Sometimes, if he thought of something else to say, he followed the first card with another one on the same day, much to Tatya's amusement. He wondered, idly, whether Dada had saved his replies, many of which Tatya had written with a wonderfully smooth ink pen from Germany. He always had enough to report about his business to fill at least a side of letter paper. The pen had been a gift from Schmidt. Wolfgang Schmidt, he of the heavy brown eyebrows. He had never met a man with sleepier eyes than Schmidt. Nor a man who was more alert. Like a sleeping wolf, Sharad would say, fascinated by the name Wolfgang. Yes, if you've ever met a wolf fond of laughing so much. For Schmidt found everything funny. He found comedy in the most extraordinary situations. What a pleasure it was, thought Tatya, to hark back to Schmidt again. What on earth had made him think of the man? Ah yes, the fine ink pen from Germany that he had used to write letters to Dada. The ink pen that had sailed in a ship from Germany, in the luggage of a laughing German, to land in Tatya's hands in Bombay, to glide over letter paper printed with his letterhead at Phadke's Paper Karkhana in Parel, to be sent by His Majesty's postal service to Dhangadh. His Majesty had retreated to England, and Phadke's Paper Karkhana had been destroyed in the pre-independence riots of 1945. But what became of Schmidt? All this Tatya thought as his eyes lingered on the white painted cabinet, looking through it, as if it were wide open, revealing its dark insides. He would get Aru, he thought, to pull out that brown leather folder for him. He will like that, he likes doing little jobs for me. It makes him feel important when *you* tell him to do things, Durga had said about her ten-year-old son. It's another matter when I tell him to do something, of course, she sniffed. Tatya had felt absurdly pleased at hearing this.

He reclined in his planter's chair in his bedroom, the bedroom door opened wide on to the balcony. It was so early in the morning that night had not fully withdrawn yet, had not given up its hold on the sky, and still hung like a deep, sulky curtain over the placid sea and the horizon now tinged with a dim pink. The night is like a glowering child, thought Tatya, a night that is unwilling to go to bed, even though it is time. He looked at his wrist to check the hour of the morning. But his wrist was bare, unfamiliarly so. He frowned. He had a habit of strapping on his wristwatch as soon as he woke. Where was it? He looked around and thought he could see the faint gleam of its gold buckle on the dressing table at the far end of the room. He had nowhere to go, he didn't need it. And so he had not remembered to strap it on. Other people were his timekeepers now; they brought him food, reminded him to nap, all at the correct time. But it was disconcerting, this forgetting of a habit. Why did one forget the habits of decades so easily? He felt as if a bolt of slippery silk were unspooling and falling through his fingers. One moment in his grasp, the next minute a soft pool of textile on the floor. He rubbed his bare wrist. What other habits would fall away from him like moulted skin? Sloughed off by this wretched state of affairs as he lay waiting to get better.

A cool, leisurely breeze wafted in from the balcony. He heard distant footsteps and low voices. The servants were stirring. Sadaa would arrive with tea in a minute and prepare a muslin-tipped bidi for him.

Waiting to get better…how unpleasant it was. It would be a long, long time till he was fully recovered. He felt thinned out and shrunk within the space of a few days. He had barely eaten since collapsing in Gulwadi. His stomach seemed to cave inwards.

Something nagged him. He tried to put a finger on it, but it remained elusive, out of reach. He liked his thoughts to be clear, straight as an arrow. If a thought was wriggling in his brain, well, he wanted to get a grip on it. He began to go over his thoughts of the last twenty minutes or so, skimming over them quickly, hovering over this thought or that for no more than a few seconds. It was several minutes before he realized what it was that had made him feel disconcerted, made his heart beat awkwardly out of rhythm, as it were. Now he'd got it—it was the phrase that had appeared in his mind: 'as he lay here, waiting to get better'. Well, he was indeed 'lying here' and there was nothing wrong with that; he was reclining on his planter's chair, legs stretched out, waiting for his tea. Perhaps it was the thought 'waiting to get better' that had given him pause. He couldn't see anything wrong with that thought either, but as he began casting about for other possibilities, he stopped. Perhaps he wasn't waiting to get better, he thought. Perhaps he was waiting to die. His mind came to a rest here, as if a musical tune had been brought to a close. That was it. He had known it, he supposed, but was only now articulating it to himself. It was the lazy narrative of 'waiting to get better' that had bothered him.

He didn't feel ready to die, though, not yet. Not today, anyway. He had things to look forward to today. He was looking forward to his morning cup of tea. Maybe even half a Marie biscuit, something he hadn't managed so far. Sadaa, small, round, grey-moustached Sadaa, would squat down and roll a bit of muslin around the tip of his bidi. And he looked forward to Durga sitting by him, talking, or quietly sewing, and wasn't Aru playing cricket at the Hindu Gymkhana this afternoon? No doubt he would come tumbling into Tatya's bedroom, breathless and sweaty and excited to tell him the score.

He felt an affinity with the low-hanging night that was now withdrawing, its moonlit fingers of indigo feebly scraping at the sky. Pushed out by a golden blanket of sunlight unrolling over the world.

He thought of Bhalerao. Bhalerao with his head of thick hair that he kept very short, though that didn't stop it from curling. With his square jaw and light brown eyes he was a handsome fellow in his dark coat and spotless white dhoti. He had reached the pedhi early one morning when Tatya was at Rose Mills, and was patiently waiting for him when Tatya arrived at the market around noon. If he had come but a month later, thought Tatya, when my head had begun cooling down about Chandu Barve and his infernal bioscope, I would probably have turned him away. He could still see Bhalerao sitting there, his back straight, neat black cap on his head. But for Bhalerao, none of the rest of it would have happened. Not the letter. Not the betrayal. Not the hunt that led him, eventually, to a room of peeling paint and the sickly sweet smell of decomposing nitrate.

CHAPTER 29

1918

'Who is this Bhalerao, anyway?' asked Tansukhrai. Tatya and Tansukhrai were walking to their iron and steel factory one afternoon. Tansukhrai had developed a rather debonair air ever since the war-time money had started pouring into the myriad pedhis of Mulji Jetha Market. The look suited him. With his pencil-thin moustache, bespoke beige coat, and white dhoti, he had acquired a languorous walk, a slow stride that seemed to signal he was perfectly in control of everything and in no particular hurry to go anywhere. Walking beside him, Tatya felt as if he were hurrying with quick, restless steps.

Tansukhrai was the only man, apart from Dada, to whom Tatya could bring himself to narrate the sorry tale of Chandu Barve and his bioscope. He could not tell Zaveri, he could not even bring himself to tell his gumastha, Kishan Mehta, about it. Tansukhrai, on the other hand, was a man whose response would be thoughtful, yet practical. And he was a reliable keeper of secrets. Not like Murari who circulated secrets and information like currency. Still, Tatya kept it short, presenting the situation to Tansukhrai mainly as an unfortunate business investment which he had misjudged. But Tansukhrai was too astute to take Tatya's tale at face value. Trying to ignore Tansukhrai's look of scepticism, Tatya then went on to tell him about a man called Bhalerao who was trying to convince Tatya that he could make a better bioscope than Chandu Barve.

'While I was watching Chandu Barve's bioscope, Bhalerao was sitting at the back of the tent, in the darkness,' said Tatya. 'He said he had heard that a film was to be tested that evening, and slipped in to watch. The owner of the tent theatre had told him that I was a new investor who wanted to make bioscopes, and so he approached me a few days later.'

'And? What did you tell him?' asked Tansukhrai.

Tatya did not reply. He had not told Tansukhrai the real reason why he was so angry. Tatya's anger was directed not just at Chandu Barve but at the universe. The debacle felt like a personal insult. He had absolutely no interest in the cinematograph. But now, foolishly, he felt as if he could not rest till he had made one. He wanted to prove to himself, to the universe, to the smiling, winking city of Bombay that he could do it. For the sting of failure was not a sensation he was used to.

He let the sounds of the city take over for a while. He wanted to think before he spoke.

There was the rattle of trams, the cawing of crows, handcarts trundling past, the languid clanging of a temple bell, the soaring lilt of a muezzin floating high in the air. A group of plump women, dark-skinned with fat gold nose rings, sat by the roadside with baskets of marigold garlands for sale, chatting in loud voices. As Tatya and Tansukhrai approached the dock area where their factory was situated, there was a strong smell of fish, and the sight of old, overturned boats weighed down by heavy black fishing nets.

'You don't need to say anything,' Tansukhrai said after a while, quietly. 'Let it be, Vaman seth.'

'No. I can't let it be,' said Tatya. 'I am a seasoned businessman. Yet I let myself be fooled by that scoundrel. So now I am seriously thinking about Bhalerao's proposal.'

'I am going to ask you something else before I ask you about Bhalerao,' said Tansukhrai, and stopped so that Tatya had to stop too, and look at him. Tansukhrai glanced up at the sky and its unshakeable blue glare. 'Let's stand over here,' he said, and moved a few steps away to stand in the shade of a bel tree. Under the leafy, low-hanging branches Tatya immediately felt his forehead cool. 'Now tell me,' continued Tansukhrai, 'the real reason why you invested in this Chandu Barve's bioscope in the first place. It's not like you. I know you want to diversify, which is why we bought the iron and steel factory. But that was after careful consideration, with a trusted foreman, and with advice from my relative, and with me as a partner. What made you give ten thousand rupees to a stranger conducting a business you know absolutely nothing about?'

'It's difficult to hide anything from you,' Tatya said, with a reluctant smile and then decided to come out with it in a single sentence, so that his foolishness would be on display for as short a time as possible. 'I gave him the money,' he said, 'because it was a story about Ganpati and it was my son's favourite story, and because my son was called Ganesh himself, and because I thought that it would be an offering to god, and a way of atoning for any sins I may have committed, and because we would release the bioscope during the

Ganpati festival, and people watching it in the theatre would be participating in a sort of community worship, and because so many people would come to see it during the festival, I thought I would also make money on it.'

It had turned out to be a longer sentence than he had planned, and a very confused one; but he was glad to have gotten it off his chest.

Tansukhrai stared at him. 'I shouldn't need to tell you this,' he said after a moment, 'but if you are going to make a bioscope, it is very important that you don't do it for religious purposes, or for sentimental reasons. And don't do it simply because you are angry or grieving. Do it the way any business is conducted: do it to make money.'

Tatya nodded. Yes. Of course. And from a forgotten recess of his brain emerged the memory of a distinct sound. He had heard it a long time ago, in a tent, next to an ice-factory. It was hidden under the clickety-clack of the magic lantern's changing slides, and veiled by the light of jewel-green forests, and the crack of a coconut split open by a devout viewer. But the sound came to him now: the tinkle of coins being poured from a brass bowl into a cloth bag.

He felt buoyant, as if he had forgotten something of vital importance, and unexpectedly remembered it again.

As if his head had been underwater all this time, his ears filled with a glugging pulse, and had now been pulled out into the air to inhale cleanly and hear clearly again.

Tansukhrai began walking, as if to save Tatya the embarrassment of being looked at directly. But Tatya felt much better now. 'What did your friend Ponkshe say?' asked Tansukhrai. 'Wasn't he the one who introduced you to Chandu Barve?'

'Ponkshe was furious on my behalf. Ready to go teach Barve a lesson, as he called it. He was sitting under the banyan tree of the gymnasium, surrounded by three or four wrestlers when I went to talk to him. Let me just catch that fellow, I'll teach him a lesson he'll never forget, he started thundering. And I was alarmed to see that the wrestlers—one was of monstrous proportions, a neck like an elephant's foot—began nodding in agreement. Have you gone mad, I said to Ponkshe, you can't go beat up the fellow!' Tatya suddenly chuckled at the thought of Ponkshe and his bare-chested wrestler-henchmen scarpering after the puny Barve like some absurd comic drama.

Tansukhrai laughed too. Then he said, 'Now what about this Bhalerao? What does he want?'

'He wants sixty thousand rupees to make a bioscope. He is confident that it will make enough profits to make another bioscope after that. And another, and another. He says the business is about to take off.'

Tansukhrai's eyes narrowed at the mention of sixty thousand rupees. 'That's big money,' he said. 'The fellow seems serious. But we need to make sure that he is not another scoundrel.'

'We?' said Tatya.

'I have heard something of this bioscope business. There is a man called Phalke who has recently made a lot of money in it. Your Bhalerao fellow could be right. Let me make some enquiries.'

'Are you interested in investing in it?' asked Tatya, surprised.

'I might be,' said Tansukhrai, with a grin. 'I have a feeling about this.'

'A good feeling or a bad feeling?' asked Tatya, a smile dawning on his face.

'A feeling that this must be investigated further,' said Tansukhrai. 'Especially since you insist that we sell the iron and steel factory. What am I to do with all that extra money, eh?'

Tatya began to laugh. Tansukhrai had a blasé manner of speaking about money which his own prudent nature could never match. 'Come, Tansukhrai, let's reach a decision about the factory and be done with it. The war in Europe is probably going to end soon. The time is right to sell.'

'That's what you said last year, when the Americans entered the war,' said Tansukhrai.

'I know. But then I thought it would probably prolong the fighting, and keep up the demand for iron and steel,' said Tatya.

'Well, it turns out you were right. It's a good thing we hung on. But what now? How do you know it's going to end now? And if that is indeed the case, why would anyone want to buy the factory from us?'

'I don't know that the war is going to end. But thousands and thousands of soldiers have died on all sides. They have released poisonous gases on each other. Entire battalions have been blown off the face of the earth. How much longer can it go on, really? I say we sell the factory and cash in our profits.'

Tansukhrai looked dubious. 'I don't know. It's giving us good returns at the moment. And we don't have a buyer anyway.'

'We do,' said Tatya, triumphantly. 'I have an Englishman based in Calcutta who wants to buy it. He heard about our factory through Matthew Wales at Rose Mills. He is a small-time businessman, about to shift his operations here. He says that ever since the British moved the capital from Calcutta to Delhi, it is not the same there anymore. He thinks that Bombay is the place to be for business, and wants to buy our factory as an investment.'

Tansukhrai frowned and then stopped walking as their small factory came into sight. The foreman was busy chivvying a group of workers into the main shed. A large pile of scrap iron was being dragged by a pair of bullocks towards the crushing shed, while two men heaved shovelfuls of coal into a wagon. The factory looked like a busy, thriving business, as indeed it was.

It was primed for selling at a premium, thought Tatya, and, looking at Tansukhrai, was fairly sure he would agree. He could see Tansukhrai's black, squirrel eyes calculating the value of the land, the structure, the equipment, the columns in their account books.

Finally, Tansukhrai nodded. 'Yes,' he said, 'I'm ready to sell. Ask your Englishman to come and look at it.'

'Not yet, Seth.'

'Now what?' Tansukhrai looked at him in surprise.

'It needs a quick coat of paint,' grinned Tatya. 'That will get us a higher price for a minimal investment on our part. Let's make it look nice.'

Tansukhrai nodded again, eyeing the factory.

'And what about Bhalerao and his bioscope?' said Tatya.

'Let's meet him too,' said Tansukhrai, clapping Tatya on the back.

Within a month, Tatya had sold the iron and steel factory to the Englishman from Calcutta at a profit of three lakh rupees. And six months later the Kaiser fled to Holland, surrendering all of Germany's machine guns, aircraft, locomotives, lorries, and submarines to the Allies. The war was over.

CHAPTER 30

Tansukhrai came back to Tatya with news that the Jubilee Cinema in Girgaon had recently made thousands of rupees by showing a bioscope made by the increasingly well-known Phalke, a film called *Shri Krishna Janma* about the birth of Lord Krishna. He also informed Tatya that when Phalke had made *Lanka Dahan* about a year ago, a theatre in Poona almost had its doors broken down by people desperate to see it.

'People went crazy over it,' said Tansukhrai. 'Phalke literally had to hire a bullock cart to carry his earnings home, that's how many coins came in.'

'Is that so,' said Tatya, thoughtfully.

'There is money to be made here, Vaman seth,' said Tansukhrai, his eyes gleaming.

And so they had a meeting with Bhalerao in the leafy courtyard of a small house near the Babulnath temple where he lived with an uncle. Bhalerao and Tatya sipped tea, while Tansukhrai declined a cup, chewing on a paan instead. Tatya smoked one bidi after another, gazing at Bhalerao as he talked, asking him a question now and then. The concern uppermost in his mind was: could Bhalerao be trusted?

Bhalerao assured them that he had learnt all the tricks of the trade from Phalke himself. 'Phalke is a genius,' said Bhalerao. 'I left his employment most reluctantly.'

'Why did you leave?' asked Tatya.

'He is too temperamental. Too exacting. He has his creative vision and won't budge from it, no matter the cost, no matter the time taken. That is no way to run a film company. I too have a creative vision, but in his company it was not possible to make films in any way but his.'

'What was your job there?' enquired Tansukhrai.

'I assisted in running the camera and developing the film at night. I even acted in a few scenes. But I was always present, whether or not I was needed. I learnt a lot that way. Phalke really is a genius.'

'You mentioned that,' said Tansukhrai, dryly, glancing at Tatya.

Bhalerao appeared not to hear him. 'Naturally, I learnt the basic rules from him,' he said. 'As you know, making a film is not simply a matter of placing a camera in front of actors.' Here he glanced quickly at Tatya as if alluding to the disaster that had been Chandu Barve's bioscope. Tatya kept his face expressionless. He had no wish to delve into that experience in any manner. 'For example, a scene can be spoilt if you place the camera too close, or too far, from the actors. You have to learn to place it in a way that the scene appears as a graceful and pleasing composition. If an actor exits to the right, he must reappear in the next scene from the left. If someone makes his exit towards the camera, then in the next scene he must enter with his back to the camera. All these techniques make the film and the story flow well. I learnt all these things from Phalke. And I also learnt other things from him which nobody else would have been able to teach me.'

'Such as?' said Tatya.

'He makes people appear and disappear on the screen,' enthused Bhalerao. 'He shows demons flying and gods wrestling with monsters. He fools you into thinking that he is filming underwater.'

'How does he do all those things?' asked Tatya, thinking back to the trickery of the magic lantern that had manoeuvred one slide over another to create the illusion of movement. What Bhalerao was describing now was, of course, a different level of trickery altogether. He was curious about how it was achieved.

'I am not sure of all of his techniques,' replied Bhalerao, 'because for the most complicated scenes either he or his chief cameraman would run the camera themselves. They would not always reveal the diaphragm setting of the camera. Sometimes when I went to have a look at it the cameraman would quickly snap the lens wide open so that I could not see the setting. Still, I learnt many techniques for lighting, directing, make-up, and so on. I know, for example, that Phalke made several avatars of Krishna appear on the same screen simultaneously, by filming over the same reel ten times, making the actor stand in a different place each time. So when we saw the final result, it was as if there were ten different Krishnas attacking Kansa all at once.'

'Incredible,' said Tatya, mesmerized. 'What else?'

'Phalke described to me in detail how he filmed the growth of a pea plant several years ago,' said Bhalerao. 'He filmed it over several days but when he ran the film quickly, the plant appeared to grow miraculously from a seedling to a plant within a minute.'

'We must see one of Phalke's creations,' said Tansukhrai, briskly. 'What is he going to make next?'

'I believe it is another film on Krishna,' said Bhalerao. 'Phalke likes to make mythological bioscopes. But please also see some of the American bioscopes that are showing in the theatres. You can see from American ones that it is possible to film all kinds of stories. And not all of them require the camera tricks that Phalke uses. In fact we can make films much faster if we keep them as straightforward stories, with as few tricks as possible.'

'We must have at least some of those tricks,' said Tatya firmly. 'Can you or can't you make a man appear to fly?'

'Absolutely,' said Bhalerao with a handsome grin. 'If that's what you want.'

It turned out that the sixty thousand rupees that Bhalerao wanted was to set up the film factory from scratch. Once that was set up, a bioscope would cost only ten thousand rupees to make and would take, Bhalerao estimated, about a month and a half.

'So we can easily make at least six films a year,' said Tansukhrai, jotting down numbers quickly on a piece of paper. 'If we recover just double the cost of making each film, at twenty thousand rupees, we will have recovered the entire cost of the factory within a year!' Here he looked up, apparently astonished at the possibilities he was discovering.

Before sealing the deal, however, Tatya determined to do his homework. He was taking no chances this time. 'Let's start slowly, Seth,' he told Tansukhrai. 'Forget about making six films in a year. Let's just think about the first one for now. And before we do even that, I am going to take you to see some bioscopes.'

And he dragged Tansukhrai to see whichever American and European films happened to be playing over the next month or so.

How is it that I knew nothing about this, pondered Tatya, as they watched *A Trip to the Moon*, *The Great Train Robbery*, *Tarzan of the Apes*, *The Tramp*, *Cleopatra*, and more, and saw the enthusiastic crowds in the theatres. Bioscopes both old and new were pulling in audiences again and again. He felt himself being swallowed whole by the melodious sounds of the musicians that sat by the screen and played their instruments to match the moving pictures, the swaying, clapping crowds, the antics of Tarzan, the diaphanous robes of ancient Egypt, the descent of nymphs from the heavens, and the impossible, yet entirely believable moon that glowered down at them with a pockmarked face and a telescope stuck into its eye. He let the screen pour its imagined realities into his soul, and let himself be dragged along like a child beguiled by a good yarn. He did not tell himself that none of it was real, that no man could leap from a moving train on to a galloping horse, that no woman could swing down from a tree into a man's arms, that all these people and lands were so far from his own existence of pedhi and looms and scrap iron as to be irrelevant; instead, he simply allowed it all to be real. And therefore it was real. He let worlds be created in his head.

How is it, thought Tatya, that so far I had seen only one bioscope in my life? He was reminded of Ponkshe's words: *I go everywhere and I do everything; that is why I am much better informed than you about what is going on in the city*. Ponkshe's instincts had been right, after all, in bringing Chandu Barve to him—it had simply been a stroke of bad luck that Barve turned out to be a scoundrel.

But there was something else that Ponkshe had said: that the bioscope was probably no more than a passing fad, and that Tatya should make some quick money on it and move on. But there Ponkshe was wrong. Surely he was wrong. The acrobatics of cowboys, the fearsome swarms of African crocodiles, the shockingly bare legs of women parading across the screen, this was not a phenomenon that would pass easily. Why would anyone turn their backs on an alternate reality where everything was bigger, better, faster, and every story more gripping and sensational than anything encountered in real life? And he recognized that what the bioscope offered was the sloughing off of old skin, and the inhabiting of a new, sparkling one, for howsoever short a time.

They watched *Lanka Dahan*, still playing at the King's Theatre in Byculla, and gazed at the tangle of bullock carts that stood outside, belonging to villagers who had travelled from afar to see their gods come alive. They found *Shri Krishna Janma* playing at the West End theatre in Girgaon, and watched, mesmerized, as the evil Kansa's head floated away from his body in a spurt of blood. The audience—Tatya and Tansukhrai included—gave a collective gasp as the blood suddenly turned a bright red. This was followed by thunderous cheers and ear-piercing whistles of a kind that Tatya had never heard in his life.

The slash of colour among the moving shades of greys and blacks and whites remained with him, coming to him in his dreams.

'How did they get colour into a grey toned film?' he enquired of Bhalerao later.

'I believe that Phalke has hand-tinted only those few frames,' said Bhalerao, thoughtfully. 'It is a stroke of genius, of course. He cannot have done that for more than a handful of prints, of which you happened to see one. He has literally taken a paint brush and coloured the blood red.'

'So I suppose an entire film can be coloured?' asked Tatya.

'I'm afraid not,' said Bhalerao, shaking his head ruefully.

'Why not?' demanded Tatya. 'If a few frames can be coloured, why not an entire bioscope?'

'Technically it is possible,' said Bhalerao. 'It has been done in the West. Though I have not seen such a film myself, I have read about it. But it would be expensive and time-consuming. Méliès, the man who made *A Trip to the Moon*, used hand-colouring for many years. But, you see, each release print of a film needs to be individually coloured, one frame at a time. One would need to train artisans to do that sort of work in India.'

'It hardly seems worth it in terms of the cost and effort,' said Tansukhrai.

'Is there no other way of colouring a bioscope?' said Tatya. He was enthralled by the idea of seeing moving pictures in colour.

'Before the war there was the Kinemacolor system for a few years. The inventors managed to produce several newsreels in colour. They even made one of the Delhi Durbar eight years ago. But the process needs the camera as well as the projector to be fitted with a rotating colour filter. It is a complex process needing specialist knowledge not only for filming but also to exhibit the film. Nobody uses it now.' Bhalerao paused. Tatya waited eagerly for him to go on, for he clearly had more to say. But Bhalerao's next words were disappointing. 'As per my reading of some of the American film magazines, the only other way to colour a film is to tint it in a single colour, like sepia.'

'What good would that do?' said Tatya, annoyed. 'Who would want to see an entire bioscope in sepia?'

'Actually, Saheb, the most common method of tinting is to immerse the film into dye baths of different colours, scene by scene, according to the mood required. One could use a blue tint for scenes at night, or a red tint for scenes of battle. But to do so, the scenes would need to be cut from the print, dyed, and then spliced—meaning put back together again—to create the final bioscope. This has not been tried in India so far. But apart from the expense and our lack of expertise, in my opinion it would weaken the quality of the print by cutting it and putting it together again.'

'You seem to have read a great deal about foreign bioscopes,' said Tansukhrai.

'A bit, Saheb,' said Bhalerao modestly. 'Phalke used to subscribe to American and British bioscope magazines to keep up with new developments.'

'Then we'll subscribe to the same magazines,' said Tatya at once. 'Perhaps we will find that there has been some new development which allows bioscopes to be made in full natural colour.'

'It is impossible, sir,' said Bhalerao, smiling at Tatya as if he were a petulant child. 'There will never be bioscopes produced entirely in colour.'

Tatya frowned. He did not like to be told that something was impossible.

'Leave it, Vaman seth,' said Tansukhrai briskly. 'Let's talk business, and what can be done, not what can't be done.'

Now that their groundwork was complete, and the endless discussions with Bhalerao appeared to be coming to an end, it seemed that they could begin their first production. It was shortly after the end of the war that the Rising Sun Film Company was formed by Tatya and Tansukhrai, with Bhalerao appointed as chief technician on a monthly salary of five hundred rupees. In consultation with Bhalerao, Tatya identified a place in Borivali as a good location for the film factory.

'It is far enough from the city to take advantage of the hills and forests nearby,' Tatya said to Tansukhrai, 'but close enough for us to keep an eye on things. It is well connected by train, we can be there within a couple of hours. Old Shahpurwala, the owner of Noor Begum Mills, has some land there. He is willing to rent it out to us.'

With guidance from Bhalerao, they placed an order from Moss & Ainsley, dealers of photographic equipment, for all kinds of things—a Houghton-Butcher camera, film stock from Kodak, a printing machine, chemicals for washing the film, a projector to view the completed film. Tins of make-up arrived one day, ordered by Bhalerao from a German company called Leichner, while Tatya arranged for yards of white muslin at a cheap price, because Bhalerao said the cloth would help to diffuse the daylight for the camera when the sun was especially harsh. Tatya could barely keep up with the number of things which had to be put in place before Rising Sun Films could actually begin making a bioscope. He began to have second thoughts when Kishan Mehta put in front of him yet another bill of a few hundred rupees, this time for cutting tools and film-developing chemicals.

'What are these cutting tools?' he enquired testily, 'are we making films or chopping wood?'

It turned out that the tools were for cutting and editing film. Tatya began to be unnerved at the amount of money being poured into something he knew so little about. But Tansukhrai was in his element, relishing the prospect of doing something entirely new, and after only a few misgivings Tatya was swept along in his partner's enthusiasm. Almost every week, the two of them made the trip to Borivali where work was progressing on makeshift sheds which would function as storage space and living quarters. A pucca studio, said Bhalerao, could easily be built once the company started making profits.

A key decision to be taken was what kind of bioscope to make.

'Let us not do mythologicals,' said Tatya, as he and Tansukhrai strolled around the Borivali property, watching the building works. 'Phalke is a master at that, so let us carve our own niche.'

The eight-acre land included a couple of large cottages with their own courtyards, and into these were moved the growing piles of equipment and chemicals. It was an idyllic plot of land, dotted with mango trees, laburnums, rain trees, ashokas, and, in a corner by a pond, an old banyan tree whose ancient roots had formed buttresses so far and wide that they created small sun-dappled rooms of vines and leaves in their midst. The sun was about to set and shot forth the last of its blazing yellow rays across the landscape, casting long shadows as it began its slow descent at earth's rim.

'What do you propose?' asked Tansukhrai, raising an arm to shade his eyes against the sun. He glanced down at a sheet of foolscap paper in his hand with details of the number of labourers already at work, and a list of other essential staff that would be required, such as a cook, a cleaner, a painter. The carpenter, who was supervising the building of the sheds, had already agreed to work full-time for Rising Sun Films.

'Which of the films that we watched did you like the best?' asked Tatya.

Tansukhrai shrugged. 'They were all good,' he said. '*Lanka Dahan* was the best, I thought.'

'Let's leave the mythologicals out of it for the moment. Why try to do something that Phalke is already doing so well?'

'Also the action and adventure films were good,' said Tansukhrai, thinking.

'My thoughts exactly,' said Tatya, stopping under the shade of a jamun tree. 'Now the advantage of producing mythological films is that the stories already exist. Nobody has to make them up. So I propose we do the same thing. Let us use stories that already exist.'

'So you want to make stories that already exist, but which are not mythological, and which are full of action and adventure?' said Tansukhrai.

'Yes!' said Tatya, the idea beginning to sound better and better to him. 'Can't you think of wonderful adventure stories that already exist?'

'No,' said Tansukhrai, baffled. 'In truth, I have not given much thought as to what kind of films we should make. I assumed that Bhalerao would come up with something similar to the films being made by Phalke. Because that is what he has been trained to do.'

'Would you have Rising Sun films become a cheap imitation of Phalke's bioscopes?'

'No, of course not, but....'

'So let's not try to ape them,' said Tatya flatly.

'What shall we make then?' said Tansukhrai, rather impatient. 'Seth, we should have discussed this a bit earlier, don't you think? What if Bhalerao wants to continue doing religious films?'

'Well, then he'll just have to change his mind,' said Tatya. 'It's our company and we get to decide the films we make. We need stories that people are familiar with, that will make them want to come and see them being enacted on the screen, something fantastic and resplendent and magical, like...something like....' And into Tatya's mind floated the image of the princess clad in the magical, sheer muslin from Dhaka that had made her seem so alluring and unadorned, the legend he had narrated to Radha so long ago, enchanting her. They needed princesses and palaces and enchantments. They needed *The Arabian Nights*.

'Well?' Tansukhrai fiddled with his papers, at a loss.

'*The Arabian Nights*,' said Tatya, looking at Tansukhrai. 'We'll make bioscopes on stories from *The Arabian Nights*.'

A smile broke out on Tansukhrai's face, just in time for Bhalerao to see it as he walked up to them, shading his eyes against the dazzle of the evening's rays.

'Bhalerao,' said Tansukhrai, turning to him, 'do you know the story of Sindbad? And Ali Baba?'

'Yes, of course,' said Bhalerao, looking with a puzzled expression at Tatya who now wore a wide grin.

'Let's do Sindbad first. Keep Ali Baba for later,' said Tatya, giving Bhalerao a clap on the back. 'After all, we don't want to start off by hiring forty thieves.'

CHAPTER 31

Once the rehearsals began, Tatya preferred to leave matters in the hands of Bhalerao.

'We have done all we could,' he told Tansukhrai. 'He has the equipment and the actors, and Kishan Mehta is looking into the accounts. Let him get on with making the bioscope and let us not interfere too much in it.'

Tansukhrai agreed. Bhalerao had earned their trust by going about the setting up of the film factory in a most meticulous manner. Every anna spent by him was accounted for, and he vetoed any plans for unnecessary expenses. He insisted that the cottages be furnished in the sparsest manner possible, rolling out his bedding at night in the room that housed the most precious equipment, like the camera. Other rooms were shared by the carpenter and tailor and men hired as actors from various theatre companies. An advertisement had been placed in the *Mumbai Samachar*, *Mouj Majah*, and the *Bombay Gazetteer*, stating: 'Able-bodied actors wanted for male and female roles for a new concern, the Rising Sun Film Company and Works, situated in Borivali. Full employment available. Must be willing to dance, fight, swim, climb trees, etc.' It was this advertisement that finally brought home to Tatya the reality of his new company. No longer was it simply a question of long discussions with Bhalerao and Tansukhrai about costs and profits. They had announced to the world what they were going to do, and that, even more than the equipment arriving at the Borivali cottages, made it real.

Khatryachi Chawl was abuzz with excitement. Tatya was going to make a bioscope! What was it about? Who was to act in it? Were Tatya and Radha, God forbid, moving to Borivali? What about his textile pedhi? Could he really manage two businesses at two opposite ends of Bombay? Rumour flew thick and fast about how much money Tatya really had, and how much it cost to make a bioscope, and how much money he might earn from it. In the midst of this excitable chatter came the news to Jamshedji Mansion that Nagesh Godse was considering answering the advertisement for he fancied himself a good climber of trees, but it then turned out that it had been more of a threat to his wife with whom he had had an argument that day.

Tatya proudly showed the advertisement to Radha and Sharad. Sharad could scarcely contain his excitement.

'I want to go and see the actors swim and fight!' he exclaimed. 'Will they have swords for the fighting, or will they use their fists? Are they going to swim in the sea? Or will you find a river? When are you taking Aai and me to watch?'

'Under no circumstances can you come to watch,' said Tatya at once. 'A film factory is no place for women and children.' And later he told Radha not to bring up the subject with Sharad again. 'I regret showing him the advertisement,' he said.

'But why?' asked Radha, surprised, looking up from kneading dough. Tatya was standing at the door of the kitchen, taking care not to step in, for he had not completed the necessary purifying rituals which would allow him to enter.

'There will be theatre actors there,' said Tatya, hesitantly. 'And I believe they are not the best company for a child to keep, nor to take examples from regarding behaviour.'

Radha stopped her kneading and looked suspiciously at Tatya. 'But *you* will be mixing with them,' she said.

'Only because I have to,' he said. 'And not more than necessary. Dealing with them is Bhalerao's responsibility. He is used to it.'

She opened her mouth as if to speak, closed it, and nodded. She peered behind her, over one shoulder, to ensure that Uma bai was out of earshot. Then she said, awkwardly, not looking at Tatya, 'Can I ask you something?'

'Of course,' he said.

'I heard that the foreign bioscopes have women in them. And that...and that...some Indian ones have started showing women as well.' She looked steadfastly down at her dough.

'Indian women do not work in the bioscope,' said Tatya, firmly. 'People would not tolerate it. Yes, there are one or two examples I have heard of. But Bhalerao would not, I am sure, indulge in any such nonsense. There are enough male actors who play female parts very well. So where, then, does the need arise for women to be included?'

She nodded, embarrassed at the thought of it.

The day finally came when the first production of Rising Sun Films was announced in the papers. Tatya was in Khatryachi Chawl. He often dropped in to see his former neighbours—they were almost like family, really—and to play an evening round of ganjifa or bezique with Dattopant Apte, Jagannath Lele, and the rest. Today he had surrounded himself with his old friends, all admiring the advertisement in the newspaper:

'COMING SOON! The forthcoming production of Rising Sun Films, the adventurous feats of SINDBAD THE SAILOR! See the ARABIAN NIGHTS come alive! A magical spectacle of giant birds! Stormy voyages! Treasures guarded by monsters! COMING SOON!'

The chawl was once again abuzz with Tatya's new venture. Nobody knew anybody who had anything to do with bioscopes—and now suddenly they all did. Again and again Tatya had to explain what a bioscope was to Lele mavshi. With all the excitement surrounding the bioscope, he hoped that it would live up to this grand and, in his opinion, over-the-top announcement. The filming had yet to commence, but the rehearsals were finished and the costumes stitched. Since the bioscope would be ready within eight weeks—nine at the most—Tatya, Tansukhrai, and Bhalerao had decided that every week in the run-up to the release, there would be an advertisement for it in the papers.

'But it sounds as if we are shouting at people,' Tatya said to Bhalerao. 'Is there any need for all these capital letters and exclamation marks?'

Bhalerao assured him that this was how bioscopes were advertised. 'We have to catch people's attention,' he said. 'Make sure they don't forget that soon they will see Sindbad come alive in front of their eyes!'

On the first day of shooting Tatya took an early morning train to Borivali, wondering what to expect. For weeks Tansukhrai and Tatya had not visited the location, both agreeing that they would keep themselves out of Bhalerao's way. Besides, business at Mulji Jetha Market showed no signs of letting up. The war was over but the war-time shortages were not. Whatever Rose Mills and Noor Begum Mills produced, Tatya sold at premium prices. Business was still booming and money was pouring in. In the midst of all this, he and Tansukhrai had decided that they were better off leaving Bhalerao to manage things as he saw fit. Now Tatya was looking forward to seeing what Bhalerao had come up with. He had sent a postcard to Bhalerao three days ago to inform him that he and Tansukhrai would be coming that day. He wondered whether Bhalerao had received the postcard, for he had left it a little too late, and he didn't know how quickly the post arrived in Borivali, far-flung as it was.

From the train station he hired a horse-drawn tonga to take him to their eight-acre plot, and the first thing he saw when he arrived there was a large, painted board with the words: 'Rising Sun Film Company and Works'. It included a picture of a vivid sun rising behind two brown hills, shooting red and yellow rays all over the wooden rectangle of the board. Tatya was impressed at this display and, standing in front of it, felt something in his chest expand. Pride? Excitement? Yes and yes, but he could detect something else too. It was the feeling of power, as if he could go anywhere and do anything because he had just proved that he could create something out of nothing. That he could launch his own boats on to the high seas. A few months ago none of this existed. He had brought it into being through sheer willpower and the wads of bank notes that he had conjured up through years of effort. Something out of nothing. Was that how the gods had created the world? Through the force of their will? Why had they done it? Just to see what would happen? He felt a bit like that now. He wanted to see what would happen.

He walked past the wooden board and through stands of palm trees. In the distance he saw the open-air set that Bhalerao had written to him about, during his regular reporting of progress at Rising Sun Films. The set was built not far from the two cottages that were being used as residence and storerooms. Tatya saw that two makeshift pavilions had been constructed, thatch-roofed but open on all four sides; one seemed to be an outdoor kitchen and dining area while the other was scattered with a few bedrolls, and was probably used for the men to sleep in at night. A young boy squatted by a wood-fired stove, tending to a pot of something boiling. He did not notice Tatya. Tatya had reached so early in the morning that hardly anybody seemed to be about. He gazed around him, enjoying the cool morning breeze. He could hear voices in one of the cottages. Perhaps the actors were getting ready.

Eagerly he walked towards the open-air set, which was built like the throne room of a grand palace. But then he stopped in his tracks, aghast. It was painted entirely in shades of green. There was a throne painted green, covered in a green velvet cloth; there was a carpet painted on the floor, made up entirely of green patterns; the pillars were moulded gracefully, with decorated plinths, but they were green too. He stood there, staring open-mouthed at this monotone spectacle. He waited for Bhalerao to appear, his heart beating fast. Did Bhalerao really know what he was doing? Was this going to be another disaster like Chandu Barve's bioscope?

Bhalerao emerged from one of the cottages and hurried towards Tatya with quick steps and a surprised look on his face.

'Namaskar, Saheb! You should have told me you were coming today, I would have sent a tonga to the station to pick you up. And I would have made sure that I was present to greet you. Please, sit down, I will arrange for a cup of tea for you and something to eat. We were all in the cottage getting the actors ready. We have been up for hours. This is going to be a bioscope like no other, I assure you.' Through the stream of words, Bhalerao pulled up a chair, seated Tatya, and hurried away before Tatya could get a word in edgeways. Bhalerao appeared to be possessed with a manic energy, not really seeing what was in front of him. Tatya had the distinct impression that his eyes were glazed, and shone bright as if looking at something that was invisible to others.

Certainly this film will be like no other, considering that it is entirely green—has the man been smoking ganja, thought Tatya, frowning.

Before Bhalerao could put in another appearance though, the actors wandered out to the set. Tatya's mouth fell open. They looked like ghosts. Every one of them, even those dressed as men, had on a dark lip colour. The skin on their face, neck, arms, and hands was coloured pink, and their eyebrows were dabbed black. A large bare-bodied man, dressed as some kind of monster with horns on his head, was painted entirely red.

Bhalerao now reappeared with the young boy hurrying beside him, carrying a cup of tea and a plate of khichadi. Meanwhile Tatya had risen from his chair and was looking around him as if he couldn't believe his eyes. When he saw Bhalerao, he strode up to him, waited till the boy had left the cup and plate and was out of earshot, and then spoke in a low, angry voice.

'What's all this?' he said, waving his arms around.

'What's all what?' asked Bhalerao, his amicable smile fading.

'You know perfectly well what I am talking about. What spectacle is this that you have created?'

'Saheb, this is the film set that I wrote to you about. And these are the actors we have hired. The camera is being readied as we speak. We have been rehearsing the scenes for days. Is something not to your liking?' Bhalerao looked astonished.

'Bhalerao,' said Tatya, struggling to retain his dignity because the question he was about to ask was so absurd. 'Why is everything green?'

Bhalerao looked at the set and back at Tatya.

'Well? Are you going to tell me or are you keeping it a secret? And why do all these actors look like pink ghosts? Why are the men wearing lip colour?'

Bhalerao was now looking at the actors milling around, here a man retying his turban, there another man dressed in some kind of flowing feminine robe, adjusting his nose ring. All at once, the look of confusion cleared on his face and he smiled broadly.

'I should have explained earlier, Saheb. This is a technical matter. What you see now, is not what you will see on the screen.'

'It's not?' said Tatya. 'I thought the camera captures everything exactly the way it is, whatever is in front of the lens.'

'Yes and no,' said Bhalerao. 'Certainly the camera will capture everything that the actors do. But colour appears differently to our eyes, and differently to the camera's eye. Eh, Shinde! Come here!' He beckoned to one of the actors dressed in a fine turban which was, of course, green, with wispy yellow feathers fanned out above his forehead, pinned together with a shiny rhinestone trinket.

The man called Shinde came forward and bowed in a deep namaskar to Tatya. 'It is a blessing to have you here on the first day of our shooting,' he said obsequiously.

Tatya returned his namaskar, looking rather uncomfortable. He was not used to being spoken to in this self-effacing manner. 'Namaskar,' he said. 'Now, Bhalerao, you were saying?'

'Shinde is our main actor for this film, Saheb,' said Bhalerao. 'He plays Sindbad.'

Tatya looked at Shinde again. He was certainly a fine looking fellow, tall, broad of shoulder, and with large dark eyes and a well-shaped nose. The trouble was, he looked like a painted mannequin. It was hopeless. This was Sindbad. Looking like a giant puppet.

Bhalerao appeared to think that he had supplied Tatya with sufficient information by telling him that the camera eye was not the same as the human eye. He was gazing at the set again with a faraway look on his face. 'We will need to do some shooting at the seashore, Saheb,' he said. 'There is a scene when Sindbad gets washed ashore on to the beach. And we'll stage a fine sword fight on the beach too. We'll also need some shots of the sea so that we can impose a toy ship on it, to show it tossing in the waves. I estimate that we can finish shooting here in about ten days, and then begin the outdoor shooting of jungle and sea. That will take a bit longer, of course.'

'Bhalerao,' said Tatya, with as much patience as he could muster, 'will you kindly enlighten me as to why everything is green, and why these actors look like ghosts? Please do not take offence, Shinde.'

Shinde, alarmed, glanced at Bhalerao and quickly took his leave, murmuring a few words about something he had to do.

Bhalerao turned to Tatya. He no longer looked worried, but was smiling happily. 'Yes,' he said, 'I will explain everything to you. You see, the film is not sensitive to a wide spectrum of colour. It does not recognize red, for example. Or, more accurately, I should say that it recognizes red as black. Do you see that monster of a man there? He is a professional bodybuilder and wrestler. I found him in an akhada in Poona. We have painted his body red. But on film he will appear as a fearsome, black, monstrous creature. You see what wonderful wooden horns Mistry has made to fit his head.'

'Go on,' said Tatya, gazing at the horned bodybuilder.

'Green, on the other hand, photographs very well. By painting the set different shades of green we will get different shades of grey on film. Different gradations of tone, in other words. You may have noticed that Shinde—our Sindbad—is wearing an outfit made of light blue cloth, with embroidery on it.'

Tatya hadn't, in fact, noticed this.

'That,' continued Bhalerao, 'is because light blue will photograph as white on the camera. So Sindbad will appear dressed in a pure white, richly embroidered robe.'

'And the pink faces?' enquired Tatya.

'Will appear as perfectly normal faces, Saheb,' said Bhalerao.

Tatya nodded, bewildered but mollified. Bhalerao appeared to know what he was doing. It had not occurred to Tatya that making a bioscope required this extent of technical knowledge.

'Are you going to start filming right away?' he asked.

'Not yet,' said Bhalerao. 'The sun needs to get brighter first. But you have arrived in good time indeed. We are going to break a coconut and conduct a short puja before beginning a final rehearsal on the set. The cook has prepared a huge platter of besan ladoos for the prasad.'

'All right,' said Tatya, nodding. Bhalerao clearly had things he needed to do. Tatya looked at his chair and the rapidly cooling tea and khichadi placed under the fan-shaped leaves of a clump of papaya trees. 'I'll sit here and wait. You carry on.'

'Yes, yes, I'll carry on,' said Bhalerao, in his element now. Tatya could have sworn that he glided away like a swan.

Half an hour later the puja commenced with an aarti to Ganpati, with the entire staff of about thirty people gathered round and singing loudly. A new, freshly painted idol of Ganpati had been bought, the deity smiling benignly under his trunk and tusks, wearing a bright crimson turban and reclining against a comfortable tasselled pillow painted yellow, gazing at everyone. It was a good choice of idol, thought Tatya, for Ganpati looked as if he had settled down to watch a bioscope, and as if they were the actors acting out their lives in front of him for his entertainment.

Bhalerao slammed a coconut on to the ground with a resounding crack, and the sweet water flew out in a spurt, scattering its blessings across the set.

Just then Tansukhrai appeared, walking quickly. He had driven up from the city in his new Buick rather than take the train. He looked around with a glowering frown on his face.

'Vaman seth,' he said, 'why is everything green?'

Tatya sighed.

CHAPTER 32

1951

The film had been a marvel. In the end they had taken all kinds of artistic liberties with the story of Sindbad. Bhalerao blithely made up large parts of it to suit his purposes, depending on what tricks he was able to play with the camera.

Apparently there was still an old camera in the store room on the terrace. Durga had found it the previous day, wrapped up in dusty old bedsheets.

'What shall I do with it?' she had asked.

That night he dreamt about the camera, that he was peering through the lens, looking for Sindbad, unable to see him anywhere. Then a horned creature came into sight and Tatya curled up in fear, but it appeared to be harmless, following the instructions of Bhalerao who made extravagant gestures with his arms. Some musical notes floated by, and carried Tatya along with them till the morning; though along the way something puzzled him, something needed solving, but he kept forgetting what the question was. He was determined to find the source of the music in his dream, for he felt that it held the key to the puzzle. He woke up with the answer on his tongue: it was the foot-operated harmonium that had once belonged to Rising Sun Films, and which stood in the gigantic living room downstairs. He thought he had heard it playing as he slept. So old was it that it had become a part of the walls. Nobody ever noticed it, nobody ever played it. 'What about the foot-operated harmonium,' Durga had enquired the day before, reminded of it by the discovery of the old camera. 'Isn't it of the same vintage as the camera? Do we need to keep it? Does it even still work?'

Lying as still as he could on his back to conserve his energies, he used all the might in one arm to fling the heavy sheets off his body. He did it so violently that most of them slid to the floor. He had started going to the toilet on his own, without any help, and soon he would be able to bathe himself. Sadaa left him on his own for longer periods of time now. But every movement was still painfully slow. He was lucky that he hadn't ended up with half his body paralysed. Now he intended to use his body

189

carefully. His body had become something that needed to be well-tended, watered, nourished, like a faltering garden, one where yellow leaves appeared with annoying regularity, though other days it grew fresh and lush as if it had just rained. It was still to be seen whether today would be a yellow-leaved day or a green-leaved one. He sat up gingerly, his head swimming a little. It was late. At least six in the morning, judging by the sunlight. Sadaa slept on the floor next to his bed every night. But his bedroll was gone. He must have popped in earlier to see whether Tatya had awakened and then returned to the kitchen.

I must tell Sadaa to wake me at four-thirty, thought Tatya, peevish. It is far too late to be waking up now, I shall feel groggy all morning.

He hobbled to the bathroom to relieve himself and then began shuffling back towards the bed, but changed his mind. He went instead to the door of his bedroom and looked out. There was a long corridor with an ochre floor, well swabbed and clean. Doors to other rooms lined the corridor intermittently. On his right was a staircase descending to the sprawling living room and the enormous courtyard, and the lively kitchen area and the suite of rooms occupied by Durga.

He peered into the stairwell and detected some movement there, shifting shapes and shadows just outside his line of vision. The morning was still hushed. A faint childish voice then, in the distance—Aru reciting his times tables to Durga. Tatya decided that Aru could spend the morning up here, in his bedroom. Aru was trying his hand at carving a small wooden boat these days, and it would be pleasant to watch him quietly whittling away.

Now he took careful steps towards a door at the other end of the room. It led out to a wide open-air balcony that overlooked the sea. Here was his planter's chair. The wonderful thing about the planter's chair was that it reclined so far back that it was almost as comfortable as lying down. He lowered himself into the chair, put his feet up on the leg-rests, and waited for Sadaa to appear with some tea.

He thought about his dream again. It was vanishing quickly from his mind, large patches of it drying up as it was exposed to the sun. In the old days he liked to idly pick out a tune on the keys of the foot-operated harmonium. But it had been years since he'd done that. And even longer since it had been played properly. It had been bought after *Sindbad* did so well. No, wait. Hadn't it been bought during the production of *Aladdin's Lamp*? He couldn't remember exactly. But he remembered what a marvel

Sindbad had been. Bhalerao had managed to show Sindbad as a tiny man in front of an enormous, horned monster. He had taken a pile of ordinary coins and made them seem like a mountain of gold towering over Sindbad. He created a model of a terrifying bird with wings that flapped up and down, and showed Sindbad trapped in its claws. The shots on the beach had Tatya and Tansukhrai on the edge of their seats when they'd first seen it: Shinde had swum out to sea and then back towards the beach, flailing about as if he were on the point of drowning, and flopped on to the sand as if he were dying. It was a fine performance. Then there was a sword fight, with the sea as the backdrop. Bhalerao had been lucky that day—the sun was a shining yellow orb in a blue sky but there had been a strong wind and high waves crashed on the shore, making for a dramatic setting and a majestic sword fight. Bhalerao had also employed an artist to paint beautiful title cards. Most films used ordinary black squares with white lettering on them. But the title cards for Sindbad were elaborately decorated around the edges: daggers and birds, roses and beaked ghouls encircled the Hindi, Marathi, and Urdu dialogues written at the centre of each card.

It was sad now, thought Tatya, to recall that the title cards of their first film were lost. They would have been discarded or painted over. Bhalerao ran a tight ship and there was no clutter or waste in his studio; all of which was, of course, as it should have been. Yet, those painted cards had been works of art. But how foolishly sentimental he was being: they were only title cards after all.

April 1919. It should have been a moment of unalloyed triumph. The war was over. Money was flowing like a mad river through his pedhi's account books and into his bank deposits. The shows for *Sindbad* were running to full capacity in the Coronation Cinema in Girgaon and the King's Theatre in Byculla. But something happened just a few days after the film released. The news oozed in. Trickles of information, counter-information, scandal, gossip, and then it all bubbled over into a vast ocean of shock and disbelief. And something in the air changed. He had felt it. He knew that Tansukhrai felt it. He knew that Dada had felt it, and so had Dada's employer, the Rajesaheb of Dhangadh. It was only a matter of time before those bubbles of information boiled over into rage. The thing that happened was far away, in Amritsar, in a place he'd never heard of before, a walled garden called Jallianwala Bagh. Something uncommon had happened in a commonplace garden where children and women and men milled about for the festival of Baisakhi. Who knew what god Brigadier General Dyer was answerable to.

But whoever his god was, Dyer clearly believed that He would be all right with Dyer slaughtering a crowd of peaceful Indians. He shot them in a walled garden, in a ghastly game of pigeon shooting. And his footsoldiers were Indian. Indians shooting at Indians because an Englishman told them to do so.

The British were always saying that the most British thing in the world was their sense of fair play. His own brother, Dada, had taught him that; taught the same thing to the princes, to his own children, to all his students. Tatya had believed him. Though the British had always done as they pleased, they didn't like to rock the boat much, sailing perilously as they did on a sea of Indians. Of course, there were scandals one read about in the papers: Europeans getting off lightly while Indians were punished harshly for similar offences; Englishmen kicking their Indian servants to death; sahibs on a shikar shooting at coolies, invariably labelled as an 'accident'.

But this, this was different.

He had felt as if his eyes had been washed out with some abrasive cleansing liquid that had left his vision clean, his eyeballs clear of motes. It didn't happen all at once—it happened as the news came through one day at a time. They read and heard about terrible things. That Dyer had stopped his soldiers from helping the injured in the garden. That he closed down the city so that relatives could not get to their dead and dying, not even with a cup of water. That he made people crawl on their bellies if they wanted to use a particular road where a British woman had been attacked. And months later, the news that Dyer would not be punished, after all, but that many British people were collecting money for him to be feted and sent off home with a jewelled sword and a hearty clap on the back. Tatya remembered that April as one of humid heat, a summer of mango juice dripping down Sharad's chin, and protests on simmering streets; and the crackle of hundreds of thumbnail-sized Sindbads and crashing waves and gold coins sluicing through clattering film projectors across the city. That was the year he had started donating generously and regularly to the Indian National Congress; felt, for the first time, that he had a personal stake in the fight for independence from British rule.

Sadaa appeared with Tatya's morning cup of tea. Tatya sipped, his hand shaking a little, his cup rattling on the saucer each time he rested it there. Sadaa watched him, hesitating, then said, 'Let me hold it for you, Saheb.'

Tatya raised a palm irritably.

Sadaa sat on the floor and brought out a tin of bidis and a small wad of muslin dampened in water. He began rolling a thin piece of wet muslin around the end of a bidi to act as a filter and waited for Tatya to finish his tea so that he could hand it to him.

The tea was scalding hot. Tatya stirred it a few times with a teaspoon, and was reminded of another kind of tea. A porcelain tea tray on Matthew Wales's desk, wrapped carefully by his fiancée in sheets of tissue paper and a cardboard box and sent to him by ship from England. The tea: the watery English kind, mixed with milk and sugar in the cup itself; he'd learnt to appreciate it. On that day, as he sipped the tea offered by Wales, he didn't know what to say to him.

He could not get involved in politics. Because, thought Tatya, I was the selling agent of a British-run mill. And so I sat drinking my English tea with Wales. And why not? Wales was still the same, after all. An honest fellow in a school-boy haircut, and good at his job.

Sir Francis Wheeler was the same, swanning about in his Bentley with his wavy white hair and ivory-topped walking stick.

They weren't pointing a gun at me, thought Tatya.

In fact, Matthew Wales was horrified by the news. When Tatya walked into Wales's office at Rose Mills that day, Wales was reading the *Bombay Chronicle*. He looked up at Tatya and it was obvious that they were both thinking the same thing. They had never discussed politics before. But now that there were things to say, Tatya could not say them.

What would I have said, thought Tatya, had I spoken? Would I have asked Wales what happened to the famous British sense of fair play? He could have told Wales that he had purchased war debentures to raise money for the British war effort. That he had done so on the behest of Tilak who proclaimed, 'Purchase war debentures but look to them as the title deeds of home rule.' Was it fair play, he could have asked Wales, to send thousands upon thousands of Indian soldiers to fight in Europe in a war that was never ours? Was it fair play to promise Dominion Status to our country in return for our loyalty and then, once the Great War was over, pretend that you never promised it?

He could have informed Wales that he had sung God Save the Queen in school, and still knew every word by heart. He could have said, 'Wales, we would sing it on the Queen's birthday and get a soft yellow pedha as a gift, to sweeten our mouths. It was always a welcome, delicious thing to receive at school. I still remember how it would crumble on my tongue, every little bite I took, and I would make it last as long as possible. I believed that the Queen of England herself had sent sweets especially for our school.' Should he have told Wales about the pedha? What exactly was that pedha supposed to be? A bribe? And what would Wales say? I'm terribly sorry about these events, but I didn't pull the trigger, I didn't give the order, I am not Dyer, I am still Matthew Wales, your friend. And he would have been right. Wales hadn't done anything himself.

And yet he would have been terribly wrong, thought Tatya, sadly. Because he was not my friend. He was a British man who I worked with, who could retreat to the 'Europeans-only' Bombay Gymkhana the minute anything went wrong. I had no doubt that he would go there that evening. What did they say there about us? Did they play a game of cricket to soothe their nerves before going home to their bungalows on Malabar Hill?

Tatya, meanwhile, had taken the tram back to Girgaon, having said nothing; for he was a selling agent for a British-run mill.

But somehow it appeared that Tatya had indeed spoken, along with Tansukhrai and Bhalerao. Unwittingly. So did that really count? Tatya wasn't sure. But a peculiar thing happened to the film *Sindbad*. The cheers reserved for Shinde's Sindbad turned into shouts of nationalist slogans. Naktode, the actor playing the giant horned monster, became equated, in the minds of the audience, with their colonial masters and Dyer. And when Sindbad defeated him and threw him into the sea, claiming the island with its mountains of gold for himself, there were reports of coconuts being broken in front of the screen, people dancing in the aisles, demanding a repeat of some of the songs from the musicians, and ending the film with shouts of vande mataram. Tatya went with Tansukhrai to the Coronation Cinema so that they could see the phenomenon for themselves.

It was no coincidence, thought Tatya, taking a muslin-tipped bidi from Sadaa, that just a few months later the British instituted a board of film censors.

'Though what the censors would have cut from a film like *Sindbad* is beyond me,' he said to a shadow on the wall, probably his own. 'For we never intended Naktode to be a stand-in for the British. It simply turned out that way. One man playing the whole British empire! Well done, Naktode!' He heard a sort of chuckle at the back of his throat. He must have dropped off for a moment and dreamt this, because it was morning and there were no shadows where he sat on his planter's chair. On the contrary, he was blinking in the sunshine.

CHAPTER 33

1924

Despite Durga's bad hand—no, *because* of it—Radha insisted that Durga, seven years old, now almost eight, help out with chores in the house as much as possible. The oils that Radha regularly rubbed on to her daughter's left arm, and the stretching movements she compelled Durga to do daily, meant that Durga could move her arm fairly well, though her elbow stuck out at an odd angle, and the fingers on her left hand were useless. But she could lift a pot of water with her right hand, using her left forearm as an additional support. She could sweep the floor efficiently, dragging her left foot along. She had even started doing a few simple stitches, using her bad hand to hold the cloth down on her lap. It was imperative that Durga excelled at these things for in three or four years she would be someone's wife. Radha felt something heavy clench in her stomach whenever she thought of Durga going away as an eleven- or twelve-year-old. Could it be possible that in another four years her little daughter would be gone? And who would marry a girl with a crippled hand and limping foot?

That was the question Mai had spat out seven years ago, that hot, still afternoon in Khatryachi Chawl, pointing an accusing finger at her as the cradle swung empty and Radha tried to quieten the thin wails of her baby. There was still no satisfactory answer to Mai's query. And so it remained floating in the air, a question mark hanging like a scythe above their heads.

Sharad, meanwhile, had recently joined Elphinstone College. His skinny frame, which had worried her when he was a young boy, had morphed into a lean athleticism. He had become a fast runner, regularly winning races and medals at school as he grew older. And she had seen him sprinting like the wind when he bowled a fast cricket ball. His limbs now had a hard strength that remained contained like tightly packed iron. He had been chosen as the vice-captain of the Elphinstone cricket team almost as soon as he joined the college. Radha was proud of her good-looking son. She understood next to nothing about cricket, or any sport for that matter, but listened to Sharad with pleasure when he poured out to her the doings of the college team.

But Tatya had become increasingly brusque with his son. His old jocular ribbing of Sharad had taken on a sharp undertone of late, and she could not understand why. It dawned on her only when Tatya himself spoke of it, late one evening. Usually after dinner he read the newspaper in the living room before turning in. But this evening she found him standing in the bedroom, gazing out of the open window. He was in his night clothes already, but made no move to get into bed. Instead, he sat down in an armchair, lost in thought, frowning, and then stood up again.

Radha looked at him curiously, as she folded a pile of clothes on the bed, but decided against speaking, unsure whether he would welcome an intrusion into his thoughts.

Then, apropos nothing, he said, 'Do you know what sizing is?'

She paused, a half-folded towel in her hands. 'What?'

'Do you know what sizing is? At the mills?'

She shook her head, mystified. 'How would I know what goes on at the mills?'

'No, of course, you wouldn't know,' he muttered. He looked worried and seemed to be wondering how to proceed. Then he said, 'Listen. I'll explain it to you. When cotton is spun into yarn, the yarn cannot be woven into cloth right away. It first needs to be strengthened. The way to strengthen the yarn is to cover it in semi-liquid starch. This process is called sizing.'

'I see,' said Radha. She was none the wiser as to why her husband was telling her this. But he wasn't done yet. He spoke with increasing enthusiasm, as if speaking to a keen but invisible apprentice.

'After sizing, the yarn goes on to the looms to be woven into cloth. And then the starch has to be removed from the cloth. The cloth goes through boiling water to get rid of the starch. And after all that, it still isn't ready—it has to be bleached, stretched, folded....' He stopped here, as if realizing that he was talking to his wife, who looked increasingly baffled. He took a deep breath. 'Don't you see? Cloth becomes what it is only because the cotton is picked apart and battered and boiled and bleached. Only then does it turn into something of value.'

Radha nodded.

'Our son,' continued Tatya, 'does not seem to understand that to gain something of value, one needs to put oneself through a certain rigour. Much like the cotton that turns into cloth. I started with almost nothing. Sharad has all the advantages that I did not. And yet he does not seem to see it.

If I have built a castle, he should aspire to replace it with a fortress. That is the kind of son I would be proud of. Why does he not want to build higher than his father? Why does he not want more?'

Radha felt this was rather harsh on her son. 'He is still young,' she said. 'He'll learn soon enough.'

'It is not a question of learning,' said Tatya. 'He has agreed to learn the trade. He comes to the mill with me at eight-thirty in the morning, before going to his college classes at eleven-thirty. But his heart isn't in it.'

Radha had an explanation for this. 'He has joined a tennis club at the college,' she said. 'And they play at seven every morning. I think he was a little disappointed that his tennis sessions had to be shortened in order to join you at the mills in the morning. That's all.'

Tatya looked angry. 'I know,' he said. 'Sharad mentioned it to me. It is not something he ought to be disappointed about. As it is, in the evenings, instead of coming to the pedhi he goes to the Hindu Gymkhana to play cricket.'

Radha opened her mouth to protest but Tatya held up a palm, as if he wanted to hear nothing more. 'Please talk to him,' he said. 'Talk some sense into your son.'

Troubled, she finished folding the clothes, Tatya's question ringing in her ears: why does Sharad not want more? In her opinion, he did want more. He wanted to win more races, more matches, more trophies. He wanted to continue learning tennis, he had told her that it was a sport that filled him with joy, that he thought he might be good enough to participate in the college tournaments in a few months. When he spoke to her of his cricket matches, he talked of creating the swing of a ball as if it were an art, something he thought deeply about, a riddle to be worked out in his head and on the field. She loved his enthusiasm, though she didn't understand most of what he said. It was all so alien to her husband's world that her arms prickled with goosebumps. She would have to find a way to talk to Sharad about it, she thought, filled with unease. Her husband was right, after all. Playing tennis and cricket could not be the focus of Sharad's life.

She decided to talk to Sharad by impressing on him the need to build on what his father had done. Sharad heard her out. It was early in the morning and they sat on the cool tiled floor outside the kitchen, sipping tea. A sliver of yellow sunlight glanced in through a window, and lay down a golden bar across their toes. He was already in his white sports clothes, tennis racquet in hand, and as she spoke he looked down at it, fingering the strings gently, a small, stubborn frown on his forehead. She talked of the family's early years at the chawl, when they had so little, and reminded him how far Tatya had brought them all since those days.

'I don't know how your father has done it,' she said to Sharad. 'Hard work, certainly. But there is more to it than that. I don't know what his secret is, but that is what you must learn. He has a way of always achieving more, being more. It is what he wants for you too.'

Finally, Sharad looked up at her. 'Shall I tell you something, Aai? The secret of more is that more is never enough.'

'What do you mean?' she said, astonished.

'Tatyasaheb has everything he could possibly want,' said Sharad. 'His wife is devoted to him. His son has only love and respect for him. He wanted me to go to the mills in the mornings with him and learn the trade. I go with him because I know it is my duty to do so. And yet he persists in being disappointed in me. Why isn't it enough, what he has? Why must he insist that I accept his definition of wanting more?'

She had no answer to that. What could she say to him, beyond teaching him to respect his father's wishes? And yet, surely Sharad's own wishes counted for something too? She decided to let the matter rest for the moment. He had only recently joined Elphinstone College. Perhaps he would settle down once the initial excitement and novelty of it had subsided.

Meanwhile, Durga's training was an issue that she could actually do something about. Her daughter must be taught how to be a good housewife. She must make up for her limp hand and crooked elbow and dragging foot by being better than other girls in every way. Recently she had taught Durga how to make salt. When Sadaa, the young boy who now worked for them, brought home a lumpy bag of rock salt, Durga helped Uma bai grind it. She had learnt that it must then be soaked in a pot for three consecutive nights, with the top water carefully poured into a clean vessel every morning, leaving behind a residue of dirt and stones. On the third morning, Radha taught her to boil the water till it had all disappeared in clouds of steam and only the salt remained, encrusting the insides of the pot. She showed Durga how to turn down the heat at this point and gently roast and stir the clean salt till it was dry. In the summer they created an impressive quantity of salt supplies in tightly packed jars, well before the monsoon months began and turned any open salt into white mud, as if it

Tejaswini Apte-Rahm

had just been scooped out of the sea. Radha then moved on to teaching Durga how to make chilli powder. 'Remove the stalks of the chillies. Dry the chillies in the sun on the terrace upstairs. Oil your hands, tie a cloth around your nose and mouth, and pound them. Turn the chillies into a fine powder. Use your right hand to pound and lean your bad arm against the mortar. Stop for a few minutes when your arm is tired. Continue pounding and remember, not even the seeds must remain visible.' Uma bai added her own knowledge to Radha's: 'My dearest, to prevent the chilli powder flying up in red hot flurries while pounding, roast the chillies in oil first.' 'And,' continued Radha, 'pound enough chilli to last a month at a time. But before the monsoon, make enough for four months because how on earth are you going to sun-dry those chillies when it's pouring rain?'

And so the lessons continued: making turmeric powder, making mango powder when unripe mangoes were cheap to buy, rolling and storing balls of salted tamarind which had to occasionally be given a turn in the sun to prevent cobwebs forming on them. Radha taught Durga how to worship the tulsi planted in a vrindavan on the balcony and how to decorate the ground around it with patterns of white rangoli: swastiks, flower petals, simple geometrical shapes like squares and triangles. Durga sat by while Radha conducted her daily puja in the puja room, slowly picking up the details of what her mother was doing; the correct way to hold the bell, the right time to light the incense sticks, how to offer fruit to the gods on special occasions by placing them on a water mandala. The stem of the fruit or flowers being offered must always point in the direction of the gods, Radha told her. Now tell me, what are the favourite foods of the gods? And Durga would recite: Ganpati likes modaks and ladoos, Surya likes rice kheer, Khandoba likes onion bhareet, Krishna likes curd, milk, butter, and ghee, and Vishnu likes all kinds of sweet things. What about flowers, Durge? What flowers will you offer to Ganpati? Red flowers, Aai, like hibiscus, and durva grass too. White flowers for Shiva, like bakul and lotus.

Durga learnt patiently. She had time on her hands after all; she couldn't always go play with the other children for often, at the end of the day, her leg ached. And when Durga complained of pain, and sat still, leaning against a wall and cradling a doll in her lap, Radha gave her warm milk to drink and talked to her, teaching her things with a fierce doggedness, for behind the ferocity lay fear.

The Secret of More   199

'Shankar? From Kolhapur? He's your aunt's son, isn't he?' Tatya said. He was in the living room, rifling through the pages of the *Bombay Chronicle* when Radha brought in the letter just before dinner. The plump, apricot-coloured sofa and armchairs were lit by a tall, wood-stemmed lamp with a fringed lampshade. Tatya had recently acquired a planter's chair made of Burma teak and in the evenings liked to recline on it with his legs stretched out on the extendable leg rests. 'I remember Shankar at our wedding, a bit younger than you. I have a vivid memory of him twisting my ear during the ceremony.'

Radha smiled, thinking back to the wedding ceremony and the custom of kaan-pili, where the bride's brothers and male cousins twisted the groom's ear to warn him to look after their sister.

'I don't think he realized,' continued Tatya, 'that the ear twisting is purely ceremonial. Rascal twisted my ear well and good. Do they already have a place to stay in Bombay?'

'They will look for accommodation once they get here,' said Radha, handing Tatya the letter. 'Just him and his wife. They have no children. Perhaps they could rent a room at Khatryachi Chawl. Can they stay with us while they are looking for a place of their own?'

'Of course,' said Tatya, glancing down at the thin sheet of paper. 'There is no question of them staying elsewhere.'

Within a week Shankar and Shalu arrived at Jamshedji Mansion. Shankar was thirty years old, and had lost his job as a clerk at the offices of the Rajesaheb of Kolhapur, caught in some unexpected retrenchments. Shalu, his slender eighteen-year-old wife, laughed with Durga all day long, stitched tiny frocks for her doll, had a great repertoire of comic rhymes, knew seven different ways of braiding hair, and willingly helped Radha and Uma bai in the kitchen. Radha was full of joy at having a full house again. Mandar, who had studied at Elphinstone College and then moved to the Victoria Jubilee Technical Institute, had recently left Bombay to take up a job in Madras. She missed him, as well as his friends who had often dropped in at Jamshedji Mansion to visit him. She was glad, now, to chat with Shankar who was just a couple of years younger than her and was full of jokes. So well did Shankar and Shalu fit into their small household that, within a month, Tatya decided it was pointless for them to go live elsewhere.

'They might as well continue living with us,' he told Radha, 'and Shankar might as well work for me.'

'Work for you?' said Radha, surprised. 'At your pedhi in the market?'

'No, at Rising Sun Films,' said Tatya. 'Bhalerao is making at least six films a year now. Sometimes seven or eight. He needs someone to look after the studio while he concentrates on making films. Someone trustworthy who can keep the accounts and hand them over to Kishan Mehta at the pedhi. Disburse the salaries, keep track of the food expenses, and so on. So far Bhalerao has been doing all that with help from Tambe, our cameraman. But we really need someone to do it full time. Shankar has had experience as a clerk at the palace in Kolhapur. He will be a good manager for Rising Sun Films.'

Radha was delighted. She had heard that a room in Khatryachi Chawl was soon to be vacated, and was looking forward to Shankar and Shalu living nearby—but this was even better, they would be at home with her. They would be part of her household.

Shankar came to her that afternoon with a solemn look in his eyes.

She was sitting on the floor of the kitchen busy churning cream to make butter. She loved making butter in the afternoons. The churning had a calming effect on her mind, almost a soporific one, and she could quietly mull over things and plan the rest of her day to the swishing rhythm of the churning stick. When the butter rose to the surface in delightful creamy chunks, she would carefully scoop it out, mould it into a ball, and then pour out the remaining buttermilk for anyone who wanted to eat it with rice. Sharad, especially, loved eating rice with buttermilk at the end of his meal. Lost in her thoughts, Radha was startled to see Shankar standing at the door of the kitchen.

'Shankrya? What is it?' asked Radha in surprise.

Shankar sat down, taking care to keep his feet from touching the threshold of the kitchen. 'Tatyasaheb has offered me a job at Rising Sun Films,' he said.

Radha smiled, starting to wipe down small covers for the containers of butter and buttermilk. 'I know,' she said, 'I'm very happy that you and Shalu will be living here with us.'

'How can I ever repay you?' said Shankar, 'I don't know what we would have done without you and Tatyasaheb. I just want you to know that I will do my very best for him. And that Shalu will help you in every way she can.'

'Shalu already helps. And the children love having the two of you here. Durga constantly runs after her Shalu mami. And Sharad waits for you to come home so that he can tell you all about his day and his cricket matches. He misses having Mandar around, and dare not talk to his father the way he talks to you. It's good for all of us that you are here.'

'Tatyasaheb said that he needs a trustworthy manager at Rising Sun Films. It means that I will have to stay at the studio in Borivali during the week.'

Radha was taken aback. 'I didn't realize you would need to do that,' she said, frowning. 'Can't you take a train there and back every day?'

'It would be an unnecessary expense. And it would take too long. I don't mind staying there at all. I just hope Shalu doesn't mind. I haven't told her anything yet.'

'You leave Shalu to me,' said Radha firmly. 'She's like my daughter. And she won't even notice you're gone during the week. I'll keep her busy here, don't you worry.'

'My wife won't notice I'm gone?' said Shankar, a twinkling smile emerging on his mouth. 'A fine lesson you're teaching her. Is this your revenge for me twisting your husband's ear?'

'Yes, very funny,' said Radha. 'Just make sure you're back every Saturday and Sunday. And don't you forget your duties as a householder. Here, have a boondi ladoo, Lele mavshi made them for her grandson's birthday and has sent some for us. And ask Shalu to come here, will you? We need to start preparing for the haldi-kunku.'

'This is going to be my first real haldi-kunku,' said Shalu, later, sitting cross-legged on the terrace, shelling peas with Radha and Uma bai. 'My mother-in-law didn't really celebrate Chaitra Gauri. She just had a small puja at home. At the most she would invite one or two neighbours. I can't believe you are inviting fifty women! I wouldn't dare to.'

'Well, I'll teach you everything,' said Radha, smiling. 'And Uma bai is a wonder, she knows all kinds of things. So make sure you learn from her too. Now, do you know how to decorate a house for haldi-kunku?'

Shalu shook her head. Radha felt a real veteran when she saw Shalu looking at her with big eyes, nodding earnestly. Radha had never had anyone listen to her so intently, accept every word she said as if it were the indisputable and final word on the subject. In Khatryachi Chawl, she had become used to following Lele mavshi's lead, while in Jamshedji Mansion she deferred, often, to the more experienced Uma bai's views. But now, as she instructed Shalu, Radha was surprised at how confidently she could state her opinions. And so she took great pleasure in teaching Shalu many things which Shalu's mother-in-law had mysteriously omitted teaching her.

The evening before the haldi-kunku, Radha, Durga, Shalu, and Uma bai made drons—small cups made of banana leaves to serve snacks to their guests. Uma bai heated the leaves on a pan to soften them, and passed them on to Radha who rapidly shaped the leaf into a square dron and passed it on to Durga who pierced it with a small twig of bamboo to hold it together. Radha expected about fifty women, but they made seventy drons just to be safe. There would be grated raw mango mixed with spicy, coarsely ground gram, cooling mango panha to drink, and sweet sugar candies called batashe. Radha had promised Durga that she would be in charge of sprinkling their guests with rose water from the long-stemmed silver gulabdaani.

On the terrace Sadaa laid out green and white paisley-patterned carpets transported from the storerooms of Rising Sun Films for the occasion. Earthen planters with pink, red, and yellow hibiscus arranged around the carpets made the terrace look like a pretty green lawn surrounded by blossoming plants. Instead of chairs, Tatya arranged for bolsters with pristine white cotton covers for the guests to lean on. One wall of the terrace was taken up with a cascading arrangement of about fifteen wooden paats so that they formed a flat-topped pyramid. At the peak of the pyramid, Radha placed a small swing made of delicate silver filigree. It moved at the lightest touch, just like a real swing. She placed her small idol of the goddess Gauri in it and swathed the goddess in a tiny crimson sari and fresh marigolds that had bloomed into soft cushions of saffron. Around the swing she placed garlands of white mogra flowers and, on either side, proudly spread out two handkerchiefs which Durga had embroidered with rosebuds. On lower levels of the pyramid, Shalu displayed some of the colourful knitted dolls she enjoyed making, as well as bowls of moon-shaped karanjis filled with coconut, bunches of bananas, little hills of apples, incense sticks in silver-petalled holders, and tall silver samais filled with oil and cotton wicks, ready to be lit with a flame.

Tatya came up to the terrace to have a look at the arrangements. 'You have created a garden up here. And all the little girls are going to look like flowers moving about in it,' he said, smiling at Durga who came up wearing a bright red parkar-polka, with a small red sun on her forehead. Tiny pearl earrings hung prettily from her earlobes. 'Which of your friends are coming, Durge?'

'Everyone from the chawl,' said Durga, her eyes lit with excitement. 'Jayshree and Munju and all the rest. Aai, will any of Sharad bhau's friends be coming?'

'Of course not,' said Radha, 'a haldi-kunku is only for women. You should know that. Even your father will not be here for more than a few minutes.'

'Oh yes, I forgot,' said Durga. 'Tatyasaheb, did you look at the handkerchiefs I embroidered? Come and see!'

Tatya allowed himself to be led by Durga to the colourful pyramid of paats covered in decorations. Radha watched as Durga enthusiastically pointed out everything to Tatya, even pointing to the little heaps of apples and informing him that they were apples. She watched Tatya laughing at their daughter's chatter and admiring everything just as Durga desired. How she wished that Durga would laugh and chatter like that for ever. But it was only in this house that everyone seemed to forget that Durga was different.

It was almost three o'clock. Nothing more needed to be done apart from getting ready herself. Durga was dressed already but needed something around her neck, perhaps a string of pearls, for she was old enough now to look after it. But before that there was something Radha needed to talk to her husband about.

'Durge,' she called, 'time to get ready. Go down and wait for me.'

'Don't you need to get ready too?' asked Tatya, looking up at the sky to gauge the time, as Durga obediently made her way downstairs, two long plaits swinging in the afternoon sunshine.

'Yes, I do, but listen to me first. There is a girl who is coming today with her mother. I would like you to take a quick look at her while she is here,' said Radha.

'You mean....'

'Yes. For Mandar. It is high time.'

'Who is she?'

'Kusum Joglekar. The Joglekars are related to Lele mavshi. I hear she is a quiet and intelligent girl. Quite good-looking too.'

Tatya nodded. 'I must write to Dada.'

'Have a look at her first,' said Radha. 'If you approve of her, we can see if the horoscopes match. Dadasaheb's health has been poor ever since Anandi vahini died. He is preoccupied and lonely. I doubt whether the thought of Mandar's marriage has even crossed his mind. Do you think Dadasaheb will change his mind and come and stay with us in Bombay?'

Tatya shook his head. 'He'll never leave his beloved school. Well, you're right. We have to think about Mandar's marriage. You're certainly collecting a houseful of people, aren't you? Shalu, Shankar, and now Mandar and his bride. That's if Mandar agrees to return to Bombay. Where is he, anyway?' Mandar was visiting them from Madras, on his way to see his father in Dhangadh.

'Downstairs, churning the ice cream with Sharad and Shankar,' she smiled.

'I should have known. He tends to show up when you are planning to serve ice cream.' Tatya and Radha exchanged an amused glance. It was an old joke. 'I have lost count of the number of times I have told him to join me at the pedhi,' continued Tatya, turning away towards the staircase that led down into their flat. 'But he is obsessed with engineering and railways.'

Radha opened her mouth to speak, but then hesitated.

'What is it?' asked Tatya, stopping.

'It's just that Mandar—well, he hasn't lost his interest in the military. Just the other day he was saying that the army needs engineers....' Her voice trailed off. She didn't want to get Mandar in trouble. But she couldn't keep it from Tatya either.

'We'll get him married,' said Tatya, frowning. 'It will knock all that nonsense out of his head.'

CHAPTER 35

1951

'I remember the first time I saw Kusum,' said Durga, smiling. 'Such a long time ago now…I thought I had never seen such a lovely girl in my life, with her fair skin and green eyes. I was only about eight years old but I remember the scene as if it were a picture in a book. Do you remember the year we brought the green and white carpets from Borivali to decorate the terrace?'

Of course, he thought, the green carpets from Rising Sun Films. At the studio they had used them to decorate the floors of the palaces and sorcerers' caves built by the carpenter Mistry. And one day it had occurred to him that they would do very well for Radha's haldi-kunku. He had an image in his mind of that afternoon, of a green garden bordered with hibiscus and leafy verdure—like a painting in a book, as Durga said—but he had forgotten that the green belonged to the carpets.

'Do you know,' he said to Durga, who sat leaning against the railing of the balcony, gazing at him as he reclined on his planter's chair, 'I have just thought of something very peculiar. It's a surprising thought, really.'

'What?' said Durga, curiously.

'Your mother hosted dozens of haldi-kunkus in her life. She loved doing it. She looked forward to it. She always described the arrangements to me in advance to check that I was in agreement. And yet, I find that I know very little about celebrating a haldi-kunku. I was never a part of it, since it was only for women.'

'Well, it's just a pleasant day for us women to get together and exchange news and talk and laugh,' said Durga. 'Don't you think, Tatyasaheb, that often women don't have much to laugh about?'

'I don't know about that,' said Tatya, 'your mother had a happy life.'

'That's not what I meant,' said Durga. 'Well, leave it, it doesn't matter much. Yes, she was happy. Especially when she was organizing gatherings and festivals.'

'She loved dressing up,' said Tatya, raising his arm and placing it behind his head so that his head rested on the crook of his elbow. 'I remember her in heavy gold ornaments at Diwali, or at the haldi-kunkus, or at weddings. But for the life of me I cannot recall the individual pieces of jewellery. Even though I ordered those ornaments myself. From Pethe.' His brow knitted together, as he tried to remember.

Durga watched him. 'You know, we still have all her jewellery,' she said.

'Yes, I know. Of course.'

'I can bring it here to show you. Then you'll remember.'

Tatya sighed. No, that was not what he had meant at all. He had no desire to see the jewellery. It would be sad to see the necklaces that had adorned her neck, the earrings that had hung from her ears, the bangles that had encircled her wrists. If he touched them he would feel like weeping. He thought about the strong-room at the end of the passageway that ran down from his bedroom. It opened with a set of five keys to be used in a sequence, each unlocking a piece of the mechanical puzzle that lay entombed inside the thick iron door. The strong-room was filled with shares, cash, ornaments studded with precious stones, ceremonial silver utensils, gold pocket watches, and what not. It would all go to his grandchildren one day, and then to their children.

But no, he had no desire to see all those things. They belonged to a past life. And to future lives, set in motion by him, but ultimately unconnected to him; unconnected to Radha's scrupulous likes and dislikes, to his careful orders at the jeweller's, to the stooping, hook-nosed man from Pethe's who came home with diamonds meticulously wrapped in little blue papers and displayed them for the serious business of selection. For now, the velvet boxes of jewellery gathered dust and waited. Like actors in the wings, waiting to speak their next lines. He wouldn't be around to hear them, to see the next act in the life of those ornaments.

'Describe it all to me,' he said, looking at Durga, wanting to move away from his own thoughts. 'What was it that you women did at your haldi-kunku celebrations? Tell me about that day, the day Kusum came for Mandar.'

'I was only eight,' said Durga. 'What I tell you will be a mixture of memory and what Aai used to tell me.'

'Even better,' said Tatya.

'And I didn't know that Kusum was to marry Mandar bhau. She was hardly three years older than me, after all. Oh, and I remember the ice cream,' said Durga. 'Mandar bhau, Sharad bhau, and Shankar mama were in the passage outside the kitchen, hand churning ice cream tinged with saffron. I wasn't supposed to have any till the guests had been served, but Mandar bhau got hold of a small bowl and gave me a spoonful of it. I remember thinking what a funny contrast it was between his big fair hands and the small little bowl of ice cream he held out to me with a wink. It looked like a toy in his palm. I ate it very quickly, before it could melt, standing right there in front of him. You know, I don't ever remember him wearing a dhoti; apart from his wedding of course. He always dressed like an Englishman in trousers and a shirt, and once I saw him in a tie, I can't remember what occasion it was for. But I remember teasing him. You've bound up your neck like an Englishman, I shouted, dancing about. I'd never seen a tie. I wanted to touch it, but he wouldn't let me.'

'Surely Mandar wasn't wearing a tie on the day of the haldi-kunku?' said Tatya.

'No, no. That was some other day. I just remembered it now, thinking of him. Well, I ate the ice cream and ran off to change into my red parkar-polka. Then Shalu mami came with a paper with lots of small shapes cut out in it. What's this, I asked. One shape was a star, another a half-moon, another like a sun surrounded by small dots. Do you know what they were? They were shapes to put on kunku! She said I was growing up, and so she was going to let me choose the shape that I wanted on my forehead. Usually my kunku was just a little dot. I pointed to the sun. Can I have that one? I asked. She took a little flat tin of beeswax and rubbed a small circle of wax on my forehead. Then she put the sun cut-out on my forehead and patted it all over with red kunku. It stuck to the wax, and when she removed the cut-out I had the most perfect little sun in the centre of my forehead, surrounded by a circle of dots. Then she did the same for herself and laughed and said, we are twins now! Shalu mami was always laughing in those days. She was hardly ten years older than me, but I felt honoured that a grown-up like her noticed me and played with me.'

Durga was lost in thought, a small smile of reminiscence on her lips. Then she took up a platter of cotton that she had brought up with her, and began rolling wicks for the evening. Tatya chuckled. What a to-do, he thought, over a small little kunku. But clearly the incident had left an impression on Durga for she described it with such clarity that Tatya could almost see the tiny figure in her red parkar-polka, looking up in delight at her Shalu mami. Well, that was not quite true, he thought. He could only see the crooked silhouette of his daughter, her elbow sticking out awkwardly, and the slender girlish outline of Shalu bending over her. But those silhouettes came alive because his other senses had their own memories. He could smell the vegetal essence of the garlands of marigolds and mango leaves adorning their home that day, smell the incense sticks lit at an odd afternoon hour, the sharp aroma of cardamom that floated out of the kitchen, and he could hear the feminine voices of the guests on the terrace mingling with the clink of their jewellery. In the midst of all that, the silhouettes of Durga and Shalu moved, he could tell who was who. But it was the visual detail that often seemed to slip his mind, as if his old eyes were tired of seeing, and were content with shapes and broad strokes of colour.

Shalu. Was she home yet?

'Is she back?' he asked.

'No,' said Durga, 'Not yet.'

'What else,' said Tatya, 'what else about that day?'

Durga gazed at him, and then said, 'I'll tell you exactly how Aai got herself ready.'

Tatya nodded.

'I loved to watch while she did it,' said Durga. 'That year she wore a beautiful deep blue nauvari saree, woven with silver threads. The padar so laden with silver embroidery that it hung immobile and heavy on her shoulder. She put a hira kanthi around her neck.'

'Which one is that?' asked Tatya.

'The long string of gold beads. Each bead has eight facets cut into it so that it looks diamond shaped. Do you know which one I mean?'

'I think so, yes.'

'Of course, she wore her gold goth-patlya bangles, and green glass bangles everyday, along with her diamond earrings. But on the day of the haldi-kunku she added two more pieces worn only on special occasions: around her neck a chandrahaar, the one made up of five long chains of solid gold—I wore it once and it was so heavy it hurt my neck—and a nose ring. The one made of pearls and a single red ruby which hung down over her mouth.'

Tatya looked at Durga. 'The nose ring you wore at your wedding?'

Durga simply laid down the oiled wicks, the job done.

CHAPTER 36

1925

My dear Dada,

I am sitting in the shade of a banyan tree at the Rising Sun studio. Nearby is a pond where shooting will commence shortly. Bhalerao has devised a scheme to make some of the actors pose as mermaids by the pond. Never mind that mermaids are said to gather around remote islands at sea. Bhalerao lets no such minor obstacles come in his way. Rambhau Shimpi is our new tailor. He and his two assistants have been busy stitching fish tails out of sparkling material. The actors will climb into the fish costumes and then be quite immobile for the duration of the shooting, for they cannot, of course, walk on the fish tails which will encompass both their legs. As I write, the actors are shooting a few scenes at the cave constructed and painted by Jairam Mistry. They will all arrive here at the pond in a while. The 'cave' is actually an open-air affair for we need bright sunshine in which to shoot. (On that note, I recently read that the reason American films are made in California is because the state has nine months of sunshine in the year. One wonders how any films are made in England at all, given its grey climate.)

I hope you have settled well at home after the wedding celebrations and the long journey from Bombay to Dhangadh. You mentioned to me at the wedding that Mandar did not seem to approve of the quick arrangements for his marriage. But I am pleased to say that I have not observed anything but polite and discreet behaviour by Mandar towards his wife. As discussed with you, we had offered for Kusum to return to her parents' home till she came of age, but her mother has requested that she live with us (I understand that their living arrangements are rather congested). Meanwhile, Radha has asked me to convey to you that she misses Vahini a great deal, for she has taken on the mantle of teaching Kusum everything that Vahini taught her as a young bride.

Given that Kusum is only eleven, I don't see the need for Mandar to make any changes in his plans just yet. Let him continue to work for the railways in Madras for now. Once Kusum comes of age, and he is a householder, he will be more easily persuaded to return to Bombay and take up work here. I know that you are rather displeased at his stubbornness in remaining in Madras, but I must admit that I am impressed by his focus on his work. He is a fine engineer, is building up his experience, and will not find it difficult to get work in Bombay in the railways.

I wish that Sharad were as serious about his career as Mandar. He is due to sit for his exams in a few months and yet shows little interest in them, doing only the minimum that is required. When I take him to the pedhi he looks through the account books and listens to Kishan Mehta's explanations, but it is clear that his heart is not in it. I had asked Radha to talk to Sharad about it, though I don't think it had the desired effect on him. I told her to explain to him that as my only son he ought to take an interest in the pedhi. (It must be the pedhi, for under no circumstances do I want him to develop an interest in the film line. That is not a business for impressionable young minds.) While Mandar lived with us as a student he was a good influence on Sharad. But since he graduated and went to work in Madras, Sharad's focus on his future appears to have slipped. So I must say that I have a selfish interest in Mandar coming to live with us in Bombay, for Sharad is fond of him and looks up to him. Since Sharad is not much interested in studies, I suspect he joined Elphinstone College mainly because they have a good cricket team.

Tatya paused to stretch his arm, which had become cramped due to his rapid writing. A sudden gust of breeze whisked the letter away and sent it dancing along the ground towards the pond. Tatya jumped up and made a grab for it but it changed course, flew over a thicket of bushes, and was lost to sight. Cursing under his breath Tatya found a narrow gap among the tightly knit twigs and leaves of the shrubbery and pushed his way through, his fresh cotton dhoti hopelessly pulled and scratched. Then he spotted the letter.

It lay in a small, quiet clearing of green ferns and red earth. From above descended dozens of thick aerial roots of the banyan tree, so long that they brushed his shoulders, dangling and swaying in the breeze like an upside-down garden, as if the sky were in motion. A woman bent down to pick up the letter, her eyebrows creasing, before she noticed him. In a reflexive motion he extended his arm as if to claim the letter, but then lowered it again. In confusion, he lowered his gaze too, but not before he had noticed that her eyes were lined with kohl, that her bun was so large that it surely meant thick black hair down to her waist, that she smelled of mogra because she had tied a chain of plump, white-petalled flowers around her wrist, that she wore a deep red sari embroidered in gold. Her feet were fair, the skin smooth as if she were used to walking barefoot on silk, and the hem of her sari offered glimpses of silver anklets dotted with bells. He thought he heard a delicate clink as she shifted one foot.

She looked at him with frank curiosity and appeared to wait for him to speak. Finally, she said, 'Is this yours?'

'Yes,' he said, reaching out for it.

She handed him the letter. Tatya said, 'I assume you have informed the studio of your visit. All our visitors are usually directed to Bhalerao, as he is in charge here.' As their films and, indeed, the films of other companies, had gained in popularity, Bhalerao increasingly had requests from people curious to see the studio. People were fascinated by bioscopes nowadays.

She nodded. 'Of course,' she said.

'I assume you are interested in how bioscopes are made?'

'It would be strange if I were not,' she said, smiling. He had no idea what she meant by that. He saw that her teeth were perfectly white and even. And her lips were tinged with a delicate pink—surely it was not colour, for no respectable woman painted her face.

'I suppose you have seen several of our bioscopes,' he said.

'I have seen a few,' she said.

Tatya didn't know what else to say, so he nodded and squeezed back through the tangle of bushes, the letter clutched in his fingers. Only then did he realize how foolish he must look, for now he noticed that a few paces away there was a rough path that led towards the clearing, hidden behind the bushes. He waited a moment to see whether she would emerge from there, but she didn't. Who could she be? As he sat down again, it seemed to him that he had glimpsed some kind of wood nymph. Gathering his pen and papers into a sheaf under his arm, he began striding away over the open grounds, past the small flower beds and vegetable patches that had been planted by the studio staff, towards the open-air cave. He looked back once or twice to see if he could catch a glimpse of her, but all he saw was his recently vacated chair, empty by the giant banyan tree. The tree's aerial roots nudged each other in the breeze, its ancient branches like so many vast arms opened as if to gather the earth to themselves.

He fished out his pocket watch and glanced at it. Eleven o'clock. Bhalerao was in the habit of breaking for about half an hour at this time, for the staff had been working since daybreak. He must be in his cottage now. Tatya directed his steps there.

He decided he wouldn't tell Bhalerao about the woman he had met. He didn't see the point of it. If she had simply wandered into the grounds from a car full of picnickers, there was the end of the matter. He did not want to create trouble for her, for Bhalerao was strict about who could enter the premises. She had said she had informed Bhalerao already, but he didn't quite believe her. Most likely she was one among the thousands of women who had thronged to see the adventures of Sindbad and Ali Baba and Aladdin and all the other characters in Rising Sun's stable of tall tales. For some reason their bioscopes were particularly appreciated by women. The good-looking Shinde's leading man act in all their films probably had something to do with it.

As he approached Bhalerao's cottage he passed the new laboratory room and film cutting room. Bhalerao, with Shankar's help, had embarked on a large-scale expansion of the facilities. There was also a large new costume room to store the dozens of costumes they had accumulated over six years. Shimpi, the tailor, worked in this room with his assistants and two sewing machines. And there was a make-up room with a mirror running the length of an entire wall. A living space had been constructed for the staff, a large bungalow with wide halls where the men could spread out their bedrolls, and also a kitchen with enormous cooking vessels, the kind that reminded Tatya of the old khanaval where he used to eat as a bachelor. Rising Sun Films now had about fifty full-time employees, including actors, technicians, and workers like cooks, carpenters, and tailors. The entire staff was male, apart from a few women who came daily from a nearby village, to fetch water from the well and to wash clothes.

Some of the men were married but it was not possible to let them bring their families with them. For one thing, there was no school nearby. The men took leave now and then to go see their wives and children. But since the work carried on at full tilt through the year, it was only in the monsoon that most of the staff could go home to their families, for when it rained, all filming ground to a halt.

Tatya never tired of admiring this miniature studio settlement with its open grounds and woods and ponds every time he walked through it. He congratulated himself on hiring Shankar, who had become indispensable to managing the place. Bhalerao had made detailed sketches of the layout of the buildings to be constructed, with plans as to how they would best be put to use. Shankar, meanwhile, had harangued the carpenters and painters and masons to stay within the estimated costs and timeframes. The expense was considerable, but the profits from their bioscopes kept pouring in and there was every reason to expand the studio facilities. They were making six bioscopes a year, sometimes eight, and theatres willingly screened Bhalerao's fantasy adventure tales which ran for weeks.

A separate small cottage had been built for Bhalerao, who was now married. It was to this cottage that Tatya directed his steps. He hoped Shankar would be there as well, for there was something he wanted to discuss with the two of them. It wasn't terribly urgent, but he didn't feel he could sit by the banyan tree and continue writing his letter after the encounter with the woman who had made his heart beat strangely and his face grow warm.

He found Bhalerao and Shankar in the dim, cool study of the cottage. Bhalerao's desk was scattered with papers. Old film cans made a miniature tower in a corner of the room, and haphazard piles of books and magazines grew like toadstools on low tables.

'You are a remarkably messy person,' observed Tatya, glancing around him and settling into a capacious armchair, 'considering that you are so meticulous with your filmmaking.'

Bhalerao, sitting behind his desk, looked around him and shrugged, good-humouredly. He looked as handsome as ever, with his dark tousled hair and charming smile. Six years on, he had grown broad-shouldered and developed pleasing crinkles around his eyes when he smiled. 'Tatyasaheb, judge me not by my mess. I hear enough about it from my wife.'

Shankar chuckled, and said, 'I won't hear a word against Suhasini vahini. I'd say she has to put up with a great deal, with you locking yourself away for hours in your study when you're not filming.' Suhasini was a quiet woman, always dressed in simple cotton saris, and had gotten on well with Radha the few times she had attended Radha's haldi-kunku events.

'I fear she must be bored living here, so far away from any entertainment or the company of other women,' said Tatya. 'But there's little to be done about it, I'm afraid, for that is the nature of the business we find ourselves in. Men pretending to be women in front of the camera. I never cease to be astonished at how well that works.'

Bhalerao cleared his throat and said nothing, looking vaguely uncomfortable. Tatya had no idea why. 'You have a woman coming in every day to help clean and cook, don't you?' he continued. 'Why not find a maid who would live with you? That would provide some company for your wife.'

'Er…yes,' said Bhalerao. 'In fact we have a cook who lives with us now. She started recently.'

'Well, that's all right then,' said Tatya, pleased for Bhalerao's wife, but still puzzled at Bhalerao's sudden discomfiture.

Bhalerao once again cleared his throat, and said, 'There's someone I want you to meet before you return to the city.'

'Who is it?' said Tatya.

'Well, I'll come to that. There's something I wished to discuss with you first.'

'Go on,' said Tatya.

'It's a pity that Tansukhrai seth isn't here today,' said Bhalerao. He appeared to be skirting around the topic he wanted to introduce.

'The market is very busy nowadays,' said Tatya. 'I'll be coming here less frequently myself, for I have too much to do at my pedhi. The same goes for Tansukhrai. We are satisfied with the profits Rising Sun Films is making, so we can safely carry on doing things the way we have done so far.' He looked at Shankar. 'Do you have anything to say about the costs incurred here?'

'Nothing new to add,' said Shankar, shaking his head. He had brought out his pencil and notebook and sat ready to jot down any points discussed. 'Our annual costs for making six or seven films a year, are about seventy or eighty thousand rupees. And our monthly earnings are forty thousand rupees. Currently we recover the cost of a film within about six months. After that it is all profits. Most of our films tend to run over eight or nine months in various parts of the country. If we try to increase the number of prints we send out we might be able to drive up our profits.'

Tatya shook his head. 'I think we are operating at peak capacity at the moment. Our bioscopes are running in theatres as far away as Calcutta and

Madras. And there is a new development. We have recently had an enquiry from a distributor who wants to ship our films to Singapore and Zambia.'

Shankar's eyes lit up in excitement. 'But this is great news, Tatyasaheb! Our bioscopes are going to cross the oceans! When does Sharangpani intend to send the films abroad?'

Sharangpani was the man who managed the small distribution office of Rising Sun Films, in a ground floor room of an office building not far from Mulji Jetha Market. From there the prints of their films were distributed to theatres all over the country, booked by distributors and sometimes directly by theatre owners.

'He will put the prints on a ship that sails in two weeks' time,' said Tatya, smiling at Shankar's enthusiasm. 'I suppose we can gradually think of new avenues to explore. In the near future, perhaps we could hire another director to be trained by you, Bhalerao? In which case we can expand the facilities here and make at least ten films a year.'

Bhalerao blinked. He didn't appear to have been paying attention to the conversation. 'Yes, yes, certainly,' he said, distracted. 'But only if we find the right candidate, of course. Why rock the boat? Everything is going very well.'

Tatya wondered what had come over Bhalerao. Was he coming down with a fever perhaps? His eyes looked bright, very much the way they had looked on that first day of shooting for *Sindbad*. He's seeing things, thought Tatya, probably envisioning how to position his mermaids around the pond.

'There's someone I'd like you to meet,' said Bhalerao, 'before you go back to the city.'

'You did mention it,' said Tatya, amused.

'We face a peculiar problem, Saheb,' said Bhalerao. 'Our competitors have something we don't have.'

'By competitors I assume you mean Kohinoor Films and Madan Films and....'

'Yes. Yes, exactly.'

'But what do they have that we don't have?' asked Tatya, frowning. 'We have ordered the latest equipment last year. Surely you don't want more?'

'It has nothing to do with equipment, Saheb,' said Bhalerao hastily. 'I also have all the film stock and developing chemicals I need. I have everything. But they have a competitive advantage over us. And it is going to be more and more of a problem if we don't do something about it.'

Tejaswini Apte-Rahm

'My dear Bhalerao,' said Tatya, 'are you ever going to get around to saying it?'

'Yes, of course,' said Bhalerao, and now he smiled brightly as if egging himself on to speak. 'What they have, you see, and we don't, is….'

'Is…what?' said Tatya and Shankar in unison.

'Is…actresses,' finished Bhalerao, and sat back looking relieved now that he had said it.

'Actresses?' said Tatya blankly.

'Yes,' said Bhaelerao. His smile faded and he looked apprehensive.

'What do you mean actresses?' said Tatya.

'Women actors. Females, you know,' said Bhalerao.

'Yes, I know the meaning of the word, but what on earth can you mean?' said Tatya in amazement. 'You know perfectly well that we are not that kind of film company. I won't have it. And neither will Tansukhrai, I can assure you.'

Tatya looked at Shankar and saw that he appeared astounded too. Clearly Bhalerao had chosen not to confide in him. Tatya got up from his armchair and walked to the other end of the room. Then he walked back and sat down. His heart was beating strange and fast.

'It's impossible,' he said, finally, to Bhalerao. 'I have a wife and children. How do you propose to run such an enterprise with any kind of decency?'

Before giving Bhalerao a chance to answer, Tatya turned to Shankar. 'What do you think about all this?'

Shankar looked startled at being asked his opinion. He twisted his pencil in his fingers and there was an awkward pause. Then he said, 'Tatyasaheb, since you have asked my opinion, I think you should at least listen to what Bhalerao has in mind.'

Tatya nodded. Of course. It made sense to at least hear him out.

'Saheb,' said Bhalerao, quietly, 'there is nothing immoral about women acting in front of the camera. It is only a convention of society. It will change. It must. Some Anglo-Indian women already act in our films, pretending to be fully Indian. I am sure you are aware of the fact that Madan Films employs an actress called Patience Cooper. A woman of great beauty. Even Phalke had worked with an actress called Durgabai in an early film. And now I hear talk of a sudden incursion of women into the business. I've heard of an actress called Gohar who is going to be launched soon, and also a Jewish girl called Ruby Myers who, apparently, has decided to call herself

Sulochana. They say she is prepared to do all kinds of roles in all kinds of costumes, and that she looks like a princess with delicate features like glass. If we do not keep up, Saheb, this will be the end of Rising Sun Films.'

'Bhalerao, I am well aware that there are bioscope companies that employ actresses. But Rising Sun Films is not that kind of company. I hardly need to tell you this,' said Tatya.

'Sultana,' said Shankar.

'What?' said Tatya, turning to him.

'Sultana,' repeated Shankar, sheepishly. 'It's just that she's an actress too. A woman, you know. She's already appeared in a couple of bioscopes for Kohinoor Films. Also there is an actress called Fatma Begum.'

'Saheb,' continued Bhalerao, 'I assure you that any actress we hire will be treated with the utmost dignity. I have spoken to my wife about it already, and she has agreed to oversee the living arrangements of any women employees.'

'I can't see her disagreeing with anything you say,' said Tatya, annoyed at Bhalerao producing extra ammunition in the form of his wife. 'She is bound to agree with you. You are her husband after all.'

'But, Saheb, surely you can see that the more women enter the bioscope trade, hired by other film companies, the more difficult it will be for us to compete. The most effeminate man cannot compete with a woman. At least you will concede that point to me,' said Bhalerao.

'Of course, there I must agree with you,' said Tatya, getting more annoyed by the minute. He felt as if he had walked into an ambush set up by Bhalerao and couldn't think of a thing to say in his own defence.

'You know, of course, of the great Natya Sangeetkar, Bal Gandharva,' said Bhalerao.

'Who doesn't know the sublime Bal Gandharva,' said Shankar. 'Even a woman cannot look as womanly as him, when he dresses in his silks with flowers in his hair.'

'There Shankar proves my point,' said Tatya at once. 'When you have male actors of that calibre, you do not need actresses.'

'But did you know,' said Bhalerao, 'that even the great Bal Gandharva refuses to employ female actors in his theatre company? Do you know why? It is because he is afraid. He knows that even his God-given skill in impersonating a woman is no match in the face of a real woman. We cannot wait any longer, Tatyasaheb, if we are to retain a foothold in this industry. We must hire at least one female actress to begin with, to play our female lead roles.'

Tatya could not think what to say in reply. Bhalerao's arguments made perfect sense. And yet, it was all wrong. He did not agree, but felt as if he were facing a stiff wind, a rising wind, that was rushing in to engulf him.

Finally, he said, 'I see that you've thought all this out, and I will discuss it with Tansukhrai. But I warn you, it doesn't sound like the kind of thing that....'

A clink of anklets. And another. They all heard it. Or had they? Both Shankar and Bhalerao appeared oblivious to it. Tatya stopped short and listened hard. There was nothing. A bird chirped outside, and the branches of a mogra bush rapped against the open window, its fragrance floating in with a warm morning breeze. Bhalerao and Shankar both stared at him, waiting for him to continue speaking.

'Well,' said Tatya, disconcerted. 'That's all I have to say for now.' And he sat back into the recesses of the wide, wing-backed chair, as if it would protect him from what was to come.

CHAPTER 37

Farmlands whizzed by him. Muddy creeks, swaying palm trees, water-soaked rice paddies, thatched huts, banana-laden trees in courtyards, white-washed walls and orange doors belonging to sturdy village temples, all rushed by. Tatya sat on the train from Borivali back to the city, eyes fixed on the landscape while his mind was elsewhere. He was preoccupied with the subject of nose rings, and how it could make a woman's face glow as if bathed in early morning sunshine.

Radha looked radiant in her wedding nose ring. Of course, he hadn't seen it on their actual wedding day, he had been too nervous to look at her. Now she often wore it on occasions such as Gudi Padwa and Diwali. But if he was honest with himself, he could not describe her as physically beautiful. She was beautiful to *him*. He could never tire of gazing on her, for she made his days begin and lulled his nights to sleep. He couldn't imagine a life without her devoted face in his home, by his side.

But to tell himself that she was beautiful would be dishonest. He liked the definition of things, the description of things, to be honest, to appeal to his rational sense as well as to his soul. To take stock of things without flinching at the truth had helped him navigate his long years in business: to recognize a bad debt when he saw it; to accept that he had made a wrong move and take steps to rectify it; to write off a poor deal as a loss and forge ahead, on to fresher pastures. To be optimistic, but not foolishly so. And so, it was clear to him that his wife was not a beauty—and that Durga was not likely to be one either, though there was, perhaps, a certain charm in his daughter's thin, angular face, and her dark eyes with their long lashes.

It occurred to him that till that morning, in that clearing of red earth and green fern, he had never come face to face with real beauty. Till that meeting...but it was not even a meeting. It was a seeing. Because he had seen her before she saw him. Till that seeing, then, he had never been in the presence of real beauty. He had seen pictures of beautiful women in magazines. He had seen the bare legs of the European actresses who walked across the screens of cinema tents to cheers and whistles. But they were different. They were foreign. They had nothing to do with him, nor he with them. But the woman in the clearing had appeared to him like a character come to life from a book or a play. Never before had he seen a woman wearing a circlet of white mogra flowers around her wrist. Suddenly it seemed to him a barren sort of living, to have never before seen the simple act of white flowers strung together and wound around the wrist of a woman. There were flower sellers outside the temples in Girgaon selling strings of delicate white blossoms for women to pin into their hair. He had never considered buying one for Radha. Not once. He couldn't think of a single reason why he would ever have done so. Radha would certainly not have approved. She would have been embarrassed on his behalf and the whole thing would have been terribly awkward.

Besides, beauty was always filtered through other knowledge. When he saw a woman in a magazine, something within him made his soul turn away from the spectacle of a woman flaunting herself in public. If he saw a good-looking girl in the neighbourhood, he almost always knew of her as someone's sister or daughter or wife. He tried to enumerate the women he had interacted with in his life. The roll call was limited to his neighbours' homely wives, his aunts and cousins, and Radha's relations. Though several had pleasant faces, he could not classify a single one of them as a beauty. Could it really be possible that he had reached the age of forty-three without ever having met a beautiful woman? Prior to this day, he had thought of beauty simply as an abstract concept; it had never once appeared to him in tangible form, in the shape of another human being.

But today, the woman in the red sari. He knew nothing of her. He did not know where she came from, who her family was, why her lips were so pink, whether the colour was natural or made that way by some womanly sorcery. His response to her beauty had nothing to do with any prior knowledge of her. She could have appeared to him in a dream, and the effect would have been much the same. A beauty in a sort of void. Beauty without any history, without any reason, without any context. It was a startling and liberating feeling, a giddy feeling to come upon beauty such that it engulfed his senses, like the strains of a gorgeous raag that might waft in through a window and demand to be heard and appreciated. He had responded to her as if she were no more and no less than a musical phrase that had played with his senses and then gone on its way. What was it about the elements that morning amidst red earth and green fern and swaying banyan roots, the air so liquid and clear, that magnified his senses?

It was as if he had inhaled the scene rather than witnessing it.

And then Bhalerao's words: *there is someone I want you to meet before you go back to the city*. Like a bride brought forth in all her finery, Bhalerao's wife had led her into the dimly lit book-lined study where Shankar sat with his mouth open. And he himself...he had no idea what he looked like. But all at once his chest felt as if a weight had been neatly and firmly placed upon it. He shifted in his seat, the armchair uncomfortable, when she threw him a sudden glance of recognition from under lowered lashes. She looked exactly as she had looked earlier, under the roots of the banyan tree—red sari, gold embroidery, a wrist fragrant with flowers, thick black hair and glowing skin—except that now she was wearing a large nose ring studded with crimson jewels that descended over her pink lips and brushed them lightly.

Her name was Kamal, said Bhalerao. She was a theatre actress, a dancer of great charm and skill.

'Namaskar.' Kamal joined her palms together and bowed her head gracefully. She waited for someone to say something.

'Er...Kamal bai has chosen to wear one of her stage outfits, to demonstrate to us how she would look when dressed as a lead character.' Bhalerao spoke in careful, almost formal tones, as if to underline the propriety of the situation. 'As you know, much of our action takes place in palaces or other royal settings, with characters who are princesses or queens. You can see that this is how she would appear, in full dress and jewellery. But since we also film in jungles and by the sea and other places of natural beauty, Kamal bai is also prepared to wear other kinds of costumes that may be required of her.'

'I can even ride a horse,' said Kamal, demurely. 'And I learnt to swim at a young age. There was a large well in our village and all of us children learnt to swim there.'

Tatya felt his throat go dry at the thought of filming a woman swimming. This was a step too far. He would not allow it. But Bhalerao was most enthusiastic.

'Marvellous,' he said, smiling in exaggerated astonishment. 'I never thought of including an actress in the action scenes. Certainly, yes, why not? We can even give you sword fighting lessons. We'll create a sensation, Tatyasaheb, with an actress who rides and fights and dances.'

'Dancing is no problem at all,' said Kamal bai. 'That was our daily bread at the Karkhanis Theatre Company.' She adjusted her red and gold sari around her shoulders. Her anklets clinked prettily as she took a small step sideways. Had she done that on purpose? To charm them? She was a vision. In the study, purposely kept dimly lit to provide a respite from the glaring heat outside, she appeared as dreamlike as she had in the wooded clearing.

Bhalerao's wife stood a step back, in the role of the perfect chaperone, listening to the conversation with a distant sort of interest, but without any other emotion on her face. Tatya wondered what she thought of all this.

'I just have a small request regarding my living arrangements here,' said Kamal. She speaks as if it were all settled, thought Tatya, apprehensively. 'I would like to bring my maid with me, and have separate cooking facilities so that I can eat on my own. I understand that there are no other female employees.'

'I can assure you that everything will be done with the utmost decency and goodwill.' Bhalerao turned to look in surprise at Tatya, for it was Tatya who had spoken. Tatya had decided that it was time he took charge of the conversation, and reined in Bhalerao's boundless enthusiasm with some straight talking. 'If we do decide to go ahead with your employment, we will, of course, arrange for separate living quarters for you and your maid,' continued Tatya, keeping his eyes averted from her, looking not at Kamal but at Bhalerao and Shankar. 'May I ask why you left your theatre company?'

Kamal only said, 'It was difficult for me to remain there any longer.' She looked as if she was about to say more, but fell silent.

'May I ask—what was the nature of your difficulty there?' asked Tatya after a pause. He wanted to get a measure of her, understand a little of her background and character, if she was to live and work at Rising Sun Films. But even as he spoke he acknowledged uneasily to himself that he was actually giving the proposal a serious thought, when really what he wanted was to mention it to Tansukhrai as a hare-brained scheme of Bhalerao's and come to a unanimous decision that this was a bad idea.

'If you will allow me to speak frankly, I have no hesitation in telling you about my difficulties,' she said, raising her chin and looking at him directly with her dark kohl-lined eyes, so that he could not help but look directly at her too. She had a wide, pale forehead emblazoned with a small but vivid crimson circle of kunku. He suddenly wished he hadn't asked her about her difficulties.

She spoke as if she were talking only to him, disregarding the presence of Bhalerao, Shankar, and Bhalerao's wife. She was succinct. 'The Karkhanis Theatre Company is owned by my brother, Manohar. It tours the larger towns like Sangli, Kolhapur, Satara, and some of the villages in between. Once we even went all the way to Belgaon. My brother is much older than me and I am his only surviving sibling. Our parents are dead. He stopped my education when I was eight years old, and put the dance master of the company in charge of me. The master taught me dancing as well as singing, and almost right away I was required to be a background dancer in the shows. As I grew up, I started dancing and singing in more prominent roles. I know that my singing skills will not be required for making bioscopes, but there are no dance steps that I cannot execute.' She made this last statement in an almost regal manner. Tatya could instantly envision her as a proud princess on screen. Clearly she had a high opinion of her own dancing skills. 'I did well at the company,' she continued, 'and my brother made good money.'

'What about you?' asked Bhalerao. 'Didn't you make good money too?'

Tatya could guess what was coming, and wasn't surprised when Kamal replied, 'No, I didn't. My brother told me that he was keeping my salary aside for me so that I would not spend it on clothes and other trifles. He said I didn't need my own spending money because he would provide me with whatever I needed. But he was often drunk in the evenings and I began to suspect that he was using my money for his drink habit. One day I told him that I simply wanted to see my money, but that he could look after it for me. I said I wanted to know how much exactly I had earned, because he wouldn't even tell me how much I was being paid per month. He shouted at me then, and told me that I was not earning my keep, and not working hard enough for the company. I shouted at him too. I told him that I spent days and nights slaving at my dancing and singing, and that most of our shows were sold out. I cried because I was very hurt at being treated that way. I began to realize that he had no intention of giving me my money.'

Here she paused for breath, and looked at Bhalerao and Shankar as if to confirm that they too were listening to her story. Then she turned back to Tatya and continued, 'Long ago, before he started drinking, he had once told a Chinese shoemaker to make delicate silk shoes for me with a thin leather sole. When I walked in them I felt that my feet were flying over the ground, without touching the earth. I was very fond of them. Now unexpectedly he said that if I wanted luxuries like those shoes I must work for them. I asked him what more he wanted me to do. He said he would let me know. I spent the whole day worrying about it, feeling hurt that he had talked about my silk shoes which he had once given me with so much love. It was his habit of drinking that turned him into a vile creature. That evening I performed in the show as usual, and after the show when I was in my dressing room he brought a man to me and left me alone with him. You can guess the rest. By god's grace I managed to run away from the room before anything bad happened.' She ended her tale in a low voice. Then, louder, she continued, 'I want to make my own life now. I ran away from my brother with my maid, Shanta. If it pleases you to give me employment I would be most grateful.'

She lowered her gaze to the floor, looking vulnerable, beautiful and yet superbly strong, thought Tatya. He couldn't imagine the courage it would take for a lone woman to run away and try to start a new life after being treated so inhumanely, and being in the wretched position of having nothing to show for her years of hard work on the stage. And yet it wasn't a surprising story in the least. He had heard enough about theatre life from Ponkshe, who still frequented lavani shows, to know what sort of thing went on there. This was precisely why he had wanted Rising Sun Films to have nothing to do with women from the theatre. And yet Bhalerao's arguments spun about in his head. If the other film companies were hiring actresses, it was hard to see how Rising Sun Films could keep up the charade of dressing up effeminate men as women and hoping for the best. He felt the ground shifting beneath his feet, as if the wind had changed direction and as if time itself had turned a corner.

Bhalerao and Shankar were looking at him. 'I will have to discuss this with my business partner,' he said gruffly, keeping his eyes on the ground, at a spot near Kamal's feet. From the corner of his eye he noticed Bhalerao making a slight gesture with his hand, and his wife led Kamal out of the room. But not before Kamal had once again raised her hands in a polite namaskar to all of them, the bangles on her wrists ringing out softly as they slid down towards her elbows.

As Tatya's train clattered along the tracks, away from the studio and towards his life at Jamshedji Mansion, he realized with a jolt that he had not mentioned to Bhalerao his encounter with Kamal under the banyan tree. He felt a mixture of acute embarrassment and annoyance at the realization. In the study she had pretended that she had never seen him before, and he had been so taken aback at her appearance that, for some reason, he too had pretended the same. So now their first meeting was a secret between the two of them. It was much too late to tell Bhalerao or Shankar anything about it; he would simply look like a fool. The only two people in the world who knew about the chance meeting that morning were himself and Kamal.

It was a name of beauty. Kamal. Lotus flower. One with delicate petals, buoyant in the water, sun-yellow and white among floating islands of green leaves. As the train lurched into the city, entering the throngs of men, a dark shape passed over his heart, for he had a vision of lotus flowers blooming wide, spreading their petals open to the sky, breathing in sunlight, but revealing their delicate, innermost parts to passing bees and gatherers of nectar.

Tejaswini Apte-Rahm

CHAPTER 38

1951

Jumbled thoughts, memories tumbled together like wet, washed clothes twisted in a bucket. Clean, but hopelessly knotted. They could be extricated from each other of course, but it took time and effort. One by one they must be wrung out, shaken into shape and hung out to dry.

He had time now. Ample time to reflect. But careful now! Ample was perhaps an exaggeration. He wondered whether this was what old people did before they died. Did all aged bodies lie on their beds and try to pluck apart one day from the next, try to remember whether it was dawn or twilight at the window because the veiling of the day looked much like the dimming of the night? On some days, when the light in his bedchamber waned, he closed his eyes and steadied his mind to sleep, only to realize it was simply a dark, water-bellied cloud passing over an undulating sun: an afternoon anomaly.

The city had a remarkable couple of days of unseasonal rain. He saw it all, for his bed was positioned so that he faced the wide casement windows which framed the coconut trees and the black rocks by the shore, the grey-green sea beyond, and the broad arc of sky above.

He noticed the different kinds of rain. When it drizzled, he was reminded of the pond by the banyan tree at the studio: playful pins and needles mocking and pricking the still water. When the water crashed down in silvery shifting columns, it created aquatic pillars in a palace for giants, and there were moments when he could not distinguish sea from sky. The sea seemed to rise in massive salty mists to create a water world. It was strangely comforting, as if this was how the planet was meant to be, the original orb, before man. And when the wind heaved, and he could no longer tell which were the sounds of the sea and which the sounds of the sky, he closed his eyes in relief and waited for the end. The end eluded him, though, and when he opened his eyes again, he was unable to rid himself of an image of Kamal coursing through the wild rain—her hair streaming down her back, the red earth squelching between her toes, the fabric of her sari clinging to her wet calves—as fast as she could, away from him.

But he was getting ahead of himself. He must place it in context. He must piece the past together, reel by reel, shot by shot, he must make his own bioscope as he lay there, and let it unspool through his head, against the backdrop of the dusk-darkened sky that hung outside his windows. For he had nothing better to do and, more importantly, more accurately, he felt he would like to live some of his life again, before it let go of him entirely.

After the day Bhalerao had introduced Kamal to him, he had avoided going to the studio in Borivali. But he had been bound to relate the day's events—minus his first enigmatic meeting with Kamal, of course—to Tansukhrai. Tansukhrai, to Tatya's discomfiture, took barely a few moments to conclude that Bhalerao was entirely correct in his assessment of the situation. There was no way that Rising Sun Films could afford to continue solely with male actors. Tansukhrai didn't seem in the least bothered by the fact that a female theatre artiste, with all that entailed, would begin living and working at the studio. On the contrary he took a rather robust approach to it, Tatya thought, considering Tansukhrai's was one of the oldest and most conservative business families in Bombay. There, of course, was the clue to Tansukhrai's views—he was a businessman after all, and, he said to Tatya: 'Vaman seth, it is a strange business indeed that we find ourselves in.' He chuckled and appeared lost in thought for a moment, perhaps lost for words. Then he continued, 'Who would have thought that you and I would get involved with actors and theatre artistes and, of all things, women performers. But now that we have found ourselves on this journey, this new modern industry of filmmaking, let us ensure that we spin as much gold out of it as we can, eh? What do you say, Vaman seth? We are, after all, businessmen. It is our job to run our businesses as successfully as we can.'

'But Tansukhrai, though I agree with you purely on business grounds....' began Tatya.

Tansukhrai interrupted him. 'Do you doubt Bhalerao's intentions?' He looked carefully at Tatya.

'No,' said Tatya, after a moment's thought. He adjusted his collar of stiff cotton fabric. It suddenly felt hot on his neck. 'Not at all. I have no doubt that he will behave with all propriety. But what about the other men in the studio? How can we give any guarantees?'

Tansukhrai considered this, and then said, 'Do you know, I do believe that these women know how to look after themselves. Add to that, Bhalerao's eagle eye and Shankar's presence, and I don't think we have much to worry about.'

These women. That's exactly what he had been afraid of. That she would be thought of as one of 'these women'. And he was even more afraid that she was indeed that kind of woman. The kind he had heard about. On the other hand, she had run away when her brother had tried to force her into that kind of life. And so, his fears were likely to be unfounded. He thought back to the days of the doomed venture with Chandu Barve and the twists and turns that had led him to this juncture. Had he ever meant for things to come this far? He didn't think so. He was a selling agent of cloth, after all. It all seemed dreamlike, as if he were living a destiny meant for someone else. But there was nothing for it but to go ahead with the scheme. Tatya waited till Shankar arrived at Jamshedji Mansion that weekend, and told him to give Bhalerao the message to hire Kamal. Shankar seemed rather in awe of the whole idea.

For months afterwards, Tatya stayed away from the studio. In any case, he was busier than ever at Mulji Jetha Market. He now had five employees at the pedhi to look after his warehouse stocks, to run errands to Noor Begum Mills and Rose Mills, and to help Kishan Mehta with the accounts. And he took on a new selling agency—a set of seven mid-sized textile mills located in Ahmedabad run by a savvy mill owner called Pratap Choksi. Choksi made sure his mills ran at high efficiency and low cost. He was keen for Tatya to take on the selling agency for the vast region of the Bombay Presidency, with a promise that Tatya would soon be the agent for sales all over the country. Scenting that Choksi was a man whose sole mission in life was the production of as much cloth as possible, Tatya threw himself into setting up new networks to sell and distribute the cottons and especially the fancy, high quality shirtings that Ahmedabad's mills were known for. He travelled frequently to Ahmedabad and, on returning to Bombay, would sit late into the night poring over and catching up on documents and accounts that he had missed overseeing while away.

Now, almost thirty years later, Tatya could still see the graceful curves of the oil lamp that lit up his pedhi in the small hours of the morning. A few times he had fallen asleep there, and had woken up with his head on a cotton-covered bolster and the account books lying open under his arm. At such times he went home to Jamshedji Mansion in the early morning simply to bathe and eat, and then returned to the pedhi.

But he was already a rich man by then. He had bought a seven-seater Buick, and hired a chauffeur who drove the sparkling cream-coloured motorcar while Tatya himself sat behind a sliding glass partition on soft leather seats. Why then, had he taken on the selling agency of seven mid-sized mills in faraway Ahmedabad, and why had he worked himself to the bone?

Well, he thought, I am now an old man and it is time to be honest with myself. I avoided telling myself the real reason I took on the Ahmedabad mills, because it would have been almost like confessing to Radha: surely she would have seen it in my eyes. (It was a fanciful notion, of course. In all his decades he had never met anyone who could read another person through their eyes.)

Out with it now, after all those years: he had spent a year shuttling between Bombay and Ahmedabad simply to avoid going to Borivali.

He had made sure that Tansukhrai, seeing how busy Tatya was, took a more active role in keeping an eye on the studio. In fact, Tansukhrai was of the opinion that there really wasn't much of a need to oversee Rising Sun Films, apart from counting the profits that came in and investing in new equipment and hiring more employees as needed.

Over the period of that one year, Kamal bai, as she was called at the studio, starred in no fewer than eight films. Bhalerao, in a frenzy of creativity, put the *Arabian Nights* to one side and rapidly wrote new tales of adventure and fantasy in much the same vein, centred around Kamal bai and the ever-swaggering Shinde. It hardly seemed possible, but Kamal had appeared even more beautiful on the screen than in reality. Her face was made for the caresses of the camera's eye. There were sword fights under a waterfall, wicked magicians juggling balls of fire, a stampede of horses hired from a travelling circus, palaces billowing with smoke, and caves encrusted with sparkling gems. Fighting every conceivable villain on the screen was not just Shinde but also Kamal bai, at his side. She rode, she danced, she swam, Bhalerao even hired a gymnastics instructor to teach her how to tumble and gracefully leap off a tree. Nobody had ever seen a woman do such things, much less a delicate-featured beauty dressed in the most gorgeous, exotic costumes all aflutter with trails and veils. And when Bhalerao created what was to become Kamal bai's trademark move on screen, the audiences went wild. There were reports of young men coming back to watch the same film six times in a row. And what a trademark it was: as the story ended, and the princess had been rescued by her prince, the last lingering shot of the bioscope was always of Kamal bai's face as she turned to look directly at the camera, at her adoring audience, bestowing on them a brilliant, knowing smile as if to say, 'Of course, I knew all along that I would win!' It was an unprecedented move by Bhalerao to make his heroine break through the seemingly unbridgeable distance between actress and audience, and smile directly into every viewer's eyes, breaking thousands of hearts at a stroke. Magazines were full of photos of Kamal bai, and newspaper reviews raved about her performances. Tansukhrai reported that Shinde had to be placated with an increase in his monthly salary, for he felt that she had stolen much of his thunder.

Thunder and rain—playing a terrible duet outside his bedroom window now, in the cloud-darkened sky. It had been one such monsoon when… yes, exactly this kind of rain.

CHAPTER 39

1927

He barely saw Radha nowadays. All his time was taken up with going back and forth between Ahmedabad and Bombay, or spending long days at Rose Mills and Noor Begum Mills discussing quality and costs, or negotiating cloth deliveries and payments with his wholesale merchants. And he took on yet another selling agency, of a large mill called Shivam Textile Mills located in Parel. He was now dealing in colossal quantities of cloth.

All this led to one undeniable fact: wealth was pouring into his coffers. But it also took up all of his time.

Guilty at not spending enough time at home, he ordered an elegant carved vanity chest for Radha, crafted in Kashmir from the wood of a walnut tree. When opened, a large mirror unfolded on a stand; inside were compartments where she could keep the small vials and bottles she used for her daily toilette. It was an extravagance he could well afford. He bought another car too, a smart red Chevrolet. Shankar sometimes drove the new Chevrolet on weekends to take Radha and Shalu, along with Sharad, Durga, and Kusum, on outings to the sea front at Worli, or further afield towards the hills and cooler climes of Lonavala where they took a picnic with a simple packed lunch of large, flaky polis and spicy potato bhaaji, green-skinned bananas and screw-top tambyas of cooled buttermilk. But never to Borivali; though the bucolic grounds of the studio would have been an obvious place for a day's outing and picnic, Tatya had forbidden Shankar from taking any of the family there, including Shalu, Shankar's wife.

And during these months of increasing fatigue and lack of time, he eventually made a bad decision, a poorly judged one. He loaned fifty thousand rupees to a man who was a relation of Zaveri, and who promised to return the money within six months at a good rate of interest. After a year, however, there was no sign of him, and it was only with an embarrassed Zaveri's persistent efforts that the man repaid part of the loan: he gave Tatya half the original amount and, in lieu of the remaining twenty-five thousand, an old property a short distance outside Girgaon. Not only had Tatya lost the promised interest, but he was now saddled with a dilapidated structure akin to a warehouse, which he had no idea what to do with.

Tatya and Zaveri went to look at the old property together. Tatya's driver stopped the cream-coloured Buick in front of the building. Across the road stood a ramshackle cattle shed. A few urchins ran about and a beggar woman wandered by. Some poor stalls selling day-old vegetables lined the street, along with a couple of shops operating out of shop-houses. Hanging in the air was a strong smell of cow dung. It was an area that Tatya had had no reason to visit prior to that day.

Zaveri and Tatya stood in front of the old building that Tatya now owned, and looked up at the two-storey structure. They took in the wide, hulking door with its peeling red paint, the blank-eyed windows that looked down on them from the first floor, and the brown patches of mould that creeped over its walls.

'This place is a wreck,' muttered Zaveri in disgust. 'Tatya, I can't tell you how embarrassed I am at my nephew's behaviour. He is utterly irresponsible. I had no idea that he owned this property. The least he could have done is to look after it so that it did not fall into a state of disrepair!'

Tatya took a deep breath and held it in his chest for a moment before exhaling. It was that old familiar feeling, not experienced by him since his disastrous foray into Chandu Barve's scheme of making a bioscope. That sickening feeling of having been taken for a ride, his hard-earned money siphoned off by some fool's lack of foresight. No greater fool than myself, though, he thought wearily, for having lent the money in the first place. But he would not let this spoil his relations with Zaveri.

'Come, Seth,' said Tatya, with a faint smile. 'Let's look on the brighter side of things. At the very least I have gotten my twenty-five thousand back, of the original fifty. I haven't lost all of it!'

'But what about the interest?' fumed Zaveri, his face turning a darker shade of brown. 'Is this any way of doing business? Is there no honesty left in the world anymore? I curse the day I introduced that idiot to you.'

'Seth,' said Tatya firmly, 'on no account must you blame yourself for this. You simply introduced him to me. After that it was my own decision to lend him the money, which I did because he promised me a good rate of interest. Of course, the fact that he was your sister's son influenced me. I will not deny it. But I blame myself entirely for this blunder, and I refuse to let this incident affect our relationship.'

Zaveri had tears in his eyes as he heard Tatya out, and Tatya felt a sudden rush of affection for the old man who stood there leaning on his walking stick. What was the loss of twenty-five thousand rupees when his bank account was overflowing with wealth, when he owned shares in a dozen premier businesses? Besides, he hadn't really lost the money. There was this old building, after all, in place of the twenty-five thousand. Though he couldn't for the life of him see what he was to do with it.

Zaveri had now regained his composure and stood a little more upright, his face turned up towards the building, appraising it with narrowed eyes. A crow flew down to inspect one of the windows on the upper storey. It flapped its wings at the window and hopped straight in. The glass was missing.

'The question,' said Tatya, thinking aloud, looking up at the structure, 'is whether I should simply sell it, or find some other use for it.'

'You could sell it,' said Zaveri, 'though you will not get twenty-five thousand for it even with a coat of paint on it. Even if you renovate it.'

'And there will be the cost of the painting and renovation,' sighed Tatya, 'which will eat into whatever little money I get for it. And it's too far from Mulji Jetha Market to be used as a warehouse.'

Zaveri shook his head in resignation and seemed to be at a loss for words or ideas. He seemed tired. Nowadays he spent not more than two or three hours a day working, and his pedhi was no longer a hub for wholesalers. A few of his trusted merchants dropped by at his pedhi now and then, but Tatya felt that the small amount of business that Zaveri acquired these days was based mainly on the remnants of old goodwill.

They went inside through the wide creaking door, which was high enough for an elephant to pass through. Inside was a large empty space with an extraordinarily high ceiling. They found a staircase and Tatya walked up alone, telling Zaveri not to bother with the climb. He found that the first floor was simply a series of three or four rooms with windows facing the road. On the other side the rooms had windows that looked down on to the inside of the large hall. Baffled by the construction, Tatya returned downstairs.

'I wonder what this building was used for,' he said to Zaveri, frowning. 'This high ceiling extends up to the roof, and there are just a few rooms on the first floor.'

'Must have been some kind of warehouse,' said Zaveri. 'The owner probably lived in the rooms upstairs. Maybe it was used for some kind of large machinery. Maybe even animals.'

There was nothing more to say. The place was a puzzle. Tatya dropped off Zaveri at his house, but did not go home himself. It was Saturday morning. He did not wish to go to the pedhi. Jagan, his driver, sat patiently behind the wheel of the Buick, awaiting instructions. A sudden weariness overcame Tatya. He couldn't possibly settle down to any work. There was no point going home, there was no one there, save for Uma bai and Sadaa. Shankar and Shalu were away in Kolhapur visiting Shankar's parents. Radha had sent Kusum home to her parents for a while and gone to Shervi to visit her mother, taking Sharad and Durga with her. It appears to be the season to go home, thought Tatya, sourly, everybody's gone, leaving me behind to stew in Bombay. This was entirely unfair, and Tatya knew it, for Radha had pleaded with him to join them at the old wada for at least a few days. But he had too much to do in Bombay. Sharad was now twenty-one years old and worked in the pedhi everyday, but Tatya had agreed to let him go visit his grandmother. It disturbed him how eagerly Sharad went with his mother and sister, how relieved he seemed to be to get a few days' respite from his work at the pedhi. Tatya could not understand it. At that age he had worked with a single-minded ferocity, day and night, constantly thinking up schemes for his own betterment. Even today, his thoughts were never far from the pedhi and the mills and his film business. Why didn't his son appreciate the effort he had put into creating all this wealth? Why did he not want to follow in his father's footsteps? It was Sharad who should have come with him to inspect that dilapidated structure, not old Zaveri. But Sharad was away at Mai's, eating her ladoos and puran polis, thought Tatya in irritation, his mind becoming more restive by the minute.

'I'll visit Bhalerao,' he thought. 'It will do me good to get out of the city. And he'll be free, I won't be disturbing his work. It's the monsoon, after all, impossible to film in this weather.' It occurred to him, too, that the studio would be practically empty, for all the staff routinely took their annual leave during the monsoon. There would be no Shinde, no Tambe, no...Kamal. It would only be Bhalerao and his wife, Suhasini, in their cottage, for they had made their permanent home there, having no other home of their own. All at once, the idea of spending the entire afternoon in the company of Bhalerao and his pleasant wife appealed to Tatya, and soothed him. He would have lunch there, and some tea, and be home in time for dinner. It was more than a year since he had been to the studio.

It was Tansukhrai who visited Borivali regularly and gave him the financial updates on Rising Sun Films, and he received detailed monthly letters from Bhalerao about the company's functioning. And, of course, Shankar came home to Jamshedji Mansion almost every weekend and told him about the day-to-day goings-on at the studio. He felt well-informed. There had been no need at all for him to go there, he thought with satisfaction. On the contrary, he had helped his own cause by throwing himself into the new selling agencies in Ahmedabad and in Bombay.

And he had watched her films. All twelve of them. Before they were distributed to theatres, Bhalerao unfailingly sent the films to the city for Tatya and Tansukhrai to watch. Karve, the technician, came in the studio lorry, causing a minor commotion on their street for on the side of the lorry was written in large bold letters, 'Rising Sun Film Company and Works'. One wall of the living room in Jamshedji Mansion served as a screen, and here Tatya sat to watch the films as they clattered through the machine, Karve fixing any hiccups and glitches that the projector chose to throw up. Tatya did not really mind his family watching along with him. They could watch, he supposed, as long as they stayed away from the strange world of make-believe that was the Rising Sun film studio.

CHAPTER 40

'Take me to the station,' said Tatya to his driver. Jagan looked surprised.

'Saheb, are you going somewhere by train? Why don't I drive you instead?'

Tatya considered this. It would certainly be a more comfortable journey. But he was too restless to sit in the car. He felt a desire to go to the studio by train, as he had done in former days, and to smell the warm odours of hot peanuts and sticky chikki at the station, to see the vibrant rush of the landscape as the train hurtled through it, and to sit anonymously among others. Sometimes he even felt a longing to once again saunter along the street smoking a bidi; but it would be unseemly now, for him to do that. People would think him strange indeed, if he chose to walk somewhere rather than sit in one of his two cars. But at this moment he felt a desperate need to get out of the Buick. And he felt relieved that there was nobody at home to whom he needed to explain his absence. He wanted a day that was a complete break from the exhaustion of dealing with the mills, and the bad loan, and the infernal warehouse or whatever that building was that he now owned.

'No,' he said to Jagan. 'I'll go by train. Drop me off, then take the car back to Jamshedji Mansion. Inform Uma bai that I have gone to Borivali and might be late for dinner. After that you can go home.'

'Yes, Saheb,' said Jagan, and began driving towards the station.

As Tatya's train sped out of the station, he exhaled, letting the weariness overtake him and turn his body limp. He passed the time smoking bidis and looking up at the fortresses of white clouds racing across the blue sky, while the cool, moist air that blew through the compartment brought half-hidden smiles on to the faces of his fellow passengers. But about half-way to Borivali, as if a child had taken a ruler and pencil and drawn a straight vertical line from the sky to the ground to divide the world into a dry zone and a wet zone, the train crossed some invisible boundary, and within seconds had passed into a soaking wet landscape, lashed by rain and whipped by winds. The crashing water almost drowned out the roar of the train. When he arrived at his station, Tatya made a dash towards the covered area of the platform through a curtain of rain, splashing through puddles so that his dhoti was drenched and clung unpleasantly to his shins. The station was almost empty; few people were fool enough to venture out in this wild weather unless they really had to. Tatya, cursing under his breath and wiping his face with a handkerchief, squinted through the rain towards the road, looking for a tonga. He was in luck: there was one just coming into the station, its black horse miserable and sodden. The person who descended from the tonga was none other than Bhalerao. He stood stock-still and stared at Tatya in astonishment, forgetting to take shelter; not that it would have made much difference, for he was already completely wet.

'Bhalerao?' called Tatya in amazement, raising his voice against the deafening rain. 'What on earth are you doing outside in such weather?'

Bhalerao suddenly remembered that he was standing in the rain, and ran towards Tatya who stood in the shelter of the platform.

'I could ask you the same question,' he said, his eyes large and worried. He drew a limp handkerchief from his pocket and mopped his face with it. 'Why this sudden visit? Has something happened?'

'Nothing at all,' Tatya assured him, 'I simply wanted to come and see you. I was going to eat lunch with you.'

'You came for lunch? In this weather?' said Bhalerao, nonplussed, and he looked up at the raging sky as if it might offer him some clues as to Tatya's behaviour.

'Bhalerao, the skies were clear when I embarked on my journey,' said Tatya, half-amused. He felt rather annoyed with himself. Perhaps it had been a silly idea, after all, to come here on a whim, simply to eat lunch. 'Why are you here?' he said. 'Are you expecting someone?'

'No, I have a train to catch. My wife has gone on ahead to her parents' home, and I am joining her there for a few days. There is absolutely nothing happening at the studio now, you know. Can't film anymore till the sun comes out again. The entire staff has gone on leave. But Gotu the watchman is there, of course.'

'I see,' said Tatya, now noticing the large bag in Bhalerao's hand. It certainly appeared to be the season for visiting in-laws. What was he to do now? The train to go back to the city didn't leave for hours. 'I assume Gotu can open your house for me? I will have to wait there till the next train.'

'This is terrible,' said Bhalerao in despair, scrabbling about in his pocket and drawing out his ticket. 'I'm going to cancel my ticket. You at Rising

Tejaswini Apte-Rahm

Sun studios—and me not there to receive you! It is unthinkable. Let us go back to the studio together. I will leave tomorrow.' He turned towards the tonga driver who was slowly clattering away. 'Hey you! Stop!'

'You will do nothing of the sort,' said Tatya at once. 'There is no need to change your plans on my account. I came because I had nothing better to do today and I wanted to get out of the city. I assumed that you and your wife would be at home, of course.'

'No, no,' protested Bhalerao, 'she would not forgive me if I let you wait in my house on your own.'

'Well then, don't mention this little episode to her,' said Tatya. He began walking quickly towards the tonga, his shoes filling with water, and climbed in before Bhalerao could change his mind. He left Bhalerao standing at the station, clutching his ticket in one hand and his bag in the other as the tonga began clacking down the road away from the station. Bhalerao shouted something at Tatya, but the rising wind whipped his words away.

'What?' bellowed Tatya, squinting through the rain.

This time a few of Bhalerao's words made their way through the sounds of the rain and the horse's hooves. 'I forgot to tell you something,' he yelled, but his next words were incomprehensible. The tonga driver drove his horse on implacably, as if he did not care whether the sky was blue or grey or black.

A surprised and rain-soaked Gotu, wrestling with a large and useless black umbrella, obeyed Tatya's instructions to open up Bhalerao's cottage. Tatya told the tonga driver to return in four hours, removed his shoes at the entrance, and made his way to Bhalerao's study, relieved to be indoors. Gotu lit an oil lamp that stood on the desk and retreated back to his guard's house some distance away.

Tatya removed his coat and hung it over the back of a chair to dry. Somehow he had escaped getting completely drenched and thought he could dry off quite easily in a short while. He was hungry. There was nothing for it but to wait it out, though. He checked his pocket for a bidi and lit up, reclining on an armchair and looking idly around the room. Bhalerao had made it a cozy, comfortable den. Not much had changed since he had been here last, but it did appear to be a little less messy. The stacks of books and magazines had disappeared and were now all neatly arranged in a large wooden bookcase with glass-paned doors. There were two or three comfortable armchairs interspersed with low, round tables covered with prettily embroidered cloths, no doubt the handiwork of Bhalerao's wife. Bhalerao's desk was a large wooden one, on which were scattered notebooks, loose sheets covered in Bhalerao's handwriting, a fountain pen, and an ink stand.

Tatya looked with pleasure at the arrangement of the room and especially at the rows of books in the tall and wide bookcase. He ought to get one like that at home, he thought; unfortunately, he rarely had time to read. Dada had inculcated in him the habit of reading at least a few pages of a book every day, but it was a habit he had fallen out of. The real readers in the family were now Sharad and Shalu, and Durga showed every sign of becoming an avid reader herself. Radha usually contented herself with her small store of religious books, though he knew she enjoyed looking through magazines and newspapers sometimes. He had arranged for a membership to the Granth Sanghralay, a lending library near Jamshedji Mansion, and Sharad often went there, returning with a selection of books and magazines for the family. Perhaps he didn't really need a large bookcase after all, thought Tatya, for his family mostly read library books.

He was comfortably dry now, and felt quite content sitting there in the dim, flickering light of the oil lamp, amid the dark wood of the furniture, smoking and ruminating. He considered fetching a magazine from the bookcase—perhaps a copy of *The Bioscope* or *Moving Pictures*—it had been a while since he had glanced through one of the foreign magazines to which Bhalerao subscribed to keep up with cinematographic developments in the west. But he was too comfortable to move just yet. He finished his bidi and lit up another one, inhaling deeply and gazing at the smoke which curled out of his mouth, enjoying its odd shapes and curlicues. His life in Bombay seemed a world away, on the other side of an ocean of wind and rain. A cocoon inside a cocoon: a watery bubble had cut him off from the anxieties and exhaustion of Bombay, and inside it was this snug nest of a room which was keeping him safe and dry. He felt his eyes closing and fell into a deep slumber.

A thundering crash jolted him awake and he jumped to his feet, startled, not knowing how long he had slept.

This was no ordinary rumble of thunder. Something had happened. He went to the window and peered out. The rain had whipped itself up into a raging storm. The glass pane shuddered and rattled in the window frame, as if the screaming wind were intent on tugging it out and catapulting it up to the skies. Tatya could just about make out the outlines of the tall gulmohar tree that had stood near the film editing cottage. It must have been struck by lightning for it was now a splintered wreck of a tree trunk, its large branches torn and flung to the ground.

There was a knock at the door of the study and he turned, expecting to see Gotu. But the person who stood there was Kamal.

CHAPTER 41

She held a tall white candle in her hand.

She wore a simple white sari, with a thin golden edge, tied not in the nauvari style but in the new fashion, wrapped and pleated around her waist, its hem reaching below her ankles and hiding her feet. It made her appear tall, and as luminous as the white candle she held in her hand.

'You? Here?'

'I live here now,' she explained, as if perhaps he might not know that she had been living and working at the studio for a year and a half.

'Yes, I know, but I thought the entire staff had gone on leave,' said Tatya. He was unnerved by her appearance. He tried to compose himself.

'I did not plan on going anywhere during my leave. I don't really have anywhere to go, except for my brother's house—but of course, I have no wish to return there.' She spoke as if she were simply carrying on the conversation about her brother that had taken place months ago. 'I could have taken a room in Bombay for the rainy season,' she continued, 'but I didn't feel like it. I'm quite happy here. I like the peace and quiet, especially now that everyone has gone away. But my maid is with me, of course.'

Tatya remained silent. Why hadn't Bhalerao mentioned that Kamal was here? He had shouted something out to Tatya at the last moment. This was probably what he had been trying to convey.

'My cottage has been built practically adjacent to Bhalerao's home,' she added, as if to explain her sudden and dry-clothed appearance.

'I see,' he said. How was it that he was having this casual conversation with her, without either of them going through the social niceties that would normally be required of them? A polite namaskar, an enquiry into the other's well-being, an invitation to sit down. All these were dispensed with, and they found themselves in the middle of a dialogue about the staffing arrangements of the monsoon season.

She did not enquire what he was doing there. Perhaps she felt it would be rude to question why the owner had arrived at his own studio.

'It will be difficult for you to return to Bombay today,' she observed. 'You saw how that tree came crashing down.'

'Actually, I have asked the tonga driver to come back here,' said Tatya, and he went over to his coat and withdrew his pocket watch from an inside pocket. But he saw that it had stopped. Perhaps it had gotten wet. He had no idea what time it was.

She shook her head. 'Impossible,' she said. 'No tonga could arrive in this weather. The horse would bolt at the sound of the thunder.'

'Yes, you're right,' he said, putting the watch back into his coat pocket. His arms hung at his sides and he didn't know what to do with them. 'I'll just stay here till the morning,' he said. 'Please don't trouble yourself about me.'

She looked shocked. 'But you must eat,' she said, her eyes wide. The candlelight danced in her dark eyes.

'No, please don't bother,' said Tatya, though he realized that he was starving. He now felt that he had been asleep for a long time, and that it must be long past the lunch hour. 'But if I could have some water to drink, I would be most obliged.' He wondered, uncomfortably, whether she had already been in earlier and watched him sleeping.

She gave an efficient nod and disappeared, taking the candle with her.

Tatya was left alone, in the dim light of the oil lamp. He remained standing, still rather groggy from his sleep, looking at the empty space where she had stood, wondering if he had been hallucinating.

When she reappeared it was about half an hour later. She came with her maid in tow. Her maid carried a large tray with a platter of food on it, while Kamal held the candle and a tambya of water.

'I could not let you only drink water,' she said. 'Please eat. I will wait in the adjoining room in case you need anything.'

The maid was a poker-faced young woman dressed in a simple green sari. Taking care not to look at Tatya, she placed the tray on a low table and disappeared. Kamal, however, had no qualms about looking Tatya in the eye, and did so in such a straightforward, unassuming manner that Tatya felt it was the most natural thing in the world. He had never been alone in a room with a woman who was not a relation. But he was surprised to find that instead of feeling awkward, he was simply focused on how hungry he was. She didn't linger, but left quickly so that he could get on with his meal.

It was a simple meal of a spicy bhaaji of potatoes and brinjals that he ate with two large, rustic polis, ending with dal and hot rice with ghee. He uncovered a final little container and saw, to his pleasure, that it was filled with thin buttermilk which he drank with relish and thirst. The delicious food spread such a wonderful warmth through his body that he wanted to simply lean back on his armchair and fall asleep again. He could not recall the last time he had felt such a sense of repose, felt so at ease with himself and the world, and he couldn't remember anymore why he had so anxiously stayed away from the studio for over a year.

He slept, woke again when it was completely dark, with the rain still a relentless patter on the window sills, and was offered a light snack of pohe with curd and mango pickle, and a large glass of hot, sweet tea. Only the maid appeared with the tray this time, so he could not protest to Kamal that the two women were taking far too much trouble over his food. He leafed through some issues of *Mouj Majah*, noting the film productions of other companies, including Phalke's latest mythological successes. He thumbed through a copy of *David Copperfield* that he found in the bookcase and read some of his favourite chapters, remembering the parts that Dada had made him underline, and recalled Dada's enthusiastic views on Dickens. He wished he could spend more quiet hours such as these in Bombay; he couldn't tell what stopped him from doing so—but there simply never seemed to be enough time.

Kamal did not make an appearance till after he had finished eating the dinner brought in by her maid—yet another platter filled with well-spiced vegetables, a sour aamti to pour over a mound of rice, and a cooling bowl of curd. When Kamal did finally appear he realized that, in fact, her presence had hung about the room all afternoon like a fragrance; he had eaten food which she must have, at least partly, prepared herself with her lovely hands; and he realized that he had been waiting for her. How pure she looked, how radiant, as she approached him with an oil lamp in one hand and a mysterious silver box in the other. And he remembered that she had escaped her brother's clutches, had managed to run away before any man had forced himself on her. He felt relief that she was now here, that his studio provided her sanctuary, a place where she could remain safe. He had imagined that no woman who danced and displayed herself to the world on the stage or screen could possibly retain an innocence in features and in manner—but she was living proof that it was so, that it could be so.

She smiled as she put her lamp down on a low table, adding to the illumination of the other lamp still burning on the desk. She sat down, and they were ensconced in a circle of yellow light.

'I thought perhaps you might like some company after being alone all

244   *Tejaswini Apte-Rahm*

day,' she said. 'Was the food to your satisfaction?'

'You have taken far too much trouble with all the arrangements,' he said. 'I've been well-fed indeed. It has been a comfortable day, thanks to you.' His eyes took in the circlet of milky-white mogra flowers around her wrist.

She saw him glance at it and laughed. 'I prefer flowers to jewellery,' she said. 'In any case, I have to wear jewellery all the time when filming, so it is a relief to not have to wear it during this season.'

'What is in that box?' he said, a little embarrassed that she had remarked on his looking at her wrist.

'I was hoping you would ask,' she said. 'It is a box I treasure greatly, for it was presented to me by a wealthy landowner in Ratnagiri when our theatre company was touring the region.' She held it towards him and Tatya leaned forward to look at it. The silver box was made with skilled craftsmanship. It had three small drawers built into its front, and a lid that was expertly moulded into figures dancing and playing musical instruments.

'It was my first show as a lead character,' she said. 'I had to do more singing and dancing than I had ever done before. So many steps to rehearse, so many words to memorize! I was terribly nervous. But the show was one of our biggest successes. We stayed in the region for weeks and made a lot of money. When we had finished our final show, and I was resting in my room, my maid came in with this silver box. I learnt that it had been sent to me by one of the big landowners nearby and that he had watched our performance several times already. I also discovered that he was almost like a prince in that region, owning vast amounts of farmland and a palatial wada; and that he was so fond of the arts that he employed his own small troupe of musicians to entertain him and his family. He was an old man by then. When I opened the box, I found inside it a single yellow rose. It is the most beautiful gift I have ever received.' She sighed in satisfaction and put the heavy box down by her side. Tatya found himself waiting for the next part of her story—she was a natural raconteur.

'Of course, I had to take it to my brother to ask whether I could keep it. I assumed that he would want to keep it for me, the way he kept my earnings for me. But he was drunk that evening and barely understood what I said to him. He had made so much money during our stay in the Ratnagiri area that he didn't care about the box. Still, I kept it out of his sight afterwards, just in case he decided to take it away. Whenever I look at this silver box I feel as if my artistry is validated, that my talents are of some worth. For it was given to me by a connoisseur of the arts.'

'That is a wonderful story,' said Tatya, moved at how much emotion she had invested in the silver box. 'But I can tell you that there is no question about your value and skill as an artiste. Not for nothing do your photographs appear in the magazines and newspapers. You have made a great success of our recent bioscopes. You don't need a silver box to remind you of your talent.'

She inclined her head slightly, in acknowledgement of his praise. 'You are kind,' she said, 'to have given me a place in your film company.' She looked down at the box and traced a finger over the delicate human shapes on the silver lid. 'Do you think,' she said, 'that bioscopes will always show humans like the figures on this box—dancing, playing instruments, full of life, but forever mute?'

'You mean will there ever be bioscopes with sound?' he said, smiling. 'We are not likely to see any such thing in our lifetimes.' He looked at her wide, intelligent forehead. She was capable of such fine feeling. Surely in another life she could have been a consort worthy of a king.

She shook her head at her own whimsy and then opened the box, displaying its contents proudly. 'The finest paan box in the land,' she said, with laughter in her eyes as she looked at him. Inside was the neatest, finest arrangement of paan ingredients that he had ever seen. There was a compartment for everything, including some exotic items he couldn't name.

'May I make a vida for you?' she asked.

He shook his head. He was not in the habit of chewing paan. 'No, I don't want one,' he said.

'I can make all kinds of vidas, you know,' she said, looking down at her array of ingredients. 'I can make a Govind vida, or a Hindustani, or a Darbari—any kind you like. And I have the finest Ramtek leaves. I grow them myself.'

He did not want to dampen her enthusiasm, but shook his head again. 'Please go ahead and have one yourself,' he said.

'No,' she said, 'I am forbidden from eating vidas by your Bhalerao saheb.'

'Why?' asked Tatya, puzzled.

'What a taskmaster he is,' she complained, but she had a humorous look on her face.

'I'm certain that is exactly what Bhalerao is,' smiled Tatya, 'I have seen few people as dedicated to their work as him. But I can't imagine why he should stop you from eating vidas, if you are so fond of them.'

'He says it will stain my teeth and lips. He says he won't have his heroine appear as a paan chewing princess.'

This seemed incredibly funny to Tatya, and he began to laugh. No wonder poor Kamal bai thought of Bhalerao as a wicked taskmaster. And laughter came easily to him, as if it had been hiding all this while in his mouth, waiting for the right moment to burst out like a song.

She laughed too, and shut the paan box and put it to one side.

'I can't remember the last time I was in stitches like this,' he said, chuckling, wiping his eyes.

She looked at him in surprise. 'I thought someone like you would have plenty to laugh about.'

He should, he thought, but for some reason he didn't.

'The push and pull of business never stops,' he said, shrugging. 'There never seems to be enough time to just think quietly, or laugh, or sit around with friends.'

She nodded. 'I will never be able to understand the demands of business, of course,' she said, 'but I am sure you are successful at everything you do.'

It was a conventional reply, a polite one. And he ought to have left it at that. But he said, in spite of himself, 'A good businessman will make a lot of money. But it is a truism that in business you cannot avoid losses. If you don't have the stomach for losing money, you shouldn't be in business. As a matter of fact, I recently squandered some money rather foolishly. I lent money to a man who promised me a good rate of interest. But I didn't make the correct enquiries about him.' He had no idea why he was telling her this. It was not something he would even think of discussing with Radha. But everything about this day had been rather unusual.

'And he ran off with the money?' she said.

'Not exactly. He returned part of it. But he is unable to pay back any more so he has left me with an old building near Girgaon instead, which I have no idea what to do with. You see how one small decision can lead to all kinds of problems.'

She stared at him, and then looked down, a small smile on her lips.

'What is it?' he asked.

'It's nothing. It's just that rich people have such peculiar problems. If I owned a building in Bombay I would consider myself a lucky creature indeed!'

He laughed again. 'I didn't think about it that way,' he said. 'Well, if you owned a building near Girgaon what would you do with it?'

She looked at him, suddenly serious. 'To answer that I'll first need to know what kind of building it is.'

He was amused at her grave tone. 'It's something like a large, empty warehouse,' he said, humouring her. 'Though I'm not sure what it was originally used for. It has a high ceiling, going up to the roof of the first floor.'

'It has a first floor?' she asked, impressed.

'Not really,' he said, and described the curious building with its enormous doorway and two or three small rooms upstairs.

'And what is the problem with owning such a building?' she said.

'It's dilapidated,' he said. 'The windows are missing glass, the paint is mouldy, the wood of the door is probably rotting, and it's too far from my pedhi to use as a warehouse. And it's in a rather poor sort of neighbourhood.'

'But is the roof falling in?' she said. 'Are the walls caving in?'

'No, they looked quite sturdy to me,' he said, thinking.

'Then why don't you want to sell it?' she said. 'It sounds as if it just needs some repairs.'

'I probably will sell it,' he said, 'though I wouldn't recover the money I was owed for it.'

'In that case it's obvious what you should do with it,' she said.

He stared at her. He hadn't asked her what he should do with it. He had simply asked her, in jest, what *she* would do with it.

But to be polite he said, 'What's that?'

'Convert it into a cinema theatre, of course,' she said. 'From your description it sounds exactly like a theatre should be. You can show the bioscopes of Rising Sun Films there. I know that it is sometimes difficult to get theatres to distribute your films. I have heard that the Madans have a monopoly on the theatre business because they own so many theatres, and that they give preference to exhibiting their own bioscope productions there. One theatre of your own won't solve all your distribution problems, of course, but it will certainly help you.'

Tatya was dumbfounded. Never had a woman spoken to him about a business matter, much less with such disarming frankness. Or such accuracy.

She smiled and looked straight at him. 'There,' she said, 'I've solved your problem for you. In return perhaps you will allow me to make you a vida?'

He nodded without realizing it. His head buzzed as if he were at the peak of a hill and was about to start rolling down at high speed.

'Good,' she said, and she drew the silver box towards her once more. As she made the vida, she talked softly, as if she were thinking aloud, her thoughts floating out as perfectly formed words and tableaus. 'Do you know,' she said, her small, graceful hands drawing out some paan leaves from one of the silver drawers, 'you could really make it a unique theatre. I know what audiences want. When I performed on stage they wanted comfort. And they wanted to be entertained. They wanted their souls renovated, buffed, polished, with dance and music. But most theatres offer comfort only to the few patrons who pay high prices for their seats. They are the ones who get the comfortable sofas, the arm rests. What if you offered every customer a high degree of comfort, no matter how much they paid?'

She took a pair of small silver scissors and cut off the tips and stems of five small paan leaves. They appeared freshly cut from the vine, for they gleamed with moisture that clung to them like dew. She unrolled a clean cloth and spread it out beside her, laying the leaves on it in a row. Then she wiped each one dry with a small square of cloth, one smooth motion for each leaf. She shrugged, a charming gesture of her shoulders, and said, 'I don't know why, but one must always make a vida of two leaves or five. Never with one or three.'

Her face acquired a thoughtful expression, as if she were mulling over this oddity, as she produced a miniature glass vial of chuna. She dipped a slender silver stick into it and applied a thin white layer of chuna on each leaf. 'Did you know,' she said, 'that in the old days princes used chuna made of pearls? Perhaps they still do, who knows.' And she smiled. Her teeth are a perfect pearly white, thought Tatya. She took up a small tin and dipped another stick in it to apply a thin beige paste of kaatha over the chuna. A wonderful scent emanated from the leaves. 'I soak my kaatha in rosewater,' she continued softly, glancing up at Tatya through her eyelashes. 'It helps to relieve the spiciness of the chuna. Wouldn't it be wonderful to sprinkle the patrons of your cinema theatre with rosewater as they entered and took their seats? Did you know that Bal Gandharva uses the most splendid perfumes on himself when he is on stage so that his audience is enveloped in fragrance and poetry and music?' She layered the leaves one on top of the other and picked up a small, round areca nut. 'The finest chikni supari,' she said. 'Don't worry, it won't give you a hoarse throat like bharda supari does.'

Vital knowledge for a singer, thought Tatya, even though it doesn't matter what sort of voice she has as a bioscope actress. And she was simultaneously using her knowledge of the stage to tell him how he ought to treat his customers in his theatre. The idea of a woman with opinions about business was a new one to him. He wasn't sure whether he should be offended or charmed. Her thoughts seemed to him as whimsical as gossamer tendrils, moving this way and that, a beguiling web of words and images. He looked at her hands moving expertly over the leaves and her silver box. Her graceful movements, the dim yellow light, her soft voice, the gleam of silver, it was all hypnotic, and Tatya felt as if he were observing the scene from elsewhere, from a far-off place of restfulness. And yet, another part of his mind ticked in time to the patter of the unrelenting rain, thinking about the old building, and her words about theatres, customers, seats. And he felt something he had not felt in a long time: the desire to run far, fast, and hard.

She took up a sharp silver nutcracker, in the shape of a dancer with an arm raised over her head, and began cutting thin slivers off the areca nut. She sprinkled these on the leaves. 'I like to cut my supari as thin as paper,' she said, 'so that it feels soft in the mouth.' She dipped the tips of her fingers into different compartments of her box, softly pronouncing the name of each ingredient as she added it to the growing layer of slivers and powders, as if to reassure him about what she was going to put in his mouth: a pinch of nutmeg, a sprinkling of cardamom seeds, mint flowers, shavings of coconut, a few strands of saffron, and rose jam from a crystalline bottle. And, after the hesitation of a split second, with a small smile on her pink lips, she added a fine auburn powder, but did not say what it was.

She folded the leaves into a dainty green pyramid and pierced its heart with a clove to hold it all together. Then she handed it to him and he put it into his mouth. It was like eating a bouquet of sweet aromas. It had been years since he had eaten a vida, thanks to some vague childhood remonstrances about avoiding bad habits. He sat back in his armchair, relishing the myriad tastes in his mouth, while she busied herself with arranging the contents of her silver box, discreetly keeping her eyes lowered so that he could enjoy himself without being observed.

But when he finished his vida, the spell broke, as if a musical fantasia playing in the background had come to an abrupt end.

And they were just a man and a woman, alone, cocooned in a rain-drenched house. He averted his eyes from her.

Tejaswini Apte-Rahm

She appeared to have realized, too, that something had shifted in the air between them, for she rose awkwardly and turned to leave. 'I've taken up too much of your time,' she said in a low voice. 'Please get some rest.'

'Kamal bai,' he said, for he didn't want her to leave without saying something to her. She stopped at the door. He could not think what to say, and so he said the first thing that came into his head. 'What was the final ingredient you put into the vida? Is that what made it so exquisite?'

She smiled down at the silver box in her hands, and he thought a flower bud was blooming in the dusk. 'Yes,' she said. 'That's my secret. It's cinnamon.' She closed the door behind her quietly and was gone.

And though the night outside was a torrential, swirling blanket of black, it was with the clarity of a full moon night that he recalled the reason why he had stayed away from the studio for more than a year.

CHAPTER 42

Tatya left the studio early the next morning without meeting Kamal. Gotu the watchman knocked at his door to tell him that an apologetic tonga driver had arrived at the studio gates and was willing to take Tatya to the station immediately. It was a while till the train's departure, and Tatya need not have left at that early hour; but he felt uncomfortable about meeting Kamal after what had transpired between them the previous evening. But what had, after all, transpired between them? Was it the way she looked at him from under lowered eyelashes? Was it the smiles that went back and forth between them like a bird carrying covert messages? Was it the astonishing moment when she spoke to him as an equal, giving him business advice? Was it that she looked him straight in the eye when she spoke? All these elements, innocent in themselves, had conspired to create an evening of intimacy, taking his heart down strange alleyways. She was intelligent, self-confident, she was as beguiling and graceful as an apsara, she was beautiful beyond compare, she was like no other woman he had ever encountered.

So no, he did not wish to see her before he left the studio.

Nor did he wish to articulate the meaning of the previous evening, even to himself. He would not let words give shape to the sensations that enveloped him like a mist of rain, leaving droplets clinging to his skin. Even so, he could not deny, in the days that followed, that he was filled with an unnatural energy, that when he looked at himself in his bedroom mirror with its wooden frame carved into twisting, writhing vines polished to a sleek black, his eyes looked bright, his forehead clear of minute wrinkles and worry lines. The world appeared freshly washed, just for him: the city was a joyous, kaleidoscopic canvas waiting for him to add to it his own audacious brushstrokes of honey and jade and other jewelled tints; when the massive sea-green waves rolled up to the shore in giant cylindrical shapes, he felt that the salt waters were rising up to meet him with a nebulous invitation; as if the sea drew his eyes to the illumined, liminal horizon and then pulled his gaze up to the sky so that he was reminded of how high the sky was, how endless its blue.

But he would not, could not, let the words of tenderness and ardour form in his head.

He could not betray Radha, nor his own conception of himself; for he felt that he would fall irredeemably in his own estimation if he followed his thoughts to their logical conclusion. And so an undefined sense of possibility hung about him like a swirling haze, a sensation of tingling limbs, a sense of somewhere he needed to go, of boats that needed to set sail from the sands into the boundless blue.

He turned his attention to the theatre; in his mind, the dilapidated building was already filled with the buzz of patrons waiting for the screen to flicker to life while sellers of candied peanuts roamed the aisles and the musicians tuned their instruments. For it was a stroke of genius, the idea of turning that building into a theatre; and she had hit upon it without even seeing the place!

He stood in front of the building on that poor road, the cattle shed opposite sending forth its usual odour of cow dung. With him were Zaveri, leaning on his walking stick, and Tansukhrai, looking dapper as usual in a navy blue coat worn over a pure white dhoti. Tatya had brought them along for a second opinion. He had just finished walking them around the inside of the building, pointing out the high ceiling, the wide open space that could be filled with seats, the wall where a large screen could be installed, the rooms above which could be used to store film reels and other equipment. Now that they stood outside again, Tansukhrai looked dubiously around at the street. The Buick was parked nearby with Jagan, the driver, shooing away some small boys who had gathered around to peer into the car.

'Vaman seth,' said Tansukhrai, 'there is no doubt that this building can be converted into a theatre. But if you want to attract the better sort of clientele, what are you going to do about these surroundings? Who will want to come to this street with its raggedy shops and urchins and smelly cattle shed?'

'First things first,' said Zaveri, tapping his cane on the ground imperiously. 'What is the situation with regard to showing Indian bioscopes? Are they really so popular that people will fill up this theatre? I would have thought there were enough theatres already in Bombay.'

Tansukhrai shook his head at Zaveri's lack of understanding, and glanced at Tatya.

'Seth, Indian bioscopes are far more popular than the American ones,' explained Tatya. 'In fact, the problem is not one of demand but of supply. Often there aren't enough theatres to show the Indian films that do get made. And the Madans have cornered the exhibition trade—they own sixty-five theatres across India, and have an arrangement with twenty more, in which they show either the films they produce themselves, or films from America and Europe. They usually refuse to exhibit films of other Indian companies.'

'If Indian bioscopes are as popular as you say they are,' said Zaveri, frowning, 'why do the Madans bother exhibiting western films?'

'They have some theatres where they have a foreign or Anglo-Indian clientele,' said Tansukhrai. 'The elite Indians go there as well. Those are the theatres where they show foreign films. The Madans are afraid that if they start showing Indian films there, they will scare off their regular high paying patrons. Indian films don't get an elite audience. Only western films do.' Tansukhrai shrugged. 'That's the nature of our business.'

'Why shouldn't Indian films attract an elite or European audience?' said Tatya, thoughtfully. 'I know that some Indian films are made in a slapdash, shoddy manner, but ours certainly aren't. They are well-made stories about exciting adventures, after all. They aren't mythological or religious films which would appeal only to Indians.'

'What are you proposing?' said Tansukhrai.

'Well, what if we included title cards in English? And made this theatre a really attractive place to which all kinds of people would come to watch Rising Sun films?'

'If you're sure about it,' said Zaveri, looking up at the blank-eyed windows. 'It shouldn't take you too long to get this up and running. You just need to paint the place, fill it up with benches, and start selling tickets! If what you say about the demand for Indian films is true, you ought to have no problem making money on this theatre.'

Tatya shook his head. 'This is not going to be just any old theatre.'

Tansukhrai looked at Tatya with narrowed eyes and the beginnings of a smile under his pencil-thin moustache. 'You see, Zaveri seth?' he said. 'Give this man a simple answer and he'll turn it into a complicated question.'

'You mean to say, give this man a paisa and he'll turn it into a rupee,' chortled Zaveri.

'My point exactly,' said Tansukhrai, grinning. 'So tell us, Vaman seth, what is it that you have in mind? What wondrous thing is this theatre of yours going to be?'

Tejaswini Apte-Rahm

'For a start,' said Tatya, enjoying his friends' ribbing, 'I'm going to buy up the shops on this street.'

Zaveri and Tansukhrai stopped chuckling and stared at him.

'Then I'm going to get them repaired and painted, and rent them out to respectable shopkeepers who want to sell wares that well-to-do people might want to buy. Like dry fruits and nuts, or sweetmeats, or fine footwear, or seasonal fruit like mangoes and sitaphals. Maybe in time add a shop selling small items of silverware and brassware.'

'Silverware?' said Tansukhrai, incredulously. 'On this street? Vaman seth, the smell of cow dung hangs in the air. Who is going to come shopping here for that kind of thing?'

'I was coming to that,' said Tatya. 'You see the cattle shed opposite us? That is the sole source of the smell. I spoke to the man who runs it. All he has are a few scrawny head of cattle. He doesn't make much from the milk he sells. His only other source of income is selling the cow and buffalo dung. I asked him whether he would agree to take on the job of a watchman at the theatre, as long as he gives up his cattle. He is more than happy to do so. I also told him that I would eventually help him set up a small shop instead of his cattle shed, which his wife and children can run, and that he would get a good number of customers once the theatre is up and running. And the point of sprucing up the street is that my theatre will cater to the elite, the people with money, as much as it caters to the common man. And for the well-off people to come here, it is absolutely vital to create an environment around the theatre which they will find acceptable. It's going to be a circle of prosperity, Tansukhrai. My theatre will attract the monied folk, who will come to the theatre to see bioscopes made by Rising Sun Films, and afterwards, will buy sweets and nuts and fruits in wonderful, brightly lit shops, and go home with their pockets suitably lightened, and come back to see more bioscopes because their families will pester them to repeat the whole experience.'

'Well!' said Zaveri, looking at Tatya in unabashed admiration. 'He's thought it all out! You see, Tansukhrai? This is the man I trained and brought up. He was a weakling of seventeen when he started with me, bringing me cups of tea and knocking together old fruit crates to make me a shoe rack. And now he talks of buying up an entire street of shops!'

Three months later, the exterior of the Kohinoor Theatre was ready. The outside walls were painted a fresh lemon yellow. Two large stone elephants flanked the wide doors, trunks raised, as if welcoming the audience. Their caparisons were painted with fanciful motifs in deep scarlet and sapphire blue, and their ornaments outlined in gold paint. The doors of rotting wood had been replaced with a solid wooden double door with massive iron locks which looked like it guarded a palace, particularly with the effect of the elephants standing by. Inside the theatre, Tatya had each wall painted with a row of dancers and musicians playing drums, horns, conch shells, sitars, and all manner of instruments, so that it felt as if one were surrounded by an ever-moving caravan of melody and dance. A mezzanine balcony was added for extra seating since the ceiling was so high. There was also a lobby through which people would pass to go into the seating area, while a small ticket booth was built in the compound.

In the early days, when Tatya had dragged Tansukhrai around the city to watch various bioscopes and get a measure of the business possibilities, he had observed the customary operating style of film theatres. Most theatres in the city lined their spaces with benches, along with a few sofas in boxes at the back. When the doors were thrown open, there was a melee to get inside with young men rushing to the benches and lying down on them to reserve seats for their friends. Then came the ticket collector collecting the ticket stubs amid the chaos, while vendors selling snacks wandered about calling their wares even while the film was playing. It was no surprise, thought Tatya, that the British and the Indian elite stayed away from most theatres, preferring to patronize the ones that showed American films, and which did not attract such a raucous crowd. He knew that there were even theatres where European audiences watched films in full evening dress, with a bar available to purchase wines and gins. Obviously, he would not sell alcohol in the Kohinoor Theatre—apart from his own aversion to the idea, it would scare away his Indian audience—and he knew that in this part of the city he would never get the sort of audience that wore evening dress for film shows. Nevertheless, he was determined that the Kohinoor Theatre would be different. He didn't care who came to see his films, as long as it was in a decorous atmosphere that didn't put off the more monied customers, Indian or European.

The first thing to do was to address the problem of reserving seats. He had seen for himself the confusion that prevailed when people tried to grab the best seats for themselves and their friends. Then there was the problem of ventilation: as dozens of people exited the theatre and dozens more entered, there hung an oily smell in the air of food and drink and bodily odours. Though one got used to the smell after a while, it was still a rather unpleasant thing to encounter. He remembered what Kamal had said about Bal Gandharva's theatre company using real perfumes on stage for the benefit of the audience—well he couldn't do that, obviously, but he could place fragrant incense sticks in the four corners of the theatre. And he could make sure that the Kohinoor Theatre was well ventilated before and after every show. The abnormally large double doors would come in handy for this purpose: they could simply be thrown open after every show to air out the place. As far as the seating was concerned, Tatya decided to do away with benches entirely. What was it that Kamal had said? Let every customer be offered comforts, not simply the ones who have paid for the sofas. Well, there was a way of offering comfort and getting rid of the chaos of the benches in one go: individual seats. He would install individual seats with armrests and numbers, and tickets would be issued with the seat numbers written on them. And on the mezzanine balcony would be the sofas and the comfortable cushioned chairs, sold for a higher price.

As for the state of the street, the problem of the cattle shed had been solved with the shed owner, Sahdev Kane, happily taking on the role of full-time watchman; and Tatya was now the owner of the three shops closest to the theatre. He had tasked Phatak & Co., the builders who were renovating the theatre, to do a quick refurbishment of all three shops. Having put it out at Mulji Jetha Market that three shops were available on rent, he was already courting enquiries about it: word had spread rapidly that there was to be a new theatre and a regular flow of customers on that street.

But he intended to vet each potential tenant carefully to ensure that the new shops fitted in with the clientele of his theatre. He had already rejected an enquiry from a vendor of wooden toys; not a good match because people didn't usually take children to the bioscope unless the film had a religious theme. And another enquiry from a man who wanted to open a shop selling kitchenware; again, not suitable because he did not want his theatre to be associated with the humdrum routines of the every day.

The shops nearby must offer the same thing that the Kohinoor Theatre intended to offer: pleasure.

CHAPTER 43

Despite being married for years, Shankar and Shalu still had no children. Radha felt ill seeing Shalu's increasingly desperate attempts at getting pregnant. She was reminded of the sickening period of her life when she had waited for her first blood to arrive. There had been nothing to do but pray, and she had conducted the myriad religious rituals with a desperation that was difficult for her to recall without a feeling of stones settling into her stomach. As she watched Shalu, the notion that she herself had had a narrow escape came back to haunt her.

Shalu began consulting the calendar for every single fast and ritual she could think of. Uma bai added her own knowledge to the endless possibilities of what to eat, what not to eat, whether to look at the moon on a particular night, or wait for first light on an auspicious morning. Shalu stitched silken clothes for the idols in the small shrine in her room, washed their feet in milk, smothered them in flowers and turmeric and vermillion, offered them sugared delicacies. There was no end to the ways in which one could pamper the gods. In all her spare time Shalu stayed in her room, praying and reading holy texts. Radha wanted to tell her to stop, that it was too much, that she should not forget to live her life, should not forget to laugh and play with Durga as before. But it also felt hypocritical to tell Shalu to stop. Radha herself had followed the rituals with the same relentless intensity, after all, and the result was that her prayers had been answered. There was no other way to reach out to the almighty. So she said nothing to dissuade Shalu, but was kind to her, urging her, when she wasn't fasting, to eat hot, nourishing food that would strengthen her thin body and help her conceive.

It seemed to Radha, though, that a large part of the problem was that Shankar was hardly ever around. How, then, could a child be conceived? He had stopped coming home every weekend, citing staffing problems, new carpentry work to oversee, a new film production to plan. There was always a good reason to not come home. She thought of mentioning it to Tatya but was afraid that he would think she was interfering in the studio's work. So she said nothing, and continued to worry.

Even when Shankar did come home, he hardly spent any time in the apartment but stayed out with Ponkshe and some other friends he had made, smoking and doing she knew not what. When he returned in the evenings he was often brusque with Shalu, though unfailingly courteous to everyone else in the house. But he didn't laugh and joke with Sharad and Durga as he had done in the past, didn't suggest driving them all out in the red Chevrolet for a picnic, and it often seemed as if he would rather be elsewhere. Sometimes it was almost a relief when he left for Borivali on Sunday evening or Monday morning, so taut was the atmosphere between him and Shalu when he was at Jamshedji Mansion. Surely he could not be angry with Shalu for not producing a son? Surely he couldn't be thinking of taking a second wife? Everything was possible, Radha knew, when it came to a woman's fate. Shalu's slight frame seemed to get even thinner, and her face grew wan through the week. When Friday came, she eagerly sat by the window waiting to see Shankar's tall figure striding from the tram stop towards Jamshedji Mansion. When she saw him, she would immediately tie a fresh braid of mogra flowers, which she had strung herself, around her bun, and rush to the kitchen to get him some tea. If he didn't arrive, she despondently gave the string of flowers to eleven-year-old Durga to wrap around her plait.

So Radha was pleasantly surprised when, one evening, Tatya looked up from a letter he was reading and said, 'I've asked Shankar to come back to live in Bombay.'

Radha had stepped into the living room, where he sat at his desk, to bring him some cooling, sweet buttermilk, for it had been a hot afternoon. 'Don't you need him any more at the studio?' she asked in surprise.

'The studio is on a steady footing now,' said Tatya, 'and he can easily train somebody else to take on his job there. But I need a reliable manager for the theatre.'

'Shalu will be very happy,' said Radha, and she paused. 'Actually, there was something I wanted to mention to you.'

'What about?' said Tatya. It wasn't often that Radha came to him with any particular petition.

'About Shankar. The thing is…he comes home less and less now. And when he does come home for weekends, he spends much of his time hanging about with Ponkshe and some other friends he's made.'

Tatya frowned. 'I hadn't realized that he wasn't coming home as often as before.'

Radha said nothing. Tatya himself had not been much at home lately, so it was no surprise that he hadn't noticed Shankar's absences.

'He is very involved with the work at the studio,' said Tatya. 'In fact, when I mentioned to him the possibility of his returning to Bombay he didn't seem too keen on it.'

Radha's heart sank. 'But why?' she said. 'Surely he should be happy to come back here and be with his wife. Perhaps you can persuade him to do so.'

'Well,' said Tatya, 'I don't want to force him. After all, looking after a theatre will not be as challenging as managing a studio. I fear he may think of it as a sort of demotion.'

Tatya was thinking aloud now and even as he spoke, Radha felt that he was rethinking the desirability of asking Shankar to leave the studio for the theatre.

'I'll speak to him about coming home more often, but it has been a busy time at the studio,' said Tatya, 'what with the new films being made with our new...staff.'

Again, Radha said nothing. She knew about the new addition to the staff. And Kamal bai was hardly 'new' anymore. Tatya had assured Radha that Indian bioscopes did not employ actresses but now Kamal bai, well-installed at the studio, was the most successful employee of Rising Sun Films. Tatya looked uncomfortable, as if he were waiting for Radha to ask him something about it. But how could she question her husband? If there was any information he wanted to give her, it must come from him without any prompting. The whole affair seemed a highly embarrassing one to Radha. She had seen the films that Karve, the technician, brought home for Tatya to watch. She could not imagine why any decent Indian woman would dress up like that and display herself for the world to see; how she could smile dazzlingly at the camera without, afterwards, covering her face in shame; how she could look so happy jumping from trees and hills into a man's arms. Radha did not want to see the films that Karve brought home. Durga was certainly not allowed to watch. But Radha couldn't bear not to watch either. She had never been to the pedhi, never been to a textile mill, never seen her husband's iron and steel factory, and had never been to the studio—nor did she wish to go to these places, for no respectable woman would ever have done so. But these films were a glimpse into a part of her husband's life that, till now, had been barred to her. And so she found herself watching them avidly.

She took careful note of the glistening pond in the grounds of the studio, the ancient banyan tree with its gigantic limbs, the gardens planted with hibiscus and sunflowers, Shinde's swagger and his dashing moustache turned up at the tips, his turban and leather boots as he strode about the screen declaiming his lines furiously, brandishing his sword. She saw the title cards displaying the dialogues in brief lines of Hindi, Marathi, English, and Urdu. And she observed the way the gorgeous silks clung to Kamal bai's hips, falling away in graceful lines to her ankles, her thick dark hair now tied up in a bun studded with fantastical jewelled designs, now left loose so that dark strands of it grazed her cheeks and lips, then again plaited demurely into two braids that made her appear like an innocent child. And above all—her smile. There was no describing that smile, wide and tantalizing, displaying perfect white teeth, as if she were laughing at herself and at the world as it gazed on her beauty. She had dark eyes with long eyelashes, her eyes made even larger by the use of kohl; fair skin made even fairer by using face paint and, perhaps, by bathing in milk; her hair was soft and long, impossible to tell whether she had attached false hair to her own. But the means by which she had accomplished her allure were, in the end, irrelevant. For it was clear that the beauty underlying it all was undoubtedly her own.

Radha felt shabby in comparison. The first time she saw one of Kamal bai's films, with the curtains of the living room shut and the furniture pulled away to leave a blank space on one wall, Tatya sat on a sofa placed in the centre of the room. Shankar sat on a low stool by his side and, behind them, Karve fiddled with the projector. Radha and Shalu stood near the door to watch, eventually sitting on the floor as the film progressed and their legs began to ache.

When the film was over, Radha washed her face clean with soap. Then she went to the corner of her bedroom where she had placed the toilette box of carved walnut wood that Tatya had ordered for her. Sitting on the floor in front of it, she opened the lid so that the mirror unfolded and came to rest on its stand. She looked at herself. Her forehead was bare from being washed: she couldn't bear seeing it that way even for a moment. She took up her small container of haldi-kunku from the box, dipped the tip of her fourth finger in the vermillion, and drew a perfect circle of red on her forehead. Her bun was tied tight and neat, but some hair stood out on her temples in untidy wisps and curls. She took a drop of coconut oil from a vial, rubbed it between her palms and smoothed the hair down over her scalp. There were three combs in the comb compartment: wood, horn, and ivory. She took the thin-toothed one, made of ivory, and carefully combed her hair down, starting at her middle parting and combing towards her ears, till there was not a hair out of place. There was a box of talcum powder in one of the compartments too, something she hardly ever used. But she took some in her palms now, and smoothed it on to her cheeks and on her neck, covering herself in the scent of sandalwood. The top layer of the box was removable. She lifted it out to reveal a second tier of compartments underneath. In a corner was a cleverly concealed drawer which she now opened. Inside was the surprise which had delighted her so when she first saw it: a small golden rose for her hair, ordered by Tatya from Pethe jewelers, and secreted in the little drawer before he presented her with the toilette box. She hadn't kept it in the cupboard with her other ornaments, but had let it stay in the box, occasionally wearing it in her bun, delighting in how it glittered inside its polished wooden drawer. She inserted it into the side of her bun now, turning her head this way and that to catch a glimpse of it in the mirror. She could just about see it, glinting prettily against her dark hair. She looked down at the array of things in her walnut wood box: a hair brush, a small handheld mirror with a carved wooden frame, the vial of oil, the box of talcum powder, a silver tin of crumbly utne with its earthy smell, which she often washed her face with, hair pins, a paisley-shaped silver container of vermillion and turmeric, a small bundle of wool which she used to tie Durga's plaits, and a clean square of cloth to wipe her face with. Then she looked at herself in the mirror and noted the differences between her face and Kamal bai's face: dark skin, a broad nose, the small dent where her nose met her forehead, oiled hair flat against her scalp. She sighed and closed the box. But she left the golden flower in her hair and, feeling fresh from her face wash, and fragrant with the face powder, went to meet the rest of the evening.

CHAPTER 44

Shankar was indeed not at all keen to return to Bombay. When Tatya pointed out that he needed a reliable manager for the theatre, Shankar said he needed time to train someone else for his job at the studio.

'I can train Jadhav for my job,' said Shankar, 'He already helps me a lot, and is the right man to take over from me. But if I leave the studio before Jadhav is ready, Bhalerao will not like it. And it will be disruptive to our studio operations.'

'Do you have any other suggestions, then?' said Tatya impatiently. In another two months the theatre would open and time was short. He should already have had a manager in place by now, but no suitable candidate had been found. Tatya himself had been looking into the final details of the refurbishment of the theatre, but there was far too much to be done still.

The theatre was to open with great fanfare, with the release of Rising Sun Films's latest production, titled *The Caravan Princess*. It was about a band of robbers led by a girl who pretended to be a princess travelling in her caravan. They waylaid other caravans and looted them till, of course, they met their match when they crossed paths with a caravan of bandits led by Shinde. Bhalerao had pulled out all the stops for this production. He had taken the actors to a plateau in the ghats where they shot with the majestic hills all around them; he took them to the banks of the Krishna river where he hired twenty sailboats and staged a battle on the water; in the studio, he created a moonlit night in broad daylight by getting Mistry to craft a silvery low-hanging moon and using clever lighting techniques like muslins to diffuse the sunlight, and tinfoil covered boards to strategically redirect the rays of the sun. And the crowning glory of the film was a fight in the jungle between two elephants on loan from the Rajesaheb of Sangli who also provided the mahouts to help stage the battle.

Tatya could not imagine throwing open the theatre without a manager to oversee it all. The theatre opening had to match the grandeur of *The Caravan Princess*.

'What about Neelkanth?' said Shankar, after a pause. 'As an interim manager, of course.'

'Neelkanth has just written his final examinations,' said Tatya. 'He is waiting for the results, after which he wants to study engineering at the Victoria Jubilee Technical Institute, like Mandar.'

Neelkanth Bhave was a poor Brahmin student who had come for his evening meals to Jamshedji Mansion for the past two years. It was common for wealthy families to support poor students in this way, and Tatya had readily agreed to it when he received a petition from the boy's school principal. So Neelkanth Bhave, then a sixteen-year-old boy, had started eating his evening meals with the family. He would then return to his chawl nearby where he lived with an old widowed aunt, and studied late into the night. He was a good-looking youngster, always neatly turned out in a white dhoti and black cap, and Tatya liked his serious, quiet nature. He only spoke when he was spoken to, and when Tatya sometimes questioned him about his studies he replied in a good-natured voice, his answers were well considered, and he was always ready to hear Tatya's advice. He was grateful for the support of the evening meal, when he could eat his fill of hot, wholesome food, but Tatya was impressed by the fact that he was never obsequious. He touched Tatya's feet in gratitude every evening but did not humble himself either in his facial expressions or his words. On the contrary, he held himself up to his full height. Everyone in the family liked Neelkanth, and Radha was especially fond of him, often giving him a parcel of sweet ladoos or savoury chiwda to take home, calling it 'study food'. You can pop some in your mouth when you stay up late studying, she would say to him, smiling.

On hearing that Neelkanth intended to study engineering, Shankar looked puzzled. 'Surely Neelkanth will not have the money to pay the fees at the institute?' he said.

'I know. I'm going to offer to pay his fees. He deserves it,' said Tatya. And so the question of finding a theatre manager remained unresolved.

But it was Neelkanth who unexpectedly solved the issue himself. When he heard from Shankar that the position of theatre manager was vacant, he approached Tatya one evening after dinner, in the living room. Tatya had a new gramophone and was examining it to see how it worked. Its sound horn looked like a golden trumpet sticking out of the contraption and the whole thing seemed larger and more unwieldy than it had looked in the shop. He had placed a thick black record on the turntable and was in the midst of screwing a needle on to the arm when Neelkanth knocked on the door and entered.

Tatya turned in surprise. 'Neelkanth? Aren't you off home yet? It's late.'

'Tatyasaheb, I am sorry to trouble you so late in the day. I heard that you are looking for a manager for your new theatre, and I would like the job if you think I am suited to the post.'

Tatya smiled at Neelkanth's direct way of speaking. No beating about the bush, no social niceties, simply an earnest question in search of an honest answer. 'I was going to offer to pay your college fees,' he said. 'Your results are sure to be good. Don't you want your engineering degree?'

Neelkanth looked startled by this offer. He thought for a while, and said, 'You are too generous. But it will be a long time before I can repay you.'

'I don't expect repayment,' interrupted Tatya.

'I would prefer to earn the money myself,' said Neelkanth. 'I could do that if you were to give me this job for a year or two. By then I assume that Shankar will be ready to take over, and I would have earned the money I need. Shankar told me you need someone urgently. Well, here I am. I promise you I will do the job sincerely and honestly.'

This impressed Tatya. He remembered the sense of triumph he had felt when he received his first pay as a young man at Zaveri's pedhi. Neelkanth was, in fact, perfectly suited for the post of theatre manager though he was young, barely nineteen. Soft-spoken he may be, but he had a determination to get the job done and a forthright manner of speaking that would keep the rest of the staff on their toes.

Tatya nodded. 'All right,' he said, 'the job is yours. But remember—the opening of the Kohinoor Theatre is going to be a grand affair. Are you prepared to work hard for it?'

Neelkanth nodded, a smile breaking out on his young, pleasant face. Tatya felt a prick of disappointment that his own son, Sharad, had never looked as eager to work as this young man.

With Neelkanth on board as the theatre manager, Tatya's burden lightened. Neelkanth ensured that every weekend for a month before the opening, there was a full-page advertisement in the newspapers announcing the new theatre. He made sure that the ticket booth was neat and well-swept every single day, even though the theatre opening was a few weeks away. He supervised the upholsterer who covered the balcony chairs and sofas with red velvet. Bhate was the man employed to sell tickets and it was decided that he would give the receipts to Neelkanth, who would ensure that the money reached Kishan Mehta at the pedhi. Neelkanth suggested to Tatya that they decorate the lobby with potted plants and strings of marigold for the opening; that they should procure an abundance of flowering plants to decorate the compound of the theatre and get the watchman, Sahdev Kane, to double up as a gardener. He also chivvied the new tenants of the three shops to display their wares in an attractive fashion. The tenants needed no encouragement to do so. Two were canny Gujarati shopkeepers and one was Marwadi. Among them was a cousin of Kailashnath Karsandas, Tatya's old business partner whose relations were in the dry fruits business. The family already owned shops selling dry fruits and nuts in other locations of the city and went about setting up their new shop in an efficient and almost clinical fashion with their rows of polished brass pots overflowing with almonds and walnuts, dried figs and raisins and dates.

Another tenant was a seller of sweetmeats and fried savoury snacks, and his shopfront display was a colourful affair of pink coconut barfis, honey-coloured anarse, and fresh white rasgullas, not to mention crisp golden jalebis and rose-brown gulab jamuns, which his assistant fried fresh at the back of his shop and smothered in sticky syrup before serving them hot to customers. Rows of glass jars filled with spicy red chiwdas and lemon-yellow shevs lined the shelves on the wall. Tatya thought that two shops offering food were quite enough, and so for the third shop he had chosen a tenant who sold glass bangles in a rainbow of colours, displayed according to shade, from grass green to dark green, rosebud pink to crimson, pale yellow to blazing orange, sky blue to shades of indigo. Tatya supplied his tenants with gleaming lanterns, and strung up lanterns outside the theatre too. All the lanterns were of the same kind which, when hung up and lit, created the impression that the theatre, the syrupy sweets, the plump nuts, and the sparkling colourful rows of bangles were all part of a single bubble of pleasure and entertainment. Conspicuous above all was the name of Tatya's theatre, in large stone letters perched along the compound wall: Kohinoor Theatre.

And when Neelkanth came to Tatya the week before the grand opening, suggesting that all the balcony guests should receive a rose as they entered, Tatya knew, without any doubt, that he had hired the right manager for his theatre. Tatya remembered Kamal's idea about perfume too, and added, 'Rosewater. Let them all be sprinkled with rosewater.' Neelkanth seemed to grasp, instinctively, that Tatya wanted this theatre to be like no other, that the shops outside were meant to be part of a sort of brightly lit pleasure palace, that the elegant décor and facilities would, in themselves, act to eliminate any raucous behaviour even from those in the cheaper seats.

The large lobby, however, seemed rather lacklustre, even though Neelkanth had lined it with potted plants and put up framed photographs on the wall of the past productions of Rising Sun Films.

And then, completely unexpectedly, an Oriental Organ entered the scene.

A man called Wolfgang Schmidt had appeared at the pedhi, as if out of nowhere. Nobody could remember the last time a European had been seen at Mulji Jetha Market, and there were many sidelong glances and wide-eyed stares as Schmidt wandered down the lanes and crossroads of the market. At any time a European strolling about in the market would have led to much surprise, but Schmidt's appearance created a positive buzz of amazement, because he was a gigantic man. With his luxuriant blonde beard and moustache, and wavy hair covering his ears and neck, he had the appearance of a shaggy but affable giant. He smiled amicably around him at the staring people, almost appearing to enjoy being the centre of attention. Tatya saw him pass by his pedhi one afternoon as he sat there examining some cloth samples, and stared in astonishment as the man paused, looked up and down the lane, and then turned back to head straight towards Tatya's pedhi.

'I am looking for Mr Govind Abhyankar,' he said politely in perfect English. His accent was not that of an Englishman, however. 'My name is Wolfgang Schmidt. Of Germany.'

Tatya and Kishan Mehta gaped up at him, feeling dwarfed. Finally Tatya said, 'You've come to the right place. How may I help you?'

'I have heard that you are in the process of erecting a pleasure palace, a place of entertainment. Am I correct?'

'No,' said Tatya, 'that is not quite correct. I am about to open a bioscope theatre, that is all.'

'But that is exactly what I mean!' exclaimed Schmidt. 'It will be a place where people come for pleasure, for recreation and relaxation, yes?'

Tatya nodded, bewildered.

'I have for you a proposition. Will you please come with me?'

'Come with you? Where?' said Tatya. 'I am rather busy you see, and....'

'I have heard you are a man of culture, who appreciates music and the arts. That you have already hired a troupe of musicians to play newly composed music, songs created especially for your films. If you will come with me, I would like to show you something magnificent, which will be of benefit to both of us.'

The man's reticence at saying what exactly he wanted to show was puzzling, but Tatya was intrigued. Schmidt seemed to think that the greater a mystery he made of it, the more likely it was that Tatya would come to see whatever it was he wanted to sell.

He went with Schmidt, who had a landau waiting outside the market. They drove to a small lane off Flora Fountain, and walked through an entrance into a building, and into a large chamber. And here was the most extraordinary contraption that Tatya had ever seen.

'This,' said Schmidt, with a flourish, 'is the thing you need to transform your theatre into a true palace of pleasure! I present to you the superlative and sumptuous Oriental Organ, made of the finest wood from the Black Forest, crafted by the renowned firm of Gebrüder Bruder in Waldkirch, in Germany.'

'An organ?' said Tatya, nonplussed. 'But I don't see any keys for anyone to play it. I don't need an organ, Mr Schmidt. I run a theatre, not an orchestra.'

'This is not that kind of organ. And once you own this, you will have no need of an orchestra, I assure you. Would you like to hear it?'

Presumably the thing plays some kind of music, thought Tatya, staring at it. It had clearly been fashioned with love and care. It was enormous, taller than even Schmidt, and took up almost an entire wall of the room. And it was shaped like a splendid oriental palace, exactly like something Bhalerao, in one of his frenzies of inventiveness, might order Mistry the carpenter to erect as a set.

Except this palace came in full colour and, apparently, with grand orchestration to boot.

It was crowned with three symmetrical domes painted a bright peacock blue, their mouldings and finer points highlighted with gold paint. Each dome was topped with a gilt spire on which hung a superb golden crescent. Every last inch of the Oriental Organ had been painstakingly covered with brightly painted geometrical shapes: small flowers inside green and red triangles, blue stripes on yellow arches, sparkling silver stars on lavish red backgrounds, delicate ivory shells on pearl blues. Tatya felt that every time he shifted his gaze, he spied some new oddity of colour and pattern that he hadn't noticed before. The palace alone would have been impressive enough, but there was also a three-arched balcony built into the front. Under each arch stood a large doll made entirely of carved wood. The doll in the centre was a bearded man of regal appearance, who looked as if he had stepped out of the *Arabian Nights*. He wore ivory white robes overlaid with a long coat of pale moss-green, silver sandals upturned at the toes, a white, feathered turban on his head, and green eyes that looked as if he wished to impart all the wisdom of the world if only he could talk. Flanking him were two female dolls painted to look as if they wore robes of heavy silks. Their large, dark eyes peered out over gauzy pink and green veils that covered half their faces. Each held a bell in one hand and a long-stemmed golden rose in the other. And on either side of the princess dolls were, curiously enough, two drums, their taut skins facing outwards.

'What are these drums for?' asked Tatya.

Schmidt looked at him with bright eyes and a broad grin, his mouth almost smothered with his thick golden beard. 'Just you watch,' he said, in that strange staccato way he had of speaking. He went round the back of the enormous contraption, fiddled with something, and brought forth a large silvery cylinder covered in curious ridges. 'See this?' he said. 'Now I place this inside the organ. So. And now I close the door. So. I turn a little key, a magic key, eh?' And here he winked and smiled so roguishly that Tatya chuckled and could not help but return that moustachioed smile.

There was a click and a whirring sound as if something were turning; presumably it was the silver cylinder since that seemed to be central to the proceedings. And without any warning whatsoever, out blasted a sound of trumpets and cymbals and all kinds of instruments tooting and honking away, with two mechanical drumsticks keeping time on those big drums. It sounded as if a band were playing, and Schmidt punched the air with glee to see the dumbfounded expression on Tatya's face.

'Do you know how many instruments are playing?' yelled Schmidt over the music. 'You can hear a tambourine, a cello, a xylophone, a violin, a flute, a piccolo, a tuba, a horn, and also....'

Tatya nodded vigorously and motioned for him to turn off the organ, which Schmidt promptly did.

'Er...is that cylinder the thing which starts the music playing?' asked Tatya, his ears still throbbing with the music. The organ sounded like an entire circus with elephants trumpeting and horses galloping in the background. He wasn't sure he liked it. It was horribly loud, for a start.

'Yes, yes, sure, it is the cylinder,' said Schmidt, his smile fading a little as he realized that Tatya was doubtful about the merits of the organ. 'The cylinder *is* the music, you understand? Like a gramophone record.'

'Do you mean to say that the cylinder works like a gramophone record and sets all those instruments playing?' said Tatya, impressed. He had never heard of most of the instruments that Schmidt had reeled off, but it certainly sounded like a comprehensive list.

'Absolutely,' said Schmidt, 'now you have understood it. It plays forty instruments. And if you don't like the music I played now, never fear. Do you know how many cylinders this organ comes with? Do you?'

'No, I don't. You haven't told me yet,' said Tatya. Of course Tatya did not know. How could he, he had never beheld such a machine in his life. But Schmidt seemed to delight in asking questions for which his audience had no answers.

'This organ,' said Schmidt, and here he paused dramatically, 'has twenty cylinders. That means twenty different tunes for you to play. You don't like this one? No problem, I have another.' He popped out of the room for a minute and was back with another cylinder, similarly grooved and ridged, though Tatya noticed that its pattern of ridges was distinctly different from that of the first cylinder.

A click, a whirring, a little bit of fiddling behind the machine, and Schmidt re-emerged. And now the organ fully came into its own. Gone was the crazy tooting of a funfair, this music soared with violins and flutes and trumpets and cellos, and who knew what other mystical combination of instruments. Orchestral music worthy of that incredible palace of blue domes and gilt and gold. Once more the mechanical drums played in time to the music, but now—Tatya could hardly believe his eyes—the arms of the veiled dolls moved too: each doll, with the most charming movement, used her golden rose to sound the small bell she held in her hand. Meanwhile an arm of the turbaned man moved up and down as if he were conducting the invisible musicians.

It was a perfect mirror of the exotic adventures and costumes of Bhalerao's films. It would be a sensation. All of Bombay would come to Kohinoor Theatre to see it.

Tatya nodded and tried to keep his words as business-like as possible. But he simply could not keep the excitement from his voice. 'It's...glorious,' he said, smiling.

'You have fine taste, sir,' said Schmidt, rubbing his palms in glee, clearly as excited to sell it as Tatya was to buy it. 'This piece is hardly fifteen years old, and has been used very sparingly by its owner. An enthusiast of clockwork items and music boxes, you know. Unfortunately he lost much of his wealth in the Great War, and, well....' Here Schmidt shrugged his giant shoulders as if to submit to the vagaries of fortune.

How curious, thought Tatya, that barely ten years ago we supported the British in killing his countrymen in the Great War; hoped that in return the British would bequeath us some kind of independence; that our men crossed thousands of miles to shoot bullets at the Germans and their allies; and here we are now, still a British colony, and here is Schmidt of Germany, selling me a musical box.

'How much are you selling it for?' asked Tatya.

When he heard Schmidt's colossal price he decided that he would never reveal it to anyone but his gumastha Kishan Mehta.

The Oriental Organ fitted perfectly into the lobby of the theatre, taking up an entire wall. It would be played at the beginning of each show, as the audience filed in. Neelkanth placed two large palms of exceptional verdancy on either side of the organ, and the illusion was complete: it was a sublime oriental palace in the midst of lush jungle-green.

CHAPTER 45

Shankar had grown increasingly irritated by his wife's religiosity. One weekend, when he came home he found that she had embarked on the kokila vrat and had not eaten for three days. She couldn't eat till she heard the kokila bird sing. She looked pale, and yet there was a gritty determination in her eyes. Radha encouraged her gently, saying that she too had done the kokila vrat as a girl and had fasted for two days before she heard a kokila.

'But where, in the middle of Bombay, are you going to hear a kokila sing?' said Shankar impatiently when he heard this. 'I know all about this vrat. Go down to any of the temples and you'll find a man outside with a kokila in a cage. Give him a few annas and he'll poke the bird with a stick so that you can hear it cry out. Then you can come home and eat your fill.'

Shalu looked so hurt at these words, that Radha intervened, saying, 'Shankrya, hurting a poor creature in a cage is hardly the way to fulfil a vow.' Then she added, 'Don't worry, Shalu, there is a way around it.' And she proceeded to show Shalu the rites to be conducted in the absence of a real bird. She brought out a small silver tree from her safe, and told Shalu to draw the picture of a bird on a stiff piece of paper. They attached the picture to the tree. Then they decorated a low table, a chaurang, by tying banana stems on its four corners. Radha put a few grains of rice on the chaurang, on which they placed a pot wrapped in a black blouse piece. On top of the pot went the tree and the bird on a platter. When this elaborate structure was complete, Radha told Shalu to worship it with flowers and incense, turmeric and vermillion. Then she prepared some hot khichadi for Shalu and made her eat it.

Radha wished she had thought of the silver tree earlier, before Shankar had had a chance to chide Shalu. But as far as possible she did not wish to interfere in Shalu's pieties, for she strongly believed that each one must worship the gods in a way that brought them peace of mind. Except that she wasn't sure how much peace of mind Shalu was really gaining from her efforts. She had become obsessed with reading religious texts. She spent days reading the Shiva Puran and the Ganpati Puran and other pothis. At the small shrine in her room, she worshipped the texts every day by lighting camphor and incense sticks and making an offering of flowers and a spoon of sugared milk which she then drank. Once she wore the same white sari for seven days, washing it in the evening and wearing the same one the next morning, as a purifying ritual before settling down to read her texts. For those seven days she did not move out of the apartment, even to water the plants on the terrace, and Radha did not have the heart to interrupt her prayers to ask her to help with the household work. Shalu seemed to be in a trance. Radha decided to let her be for a while and got Durga to help her instead.

While Shalu prayed and fasted and counted out exactly a thousand and one tulsi leaves, a thousand and one bel leaves, and a thousand and one marigolds to offer to the gods, Durga learnt about the myriad things she needed to have knowledge of, to prove her worth to her prospective in-laws: how to make tooth powder cheaply using almond husk and charcoal powder, with the option of adding a bit of salt and camphor to it; how to stir drinking water with a piece of alum so that any residue settled to the bottom, and how to then strain the water with a clean cloth; how to make lime pickle in large quantities, using one hundred limes along with cleaned, finely ground salt, red chillies, turmeric and other spices; how to roast each spice separately, pound it into a powder and mix it with the salt. Durga spent hours making crossed incisions in the one hundred limes to create four sections—the work was slow with her bad hand—and stuffing each lime with the ground spices. Under Radha's watchful eye, she took a big clean china jar and held it upside down over a piece of burning coal to get rid of any smells inside it. She filled the jar with the limes and shut it tight, binding the lid down with a cloth; after two days she juiced fifty limes, strained the juice and added it to the jar; diligently, she stirred the jar every morning for a week; and Radha was satisfied that her daughter had learnt how to make a good lime pickle in substantial quantities. It would be an essential skill if she were to be married into a large family. She taught her the delicate art of preparing banana flowers to cook them, gently peeling each one, and soaking the chopped white flowers in salt water to stop them turning brown. She taught her that the secret of making the softest, fluffiest saboodanyachi khichadi was to cook it only after leaving the washed, moist pearls of sago overnight; that the most feather-light, sugared chirote were made by rolling out the layered dough into thin, delicate circles to be fried;

and she taught her how to make cooling salads of tangy cucumber and peanuts, or chopped, spiced guavas. In Radha's opinion, a good salad or koshimbir, even though eaten as a side accompaniment to the main meal, could brighten up the dullest of meals and elicit praise for the cook. She was determined that Durga knew every trick in Radha's own personal armoury, to compensate for her dragging foot and her slow pace of working.

For all her efforts at making Durga as eligible as possible for a good marriage, Radha was increasingly worried about her daughter's future. She confided her fears to Lele mavshi one day at Khatryachi Chawl, a few days before the opening of the Kohinoor Theatre. Lele mavshi had asked her to come and help roll out papads because it was blazing hot during the days, and was a good time to dry papads in the sun.

'Mavshi, he is so preoccupied with the new theatre, that he doesn't have the time to think about anything else,' began Radha, kneading the papad dough as they both sat on the floor in the shady balcony of the chawl.

'My dear child, you can't really blame him, he has a great deal to manage,' said Lele mavshi, ever ready to defend Tatya, her favourite.

'But what about Durga's marriage? She is almost twelve years old,' said Radha, sighing. 'And she's still in school. It's time to pull her out and get her married.'

'Haven't you had any proposals?' said Lele mavshi in surprise. 'Who wouldn't want to marry a successful businessman's daughter?'

'You don't see her limping foot and her frozen hand anymore, because you love her. But don't think other people don't notice it. I've seen the way other women look at her. I know what they're thinking: who's going to marry that poor girl. And there are other malicious women who will say that despite all her father's money, her fate is sealed,' said Radha bitterly. There was also something else playing on her mind, which she did not mention to Lele mavshi: that they had recently had a letter from Durga's school principal, Nadkarni bai. In it, the teacher said that she was writing to the parents of all the students, imploring them not to remove their daughters from school, because many girls were pulled out at the age of ten or eleven. She wrote that Durga was an especially good student and should continue her studies, that she was one of a handful of students in her class who really shone.

'It's certainly time to stop her schooling,' said Lele mavshi firmly. 'As you say, it is going to be difficult to find a good husband for her. If you educate

Tejaswini Apte-Rahm

her too much, that will end up being a further handicap to her marriage prospects. Nobody wants an educated girl. It gives girls too many opinions and prevents them from settling down well into the husband's family.'

'She has started saying that she wants to learn English,' said Radha, troubled.

'You see what I mean?' said Lele mavshi, alarmed. 'I say put a stop to all this immediately. Who is going to marry a girl who knows English?'

'It would mean that her husband would have to know English too,' brooded Radha, 'which narrows our choices down even further.'

But it would be difficult for her to say no to Durga. Durga was so bright, so keen on learning, that Tatya was inclined to keep her in school for now. And whenever her class started learning English—not soon, hopefully—Radha knew exactly what Durga would do. She would rush in to her mother, laughing excitedly, showing off her new copy of Tadkhadkar's English textbook, delighted to be learning from the same textbook that Sharad had once used. Durga found every little thing amusing, especially when she met her friends from the chawl. She laughed too much, and Radha was fearful that life would find a reason to mute her laughter. Durga was such a cheerful girl despite her handicap, which nobody in the family seemed to notice anymore, least of all Tatya. But she knew that other women looked at the arm that Durga held close to her body, they looked at her foot which she dragged across the floor when walking, and Radha saw the pity in their eyes. They knew that the smiles of her father's house would last only so long; that sooner or later she would be married, go to an unfamiliar house, and hear the taunts of other women in her marital home. It was as if all the women in the neighbourhood knew this, as if they all shared in one gigantic secret, but nobody ever said anything. And where will we find a man who will want a wife with a half-broken body, thought Radha. Tatya and Radha would have to offer a large dowry for her—which Radha did not mind, for they had all the money in the world for it—but her heart broke to think that they would have to use money to persuade strangers to take darling Durga into their home.

Lele mavshi spoke again, breaking into Radha's thoughts. 'What does Tatya say?' she asked. 'Have you spoken to him about it?'

'Yes, I have,' said Radha, sighing. 'But he is stubborn. He says he is not going to give Durga in marriage till he has found a groom worthy of her. My husband has such a high opinion of his own daughter that I fear he will never find such a groom. And in the meantime, the years are slipping away. Soon she'll be too old, and then we'll either have to take any match that comes our way, or leave her unmarried.'

Lele mavshi looked as if she didn't know what to say to such a dire prediction. Then she said, in soothing tones, 'It won't come to that. And even if she does stay unmarried, her brother will always look after her. He loves her very much.'

'Yes, she'll have to live with Sharad and his wife, whenever he gets married, suffering his wife's scorn,' said Radha, bitterly. She could not bear to think of Durga leading that sort of twilit life. Lele mavshi said nothing more, but patted Radha gently on her arm. They returned to their task of rolling out papads. Both women knew that for now, there was nothing to do but wait to see what fate had in store for them.

Meanwhile the arrangements for the opening of the Kohinoor Theatre were gathering pace. There was to be a puja in the morning and the first screening of *The Caravan Princess* that evening.

Shankar arrived from Borivali the previous night looking tense and preoccupied.

'What's the matter?' said Radha. She sat by him on the floor as Shalu bent down to serve her husband rice, lentils, and vegetables. It was late and everyone else had already eaten.

'I have a lot of work, Tai,' said Shankar, as he gulped down mouthfuls of rice. He ate as if he hadn't eaten in weeks. He had lost weight and wouldn't look at Shalu directly even though she stood nearby waiting to see what he might need on his plate next.

'But you've just completed the film that is going to be released tomorrow,' said Radha, glancing at Shalu's downcast face. 'Surely things have slowed down at the studio for now?' She would have to speak to Tatya, for the situation between Shankar and Shalu seemed to have worsened. It was getting out of hand. She suddenly wished she had mentioned it earlier to her husband; he could have spoken to Shankar about it, persuaded him to make more of an effort, resolve whatever was troubling the marriage.

But that must wait. For now, all talk in the house was about Kohinoor Theatre.

CHAPTER 46

Khatryachi Chawl, situated just behind Jamshedji Mansion, had assumed a festive air, for Tatya had reserved two rows of seats in the theatre for the menfolk of the chawl who would attend the opening. None of the women of the chawl would go, of course, and neither would the children. But Radha's neighbour in Jameshedji Mansion, the footloose Mrs Kanhere, would not think of missing it and had already bought balcony tickets for herself and her husband; she would not hear of Tatya's offer of complimentary seats.

Radha knew that there was no question of the women of the family being present at the opening: Radha, eleven-year-old Durga, Mandar's thirteen-year-old wife Kusum, and Shalu would stay home along with Uma bai. Sharad would go, and some of the key studio staff would be present, including Tambe the cameraman and Shinde the leading man, in addition to Bhalerao and Shankar. Of course, Tansukhrai would be there too; for though the theatre belonged to Tatya, the fortunes of the film company were closely linked to Kohinoor Theatre, which would almost exclusively show bioscopes produced by Rising Sun Films. Wolfgang Schmidt would be present as well, to work the Oriental Organ till Neelkanth was fully trained in using and maintaining it. In a year or two Neelkanth would begin studying for his engineering degree, and he had told Radha how wonderful it was to already have access to a machine as fascinating and intricate as the Oriental Organ, and to learn how it functioned. He had struck up a friendship with Schmidt, whom Radha had seen only from a distance. She marveled at his jacket and large brown boots and shaggy mane of golden hair under which lay a pale, freckled face. She had never seen the likes of him. Indeed, most people felt the same way about Schmidt: he was like no one they had ever seen.

'Aai, how does Neelkanth dare to talk to Mr Schmidt in such a familiar way, and laugh and joke with him? And Sharad too?' said Durga in wonder. When she heard that Schmidt talked to the young men about Germany, she pestered Sharad and Neelkanth to tell her what he said, while Radha listened avidly to their tales as well: descriptions of a mighty, swirling river called the Rhine which was as cold as ice, and, on its banks, dark forests and ancient fortresses, towering churches called cathedrals and undulating hills planted with grapevines. Schmidt described to Neelkanth, who had a passion for engineering, even more elaborate and inventive musical boxes than the Oriental Organ: richly costumed mechanical monkeys that slid across tracks in time to the music, fine casings made of mahogany and walnut, cymbals that clashed, and pneumatic mechanisms which made real violins play themselves.

'He even told us of a pistol he had once seen in a renowned workshop, made of gold and silver, encrusted with precious stones. And when the trigger is pulled, do you know what happens?' asked Neelkanth, conspiratorially to Durga and Radha.

'It shoots out a golden bullet,' breathed Durga in awe.

'No,' said Neelkanth, 'even better than that. It shoots out...a small singing bird.'

'And when it has sung its song, the bird disappears back into the pistol,' finished Sharad, grinning at Radha's and Durga's astonished faces. Radha accused the boys of making up stories, but Durga fell about laughing so hard that she developed hiccups, and Neelkanth hurried off to fetch her a glass of water; he was very fond of her.

'It's absolutely true,' Sharad insisted to his mother. 'Ask Schmidt yourself if you don't believe me.'

'You foolish boy, am I going to go and start chatting with that Schmidt?' admonished Radha.

On the morning of the grand opening the whole family was present at the puja which took place in the theatre lobby. Radha wore a crimson and gold paithani sari, a dark green silk stole around her shoulders, and her diamond nose ring. Durga and Shalu were dressed up too, Durga excited to be wearing a silk nauvari sari for the first time, a step towards leaving behind her girlish days of wearing a parkar-polka. Tatya and all the men were in fresh white dhotis. Tatya and Radha together completed all the rituals as directed by the priest. The place was bedecked with strings of marigold flowers and mango leaves and Uma bai had made quantities of sweet shira to be distributed as prasad to the gathering, including many of Tatya's well-wishers and wholesale merchants from Mulji Jetha Market and, of course, Zaveri, Tansukhrai and the tenants of the new shops around the theatre. Radha glanced around nervously as she went through the rituals of the puja, wondering whether Kamal bai would appear. She half-hoped that she would, for she had never met her, and half-hoped that she would stay away so that she would not need to talk to her. Radha repeatedly scanned the faces of those gathered, but did not glimpse the beauty that she had seen on the screen.

Schmidt, who watched the proceedings of the puja with the greatest curiosity, later set the Oriental Organ playing, so that Radha, Durga, Shalu, and Kusum could hear the orchestral music of forty instruments and see the exotically dressed mechanical dolls move. They were so enchanted by the spectacle that at the end of it, Radha went so far as to nod and smile at Schmidt, something she would not have normally dared to do.

The festivities of the morning were followed by the frantic bustle of getting the theatre ready for the grand evening show. Radha wondered where Shankar was. She hadn't seen him after the puja.

Tatya also wondered where Shankar was, and assumed he was running some last minute errand for Bhalerao. That evening, the new Kohinoor Theatre appeared picturesque and inviting, strung up with lanterns. People came on foot, others came on trams, and yet others in landaus and cars. Those in cars and landaus didn't linger on the road. They were the ticket holders for balcony seats and were let into the lobby ahead of time, for a preview of the Oriental Organ. A velvet rope had been strung around the organ so that no one could get close enough to touch it, for it was a delicate object. When Schmidt started up the organ and the veiled dolls began striking the bells with their golden roses, there was a collective gasp of admiration and such a loud murmuring started up that for a moment it threatened to drown out the music. Everyone craned their necks to see the Oriental Organ—elegant Parsi ladies in their pearls, the prosperous merchants of Mulji Jetha Market, even Matthew Wales who was there with a delicate English girl on his arm. The electric lights in the lobby lit up the vivid colours of the musical palace so that it seemed a charming and wondrous thing.

Tatya moved about in the crowd in the lobby, greeting the many people he knew, looking rather regal in his white dhoti and long dark coat buttoned up at his neck. On his head he wore his red and gold pagdi, and a white, gold-trimmed shawl was thrown over his shoulder. In truth he felt rather anxious; this was entirely new territory for him, this business of providing entertainment for people in the here and now—quite different to creating a show for them from a distance, by producing bioscopes. But he managed not to show his anxiety, for at the worst possible times he had the ability to

The Secret of More 279

look calm and confident. After the first few nights he would not be going to the theatre himself, for greeting people and mingling with strangers was not something he enjoyed doing. But for now there was no denying the thrill of doing something entirely new, of waiting to see what would become of this night that he had planned so meticulously over months. The world's first glimpse of his theatre had to be perfect to ensure that there were good notices and reviews in the next day's papers. And he had to keep reminding himself that it wasn't simply the first show for the theatre, but also the first show of *The Princess Caravan*.

A separate little staircase had been built to lead up to the balcony seats, and here all the elegantly dressed folk went, after Schmidt had played two tunes on the Oriental Organ. When they were seated on their velvet-covered chairs and sofas, Neelkanth courteously handed each of the patrons a rosebud from a silver tray and sprinkled them lightly with rose water, eliciting surprised and delighted smiles. There was no other cinema theatre in the city where people in the best seats were treated in this way. Following that came trays of cool lime sherbet which they all sipped as they waited for the rest of the theatre to fill up.

Meanwhile the crowd of people waiting outside the theatre milled about buying bangles for their wives, and hot syrupy jalebis, and small paper cones of salted cashew nuts. As they filed in through the lobby, the Oriental Organ played once more, and the sight of the gigantic Schmidt in his tawny waistcoat and big brown boots was enough to quiet the loudest customers. In fascination they watched the turbaned doll beating his wooden arm in time to the music, they grinned and nudged one another as they saw Schmidt swaying along, enjoying himself thoroughly, and as they entered the hall there were three or four attendants to show people to their numbered seats—a novel idea for a bioscope theatre. They gazed around at the murals of singers and dancers and musicians that encircled them, the hum of voices buzzing like a swarm of bees as they looked expectantly at the blank white screen and waited for the bioscope to begin.

It would begin any moment now. Tatya and Bhalerao stood at the back of the theatre downstairs, while Neelkanth stayed up in the balcony. The troupe of musicians was ready and waiting to begin. There was a narrator to read out the title cards since many in the audience would not be literate. The narrator was also going to mouth some of the crucial dialogues of the film. The music had been written especially for *The Princess Caravan* and

Bhalerao was waiting with bated breath to see how it would be received by the audience. In other theatres, the music tended to be whatever the musicians of that theatre could provide, but Tatya had suggested that original music be composed and performed for the shows at the Kohinoor Theatre, so that it matched each scene perfectly. Bhalerao had been most excited by the idea that Rising Sun Films would, from now on, boast of original music to be played exclusively at the Kohinoor Theatre. There were four musicians to play a tabla, a harmonium, a sitar, and a sarangi, and there was an additional man whose sole job was to create sounds with his hands and feet to match the movements on the screen. When somebody ran in the film, he too ran, but on the spot, on a hard plank of wood, so that his steps echoed out across the theatre. When there was a battle he clapped, stamped, banged pots and pans to match the clang of swords, and produced a general hullabaloo in tandem with the musicians to recreate the sound of dozens of people battling it out. He had other props too: for the galloping sound of horses' hooves he banged two coconut shells together, and when there was a storm he vigorously flapped in the air a thin sheet of corrugated iron to simulate thunder. In addition, there were a male and female singer to sing short songs sung on screen by Kamal bai and Shinde. Tatya knew that Hollywood films were often screened with a small orchestra playing; but it was unheard of for an Indian film to have such a vast troupe of musicians, and the effect was spectacular. A wonderful side effect of that crescendo of sound was that the noisy whirring of the film projector was effectively drowned out. It seemed as if the images on the screen had indeed come to life and were singing, dancing, galloping, and fighting with full sound.

The greatest spectacle of the night, though, came at the end of the film: after that dazzling smile at the camera which was Kamal bai's trademark, and after the screen had gone blank, the musicians didn't stop. They continued playing as the ceiling lights came on, as if the show hadn't yet ended. And what should emerge in front of the audience but a palanquin, the exact one that had been used in the film as Kamal bai's mode of transport, carried by the same men in costume. The palanquin came to rest directly in front of the screen, and when Kamal bai emerged from the palanquin, in full costume and jewellery, she brought the house down. She bowed and waved and did pretty namaskars to all present, and then got back into the palanquin and was carried out again. This sudden appearance of the gorgeous Kamal bai, almost as if she had stepped straight out of the exotic, adventurous lands of the bioscope into more earthly abodes, was the talk of the papers the next day, and Kohinoor Theatre's success was assured. Her appearance was not something that would be repeated, but it ensured that Kohinoor became known as the theatre to go to for a unique form of entertainment.

Even Schmidt benefited, for there were several enquiries from the wealthier patrons of that evening, about other music boxes he might procure. A few days later he told Tatya that he had sold an ingenious wooden chair which began to play music when someone sat on it, and a musical box that opened automatically to reveal a rotating stand of cigarettes, and that he had also had an order for a piano that played itself, the correct keys going up and down according to the score; in fact, he said, he was leaving for Germany on the next ship to bring the piano back to India. Before he left he promised to bring back the famous wines of the Rheingau vineyards for Tatya. Tatya hurried to inform him that on no account must he do so.

'I don't drink alcohol, Schmidt,' he said, 'but I do appreciate the thought.'

'Well, then,' said Schmidt with a smile that made his white teeth gleam through his golden beard, 'I will think of something else to bring for you. You are a good friend Tatyasaheb, you have given me a wonderful opportunity by buying the Oriental Organ. People in this city know me now.'

But through the stunning success of the evening there was one unanswered question on Tatya's mind: where was Shankar? Bhalerao and Neelkanth too had no idea where he was. He had been present for the morning puja at the theatre. In the afternoon he disappeared. Tatya had thought that he was helping Bhalerao with the arrangements for Kamal bai. And Bhalerao assumed that he was with Tatya and Neelkanth at the theatre. But the truth emerged after Tatya returned home with Bhalerao and Neelkanth in tow: Shankar had vanished. Nobody knew where he had gone.

Shalu looked as if she was going to collapse. Radha, scared out of her wits, thought the shock would expel sanity from Shalu's head. She didn't care about Shankar at that point, she focused on Shalu. When it became clear late that night that he was truly nowhere to be found, Shalu simply sat down in a daze on a chair, and looked as if she didn't know where she was. And the most frightening thing of all was that there was a small smile on her lips. What did that smile mean, thought Radha. Was it the smile of a crazed mind? Shalu looked confused but that peculiar, knowing smile on her lips remained. Her eyes were sunk into her face, like drowned boats, and her cheeks seemed to collapse into the sides of her mouth, making her look like a skeletal doll. And still that smile, that horrible haunting smile.

When she finally spoke, she said in a low, quavering voice, 'I know he's gone. I've been waiting for him to go. I knew he would go.'

'You knew?' Radha said, in a voice that was almost a screech. 'You knew that he was going? So where is he?'

'He has gone somewhere where nobody will ever find him,' she said, tears starting to moisten her eyes, but that maddening smile still on her lips.

'What do you mean?' Radha gasped. 'Has he left you a note that he is going to kill himself?'

'I have no note,' Shalu said.

Tatya was standing at the door of the room, staring at the two women, trying to comprehend the scale of what had happened. Radha could hear Bhalerao's voice in the background, hollering into the telephone, and Uma bai quietening down Durga who had woken up and had started asking questions in a high, wailing voice. Sharad and Neelkanth were out; after repeatedly circling the neighbourhood they had begun driving towards the train station, in the wild hope that they would see Shankar somewhere.

'He will not kill himself,' said Shalu. 'He is alive. But he won't come back.' And then she fainted.

CHAPTER 47

1952

Makar Sankranti. Already mid-January, a month since Tatya's stroke. He was recovering remarkably well. The big house resounded with the laughter of children, the hum of voices. It was a holiday. Durga had made quantities of tilgul—small, spiky sugar shapes—to distribute to everyone. Aru was the most enthusiastic of all the children. '*Tilgul ghya, god bola!*' he crowed as he danced from one room to the next, exchanging fistfuls of tilgul with everyone and liberally sprinkling them into his mouth—*Eat some tilgul and speak sweet words!* Kumi was even more amusing. She consumed one tilgul at a time, with a look of ecstasy on her face, her eyes closed, as if she were a connoisseur of sugar. And Mukund had his own way of eating them: some he sucked, others he crunched up greedily. Smiling family members and children had streamed into Tatya's room one after another, through the morning, to offer him tilgul, get some from him in return, and bend down to do a namaskar and receive his blessings. Sadaa had kept a small platter of tilgul by Tatya, where he reclined on his planter's chair. Every so often Tatya popped a few into his mouth and chewed contentedly. After a while, everyone went back downstairs to allow him to rest. He could hear the clatter of a ball hitting a pile of stones as Aru started up a game of lagori in the garden with Balu, Khandu, and the boys from next door. He asked Sadaa to bring him some cashew nuts. He liked eating tilgul mixed with cashews, and when Radha had been alive she had, every single year, commented on this peculiar habit. The whole world is content to eat just tilgul, she would tease him, but you always need something special, you must eat them with handfuls of cashews!

'The whole world?' he had parried once. 'What do you know about the goings-on in the world?'

To which she had said, 'Then why not take us somewhere else so that we know more about the world? You never take us anywhere!'

And little Durga had chimed in, 'Yes, Tatyasaheb, you never take us anywhere!'

Laughing, he agreed to plan a holiday, and they all went to the cool climes of Mahabaleshwar where Radha, Shalu, Durga, and Kusum had tried their hand at horse-riding down the narrow green-leaved lanes, and Shankar, Sharad, and Mandar had sent everyone into splits by rowing a boat out on to the lake and deliberately falling into the chilly water. True, Mahabaleshwar hardly counted as showing his family the world, but they had been fun-filled days which he remembered with fondness.

But Shankar's vanishing had cast a shadow over the days of contentment woven together by Tatya and Radha. Tatya had seen it as a betrayal. He had taken Shankar and Shalu in, given him a job when he needed one, come to depend on him at the studio, and Shankar had repaid him with his foolish disappearance. Shankar had marred the triumph of the opening of the Kohinoor Theatre. Since Shankar wasn't there to bear the brunt of his anger, he took it out on Radha, blaming her for her feckless cousin, blaming her for not keeping an eye on things. When she told him that she had, in fact, mentioned to him that Shankar was increasingly absent from home, he became even angrier saying that she understood nothing about the demands of running a bioscope studio.

It emerged that Shankar had, after all, left a note, one that they found on Tatya's desk in the living room later that night. The note said that he could not live two lives at once, that he valued his independence too much, that he was afraid that Tatya would insist he come back to Bombay to manage the theatre, that returning to the city was something he could not countenance, and that he was leaving because he knew that Shalu would be well looked after.

The full meaning of this letter became clear when, one week later, Kamal bai's maid ran away.

It was then as clear as day that she and Shankar had carried on a secret liaison at the studio in Borivali. But it seemed that they had managed to keep it so secret that not even Shinde, who had become a good friend of Shankar's, knew anything about it.

Tatya had heard that men who disappeared, often returned years later as sadhus, ascetics. Full of remorse, they would matt their hair, smear ash on their bodies, and eventually their footsteps took them home, only for them to run away again, renouncing everything, even responsibility for what they had done. For many years he had wondered whether Shankar would perhaps return in such a guise. But he was never seen again.

The Secret of More

Nobody in the studio had been able to give him the slightest clue as to where Shankar had gone. As for Kamal bai's maid, Tatya had driven to Borivali early in the morning, following Bhalerao's sombre phone call of the previous night, informing him of her disappearance. He meant to get to the bottom of the whole sordid business. He was furious. How dare Shankar run off with a woman, and how was it that the staff—including Bhalerao—were so lax at Rising Sun Films, that such a liaison could pass unnoticed under everybody's noses? Or worse—and here his heart stilled—was it really possible that people knew about it and nobody had said anything? And what about Kamal bai? Surely she would have some information about her own maid, who had been with her for years, ever since her days at the Karkhanis Theatre Company? But his trip yielded nothing. He had interview after interview with Shinde, Tambe, Karmarkar, Mistry, and the other men, with Bhalerao at his side, but one after the other they all professed to know nothing. He felt sure at least one of them was lying and was too scared to admit it. In Bhalerao he had complete faith; Bhalerao would not lie; in truth, Tatya did not really hold him responsible, for he was busy night and day with the production of films, and could not have been expected to know about Shankar's private life. Still, Bhalerao was subdued, as if he felt he was to blame for not being more vigilant.

And then, finally, the interview with Kamal bai. The one he should have had first, considering that it was her maid who was missing; but Tatya had put off the meeting till after he had spoken to all the men. He hesitated to confront her, wanted to delay bringing into their conversation this unpleasant situation.

He thought back to that rain-soaked day when he had made his impulsive trip to Borivali to eat lunch with Bhalerao, and had ended up stuck there overnight in the midst of a raging storm, in Kamal's luminous presence. Before then he had stayed away from the studio for over a year, for reasons he was afraid to fully articulate to himself, but that night had broken his resolve and his self-imposed absence. In the following months he visited the studio often, on one pretext or another, but always with the keen anticipation of meeting her.

They talked, they took chaste walks around the grounds of the studio. He watched her, entranced, as she talked of the latest films released by other Bombay studios and by Hollywood, of her views on the dashing Douglas Fairbanks, of storylines she had invented and tried to get Bhalerao to hear; in a light-hearted mood, she gossiped about the other employees of the studio, making Tatya laugh with her anecdotes and mimicry. They were short walks: propriety demanded it. She astonished him with her knowledge about the bioscope business. She knew the difference between block booking, where an exhibitor contracted to take all of Rising Sun's films for the year as long as Kamal starred in all of them, and blind booking where an exhibitor agreed, for a cheaper rate, to contract for a few films starring Kamal and a few other short comic reels which Bhalerao's assistant sometimes made with the male actors.

If he discussed with her the percentage of gross receipts from an exhibitor, say of Sharada Theatre in Parel, she would charm him by making a precise comment such as, 'Rising Sun currently gets 40 per cent, does it not? So you could either demand 50 per cent of the takings of Sharada Theatre, or negotiate a block booking with them if they want to retain the 40 per cent arrangement.' Even before Bhalerao could raise the subject with Tatya, Kamal enumerated to him the details of Kodak's new panchromatic film. 'Look at this,' she said, putting the latest issue of *Bioscope* in his hands. 'A new kind of film stock that is sensitive to all colours.' And they discussed the welcome changes it would bring to make-up and set design. They talked, too, of the costs incurred due to poor handling of film by exhibitors, where prints that should have lasted four months were returned to Rising Sun Films in four weeks, worn out and scratched, their sprockets split; and she couldn't help but giggle over Bhalerao's famous temper on such occasions.

Tatya would watch her as she practised riding her sleek brown horse with the horse trainer, or practised pulling herself up a rope dangling from a tree, then jumping off a branch on to soft mattresses piled up on the ground. When her black hair curled in tendrils on her perspiring neck, when she whooped in delight on executing a difficult move on her horse, when she whisked a practice sword through the air, when her skin glowed in the honeyed rays of the setting sun and the shadows lay long and sun-singed on the grass, Tatya wanted to look at her forever. Often she glanced at him as if to reassure herself that he was still there, and when she caught his eye a secret smile hid in a corner of her mouth.

'A film should last even up to six months if handled carefully,' she had observed one day, as she took a break from filming. Shinde and a cast of thirty other men were shooting a fight scene that day, and she wasn't needed. She had a relaxed look on her face as she reclined on a cane chair under a sprawling gulmohar tree, its thick brown branches ablaze with orange blossoms. Far in the distance stood Tansukhrai, surveying the mayhem created by the thirty men charging at each other. Bhalerao was engrossed in peering through the camera.

'That would depend on how many times it was put through the projector over six months,' said Tatya. He sat nearby, also on a cane chair, with a cooling glass of lime sherbet in his hand.

'But what if a film was never projected, and simply put away carefully in a can? Would it last for a hundred years? I think it would. I imagine my films being watched a century from now. What kind of people will they be, who see me on the screen after a hundred years? What year would it be?'

'It would be the year 2027,' said Tatya, amused at her flight of fancy. She hardly seemed to hear him. She leaned her head back and looked up at the blue sky, through the jigsaw of the tree canopy. Her neck stretched out white and swan like.

'How mystifying,' she had murmured, 'I'll have ceased to be…and yet I'll live.' She closed her eyes. Often she said things like that. Whimsical things, fragments of poetry, which needed no answer, as if she were simply conversing with herself. She was draped in a pale cream saree that day, the soft, delicate cotton light enough, it seemed to him, to float up with her to the sky.

There was no one else on the face of the earth who spoke to him the way she did.

But on the morning when he arrived at the studio determined to solve the mystery of her maid's disappearance, he knew that he could not afford to let their strange, undefined relationship intrude on his questioning of Kamal. He needed answers.

Bhalerao had assured him that Kamal bai knew nothing about her maid, that he had already questioned her. But Tatya told Bhalerao that he would like to ask her some questions too; and that he would like to meet her alone as he did not wish to give her the impression that she was being interrogated by both men together.

So it was that once again, Tatya and Kamal bai met in Bhalerao's study. Neutral ground on the face of it, but in reality a constant reminder of the evening of the storm. When that evening came to him in his dreams, the raindrops on the darkened window were always silver, and the orb of light which enveloped them in the room was flecked with golden dust.

When she entered the study she looked forlorn, and yet defiant, as if she knew she would be blamed for the conduct of her maid.

Tatya decided to begin on a conciliatory note. 'I hope you don't think I blame you for any of this,' he said.

'No,' she said, 'I didn't think you would.' But she looked on edge, as if he might change his mind at any moment.

'Please sit down,' he said. She sat down on the edge of a chair, her back straight and graceful. She didn't relax, but maintained a sort of formality in her demeanour, her gaze directed at a spot near Tatya's feet. 'This is a serious affair for my household, because Shalu—I am sure you have heard her name—has been abandoned by her husband. Though we have no proof that Shankar and your maid have run away together, it is fairly obvious that that is the case. What can you tell me of your maid's behaviour over the last few months?'

'Her name is Shanta,' said Kamal, raising her eyes to look at him. 'She was with me for years. When we were at the theatre company, my brother would sometimes call her to his room in the evening. I couldn't help her then. But because of it she was glad to run away with me.'

Taken aback, Tatya stared at her, a cold sensation creeping over his skin. He could hardly believe that Kamal had conveyed such a ghastly fact to him in this bland manner. So that nondescript young woman who had brought him food through the day of the storm, the small, slight creature in a green sari and a few glass bangles, had been Kamal's brother's...what? Plaything? He didn't know what to say to this revelation. Kamal assumed an ironic expression on her face, as if surveying some weakness in him, observing his discomfiture, his lack of knowledge of the world. What was the weakness she saw in him? The inability to imagine lives far different from his own? He simply cleared his throat and waited for Kamal to continue.

'All I can say is, that Shanta had no life of her own,' said Kamal. 'I don't think she ever expected to marry. She was with me all the time, except when I was filming. Which means that of late she had a lot of time on her own, in my house, while I was in front of the camera.'

'Are you defending her actions?' said Tatya. 'You say that she had no life of her own, as if you speak in her defence.' He didn't wish to antagonize Kamal, but the words left his mouth before he could stop himself.

But Kamal didn't look in the least offended. She smiled a small smile and said, 'I am not defending her. I suppose what I am saying is, that we all have to take whatever little happiness life offers us.'

'I don't agree,' said Tatya. He felt his temper rise at this casual justification of her maid's actions. 'If she wanted to get married, it would surely have been possible to arrange a suitable match for her.'

'I didn't want her to get married,' said Kamal.

'Why not?'

'Because I wanted her with me. I wanted her to look after me and my needs.'

'So on the one hand you say she had no life of her own, and on the other you say that is exactly what you wanted? To forever keep her with you?'

'I'm being honest with you about my motivations. I do not say that I stopped her from getting married.'

'But you didn't encourage it either?'

'What was there to encourage? I felt she had a good life with me. A decent one. One where she wasn't being called to my brother's bedroom whenever he felt like it. Even if she had ever married, what kind of marriage would it have been? To whom? Do you think it could ever have been to a man who would have provided for her the way I did? Who could have given her the life I offered her? With me she was protected, well fed, cared for. She was master of her own domain, nobody to tell her what to do. Her duties with me were circumscribed and limited. We could have lived out our days here in this studio. You don't understand! You don't understand what it is like! She was a fool,' said Kamal with a sudden vehemence. 'A fool to trust a man so entirely, to put herself so at his mercy that he is free to use her and throw her away like a crumpled piece of paper.'

'Shankar wouldn't do that,' said Tatya. 'He will look after her.'

'The way he looked after his wife?' shot back Kamal.

Tatya was silent.

'She could have had the best of both worlds,' said Kamal, her words bitter. 'If only she had been content to let things continue the way they were going.'

'I see,' said Tatya, angry now. 'So even if you had known about her affair with Shankar, you would have let her carry on with it? Destroying a man's marriage, his integrity, his reputation?'

'I don't know what I would have done had I known about it,' said Kamal quietly. She said it after a pause in which she genuinely seemed to ponder what she would have done. 'In any case, I suppose it became impossible for her.'

'What do you mean?' said Tatya.

'I mean that…' Kamal looked at him and hesitated. A silence enveloped the room, like a cloak that smothered everything out around the two of them. 'I mean that a woman has many needs. All her needs are unlikely to be fulfilled by the same person. Only a few women are fortunate enough for that. The most basic thing of all—fulfilling hunger of the stomach with rice—that is one thing. But a person also hungers for other things. A second hunger, a physical need. It may be obvious what I am talking about.'

Tatya could not look at her, though he could tell that she was looking directly at him.

'And there is a third kind of hunger too. Not of the body, but of the mind. The hunger to be with someone who understands you, who nourishes not merely your body but your soul. A connection between two minds is so rare that when one finds it, one would be foolish indeed to throw it away.'

In spite of himself, Tatya was held in thrall by her words, her observations, her precise articulation. Words which should have created in him a feeling of revulsion—she was, after all, talking in a way that no woman ever should—sounded simple, elegant, true.

'This third kind of hunger,' said Kamal, 'can't be fed in short bursts of time, a stolen afternoon, an hour of the night. It is the kind that is the most demanding. The kind that needs entire lives to be given to each other. The most rare. The most elusive. Perhaps that is what Shanta found. Perhaps that is what she gave in to. And if so, who can blame her?'

He wished that he could listen to her talking for hours, for days, forever. That they could both lie together, in some far away forest glade among green ferns and buttress roots, with nothing but the red earth below them and a vault of verdure above; they would lie there, suspended on a zephyr; she would rest her head on his chest, and simply talk to him. Only after the talking would he take her fully in his arms.

He felt, in a mad moment, that Shankar had succeeded in doing what he himself would have liked to do. As if Shankar had held a crazed mirror up to him in which he saw himself with Kamal far away, elsewhere. But what that far-flung place might be he could not imagine; it was a void, with no context.

He struggled even now, after decades, to articulate what he had felt then. Now, of course, was the time of reckoning, a time when no man should be dishonest with himself, for the end was in sight; and he did not like the idea of departing this world with his thoughts in disarray. And so, he must finally say to himself, clearly and without any obfuscation, that he had loved Kamal. There, he had said it to himself. And what of it? He had known it all along, simply never put it into words. He felt a curious sense of anti-climax at his thoughts. The thing he had struggled with for years—the years of Rising Sun Films, of the Ahmedabad mills, of the brilliant success of the Kohinoor Theatre—boiled down to a few words, pale as milk, that held no meaning anymore.

CHAPTER 48

1928

Radha did not think that Tatya would shield her from the truth, however unpleasant it might be. Nobody at the studio, he had told her, knew anything about the disappearance of Shankar and Kamal bai's maid.

But from then on, she developed a great resentment and dislike of Kamal bai. Up to now, she had only felt a sense of disquiet; she had felt unsettled because Kamal bai was so beautiful and she wondered what Tatya really thought of her. But, perhaps out of a sense of fairness, Radha had not judged her harshly. Now, though, she felt that Kamal bai was to blame for Shankar's actions and for Shalu's misery. Kamal bai was the source of trouble in Shalu's life because she had not been able to do a simple thing like control her maid and observe what was happening in plain sight; or, worse, she had known about the affair but hadn't troubled herself to do anything about it.

All those missed weekends when Shankar hadn't come home to Bombay now made perfect sense. And could it be that like maid like mistress? If she had such loose morals as to know everything and yet do nothing, she was a dangerous woman indeed. And Radha longed, suddenly, for her husband to leave behind everything to do with the world of bioscopes. They had been happy and content when he simply had his textile pedhi to look after, even his iron and steel factory. They had become prosperous, their family had flourished. What madness, what twists of fate, she thought, had led them into this world of actors and dancers and face paint and vile make-believe? It was incomprehensible to Radha that a respectable family like theirs had become involved in this sort of shabby, tawdry affair of lovers disappearing together.

She remembered, too, that ever since Kamal bai had joined the studio, Tatya, like Shankar, had been less frequently at home. Of course, there had been all the trips to Ahmedabad that had kept him away. But still, could it be that he too had been taken in by her extraordinary allure, taken in by a woman who knew how to be beautiful? I don't know how to be beautiful, thought Radha. I know how to be neat, dress correctly, I know which jewellery is appropriate for which occasion and how to wear my sari so that it is convenient to sit and stand and squat and stir pots and ladle out dal and kadhi, for even when women wore their finest sarees, these were jobs they had to do. She could not think of setting her hair into different styles like Kamal bai, only a khopa would do, a small traditional bun. She would have looked foolish in any other kind of hair, or in those exotic long robes that Shimpi the tailor designed for Kamal bai by drawing and painting over full-length photographs of her. There was no question of competing with her. She can show off her beauty in the most entrancing way possible, whereas I, thought Radha, am happy in my day-to-day life, being plain. Before this Radha had perhaps envied another woman's fair skin, or clear green eyes, but never dwelt on the matter. What mattered was that Tatya loved her and looked after their family. Even now, she did not aspire to look beautiful like Kamal bai, and even if she had been foolish enough to want it, it would have been impossible. How could her tightly bound khopa compete with Kamal bai's flowing tresses? How could her blunt nose be compared with Kamal bai's fine and fair features? What occasion did Radha have to smile in that scintillating manner at anyone, and what good would it have done, for her teeth had slowly acquired a brownish tinge over the years. Also, Radha was by now thirty-six years old, the mother of two children, one of whom was a grown man, whereas Kamal bai was at least ten years younger than Radha.

It troubled Radha that Tatya never spoke of Kamal bai. It was as if he were keeping something from her. There was no reason to not bring Kamal bai into conversation, particularly when he talked to Radha about happenings at the studio. But though he alluded to the men by their names, names which Radha had long become familiar with, he never talked of her. It was as if they were playing an elaborate game of pretence that Kamal bai didn't exist, though every two months Karve came home to show a new bioscope in which she dazzled all over again.

It seemed that Tatya wanted to curtain the actress off from Radha. And what was behind that curtain? Radha didn't know.

A month after Shankar's disappearance, Shalu found that she was pregnant. This led to another frantic search for Shankar, more telegrams to his parents in case he had been in touch with them, repeated calls to the police. It led to nothing. Eight months later she gave birth to twin boys. It was as if the gods, guilty at taking her husband away from her, had decided to give her a double dose of happiness in return. Both boys lived. Radha had assumed that they wouldn't, for Shalu herself was so wasted away that Radha could not imagine what life could possibly emerge from her frail body.

During Shalu's pregnancy, Radha and Uma bai had both put their foot down and refused to allow her to undertake any more fasts. Shalu, still not in a sound state of mind, had insisted on continuing her gruelling pieties in the hope that it would bring her husband home. Only when Tatya intervened and told her firmly that she must eat well during her pregnancy, did she relent. She would not disobey Tatyasaheb. But she continued reading her religious texts as if she were studying for an examination. Twelve-year-old Durga hovered around her anxiously like a flitting butterfly, tried to make her laugh, tried to draw her into her games, but Shalu turned inwards, simply going through the motions of the day, eating her meals, and sleeping so soundly and so still that an absurd worry grew in Radha's mind that at night she might simply stop breathing. But slowly, flesh returned to her bones, and by the time she gave birth to twins, Radha could see that she had reached a more tranquil state of mind where she felt some happiness at gazing weakly on the two boys who had emerged from her.

Radha employed a stout, middle-aged woman called Subhadra who came in for a few hours everyday to look after the new mother and the babies. She gave expert oil massages to the twins, set up a crock of live coals under Shalu's bed and made her lie on the bed without a mattress to heat and soothe her back. She then gave Shalu an oil massage and bath, made up her bed with clean sheets, and bustled out, only to repeat the whole process the next morning. Uma bai prepared nourishing food for Shalu to regain strength, and Shalu especially liked Uma bai's crunchy dinkache ladoo, full of restorative ingredients like dates, almonds, poppy seeds, bibba seeds, jaggery, and crystals of plant resin. Uma bai also insisted that Shalu drink sweetened milk everyday, mixed with almond paste and spiced with saffron and cardamom. Radha kept Shalu's room in a semi-darkened state for a month after the delivery, creating a restful cocoon where all Shalu had to do was feed her babies and regain her strength.

Now Shalu had neither the time nor the desire to read her holy texts or to think of all the rituals with which she had previously burdened herself. Radha was relieved; it was clear that Shankar could not be found, and no good would come of Shalu torturing herself with hopes of his return. She seemed to have come out of her trance, and looked increasingly clear-eyed and alert. Radha sat by Shalu's bed one afternoon, after Shalu had fed her babies. Radha rocked the cradle gently with one hand so that the twins would drop off to sleep, and stayed silent so that Shalu would sleep as well. The curtains were closed and only small chinks of the afternoon sun darted in to spot the floor with golden speckles. Tatya had installed a new electric fan in Shalu's room and the blades of the fan rotated gently, cooling the air into a pleasant stupor. But Shalu didn't sleep. Instead, she began to talk.

'Tai', she observed, quietly, lying on her back and looking up at the ceiling, 'everything has changed now.'

'Don't trouble yourself about it,' said Radha in a soothing voice. 'Go to sleep.'

'I haven't spoken about it for nine months,' said Shalu, 'let me speak now. I just want to tell you how I feel. I feel calm. I am not troubled. I like Subhadra bai who comes every day. I like the special foods you and Uma bai make for me to eat. I can never repay you and Tatyasaheb for treating me like your own daughter.'

'Come now, you don't need to...' interrupted Radha.

Shalu continued talking quietly as if she hadn't heard Radha. 'Do you know, I have spent weeks letting my body sink into this mattress. I listen to the warm breathing of my boys lying in the crook of my arm, or I listen to the small sounds they make in their cradle. And I think. I think about my husband. About the woman he ran away with. About my own life, and about the future of my boys. And I sleep. I have never slept so well, so soundly, so peacefully. I won't be fasting anymore. I will not immerse myself in rituals anymore.'

'I'm glad to hear it,' said Radha, relieved.

'But do you know why? It's because my prayers have already been answered,' said Shalu. 'I have not one child, but two. My prayers have been answered two-fold. And now it is time for me to look after my children. By myself.'

At these words Radha turned to look at Shalu in alarm. What new madness was this? 'What do you mean by yourself?' said Radha, frowning. 'This is your home. We are all here to help you with your children.'

'Of course,' said Shalu. 'But what about the future? Am I to live out the rest of my days relying on everyone but myself?'

'What do you mean, Shalu?' said Radha, worried at these cryptic, quiet words coming out of Shalu's mouth. She had never spoken like this before.

'I mean that I want to complete my schooling. Complete my matriculation. Then think about what else I could do. Please, Tai, will you talk to Tatyasaheb about it?' Shalu had tears in her eyes, as she turned her head on her pillow and looked at Radha.

Radha didn't know what to say. But she nodded.

'It is simply a new obsession,' Radha said to Tatya later that night. She was deeply troubled. 'What can Shalu mean by wanting to complete her matriculation? What purpose could it possibly serve? She ought to be looking after her children now, not going back to school herself.'

Tatya thought for a while, not knowing how to respond. It was a novel idea, for an abandoned woman to study further. And yet it was not without precedent. There were women who had done it. He had just never thought that such a woman would emerge in his own household. He frowned, and said, 'I don't like the idea myself. On the other hand, Shalu has had a shock. It is better that she keeps her mind occupied with studies rather than falling back once again on religious rituals.'

'And,' he continued, a new idea occurring to him, 'once her boys go to school, she will be able to help them with their studies. So her matriculation may not go waste after all. It may turn into something more useful than a mere way of passing the time.'

Radha paused. This was a new notion indeed, for Shalu to learn so that she could later help her own boys with their schooling. It would not be a bad outcome. 'But which school is going to accept a grown woman?' she said.

'That's the next step,' said Tatya, 'leave it to me. But the important thing is that we make the decision to support Shalu. It will focus her mind and be a welcome distraction from her grief. And who knows, she may find that she does not like the rigours of school after all.'

Radha nodded, still feeling rather uncertain, and turned to leave the room. But Tatya stopped her.

'And there's another thing that will take *your* mind off things too,' he said.

'What's that?' said Radha in surprise.

'I want us to move house,' said Tatya. He spoke decisively, as if it were all settled. 'Our family is growing. Soon Mandar's wife will have children too, and Sharad will get married. We need a bigger house.'

'Why move houses?' said Radha, alarmed at her world being turned upside down. First Shankar's disappearance, then Shalu wanting to return to studying, Durga still unmarried, and now this. 'Why not rent one more apartment within Jamshedji Mansion?'

'You'll love the new place, don't worry,' said Tatya.

'What? You've already chosen a place?' said Radha, taken aback.

'Well, I've identified a new place,' he said. 'But I won't make the final decision before showing it to you, of course.'

'Where is it? Which apartment block? Is it nearby?' said Radha anxiously.

'Not an apartment block,' he said, 'and quite nearby. It is a mansion with enormous grounds. We can afford it now. It is on Peddar Road. Overlooking the sea.'

'A mansion?' said Radha, incredulous. 'What do we need a mansion for? And Peddar Road is outside the town, beyond Chowpatty and Babulnath, so far away that hardly anyone lives there. Why would we want to move there?'

'Let's call it a bungalow, then. We'll visit it tomorrow,' said Tatya, smiling at her.

'I don't want to move,' said Radha. 'I already know that I'm not going to like it. What could be better than living in Girgaon, among all our friends?'

Part III

Part III

CHAPTER 49

1930

Durga strolled through the grounds of Greenglades and came to a stop at the sturdy and ancient banyan tree at the periphery of the property. The gardens and mansion of Greenglades were sprawled out over a small hill. A path ran down the slope towards the tree-lined road which was dotted with large mansions belonging mainly to Parsi and British families. From the banyan tree she could look straight out to the sea and hear its gentle swishing sounds. Apart from a faint rustle of leaves and branches, there was not another sound to be heard. It was early morning, and a lemony half-light dropped from the sky over the water. The blue horizon swept across in an arc in front of her, and she often imagined it to be the circular rim of a giant saucer of sloshing water. Neelkanth had told her that in the old days people thought the earth was flat, that if you sailed far enough you would simply fall off its edge. It was a proposition that enthralled her. She loved talking to him, for he was full of interesting titbits of information. This morning, looking out to sea, she imagined that the horizon was the top of a gigantic waterfall, which, if one happened to slide down it, would take you goodness-knows-where. It was a hair-raising idea. She decided to tell Neelkanth about it that evening.

Even after the family had moved to Greenglades almost two years ago, he had continued eating his evening meals with them. Though he was no more a student and was earning a salary at the theatre, he had become so much a part of the family that it was unthinkable that he should eat anywhere else. Durga had once heard Neelkanth mention to Aai, in a hesitant manner, that perhaps he need not have his evening meals with them anymore. Aai had said, bluntly, 'Don't you dare think of going and eating at some khanaval. I expect you to come here as usual.' And that was the end of the matter.

Durga was pleased that Neelkanth was a regular at Greenglades. Kusum, Mandar's wife, was a good companion, though at sixteen she was two years older than Durga. But she went off to look after Shalu mami's twins every spare moment she had. Durga liked the toddlers too, but soon got bored

301

of them and wandered off while Kusum, in her adoration, made up all kinds of games with them, and even stitched them tiny clothes. Mandar was constantly busy too. He had moved back from Madras a couple of years earlier and now worked for the railways in Bombay; when Kusum had come of age, Tatyasaheb had told Mandar that he must return to Bombay and begin life as a householder. Though the two girls still chattered together as before, things were not the same since Mandar's return. Durga could not put her finger on what had changed. Kusum had embarked on her own journey to a place Durga could not follow, and did not really understand.

Her brother Sharad was annoyingly uncommunicative, and it was difficult to be chatty with him. He was either at the pedhi or the gymkhana, or listening to the cricket commentary on the radio, or gathering his friends to play tennis; he had been delighted to find a tennis court on the Greenglades property. Much to Aai's exasperation, Sharad went to the Hindu Gymkhana directly from work, heading there from the pedhi every evening to play tennis and cricket. He appeared at home only when it was time for dinner. Shalu mami was usually busy with her twins or her studies. That left Durga only Neelkanth to talk to. He was closer in age to Durga than Sharad was, and always ready for a chat. In fact, since they had moved to Greenglades, the family saw much more of him. He arrived in the mornings, before Durga and Shalu left for school at ten o'clock, to give a report to Tatyasaheb about the previous evening at the Kohinoor Theatre. Her father hardly ever went to the theatre, being too busy at the pedhi. So Neelkanth conscientiously turned up everyday to let Tatyasaheb know how things were going, and often ended up eating his morning meal with the family as well. He invariably had time for a quick chat with Durga before she went to school. She wasn't allowed to visit the theatre, and the only time she'd been there was for the inaugural puja. She longed to go back and listen to the Oriental Organ. What tune did you play last night, she would ask Neelkanth. And he'd say something like 'Dance from Alsace' or 'The Merry Schuhplattler'. Schmidt had translated the names of all the cylinders into English for Neelkanth. Where's Alsace, she would ask, and what is a Schuhplattler? Neelkanth knew all kinds of things, so she was constantly asking him questions. Sure enough, he had already asked Schmidt the meaning of all the words. Alsace, he told Durga, used to be a part of the German Empire, but after the Great War went to France; and the Schuhplattler, he said, is a kind of German dance where the men leap about and slap the soles of their shoes.

But Durga's credulity had limits and she drew the line here. 'You're making fun of me,' she pouted. 'Whoever heard of a dance where people slap their shoes.' Neelkanth chuckled, partly at Durga's pout, and partly because the idea of such a dance tickled him no end.

They would often take a stroll through the greenery of Greenglades, exchanging information and laughing—they were always laughing when they were together—and Neelkanth was most interested in Durga's tales about her class and Shalu mami's progress at school. He got on well with everybody in the house though he didn't joke and laugh with the others the way he did with Durga. He treated Durga as an equal, though she was fourteen and he was almost twenty-one. And he treated Mandar's wife, Kusum, as if she were a child, though she was older than Durga. Indeed, thought Durga, Kusum doesn't go to school, so I know much more than her. That's why she seems younger than me.

This morning, as she stood by the banyan tree imagining the waterfall at the rim of the sea, she heard voices in the distance and peered over her shoulder, across the large lawn, to see if it was Neelkanth arriving at the house. But she couldn't see anyone. These days, whenever Durga thought of Neelkanth, it felt as though she were eagerly waiting for him, because there was always something interesting or humorous stored away in her mind that she wanted to share with him. She pulled at a low branch of a nearby frangipani tree and shook it, turning her face up in pleasure towards the white blossoms as they showered over her.

A delicious toasty smell wafted by, from behind the magnolias. A few steps away an abundance of pink and white magnolias bloomed on shoulder-high bushes, concealing a small, low hut in their midst. Durga walked over to peep through the large-petalled flowers and saw Tai bai—she didn't know her name, everybody just called her that—tending a small wood-fired stove, and rolling out and roasting large, delicious-smelling polis. Next to her sat her son, Ramya, sorting out fresh magnolias that he had picked, tying them into small bunches. He was mute. He spent most of the day at the market, selling the magnolias that his mother grew, carrying with him the polis that she made for his lunch. When the family had moved into Greenglades, Tatyasaheb found that Tai bai had been living at the edge of his new property, in her hut, for the last several years, growing and selling her magnolias. He had decided not to interfere with this arrangement, and let her continue living there.

Durga watched Ramya eat a poli, hot off the pan. He was about the same age as Durga, but of a hefty build. The wood crackled in the stove, and Tai bai slapped another poli on to her pan. Durga wished she could eat one. Her mouth watered. But, of course, she would never eat anything outside her house. Her mother was strict about it. She remembered the terrible caning Aai had given Sharad when he was a schoolboy, when Aai found out that he had bought and eaten some peanuts on the road. She didn't care to be caned, thank you very much. She knew her mother wouldn't hesitate to do it, though her father was more inclined towards leniency in these matters.

She heard footsteps behind her and turned around. It was Mai. She was visiting them. She now lived with her son, Raghu mama, in Poona in a house with a large kitchen garden where she spent her time growing all manner of fruits and vegetables. The household of the old wada in Shervi had broken up when Narayan Bhatt, Mai's brother, had died. The crumbling old wada had finally been demolished, and his sons now lived there with their wives in a small new bungalow. That was when Mai had decided to go live with Raghu mama, who was a senior civil engineer in the railways.

Mai hobbled up to Durga, her shaved head tightly wrapped in her red padar. She had arrived at Greenglades the previous day, her chauffeur-driven car filled to the hilt with dozens of sweet limes, bags of fresh chickpeas, tomatoes, a sack of green peas in their pods, five boxes of guavas and several large watermelons, all freshly picked from her kitchen garden and nearby farmsteads. In the midst of this cornucopia sat the diminutive figure of Mai. Despite her age, her personality had not diminished over the years. She often had painful feet but that didn't stop her from hobbling around all day. When Aai told her to rest her legs, she would mutter, 'If I had let pain stop me from living my life, I would have come to a standstill when my husband died.' Durga was fond of Mai, though most people found her stony gaze unnerving. Shalu, in particular, was greatly in awe of her, and made herself scarce as soon as Mai appeared. But Durga liked the way Mai spoke to her, as if she were not still an unmarried child, but an adult.

'What are you looking at, peeping through those flowers?' said Mai. 'Wandering about all day as if you had wheels instead of feet. At your age I was already helping to run a household, not walking about with my head in the clouds.'

Durga paid no attention to the admonishment. Mai was constantly saying things like that: how terrible things were earlier, and how cushy

Durga's life was in comparison. She wasn't sure whether Mai really meant it, or whether the grumbling had just become a habit.

'Mai, I want to learn to make wonderful-smelling polis like that!' she said. 'Why don't we use a wood-fired stove in the house? Don't you think the food would smell better than using gas? Is it time for me to come in already? I just wandered here to look at the sea. This banyan tree is my favourite. It's so ancient. It would tell stories, if only it could talk.'

'Talking trees, eh?' said Mai. Then she looked up at the silent, spreading tree and said, 'Tai bai knows all about this tree. She would. She lives right next to it after all.'

'What does she know?' said Durga curiously, also looking up at the tree.

'Look at your feet, instead of sniffing the air like a dog.'

Durga jumped involuntarily and looked at her feet. 'Why, what's at my feet?' she said warily.

'A hairy snake lives in the roots of this tree,' said Mai, grinning at Durga's expression. 'A snake with a bearded human face.'

Durga gasped, looked closely at her grandmother's expression, and then laughed. 'You're teasing me,' she said.

'Whether you believe it or not, remember to put some milk out for it on Nag Panchami,' said Mai, her grin vanishing. 'The snake is the guardian of this property. These stories are told to us for a reason.'

Durga nodded.

'Now,' said Mai, suddenly businesslike. 'Tell me about that Shalu. She runs like a scared cat when I enter the room. A mother of two and she's in school with you, isn't she? The world is turning upside down.'

'She's already in a class ahead of me,' said Durga, 'So no, she's not with me exactly.'

'But she's in your school, so it's the same thing,' said Mai, scowling. 'How did she end up there?'

'Aai was sure that no school would take her. But Tatyasaheb spoke to my principal, Nadkarni bai, and she agreed right away.'

Mai said nothing, but simply nodded, rather grim.

'No woman should be denied an education,' added Durga, as if quoting from a book.

'And who taught you that? Don't tell me such an idea came out of that hay-stuffed head of yours.'

'Nadkarni bai taught me,' said Durga, with a reverential look on her face.

'What else did the divine Nadkarni bai say?' said Mai.

'She said that Shalu mami could sit at the back of the class every morning, and take work home with her in the afternoon so that she would also have time to look after her boys. They are two years old now. And do you know, Shalu mami has completed the examinations of two classes in one year. That's why she's already ahead of me. At this rate she'll be able to matriculate next year! She studies late into the night after the twins have gone to sleep.'

'And what is she going to do with all the knowledge that she's cramming into her head?' said Mai, narrowing her eyes.

Durga pursed her lips. 'Can you keep a secret?' she said after a moment, whispering even though the banyan tree was the only thing that could have heard her.

Mai's stony eyes at once glittered with interest. 'Of course.'

'You mustn't tell Aai or Tatyasaheb, otherwise Shalu mami will get into trouble,' said Durga. She knew she could count on Mai not to say a word. Mai loved an intrigue. In fact, for all Mai's stone-cold stares and ominous silences, Durga found it easy to talk to Mai.

'What is it?' said Mai, impatiently.

'Shalu mami says that after matriculating she will ask for Tatyasaheb's permission to do a nursing diploma and work as a nurse,' said Durga.

Mai stared at Durga as if she couldn't believe her ears. 'Step out of the house and go to work? Your father will never agree,' she said thoughtfully.

'But what about you? Do you agree?' asked Durga.

'What does it matter what an old woman like me thinks,' said Mai. 'What do *you* think?'

'Me?' said Durga. Mai was the only person, apart from Neelkanth, who ever asked Durga what she really thought.

But before she could tell Mai what she thought, the sound of a motor car filled the quiet morning. It came from across the road. They stepped closer to the low branches of the frangipani tree to peer through its leaves. Durga plucked one of the creamy white flowers and stuck it in her braid. They saw a long, sleek car, coloured a deep magenta, turning into Bell House.

Bell House was the palatial, onion-domed mansion that stood across the road from Greenglades. Greenglades must have been a hundred years old, but Bell House was older. It was built of solid, hefty blocks of grey stone. Its windows were graceful arches, decorated with white stucco. The three domes that crowned the roof were a rosy red brick, each topped with an intricate spire which Durga thought looked like a bird standing on tip-toe, pointing up to the sky. The place had been empty since before Tatyasaheb bought Greenglades, and the family had often wondered who might come to live there. It belonged to a Sir Noshir Vakil, but apparently he lived in faraway Simla. So who did this grand car belong to? Just behind it were two smaller cars, both dark blue. The procession of cars disappeared elegantly into the gates of Bell House and were lost to sight behind the shrubbery and wrought-iron fencing of the gate.

Durga heard Aai calling. She turned and saw that her mother was halfway down the expansive lawn that fronted the house. 'There you are,' she called to Durga, 'Uma bai has just boiled some milk for you, come and have it while it's hot.'

'Aai, has Neelkanth arrived?' called Durga, but Aai was already hurrying back inside over the closely cropped grass.

'Go on,' said Mai. 'I'm going to pick some flowers.'

Durga limped home at a leisurely pace. She couldn't walk fast anyway, what with her foot dragging along the ground. She took in, with pleasure, the flaming, flowering gulmohars that spread their branches over the grounds in vast, uneven canopies. When they had moved in, the garden was a tangle of greenery, and she had gone around spotting dozens of flowering and fruiting trees: chickoo, cashewnut, tamarind, drumstick, banana, jackfruit, and more. Coconuts lay scattered under a stand of coconut trees. Since then, the grounds had been pruned, with two gardeners looking after the place every day, bringing in fruits and flowers to the house as needed. There was also a kitchen courtyard behind the house, and there Aai had told the gardeners to plant flowers for the daily puja: bushes of red hibiscus, clumps of orange marigold, delicate white parijat flowers, and also bushes of mogra flowers which could be strung and woven into the women's plaits or buns.

In the apartment in Jameshedji Mansion, Durga had been used to helping out regularly in domestic chores, including sweeping the rooms. Her mother had insisted. But here in Greenglades, there was a retinue of about fifteen servants employed to look after the mansion, the sprawling grounds, the stables, the lawn, the tennis courts, the cars in the garage. She didn't need to do much—she woke up early in the morning to study, ate her lunch, and headed off to school at ten. Even routine tasks like boiling and straining the drinking water no longer needed to be done, because they had a brand-new Chamberlain and Breakfield water filter. Tatyasaheb had gone ahead and bought it despite Aai's belief that it would only serve to pollute the water. She refused to have it in the kitchen, and it stood in the passageway outside the kitchen for anyone who wanted a drink. Despite the reduction in most daily chores, Aai still wanted Durga to sit and cut vegetables with her and Uma bai and Kusum every morning, which Durga didn't mind in the least. She liked carefully cutting long beans into fine slivers and lady fingers into star-shaped slices.

Tejaswini Apte-Rahm

CHAPTER 50

1952

'Tell me about the princess. That was a strange beginning, wasn't it?' said Tatya.

'I'm not sure whether you know what exactly happened,' said Durga. 'I told Aai. How much did she tell you?'

'The bare bones,' said Tatya. 'Not more than that. Because, after all, it had a happy ending, didn't it. Once you know the end of the story—especially if it's happy—you don't necessarily need to hear the story itself.'

Durga looked at him with interest. 'Really?' she said. 'I'd always want to know the story.'

Tatya chuckled. 'You were always one for stories.'

'Like the story Mai told me about the hairy snake.'

'Ah yes. The famed hairy snake. The one which definitely exists, on this very property, but which no one has ever seen,' he said.

'It will be seen only if the banyan tree is cut down,' said Durga. 'That's what Tai bai used to say. On the other hand, she also claimed to have seen it. I wonder what happened to Tai bai and her son. Do you remember why they left?'

Tatya shook his head. 'Your mother knew,' he said. If only she were here, he thought, and we could tell each other our stories. Each of their stories would be different, though they had lived a life together. It occurred to him that it was certain that one day even the ancient banyan tree would fall. An unexpected sorrow gripped his heart at the thought.

He cautiously pulled himself out of his chair and stood up to peer over the balcony railing. Below him lay the vast gardens of Greenglades. He could see Sadaa picking long blades of lemongrass to brew with tea. Every day Tatya felt himself getting stronger. Perhaps he'd be able to visit the pedhi sometime soon. See what Sharad was doing, look over the accounts, lean on the pristine white bolsters and receive his merchants and wholesalers just as in times past. He really felt as if he might be able to do it one of these days. Many young faces now, of course. The old timers had gone:

the genial Zaveri who, in the end, had forgotten his own name; Zaveri's gumastha Govardhanji and his fortress of account books and incense sticks; Tansukhrai whose business had been torn apart by warring sons; Jamnalalji with his miraculous memory for numbers and who never needed to write down a thing; Nattubhai with his pot belly; the Mehta brothers. All dead and gone. Kishan Mehta, his own gumastha, remained with Sharad, but not for long. The assistant gumastha would soon take over, and Kishan Mehta had also trained a new accountant, a youngster in his twenties. The reed pens had been replaced by fountain pens, electric lights lit up the market. It was all different now. But still, he would like to visit the place where he had once felt like running so hard and so fast, where he'd heard the buzzing of bees and witnessed the making of honey, partaken of the spoils himself.

Durga put aside her sewing, and stood up to join him at the balcony railing. She was short, exactly her mother's height. She looked out over the tree-filled grounds and the banyan tree and the road. Across the road stood Bell House. It was empty now. But on the day she had met the princess, it had been a rather different house.

'Wasn't it very early in the morning that you happened to meet her?' he said.

'Yes,' she said. 'The darkness had barely lifted. Only the faintest light appeared in the sky. It was hot and still, and my bedroom felt stuffy even with the windows wide open. I decided to go out into the garden and walk over the grass and feel the cool dew on my feet.'

'How old were you then?' said Tatya, interested in her tale, almost as if he were a child and she was narrating a story from a book.

'I was fourteen,' said Durga, smiling, 'already getting too old to be married! Weren't you worried I'd remain unmarried?'

'Your mother was almost frantic by then,' he said, 'though she tried to hide it from you. But I didn't want to give in to worry and haste. If there's one thing I've learnt from business, it is to avoid making a decision when one is hot-headed or overly anxious.'

'Give me an example,' she said, 'of a bad decision you made when you were anxious.'

Tatya wondered whether to tell her about that charlatan Chandu Barve and his mad scheme of the Ganpati film. Had it not been for Chandu Barve and Ponkshe, and his own confused and emotional response to Barve's proposal, none of the rest of it would have happened. Not Rising Sun Films, nor Kohinoor Theatre, nor Kamal bai. A large chunk of his life would simply not have taken place. It was a curious thought. He decided against telling Durga about Chandu Barve.

'Maybe another time,' he said. 'Suffice to say that I had no intention of getting you married in a hurry, just because of your age. An unconventional view, I know, and I'm not sure your mother ever forgave me!'

'Not even after what happened eventually?' said Durga.

'I suppose she did forgive me, eventually,' said Tatya, smiling. But now he wanted to hear Durga's tale. Why didn't he know it already? Well, he knew the answer to that. Daughters and fathers did not talk. Not openly, not frankly. A convention which had fallen by the wayside after Radha's death. Since then, he and Durga had sat together often. He liked her company, liked her conversation. Wanted to hear her stories, her opinion on this and that. He looked forward to the time when Aru would be old enough for Tatya to talk to him about things in a way that he had never been able to with Sharad. Durga had three girls older than Aru. But Durga's youngest—earnest, quiet, innocent Aru—was his favourite.

For years, Sharad had worked with Tatya at the mills and the pedhi every day. They ate their evening meals together with Mandar and Neelkanth, just the four of them, for the women of the house ate later. There had been ample opportunity to talk, and they spoke not only of business matters but also related amusing anecdotes to each other and exchanged news about friends and business acquaintances. But it was all to the point. Every conversation with Sharad had a full stop, precisely punctuating its end. There were no relaxed meanderings of thought through unmarked pathways. Those were the sorts of conversations he could have with Durga, the sort where he could form his thoughts even as he spoke. But the bridge between his own soul and his son's was marred by a missing link. An architectural folly that meant that they could walk towards each other over the bridge, even sense the love each had for the other, but were unable to overcome that final missing piece, always just too wide to step over. In the days since he had been rushed back to Bombay from Gulwadi, after the stroke, Sharad came to his bedroom every day without fail, once in the morning and once in the evening. He was an affectionate boy. Sometimes Durga was present too, and at such times the conversation flowed easily. But when Sharad was alone in the room with Tatya, there was less to say. Sharad usually gave him a general update on the pedhi and the business; he sometimes carried a cup of tea and sipped it as he sat with his father. The ship sails steady, thought Tatya, as he lay in bed listening to his son, though after I am gone it will never again venture into uncharted waters. As usual, his feelings swung between a weariness at his son's lack of ambition, and relief that, at the very least, Sharad would not diminish what his father had built.

Perhaps his grandsons…but here Tatya brought his thoughts to a halt. Who knew what paths his grandchildren—and *their* children—would take? Sharad had three boys and a girl who filled the house with chatter and schoolwork and racquets and tennis balls. He tried to picture young Balu or Khandu or Dilip sitting in the pedhi, conducting their business amid ledgers and samples of cloth. But he could not imagine it; it was like trying to look through a mirror. It had nothing to show him but himself. A fool's game.

He turned to Durga who stood next to him, contemplating the leafy grounds and the sea beyond.

'You were saying,' he said. 'The dew under your feet. The early morning when you met the princess.'

'Yes. I felt refreshed. It was like walking on cold silk. It was so tranquil and then I heard the most unexpected sound. The clip-clop of hooves. Who could be out at that time of the morning? And then the sudden neigh of a horse, and a thump. Like someone falling. I heard a faint cry as well. I was near the jackfruit tree, at the top of the slope. I had a clear view of the road. I saw a girl lying on the road, trying to pick herself up, and a lovely white horse standing next to her. He was skittish and pawing the ground. I went down the slope and helped her up. She was taller than me and so beautiful! She had a long black braid that hung down to her waist, and she wore riding trousers. I had never seen an Indian girl in trousers before. I asked her where she lived, whether she was hurt. She said she might have sprained her ankle, and that she lived at Bell House. That's not possible, that house is empty, I said, confidently. She must have thought I was a half-wit! Especially when I started giggling as the two of us limped across the street, and I said, look at us, two lame girls! She looked at me then as if I was the strangest creature she had ever met.'

Durga laughed, but Tatya didn't smile. 'Go on,' he said.

'I think you know the rest. I helped her to Bell House, she asked my name, and thanked me. By the time we reached Bell House, a couple of lights had come on in the windows and two men in uniform came running out. One salaamed the girl, the other ran to get the horse. And then I left.'

Tejaswini Apte-Rahm

'And the next day came that enormous basket of mangoes for us,' finished Tatya.

'Later she complained to me that I got the mangoes and she got the scolding,' said Durga.

'And with the basket of mangoes came Jaikumar Raje, young and handsome and so extremely formal. I'd never seen a young man so well turned out before.'

Durga said nothing. Tatya knew that this was where Durga must stop, because a daughter can tell a father only so much.

And only so much that a father could tell his daughter. There were things which he must think through himself, turn over in his mind, on his own, in solitude.

CHAPTER 51

1930

Durga could hardly believe her luck. She, who never went anywhere at all, much less alone, had been given permission to visit her new friend at Bell House. Aai didn't like the idea one bit. Tatya had frowned, and hemmed and hawed, though he had been most cordial with Jaikumar Raje, who arrived accompanied by a liveried man carrying an enormous basket of mangoes. The basket itself looked rather grand, for it was wrapped in a deep red cloth tied like a sash, with a pyramid of ripe mangoes arranged inside.

It turned out that Jaikumar Raje was the prince of Sonpur, a small state in the southern regions, beyond Poona. And the girl that Durga had so dramatically saved in the early hours was his younger sister Gitanjali Raje, the princess of Sonpur. (Durga knew there wasn't anything terribly dramatic about what had happened, but she liked to think of it that way.) Jaikumar had been instructed by his parents to deliver the basket of mangoes to Tatyasaheb with a personal message of thanks for helping their daughter, and to say that the princess, Gitanjali Raje, would be most pleased if Durga would join her that afternoon to spend an hour or two together.

It had been impossible to refuse such an invitation. As soon as the prince left, Durga was summoned by Aai and made to recount the early morning incident once again, this time in detail. Then Aai went off to talk to Tatyasaheb, Durga anxiously following close behind. Was she in trouble? Normally she wouldn't have dared to follow her mother into her father's presence, but something crackled in the air and made everything piquant and unfamiliar; she realized it was because she had never seen her parents as flummoxed as they were that morning.

'Did you know that the Rajesaheb of Sonpur had rented the bungalow across the road?' demanded Aai. She didn't like to say Bell House; she was uncomfortable using English words, Durga knew. She had taught Aai, when they moved in, how to pronounce 'Greenglades'.

'I had absolutely no idea,' said Tatyasaheb, defensively, as if he ought to have known what was going on at Bell House and had somehow missed a beat.

'What are we going to do about this invitation?' said Aai.

'There's nothing to be done. I've already said that Durga will go,' said Tatyasaheb, clearly not pleased that events had somehow slipped out of his control. 'I could not say no, since it was Jaikumar Raje who came with the invitation.'

'What do we know about princes and such big people? What if Durga makes a mistake there and causes some offence?' said Aai. She glanced back and saw Durga standing just behind her, but instead of admonishing her and telling her to leave, she barely seemed to notice her presence. 'When have we ever sent her out alone, anywhere? Let Shalu go with her.'

Tatya shook his head. 'We can't do that. This is not like getting an invitation from someone at Khatryachi Chawl. The invitation is specifically from the Rajkumari to Durga. She must be of a similar age and probably has no friends nearby.' Tatya sighed and then looked at Durga standing timidly behind her mother. 'It's usually best to stay among people of our own standing,' he said. 'The princess may become your friend, but remember that she is a princess and you are not. Be aware of what you do and say at all times.'

Durga nodded. She knew that Dadasaheb, her uncle, had served as tutor to the royal children in Dhangadh, and she had overheard enough to know that the ways of royal families were different. Still, wasn't her father the owner of the grand mansion of Greenglades? Wasn't he one of the most successful and wealthy businessmen in Bombay? Why should she feel that she was somehow lesser than the princess? And if the princess had been standoffish about her status, she would never have invited Durga over. So Durga wasn't nervous, but simply very excited.

Durga dressed in a fresh, simple nauvari sari of dark blue with a bright orange border, carefully chosen by Aai after much deliberation. For the first time in her life, she made her way on her own across the road, accompanied by no one at all, and stood in front of the tall wrought-iron gate of Bell House. It had been thrown open for her arrival and two soldiers standing inside the gate salaamed her. A servant, dressed in a pristine white dhoti, sadra and turban, ushered her in through the stone arched doorway, up a low flight of marble steps, and through another door.

She found herself in a room filled with carved wooden furniture. On the walls were portraits of important looking personages, men in impressive turbans and military moustaches. She was led further into another living room, a smaller, less severe one, its furniture upholstered in delicate pink material, and with large canvases on the wall depicting Englishmen playing cricket in bucolic surroundings. Then she spotted the princess writing at a slender-legged desk at the far corner of the room, by a window that was so large that it ran from the floor almost to the ceiling. Indeed, the princess looked as if she herself was one of the paintings, framed by the green shrubbery outside the window, the daylight streaming in on her beautiful features bent gracefully over an expensive-looking fountain pen and paper which was covered with her handwriting. For a moment she didn't notice Durga, but then the man who had ushered her in said, softly, 'Maharaz...' Then she looked up and a smile spread over her face revealing perfect white teeth. Her large dark eyes looked so friendly that Durga forgot her feeling of awe at her surroundings and went up to her, smiling.

'Oh good, you've arrived,' said Gitanjali Raje. She limped across to the sofa. She wore a pale sari of lemon yellow, a simple cotton one, and Durga felt she had overdressed in comparison. The princess raised her hand slightly, an almost imperceptible movement, and the servant left the room after a deep bow and a salaam.

'My foot is much better already. And I think it was a good thing that I fell off the horse yesterday,' she said.

'Why is that?' said Durga.

'Because I met you! I have no friends nearby. Tell me, how old are you?'

'I'm fourteen,' said Durga.

'So we're almost the same age,' said the princess, with a satisfied smile, 'though you seem a bit older. I'm sixteen. Do you like this room?'

'It's beautiful,' breathed Durga, looking around her in wonder. A crystal chandelier hung from the ceiling. There was a small carved bookshelf which held volumes with gold lettering embossed on their spines. A tall glass vase of translucent amber was filled with slender stalks of rajnigandha blossoms. On a cabinet stood three porcelain figurines of slim European women in pale rose and lavender ballgowns. And a soft carpet in shades of crimson, covered in intricate swirling designs, lay under her feet. The princess politely gestured for her to sit, and Durga sank down into one of the pink upholstered chairs. Greenglades was bigger than Bell House, it was a massive mansion with rooms upon rooms over two floors, and three vast terraces on the roof, but its interiors were not half as plush as Bell House. Tatyasaheb had filled their new home with expensive but simple wooden furniture, some of it from

Tejaswini Apte-Rahm

Jamshedji Mansion; the curtains had been stitched by Aai, Kusum, Shalu mami, Uma bai, and Durga; they certainly had no paintings or chandeliers, and there were only a few new carpets scattered about the house. Bell House, in comparison, was decked out like a small, exquisite palace.

'This is my brother's favourite room in Bell House,' said the princess, leaning back comfortably on the sofa. 'It's because of all these cricket paintings on the walls. He's mad about cricket. We don't have such paintings back home, you see. We only have pictures of battles and royal hunts and portraits of our ancestors. My favourite is that one.' And she pointed to a canvas washed in a pale green light, in which a small group of women in elaborate hats and long flouncy skirts played a game with an odd curved bat and a ball. 'Women playing cricket in the olden days in England!' she said.

'Women play cricket?' said Durga, in wonder.

'They used to, anyway,' said Gitanjali. 'My brother knows more about it. My father would probably approve. He's very progressive. We used to have the purdah system in my family. But my father abolished it shortly after he married my mother. He faced a great deal of opposition, especially from my grandmother, and some of his advisers. But he was adamant. Now people say that he is a modern ruler.' Gitanjali had been casual when talking about her brother, but when talking of her father she spoke seriously and sat up straight, as if the mention of her father's name called for a different kind of propriety.

'I would hate to live under a veil,' said Durga, flatly. 'So I'm very glad he did that.'

The princess smiled and looked at her. 'I love the way you say what you think,' she said. 'I've always been taught to watch my words. When you said we were two lame girls crossing the street, I just knew I would like to have you for a friend.'

'Oh, I've been taught to watch my words too,' said Durga quickly. She didn't want the princess thinking that her mother had been lax in Durga's upbringing. 'My mother is very strict with me.'

'Is she really?' said the princess with interest. 'So is mine. I've had to learn all kinds of things, especially before my first trip to England. She hired a special tutor for me then to make sure my English was perfect.'

'You've been to England?' said Durga, in awe, and she couldn't think what else she could possibly say. What could she say to a girl who had been to England, who rode a horse wearing trousers, who knew about women playing cricket? She sat quietly.

The princess seemed to sense Durga's discomfort, and began to talk very prettily, with a polish of manners and language that Durga found enchanting.

She went on to say that Durga must call her Gitanjali, that she was bored on her own all day, that Durga must visit her often, and that her family had rented this house because she would soon be joining St. Xavier's College in Bombay, after the summer holidays. She was so free, so open in the way she talked, that Durga soon relaxed, forgot about the grand surroundings, and began chatting with Gitanjali the way she chatted with her school friends.

'Are you really going to college?' she asked Gitanjali. 'My father would never allow me to do such a thing. Most of my friends are already married, but I'm still in school.'

'And it's a good thing too,' said Gitanjali indignantly. 'Who wants to get married, when there is so much to learn and do. Marriage can wait.'

'I can't believe you would tell your parents such a thing,' said Durga, astonished at the casual way in which Gitanjali talked of marriage. And she had never met a girl who would be going to college. She looked at the princess in admiration.

'No, of course I wouldn't tell them,' said Gitanjali, with a grin. 'But I need to tell someone. That's why I'm telling you!' And the girls burst into a delightful conspiratorial laughter.

The princess took Durga around the palatial mansion, much of which was still in the process of being redecorated with the family's own things from Sonpur. 'But some of the furnishings are already so lovely, my mother says we don't need to replace everything,' said Gitanjali. There was a large reception room which Durga only dared to peep into, though Gitanjali urged her to come inside. The walls were covered in large mirrors elaborately framed in gold, and the smooth white marble of the floor gleamed as if it too were a mirror. The garden behind Bell House was different from the one at Greenglades. Greenglades had a wide expanse of neatly cut lawn, bordered with stands of fruit trees and vegetable patches. This one was wild, a press of green leaves and stalks and tree trunks, full of hidden corners and drooping stands of bamboo, a mango tree ripe with fruit and a tangle of pink bougainvillea creeping up its trunk, golden shower trees shimmering with yellow clusters of blossoms, and narrow stone-paved pathways that disappeared into the greenery and suddenly emerged on to a sweeping view of the sea. Finally, they came upon a jacaranda tree under which stood a wrought iron table and chairs, covered in purple bell-shaped flowers.

'We've been using this table for breakfast,' said Gitanjali, and Durga had a vision of the beautiful Gitanjali drinking tea amid a shower of purple petals. 'Just a minute, I'm going to get you some lovely flowers to take home. Wait here.' And she squeezed through some bushes next to the jacaranda tree before Durga could say anything. Durga heard her poking around there, and then there was a silence. She heard the waves rolling up gently towards the shore, retreating with a sigh, and then gathering pace as they rolled up again. The sound of the sea was louder here than at Greenglades, for Bell House was almost on the waterfront.

A rustle of leaves and the sound of crunching gravel. Gitanjali making her way down a different path. Durga called out, 'Gitanjali, don't worry about getting me flowers, I have plenty in my garden at home.' She stretched out an arm and idly began picking up the purple flowers from the wrought iron table, balancing them on a row on her outstretched arm. The crunch of gravel grew louder and stopped right behind her. Durga continued covering her arm with flowers. 'Look how many I've balanced,' she said. 'Try it, it feels lovely and cool on the skin. Sometimes I wonder what it would be like to bathe in flowers instead of in water, don't you?'

'Not really,' said a male voice, and Durga turned. It was a young man in a white churidar-kurta. He was cleanshaven, so fair that he looked almost European, and the combination of dark hair and green eyes made him the handsomest man Durga had ever seen. He was smiling in amusement, but his smile faded when he saw that Durga was tongue-tied. 'I'm sorry, I didn't mean to startle you,' he said, 'please continue your game with the flowers.'

Durga realized that she was still standing with one arm outstretched, like a flower-bedecked scarecrow, and she quickly brought her arm down to her side. The purple flowers slid off her arm and scattered at her feet. She looked around for any sign of Gitanjali, but the greenery pressed in on them from all sides. She couldn't see a thing beyond the dense shrubbery and dared not call her name. So she simply stared down at the young man's feet. She felt that she was about to be questioned by him about her presence in the family's private garden.

'I see my sister has absconded,' he said.

'Your sister?' she repeated dumbly, realizing all at once who he was. She hadn't seen him when he had come to meet Tatyasaheb with the mangoes and the invitation. A smile of relief broke out on her face. 'Oh, now I know who you are, you are the brother!' she said, and then immediately wondered how she could have said something so direct, and possibly offensive, to a prince.

Jaikumar Raje looked rather taken aback at this direct way of speaking.

Gitanjali appeared, holding dozens of mogra flowers in her padar. 'Jai? I thought you were at…at the…I mean not coming back till….' She stopped herself and looked a bit self-conscious. The prince smiled again, though this time it seemed rather forced. Durga wondered where he had been.

He said, 'I've just met your friend. Isn't it time we all had something to eat?'

We? Did that mean the prince was going to join them for the rest of her time here? Durga felt uncomfortable. She would much rather have spent the afternoon with Gitanjali on her own. What would she find to talk about to the prince? Why was he joining them? He must be about Sharad's age, and Sharad wouldn't have dreamt of joining Durga's friends for anything more than a minute. She remembered that Tatyasaheb had told her that royal customs were different. This must be one of those customs. Like Gitanjali riding about wearing trousers. Gitanjali had been so friendly and open, that part of Durga had almost forgotten that she was a princess. Now, with the prince, who was so much older, and whose good looks were rather intimidating, she felt that she had better choose her words carefully. Or better still, not talk at all and let Gitanjali do the talking.

But it was impossible to be silent with the two of them. 'These are for you,' said Gitanjali as they walked back down the stone-paved path towards Bell House. 'Take a large bowl of water tonight, float the mogras in it, and keep it by your bed. I promise that your room will be filled with scented air, and you'll have the most wonderful dreams!'

Durga thought this was a lovely idea, and she spread out the end of her padar so that Gitanjali could tip the flowers in. But Gitanjali shook her head. 'I'll have someone wrap them up for you to take home.'

What did they talk about at teatime? Later, walking back to Greenglades with a royal servant carrying her flowers for her, Durga had the sense that it had all been a dream. They had returned to the light-filled room of pink upholstery and cricket paintings. The prince, Jaikumar Raje, had been so courteous towards her as to make her feel simultaneously embarrassed and flattered. He had an elegant way of gesturing to her chair to ask her to sit down. He didn't sit down himself till both girls had taken their seats.

Nobody ever did that at home, thought Durga. When his sister got up to fetch her handkerchief from a drawer in her desk, he stood up politely till she had sat down again. Durga could scarcely imagine Sharad or Mandar scrambling to their feet for her. A servant entered with a silver tea tray, and placed it in front of Gitanjali. She poured out steaming hot tea into the most delicate china teacups that Durga had ever seen, decorated with pale pink and yellow flowers and rimmed with gold. Even the handle of each teacup was a delicate curl of porcelain. Durga couldn't help but say how gorgeous it was, to which Gitanjali replied, without the least affectation, that it was her favourite set, ordered especially from Paris, and that she used it every afternoon. They ate the most exquisite, fluffy pohe sprinkled with fresh white coconut, in silver bowls, with silver spoons, drank cool lime water in slim silver goblets, and Durga was given a small, white, lace-edged napkin which she wasn't sure what to do with till she saw Gitanjali use hers to pat gently at the corners of her mouth.

Where have I come? thought Durga, in bewilderment. Why am I here, and not at home, sitting on our balcony with Aai and Shalu mami drinking tea out of our plain, sturdy cups? Her father had all the money in the world and they lived just across the street, but the style of Bell House and its royals was a world away from her own life.

They mainly talked about Gitanjali's upcoming college term. Jaikumar had finished college a few years ago, and was now busy helping his father administer their small state. But for the next few months he would be mainly in Bombay, he said, because he liked it here, and also so that he could keep an eye on his sister, as his parents would often have to go to Sonpur.

'I don't need anyone to keep an eye on me,' said Gitanjali regally, her nose in the air. 'Though I shall be glad of your company. But I won't have much time for you once I begin college, you know.'

'She certainly does need me to keep an eye on her,' said Jaikumar ignoring his sister and speaking amiably to Durga. Durga didn't know where to look when he spoke to her directly like that. She tried to look away but often found herself looking straight into his green eyes. 'Do you think a girl can stay alone in a big house like this and go to college?' he said.

'I certainly can,' said Gitanjali. 'Women should be given more freedom, that's what you always say. That's why our father abolished the purdah system. So why not put your ideas into practice?'

'I can't imagine why you would want to live here all on your own, anyway,' he said.

'It would certainly be lonely,' said Durga, unwillingly, because the prince was looking directly at her, as if waiting for her to contribute to this spirited back and forth between brother and sister.

'I don't *want* to live here all on my own,' said Gitanjali. 'But I don't want you to be here just because you think I need looking after, as if I were some helpless creature.'

'Oh I see, it's the intention that's bothering you is it?' said Jaikumar, laughing. 'You see what a difficult new friend you've made, Durga.'

'I have no intention of being difficult with Durga,' said Gitanjali. 'I think she's adorable, and I like her very much.' She said this last sentence in English, and Durga looked bewildered. Jaikumar noticed her discomfiture and translated. Then he said, 'You see, only nice things about you will ever be said in this house.' His smile held such a cordiality of feeling, such a frank friendliness, that Durga couldn't help but return a cautious smile. There was something fluttering at the back of her mind, something pleasant but unfamiliar. Was it something she meant to say, but had forgotten when it was on the tip of her tongue? Was it the odd feeling that Jaikumar, the prince who was so perfect in looks and speech, seemed to have emerged out of a charming storybook? Was it that he always looked as if his mind was occupied with thinking deeply about something, even when he was exchanging flippant banter with his sister? Or the feeling that he was looking at her even when she wasn't looking at him?

There was a distant clang of a clock striking. 'I must leave now,' said Jaikumar, abruptly, quickly finishing the last of his tea and setting down his cup. 'I hope you'll visit us again,' he said in courteous tones to Durga. He exchanged a quick look with his sister, and left.

'Isn't my brother wonderful?' said Gitanjali, pouring out another cup of tea for Durga. 'Do you have any brothers?'

'Sharad. He's much older than me. I think he'll get married soon. And my cousin Mandar lives with us too with his wife. And there's my aunt, Shalu mami, who has twin boys. And there's Neelkanth, he's almost a part of the family, he has his evening meals with us, and works at my father's Kohinoor Theatre.'

'Oh, you have a full house!' said Gitanjali. 'Just as well, you need people to fill up Greenglades, don't you? Otherwise it would be much too big.'

'I agree,' said Durga, wholeheartedly. 'I love having a big family. And sometimes my grandmother Mai visits us, either on her own or with her son, my mother's brother. My mother loves a full house too! You should see her haldi-kunkus. It was always a big affair, even when we were at Jamshedji Mansion, but ever since we came to Greenglades, she has done it on a really grand scale in our garden. It's such fun, we usually make our own ice cream for the occasion. I hope you'll come to the next one, next year.'

'I wouldn't miss it,' said Gitanjali, smiling. Then she said, 'We'd better go to my mother. She'll want to see you before you leave.'

CHAPTER 52

Durga now entered a most delightful few months. She would sit for her studies starting at daybreak, then help with any chores that needed to be done, and head to school in the late morning; she returned home in the afternoon, and almost immediately walked over to see Gitanjali for at least half an hour every day, and often longer. Sometimes she felt guilty that she was spending less and less time with Shalu mami and Kusum, but the two of them didn't seem to notice. Shalu mami was either busy with her studies or with looking after her twins, and Kusum was like her shadow. Durga talked to Neelkanth in the mornings and evenings, telling him all about Gitanjali. Neelkanth was most interested in hearing about Jaikumar Raje, for he had glimpsed the handsome prince on the day he had visited Greenglades with the basket of mangoes. Durga enthusiastically relayed the events of Bell House to Neelkanth, though he often went rather silent in the middle of her tales. But Durga was too busy and happy to dwell on it.

Gitanjali was always home in the late afternoons, having returned from her classes at St. Xavier's College, and Durga would listen to her stories of college life, entranced by the wondrous new world of boys and girls attending classes together, often talking to each other without chaperones, and the different clubs that one could become a member of. Gitanjali told her that the college was a grand Victorian structure, all old stone and charming arches, that the girls and the boys were allocated separate areas outside class, that the girls had a women's room for their leisure hours, but that they often saw boys hovering outside, waiting for the girls to emerge. Most of the students were male, and the few girls that had enrolled as students had the front two rows of each classroom reserved for them. Gitanjali, being a princess, could not be as free as the other girls. Her mother, the Ranisaheb, sent a chauffeur-driven car every afternoon to bring her home. She had to report to her mother as soon as she arrived home, and if she was late, had to explain in detail why she hadn't come home at the usual hour. The great event at St. Xavier's College during those months was the Dramatic Society's rehearsals for the play *Macbeth*. There was no question of Gitanjali participating in it, but she had already taken permission from her mother to watch it. How Durga wished she could watch it too. There was a college picnic organized in Lonavala during the monsoon months, to which, after much negotiation, Gitanjali had been allowed to go accompanied by Jaikumar. She came back with tales of raucous singing, freshly roasted corn cobs, long walks through the green, hilly pathways, and incessant giggling with her girlfriends. Jaikumar noted wryly to Durga that he had no idea that girls could make so much noise, and declared that was the last time he was chaperoning Gitanjali to any such outing. Brother and sister had a fine old argument, with Jaikumar making such funny comments in his defence that Durga couldn't help going into peals of laughter.

A society that Gitanjali was allowed to join without any objections from her mother was the Women's Debating Society. The society met once a week, after classes, and discussed subjects of interest to women. Durga was fascinated to hear of the topics that were debated there: the role of women in social work; the question of the modern woman; the duties of a mother; the education of women. There were also lectures by guest speakers on subjects like teaching as a suitable occupation for women; arts and crafts of India; women poets in England and America; and so on.

Gitanjali's account of each talk or debate was a revelation for Durga. She had no idea that there was so much to talk about, so much to think about. How she would have loved to go to college herself. But it was when Gitanjali talked about women reformers in India that the princess spoke most passionately, and when Durga found herself listening with the most interest. Gitanjali spoke of the career of the extraordinary Parvatibai Athavale, who had been widowed at the age of twenty and taken on the red garb of a widow while her shaved hair and bangles were cremated with her husband; but who then went on to challenge age-old traditions that oppressed widows. Parvatibai's sister, who had been widowed at the age of nine, was taken as a wife by the social reformer Professor Karve, even though widow remarriage was forbidden. And, for this marriage of defiance, their family had been excommunicated by their village, with even the barber and washerman refusing to provide them services.

Durga listened avidly. 'My grandmother, Mai, also had to go through the same rituals as Parvatibai,' she said. 'And also Uma bai, our cook. The barber visits Uma bai once a fortnight to shave her head. Once I came upon her by accident, when I was younger. She looked so small and ashamed, sitting with her knees curled up against her chest, as the barber went about his work, that I ran away in fright and burst into tears.' She shuddered. 'God save us from such a fate,' she said.

Gitanjali looked at her intently. Then she said, 'God can't save us. Only we can save ourselves.' And she went on to tell Durga how Parvatibai had gone to work at Professor Karve's home for widows in Poona, how she had decided to grow out her hair in defiance of social customs, and had even travelled to America to study English. Gitanjali's father, the Rajesaheb, was a great supporter of Professor Karve, said Gitanjali, and in fact she had had the honour of meeting him when he had visited Sonpur. Gitanjali spoke, too, of Anandibai Joshi, the first Maharashtrian woman doctor, and how she and her friend Kashibai Kanitkar had been stoned for daring to wear shoes and carry an umbrella in public because only men were allowed to do so.

Who is Kashibai, inquired Durga, and felt uninformed and ignorant when Gitanjali replied that she was Maharashtra's first woman novelist, who had started writing more than thirty years ago. She talked of Sarojini Naidu who had spoken about women's education as an ancient right, and who had been the first woman to be arrested in Gandhi's salt satyagraha just a few months ago; of Madame Cama who said that the independence movement would fail without the participation of women. And when Durga left Bell House that afternoon to walk back to Greenglades, Gitanjali pressed into her hands a slim volume written by Parvatibai Athavale. 'It is her autobiography,' said Gitanjali. 'She wrote it very recently. Read it and tell me what you think.'

Durga looked fervently at the book in her hand, honoured that someone as well-informed and well-read as Gitanjali should ask for her opinion on a book. She would read it in one sitting, she decided, and be ready to discuss it with Gitanjali the very next day.

Whenever Durga visited Gitanjali, Jaikumar, in his immaculate white churidar-kurta, was sure to look in on them for at least five minutes, and sometimes strolled with them in the garden. Durga found herself waiting for his handsome face to appear as she chatted with Gitanjali, and when he returned to Sonpur for a few days now and then, she felt that her visits to Bell House lacked something.

She asked Aai whether she could invite Gitanjali to Greenglades, and after much discussion with Tatyasaheb, her mother said that Gitanjali could visit the following week on any day that was convenient to her. On the day that Gitanjali visited, her mother and Uma bai prepared a veritable feast to go with their tea, and everyone in the house suddenly took on a neat and scrubbed appearance, even Sharad and Mandar who weren't even supposed to be present for the event. It was a tea only for the ladies, so Tatyasaheb did not make an appearance either. Aai was a wonderful hostess, speaking to Gitanjali as if the princess were an adult. Indeed, Gitanjali gave the appearance of being as elegant as an adult woman, and everyone in the house was much impressed. She admired the twins, spoke to their mother in such friendly tones that Shalu mami forgot her own shyness, and she asked Kusum all kinds of questions about her embroidery and sewing projects. Do you make your own gulkand, she enquired of Aai at one point, and when Aai said no, she had never made it herself, Gitanjali asked her permission to show Durga how to make it. Aai readily agreed that it would be a most useful thing to know.

So the next time Durga went to Bell House, she was confronted with a large bunch of roses that Gitanjali had ordered her gardener to pick from the small rose garden that was now blooming behind Bell House. Durga had a wonderful afternoon with Gitanjali that day. They gently plucked the bright red and pink petals off the roses, dropping them into a bowl of fresh water to wash them. They patted them dry, and then Gitanjali produced a clean jar. She took some large sugar crystals which sparkled like glass, and crushed them in a mortar and pestle. Then she showed Durga how to layer the sugar and the rose petals in the jar: a thick layer of crushed sugar, followed by a layer of rose petals, followed by another layer of sugar, and so on, till they had filled it to the top.

'Now close the lid,' said Gitanjali, 'and put the jar out in the sunshine every day for a month, and then the gulkand will be ready. Eat a spoonful every morning and you'll feel refreshed and healthy.'

'How wonderful,' said Durga, 'I didn't imagine it would be so easy.'

'And remember, the older the gulkand the better it tastes,' smiled Gitanjali, handing her the jar.

Durga had never eaten gulkand and was enchanted by the idea of eating sugared rose petals; she waited eagerly for the month to end so that she could taste it. And when she had her first spoonful, she thought that only Gitanjali could have taught her how to make something so exquisite.

CHAPTER 53

Tatya splashed his face with cool water in his bathroom at Greenglades. He had recently had its floor tiled in slabs of soft grey-black marble, with a natural pattern of white veins running through it. The ceramic fittings shone a polished, pristine white and the copper taps gleamed. The bathroom was twice the size of the room he used to rent in Khatryachi Chawl, as he never tired of pointing out to Sharad and Durga. He didn't want them to take their luxurious surroundings for granted, did not want Sharad, especially, to forget what it had taken his father to make the move from Girgaon to Peddar Road. He spoke to Sharad less and less these days. There was little to speak about apart from business at the pedhi. And the business was on an even keel: Sharad was perfectly competent and worked regular hours, visiting the mills in the morning and working at the pedhi in the afternoon. When he needed to travel to Ahmedabad or Calcutta to visit other mills or dealers, he did so without complaint. Despite all this, Tatya found himself increasingly irritated by Sharad's attitude, but could not put his finger on the reason. Perhaps because Sharad visited the Hindu Gymkhana every evening without fail, and was more interested in sports than in business; or because Sharad was not as appreciative of Tatya's efforts as he should have been; perhaps he took for granted that the family had risen in the world, as if in a balloon, floating effortlessly up, barely acknowledging that Tatya had slogged for years to finally arrive at this palatial mansion with its Burma teak staircases and marble bathrooms. Or perhaps Sharad did appreciate it, and simply did not express it. It made Tatya glum. There was no spark in Sharad. There was no fight. No desire to set sail his own boats on the high seas of his ambition. With an increasing sense of disappointment, Tatya had slowly come to realize that Sharad's passivity reminded him of his old friend Nana. Nana was perfectly content. He still lived in Girgaon, still worked at the silver shop, still lived in a chawl with his family and often came to see Tatya, full of his old dour wit; they would drink tea, smoke bidis and laugh about the old times, exchange news about the families at Khatryachi Chawl. Tatya loved Nana's visits.

But he had always felt there was something wrong in Nana's contentment. It didn't feel right to him. And now Sharad....

He wiped his face with a sigh, and changed into a loose white cotton sadra-pyjama to sleep. He didn't want to be harsh on Sharad. But he found it impossible to relate to his son's lack of ambition to do more. He rubbed his eyes, tired at the end of a long day of endless discussions: he had met with Bhalerao, who had come down to the city to see Tatya and Tansukhrai, had attended a meeting with Matthew Wales and the new sizing master of Rose Mills, and spent hours at the pedhi explaining a new schedule of cloth delivery to a dozen merchants. All he wanted to do was sleep. He threw the windows open, heard the waves rolling gently to the shore, and breathed in the cool night air. He settled down on the enormous bed and wondered where Radha was.

She entered the bedroom just then, and he said, 'Turn off the light, will you?' but then realized that she hadn't yet changed into the sari she wore to sleep, and that her eyes were red.

'What's the matter?' he asked, sitting up.

'It's Durga,' said Radha, quietly, standing in front of him. In her hand was a wet, crumpled handkerchief.

'Is this about Gitanjali?' said Tatya, after a pause. Radha nodded and he sighed. 'We've spoken about this before, and I don't see a solution. We can't simply stop Durga from going there. It would be seen as an insult to the Rajesaheb. Not to mention a disappointment for Durga.' He could see fresh tears starting up in Radha's eyes. 'What's happened now?'

'She...she asked me about Mai,' said Radha, her voice quavering. 'About...about her condition.'

Tatya lowered his eyes. He did not want to look directly at Radha when she was talking about a subject best avoided. Something about Durga's friendship with Gitanjali had begun bothering Radha. Perhaps it was the feeling that she was losing a grip on Durga, that her daughter was being pulled into a bewildering new milieu over which Radha had little control. She had previously told Tatya that Durga was coming home from her visits to Gitanjali full of nonsense in her head. She had started talking about women like Parvatibai Athavale and Madame Cama and other women who had chosen strange and difficult paths for themselves. Meanwhile her Nadkarni bai at school was writing letters home to parents every year, encouraging them to let their girls study rather than get married. It was too much.

Durga would never marry, Radha said, if she continued with such thoughts in her head.

'It must be stopped,' said Radha, bringing her voice under control and speaking in low, but determined tones. 'Her schooling must be stopped. Has my training of Durga been all for nothing? I've taken into account her misfortune of being born with a lame leg and a paralysed arm. Despite that I have taught her to do everything, all household tasks, so that she can marry into any family and hold her head high. But we are being punished for some sin committed in our past lives. We can't let Durga suffer any more than she has.' Radha's voice shook, and she wiped a tear from her cheek.

Tatya sat still on the bed, not knowing what to say. The ceiling lights dimmed, going from golden to a dull yellow, a fluctuation in electricity. Had he been wrong in allowing Durga to go on as she had? Could it really be that with each passing month, each passing year, Durga's chances of getting married were dimming, like a row of street lights going off one by one, that would leave behind only a dark and lonely road? He felt a weight descend on his heart, and he rubbed his chest to alleviate the sudden feeling of tightness and darkness.

'They will soon start to learn English in school,' sniffed Radha. 'And what is she going to do with all that education? Don't you see? Don't you see the problems it will cause?'

Tatya looked gloomily down at his bed sheet. He had been making enquiries for a suitable match for almost four years now, but he could not find any leads. His circle of friends and acquaintances in Girgaon had tried to help by making enquiries among their relatives, but as soon as people heard about Durga's arm and leg, they hesitated. They wanted a strong, healthy bride for their sons, one who would help in the house and bear him many children. And here was Durga who worked slowly, though she worked with a will, who was used to a comfortable city life and would find it difficult to adjust to, say, a rural setting and its physical hardships. There had been a proposal from a family in Parle, but they owned farmland near Sangli and their son lived there most of the time. There was a proposal from another family from Girgaon itself, with impeccable credentials and a son who was studying law, but they lived in a chawl which was even more crowded than Khatryachi Chawl. Tatya was not going to let Durga slide back into the world he had worked so hard to escape from, and nor would he give her away to a family who would expect her to work on the land and look after cattle, no matter how light her farm duties might be. It didn't matter how respectable those families were, he simply would not do it. He knew he was being choosy, he knew that the correct way to go about it was to simply look at the reputation of the family, at the education of the boy, and to match the horoscopes of the boy and girl; wealth did not, conventionally, come into the picture too much.

As far as pulling Durga out of school was concerned, he wrestled with the idea. He thought it would be a waste of her time to sit at home; but there was no doubt that the more she studied the less eligible she became for marriage. Her friendship with the princess was an unexpected development. He didn't know quite what to make of it. The prince, Jaikumar, had made a great impression on Tatya on the brief occasion that they had met, while Radha had initially been full of praises for Gitanjali, after her successful teatime visit to Greenglades. On the one hand, Durga was in fine company indeed; but on the other hand, the princess appeared to be filling her head with talk about all kinds of women reformers, and he knew that Durga had come home one day with a book which argued against the practice of widows shaving their heads.

'What did Durga say about Mai?' he asked Radha, finally.

Radha's face paled, and she looked away in embarrassment. 'She... she started asking me whether I thought it was right for widows to have shaven heads. And she asked how it had happened to Mai. Is this the sort of inauspicious thing that a young girl should be talking about? Who knows why the cursed practice began, but is it something she should think about, in her youth, before even getting married?'

Tatya was silenced. He didn't know what to say.

'Apparently,' continued Radha, 'the Rajesaheb of Sonpur is a great supporter of Karve and his home for widows. That is where the Rajkumari gets her ideas from. But she lives a different kind of life. She even goes to college. We can't have Durga wanting to emulate her. It's best to pull her out of school, I tell you.'

Tatya sighed, and nodded. 'Perhaps you are right,' he said. 'But you've forgotten about Shalu. She will sit for her matric next year. How can we tell Durga that it is all right for Shalu but not for her?'

'Shalu is a married woman,' said Radha firmly. 'Her studies are not going to affect her prospects in life one way or the other. It takes her mind off her wretched husband's disappearance, that's all.'

The Secret of More   331

'But what will we tell Durga?' said Tatya, worried.

'Exactly what I have told you,' said Radha. 'If Durga finds a husband who lets her sit for the matric after marriage, then that is her own business, I will not stop her. But marriage comes first.'

Tatya put off the subject for another month, unable to bring himself to tell Durga. But when Sharad's marriage was fixed rather suddenly, Radha put her foot down. 'There will be more than enough for her to do at home in preparation for the wedding,' said Radha. 'And it will take her mind off school. She will have a new playmate at home too.'

Suruchi Bhide was a small, shy twelve-year-old, whose family lived in Girgaon. Sharad was already twenty-four, and ideally he should have married a couple of years earlier. There was no way now to avoid telling Durga that she would have to leave school. Shalu was taking a month off from school to help with the wedding, and Tatya hoped that this would soften the blow somewhat for Durga. He loved his daughter's expression of open cheerfulness, her little chin perpetually turned slightly upwards as if she were tilting her face to the sun. He was glum as he spoke to her and saw her smile vanish, her cheeks sink into her face, a look of disbelief grow in her eyes. But she didn't say a word to him. She simply looked down at the floor, nodded her head obediently, and left the room. She behaved, in other words, exactly as she ought. And yet he felt deeply guilty that he, of all people, should have been responsible for wiping the smile off her face. There was nothing to do about it, though, and little else to say. She would have to cry in her mother's arms or, more likely, alone somewhere on the vast grounds. He had a feeling that Radha would not be able to find more than a few words of sympathy for Durga.

Still, it was a relief that Sharad, at least, was getting married. The wedding, hosted by the Bhide family in the Phadkewadi Ganpati temple in Girgaon, went off smoothly. Radha suggested that Suruchi be renamed Sharada, to match Sharad's name, and Tatya agreed. As per the custom, Sharad traced out her new name on a platter of rice at the wedding. Radha made arrangements to sleep with Suruchi in a separate bedroom, for the new bride was not yet of age.

The wedding ceremonies went on for a full five days, which Tatya found rather tiresome, but did not comment on it, for the Bhide family had turned out to be staunch traditionalists. Now, the morning after the final day of the wedding, Tatya exhaled in relief as he settled into his planter's chair for his tea and put his feet up on the leg rests. Sharad would be going to the mills this morning as usual, but Tatya had decided to stay home and catch up on his correspondence which he had barely looked at for the past two weeks. He would go to the pedhi later in the afternoon. Sadaa had arranged his letters in a neat pile on a low table next to his chair, alongside a steaming cup of tea. Tatya looked forward to a peaceful morning after five days of chattering crowds and the endless chanting of prayers.

He picked up the first letter on the pile and opened it. It was from a company called Universal Sound Systems. It was a rather insistent letter. Hollywood's increasing successes with sound film, it said, had changed the game for all theatres and bioscope companies. The letter urged him to immediately, and without delay, refit his theatre with the latest and 'world-beating' sound equipment from Universal Sound Systems. What on earth did they mean by world-beating, he thought, testily; this new, aggressive language annoyed him. In fact anybody who blew their own trumpet too much made him suspicious. But, he thought, glancing through the letter again, there was no getting away from the central truth of the matter. He would have to meet Tansukhrai without delay and come to a decision. The talkies, it seemed, were coming to India.

CHAPTER 54

After Tatyasaheb had written to Nadkarni bai, withdrawing Durga from school, Durga managed to push her grief aside for the space of a month. She kept her mind occupied with Sharad's wedding, the new blouses to be stitched, the new saris to be bought. Large bundles of Paithanis, Nagpuris, and Narayan Peths were delivered to Greenglades by the famed Athavale & Shahade sari shop. Not content with this array of choice, Aai asked the Laghates to send piles of saris from their shop in Girgaon as well. A man came from Pethe's with a selection of diamonds wrapped in thin blue paper, and Tatyasaheb ordered diamond earrings for all the girls and women. Tatyasaheb then decided that this was a good occasion to expand on the jewellery owned by Aai and the girls, and ordered identical nose rings set with pearls and a single emerald, as well as eight gold bangles each. For Sharad, he ordered a gold ring with a delicate filigreed band, set with a large diamond, and a wrist watch imported from Switzerland.

Durga enjoyed the hectic preparations, and wearing her new saris and jewellery, but after the festivities of the wedding were over, after the excitement of welcoming a new bride into the house had subsided, she was left feeling empty. Meanwhile, Shalu mami had returned to school, for she was going to sit for her matric the following year. Durga could hardly bear to hear her tales of their school, and yet wanted to know exactly what went on there, and what Shalu mami had learnt. Enviously, she heard about how her friends had started learning English, and how Nadkarni bai had taught her class to sing an abhang by Sant Tukaram. The class was much diminished, to be sure, for most of her friends had been pulled out of school over the past two years or so. But the ones who were still there were learning new things every single day. She was missing it all. And for what? So that she wouldn't become too clever. Too clever for marriage. So that she would remain an innocent like Kusum and Suruchi, both of whom had left school long before getting married. Kusum's reading, in fact, was far from fluent, though she was two years older than Durga.

Aai had not specifically mentioned Durga's marriage prospects, but had simply told Durga that there was a limit to how much one could educate a girl. 'What about Gitanjali?' Durga had said at once. 'She even goes to college, and she's not married!' She was taken aback when Aai lost her temper, and told her sharply that she should stop trying to ape the princess. That was that. No other explanation was forthcoming from Aai, and Durga did not dare to ask why Shalu mami could continue going to school. Presumably it was because she was already married.

This morning, Durga, Kusum, and Suruchi—now Sharada—were entertaining themselves in the small courtyard behind the Greenglades mansion, playing games. For some reason, the name Sharada did not stick, and everyone except Aai continued calling Sharad's new bride Suruchi. The three girls had spent almost an hour playing sagar gotya. Durga had a set of five large seeds, like smooth grey pebbles, of the sagar gota tree. She enjoyed tossing the seeds into the air one after the other and catching them while quickly gathering the rest from the floor, all with one hand. She was quite good at it, though she couldn't manage the moves which allowed the use of both hands; when she was younger Aai had encouraged her to play the game to improve the skill and agility of her good arm. Suruchi proved to be most adept at the game too, showing Kusum and Durga the best way to do the scissor move where she neatly caught a sagar gota on the back of her hand, between two fingers, in a pincer movement. Durga tried her best to make friends with Suruchi, and between Kusum and Durga, they had managed to make her feel at home. Every day the twelve-year-old laughed a little more, learnt a little more about the ways of her new home. This morning, Kusum had even entertained Suruchi by dragging her around the courtyard on a large coconut tree frond, with Suruchi laughing as she sat cross-legged on it, trying to keep her balance. But through all their games, Durga's mind kept wandering. It was eleven in the morning. All the girls in Nadkarni bai's class would be hard at work in the classroom. And here she was, playing sagar gotya in the courtyard.

'Maybe Suruchi would like to play with the children this morning,' she heard herself saying. 'Kusum, why don't you take her to them? They would have woken from their nap by now.' She was, all at once, overcome with a sort of misery, and a desire to be alone, but she did not want to simply get up and leave; the other girls might think it rather odd and unfriendly. Kusum, ever delighted to be going to the twins, jumped up and urged Suruchi to come along; perhaps they could help feed the boys too. Durga managed a wan smile before they ran off into the house. She looked around at the plants and saplings that Uma bai and Aai had planted around the courtyard, useful ones, vegetables and herbs like fenugreek, coriander, green chillies, and ladyfingers. What could she do with her days? Perhaps she could help with a bit of gardening. It might be useful to know how to grow vegetables. She would ask Uma bai about it later.

Now she wandered around the side of the house, towards the lawn at the front. She could see the gardener in the distance, walking off with a hose pipe. He had just finished watering the lawn. She stepped on to the springy, wet grass with her bare feet and enjoyed the sensation of the soft water droplets enveloping her skin.

She saw a figure walk up the steep slope of the hillock on which Greenglades stood. It was Neelkanth. He was later than usual. She stood still, looking at him approaching. Just the person she wished to see, though she hadn't known it till he appeared. She had hardly had time to talk to him over the past month, with the wedding preparations in full swing. Now she looked forward to seeing him regularly again, in the mornings when he came to report to Tatyasaheb, and in the evenings when he came for his meal. In his white sadra and white dhoti billowing in the breeze, he looked fresh and full of energy, despite the sun that was slowly getting hotter and despite his tram ride from Girgaon to Gowalia Tank and the walk from there up to the house. He grinned and waved when he saw her, and she waved back, waiting for him to come up the lawn. It occurred to her that Neelkanth would probably be equally cheerful even if soaked in a rain shower.

His expression changed into one of surprise as he came up to her.

'What's this?' he said. 'Not at school today?' Durga's smile faded. Of course, he had assumed that she, like Shalu mami, had simply taken a month off school prior to Sharad's wedding. She had not told him the truth yet. In fact, she hadn't spoken about her disappointment to anyone at all. And now, when it came to telling him, the words were stuck in a sudden lump in her throat. Her eyes filled with tears, and she lowered her head in embarrassment.

'Tell me what the matter is,' he said, startled.

She took a deep breath, only for it to turn into a sob. The tears spilled over her cheeks, and she looked up to see Neelkanth distressed and alarmed.

'Shall I call Aaisaheb? Shall I take you in? Did you get a scolding from someone?'

Durga shook her head. 'Nobody can help me,' she said, wiping her tears away, only for them to be replaced by fresh ones. 'I don't go to school anymore. Tatyasaheb wrote a letter to Nadkarni bai. I wanted to learn English. I was doing so well. I used to get good marks. Now I know it was all for nothing.'

'But why…' began Neelkanth, and then stopped, as if he understood. 'Don't say it was all for nothing. You're an educated girl. You learnt a great deal in school. And you were lucky to not have been pulled out earlier.'

'Lucky?' said Durga angry. 'How can you call me lucky? So you agree with this too! You too think it's right for me to stop going to school!'

'Not at all,' said Neelkanth, hurriedly. 'I don't agree with it at all. I don't see why girls shouldn't sit for their matric if they so wish!'

'What about college?' demanded Durga, as if she wanted to test the limits of his tolerance and his ideas.

'What about it?'

'Do you think girls should go to college?'

'I don't see why not. Many girls do go to college, in fact,' he said.

Durga sighed, satisfied that at least Neelkanth was on her side. 'That doesn't help me though,' she said miserably. 'My parents think otherwise.'

'You must respect your parents' decision,' said Neelkanth. His voice was gentle. 'They would never do anything that would hurt you.'

'But this does hurt me,' said Durga, with vehemence. Neelkanth looked troubled. He clearly did not wish to say anything that he considered disrespectful of Tatyasaheb or Aai.

'I have an idea,' he said, his face slowly clearing.

'What?' she said.

'If you wish…and if it wouldn't offend you to learn from me…I could teach you English. I can also teach you some other things.'

'Like what?' said Durga, letting his words sink in.

'Like…like chess,' said Neelkanth, smiling now. 'I know how to play chess. It needs a lot of thought and skill, I assure you. A wonderful thing to learn.'

'Really? You would teach me English?' said Durga, a smile turning up the corners of her mouth and a light beginning to shine in her eyes.

Neelkanth nodded. 'And chess,' he said.

So every morning after helping Aai with her household chores, she pulled out Sharad's old copy of Tadkhadkar's English textbook and waited for Neelkanth to finish talking with Tatyasaheb. For an hour every day they sat together and he began teaching her how to write the alphabet, and how to put the letters together in simple combinations for words like dog and cat and mat. Afterwards, she practised writing out the words and letters again and again, repeating the unfamiliar sounds to herself. There was no time to learn chess, but they would come to that. She wasn't terribly interested in learning it, in fact. She simply wanted to learn English, to speak and read and write it so that she was as proficient as Gitanjali and Jaikumar.

CHAPTER 55

Coral, tree-brown, ocean-blue, and fern, these were the earthy colours of the murals of swaying dancers and musicians which encircled the inside of the Kohinoor Theatre. Drums tattooed, anklets clinked, hands clapped, curved pipes and horns bellowed into the air, feet stamped in ecstasy, and nobody heard a thing.

But it appears, thought Tatya, that the silence is about to be broken.

The three men sat on the velvet-covered sofas in the balcony of the theatre. Empty glasses of lime sherbet stood on a tray on a small table. The rattle of the cans containing Rising Sun's new film, *The Secret of Baghdad*, died away as Karve finished stacking them up. Tatya, Tansukhrai, and Bhalerao had viewed the film as a routine check for quality and defects, and found that all was well. It would release in two weeks' time. Meanwhile, there were things to discuss. *Melody of Love*, said Bhalerao, had changed everything.

'Everything,' he repeated pointedly, as if Tansukhrai and Tatya might not have understood the gravity of the situation. 'Hollywood has increasingly been experimenting with using sound in their pictures. A film called *The Jazz Singer* was very popular. The first talkie to release in India is, as you know, *Melody of Love*—and it won't be the last. We need to adapt. This discussion is long overdue.'

Tatya and Tansukhrai exchanged a glance. Tatya had never seen Bhalerao so agitated. Or nervous.

'How can you speak with such certainty?' enquired Tansukhrai, crossing his arms and narrowing his eyes as he looked at Bhalerao.

'The Elphinstone Picture Palace in Calcutta was the first theatre in India to install sound equipment,' said Bhalerao. 'That's where *Melody of Love* released. But it didn't stop there. After that the Excelsior Theatre in Bombay also installed sound and exhibited the same film. Mark my words, this is just the beginning.'

'Gentlemen, let's not make any hasty decisions,' said Tansukhrai. 'These so-called "talkie films" aren't going to take over anytime soon.'

Tatya said nothing. He did not want to commit to a firm opinion right away, with the sparse information that they had. A few films which used

339

sound had released in America in the past couple of years, but reactions had been mixed. Though they did good business, he had also read reviews ridiculing the development, comparing the sounds of the films to the distasteful grating and whirring of a machine. He had even read an interview of Charlie Chaplin, where the great filmmaker had dismissed talkies, saying that the voice of one of the heroines had sounded as if she were speaking through sand; and that the simple turning of a door handle had boomed out like a farm tractor. As far as *Melody of Love* was concerned, the American paper *Variety* had described the talking sequences as 'brutal' and the voice of the hero as 'metallic'. If even America had not solved the technical challenges of sound films, he could not foresee their entrance into India anytime soon.

'The high cost of refitting theatres for sound,' Tansukhrai was saying, 'will defeat these talkies once and for all. They will simply not be able to release in India. What do you think, Seth?' He turned to Tatya, eyebrows raised.

'On the other hand,' said Tatya thoughtfully, 'if Excelsior Theatre has done it, why not others?'

Tansukhrai remained unconvinced. 'Would you refit Kohinoor Theatre for sound?' he demanded.

'No,' Tatya admitted. 'Not now, anyway. I had a letter from Universal Sound Systems with an offer, but the cost is rather steep.'

'There you go,' said Tansukhrai in satisfaction. 'If you, the owner of a successful theatre, are unwilling to do it, why would others do it? And we haven't even talked about film studios. Which Indian studio is going to buy all that costly equipment to start making talkie films, when there are no theatres to release the films in?'

Bhalerao shook his head. 'Listen to me,' he said. 'Talkies are not going to disappear. Rising Sun Films risks being left behind. In fact, I have heard rumours that some other studios have already started buying sound equipment. We too should invest in sound technology.'

'We don't make business decisions based on rumours, Bhalerao,' said Tansukhrai briskly. 'I've made my opinion clear. What do you say, Seth?'

Tatya hesitated. On the one hand he agreed with Tansukhrai. It would be foolish to rush into investing in making talkie bioscopes or, indeed, refitting Kohinoor Theatre when the costs were so high. It didn't seem to him that these 'talkies' would become an industry standard. At the most they might be a curiosity that stayed on the side lines, and would perhaps eventually be shown as short films prior to the main bioscope screening;

or imported feature films might be shown now and then as a novelty in a couple of theatres, like Excelsior, whose owners cared to make the investment in sound equipment. And yet…though all the indications pointed to the continued reign of silent films, Tatya had felt a strangely familiar sensation when he first heard about *Melody of Love* releasing in Calcutta. A feeling that he had ignored, but that refused to go away. The sort of feeling he had experienced when he stood inside a vast textile warehouse for the first time and inhaled the smell of the cloth pyramids around him; or when he had heard the first hot strike of hammer against metal in his iron and steel factory; or when he'd seen the magic lantern show all those years ago and heard the clink of coins falling into a cloth bag and the crack of a coconut offered up by the devout to the moving images. The feeling was that of a salty wind rushing by him, beckoning him to sprint along with it towards a marine horizon, over sunlit water and its golden glint of honey. He sensed the thing behind the new sound technology of talkies: it was hunger. Whoever had invented it wanted more. It was a sensation he knew well, could recognize the different forms it took, this hunger for more, the kind of hunger that would not rest. The question was, how long would it take for talkies to spread across the world? It might take a year, or it might take ten. He could not predict which way the wind would blow. There was no point rushing into something that required a large investment of money. So he said nothing.

And Bhalerao, after waiting a few moments for him to speak, pursed his lips. 'So your mind is made up?'

Tatya and Tansukhrai looked back impassively at him, and Tatya gave an almost imperceptible nod of his head. Bhalerao sighed. 'All right,' he said, 'but can you at least reconsider the matter sometime soon?'

'Plenty of time for that,' said Tansukhrai smoothly. 'Now, what was the other thing you wanted to discuss?'

'Well,' said Bhalerao, 'talking of being left behind…I think we need to hire at least two more actresses.'

'More actresses?' said Tatya, frowning. 'Why?'

'Kamal bai has played the lead role in our films for almost five years. I feel that people will start getting tired of seeing the same face. There has recently been a surge of new actresses being hired by other studios. I'm sorry to say that….'

'Sorry to say what?' said Tansukhrai.

'That…Rising Sun Films is probably the only studio to rely so heavily on one actress. And we are still using men dressed as women for the minor characters. It is true that we have hired new male lead actors to freshen the look of our bioscopes recently, but it is not enough. The situation is not as it used to be. Plenty of women are available these days, and if we want to continue expanding our production….'

'Stop right there,' said Tatya, sharply. 'I don't like your phrase about women being "available". We are not a cattle yard. We are a respectable concern and Kamal bai is the face of our films. There is a certain dignity in that, I'm sure you will see. I cannot have women being drafted in like factory workers, where it eventually becomes impossible to tell who may or may not behave with propriety. There will be no end to that business. I won't have it!'

There was a silence. Tansukhrai and Bhalerao both looked startled at this outburst. Tatya closed his eyes for a moment and then said, in calmer tones, 'I'm sorry. I'm rather tired. Let us continue this discussion another time.'

'Another time…soon?' Bhalerao ventured to ask. But Tatya only looked at him wearily, and Bhalerao said no more. He looked worried.

Early next morning, Tatya sat on a wooden bench by the Greenglades stable. The stable had been empty when he had bought Greenglades, but now housed two handsome cows of the Hansi breed, swan-white and dark eyed, that provided fresh milk to the household. He had hired a gawli to look after them, and often crossed the lawns towards the stables early in the morning for a glass of fresh milk, still frothing and warm from the cow. He leaned back, sipping the milk, listening to the sounds of dawn: the quiet rolling of the waves, twittering of sparrows, and distant screeches of circling kites. He thought about a newspaper article he had read a couple of days ago. It probably explained his vehemence in addressing Bhalerao the previous evening. A film actress called Sultana had sued the son of the ex-president of the municipal corporation. She claimed that she was his lawful wife, that they had been married secretly in a room at the Taj Mahal Hotel, and was now demanding five lakh rupees from him as maintenance. The papers were full of the scandal. And though he had nothing at all to do with it, Tatya felt as if he too had been tainted by association with the bioscope business.

He knew all too well what went on in some other bioscope studios. Actresses were treated as keeps by the men who ran the company. It had all begun when the practice of men dressing up as women in front of the camera had started fading away. It was what he had been afraid of when Kamal bai joined Rising Sun Films, though it was his good fortune that she had proved trustworthy in that regard. But with scandals such as these in the newspapers, the whole bioscope business appeared to the world as sordid. Not respectable. And now Bhalerao wanted to hire more women. It was an impossible request, and yet, if the studio was to run as a profitable concern, it was equally impossible to continue relying on Kamal bai. What was to be done? He felt indecisive and restless. The old way of doing things was clearly just that: old. He felt as if he were witnessing the end of something. He thought of Durga. She was fourteen. How could he possibly employ young girls to act in front of the camera and justify it to his own daughter if she ever asked him about it? He would be ashamed. And there had been the ghastly business of Shankar running away with Kamal bai's maid; if anything like that took place at Rising Sun Films again, this time, God forbid, involving an actress who could be named in the press, how would he be able to hold his head high in his own pedhi, among his wholesale merchants, among the textile community, even among his friends at Khatryachi Chawl?

Meanwhile, Rose Mills was expanding, setting up new looms in new premises, to increase production. Noor Begum Mills was booming; old Shahpurwala had passed away a few years earlier but his eldest son had taken over expertly, expanding into new weaves and keen on finding an export market. Even Sharad, Tatya was proud to note, had acquired the selling agencies of three mills in the nizam's state of Hyderabad. Though it was Tatya who urged him to pursue those mills, Sharad had worked with a will and won the selling agencies. Tatya's textile business was thriving and he was busier than ever.

He didn't need any distractions now.

But the scandal in the papers about the actress called Sultana shook him. It made him think, unaccountably, of Kamal bai. What was it, really, that he was doing with Kamal? What name could he give to the intimacy that was built on their conversations and their walks and the feeling of elation she inspired in him, as if a missing piece in his life had fallen into place? He had done and said nothing that made him guilty of infidelity; and yet there was nothing about it that he could ever admit to Radha. He wanted everything to go on as it was. He didn't want more actresses being hired by Rising Sun Films; he didn't want to get into talkies; but nor did he want a loss-making studio on his hands.

Just a few months later, the decision was made for him. Tansukhrai came to his pedhi waving a newspaper in the air.

'Look at this,' he said. 'Bhalerao was right. Imperial Movietone is soon releasing a talkie called *Alam Ara*. And Prabhat Films in Kolhapur is also making a talkie, not just in Marathi but also one in Hindi.'

Tatya took the paper from Tansukhrai and scanned the article. So it was final then. The talkies had truly come to India.

'There is no need to panic,' said Tansukhrai, though he looked rather agitated, and repeatedly stroked his thin moustache. 'I don't see why two forms of entertainment cannot coexist. We'll simply go on making our silent films. People will still want to see them, and theatres will still want to release them.'

Tatya looked up from the paper. 'May I ask you something? How is it that you haven't come here arguing for an investment in sound technology? You're always one for new ventures.'

Tansukhrai shook his head, removed his shoes, and climbed on to the white mattress of the pedhi. He leaned back on a bolster. It was late afternoon and Mulji Jetha Market was uncharacteristically quiet. Kishan Mehta, several grey hairs now lacing his temples, worked away steadily at the back, sitting cross-legged at his low desk. He greeted Tansukhrai courteously and then went back to writing.

Tatya put the newspaper down and said with concern, 'Is all well, Seth? What's bothering you?'

Tansukhrai looked down at the white sheet, glum, absently rubbing a finger on the weave. 'Do you know, I used to be proud of the fact that I have three sons. Everybody always said how fortunate my wife and I were. But now...now I think you are the lucky one, to have only one son.'

'Don't say that, Seth,' said Tatya, shocked. 'You are fortunate indeed to have three fine sons.'

'Sons that go to war with each other even before their father is dead?' said Tansukhrai, his eyes sombre. 'Not one of them trusts the other. They say I should make it clear now as to how I want to divide my business between them. The youngest is interested in neither the film trade nor the textile trade. He simply wants me to give him a lump sum of money so that he can start his own business.'

'His own business doing what?' said Tatya. He could hardly believe what he was hearing. Tansukhrai's was one of the oldest business families in Bombay, let alone in Mulji Jetha Market. How was it that he had lost his grip on his sons?

'He wants to set up a business importing Burma teak into India. He says he has found the correct contacts for it, and the only thing holding him back is my stubbornness in not giving him the money.' Tansukhrai, normally so dapper and upright in his bearing, looked utterly miserable. 'It is foolishness,' he said, 'to throw away the business I have set up and go on a wild goose chase instead. What does my family know of Burma teak? Nothing. I have no way of guiding him on his way.'

'Seth,' said Tatya, gently, 'what did we know of bioscopes when we made our first film? It might be best to let him find his own way.'

Tansukhrai nodded. 'Even if what you say is right, it will mean withdrawing a large amount of money from my business to fund my youngest son. His brothers are completely opposed to his scheme. They both want large stakes in my pedhi. So tell me, Seth, what am I supposed to do with these wretched sons of mine? Being preoccupied with all this, I find it difficult to think of investing in talkies.'

Tatya looked down at the newspaper that Tansukhrai had been waving excitedly just a few minutes ago. 'Is either of them interested in a stake in Rising Sun Films?' he said.

Tansukhrai shook his head. 'Not in the least.'

'In that case,' said Tatya, quietly, 'the decision is probably clear… especially in the light of a rather interesting meeting I had with Shahpurwala's son this morning. I was going to telephone you about it tonight.'

'Shahpurwala?' said Tansukhrai, puzzled. 'What does he have to do with any of this?'

'Rather a lot. You forget that old Shahpurwala had leased out the studio land in Borivali to us. You know that ever since he passed away, I have been dealing with his eldest son, Altaf. We have excellent business relations. He came to see me this morning. He said he regretted to inform me that due to some legal wrangles within his family, he needs to sell the studio land that has been leased to us. He said that Rising Sun Films is welcome to buy it. But if not, he will need to end the lease and find another buyer.'

Tansukhrai's expression changed to one of disbelief. In truth, Rising Sun Films had leased the Borivali land from the Shahpurwalas for so long that it had been easy to forget that the film company was a tenant there, and not the owner.

'The price of the land is considerable, but well within the capacity of our finances,' continued Tatya. He too, like Tansukhrai, was still digesting the significance of this sudden development. In fact, he sounded far surer of himself than he felt. 'Therefore, we must make a decision about whether we want to buy the land. Normally I would not have hesitated to buy it. But with the arrival of these new talkie films, I am not sure it is prudent to necessarily count on silent bioscopes lasting for much longer.'

'What are you saying?' said Tansukhrai, the old, shrewd look back on his face. 'What are our options?'

'Our options,' said Tatya, 'are either to make a large injection of cash and buy the land, as well as upgrade all our equipment to sound technology— which, by the way, will also mean building a fully sealed studio to keep sound disturbances to a minimum—or....'

'Or what?' said Tansukhrai.

'Or...' Tatya could hardly bring himself to say it, though he knew, in his heart of hearts, that the sense of an ending he had been feeling was finally upon him. 'Or...we cash in our profits, and close Rising Sun Films. We are a bioscope company, one that makes silent films. We need not be a talkie film company. We might as well recognize, Seth, that we are either at a crossroad, or....'

'Or at the end of the road,' finished Tansukhrai.

CHAPTER 56

1952

Still, Tatya had not been able to think of the decision as final without talking to Kamal bai. He wished, now, that he hadn't done it. Too late to think about that, decades later. But even now, when the time for hoping and regretting was long gone, and the end of another kind of road well within sight, he looked back on that rain-soaked journey to Borivali to see her, to ask her opinion about everything, and thought: I shouldn't have done it.

He wished that Radha were with him, or somewhere in the house, perhaps in the kitchen cutting vegetables or in the courtyard picking flowers for her puja. His chest ached. She was out of reach, though he wanted her just for a moment, just for an hour, just so that he could confess everything to her. A confession, though he had never touched so much as Kamal bai's finger, never felt even the most fleeting sensation of her skin upon his, not even the accidental grazing of an arm. But much more than that: he had loved her.

Old fool, he heard a voice inside his head. Perhaps, he replied.

He opened his eyes a slit. He'd been asleep. Had he been dreaming of Kamal and that fateful visit to the studios of Rising Sun Films? Whose voice was it that had called him an old fool? He thought it was his own; then, his bedroom swimming into focus, he thought perhaps it was Tansukhrai's voice. His arm struggled against the weight of the blanket and he finally succeeded in bringing his fingers to his face. He groped the skin of his cheeks, and the nape of his neck, checking for rivulets of rain. Nothing. Bone dry. Of course—he was safely in bed, almost twenty years past that night of crashing rain. And yet his fingers wouldn't stop scrabbling at his face.

'Saheb. Saheb. Wake up.' It was Sadaa. He took hold of Tatya's fingers and laid them on the blanket. 'It was a dream.'

'No,' murmured Tatya, his eyes open now. 'It wasn't a dream. It was all real.'

Sadaa looked anxious. 'Shall I call Durga tai?'

Tatya frowned. When he spoke, his speech was still slurred with sleep. 'Eh? What for? Get me up.'

Sadaa supported Tatya's back to sit him up. He helped him walk to the bathroom and waited outside as sounds of water trickled from within, followed by the splash of the tap running. Tatya emerged, his face wet and the sleep washed from his eyes. A rough stubble covered his chin. Sadaa would shave him later.

'Towel, Saheb,' said Sadaa, handing him a pale green hand towel. It had been scrubbed and washed so often that it was now a sturdy, rough square. Tatya liked using old things.

'Your Radha vahini bought this set of towels many years ago,' he observed to Sadaa, though he knew that Sadaa was well aware of the fact. But he liked reminiscing with Sadaa, reminding him of things that they both already knew.

'Yes, Saheb,' said Sadaa. 'I remember they used to be so soft.'

'We have all become toughened with age,' said Tatya. 'Except you. Look at that stomach of yours, as soft as a rasgulla. You were a skinny chap when you started with us.'

Sadaa grinned. 'You always tease me, Saheb. But it is Radha vahini's fault, you see, for feeding us so well. Whenever there was a sweet prepared in the house, she would make sure there was enough not only for the family but for all of us as well.'

'And she certainly used to prepare a lot of sweets.'

Sadaa shook his head. 'And ever since Uma bai left us...nothing is the same.' He wiped his eyes. He cried easily.

Uma bai had died a year after Radha. Till the end she had staunchly kept the kitchen running in exactly the way Radha liked. It was strange, thought Tatya, but when Uma bai died it felt as if the last little bit of Radha had gone as well.

'Come, come,' he said, briskly. 'Never mind all that. Bring me my tea.'

But it wasn't Sadaa who came in with his tea. It was ten-year-old Aru, his eyes shining with mischief. 'It's me, Tatyasaheb,' he announced. 'I told Sadaa that I want to bring you your tea today. I didn't tell Aai. She would have said no.'

Well, this was a pleasant surprise. Tatya smiled and held out an affectionate arm. He was back in bed, sitting up with his soft pillow behind him and the blanket pulled up to his waist. He felt too tired today to sit in the planter's chair. His back ached. His large bedroom was flooded with

Tejaswini Apte-Rahm

sunlight and the sea glinted blue outside the window.

'Just the person I wanted to see this morning,' he said. Aru put the tea on a table and bent down to do namaskar to Tatya. 'The match is on today, isn't it?'

'Yes, Tatyasaheb,' said Aru, his eyes bright with anticipation. 'I'm sure we'll hear the cheers from the ground all the way up to our house. When I grow up I want to watch every match that is played. I won't miss a single one. And I'll come and tell you about all of them.'

'Well, I won't be around to hear about the matches when you've grown up,' said Tatya. 'It's a pity, isn't it. I'd have liked to see what you look like as a young man.'

'Don't worry, you will,' said Aru, nonchalantly.

Tatya smiled. 'I wanted to tell you something. I know that your Aai likes to listen to music on the big radio downstairs, and you like to listen to the match commentary. The two of you need not sulk at each other today. You can take my radio and listen to the commentary in peace.'

Aru's face lit up. 'I'll return it to you as soon as the match is finished, Tatyasaheb,' he promised.

Tatya nodded. And then he shook his head. 'No,' he said, 'keep it. It's yours.'

Aru looked as if he couldn't believe his ears. 'But don't you need it in your room?' he said.

'No,' said Tatya. 'If I need it, I'll ask you for it. But I hardly listen to it anymore. I used to listen to some music. But I don't feel like it these days.'

'What about listening to the news?' said Aru.

Tatya looked with fondness at the small, serious face in front of him. He wondered what profession Aru would choose to follow. Medicine, perhaps, since he was always concerned about others. Though concern for others was needed in any profession. At least that was the old way of doing things. He didn't know what people thought these days.

'I have the newspaper for news,' said Tatya.

'I'll ask Aai whether it's all right for me to take it,' said Aru. 'She might get angry that I took your radio.'

This was going too far, and Tatya's brow furrowed. He felt rather annoyed at Durga for keeping such a tight leash on her children. 'Now look here,' he said. 'If I say you take it, you take it. Your mother has nothing to do with this.'

Aru nodded, and his anxious face melted into a broad smile.

'Now come here and press my feet,' said Tatya. 'Five minutes and then off you go. I want to read the papers.'

Aru felt around on the blanket till he found Tatya's feet underneath, and began to press them gently. Tatya opened the newspaper. It was a Sunday and the paper featured several advertisements for films. There was a new film called *Awara*. Tatya looked idly at the credits. Somebody called Raj Kapoor. He gazed at the picture of a man nuzzling his face into the bare shoulders of a woman.

And he thanked his stars that he had shut down Rising Sun Films.

'That's enough, Aru,' he said, shortly, and looked again at the advertisement as Aru skipped out of the room.

He wondered whether Kamal would have bared her shoulders for a film. Of course, twenty years ago she would not have been required to. But nor could he imagine her acquiescing to it. No, she was full of action. She had danced, leaped, fought, dangled off a bridge; even when she romanced Shinde, the chemistry between them was full of verve and good humour. She had not been the type to stand passively while the hero made love to her. That was the whole point of her; the whole point of Kamal bai.

CHAPTER 57

1932

The pedhi in Mulji Jetha Market was booming. It was as if a giant wave from the sea had emerged under Tatya's feet, and he rode the wave like a marine charioteer, reins in hand, expecting to crest at any moment, the surf foaming around him as he waited for the wave to crash on to the wealthy shores of Bombay. And still, Tatya felt he was on the brink of something even bigger.

The immediate reason for that was Altaf Shahpurwala.

For in the same breath that Altaf had informed Tatya that he wanted to sell the studio land in Borivali, he told Tatya of two other developments. The first was that he wanted Tatya to take over as the sole selling agent of Noor Begum Mills. So far, Tatya had shared the selling agency with old Shahpurwala's son-in-law, but Altaf had ousted him from the family business, calling him a useless, scheming fellow. Who knew what the inner workings of a large and complicated family really were? But the outcome was that Tatya would now sell every single piece of cloth that emerged from Noor Begum Mills. It meant a prodigious increase in business.

The second development was even more momentous. Altaf wanted to expand and he wanted Tatya to be his partner in a mill in Dadar that he was going to buy and modernize. Tatya felt not the slightest hesitation in going into business with Altaf; like his father, old Shahpurwala, he was a shrewd operator.

Meanwhile, Imperial Movietone's *Alam Ara* had released at the Majestic cinema—it now called itself Majestic Talkies—and the country's first talkie, in Hindi, was a runaway success. Its heroine, Zubeida, was the talk of the town for her daring costumes and her dark-eyed, lingering gazes. Soon after, Madan Theatre's *Shirin Farhad* had released to even greater success, and Prabhat Films had raced to release the first Marathi talkie, a mythological film about the king of Ayodhya, and then released the same film in Hindi. It was as if a dam had burst on to the film industry. And yet, debate raged on about whether talkies would overcome the might of the old silent bioscopes. Actors, filmmakers, cameramen, theatre owners, all waited with bated breath to see who would be washed away and who would be saved.

For Tatya, there was only one rational response to the situation: it was time to get out of the film business, focus on his pedhi, buy the new mill with Altaf Shahpurwala, become a mill owner himself.

There was no room for distractions, no room for taking a risk with investing in talkies. No room to stay in a business that was increasingly casting a shadow over his heart. He knew the shape of that shadow, he had seen her in his dreams. He felt as if he had been playing with a wisp of smoke, a smudge of colour, a drop of sun on water. A thing forever out of reach.

He must break the news to Kamal himself. Would they, in time, keep up a correspondence of some sort? Meet, perhaps? He could not conceive of any kind of social situation where their paths might cross, once Rising Sun Films had shut its doors. There was an ache within him, which he kneaded further, teasing at it, twitching it like a broken finger nail that neither held fast nor broke loose. He thought of Kamal over and over. He knew how she looked from every conceivable angle. The camera had made sure of that. He knew how she looked in a small photo print, and how she looked when her face was blown up across the giant screen of Kohinoor Theatre; how her body moved like a jerky marionette when the film ran rapidly through the projector, how her movements were slowed, arrested, when the film ran slowly, as Bhalerao examined it for defects. He knew how she looked with sea spray on her radiant face, the toss of her head as she threw an alluring smile over her shoulder, how the wind played with her black hair till it was all curls and tendrils. He knew her body intimately, though he had never touched her.

He didn't know Radha in the same way. He had never even seen her throw back her head and laugh without reservation; she wouldn't have dreamt of behaving in that manner in front of her husband. He had never seen her run or hop or, God forbid, dance, and hardly ever with her hair let loose from her tight bun. She rarely sat down in his presence. It was as it should be. Quiet lives lived decently.

And yet, there was nothing in the least indecent about Kamal. There was wit, there was business acumen, there was the flow of words, acute observations about the news, conversation that flowed like a stream and sometimes came to a standstill like a silent pool of clear rainwater and swaying underwater ferns; even their silences were full of life.

Perhaps she would be employed in whichever studio Bhalerao went to. He might see her if he ever visited Bhalerao, and surely he would visit Bhalerao, for old times' sake. But he also knew that this was a story, a fiction, the kind told to pacify a child.

It was a long journey in pouring rain. His chauffeur, Jagan, stopped the Buick at the gates of Rising Sun Films. The board outside, with its vivid painting of a red and yellow sun rising behind two hills, had faded. Squinting through the rain, Tatya could see that the sun was now the colour of an old lemon, and the reds had taken on the hues of brown earth. We must get it repainted, he thought, and then remembered it was no longer necessary to do so. The guard's shed stood soaked and forlorn. Jagan honked a few times, muttered a curse, and got out of the car to push open the large gates himself. Tatya couldn't remember a time when the guard had been missing from his post. The seams were unravelling. Did they all know that it was all falling apart? But it hadn't been announced yet. Nobody but Bhalerao and Tansukhrai knew that Rising Sun Films was on the verge of closure. Jagan got back into the car, raindrops clinging to his white uniform and peaked cap. The noise of the rain was deafening. As they rolled in through the gates, there was a distant shout, Tatya couldn't be sure from where. Then a thud on the roof of the car, and a scrabble of claws; a bird, floundering, tumbled down on to the bonnet before its soggy wings flapped away. It unsettled him. What was a bird doing flying about in the middle of lashing rain? Jagan drove slowly, the windshield obscured with streams of water despite the wild swiping of the wipers. The grounds of the studio looked ghostly under the darkening sky, as if drowning in a lake. A dark, twisting form loomed ahead of them, through the depths of the water. It was the old banyan tree, sculpted from black mist. The shrubbery, the lawns, even the staff cottages which had expanded over the years to hold almost sixty men, all had a derelict air about them, as if time had folded into itself, like an envelope, and sent him a missive from the future, from a time when Rising Sun Films had ceased to exist, when its miles of footage would remain coiled in cans, the faces on the frames looping round and round inside, in a sequestered whirlpool. He tried to brush away these thoughts as foolish and morbid. Nobody here apart from Bhalerao knew, he reminded himself, that the studio would close.

But when he was shown into Kamal's cottage, into her small living room, by her maid, he knew at once that she had already heard. He would not be able to break the news to her as he had planned. Why had Bhalerao told her?

Her living room was built almost identically to Bhalerao's. Except that there were no bookshelves and sheaves of paper. Instead, a low mattress with some large bolsters and cushions scattered across it, a sofa on which lay a pile of glittering costumes, a table with an empty teacup. And there was a large dressing table with a full-length mirror, an incongruous item of furniture in a living room.

A magazine lay open on Kamal's lap but she wasn't reading it. Seated by the window, she looked out at the grey rain. She turned to him as he came in, but did not get up to greet him as she normally would have done. Instead, a pallid smile appeared on her face, and she did not stir, as if there were no point anymore in keeping up pretences.

She held up the magazine to show him the cover. It was *Cinema*, a popular magazine from Lahore. A writer from the magazine had visited Rising Sun Films a couple of years ago and published a piece on the studio along with a photograph of Kamal.

'Have they written about you again?' he enquired. Her expression was unreadable, her eyes wide.

'No,' she said, 'but it's an issue worth reading, if only for the advertisements. Look at this page here.' She thumbed through the magazine till she found an announcement from Famous Pictures, a film distribution company. Tatya knew it well, it was based on Lamington Road and often distributed Rising Sun Films to theatres.

He squinted at the page in the dim light of the room.

'According to Famous Pictures, talkie films are just a passing fad,' she said. 'They say that jumping on the talkie bandwagon will be ruinous for studios and theatres. That silent pictures will rule forevermore. Hopeful words, don't you think?' She rifled through the magazine again. 'Now look at this full-page advertisement from a company called Swan Sound. They have mighty differences of opinion with Famous Pictures. Swan Sound says that every theatre must immediately install sound equipment, or face ruin. Two extremes. Who is one to believe?' she asked.

Tatya sighed. He shook his head. 'It's difficult, Kamal bai, to predict what will—'

She interrupted him with a mirthless laugh. 'And look at this,' she said, opening up the magazine to yet another advertisement. 'Prabhat Film Company thinks that talkies are just some newfangled invention, that people will realize its worthlessness soon enough. But look how clever they are, for while the talkie craze lasts, Prabhat says it is ready to offer talkies to the audiences.' Here she adopted an ironic tone as if delivering a dramatic dialogue, while reading out the words of the advertisement. '*Prabhat's perfect talking, dancing, singing pictures are coming!*' Her voice rang out in the small, still room.

Then she said, 'So, Tatyasaheb, where does that leave us? The world in a tumult. Nobody knows whether we ought to speak or stay mute, sing or mouth silent lines. Tell me, what should I do? Shall I talk or stay silent?'

When he did not reply, she said, 'It is all over.' A statement, not a question.

He nodded. 'I'm sorry. I see that you already know. I came here to tell you myself.' He found that he could not look at her, so he fixed his eyes on the magazine that she had tossed on to an armchair. She had accurately analysed the turmoil enveloping the bioscope industry by reading through a few advertisements. She could have triumphed in business, had she not been a woman.

She gazed at him. 'Were you planning to tell all the employees personally? One by one? In private meetings?'

'No,' he said. 'Of course not.'

'Why did you want to tell me yourself? I'm just another employee of your bioscope company, like Shinde and Bhalerao and Mistry. On a monthly salary. One cog in the machine.'

Tatya stared at her. 'Surely you know you are more than that,' he said.

'No, I am not. None of it could happen without all of us doing our best,' she said, shrugging. 'We all switch jobs when required. Mistry the carpenter has donned a costume and acted with me in a few scenes. I've often fed the horses hay when the horse trainer couldn't do it. Shinde rolls out the bedding for the men when he's not required to act. So why the special treatment for me? Or did you think that your entire business hinges on my famous smile? You know the smile I mean. The last one, the lingering one. The one that makes every man in the audience feel that I'm smiling just for him. Is it that smile that merits this personal visit to break the news to me about the studio's closure?'

She was perfectly composed. She might have been reciting the lines of a poem she had memorized.

He did not know what to say. But he said, in a low voice, 'You know you are different.'

'No.' She shook her head. 'I'm no different from the rest of them. But what is different is what has passed between the two of us. Tell me, what am I to you?'

He looked at her wearily.

She sighed, and her arch manner fell away. She looked down at her hands, and clasped them tight together. 'I thought it would go on forever.'

'I thought so too,' he whispered. He still remained standing in the middle of the room, not knowing what to do with his hands which hung at his side. An oil lamp flickered on the table. She did not move from her seat by the window. He had not expected this. He had come unprepared for this conversation. What a fool he was.

'All I wanted,' she said, 'was to talk to you, spend time with you. I would wait for you to come and watch me rehearsing, riding, climbing trees. You made everything seem joyful. My heart always wanted more, but I beat it back, argued it into submission. And now, even the little that we had is gone.'

Tatya flinched on hearing her use the word 'we'. To hear it stated so baldly, jolted him. She included him, without hesitation, in the equation of desire that they had both toyed with. He felt a coward for being unable to speak, even to himself, as honestly as she was capable of doing. He had come here thinking he was undertaking a noble task, in gently breaking the news to her; but here she was, throwing his cowardice in his face. He couldn't say it, though. He would not betray Radha.

'You're thinking of your wife, aren't you?' she asked him, looking hard into his face. 'You're thinking that you don't want to betray her. It's too late for that, Tatyasaheb. The betrayal took place long ago. At least admit that much. If not to me, then to yourself.'

He felt that till he spoke, said something, the torrent of her words would continue and would not stop till he drowned.

'Do you see what you've done?' she said. 'You made me feel as if I were a river in full flow, unrestrained, blissfully swirling any way I wished, all the while protected by the sturdy river banks on either side. And now I see that I am merely a stream, a rivulet, unclaimed, anonymous, unexpectedly let loose upon the sea. I am on my own. And you? Where are you?'

The rain thundered down on the roof.

'I am here,' he managed to say. 'You are not alone. Rest assured that I will help you in any way I can. I...I trust you know that your presence has been a special one, and your company has been something I would have found it difficult to do without. The loss is all mine. It has been a source of happiness for me to see you thrive here. But perhaps I cannot say what you really want me to say. I am...I am in an impossible position.'

She looked at him with a combination of pity and contempt. 'An impossible position? You?'

Tatya felt his temper rising. He did not deserve this onslaught. What did she wish him to say? What role could she possibly hope to play in his life?

'It's as clear as day,' he said, shortly. 'If you don't already see it, I do not know how I might explain it to you.'

'The rain crashes down on the roof, the clouds are a kingdom of dark towers, and you claim that it is as clear as day,' she said, a sad smile on her lips. 'All right then. Let us say that the sky is full of sunshine. But before you go out into that happy, dappled light, let us talk about which of us is really in an *impossible position*, as you put it.'

Tatya shook his head, regretting his sharp tone. 'I didn't mean to say...' he began, but she cut him short.

'Perhaps there were a great many things that you did not mean to happen,' she said, 'but they did, and nothing can change that. Let me tell you something that *I* didn't mean to happen. Do you remember what I told you about my brother? I said that when he tried to force a man on me, I resisted and ran away with my maid before anything bad could happen. That was a lie. Listen to the truth now, and then talk to me about *impossible positions*.' Here she paused, as if to control her voice, which had started to waver. 'I could not run away in time. That man overpowered me. And afterwards he gave money to my brother. There were three other men whom I had to lie with before I picked up the courage to run away. My brother has written me letters ever since he saw me on the screen and found out where I was, threatening to come here and break my legs if I did not send him money every month. I was terrified, and did as he said. I didn't care about the money, but I did not want him to come here and reveal the truth and spoil the life I had built for myself. I could not save any money till last year, when I heard that he had finally drunk himself to death.'

A rash of goosebumps crawled over Tatya's body as Kamal's story came tumbling out. 'Why didn't you say anything before?' he said, his voice trembling. 'Why didn't you tell me? I would have handed him over to the police!'

She looked sadly at him. 'Tell you? Would you have kept me on in your film company? You, who are so terrified of immorality and impropriety? Would you have looked at me in the same way? No more the pure, innocent Kamal who exchanges smiles with you, but one who has been dragged through the mud. No, you would not have tolerated it. And I would have lost what we had between us. I would have lost the very thing which made me feel alive.'

Tatya's throat was dry. But she wasn't finished yet.

'When I came here,' she said, now looking away, 'and Bhalerao approached me, I let it happen again. I thought it was expected of me. And I was relieved to be under his protection. It is better, I thought, to be with one man than to be the plaything of many. Not a single man in Rising Sun Films has dared to raise his eyes and look at me disrespectfully, because of Bhalerao. And that is why, whenever he comes to me, I let him.' Then she looked up defiantly at Tatya. 'And let me tell you one last thing. He fulfilled a hunger in me too. A physical need. Not to be mistaken,' she said, 'for love.'

She looked straight into Tatya's eyes. Her voice was calm. There had been no wailing, no distasteful display of passion. Simply a baldly stated position. And a declaration of love.

'I have never,' she said, 'met a man as intelligent as you…nor as naive.' Her eyes filled with tears.

Tatya felt as if something had punched him in the gut. Bhalerao too? How could he forgive himself for being so blind? He had imagined that Kamal was living safely in the haven of Rising Sun Films. But Rising Sun Films had turned out to be like any tawdry theatre company in the end. He felt his body would crumple up in shame, that such a thing had happened under his watch, that Kamal had allowed Bhalerao to sleep with her simply because she thought it was expected of her, simply because she felt she needed his protection. He wished bitterly that he had shut down the bioscope studio before ever laying eyes on Kamal. And he could not fathom what she had said about Bhalerao fulfilling her hunger. It was impossible, it was not—could not—be decent, and yet it was the truth.

'I will ensure you get the best employment possible,' he managed to say. It seemed to come out all wrong. He found his mind turning, incomprehensibly, to practical matters right away. He clung to these prosaic details as if he were flailing in water and they were his only anchor. He didn't mean for his words to take on this stiff formality. But he seemed unable to form his words in any other way. 'I will write to Prabhat Films and arrange it. And don't worry about the money you lost to your brother. I'll make it up to you. Every last rupee. I... rest assured, I will send you a sum every month, enough that you can live at peace in a house wherever you please, whether or not you wish to work.'

Kamal stared at him as though he were deluded. 'Do you really think,' she said, 'that I would be left alone? There will always be men who would think they could have me, promise me things, take advantage of me.'

'You will call the police if anyone ever does that to you,' Tatya said, anger and shame burning his cheeks. 'It is no crime to live quietly on your own, whatever your past may have been.'

'And you plan to send me money every month, do you?' she said. 'To make up for the loss of money I have suffered?'

He nodded. 'Yes,' he said.

'And what does that make me?' she said. 'What will you call that relationship? Will there not come a time when you come to me, because you think it is your right?'

'I would never do that,' he said, taken aback.

'And I would never do that to you,' she said. 'Listen to me. There will come a time when you want something else, something different from the life you are leading. At that time you will come to me. It may be in a moment of weakness. And I will have no choice but to give you whatever you ask for, because of the money you send me every month. Afterwards you will hate yourself. And I do not want any part in creating that kind of discord in your life. You are a good man. But you are a man after all and, believe me, I know something of men.'

There was nothing else to say. I must leave, he thought. I must leave before I say anything further; before I take her in my arms; before the world turns upside down.

CHAPTER 58

1933

Neelkanth was in Greenglades, but Durga had not yet seen him that morning. He must be giving his daily report to Tatyasaheb. It was almost a year since Tatyasaheb had closed down the film studio. Kohinoor Theatre used to screen only Rising Sun Films, but for months now, Neelkanth's job had included acquiring films from other studios to show at the theatre. She felt impatient this morning as she did her chores for Aai. She wanted to go and look over her notebook before sitting down with Neelkanth. They were supposed to move to a new section of the Tadkhadkar textbook today.

But Durga had barely finished her daily task of slicing and chopping vegetables when Aai said that she wanted to clean out the silverware cupboard, and that Durga must help her. They ended up looking at all the brass and copperware too, and began making a careful inventory of everything.

'Aai, why are we suddenly making lists of these things now?' said Durga, as they stacked up dozens of silver bowls and platters, piled up the puja silverware separately, and began counting it all. Durga wrote everything down neatly in an exercise book.

'Everything has become disorganized,' said Aai, picking out a few pieces that needed polishing. 'Especially since Sharad's wedding, when many silver items came as wedding gifts, and your father ordered several new things as well. I've lost count of what exactly we have. Before Diwali, I want to have these cupboards in order again. Now write down five silver ladles and five silver serving bowls.'

The morning passed in this way and Durga, bored, waited for the large grandfather clock in the hallway to strike ten. She knew that Aai would stop then, to make preparations for lunch at eleven, and to look in on Kusum who was pregnant and afflicted by such terrible morning sickness that she rarely left her room before noon. By ten, Neelkanth, too, would have finished his daily reporting to Tatyasaheb, and would have an hour free for her daily lesson with him. Meanwhile, as they sorted through the

360

cupboards, Aai talked of the correct manner of looking after metalware, for Durga's edification.

'You need to clean brass and copper pots with wet ash or soil, and then scrub them with a cloth or with coir,' she said. 'If they are stained, apply tamarind or lime or sour buttermilk on them, and then scrub it all off with ash. Now silver has to be treated differently. You must soak silver pots in water, apply a thick limestone paste on them, let the paste dry and then polish the pots with a flannel cloth. Make them sparkle. Of course, delicate silverware with design work on it, like attardaanis and gulabdaanis, must be cleaned with a soft brush. Do you understand?'

Durga nodded, only half-listening.

'And mind,' said Aai, 'if you are cleaning German silver, don't scrub it with anything rough, otherwise you will scratch it. Use something soft to clean it, like chickpea flour or soft white wood ash.'

Durga's ears pricked up at the mention of German silver. 'Why is it called German silver?' she asked. 'Do we have any?'

'Who knows why it is called that,' said Aai, briskly pulling open yet another cupboard full of utensils. 'It's actually mainly copper. We don't have more than a few old pieces of it, bought when we were still at the chawl. But you might need to know how to clean it in the future.'

'The Future', Durga knew, was a euphemism for when she would be married, though it was clear to all concerned that it was getting rather late for her to marry. She had already come of age more than three years ago, had been initiated into the mysteries of the room that her mother and Shalu mami and Kusum and Uma bai retreated to once a month. And here she was, still in her father's house. At seventeen, she had stopped bothering about it. For all she cared, she would never marry. At this moment, what piqued her interest was the German silver. She wondered why it was called that, and made up her mind to ask Neelkanth whether he knew. Neelkanth had told her that he and Schmidt were still writing to each other, since both were passionate about mechanical engineering.

Neelkanth was looking forward to earning his engineering degree, a prospect which was imminent. Since shutting down Rising Sun Films, Neelkanth informed Durga, Tatyasaheb had lost interest in the Kohinoor Theatre too and had mentioned to Neelkanth that he would soon sell it. Once the theatre was sold, Neelkanth planned to enrol for his degree as soon as possible, paying his way with the good amount of money he had saved up. In the intervening years he had kept up a rigorous self-study programme by borrowing Mandar's old engineering textbooks. He also kept up a correspondence with Schmidt, who appeared to spend all his time travelling around Germany in search of old automatons and music boxes, and had most recently written to Neelkanth from a city called Stuttgart. Neelkanth had been very excited about this letter because it described to him the Daimler-Benz automobile factory which Schmidt, with his keen interest in cars, had toured. Neelkanth's enthusiasm was infectious, and Durga found herself listening avidly to Neelkanth's translations of Schmidt describing the range of Mercedes cars made at the factory, not to mention the thoroughly modern cities he passed through, and his long description of the festival of Christmas which he had spent at his home in the Black Forest, a name full of mystery which fired Durga's imagination no end.

How Durga longed to travel to another land. I shall never travel, of course, she would tell Neelkanth, but Schmidt's letters are the next best thing. Who knows what the future will bring, Neelkanth often said, perhaps one day I shall travel there and send you letters about all that I see! Together they talked about Germany and thought up new questions to ask Schmidt, who proved to be a most obliging and prolific letter writer, and seemed to enjoy answering Neelkanth's many questions. Of course, the main part of their letters was to do with all things mechanical, and that was Neelkanth's chief purpose in writing to him for he was in awe of what he called 'German engineering'. Durga didn't care much for the subject, but she listened, simply to share in Neelkanth's fervour, and because she picked up some interesting English words as he talked about it.

When Aai had heard that Neelkanth was teaching Durga English, she had informed Tatyasaheb at once. He had called Durga to him one evening to ask her about it. She went to him, miserable and afraid that her father would put a stop to her lessons with Neelkanth. But instead, he had simply asked her why she was so keen on learning English. She was careful not to say that she wanted to be able to speak in English to Gitanjali and Jaikumar; if she had mentioned the royal brother and sister, she would not have been able to conceal her utter admiration for the lazy familiarity with the language that they possessed, casually bantering with each other in words that were slowly becoming comprehensible to her. She didn't want Tatyasaheb to tell her angrily, as Aai had, that she should not ape Gitanjali. But she would not lie to her father either. So she simply said to him, 'I like to learn. My

Tejaswini Apte-Rahm

brain feels sharper when I am learning something new. I feel happier.' And she waited for the rebuke that was surely coming her way.

But instead, her father had simply gazed at her, his eyes inscrutable and sad. She felt guilty, and was about to assure him that since Neelkanth wasn't a real teacher she probably wouldn't learn all that much from him. But before she could say anything, Tatyasaheb nodded. 'All right,' he said, 'I have no objection to it. Learn if you must.' And Aai, looking disapproving and worried, had later said, 'Remember all this is only a hobby, a way to pass your time. Your real life will begin when you are married.'

The clock struck ten and Durga heaved a sigh of relief at escaping the inventorying of the silverware. It was a quiet sigh though, for Aai could be rather sharp if Durga displayed any signs of weariness with household tasks.

'That's enough for now,' said Aai, getting up. 'We'll finish this later. I suppose you want to go look for Neelkanth now?'

Durga nodded, unable to stop a broad smile. Aai raised her eyebrows in mock exasperation, and went on her way. Durga limped off to her room as fast as she could to fetch her books, and then found Neelkanth waiting for her in their usual corner of the sprawling living room. The room was so vast that there were three sets of sofas arranged around it in clusters, a large desk which Tatyasaheb used, a couple of bookcases, and a foot-operated harmonium from Rising Sun Films that had been brought here when the studio shut down. She had seen Tatyasaheb sit idly at it now and then to play a few notes, trying to pick out some old tune, though neither he nor anybody else in the house knew how to play it. Neelkanth smiled as Durga approached him.

'Are we starting a new section today?' she asked, as she made her way towards him across the living room.

'I never met a student as eager as you,' he said. 'But I have something to tell you before we begin. I had another letter from Schmidt. He says that after I have done my engineering degree, if I get high marks, he might be able to arrange a job for me in Germany at one of the automobile factories. Which means they would even pay for my passage there. Can you imagine me on a ship?'

Durga's mouth fell open. 'Are you really going to Germany?' she breathed.

'No, you silly creature, I am merely dreaming of it,' said Neelkanth. 'Nothing wrong with that, is there?'

'But it sounded so real when you said it, as if it could really happen,' she said.

'It could, I suppose. Well, what if it became real?' He sat back and crossed his arms. 'What would you say then?'

'I'd say I was going with you,' she said promptly, and they both burst out laughing.

They began turning the pages of the textbook, and arrived at the new section that Durga was so keen on starting. She had finished learning how to use simple nouns and verbs in the present tense and had started formulating short sentences in the past tense. They were moving, now, to lists of words that were five or six letters long. This list was related to homes and gardens. Durga thought it would be fun to be able to name all the things she saw in her daily life at Greenglades. The hour seemed to end almost as soon as they had started. When Durga heard the clock strike eleven, she clicked her tongue in annoyance.

'I wish we could do two hours a day,' she grumbled. 'Now we have to stop just as we were beginning.'

Neelkanth looked as if he wanted to speak, but hesitated.

'What?' she said. 'Were you about to say something?'

'Yes,' he said, 'but you might feel bad about it, so I didn't want to say anything yet.'

Durga blinked in surprise. 'What could you possibly say that would make me feel bad?'

'Well….' Neelkanth hesitated once again, but pressed on. 'Tatyasaheb has finally found a buyer. He is selling Kohinoor Theatre. He told me last week, in fact.'

'But what does that have to do with me?' said Durga. And then the realization came upon her in a flash. 'Oh, but that means you won't be working at the theatre anymore…and you won't be coming every morning to report to Tatyasaheb…and that means you won't be here to give me my English lessons!' She stared at him in disbelief. His lessons were the one thing she looked forward to more than anything else during her day. And now it was all coming to an end. Of course, it had to end. How could she think that a young man like Neelkanth would endlessly find the time and the patience to teach her a poor bit of English? She had been embarrassingly presumptuous in expecting him to devote so much time to her. And now he was going to do other things, enrol for his degree, move on to live the rest of his life. It was as it should be. How foolish she had been to think that their lessons would continue indefinitely. And, hoping he did not take her to be a greater fool than she felt, she managed to smile gaily at him and said, 'So finally, the Victoria Jubilee Technical Institute will receive its greatest scholar yet! I wish you every success in your engineering degree. Don't worry about me, I know you won't have the time to teach me anymore. It's just a pastime really. Perhaps I'll try learning a bit more on my own.'

Neelkanth looked taken aback. 'A pastime? You've hardly approached this whole thing as if it were just a hobby. You're a talented student, you know. And what's all this about my not having the time to teach you? Did I ever say that I would stop?'

'But…I thought you meant….' Durga stammered, afraid that she'd offended him by referring to their lessons as a mere pastime. 'I mean… how will you have the time if you go to college?'

'I'll make the time,' shrugged Neelkanth. 'I might not be able to come at ten every morning, but we'll find another time. Before dinner perhaps. Aaisaheb will still expect me to eat here every evening.'

Durga exhaled in relief. Neelkanth would continue to teach her. And she had forgotten that she would still see him at dinnertime every day. Everything would still be the same, after all. Like a fool she had jumped to all sorts of conclusions. Then she frowned. 'Wait a minute,' she said. 'You said that you were going to tell me something that would make me feel bad. But so far you've only given me the good news that you will soon be able to start college.'

'I wanted to tell you that we will have to stop our lessons…just for a while.'

'Why?' said Durga in surprise.

'The new term at the institute doesn't start for another few months. Mandar had told me that as soon as my role at Kohinoor Theatre came to an end, he would arrange for me to join a railway contractor for work experience, before college begins. The railway contractor is in Madras. I will be away for four months.'

'Four months!' Durga said in alarm. 'But I'll miss you!' She had spoken without thinking, and as soon as the words left her mouth, felt dreadfully and unaccountably embarrassed.

Neelkanth looked at her quietly. 'Will you really?' he said.

Durga looked away in confusion. 'I meant to say…we shall all miss you. All of us at home.'

'I shall miss all of you too,' he replied softly.

She still wouldn't look at him. He made as if to get up and leave, but she felt that she must dispel the odd awkwardness in the air, and found herself filling the silence by saying, 'I shall practise a lot while you're away. You'll see! I'll practise with Gitanjali and Jaikumar, and even start to speak with a proper accent like they do!'

She looked at Neelkanth, smiling into his eyes to show him that everything was just fine. But he simply looked at her with an undecipherable expression.

The door of the living room was thrown open at this moment. It was Kusum. 'There you are!' she called. 'Hurry and come for lunch. Neelkanth, are you staying to eat? Durge, it's a miracle, I actually feel hungry today!'

CHAPTER 59

Telegrams were exchanged. Dates were fixed. And one day Neelkanth told Durga that he would leave for Madras in a week. Aai started making various snacks for him to eat on the long train journey, and to tide him over during his first few days in Madras. 'Madrasi food' became a topic of conversation in the house, to which Mandar, of course, could contribute a great deal, describing to them fiery preparations like the hot 'rasam' drink which was so spicy it made your eyes water, and names which sounded odd on the tongue like 'dosa' or 'idli'. Uma bai concluded that an idli was simply a minor version of saandan which was soaked in mango juice before steaming, and which she often made in the summer months.

Neelkanth had become such a part of the household that nobody batted an eyelid at Aai's and Uma bai's elaborate measures for his journey. 'I don't remember you making such preparations when Mandar used to travel to Madras,' said Durga mischievously, eyeing the spread of ingredients in the kitchen where Aai was making chiwda packed with coconut and peanuts, sweet ladoos dotted generously with raisins, not to mention stacks of puran polis. Aai did not rise to the bait and simply continued her assiduous kneading of dough. Everyone knew that Neelkanth was a favourite with Aai ever since she had found out, when he started coming for meals as a poor schoolboy, that he had lost both his parents. Neelkanth, in turn, held her in high regard and had an annoying habit of defending her if Durga ever happened to grumble to him about her mother.

Five days. Four days. Three. Neelkanth would be gone in three days. Early in the morning, Durga sat slumped on the ground, her back against a coconut tree. From here she had a view of the tennis court. It was a Saturday. There would be no more lessons before Neelkanth left. Her English textbook lay on her lap, unopened. Sharad was playing an energetic game of tennis with Mandar and two of Sharad's circle of friends from the Hindu Gymkhana. The thwack-thwack of the ball was interspersed with the screech of kites circling the sky and the swish of waves before they broke with a crash on the black rocks on the shoreline. At that early hour, the sun shone as if through a veil of milk. The petite night jasmine tree had spilt its white, star-shaped flowers on the brown earth during the night. Creamy yellow coconut blossoms lay scattered around Durga. The red hibiscus bushes had bloomed at first light, each five-petalled flower spread wide open to reveal a long yellow-powdered stamen waiting for a bee. A gentle breeze rolled in from the sea and a handful of crimson, paper-thin bougainvillea flowers tumbled across the manicured lawn. It was as pleasant a morning as any at Greenglades. But all Durga could think of was how she couldn't bear to work through the textbook without Neelkanth. She had brought it out to the garden full of good intentions, determined to devote an hour or so to memorizing a list of words. But she could hardly bear to look at it. It seemed drab, the text faded. She noticed, for the first time, how dog-eared it was and felt a sudden annoyance at Sharad for having looked after his book so poorly.

Four months stretched wearily ahead of her. Everything was changing. People were getting on with their lives, yet she remained stranded in the midst of it all, like a stagnant pool of water. Mandar and Kusum would leave for Dhangadh next week. They would be away for a month, visiting Dadasaheb, and from there Kusum would go to her parents' house in Thane to complete her pregnancy there. It was the custom, Durga knew, for girls to be looked after by their mothers during the last difficult months, especially if it was a first child. Durga would miss Kusum's company and when she returned, Kusum would be busy with her baby. Shalu mami, meanwhile, had sat successfully for her matric and then miraculously obtained permission from Tatyasaheb to train as a nurse. Tatyasaheb had written to his friend, Dr Patwardhan of Patwardhan's Maternity Clinic in Girgaon, and the doctor had suggested that Shalu gain experience as a trainee at his clinic in the mornings. She would then be free every afternoon to go home and study for a nursing diploma from the books he would recommend. Even Aai had fallen in with the scheme. Shalu, Kusum, Neelkanth, everyone was moving ahead, everyone had plans.

Even Gitanjali had been busy, studying for her exams and then sailing to England with her family for a holiday of three months. After returning, they had immediately left for Sonpur. It was months since Durga had seen her. She felt left behind, her life a loose end, fluttering aimlessly with every passing breeze. She was stuck with Sharad's wife, Suruchi, who was a nice girl but rather immature; perhaps Suruchi felt lonely too, for she had no one of her own age to be with. Durga couldn't be sure. She knew she ought to go and see what Suruchi was doing, offer to do something together like sewing or cutting out patterns. But this morning she could concentrate on nothing.

She looked forward to finally seeing Gitanjali, though. She felt certain that Gitanjali had returned the previous day, for she had seen two magenta-coloured Rolls-Royce cars, the royal pennant fluttering at the head of each bonnet, pulling into the gates of Bell House. She knew that the family travelled in one car with another following behind with luggage and servants. Sounds had begun floating across the road indicating a general increase in activity there. It could only mean one thing—the royal family was back in residence. She wondered whether Jaikumar had returned to Bombay as well. Sure enough, a message came with a servant later in the morning, inviting Durga to come to Bell House at three o'clock that afternoon.

On edge and yet unaccountably fatigued, not able to settle to any task, Durga eventually made herself lie down for a short post-lunch nap which, however, failed to dispel the morose lethargy that had settled over her since the morning. Indeed, the nap made it worse. She felt heavy-lidded when she woke up to the heat of the afternoon. She splashed cold water on her face but it didn't help. Despite the promise of the longed-for meeting with Gitanjali, there was a weight in Durga's throat, a heavy lump of tears waiting to explode. She felt that if she as much as stubbed her toe this afternoon, she would burst into tears, because it would be proof that the universe was conspiring against her.

As she limped down the Greenglades slope and made her way across the road, the shade of Bell House's gulmohar tree with its extensive canopy of flowering branches crept over her. She breathed in deeply and exhaled. A few orange-red petals twirled down. Under the shade of the tree, the day changed into one of cool restfulness. Indeed, Bell House seemed to extend its royal command over the weather itself, for the rather hot, itchy afternoon in the Greenglades bungalow fell away as she was shown into the lobby and then into the cool, high-ceilinged room where she had spent her first afternoon with Gitanjali, and where they often sat together—'the room of cricket paintings' as Durga called it—a place sequestered and tranquil. Pink rose petals floated in still circles of water in ornate silver bowls scattered about the room on various tables. A leafy light shone through the floor-to-ceiling window and it pulled her forward in a kind of quiet exultation. She breathed in the rose-scented air as she walked over to the window and gazed out at the thick green shrubbery, neatly trimmed. Tendrils of some kind of vine, sprouting purple buds, lapped delicately at the clear window panes. The sky was pale and sea-green as if mirroring the ocean beneath. The calm of the room stilled her mind, she felt her worries fall away, and a small smile of peace formed on her lips.

Gitanjali was usually already in the room when she arrived, and now Durga wondered where the princess was. If simply being in the same house as Gitanjali could bring her such joy, how wonderful their afternoon together promised to be. A photograph in a silver frame stood on the desk next to the window. It was a new one, Gitanjali must have brought it with her from Sonpur. The family crest, of two roaring lions and an eagle swooping down between them, was moulded in silver at the top of the frame.

It was a fine family portrait; the Rajesaheb with his fearsome black moustache and large silk turban, the Ranisaheb regal and upright, her silk padar framing her face. The royal couple sat on a low wooden settee, while their children stood behind them. Gitanjali had a soft, delicate beauty, unlike her mother's sharp features; her thick black plait snaked down to her hips, past her pearl earrings, the jewelled necklace that fanned across her throat and the diamond circlets around her slender wrists. But in Durga's opinion, it was Jaikumar, standing next to his sister, who stole the thunder in the photograph. He stood upright in a striking pale silk turban set off by a glittering jewel pinned to its front. It appeared to be a large emerald or ruby encircled with diamonds. He wore a long string of gold beads around his neck. His eyes looked straight at the camera, not in a sideways glance like his sister, not with bored, heavy-lidded eyes like his father, nor the otherworldly gaze of his elegant mother. He looked out of the silver frame with a heart-breaking simplicity that made his finery seem a plaything of no importance. Durga gazed entranced at him, mindful of the fact that she had never seen a photograph or portrait of him before, and so had never had the opportunity to examine his face closely; she had always kept her gaze slightly averted from him during the times he had joined her and Gitanjali. The more she examined the prince with his regalia and his handsome gaze, the more embarrassed she felt at having spent so much time in the company of so fine a person. How silly and young he must think her; and her face grew warm as she recalled some of the scenes he had witnessed, of her laughing without inhibition with his sister, or recounting droll schoolroom happenings, incidents amusing only to Gitanjali and herself, no doubt. How on earth could she have mistaken his politeness for real smiles, how could she have been so foolish as to say those things in front of him?

The door opened behind her and she turned eagerly to greet Gitanjali. But it was Jaikumar. He entered the room, smiling at her.

'I do apologize for making you wait,' he said.

It was rather a shock to be confronted by him in the flesh when she had just been examining his photograph so closely. Why was he apologizing? His manners were overly polite, often catching her off guard and making her uncomfortable. She looked down at the carpet, awkward, but couldn't resist glancing at him for a moment. He seemed different. He radiated fresh air and health, as if he'd galloped on a horse for miles. His face glowed so that his fair skin seemed tinged by the sun. He even looked taller, and yet that was impossible. A young man in his twenties did not grow over the holidays like a schoolboy.

'London has done you good,' she found herself saying. 'How different you look!'

'Do I really?' he said, a strange light in his eyes as he looked at her. 'Yes, the trip was a great success. I'm sure Gitanjali will tell you all about it.'

Durga nodded.

'I came to tell you,' he continued, 'that she is lying down with a headache, and will come down in about half an hour. Till then....'

'I can always come back tomorrow,' said Durga. 'She mustn't get up on my account. Let her rest.'

'Oh no, don't come back,' he said and, seeing Durga's startled expression, added hastily, 'I mean, don't come back tomorrow. Stay today.'

'But....'

'She's already much better, I assure you,' said Jaikumar. 'She just needs a while to freshen up. Meanwhile, shall we walk in the garden? I shall try my best to entertain you.'

'I don't need entertaining,' said Durga, bewildered by his stream of clumsy words. 'Please don't trouble yourself. I'll wait here.'

But Jaikumar was already unlatching the glass door that opened from the room directly on to the garden. They walked side by side in the yellow-dappled afternoon, through the winding pathways of the whimsical garden, twisting and turning through greenery and slender bamboo, now in the shade of a jamun tree, now under a sweet-smelling mango tree, and then so close to the sea that she felt the salt on her lips. They had never walked together before without Gitanjali. But he did not give her a chance to feel embarrassed; he never once looked directly at her. He spoke fluently and knowledgeably about all kinds of things, telling her of the enormous ocean liner that had taken his family to Liverpool via Aden, of the thousand-year-old Sira Fortress near the harbour of Aden where they had disembarked for a day, of the genteel expanse of the Hyde Park in London, of the house they had rented for two months in Chelsea; and he spoke of other, older times, telling her of the royal military college at Sandhurst where he had once spent a year, and of his boyhood hunting trips in Sonpur. Durga could not help looking again and again at his handsome profile as they walked, enthralled by how he made the world seem so large, and yet so easily within his grasp.

When Gitanjali finally appeared, all smiles and a warm hug for Durga, she led her in to a sumptuous spread of tea and sweet things to eat. Jaikumar courteously excused himself.

'Oh, don't worry about him, you'll see him later,' she said, when Durga looked surprised that Jaikumar was not joining them for tea. 'I hope you haven't been boring her,' she said mischievously to her brother, and escaped his exasperated look by pulling Durga in through the glass-paned garden door. 'I have so much to tell you,' she said. 'You will not believe my stories about what happened on board that ship to England. There was this complete bore of a brigadier who kept wanting to talk to my father while his wife constantly....'

Durga barely heard the details of Gitanjali's story though she laughed in all the right places and heard about the shopping that Gitanjali and her mother had done in London, which all seemed positively extravagant. She sipped tea and ate some sweet shankarpalya, and in reply to Gitanjali's questions about the goings on at Greenglades during her absence, told Gitanjali about her progress in learning English. For some reason her thoughts kept returning to Jaikumar, and she kept looking at the door to see whether he might enter and join them.

And she did not feel fully at ease with Gitanjali. Despite the usual chatter and the laughter, Durga felt that something had changed. Perhaps it was the effect of travelling, but Gitanjali looked more grown up. Was it that there was a certain new polish in her mannerisms? Or that she had worn her hair somehow differently? Was she wearing some new piece of jewellery? Durga could not put her finger on it. She felt inexperienced, naive, as if nothing she could contribute to the conversation would be half as interesting as the stories that Gitanjali had to tell. She almost wished that Gitanjali would revert to talking about something more familiar, like St. Xavier's College. It occurred to Durga that Gitanjali had missed a large chunk of the new term because of her trip to England.

'Gitanjali, when are you going to resume college again?' she said. 'You've missed weeks and weeks already. Will you be starting from Monday onwards?'

To her surprise, Gitanjali was silent for a moment. Then she clapped her hands twice and a servant entered the room.

'Bring some hot tea,' she said. 'This is cold, take it away.'

While the servant gathered up the tea tray and the used cups and napkins, Gitanjali appeared to be arranging her thoughts.

When the door closed again Gitanjali said, 'There's something I want to tell you. We are giving up Bell House and returning to Sonpur. I won't be rejoining St. Xavier's College.'

Durga stared at her, speechless.

'I won't stop my studies, of course,' said Gitanjali. 'I'll probably get a private tutor in Sonpur. I'll be able to get back to some other things that I haven't had much chance to do in Bombay. Riding lessons. Music lessons.' Her voice was subdued, as if she knew the effect her news would have on Durga.

'I...I thought you would be here for at least another year,' said Durga, her voice quavering. She couldn't bear to look at Gitanjali, and looked down at the tea table instead. 'Till you finished your degree, I mean. I was so looking forward to hearing more stories about your college. And...and continuing our discussions about women. And your debating club, and....' Durga felt tears pricking her eyes, and tried to blink them away. She would feel foolish, crying in front of Gitanjali. Like everyone else, Gitanjali too was moving ahead with her plans. She didn't mind having to give up her college because she would continue her studies with a fine tutor at home. She would go back to learning music and playing her sitar, she would visit her stables every day and choose the horse she wanted to ride, she would travel to Europe many more times. What else could she have expected of their friendship after all? Sooner or later they would have parted. The day had come sooner than expected, but the outcome was the same. Her friend was a princess. She would soon marry someone from another royal family. She had a full life to look forward to.

In Gitanjali's company Durga had felt free, as if Gitanjali were flying on the wind and all she herself had to do was spread her wings and fly on the currents behind the princess. Now she felt a twilit evening closing in on her, while everyone else she knew strode ahead towards sunlight, towards life.

To Gitanjali, she simply said, 'I shall miss you.' And she managed a smile.

But she saw not the least regret on her friend's face. In distress, she looked down again, at her hands, nervous and twisting on her lap, and saw a tear drop down from her cheek on to her wrist. Had their friendship been nothing more than an amusing distraction for the princess? She looked again at her friend, and saw that Gitanjali appeared thoughtful, as if there was something more she wanted to say.

'Jaikumar...' began Gitanjali, hesitating, 'is very fond of you.'

Durga stared at Gitanjali through eyes cloudy with tears. She was so bewildered at this statement that she could not blink the tears away and they rolled down her cheeks.

'Normally this would not be a matter for us youngsters to talk of,' said Gitanjali, looking uncomfortable. 'But the situation is such that...well, my father will approach your parents only if you are in agreement.'

Time slowed, became thick and inert. As if the sun had halted its descent into the sea, as if the oceans had stilled and their waves stopped rolling. 'In agreement to do what?' she heard herself say, her voice cracked and trembling.

'In agreement to be my brother's wife,' said Gitanjali, softly. 'And to be my loving sister.'

And Gitanjali told her everything; about why they had travelled to England and the gifts she had bought for Durga there in anticipation of this turn of events; she even talked of the conversations that had taken place within the royal family, of which Durga could hardly believe that she had been the subject. Gitanjali told Durga of how, as Jaikumar's wife, she would be able to continue studying with the best of tutors, travel to Europe, learn things like riding and hunting and music, or even learn to drive a car if she so wished. She would be at the centre of palace life in Sonpur and would reign as the wife of the heir to the throne.

Sitting motionless, bathed in green light, Durga saw one part of her life close down like a wilting flower and another part open up like a vast eternity. She told herself that she did not deserve this, that she was destined for other things. That her footsteps had taken her mistakenly to Bell House, that this was never meant to be, could never be. But despite it all, her breath shuddering in her chest, she nodded. She said yes.

CHAPTER 60

Mulji Jetha Market closed at seven in the evening. But this Saturday evening Tatya was on his way home at five-thirty, having left Sharad in charge. Sharad would, he knew, head to the Hindu Gymkhana on the dot of six, leaving Kishan Mehta to lock up. Nothing short of a fire at the market would make Sharad focus on the pedhi more than he already did. Sharad did his work, and he did it diligently, and Tatya would have to be content with that. But it was hard to resign himself to Sharad's passive nature; it often made him cantankerous with his son. That afternoon, a remark by Sharad had elicited a sarcastic comment from Tatya about the allure of going to the club. He did not like himself when he spoke like that and, sitting in the car as Jagan drove him home, he regretted it. He felt tired. He would have liked a short rest, but had left the pedhi early to look over the papers of Kohinoor Theatre, and keep them ready to hand over to the theatre's new owner on Monday.

On Monday evening, Neelkanth would leave for Madras and would be gone for four months; Tatya wanted to make sure one last time that the papers were in order before Neelkanth left. He had to admit that he would miss the boy. Neelkanth was insistent on paying his own way through college, though Tatya would have been glad to pay his fees. His ambition was admirable, as was his willingness to work hard. Let him get his degree, thought Tatya, and I'll set him up in a good job. With his extensive business contacts, it would be easy for him to do so.

As his Buick drove up the leafy slopes of Greenglades and stopped at the porch of the mansion, Tatya was taken aback at the sight of a servant in royal livery waiting by the marble steps that led up into the house. Durga was sometimes escorted home by a Bell House servant carrying some gift from the princess—fruits from her garden, usually. But those servants were always dressed simply, in white cotton sadra-pyjamas. This man, however, looked more like a soldier. He wore the distinctive three-cornered cap of the state of Sonpur, black boots, and a smart uniform with a red sash tied diagonally across his chest. He was holding a silver platter. Jagan hopped out to open Tatya's door, and as Tatya emerged from the car, the royal servant bowed deeply, holding out the silver tray in front of him like an offering. There was a letter on the tray addressed to Tatya. He picked it up, perplexed. It was a thick, cream coloured envelope with the royal crest of Sonpur embossed in gold on the upper left corner. Still standing at the bottom of the steps, Tatya opened the envelope and read the letter. It was in the Rajesaheb's handwriting. In simple and polite language it said that if it was not inconvenient to Tatya, the Rajesaheb and the Ranisaheb would like to visit him at four o'clock the following afternoon on a matter of some urgency.

This was baffling indeed. In the many months that the royal family had been in residence at Bell House, the Rajesaheb had made no attempt to contact Tatya. It was an honour, of course, that Durga was deemed a suitable friend for the princess, for she had been welcomed repeatedly at Bell House. He understood that the prince too had met Durga on occasion. The royal family clearly approved of Tatya's family as one worthy of association. But despite the friendly contact between the children, Tatya hardly expected the Rajesaheb to extend that acquaintance towards himself. And what could possibly be so urgent that he wanted to visit Greenglades the very next day? Why was the Ranisaheb coming too? It dawned on him that if she was coming then perhaps Radha would be expected to be present too. He had no idea what the protocol was for such an occasion, but one thing was clear: he must inform Radha immediately for there were preparations to be made. He hurried inside to the living room and sat at his desk. He opened the drawer where his letterheads were kept and wrote a brief, formal reply to the Rajesaheb saying that it would be an honour to receive the royal couple the following afternoon.

All thoughts of the Kohinoor Theatre papers gone from his mind, Tatya washed his hands, face, and feet with cold water, changed out of his dhoti and coat, and wore the loose white sadra and pyjama that was his usual evening wear at home. He wondered where Radha was. From his bedroom he stepped out on to the balcony into the cool evening. A red sun had begun its descent. The arc of the glowing sea lay spread out before him and he gazed at it, thinking rapidly. In the garden below he spied Mandar.

'Ay Mandar! Where is she?' he called. Neither Radha nor Tatya ever called each other by name. But when Tatya said 'she' it was clear to everyone who he was talking about.

'I'll find her and ask her to come up, Tatyasaheb,' said Mandar, looking up at the balcony and then hurrying inside.

Tatya settled himself on his planter's chair, lit a bidi and then immediately stubbed it out. What on earth am I doing, he thought, annoyed at his fumbling. He didn't like smoking in front of Radha. He inhaled the soothing smoke of the extinguished bidi. He hadn't taken a single puff. It would have to wait.

Radha emerged on to the balcony a few moments later, looking surprised. 'What's the matter?' she said. 'You're home early. Shall I send Sadaa with some tea?'

'The Rajesaheb and Ranisaheb of Sonpur are visiting us at four o'clock tomorrow,' he said. 'We'll need to make some preparations.'

Radha opened her eyes wide. 'Tomorrow? But...what can I prepare on such short notice? I will need to organize something really special to offer them. I must tell Uma bai. Don't worry, we'll think of something,' she said.

'Just a minute,' said Tatya. 'I've given the matter some thought. There is no need, I think, for you to prepare anything very elaborate. We will offer them pohe and saboodanyachi khichadi. That would be safest, since we do not know their tastes. Prepare fresh curd in a silver bowl and put out some of your mango pickle and lime pickle.'

Radha nodded, frowning. 'Yes, of course. They may prefer something simple after all. But we can't offer them only that. We must have some other sweets and savouries. And what if they don't drink tea? We have a good supply of unripe mangoes at the moment, I'll make some sweet panha. I'm sure the Ranisaheb would like that. It will be refreshing on a hot afternoon. I'll also keep some salted buttermilk ready. Shall I make some sweet shira with banana and saffron and almonds? Or what about....'

Tatya shook his head. 'Just prepare what I have told you to,' he said. 'For the rest, I've decided to order cakes and sandwiches from the Taj Mahal Hotel.'

Radha looked at him in consternation. 'What is wrong with the food we prepare at home?' she said. 'It is the first time they are coming to our home. And you want to serve them food from outside?'

Tatya sat up on his chair and said, 'Listen to me, royal ways are not like ours. Their tastes are bound to be different. I recall Dadasaheb telling me that the princes, whom he used to teach and who are grown men now, like to dine at the Taj Mahal Hotel when they are in Bombay. I am certain that the Rajesaheb of Sonpur too eats there. They probably like that kind of food.'

'But they are Brahmins like us, and we must offer them food prepared in sohle!' said Radha indignantly. 'What will they think of us, if we put outside food under their noses. Even the good homemade food will be polluted, sitting next to those cakes and sandwiches.'

'It's time you moved on from the customs of sohle and purification,' said Tatya impatiently. 'The world is changing in front of our eyes. We cannot cling to those rituals forever.'

Radha swallowed hard and said in a low voice, 'I have never disobeyed you. But what you are asking me to do is…it is…simply not possible.'

Tatya immediately regretted his hasty words. 'I don't mean that you should change your ways entirely,' he said. 'I don't wish to interfere with how you run your kitchen. But there are some situations where it is prudent to bend a little. If one does not bend, one is likely to break. These people travel back and forth to Europe. Do you think they eat food prepared as per the customs of sohle over there?'

Radha said nothing, but her mouth was set in a firm line and she kept her eyes averted, towards the ground. Tatya sighed. He had not meant to offend her, but there was no time for arguing over trifles.

'Where is Neelkanth?' he said. 'Shouldn't he be here by now for dinner?'

Radha shook her head. 'He was invited to eat with some friends in his chawl tonight, since he is leaving the day after tomorrow.'

Tatya got up and leaned over the balcony railing. 'Arre, where is the driver?' he shouted.

Hearing this, a couple of servants ran out from the house towards the garages. Jagan hurried up, his cap askew. Clearly he had not expected to be called upon anymore that day. 'Yes, Saheb,' he said, peering up towards the balcony.

'Drive to Neelkanth and tell him that I want him here first thing in the morning,' instructed Tatya.

'Why do you want him here tomorrow?' said Radha in surprise. 'Surely he will be busy getting ready for his trip.'

'He only leaves on Monday evening,' said Tatya. 'Tomorrow is Sunday, he will be free. I need him to go to the Taj Mahal Hotel and place an order for the snacks. I don't trust anyone else to do it.'

At the mention of the hotel, Radha descended into a sulky silence again. 'What about the buttermilk and the panha to drink?' she said, at last. 'Shall I make that?'

'Certainly,' said Tatya. 'It is a good idea.'

'I'll serve everything in silver,' she said, and then added, 'May I ask you something? Why are they coming here?'

Tatya shook his head. 'It's a mystery. The Rajesaheb's letter merely said that he wanted to discuss something urgent with me.'

'Durga might know something about it,' said Radha, thinking. 'She was with Gitanjali just this afternoon.'

'What can she possibly know,' said Tatya dismissing the idea with a brusque movement of his hand. 'In all these months she has met the Ranisaheb only a few times, and was just introduced briefly to the Rajesaheb. This has nothing to do with the children.'

'Will I need to be present?' said Radha, suddenly, as if it had just occurred to her. 'I mean, since the Ranisaheb will be there....'

Tatya did not know the answer to this. It was not the custom for Tatya and Radha to sit together or go anywhere together. Even if they did go somewhere, say to a wedding, there were always other family members with them, with the men and women sitting separately and even travelling in separate cars. Radha hardly ever sat down in front of him. The rare occasions on which she had done so, she had been fidgety and awkward. But the situation now was unprecedented. The royal couple would sit down side by side, and eat and drink with Tatya. What was to be done about Radha? He decided that on the whole it would be better for Radha not to join them, but stay prepared in case the Ranisaheb insisted on it. They would have to play it by ear. When he told Radha this she looked relieved.

'Yes,' she said. 'I will be ready, of course, and I will be present to greet them, but after that I will stand outside the door waiting to hear whether you need anything, or whether you want me to come in.'

The choreography of the whole occasion was paramount. Nobody apart from Radha was to be introduced to the royal couple, but Tatya expected the entire household to be smartly turned out, just in case the visitors asked to meet any other members of the family. At the crack of dawn on Sunday, the full contingent of fifteen Greenglades servants was scurrying around the mansion, polishing the wooden bannisters of the marble staircase, wiping down the marble floor, dusting out Persian carpets in the garden and laying them down strategically in the living room where the meeting was to take place. The gardener brought in so many tuberoses to arrange in vases that the fragrance in the living room was quite overpowering, and Radha threw open the windows so that the perfume was suffused with the bracing air of the sea and the smell of fresh green grass that drifted in from the lawn. She noticed that Durga was uncharacteristically quiet during these preparations, but thought no more of it for she had too much to do. She didn't need Durga helping in the kitchen today, for everything needed to be done as quickly as possible and Durga was a slow worker.

Neelkanth arrived promptly first thing in the morning, went with the driver to order the cakes and sandwiches from the Taj Mahal Hotel, and then retreated to pore over the Kohinoor Theatre papers yet again, to reassure Tatya that they were all in order. Radha saw him in one of the upstairs spare rooms which was furnished only with a table, a chair, and some cupboards, occasionally used as an office space by Kishan Mehta or one of the other accountants. He was scribbling away assiduously, and Radha left him to his own devices. She was of the opinion that Neelkanth should have been resting at home ahead of his journey, especially since it was a Sunday, but once her husband had decided on a course of action, there was little point in suggesting anything different to him.

As four o'clock approached, Tatya wore his red pagdi on his head, and draped his white gold-edged uparna around his neck with one end of the cloth thrown over the shoulder of his long coat. His dhoti was freshly laundered and ironed, and even his small round glasses, newly acquired due to age, were polished till they gleamed. In his anxiety to ensure a smooth visit, he had not really dwelled on why the Rajesaheb had written to him and what the urgent matter could possibly be. Now that everything was ready, he once again ran through all the possibilities in his mind but still could not fathom the reason for the sudden visit.

Finally, the Rajesaheb and Ranisaheb sat in front of him in the living room, a striking looking couple. She wore a sari of fine crimson chiffon dotted with small golden flowers, her padar draped over her head and a string of pearls around her neck. The Rajesaheb wore a pale pistachio-coloured turban which matched his light green eyes. On an array of side tables was laid out a spread of spiced yellow pohe dotted with chillies; fresh grated coconut sprinkled over a mixture of soft sago beads and roasted peanuts; delicate silver bowls of curd and pickles; chilled jugs of buttermilk and panha. And, carefully segregated from the homemade food were pink-and-cream-topped pastries, along with sandwiches made of soft white bread, the edges cut off, filled with sliced cucumbers and green coconut chutney and ripe tomatoes. There was even a plate of cheese sandwiches; nobody in the house had ever tasted cheese but Neelkanth had reported that it was a speciality of the Taj Mahal Hotel.

Radha, having greeted the visitors, was waiting outside the living room door which she had kept slightly ajar. Everything and everyone was in position, and it only remained for the couple to enlighten Tatya as to the nature of their visit.

The Ranisaheb began the proceedings by observing how pleasing the mansion and garden were. She had a soft but firm manner of speech, her diction precise and controlled. She admired the tuberoses, asked whether the Greenglades gardener might be permitted to give a few tips to her own gardener, and said the food and drink had been laid out in the most charming manner. But even as Tatya thanked her, and said it was an honour to host them, he wondered whether Radha ought to be in the room after all, to exchange these womanly pleasantries with the Ranisaheb.

It turned out, however, that these were only the preliminaries. The Rajesaheb then took charge of the conversation.

CHAPTER 61

'It gives me great pleasure,' said the Rajesaheb, 'to note the friendship between our daughters. Gitanjali tells me that your daughter is a delightful girl. She would have been lonely without Durga's company.'

'Durga always looks forward to her visits to Bell House,' said Tatya. 'She seems to have learnt a great deal from Gitanjali Raje.'

The Ranisaheb took a sip of tea. There was an odd silence. Tatya wondered what was to come next. Surely they had not come here to make small talk. The Rajesaheb's next words were most unexpected.

'You may be aware,' he said, 'that the British government has enacted new legislation with regard to sugar.'

'Indeed,' said Tatya. 'I have been following the news with some interest. There appear to be good opportunities to invest in sugar at the moment.'

At this, the Rajesaheb's face lit up in appreciation. 'I expected no less from one of the outstanding businessmen of Bombay,' he said. 'Naturally you are up to date on news of this sort. If I may, I would like to tell you how this affects my state of Sonpur. As you know, it is an arid country. We have fields of millet and sorghum along the banks of our rivers—but there are also large swathes of dry, dusty land. We do not get much rainfall in Sonpur.'

Tatya nodded.

'Many years ago,' the Rajesaheb continued, 'the British built a network of canals that branched off from our largest river, the Shaurya, to provide irrigation to the farmers. Some farmers started growing sugarcane, because they found it grew well with the irrigation from the canal water. I'm sure you are aware, however, that sugarcane has not really been a lucrative crop in India.'

'Of course,' said Tatya. 'Because India imports sugar from Java and Mauritius. It is far cheaper to buy imported sugar than to buy Indian sugar. There are just a handful of sugar factories in India at the moment.'

'But the entire situation has been changed with the stroke of a pen,' said the Rajesaheb, with an enthusiastic nod of his head.

Tatya could tell that the Rajesaheb was making an effort not to appear too effusive, but clearly this was a subject close to his heart.

'Earlier this year,' continued the Rajesaheb, 'the government imposed a tax on imported sugar. Imported sugar will, from now on, be much more expensive to buy. Which means that Indian sugar factories have suddenly become an excellent business opportunity. It is now possible to make sugar in India which can easily compete with imported sugar in terms of price.'

Tatya listened with great interest. He had read about the new legislation, and had been considering buying shares in one of the larger sugar factories up north, in the United Provinces. But the next words of the Rajesaheb put all thoughts of shares out of his mind.

'I am interested in developing a sugar factory in the state of Sonpur, and I would like the venture to be undertaken by a trusted businessman,' said the Rajesaheb. 'I have heard many things about your trading skills, Tatyasaheb, and about your vast business interests, and your standing in the business community of Bombay. All I ask is, that you bring a team of your trusted advisors to Sonpur—let us call it a fact-finding mission—to look at the opportunities that exist. You understand that the court of Sonpur would have no financial stake in your sugar factory. The investment as well as the profits will all be yours. My interest in the venture is simply to create a successful industry in my state, and the general prosperity that will come with it.'

Tatya stared at him in surprise. A sugar factory! He didn't know anything about sugar. But that was no excuse for not looking further into this proposal. He had had no experience in bioscopes either, nor in iron and steel—and yet, with the right expertise by his side, he had managed to run successful enterprises for both products, even while continuing to expand his textile business. Why not a sugar factory? He felt somewhat dizzy, and took a large sip of hot, sweet tea to steady his mind.

'I will certainly visit Sonpur,' he said, finally, looking with new respect at the Rajesaheb. The Rajesaheb was clearly no idle prince, and was intent on engaging with the newest legislation, the newest ideas. A sugar factory in the princely state of Sonpur could not be an ordinary one; no doubt the ruler would expect the latest state-of-the-art technology to be employed. It would be, thought Tatya, his heart beating fast, a magnificent challenge. 'You will not object if I talk this over with some of my trusted contacts who might be potential investors?'

The Rajesaheb nodded. 'Of course, please talk it over with whoever you think appropriate. I can assure you that the state of Sonpur will offer tax concessions and farmland at competitive rates.' The Rajesaheb sat back, and took another sip of tea.

The Ranisaheb, meanwhile, had been putting delicate spoonfuls of pohe into her mouth. She now laid her spoon down.

So that was it, thought Tatya. The purpose of the visit was now clear. The ruler of Sonpur wanted, without delay, to set up a sugar factory in his state. He wondered why the Ranisaheb had come along for what was, essentially, a business meeting. Perhaps she had been curious about Greenglades, the largest property on the road, and the most hidden due to its thick cover of trees and its position on a hillock.

His mind raced ahead. The Rajesaheb had probably extended similar invitations to other businessmen in Bombay too. The court of Sonpur would assess which investor was the keenest and most well-informed, and negotiate with him. It was imperative to move quickly. He would send Sharad and Kishan Mehta to Sonpur to find out the preliminary information, while he made some enquiries of his own in Bombay.

When he heard the Ranisaheb's clear voice slice through the air, he did not at first understand what she meant.

'There was one other matter,' she said, 'which we wished to discuss with you.'

Tatya looked at her. He had been about to call for Sadaa to...bring more tea? Lower the blinds against the sun? He could not recall, having heard her next words, what it was that he had meant to say or do.

'It is the matter of your daughter,' said the Ranisaheb, putting her plate down on the table next to her.

'Durga?' said Tatya, nonplussed.

'You could say,' said the Rajesaheb—were his eyes really twinkling?— 'that it is the real reason for our visit today. Of course, you cannot blame me for indulging in some business talk too. But if you accept, we will be joined together not only in business but also by familial ties.'

Tatya sat dumbfounded. He stared first at the Rajesaheb who now looked rather genial, and then at the Ranisaheb who sat upright and looked straight back at him, her cool expression unchanged but for the hint of a smile.

'Do you mean to say...' began Tatya, and cleared his throat, for his voice was hoarse.

'Our son, Jaikumar,' said the Ranisaheb, 'has met Durga on occasion.

Tejaswini Apte-Rahm

We bring this proposal to you with his full agreement; indeed, with his full support. We would like to welcome Durga into our family as our daughter-in-law. We are impressed by the way she conducts herself. Her manner is just what one would expect of a refined and educated young girl. I must commend you for the way you have brought her up.'

Here the Rajesaheb intervened. 'Jaikumar is our only son. He is my heir, the yuvraj of Sonpur. This means that Durga will be the future Ranisaheb of Sonpur.' He paused a moment for the import of this fact to sink in, and then continued, 'I understand from Gitanjali that Durga is a girl of wide interests and keen on learning. I am a believer in women's education, Tatyasaheb. With your permission, Durga will be free to continue her education if she so wishes. We could not have asked for a better match for the yuvraj.'

Durga? A consort fit for a prince? And the handsome Jaikumar himself in full agreement with the proposal? How was it that the royal family did not see her limp and her frozen arm? How was it that they did not mind that she was already seventeen? Tatya felt as if his heart might burst with joy. Durga, who had anticipated spending the rest of her life under her father's and brother's roof would be part of the Sonpur royal family, she would be the mother of princes. He heard a loud clink of bangles at the door and knew that Radha had heard everything. The gods themselves were hovering over Greenglades this day, raining down blessings on his family in shards of light and gold.

The Rajesaheb was looking intently at his face. He said, 'Tatyasaheb, before you say anything, I feel I must explain the circumstances to you.'

'You must not take my silence as hesitation,' said Tatya, managing to force the words out before he could cause any offence. 'I am simply overwhelmed....'

But the Ranisaheb interrupted. 'Please,' she said softly. 'Let us explain.'

Tatya nodded, baffled. What explanation could possibly be needed? Durga had a proposal to marry the prince of Sonpur. He didn't need any other information. He could not wait to rush out to Radha and see the exhilaration on her face. A lump rose in his throat. His darling child, his clever, sensitive, limping daughter with her love of life, who wanted to experience more, learn more, be more, would have everything she could possibly desire. The gods would pour golden nectar into her lap with abandon. But the Ranisaheb had something she wanted to say. Perhaps it was royal protocol to affix information on to a proposal, perhaps reel off the names of their ancestors, or enumerate Durga's duties as a member of their family, who knew, it didn't matter. Durga would marry Jaikumar Raje! Durga would marry Jaikumar Raje!

And his mind repeated these words over and over in his head as if they were a divine mantra which, if repeated often enough, would come true and make everything maleficent go away. Make the words of the Ranisaheb go away.

For she was talking about Jaikumar, about the real reason why they had rented Bell House and lived in Bombay for months on end. Something about his heart. Something was wrong with it, and…

'…And we decided that the only way forward would be for Jaikumar to follow the doctor's advice and stay in Bombay for a full course of medical care, followed by further treatment in England,' the Ranisaheb said.

'The Ranisaheb did not wish to be parted from Jaikumar. A mother's love for her only son, you understand,' continued the Rajesaheb, a subdued smile on his face. 'And so we decided to all decamp to Bombay, rent Bell House, take the opportunity for Gitanjali to enrol in college here. In other words, try to lead as normal a life as possible, while Jaikumar was undergoing treatment.'

'So your trip to London…' began Tatya. They were shedding light on the situation, such a harsh light that his eyes burned. All he could think of was Radha standing outside the door. Not a sound from her. Had she turned to stone?

'The purpose of our trip to London,' said the Ranisaheb, 'wasn't a holiday, contrary to what we led people to believe. We sailed in the company of a physician, who looked after Jaikumar during the voyage.'

'The point is,' said the Rajesaheb in a decisive tone, as if to bring the conversation to a conclusion, 'that the treatment was a success. And it has added years to his life. Jaikumar has returned from England in excellent health.'

'Added years to his life?' said Tatya, numb. This was a strange way indeed to talk of a young man in his prime. 'What do you mean?'

'It means,' said the Ranisaheb, and for the first time her voice shook, but she brought it back under control with a visible tightening of her throat, 'that he will live for another ten years. More if he is lucky, and if god so wishes. Ever since we found out about his condition five years ago, I have been conducting a yagna every year, to pray for his long life. It would seem my prayers have been answered. I will go on praying,' she said, quietly, 'to extend the ten years into twenty. A mother's prayers are powerful, Tatyasaheb.'

A mother's prayers? Was Durga's future to rest on prayers and a capricious god? He must say something. They were waiting for his answer. And what could he say but yes? Durga would be looked after for the rest of her life in the royal household, even after her husband was no more. But to anticipate death at such a moment, a moment which should have brought plain and simple joy, turned his tongue into something heavy and dead in his mouth. He could not trust himself to speak.

He heard himself saying, 'May I...speak with my wife?' He was hiding behind Radha, coward that he was. But he couldn't think what else to say. He would agree to the match, of course. It would be madness not to. But he must talk to Radha first.

The Rajesaheb looked a little disappointed, but not entirely surprised. He nodded. 'Of course,' he said. 'You must speak to her.' The Ranisaheb's expression had reverted to her cool, regal demeanour.

Her husband looked as if he was about to rise from the sofa, but he hesitated, and merely shifted to the edge of his seat. He looked at Tatya and there was a sad smile on his lips. 'You know everything now, Tatyasaheb. We have hidden nothing from you. Since Jaikumar is my only son, he must marry and produce an heir to the throne. I can think of no one more worthy than your daughter to be the mother of the future rulers of Sonpur. And she will be a daughter to us in our old age.' He looked like he wanted to say something more, but then simply brought his palms together in a namaskar. The meeting was over.

There was no sign of Radha outside the door of the living room. The magenta Rolls-Royce glided off and Tatya was left alone at the bottom of the marble steps that ran down from the porch, staring at the dust raised by the car. He stood there for a long time before turning to go back into the house.

He returned to the living room without knowing why. He found Radha sitting there, amidst the remains of the cakes and sandwiches. She did not get up when he entered, but remained seated while he stood in front of her like an errant child. The slanting rays of the setting sun fell in through the open windows like a solid block of gold, making the rest of the room look dim, a room of swirling dust motes and faded sofas.

'So this is her destiny,' said Radha, so quietly that he could barely hear her. Her face was in shadow, he could not see her expression. 'When god gives you too much, he does not forget to take something away. Our daughter will be a princess of Sonpur. She will have the wealth of Lakshmi at her feet. And after ten years she will have to pay the true price of her prosperity. She will have to pay it in tears. She will be a widow...like Mai.'

'She will not be like Mai,' said Tatya, in a low voice. 'They do not follow those customs in the Sonpur royal family. You heard what the Rajesaheb said. She will continue an active life of plenty. In time she will become the Rajmata, and possibly regent to her sons.'

Radha said nothing. He knew she was crying.

He left the living room. He walked towards the wide marble staircase that led up to the bedrooms. He walked up, one step, another step, each step a journey that must be undertaken. He walked the length of the corridor that overlooked the garden, but did not stop at his bedroom. He climbed up another flight of stairs to the open terraces and looked down over the tops of the coconut trees and frangipani trees and out towards the swelling sea, everything swaying on the evening breeze. His chest felt tight, like a knot pulled taut. He walked downstairs again and found himself at the entrance to the puja room. This was Radha's domain, a place where she did her daily puja, recited shloks, offered flowers, lit incense to enwrap the gods in wreaths of sandalwood smoke.

He looked at the idol of Ganpati enthroned on his seat, surrounded by orange marigolds and pale pink hibiscus. Durga would have the world in her grasp but in return she must drink of everything that life had to offer her in ten short years. It's a cruel trick, he thought, gazing at Ganpati. Ganpati stared back at him, round-bellied and genial, waiting to see what Tatya would do next.

Tejaswini Apte-Rahm

CHAPTER 62

A bird fluttered in Durga's chest. It flapped its wings hard, trying to get out. This was no sparrow nestled in her breast, it was a crow with a hard, black beak, it pecked at her from within, to let itself loose. It was trapped inside. She felt its panic rising within her, felt as if she too were confined, her voice muffled, her breathing ragged. It had been a full day since Gitanjali had told her about Jaikumar. Since then the earth had made a full rotation on its axis, producing a thousand sun rises all over the planet. But she felt she was stuck in resin, an ancient animal trapped in amber at one of the dark poles. She would be a princess. She would no longer lead a twilit life of waiting. She had agreed to it yesterday afternoon; and within the hour a message from the royal family had reached Tatyasaheb. And at this very moment, Jaikumar's parents sat with Tatyasaheb in the living room, making the marriage proposal which she knew would be accepted. In ten years she would meet her true fate. But for now, she was to wed a handsome and gentle man. Gitanjali wanted to be not just her friend, but her sister. Jaikumar wanted her to be his wife.

But a slow and inexplicable anger had begun burning inside her.

A hush lay over Greenglades. The household knew that Tatyasaheb was hosting the royal couple of Sonpur in the living room. Nobody must make a sound, and everybody must remain ready in case they were called upon. But if they called for her, she wouldn't be there. She was not afraid of her parents' wrath, were they to find her missing. She was not afraid of her prospective in-laws' disapproval, for she had her whole life ahead to get to know them and to appease them.

She wouldn't be found because she wasn't sitting with Shalu mami and Kusum and Suruchi in the small women's living room adjoining the kitchen, where they had been instructed to wait. She wasn't even in her bedroom anymore, where she had retreated as soon as her mother went to greet the royal couple. Her footsteps had carried her down to the garden. Then, the crow that was pecking away inside her, took her towards the old banyan tree. She looked up at its tangle of dangling roots. They brushed her cheeks and she thought what a curious tree this was, for it saw the world the wrong way round, sending its roots sprouting through the air. But this tree was an ancient, it outlived everything else. Perhaps it was everything else, and not the tree, that was upside-down. She walked on. Down the slope, across the street and through the gates of Bell House. Straight into the room of the cricket paintings and floor-to-ceiling windows and silver bowls of rose water. And now she stood in front of Gitanjali, who looked up from her book in surprise.

'Durga?' Gitanjali said in wonder. 'You, here? But my parents are at Greenglades!'

Durga nodded.

'Shouldn't you be there too?' said Gitanjali. She looked anxious now, a little afraid, for Durga stared at her, mute.

'I have something to say to you,' said Durga. Her voice was steady, but she felt as if her eyes were clouded over so that the room receded into mist and the only firm outline that remained was Gitanjali's. Gitanjali's eyes were wide as she looked up at Durga. She did not move from her position on the sofa.

'You made me feel as if anything was possible,' said Durga. 'As if all we had to do was read and talk and learn, and watch the world flower around us. I thought that in time I would convince my parents that since I would not be married, they might as well let me attend college. I was determined that day would come. I had laid my plans. If Shalu mami could continue learning, then so could I. I imagined us writing letters to each other, and this time it would be me describing to you my life in a college, attending debates, developing my ideas and thoughts. Till then, I thought, I would spend my time with you, learning, living through your stories about Paris and London and English country-houses and your life in Sonpur with your pig-sticking on horseback and your cheetahs and your tea-parties. You opened up a new world for me. You made it all seem so real.'

'It *is* real,' said Gitanjali, eagerly. 'And now you will be a part of it all!'

'It's strange,' said Durga, 'that it sounded more real when you talked of it and I listened adoringly to you. Now it seems like an illusion.'

Gitanjali stared at her, uncomprehending.

'My mother began teaching me many things from a young age,' said Durga. 'She said that I had to be better than all the other girls. She told me that I was no less than any of them, but that I would have to prove myself over and over again to the world. Finish your tasks even if your leg

Tejaswini Apte-Rahm

hurts, she said, do your work even if your arm tells you it does not want to move. Do it slowly, but do it. You are no less than anyone else. And do you know what? I believed her. I never felt as if I was inferior to other people. I never felt I was disabled. But you have made me feel disabled and worthless for the first time in my life. Would you have suggested I marry your brother if I had been healthy and whole? So much for all your talk of women's progress and emancipation!'

There was such scorn in Durga's voice that Gitanjali shrank back into the sofa.

'Don't I deserve a life of happiness that I can call my own? Am I only to be a producer of heirs and a widow-in-waiting?'

Gitanjali flinched. The word widow was inauspicious, as if to articulate it was to contaminate the very air with its ill-tidings.

'How much is the life of a disabled girl worth?' said Durga, her face hot and tears in her voice. 'How much unhappiness can she be expected to take? She knows suffering, she will not mind a bit more. She is disabled, she will feel grateful for this opportunity. She is seventeen already, but all the better, for she can produce some heirs right away, for time is short. Isn't that what you thought? She is intelligent—she will fill her life with education and books; she is innocent—she will love her husband forevermore, even as he lies dying; she is large-hearted enough to love a man whom she will lose like smoke passing through her grasp. So let us sacrifice her on the altar of love, and she will carry its flame forevermore, garbed in white, her face like ash in her grief. She is strong. She has borne suffering bravely already. She can bear a little more. After all, she is disabled. She is getting so much more than she really deserves. This much is enough for her. This much and no more. She has no right to expect anything more. Because she limps as she drags her foot across the ground, and her elbow sticks out and the fingers on that arm are useless. All things considered, she is getting more than she could ever have dreamt of. Even dreams have limits after all. What more could she possibly want?'

Gitanjali's face had gone white. 'I am your friend, Durga,' she said, in a choked voice.

'I thought you were too,' said Durga, her eyes finally filling with tears. 'But if you had been my true friend you would not have wished upon me the sadness and darkness that waits for me like a scorpion poised to strike. I would certainly not have wished it upon you.'

Gitanjali looked away at these words.

'At the very least, I would have expected you to urge me to take some time to think about it,' said Durga. 'But you failed me. I was so overwhelmed that I accepted without thinking it through.'

'Does that mean...' began Gitanjali.

Durga shook her head, her face grim. 'No. It does not mean that it will not happen. All of it will happen. Your parents are at this moment with my father, making a proposal which my father will no doubt accept. I will honour his promise. I will honour the marriage. You will not hear another word from me on this matter. Nobody will have any cause to complain about me. I will behave with perfect decorum. But I did not want to begin my new life with a lie. So I came here today to speak the truth. In honour of our friendship, surely you will not mind that I have spoken to you from the heart.'

With this parting shot, Durga turned and limped out of the room and out of Bell House. Her face burned hot and she breathed quick and shallow as she crossed the road towards Greenglades, but slowly she began to feel wretched, her insides torn apart. What had she done? She had destroyed any hope of friendship with Gitanjali. She would begin her married life on a note of bitterness. And yet, every word she had spoken had come from the depths of her being. If she had not spoken them, gotten rid of them, they would have gnawed at her forever, consumed her.

The loss of Gitanjali's friendship made her want to weep. After months of doting on Gitanjali's every word, the princess had repaid her by pushing Durga towards a life of hopeless prayers for a dying husband, had not thought Durga fit for anything better than that.

Now she was hollow. The hard-beaked crow had vanished. As she made her way up the Greenglades hillock along its narrow footpath, she saw a magenta Rolls-Royce drive down the slope that exited the property. She saw her father standing at the marble steps of the porch, his back towards her, watching the car drive away. She saw him turn and go in. Then she went up to her bedroom. The house had started to stir. She heard a voice float up, and a clatter of utensils. A crunch of feet outside, and a low mechanical hum as the driver began tinkering with one of the cars. The royal occasion was over. But for her, it was just the beginning. She spied her English textbook on her bed and picked it up, and smoothed her palm over it. She wouldn't need this anymore. She would have new books. A new tutor. She would have children. They would know their father for less than ten years. She could not imagine the horror of her own father dying and leaving her behind: the tears would seal her nose and eyes and throat till she drowned in them. Yet, this was the event that she would have to preside over in her own children's life. And she would spend the next ten years counting the days like a dreaded clock winding down. But it was all decided now. The announcement to the household was imminent. Her parents would be subdued at the painful reality of the match, but they would make the rational decision. And in the household there would be surprise. There would be jubilation. She was ready.

She spied an envelope on the floor. It had been slipped under the door. She must have stepped over it when she entered the room. Her name was on it, and it was in Neelkanth's handwriting. Of course. He was leaving. Perhaps it was a note listing out the exercises he wished her to complete in the textbook before he returned.

But this was no list.

'I was encouraged when you said you would miss me,' said the letter. 'How do I express myself? I am not a painter who can paint the colour of his soul on to canvas nor a poet who can twist your soul with mine in one or two lines. So this letter must suffice. If you think favourably of me, let me know by any sign you think fit, and it will give me the courage to approach your father. If this letter finds no favour with you, then tear it up and I will never mention it to you again. When I return from Madras, I trust the matter will have vanished from your mind, and that you will have forgiven me. Your nature is too good and innocent to hold it against me, I know. I have very little to offer you. But I will make something of myself in time, and strive to make you happy.'

Her eyes filled with tears. And she realized that she had been pulled into the darkness before she could step into the circle of sunlight that was waiting for her.

CHAPTER 63

1952

He opened his eyes. Again, the same view: cream-coloured ceiling, white fan rotating quietly. He must have fallen asleep. He sat up, put on his glasses and reached for the brown leather folder that lay on a table beside his bed. Old letters. He liked rifling through old things these days, replaying some of the old episodes. Some of it he had forgotten. It was always a surprise coming across a letter, from Dada for instance, of which he had no recollection. It was like reading it anew, as if it had recently arrived in the post from Dhangadh, as if Dada had penned it just a few days ago. Whenever an old letter created this illusion—whenever he allowed it to create this illusion—he was enveloped by melancholy and a hollow, tugging feeling behind his belly button as if the past were pulling him backwards. Or as if the dead, including Dada and Radha, were pulling him forwards. Willing him to join them. Sometimes this was a comforting thought. At other times he recoiled from it and clung to his life.

What if, one of these days, he closed his eyes and found that he could not open them again? What would it be like to fall willingly into slumber and find that one had, in fact, died? Would he realize it, a corner of his brain trying to drag him back into the reality of his bed, while his body began to shut down like the light bulbs being turned off one by one in an empty house? Would dying be a process or a pinprick in time? Perhaps he was, in fact, in the midst of the dying process: this lying in bed day after day, a sore throat one day and stiff muscles the next, this descent into eating birdlike quantities of food, this desire to sleep, to rest.

He ought not to mind. All the pieces of the puzzle had fallen into place. All except one.

Kamal.

A story half-told, even to himself. If he could write a letter to Kamal it would be about a story that had run its course, with no neat ending. Where would he send such a letter? No matter. He would compose it in his head. It would stay buried in his own skull, for there was no one on this earth to whom he could talk about Kamal. And so he must talk to himself. He must tell himself that old story, untangle the knots that remained. Dear Kamal, he would write, what is this concept of love? When you and Shinde fought alongside each other, saved each other from the jaws of disaster, ran hand in hand to leap over streams and mountains and caves, we called it love. People bought tickets to see it. How easy we made love seem! But when I loved you, I was chasing a silhouette—a mirage, shifting about just outside my field of vision. When I turned to look at it, it reappeared elsewhere, always just out of sight. It was the shadow of a wisp of a dream. What were we doing, and what did we expect would happen? It was outside the limits of my imagination. It could not be. Yet, the sun rose anew whenever I was in your presence.

And what did you want? I do not know. For I never asked. Desire bound us together. A shuddering sensation of life and love running in my veins. An unspoken understanding. Something about forever. And something about never. I felt something ethereal multiplying within me, my soul perhaps. And what did your soul endure? I do not know. For I never asked. Forgive me, Kamal.

A phantom letter.

But he had written another letter, two decades ago, a real one, to help her. It was in Bhalerao's pocket when the director left Rising Sun Films and journeyed with bag and baggage to Kolhapur, to join the Prabhat Film Company. There is hardly any need for this recommendation, Tatya had written in that letter, for Kamal bai's achievements on the screen are clear to all. She has excelled in silent films and I have no doubt, he wrote, that she will shine in talkie pictures as well. He urged the company to put her on their payroll of actresses.

After that, he kept expecting to see Kamal's face splashed across some newspaper advertisement or the other, featuring in the latest Prabhat production. But there was no advertisement, no mention of her in the press. Then he put it down to production delays due to the Prabhat Film Company's move from Kolhapur to Poona. When he slept he dreamt he was on the train to Borivali. It chugged on at a furious pace for hours while he stared out of the window at a landscape that was now barren, now leafy jungle, now lit by stars, now humming with rain, and then he turned to see that the presence by his side was Kamal. She was translucent, he could see right through her, she flickered in and out of focus, a ghostly fragment.

The dream visited him several nights in a row before it vanished.

Then, after almost a year, he had received a letter from Bhalerao.

Later that day—or perhaps it was the following day, for often one day folded into the next with little by way of distinction or demarcation—Tatya found it among the sheaf of papers in his brown leather folder. He read it as he sat up in bed, leaning back on a mound of pillows. Bhalerao's handwriting in precise blue ink. Always respectful towards Tatyasaheb. Tatya could not, even after Kamal's confession about the real state of affairs between her and Bhalerao, hold any ill will towards him. I would have been a hypocrite to have done so, he thought, as he held the letter in his hands. He looked not at the words on the paper, but at the shape of the letters, the length of the sentences, the composition of the whole on the page. He fancied he saw Bhalerao himself in these clues: as charming as the curlicues of blue ink, as matter-of-fact as the short sentences, as clear-headed as the ample spaces between his lines, a man confident about his place in the world. Now he wrote not as Tatya's employee, but as a film director at the Prabhat Film Company, immersed in the new technology of sound. A man moving on a different trajectory. He was talented, he deserved it. But he should not have lost track of Kamal. He, of all people, should have been heedful of her.

'I hardly know how to express this,' Bhalerao wrote, 'but I am afraid that Kamal bai is now seen as too old for a lead role. Nor does her voice appear to any good effect in the few trials they have conducted. She is not used to speaking while acting, and though she trained as a singer in her early years on stage, she is out of practice. There are other actresses here who have trained continuously over years to reach a level of musical proficiency which Kamal bai will not be able to achieve. In short, her voice is simply not suited to make the switch from silent pictures to talkies. So far she has been able to get some minor roles at Prabhat. However, she left Poona several months ago without leaving any forwarding address. Unless she contacts me, I am afraid I have no way of tracking her down. Perhaps she has gone to explore opportunities with some other film companies that are still producing silent films, though I doubt they will remain in business for long.'

A story with no ending. It yawned open like a black space into which he could not shine a light.

Tatya shut the brown folder and glanced at Aru who sat on the cool terrazzo floor tiles of Tatya's bedroom, for it was a hot afternoon. Tatya liked to have him there, messing about with his Meccano set.

'What are you building?' enquired Tatya after a while, looking at the clutter of nuts and bolts, axles and metal strips and pulleys.

Aru held up a half-built model. 'I'm building a tank,' he said. 'Did you see any tanks during the war?'

'No,' said Tatya, 'but there were ack-ack guns lined up along Marine Drive, their barrels pointing towards the sea.'

'On Marine Drive?' said Aru, surprised. 'But that's where the cricket matches take place. At the Hindu Gymkhana and Parsi Gymkhana.'

'Well,' said Tatya, 'in those days, instead of cricket matches there were guns.'

'Why were they pointing at the sea?'

'The British thought that the Japanese might attack us. And if they did, they would come across the Arabian Sea.'

Aru digested this fact for a moment, and then said, 'Aai says that I was born during the war.'

'That's right. You were born in 1941, in the middle of the war.'

'What was it like? Apart from the ack-ack guns pointing at the Japanese?'

'It was rather unpleasant,' said Tatya. 'I lost a friend in the war, you know. His name was Schmidt. Once he brought me a beautiful fountain pen from Germany. I still use it.' He thought, with grief, of Schmidt's infectious smile and bushy golden mane, his gigantic frame, his big brown boots, his magnificent mechanical oddities. Years ago, he had received a final letter from Schmidt from his new home in Dresden. Later he learnt that Dresden had been bombed to smithereens by the Allies.

'But what about in Bombay? What was it like here?' said Aru. Stories of unknown German friends held no fascination for him.

Tatya roused himself to try and provide an interesting account for his grandson. 'It was a time of night-time blackouts, you know,' he said. 'We had to cover window panes and car headlights with black or brown paper. So that the enemy wouldn't see us from the air. There were air-raid sirens. Sand bag barriers appeared around the city. And I'll tell you something interesting about Krishna Nivas, the building just next to Greenglades. The third floor was taken over by British Navy officers who practised signalling to ships at sea. Royal Air Force planes conducted practice flights in twin-engine propeller planes, flying low over the city. I even wanted to build a bomb shelter at Greenglades, but in the end it was not necessary.'

'Who won the war, Tatyasaheb?' said Aru, listening avidly.

'Don't you know that by now? Hitler lost the war. The British and the Allies won.'

'And then? What happened after the war?'

'And then...well, then the British left India. Two years after the war ended, India became independent.'

'Oh I knew that. I had forgotten. My teacher told us, the British won the war but lost the empire.'

'Well said,' smiled Tatya. Aru began fiddling with his Meccano set again. He had lost interest in the subject of the war and the old days. Those momentous years held no relevance for him.

Of course, sooner or later everything became irrelevant, thought Tatya. Even the things which had once seemed eternal had come to an end. Like the British, with their grand edifices and their Sir Francis Wheelers dotted about the country. Who would have thought that the British would finally up sticks and leave? It had been an illusion of permanence after all. Everything, he supposed, might very well fall into that category. Like the long afternoons on the Jamshedji Mansion terrace that would mellow into the soft glow of lanterns brought upstairs to beautify the evening. It had seemed as if those afternoons would go on forever, repeated week after week, folding in on themselves infinitely, forming an evergrowing wad of cooling afternoons, something physical that he could gather up and put into his pocket. When Murari whispered secrets in his ear amid the bee-like buzzing of the market it had seemed as if Murari would be there forever by his side, like an omniscient genie; Zaveri only a few steps away leaning comfortably on his bolster. Both men were long gone now, Zaveri dead—it was almost twenty years since he had attended that funeral—and Murari vanished into thin air on the day of the Hindu–Muslim riots of 1936, never to be seen again in the market.

As for Kamal, she had passed from his life like a moon obscured, blotted out by a cloud that threw the shapes of all things into shadow.

Tejaswini Apte-Rahm

CHAPTER 64

1933

Radha remained seated among the dirty plates and teacups after Tatya left the living room. Everything was still, save for the late afternoon breeze which rolled in through the large windows. I am sitting, she thought, among rose-patterned upholstery, silverware, Persian carpets, fine window casements, all the inert, foolish things that make up my home. These things are now revealed to be hollow. Durga will be a widow, and this truth makes everything else a worthless lie.

She rose to her feet. Birds chirruped in the garden, and the sound made the hairs on her neck stand on end. The breeze touched her forehead and a clammy perspiration broke out across her skin. She began walking to the door, aware that something had shifted in the air. The sunlight was a miasmic yellow, the floor tiles under her bare feet felt hard and foreign to her soles, the steady ticking of life had slipped, changed its rhythm.

She found herself walking towards the rooms at the far end of the mansion. A self-contained suite of rooms which overlooked a quiet corner of the garden. There was a bedroom, a small sitting area, a bathroom, and easy access to the kitchen. This was where Mai set up whenever she visited, arranging her meagre store of religious texts and clothes and ayurvedic tonics in the cupboard. Radha found Mai seated in her favourite chair by a window. She was threading beads on to a string. She looked up as Radha came in.

'I see that the grand people have left. I saw them going off in their car a while ago,' said Mai.

Radha nodded, mute.

Mai held up the beads. 'I found some glass beads. I'm making a necklace. I doubt anyone will want to wear it, but you never know,' she said, her mouth twisted. The years had raked hundreds of lines across her face, but her pale, stone-grey eyes were the same. She cast a steady gaze on Radha. 'You've been crying,' she observed.

Radha drew the curtains, throwing the room into semi-darkness, and sat down. Mai frowned, looked mystified. Radha's head had started throbbing and the light hurt her eyes. She did not have the courage to tell Mai the outcome of the royal visit. And yet, there was nothing more she wanted right now, than to tell Mai everything.

So she did.

And Mai let the necklace of beads fall from her hands, and they both watched as the blue and green beads rolled this way and that across the cool, speckled tiles.

'The question,' said Mai, eventually, her pebble-like eyes fixed on Radha, 'is whether it is better for Durga to remain unmarried, or marry a prince knowing she will soon be a widow.'

Radha spoke as if in a daze. 'She will be a princess. They do not shave widows' heads in their family. She will be looked after for the rest of her life. She will be the mother of princes. And yet....'

'Yes,' said Mai. 'And yet.'

Radha had no more words and simply stared at her mother with dry eyes. 'Doesn't she...deserve better?' she whispered.

'After all that I have endured,' said Mai, with a weary smile on her lips, 'how can you ask me that question? If there is one lesson I hope I have imparted to you, it is that a woman must die before her husband. You, Yami, must die before your husband. You must be cremated with your forehead ablaze with red kunku. That is the way to die. A widow has no dignity even in death. A married woman is cremated with rituals of honour and respect, but a widow's body is simply covered with a coarse cloth and burned.'

Radha nodded, blinking back tears. She felt like a small child again, crushed under her mother's grief. Mai's enduring lesson was that she must die before Tatya. She knew that. Mai had made sure that Radha knew it not simply as a bald fact, but as a hard knot entwined with her soul. She must not risk being widowed. She must not take upon her head the horror of seeing her husband's lifeless body, and wiping the kunku off her forehead, and passing into a life that existed only in hues of grey and white. She must not be like Mai. But could it be that this was Durga's destiny? For how could it possibly be right to let her remain unmarried?

'You say that these people are progressive, and that they do not believe in shaving the heads of widows,' continued Mai. 'But they are rulers. They can afford to behave how they like. But what about their subjects? What about the men and women who work in their palace? Do you think that the rulers can dictate beliefs on such matters? The people will point fingers

Tejaswini Apte-Rahm

at Durga. There goes the shameless woman who will not shave her head even though her husband is dead. There goes the woman who clings to her youth and shows herself in public. They will whisper behind her back. And others will deliberately whisper loud enough for her to hear. It is believed that it is unlucky to see a widow's face first thing in the morning. A person setting off on a journey will postpone leaving if he crosses paths with a widow at the time of departure. Why would people suddenly discard such beliefs? Mark my words, Durga will not be able to participate in pujas and religious rituals. Palace festivities will be closed to her. You say she will be the mother of princes, and will therefore be treated with respect. But have you considered what will happen if she gives birth only to daughters?'

Radha gave a start, for this had not occurred to her.

Mai spoke in harsh tones. 'A widow with sons has at least some merit in the eyes of the world. But one who has produced only daughters is worthless. If that happens, what will be her standing in a royal family that wants, above all else, an heir? Do you think that woman in her pearls and chiffon saris will forgive her daughter-in-law? No, she will accuse her of hastening Jaikumar's death.'

Mai continued, 'When I went back to my father's wada as a widow, holding Raghu by his hand and with you in my belly, people said an unlucky shadow had darkened the house. They said I caused my own father's death by returning home. And that is what I taught you never to forget. Do you remember?'

'Yes,' said Radha, in a low voice. 'I remember. A widow is inauspicious. Unlucky. Unwanted.'

'Not because that is what I believe,' said Mai, her voice unexpectedly soft, 'but because that is what the world believes. And because that is the fate of every widow.'

'I must go to him,' said Radha at last.

Mai nodded. 'Yes,' she said. 'Go find your husband.' She sat staring at the blue and green glass beads scattered across the floor, a small, bent figure wrapped in red cloth, as her daughter's footsteps faded away.

Tatya was in his bedroom mulling over the royal visit. Why had the Rajesaheb begun the meeting by talking about the sugar factory when it was clear that he really wanted to talk about the marriage proposal? It occurred to him that the sugar factory was a sort of sweetener. The Rajesaheb had eased his way into a thorny subject by speaking of something that Tatya would be comfortable with, something that would excite him. Talking about the sugar factory would create the sense of a business alliance, a context for the hoped-for family alliance.

In spite of himself, Tatya was impressed by the Rajesaheb's skill in conducting the difficult conversation in the living room. He was an honourable man, thought Tatya, for it would have been all too easy to conceal the true state of his son's health to find him a wife.

Radha came in. Her eyes were swollen and her face was pale. For a moment they simply looked at each other helplessly. Then she spoke.

'Tell them,' said Radha, her voice hoarse and cracked. 'Tell them to go back to their palaces. We can look after our own daughter.'

He looked at her in silence. Then he went up to her and placed a hand on her head.

He had turned down alliances for Durga in the past. He had refused to send her back to Girgaon to live in a chawl, no matter how respectable the groom. Nor would he send her to a rural family, however prosperous they might be, to pick her way through fields and feed cows and buffaloes. And now, against all expectations, she had received a proposal from a fine royal family, an offer to live a charmed life. But he would not marry her to someone who was condemned to die a young man. Even if the suitor was a prince.

He would not be the author of visiting that calamity upon her head.

'Where is Durga?' he said, quietly.

Radha gave him a watery smile. Then she turned and walked out of the room as if she were afraid that Tatya would change his mind.

From the bedroom window, Tatya saw Radha go into the garden. Durga was on the lawn, sitting on a bench, a book on her lap. The eternal English textbook. It was months since he had seen Durga without it. She would have time enough on her hands, now, to persevere at it. His chest felt heavy at the new reality to be confronted. Hopeless, now, to think it would be any other way. His daughter would never know the happiness of married life. He saw Radha approaching Durga and sitting down beside her. He saw the backs of their heads. They were deep in conversation, the two women he loved.

All at once, Durga stood upright, and began limping towards the house. He heard her steps on the stairs. Was she coming to talk to him? He went to the door of his bedroom and waited in anticipation. Perhaps she would be disappointed that she had been robbed of the chance to be a princess of

Tejaswini Apte-Rahm

Sonpur. But she was still young: she could not fathom how short ten years could be, nor what it would be like to lose a husband she had come to love. And Tatya stood there, at the door of his bedroom, waiting to soothe her, explain things to her.

But when she reached the top of the stairs, she did not notice him standing there. Indeed, she did not even glance in his direction. Her steps took her to the little room further down the passage, away from his planter's chair, away from him; she limped away down the sun-dappled corridor and Tatya had the strange sensation that he was watching her slip out of his reach. She stopped at the spare room. The small spare room which was sparsely furnished and often used as an office space, the place where, he knew, Neelkanth was sitting at this moment. She stepped towards the open door of the room; and looking in, she flashed a smile of such beauty and happiness that Tatya's breath caught in his throat.

CHAPTER 65

1952

It was his birthday. Durga had insisted on preparing a feast to mark the occasion.

'Are you out of your mind,' he said, 'to celebrate the birthday of a seventy-year-old man?' His voice was hoarse, for he had caught a bit of a cold. It hurt him to swallow.

Durga looked stubborn, standing in front of Tatya's bed with Aru next to her. She was a wily one, thought Tatya, bringing Aru with her. It was a wonder she hadn't brought along her twelve-year-old daughter, Chhabi, and Sharad's daughter, Kumi, as reinforcements. Kumi was just a year younger than Chhabi and the two girls were constantly together whenever Durga and her family were in Bombay.

'Do you mean to say that you don't want all of us to eat the wonderful delicacies I have planned?' she said.

'Eat all the sweets you like,' countered Tatya, 'but for god's sake don't make it about my birthday. I'm not a child.'

'But do it for the sake of all the children in the house, Tatyasaheb,' said Durga. 'Everyone is so keen to celebrate your birthday.' Aru nodded and smiled charmingly at these words.

Tatya frowned at him. 'Are you a puppy, that your mother snaps her fingers and you wag your tail?'

Aru giggled.

He knew why they all wanted to celebrate his birthday. It was because it would be his last one. He sighed, and closed his eyes.

How long ago it seemed now, his worry that Durga would remain alone and unmarried. And here she was, a mother of four children. He wondered whether he had kept a copy of the letter he had written to the Rajesaheb, surely one of the most tortuous letters ever written. He could remember some parts of it word for word, even after all these years. No wonder, for he must have rewritten it fifty times before settling on the final version. 'It was a great honour to receive you and the Ranisaheb in our home. I thank

404

you for doing me the honour of proposing marriage between Jaikumar Raje and my daughter. I do not need to tell you that I have the highest esteem and regard for you and your family, and therefore it is with great regret that I must convey to you that we do not think the match a suitable one.'

Or some such convoluted lines. He couldn't remember the whole thing.

And the sugar factory? An opportunity turned down in the same letter, for he understood well enough that the marriage and business proposals were tied together. He had been determined, though, not to miss the sugar boom entirely: he knew something about the gathering of nectar and the storing of sweet things, after all. (Even now he had a bee-buzzing soul, though the hum grew ever dimmer.) He had bought large and valuable shareholdings in two new sugar businesses, including the Gulwadi Sugar Factory where Neelkanth later found a position as chief engineer. Gulwadi was a bit too far for his liking—six hours by road. He didn't like Durga living so far away from Bombay. But she had set up house in a fine bungalow there, built in the modern style. He and Radha had visited the couple often, revelling in the fresh air of the countryside and the strange, still beauty of the acres of sugarcane plantations. There had been hurda parties in the winter—excursions to nearby farms where cobs of young, green sorghum or hurda were roasted by the farmers and the grains mixed with lemon, salt and chilli powder—and cool pitchers of sugarcane juice in the summer.

He wished he could do it all again.

The entire family gathered for lunch, dressed in their finery. All for the sake of his birthday. At the appointed hour, they came to his room and bent down to do namaskar to him one after another, smiling as he blessed them. He was touched by their regard and affection. What a brood of children and grandchildren he and Radha had managed to raise! For he quite thought of Mandar and Shalu as his own children. Here came Mandar with his wife, Kusum. He remembered seeing Kusum for the first time at Radha's haldi-kunku on the terrace in Jamshedji Mansion, a fair girl in a nauvari sari, so chubby-cheeked that she looked like a baby swaddled in silk. Now she was a brisk matron, still rather rotund, with three children. Her eldest, Malti, had married the previous year, and Tatya was gladdened to see that Malti had made the effort to come to Greenglades today from far-off Parel. How are you getting on, he asked her, and when she said that everything was splendid, he hoped it was really so. For in his experience, women often said that everything was fine, even when it wasn't. Next came Mandar's younger boys, Milind and Mukund, to do namaskar to Tatya.

Then Sharad and Suruchi, and their three boys of seventeen, fourteen, and twelve—Balu, Khandu, and Dilip. He never saw Sharad's boys without a racquet or a bat or a ball in their hands. They had a way of filling up a room with their long arms and sturdy bodies. Mad about sports, just like Sharad. All itching, no doubt, to run out on to the lawns of Greenglades and start a game. And here was their sister, Kumi, Sharad's youngest child.

'Tatyasaheb,' said little Kumi of the big eyes, 'Chhabi and I are wearing matching clothes for your birthday, look!' And she dragged Chhabi forward, wearing an identical blue parkar-polka.

'Both you girls look mighty fine,' he said, a bubble of joyous laughter in his mouth. Chhabi, Durga's youngest daughter, was just like her mother, with her thick dark plait dangling to her waist. Now Durga pushed forward her two older daughters, Indu and Saroj, both in college, and no sign of their parents looking for a suitable match.

'What, you two still here? Not married yet?' His usual gruff joke when he saw the two girls: always well received with a giggle and a titter. There was no point trying to persuade Durga and Neelkanth that the girls were really getting rather old. Both parents were unanimous in their determination to put their daughters through St. Xavier's College. The two girls had taken up residence at Greenglades for this purpose, while their parents and younger siblings lived in Gulwadi.

And finally, here was the formidable Shalu, almost fifty years old and head nurse at Dr Patwardhan's Maternity Clinic. With her, the twins, gangly young men who loped in on long limbs. Bhaskar, the steady one, with his bank job; and Nandu, gregarious and quick-witted, who worked as a journalist at the *Times of India*. The children called him Newspaper Nandu, the cheeky rascals.

Greenglades was now a mansion filled with young people, doing the things that young people did nowadays. How joyful Radha would have been to see the house filled with laughter and activity. For the young people constantly laughed. He couldn't ever remember himself, as a young boy, guffawing or collapsing into peals of laughter the way they did. Indu played cricket in college, he was reliably informed, though Durga apparently insisted that she play wearing a sari. Sharad's and Mandar's seventeen-year-old boys, Balu and Milind, were allowed to go off on picnics to Khandala with their school mates, a group which, Tatya was taken aback to note, included unchaperoned girls. At seventeen, thought Tatya, I was scampering up and down Zaveri's backstairs to the mezzanine floor, fetching cloth samples and getting an earful from the gumastha.

He felt, sometimes, that the globe didn't rotate calmly around the sun year after year, but that it rolled along like a marble, out and away, careering along crazy and wondrous paths, leaving behind entire eras to settle as dust. And it was marvellous, really, that it should be so, he thought. What new highways and thoroughfares would these children traverse?

He distributed envelopes of money to the children as he blessed them, affectionately patting the younger ones on the head as they bent down in front of him. In the end, he enjoyed his birthday celebration tremendously. The pièce de résistance, engineered by Durga and Suruchi, Sharad's wife, was the grand entrance of a silver tureen of aamras, and a platter of freshly made mango vadis cut into stolid squares of a burnt-orange hue. Everyone cheered and clapped and laughed on seeing the look of utter amazement on his face.

'Mangoes in January?' he said, in astonishment.

Durga's look of triumph was a sight to behold, and his shoulders shook as he started chuckling, aware that he was the target of some delightful joke. A dozen voices then competed to explain it to him, and finally he understood that the miracle was thanks to the new General Electric refrigerator-freezer he had imported from America a year ago. Apparently, one could freeze food in it for months. Durga had conspired with Suruchi, all the way back at the height of summer, to freeze large quantities of mango pulp for precisely this occasion. Well, well, it was a brave new world that could offer mangoes in January. If only Radha could have enjoyed the meal with him. By the end of the mango-themed birthday celebration, he was rather proud to note that he had managed a large bowl of aamras, three puris, and even a couple of pieces of the mango vadis. In his view, the thing that was worth celebrating was not the fact that he was still alive, but that he hadn't lost his taste for mangoes.

CHAPTER 66

1935

Tatya was away in Ahmedabad. Sharad had gone to Hyderabad. When the post came, it lay in a pile on a table in the living room, unattended. Two days later the pile had grown much larger and had turned into an untidy pyramid. Radha decided to organize the envelopes and put them on the desk in the corner of the living room. A wedding card, an invitation for a thread ceremony, newsletters from charitable organizations, bills, a letter from Dadasaheb in Dhangadh, some governmental envelopes for Sharad. She sorted them all out, one pile for Tatya and another for Sharad. Then she came across a small cream-coloured envelope with Tatya's name on it, written in an unfamiliar hand. It was slim and delicate and had been hidden under a sturdy, official envelope. She flipped it over, and on the back it said 'Kamal'. The return address was a guesthouse in the Fort area.

She put it on top of the pile of letters for Tatya and stood looking at it for a while. She picked it up and stared intently at it, as if she might be able to see through the envelope and read the writing inside. She put it down again. Then she left the room and went upstairs to Durga's bedroom.

'Where is Neelkanth?' she asked her. Durga was playing with her one-year-old daughter on the bed, gently tickling her tummy and laughing at her toothless grins. The maid hovered nearby with her clothes. Little Indu had just had a bath.

Durga looked up. 'Aai, see what a funny expression she makes when I tickle her nose!' Durga was already regaining weight, for she was pregnant again. Her face looked full and content. Like a lovely moon, thought Radha. Why had that letter come in the midst of this busy, happy time?

'Durge, I'm looking for Neelkanth,' she repeated.

'He is in the office room, studying,' she said, looking down again, intent on her game with her baby. 'He'll leave for college soon.'

Radha nodded, and made her way to the room which was formerly used as an occasional office space, but now used mainly as Neelkanth's study. He sat there in the early mornings and in the evenings with engineering textbooks and exercise books filled with his notes and diagrams. Neelkanth had no family of his own to take Durga home to. It was a sensible, if unorthodox, decision that he should live with his wife's family for now.

She looked into the room and saw that he was gathering up his notes and papers. She had caught him just in time. But how was she to broach the subject?

'Aaisaheb?' he said, his eyes looking at her in that slightly unfocussed way he had after being immersed in his books. He had acquired glasses within the last year which gave him a rather professorial look. Radha liked it very much. She was proud to have a learned son-in-law.

'Neelkanth, I have made some saboodanyachi khichadi. Come and have some before you leave,' she said. This was not the reason she had come to find him. But she couldn't think of what else to say. She felt rather hesitant, as if she were going behind her husband's back. But the letter had made her...what? Afraid? Nervous? Confused?

He looked at his wrist watch and readily came with her, saying that he had time to spare and would have some tea with his khichadi as well.

Radha hurried on towards the kitchen, calling out to Uma bai to pour some tea from the big pot boiling on the stove. She settled down with a cup herself, though she didn't particularly want any.

'So your final exams are only weeks away,' she said.

Neelkanth sighed. 'Yes. I'll be glad when they are over.'

'Your work is very different compared to what you used to do at Kohinoor Theatre.'

'It certainly is,' laughed Neelkanth. 'But I also miss it sometimes. I learnt a great deal from Tatyasaheb.'

'You are far beyond that kind of work now,' said Radha, brushing aside his words. 'But still, you do sometimes go to see films with your friends. I can't imagine why.'

'It's just timepass, Aaisaheb,' said Neelkanth, putting spoonfuls of the spiced sago and peanuts in his mouth. 'A good way to relax. You remember how entertaining some of them were when you used to watch the films at Jamshedji Mansion.'

'I watched them because they were our own productions. Now that Rising Sun Films has closed down and Kohinoor Theatre is also sold off, I don't find anything of interest in all that.'

Neelkanth nodded, as if he understood what she was trying to say. He continued eating and taking sips of his sugary tea. Radha observed him. Then she said, 'We had invited Bhalerao to your wedding. But he couldn't come. There is hardly any contact with him now. His wife was a nice lady. I wonder if she is happy in Kolhapur.'

'In Poona,' Neelkanth corrected her. 'Prabhat Films have shifted their studio to Poona. So that's where Bhalerao and his wife will be now.'

'I see,' said Radha. She hadn't known this fact. 'And...what happened to that actress? Kamal bai? Is she at Prabhat Films too?'

Neelkanth shook his head. 'Not as far as I know.' Then he looked puzzled. 'You know, I never really thought about it. I haven't seen her in any bioscopes since Rising Sun Films closed down. Neither in Prabhat films nor in any other ones. I wonder why. She was very talented.'

'And very beautiful.' The words escaped her mouth before she knew what she was saying.

Neelkanth looked at her with a smile. 'Yes. That too,' he said.

'So you have no idea where she is?' said Radha, choosing her words and her tone carefully.

Neelkanth shrugged. 'No idea. Why do you ask?'

'One wonders sometimes where people go,' said Radha. 'What paths they take and why.' Neelkanth had nothing to say to this. He took a last gulp of tea in a motion that indicated he agreed with her entirely, and that it was now time for him to leave.

She felt guilty about having prodded Neelkanth for information. It seemed manipulative, asking him careful questions while he innocently went about eating and drinking. But she needed to understand the motive behind Kamal writing that letter to her husband. Why was she in a guesthouse in Bombay? Which decent woman stayed in a guesthouse in the first place? What could she possibly want, more than three years after the closure of Rising Sun Films, and two years after Kohinoor Theatre had been sold? The family had nothing to do with the bioscope business anymore. She had no right to contact Tatya. A suspicion entered her mind—had she and Tatya been in touch all this while, without Radha's knowledge? Perhaps this wasn't the first letter that Kamal had written to him, after all. Radha never looked at Tatya's post. She had only looked at it today because neither he nor Sharad were in Bombay to look at it. Immediately, though, she berated herself for thinking badly about her husband. For to admit the possibility that he and Kamal corresponded with each other, was to admit that he might have a hidden motive for doing so. No, he would never do that. She went back into the living room and looked at the letters she had arranged on the desk. One pile for Sharad, one for Tatya. And the cream-coloured envelope, posted by a lone woman in a guesthouse in Bombay.

Greenglades rose up above her, sprawled out around her. In the garden, Kusum, heavy with her second child, played with her daughter under a tree. Suruchi was finally pregnant. She spent her days resting on the cool balcony outside the bedroom she shared with Sharad, embroidering one handkerchief after another. Radha could hear Shalu's twins getting ready for school. Shalu would be fussing around, feeding them, before she made her way to Dr Patwardhan's clinic in Girgaon. She had earned her nursing diploma and was a part-time nurse at the clinic. Durga had dodged a cursed fate and risen like a soul reborn. Sharad, Mandar, Neelkanth, Tatya, the men of the family were all busy in their respective endeavours. Festivals came and went, the seasons rolled by. They all had full, busy lives.

And in the midst of all this, the letter. What was the point of this letter in the world that she and Tatya had built up together? At best, it might be an inane attempt to keep in touch, a mere enquiry as to Tatya's well-being. For old times' sake. Or it might be that this letter would pull Tatya back into the world of bioscopes, one way or another. The same world that had robbed Shalu of her husband and had created in herself a bitterness about Kamal bai's beauty. It was years since she had thought of it. But now she remembered how she had felt as she sat huddled in a corner of the living room at Jamshedji Mansion while Kamal bai danced and smiled and stretched her limbs with abandon on the walls of their home. She had a vivid memory of a scene where Kamal bai was riding a horse. She galloped on the horizon, across an endless and barren landscape. Her dark curls streamed out behind her. Radha remembered watching, mesmerized, as Kamal bai reached the edge of the frame and galloped out of it entirely, as if she had vanished through the wall of the apartment and taken a leap into thin air, continuing her gallop above the city lights, through the night, constrained by nothing. Kamal bai could go anywhere, do anything, smiling bewitchingly all the while.

CHAPTER 67

It proved unexpectedly easy to put the letter out of her mind—though it did gnaw at her for several days. But slowly it slipped so far away from the happiness of the day to day that it became irrelevant. The next few years at Greenglades were full of the joy of faltering baby steps, the prattle of toddlers, first days at school, and continual pregnancies. Radha was at the centre of it all, supported by the implacable Uma bai and the new maids hired to look after the growing contingent of children.

Shalu's twins, the oldest of the lot, took the lead in organizing riotous games on the lawns, and were followed around adoringly by all the younger children. Mandar, now a senior engineer in the railways, had a daughter and then two sons. And though Radha loved Mandar and Shalu as dearly as her own children, she felt a special elation in welcoming Sharad's first child, a baby boy named Balu.

'Barely had I caught my breath,' Radha would say in later years, 'when Balu was followed by Khandu, and Khandu was followed by Dilip.' It was a story she loved relating to her friends, glowing with pride at having a daughter-in-law who produced three grandsons in quick succession. Indeed, by the time her third grandson, Dilip, came along, Radha was so jubilant that she insisted on distributing gold chains to the entire household staff. Tatya needed little persuasion on that point. She knew that three grandsons were enough to make any man's chest swell with pride.

Durga, on the other hand, gave birth to three girls in a row. Radha was perplexed to observe that neither Durga nor Neelkanth seemed to mind the lack of a son. But in the end this turned out to be merely the prologue to an even better story that could be told and retold: how they all laughed when Suruchi, after three boys, finally gave birth to a girl, and just a few months later, Durga, after three girls, finally gave birth to a boy! It was a fine tale, guaranteed to raise laughs of appreciation from Radha's listeners, as she endlessly repeated it at weddings, at haldi-kunkus, at thread ceremonies. When Durga's son, Arvind, was born, creating that strange and perfect symmetry between the two sets of cousins, he immediately became Tatya's favourite. He was, after all, the youngest of all the children, and Tatya had no qualms about announcing to all and sundry that Aru was the best and brightest child he had ever seen. Radha sometimes reproached him for this blatant partiality, but nobody in the family really seemed to mind. For who had the time, in those days of endless sunlight and maternal fecundity and the patter of childish feet, to sulk or be at odds with anything or anyone?

Even when Neelkanth was appointed chief engineer at the Gulwadi Sugar Factory, a six-hour drive away, and Durga joined him there along with her four children, Greenglades was hardly any quieter: it was still a house full of nine children of varying ages, while Durga made sure that she and her children spent every school holiday and festival at Greenglades. Mai, though older and slower, continued visiting Greenglades for weeks at a time. She was known to be rather disapproving of the sheer number of children that Greenglades had managed to produce, but readily participated in everything in her customary crotchety manner. As the small girls got older, progressing from frocks to parkar-polkas, they would sit with Radha, Kusum, Suruchi, and Durga, learning what the older women had to teach them about filling karanjis with sweetened coconut at Diwali, and making spiky sugar jewellery at Gudi Padwa. Tatya and Sharad took the entire platoon of children to the pedhi for the Lakshmi Puja, while Bhau Beej was an occasion that demanded an extraordinary degree of organization, given the number of brother–sister combinations to cater to. At Holi, the children would collect all the fallen branches and leaves they could find in the grounds of Greenglades to make a fine holi fire under the large tamarind tree, and Radha would give them all a coconut or a one-paisa coin to throw into the fire. There was always a reason to gather for gossip and old stories, always an occasion to dress up and prepare hand-churned ice cream flavoured with saffron and cardamom, or shrikhand made in such abundance that it was poured on to plates rather than served with a spoon.

It was 14 August 1947, late at night, when the spell broke.

The large Grundig radio was given pride of place in the centre of the Greenglades living room and they had all gathered around it. A light monsoon rain pattered down gently over the dark garden. The older children, the ten- and twelve-year-olds, were still awake, excited to be up so late but unable to stop themselves from rubbing their sleepy eyes. Milind had his arm around his younger brother Mukund, propping him up to prevent him from falling asleep. Their mother, Kusum, hovered near them. Sharad's sons Balu and Khandu remained resolutely upright, as if to prove that they were adults. Durga's girls, Indu and Saroj, perched on the low windowsill with their mother and Suruchi, their aunt. The men, Sharad, Mandar, Neelkanth, and Tatya, sat solemnly in armchairs directly in front of the radio. Across the airwaves came Nehru's speech anticipating India's independence at midnight, his earnest voice filling the room.

Standing behind Tatya's chair, Radha's eyes were intent on the radio, trying to imagine the momentous scene of the speech being played out in faraway Delhi. And then she noticed Tatya slump in his chair. He slid down in his seat, his shoulders sagging, and he put a hand to his face. Then he put his palm on his head as if to soothe a headache. But the next moment he sat up, squaring his shoulders. Mandar, sitting right next to him, hadn't noticed a thing. But Radha saw Tatya's fingers scrabbling for the arm rest and clutching it as if it would slip away from him.

And she saw with a shock that his fingers were wrinkled. Like an old man's.

When they settled down to sleep late that night, the bedroom windows thrown open towards the dark sea, she said, 'What happened?'

'Eh?' said Tatya, frowning at her, already reclining on his pillow and half asleep.

She sat next to him, on top of the bedclothes, making no move to get under the sheets herself.

'In the living room,' she said. 'You didn't seem well.'

'Nothing happened,' he said, closing his eyes. He lay very still, on his back. But she could tell that he was more alert now than when he had settled into bed. He was deliberately keeping his eyes shut.

'But I saw you,' she said. 'You slumped in your seat. Did you feel dizzy?'

'Tired, I suppose,' he said, his eyes still closed. It was obvious that he wanted her to stop talking.

'It didn't seem that way to me,' she persisted. 'Your shoulders...it didn't look right.' He made no reply. He had fallen asleep.

Radha felt tears rise in her throat. She sat looking at him in the dim yellow light. She could not forget the scrabbling motion his fingers had made on the armrest of his chair. As if something was falling away and he was trying to hold on tight. She could not tear her gaze away from her husband's still, prone form. The ghastly thought overtook her that this was how he would look when he lay dead. She squeezed her eyes closed to shut out the thought. When she opened them again, she found herself examining Tatya closely. The years go by and stop us from noticing each other, she thought. He is old. How did my husband suddenly become old? His face looks brown and wrinkled. On his neck the skin lies loose. His lips have thinned and look dry. His crumpled fingers, clutching the sheet on his chest, are fragile. She held up her own hands and looked at them. They too were the hands of an old person. What else did she expect? She was fifty-six.

And Tatya was sixty-five.

A new country is born tonight, she thought, but our time is coming to a close.

The next morning she confided in Shalu. Shalu had not been in Greenglades the previous night, for she had been overseeing a complicated delivery at the maternity clinic. But when she heard Radha's description of Tatya's symptoms, she went straight up to him and informed him that she was calling for Dr Kelkar. Tatya had little choice in the matter and, indeed, when the doctor arrived, he seemed to lose the will to feign ignorance.

'I'm rather weak this morning,' he confessed as he lay on his bed. Dr Kelkar sat on a chair, a stethoscope in his ears, listening to Tatya's chest.

'What did you feel last night?' the doctor said, frowning. Radha stood by the bed, anxiously observing the doctor's movements. She felt that Tatya was avoiding looking in her direction.

'I felt a sort of tingling in my arm, a numbness,' said Tatya. Still he wouldn't look at her.

The doctor nodded, wrapping a blood pressure device around Tatya's arm. He began rapidly squeezing at the attached rubber bulb in his palm. It made a gasping, panting noise, an alien sound of sickness. 'And?'

'And a sharp pain behind my eyes,' said Tatya. 'I found I had suddenly slid down in my chair, with no idea as to how I got into that position. But it was probably just tiredness. It was only for a moment, after all.'

The doctor took out a pad and started scribbling on it. Then he looked up at Tatya and said, 'I don't think it was just tiredness. It may have been something to do with your heart.' He smiled at Radha, as if to reassure her. 'At our age it is best to be careful, eh? Take complete rest for a week, Tatyasaheb. Stay in bed, eat light meals. And take these tablets.'

Tatya finally looked at her, meeting her gaze with his soft brown eyes. A smile, a nonchalant shrug, as if to say nothing much was the matter. But he looked tired. She gave him a small smile too, though her insides shrivelled with apprehension.

She felt a curious change come over her in the following days. A feeling of distance from the activity of daily life. As if time had begun slipping away so fast that the things around her—the four-poster bed with white sheets neatly tucked in at the corners, the shushing of the waves as they broke on the black rocks by the shore, the smooth ochre tiles of the corridor outside the kitchen, the moist smell of the red earth in which she had planted ladyfingers, and even her own face in the dressing table mirror—as if all these things had already passed into scenes of remembrance, a story to be told by someone else to strangers. When she was in the same room as other people, she felt as if she wasn't really there, but merely peering in through a window at an old scene that had already taken place in the past. Unaccountably, she thought of the old silent productions of Rising Sun Films. As if her own life, playing out on a screen, had been marred by a rip in the fabric of the screen and shown to be an illusion, a play of lights that had started a slow process of dimming.

Needle-sharp shards of fear lay perpetually lodged in her throat. The slide into old age has begun, she thought. The heart that pumps life to the rest of his body has grown old. She did not want to lose him. She did not want to be a widow. Not like Mai. No, never.

How stubborn her husband was. How unwilling to accept this reminder of his own mortality. How annoyed and brusque when she tried to convince him to spend fewer hours at the pedhi, cut down his visits to the mills, to slow down, to let Sharad take over the business entirely. To rest.

When he was at home she contrived to be as near him as possible, watchful for any sign of fatigue, any twitch of his muscles, any sagging of his shoulders, or weariness in his brown eyes.

She meditated, taking up the practice to calm her fretfulness. It was hard at first, and her mind wandered this way and that, like an errant child or a tired old woman too aged to learn new tricks. She found a quiet corner of the garden, a small stone seat by a wall, over which twisted heavy, laden creepers of a deep crimson bougeanvillea. Here she sat early in the mornings, the new balmy sun touching her forehead, and late in the evenings when the moths fluttered against her cheeks. Here she closed her eyes and brought into her mind's eye the image of Ganpati. She imagined that he was waking up along with the sun: she made assiduous preparations to bathe him. She laid out a low chaurang, on which he took a seat, sitting cross-legged and expectant. Gently she rubbed oil on his body, and fragrant utne paste. He remained immobile, as still as an idol. But she sensed that he was well pleased. He was a small Ganpati, a baby really. She mixed curd, milk, honey, sugar and ghee, and poured a small quantity of the sacred mixture on his head. And then she poured silver tumblers of warm, soothing water over him to wash it all off. She patted him dry with a soft cloth, admiring the magnificence of his curling trunk, the span of his ears, his healthy rotund belly. She dressed him, on some days in soft cotton cloth, on other days draping heavy embroidered silks over his shoulders. Next, dabs of rich sandalwood paste on his arms and on his chest. A garland of mogra around his neck, and bracelets of parijat blossoms tied to his wrists. *With these offerings, I worship you.* She took pleasure in stringing together the small white flowers one by one, to the calming rhythm of shlokas murmured under her breath.

When he was dressed in fine clothes and flowers, she served him food in a silver platter on which were arranged small mounds of aromatic dishes: vegetables and pulses, rice and koshimbirs, puris, chutneys, and savoury bhajis. *I serve to you the very same food that you have provided in your beneficence.* Every day she varied the menu, serving, for instance, different kinds of rice: vaangi bhaat with aubergines, tondli bhaat with ivy gourd, batate bhaat with potatoes. The sweets varied too: basundi, aamras, jalebi, modaks, different kinds of ladoos. And to close the meal, always a cooling scoop of rice mixed with curd. Close by, so that he could reach it easily, she placed a silver tambya of drinking water, and lit incense sticks to wreath him in scented smoke. And then Ganpati prayed, and sprinkled water around his silver platter, and when he began to eat, a holy joy filled her. After the meal she poured water over his fingers to wash them. Then she offered him the fruits of the season, peeled bananas or soft, creamy figs, bunches of pale green grapes or wheels of pineapple. She gazed at him as he ate.

After his meal she bedecked him in all manner of jewels, till he looked like a king: a noble crown, a necklace shining with diamonds, golden arm-bands emblazoned with emeralds, and ruby rings on his fingers. She strewed the ground at his feet with flowers: hibiscus and parijat, frangipani and chrysanthemum. Finally, a bell ringing out in one hand, and a lamp ablaze with yellow flames in the other, she recited aartis, worshipping Ganpati. He had come alive in her mind as she sat on the stone seat in a corner of the garden, meditating, her eyes closed, her lips unmoving. The two of them, together, breathing life into each other.

She stilled herself in this way. She was calm. She was unhurried. And she prayed: don't let my husband die. Let me die first.

CHAPTER 68

1952

The country was in the midst of its first election. Bombay had already voted. Of course, Tatya had not been well enough to go and vote. He was annoyed at this. It was obvious that Nehru would win, but he would have liked to cast his vote into the fray in any case, a vote for the winning side. Outside his window, across the great old city of Bombay and across the country, a churning that had begun many years ago appeared to him to be in its last throes. Surely after this set of political speeches and rallies and splashes of newspaper headlines, the country would settle into a sort of calm, a golden age. He couldn't tell whether he was being prescient or foolish. The violence that had brought all of them to this point in time must, surely, beget peace at last.

'You voted for the Congress, didn't you?' he asked Durga, who sat sewing by his side. It hadn't occurred to him to ask her before.

'Naturally,' she said, without looking up.

He grunted in approval. He lay in bed, his unshaven chin resting on the cool blue sheet that he had drawn up to cover himself.

'If only your mother were here to see this,' he said.

'She would have liked to vote,' said Durga. 'Do you remember how we all sat and listened to Nehru's speech the night before Independence Day? Aai used to follow the newspapers so keenly those days. But the shock of seeing Mai...' Durga exhaled quietly. 'I wish she had not seen it.'

'I am glad *you* were not here to see it,' said Tatya. 'Of course, Gulwadi was no better. Thank God you escaped.'

But it was a mystery to him where God had been in the last days of January 1948 when Gandhi was murdered. The last words to leave his lips as he fell to the ground were 'Hey Ram'. But Ram was busy elsewhere that day. So were the hundreds of other gods that the country prayed to, day in and day out. Sometimes Tatya thought of gods as being on-duty and off-duty. There were months when they all seemed to take leave en masse. The months of disaster before and after Independence were a case in point. Not content with the slaughter of Partition, the country added Gandhi's murder to the tally. Followed by yet another round of killing and destruction, as if the cycle would never end.

And the scenes from Gulwadi appeared in his mind, raising goosebumps at the nape of his neck. So vivid was Neelkanth's description, that even as Tatya had strained to hear his son-in-law's voice crackling over the intermittent phone line, it was as if he had been a witness to the events himself, impotent and trembling. Mobs of men out to take revenge on Brahmins, for Gandhi's killer was a Brahmin. Neelkanth's assistant in the sugar factory, Kulkarni, had been dragged out of his home and beheaded. Neelkanth's dash to Kulkarni's house, a watchman in tow, a single rifle between them. The mob was frozen, Neelkanth told Tatya, as it stood around Kulkarni's headless body and the blood-soaked earth, staring down at its handiwork in shock and a sort of simmering triumph. *In that moment they were quenched...a few seconds more and they would have turned on me...I screamed at them to stand back...the watchman, terrified, pointed his rifle wildly this way and that...a single twitch of his finger and another man would have lain dead...Kulkarni's wife, screaming and vomiting...I think they did it in front of her...I managed to drag her and her son back to our house... Durga and the children locked in there....* He could still hear Neelkanth's ragged voice, the exact phrases he used, the clammy chill in his own chest as he thought of Durga and the children trapped in Gulwadi amid roaming packs of men. And because the factory owner was a Brahmin too, acres of standing sugarcane set alight, the factory's machinery attacked with hammers, the sugar godown ransacked, the sacks of sugar slashed open and left to the rats and birds.

'I could not fathom, at the time,' said Tatya, 'why Mai chose the day of Gandhi's murder to travel from Poona to Bombay. What could have possessed Raghu to let his mother set out on that day? Later he told me that the news hadn't reached them before she left. When the rioting began she was already on her way.'

And who could have imagined the scale of the violence? An old and great man had been shot—surely it was a time to mourn, not to go rampaging through the streets after innocents? And Mai had arrived in her car surrounded, as usual, by a miniature cornucopia of fruits and vegetables grown on her own little plot of land: pumpkins and figs and custard apples and coconuts and bags of ladyfingers and beans and tomatoes, all for Radha.

They were all used to seeing Mai arrive at Greenglades in this style. Except this time, her driver was racked with sobs, barely able to breathe, the whites of his eyes a ghastly pink, his face streaming with tears. He had somehow managed to drive the car upto Greenglades, dented and scratched, its rear window smashed with a rock. Mai sat at the back, her eyes closed, looking as if she were merely resting, but for the gash of blood at the back of her head where the rock had struck. The car had been stoned mercilessly by a group of red-eyed men; they were drunk and sobbing, the driver said, when he at last managed to speak.

And Radha had dashed out of the house, down the marble steps, and gone running along the driveway, for the driver had lost his courage as soon as he entered Greenglades, and simply halted the car at the top of the slope that led up from the road. Radha took one look at her mother sitting amongst the bloodied vegetables, and fell to the ground in a faint.

'Your mother never recovered from the shock,' said Tatya, staring up at the ceiling. 'That is why she contracted tuberculosis. She never got over the shock, though she lived for many months with the illness.' Why was he telling Durga all this? She already knew it. But there was a comfort in reciting old stories to each other.

'One day she told me,' said Durga, 'that Mai's death reminded her of how frail we all are, of how old the two of you were. I said, Aai, you are not old, you are younger than Tatyasaheb. And look at him, he still oversees the business at the pedhi and at the textile mills. She brushed aside my words. She told me you would continue working till your last breath, no matter how old you were.'

Tatya smiled weakly. He could not dispute that assessment of his character.

'Mai used to warn her again and again to never become a widow,' said Durga. 'She wanted to go before you. And she got her wish.'

Tatya felt his head pressing slowly back into the bed, as if his pillow were pulling him in, his head a heavy and inanimate object. He blinked back tears. Yes, you got your wish, he thought. But you did not give a thought to what I would feel like, left behind, on my own. The memory kneaded itself against the inside of his skull, a deep and physical pressure. He took a long, ragged breath, and when he let it out, he found he was whispering words to Durga.

'She was in a delirium at the end. I don't know whether she realized what she was saying. Her eyes were unfocused, yet they rested on my face. She said she saw the sickness as a gift from god. She spoke in a feathery, rasping voice, a voice that seemed to live on the tip of her tongue, because the rest of her body was too weak to house it. Her cheeks were sunk against her teeth, her body was shrivelled inside her blouse. I did not take care of myself, she said. Her eyes kept wandering from my face to the window. Again and again she looked at the window as if someone was waiting there for her, or coming in for her. Stop talking, I said, you will tire yourself. But she would not stop speaking, she wanted to use her last few breaths to create words. Sometimes I woke up in the middle of the night, she whispered—there was a ghoulish smile on her face as she said this—and I bathed in cold water. I lay down again without drying myself, though I shivered and trembled. Sometimes I lied. I said I did not want to eat, though my stomach craved food. You all looked after me with care. But I did not want to get better. I want to die a married woman, my forehead ablaze with red kunku. I do not want to be like Mai. Not like Mai, no, no, no, she said. Her neck was as thin as a twig, as if the final bit of her breath had been squeezed out of it along with the last words she would ever say to me. And I…I cannot wipe away the memory of that ghastly smile on her face as she spoke. It torments me, Durge.'

He saw Durga leaning over him, her eyes wide. It was almost three years since Radha had died in the summer of 1949. But he had not told Durga before about his last conversation with his wife. He had not told her that when Radha slipped away, the afternoon sprawled outside like a hot, still desert of dead and dying things.

CHAPTER 69

1949

There was the sound of surf pounding on the black rocks. There was the spray of salt water under the hardy coconut trees clustered by the shoreline. The stretch of light brown sand was strewn with washed up pebbles and seashells. Further inland, a broad, leafy road ran along the length of the seashore, lined with bungalows and mansions, their roofs, terraces, and gables visible among the foliage. One mansion stood out amongst these, for it was built on a small natural hillock that looked out to sea. The tree-filled grounds of this mansion habitually attracted flocks of bright green parakeets. Often the young parakeets were easy prey for the kites that roamed the sky, the majestic span of their brown wings dipping and soaring with the wind. Now, high up above the grey-green sea, a kite gave a single lazy flap of its wings, and then turned its hooked beak towards the mansion in a soundless, ferocious dive. There was a green flutter of small wings just outside the bedroom window, and then silence.

In the bedroom stood Tatya, his back turned towards the window and the dusk. In front of him, the giant four-poster bed, twice the size a married couple needed. He was struck, for the first time, by the absurdly enormous proportions of the room. He looked down at the floor, covered in mangoes. A carpet of mangoes. And crates of mangoes stood stacked up by one wall too. Their heavy, sweet, drowsy scent filled the room utterly, the fragrance ripening and expanding in the warm air so that it seemed as if the room might burst at the seams. It was all for his wife. Tomorrow was the thirteenth day since her death. In the morning there would be rituals, priests, and a crowd of family members and close friends. His mind had fixated on the thirteenth-day meal, when it was customary to prepare a sweet dish that was a favourite of the person who had died. It had to be aamras, it was imperative that everyone ate their fill of it. What would he have done had she gone not in the summer but in the monsoon, or winter? Neither his lakhs of rupees, nor all the will in the world, could have produced this fragrant carpet of hapus and pairi mangoes.

422

His sense of self had remained the same over the decades—till the day she died. His body had aged, his responsibilities had changed, but he had still felt a sense of youth, a sense of sameness, as if she were keeping time at bay, like a resolute boulder blocking it from flowing by. But now that she was gone, that terrible reservoir of time had turned into a torrent, crashing by him, and within a period of twelve days, all their decades together had emptied into the sea. Now all that was left was this mansion, these mangoes, and a flutter of wings at the window behind him.

In the darkening room, as the evening breeze from the open window brushed against his bent neck, came that unspeakable thought again, the one that made him feel like he was being strangled: her body had wasted away, infected with tuberculosis, but her mind had been active. Which was why, in her last days on earth, she had betrayed him.

She had made the decision to leave him behind. To go on ahead, to hasten her own passing because of her deep and abiding fear of widowhood. Even though nobody would have compelled her to shave her head, or wrap herself in a red sari, certainly not in Bombay at any rate. But Mai's life of suffering and abstention had placed a hard, black terror in her heart. Mai was apt, in her old age, to mournfully foretell her own impending demise; *at this age*, she used to say, *you really cannot tell*. And after Mai died, Radha had started parroting those words. 'At our age,' she would say, referring to herself and Tatya, 'nobody can be sure of anything.' It became her catchphrase to express her worry about every little thing. If Tatya was late coming home, she would stand at the balcony overlooking the driveway and the garden, watching for him. On other days, in the late evening, she wandered across the lawn towards the slope of the hillock: he would see her dark silhouette among the dangling roots of the banyan tree, waiting for his car. She became anxious about all things, significant and insignificant, after the day she had seen her mother motionless and bloody on the back seat of the battered car. She started scanning the newspapers obsessively. A mill strike, a political rally, monsoon flooding, every little thing caught her attention and made her question Sharad and Mandar relentlessly—was it safe to go out? Perhaps it would be better for Tatya to stay home today? Why drive to Gulwadi in the pouring rain? Why risk the treachery of the ghats? Why, when we have enough of everything? She waited, fretful, for letters and phone calls from Gulwadi, from Durga and Neelkanth. When Tatya was diagnosed with diabetes and started giving himself insulin injections, she stared in horror at the needles and syringes that appeared in the bedroom. When Tatya caught a particularly nasty chest infection, she was beside herself with worry, staying up nights by his side even when he was asleep—was it simply to watch him breathe? And then she had fallen ill herself.

He was bewildered that he had to strain to remember, now, the minutiae of the long days of her illness. Details that were ingrained into the hours of the day, and had imposed a new regime of sickness and silence in the house for months, had suddenly evaporated as surely as Radha herself had vanished off the face of the earth. The daily visits of Dr Kelkar with his shiny black case full of vials and tubes. The hired nurse supervised by Shalu. The trays of food fit for an invalid, carried upstairs. The constant quiet hum of activity around Radha's sickroom, not far from Tatya's own bedroom, as Shalu and the nurse did everything they could to ease Radha's weakness and discomfort.

What a sleight of hand, Radha, to be able to deceive two alert nurses. I underestimated you, he thought, as if talking to her directly; as if she lived, now, among the mangoes on the floor where his eyes rested. He remembered her tired, wrinkled cheeks in the months of her illness, her religious texts and pothis by her bedside, her expression oddly resolute even though her body diminished a little more with each passing day. 'She is determined to get better,' he had told Sharad confidently, trying to lift up his son's—and his own—spirits, when all along it had escaped him that she had been determined to die.

CHAPTER 70

A month later, Tatya still did not have the heart to go through Radha's things. Her possessions remained in the bedroom. Her saris were stacked neatly in her cupboard. Thin cottons of mustard yellow and pale green, glowing silks of crimson and indigo. The saris smelled of fragrant khus, for among her clothes Radha had stored little muslin pouches filled with the aromatic grass. In a drawer lay some green glass bangles, a couple of keys, a comb, a half-empty packet of incense sticks. In a small wooden cabinet, some books, assorted magazines, newspaper cuttings; he peeped inside before quietly shutting its door again. He touched nothing. Her carved Kashmiri toilette box was stowed away on a lower shelf of another cupboard; it had been put there months ago, shortly after she was diagnosed with tuberculosis. All her things were still in it. Her bottle of hair oil, the box of red kunku for her forehead, a vial of rosewater, a handkerchief. The golden rose for her hair must still be in its little concealed drawer. Inside were things last touched by Radha's fingers. When he finally opened the box and touched the things, would it be as if their fingers were meeting?

'Tatyasaheb,' came Durga's voice at his bedroom door. It was late evening. 'Shall I turn on the light?'

He opened his eyes and was surprised to see how dark it was. She flicked the switch on without waiting for him to answer. He must have fallen into a light, exhausted sleep. He was seated on his bed, leaning back against a pillow, his glasses upturned by his side.

'I think in another day or two I should return to Gulwadi,' she said. 'The children's school....'

Something heavy dropped inside his chest. He didn't want her to go. He depended on her presence the way he had depended on Radha's presence. She had been at Greenglades for months now, through Radha's illness. Neelkanth visited often. Her children, Indu, Saroj, Chhabi, and Aru, had been temporarily enrolled in a school in Bombay. But now that arrangement must come to an end.

'So soon?' he said, after a pause, blinking in the yellow brightness.

'Do you want me to stay? I'll stay if you want.'

'No. No. You must go to your husband, of course. But....'

'But?'

'Stay just another few days,' he said. There must be some excuse for her to stay, something that needed to be done. Then it came to him. 'Look through your mother's saris. Sort them out. Give away whatever you don't want. Sort out her jewellery too.'

She nodded. 'Of course,' she said. 'I thought you didn't want....'

He took a deep breath in, and slowly let it out. 'I didn't want to do it so far. But...it's not healthy to live in this state of suspension. We must move on. There is no point in all her things being here, unsorted, untidy.'

'What about her other things?' said Durga.

'I'll look at the rest,' said Tatya. 'There are some books and papers of hers in that cabinet there.'

Durga took another step inside the room. 'Will you be all right when I return to Gulwadi?' she said.

He looked at her sweet, concerned face and had the urge to weep. It was too still, too silent outside the darkened window. Not a breath of air, and the sea becalmed. He nodded. 'I'll see you in Gulwadi soon,' he said. 'I could spend more time there, perhaps. Sharad will look after things here.'

She smiled broadly, then, and said, 'Do you think you would like to live permanently in Gulwadi? In the fresh air? What is there for you to do in Bombay, after all? Sharad already looks after most of your business here.'

How like Durga, to be carried away by enthusiastic ideas. She reminded him of a small bird spreading its wings in a high wind. He shook his head. 'Greenglades is my home, and so is the pedhi at Mulji Jetha Market. So is Khatryachi Chawl, come to think of it, and Jamshedji Mansion. And the mills. I could not live away from all this. Some of it I created, some of it created me. Here I must remain. Here I must work.'

'Also, I think I'd miss the sea,' he added, after a moment. 'And I like to think that it would miss me too. We have things to say to each other, the sea and I.' He smiled, as if to tell her not to take his whimsical words to heart.

'I thought you'd say something like that. But I'll wait for your visits.'

'And I'll wait for yours,' said Tatya. 'Every school holiday.'

'Every school holiday,' she promised.

He delayed looking into Radha's cabinet till after Durga had returned to Gulwadi with the children, and a sudden and new quiet had descended on his heart. But while she looked through the cupboards, he had sat perched on the bed, observing her. They exchanged quiet comments with each other, like 'That was the sari she wore at the first haldi-kunku at Greenglades' and 'She always liked this colour'. Suruchi and Kusum came to help too, but they maintained a respectful distance from Radha's things, only picking up or touching things when Durga asked them to. When she asked them to sort out a large pile of assorted pieces of cloth, they sat on the floor, working rapidly. They separated out pieces that could be used to sew something from pieces that were too small to be of much use. Tatya simply sat and watched them. After a day or two he began standing at the door to the balcony overlooking the sea, puffing on his bidis, now looking at the open water, now looking inside to see how the women were getting on. As the shelves and drawers emptied out, he felt better. It felt good to see the wooden shelves wiped clean, the few remaining things rearranged neatly.

On the day that Durga left Bombay, he went back to work.

He went to the pedhi, met with his merchants, received a warm welcome at the market along with condolences. The next morning he visited Rose Mills. Matthew Wales had returned to England shortly after India declared independence, barely two years ago. The British management of Imperial Industries were still in the process of returning home; a few old hands remained, intent on quickly finalizing new arrangements of ownership and shareholding. The person who replaced Matthew Wales was Ram Sapre, a capable fellow trained by Wales himself. It was Ram Sapre who now received Tatya at Rose Mills. On the third day Tatya visited Noor Begum Mills and also went with Sharad to the New India Mill which he co-owned with Altaf Shahpurwala. Back at the pedhi he sat with Sharad to get a full overview of cloth deliveries, payments, and new products and weaves on the market.

He eased himself back into his routine, invited Nana and Joshi and other old-timers from Khatryachi Chawl to come to Greenglades as before, for a Sunday game of ganjifa when they sat holding the round, brightly painted cards in their hands till the sun began sliding into the sea. He stopped by at the chawl too. Lele mavshi had died years ago, and so had Dattopant Apte, the lawyer. But Nagesh Godse and Jagannath Lele and some others were still there. The chawl was more crowded nowadays, and noisier. He ran into Ponkshe too, now the owner of the Hanuman Vyayamshala and a string of other gymnasiums across the city; he was known for organizing high profile wrestling matches between participants from competing mills.

At home, now and then, he opened the door of Radha's small wooden cabinet, extracted a few papers, put them back without looking at them. It was months before he finally got around to examining the contents properly. It had poured down for days, and on the Greenglades hillock the wind caused a wailing tumult. Tatya could taste salt on his lips as if the sea had mingled with the rain to create a salty mist that crept over the city. Alone in his bedroom, lit by a yellow bulb even though it was early, he sat thumbing through his copy of *The Pickwick Papers*, the one that Dada had gifted to him decades ago. He missed Dada. It was almost five years since he had died. The thin pages of the book had soaked up moisture and were damp; some of them had taken on a greyish mouldy hue. It occurred to him then that he ought to look at Radha's papers before the mould got to them. The instinct to avoid her things had receded. He felt he might be up to the task now.

He dragged a chair over to the cabinet, sat down and opened the door. The cabinet was so low that he had to lean over considerably to reach inside.

He pulled out a sheaf of papers. There were letters from Mai to Radha, written on thin blue paper. He put them in a separate pile and decided to go through them later. There were old newspaper cuttings of Sharad's victories in club tennis tournaments that had been reported in the local press. There was a cutting about his gymkhana cricket team winning an important match. Another one about Sharad captaining the Elphinstone cricket team and winning an inter-college cup. He paused over these. He did not know that Radha had kept them. He imagined her using her sewing scissors to cut out the little boxes and rectangles about her only son, carefully putting them away in her cabinet. He felt sad and guilty. He had never made much of Sharad's sports tournaments, dwelling instead on his minimal interest in business. He could not relate to his son's lack of ambition, but Sharad had done no wrong. He worked conscientiously, had never caused a loss to the business. His only fault was that he didn't want more. Tatya felt he should apologize to his son, but knew he would not. Sharad was a grown man, he had children of his own. What purpose was served now, by these clippings from his youth? But he would keep them aside and hand them over to Sharad.

He reached into the cabinet and brought out another handful of paper. A pile of women's magazines. A booklet of knitting patterns that was so old, its binding had fallen apart. He threw the magazines and pattern book in a wastepaper basket. More letters, several from Durga written after she had moved to Gulwadi. A dog-eared photograph of Durga, Neelkanth, and their first baby. He gazed for a moment at the picture and placed it on his bedside table. Perhaps he would get a frame made for it.

Then a small, thick diary emerged, and in it was Radha's handwriting: measurements for blouses and frocks, the odd household list of provisions. He held a wad of pages between thumb and forefinger and let them flip back rapidly with a low whirring sound.

A small cream-coloured envelope fell out on to his lap. It was stamped and addressed to him. Yet he had never seen it before. He frowned. What was it doing in Radha's diary? He turned it over and saw that it was still sealed. And then he read the name of the sender.

CHAPTER 71

Dear Tatyasaheb,

Where shall I begin? For days I have wondered whether to write to you at all. I began letters, tore them up, threw them away, began new ones. I do not yet know whether I shall complete this one, and if I do, whether I shall send it to you. I regret that our last meeting was an unhappy one, for I was sad and afraid at the time. Why am I writing to you? Do not expect a window into my soul. This letter is not that. It is simply a request for money. I know I must be among many others who ask you for money, you must be used to it. When you came to the studio to tell me that you were closing down Rising Sun Films, you had offered to send me a sum every month, for I had used up all my earnings to keep my brother quiet. I refused you then, for I could not bear the idea of being supported by you month after month. That is not what I wanted our relationship to be. I will explain why.

The years that I worked at Rising Sun Films I count as the happiest years of my life. I was free of my brother. I could work and be proud of my work. The thrill of riding or climbing, dancing or leaping is not something that daily life offers to anyone at all, except the lucky few who do so in front of the camera. I will not lie: I also enjoyed being beautiful. I would have been happy enough with the life of freedom and work that the film company offered me. When Bhalerao approached me, I did what I thought was expected of me, which then merged into a desire similar to putting food in my mouth to satisfy my hunger.

Your presence, however, made everything different. The days became more real, in a wondrous way. As if I had been in a dream before, and woken up under a sun that was yellower, the outlines of things clearer. The nights were a cooling blanket, the rain was a shower of pearls, the very salt in my food danced on my tongue. I would wait for your visits to the studio, though your visits were too few as far as I was concerned. I was honoured and astonished that though you were the owner of the film company, and I was a mere employee, a dancing girl of the stage, you spoke to me as an equal. Speaking to you was to feel elevated, as if I could accomplish great things, though I did not know what they might be. I wished to be yours. I also knew that the wish was a foolish one. You were too honourable to do or expect what Bhalerao did and expected.

But you are also too honest to deny what passed between us. Nothing happened. And yet, everything did. When we were together, we were happy. It is a simple emotion, happiness. It is easy to recognize. I felt there were small colourful butterflies inside me, flapping their fragile wings, always about to take flight towards I knew not what destination. When we spoke, you understood my meaning even before I finished expressing myself. I discovered that I could say witty things and make an intelligent man like yourself laugh. What a revelation that was! I began reading. I had paid little attention to magazines and newspapers before but now I actively looked for them when they arrived in the post at the studio. I felt I could improve myself, be better, and all because you showed me that I was equal to you. And so, I did not wish to take a monthly sum from you, for you owed me nothing. Taking it would have curdled the love and friendship between equals. I would have become a creeper, the kind that entwines with a tree, becomes enwrapped in its leaves, its flowers resting their petals on the broad branches. A pretty creature, but a dependant one.

What a strange woman Kamal is, you must think! Why, then, does she write me a letter asking for money!

Let me tell you what happened after I left Rising Sun Films. In a word, I failed. Your letter of recommendation to the Prabhat Film Company was well received. But when I spoke into their recording machine my voice sounded hoarse, peculiar, and devoid of emotion. I couldn't believe my ears when they played it back to me. They said my pronunciation was all wrong and that my singing showed that I had not had much classical training. All true. They did not lie. The actresses that were already employed by them were younger than me, and yet more accomplished in the way they acted and spoke. Talkie films need dialogues, not endless action like silent films. But I was of no use for I had never learnt to deliver a dialogue. They took pity on me and filmed a few trial scenes. Perhaps she will sound better when she acts in front of the camera, they thought. But no. When I tried to speak and act simultaneously, I was like a child learning its first words. I was not used to it. I could not remember the lines. I was like a doll trying to be a human being. And, in contrast, how fluently the other girls spoke, while expressing a range of emotions on their faces. How confidently they sang and enunciated lines, and how young and fresh they were!

Would you believe, Tatyasaheb, that the heroine of your hit pictures like *Jungle Queen* and *The Princess Caravan* has, in the talkies, played a bystander, a serving girl, one among a clutch of dancers? Bhalerao could not assist me, for he was new himself, and trying to find a foothold with his new employers. After a year I could not bear to stay there. I heard that there was a film company in Madras that was still making silent films. I went there and acted in a silent film. Though I was not the lead, it was an important role. It took a long time to make the film for there were many delays. I stayed in Madras for more than a year. Filming kept starting and stopping as the company was constantly short of cash. Finally, when the film was ready, they could not find a theatre to release it in. All the major theatres had installed sound equipment. These theatres were not interested in silent films, and they no longer employed musicians to provide the musical accompaniment either. Eventually the film played briefly in a couple of small theatres in Madras, and then the reels were sold to some rural touring bioscope company. There was no more work for me.

I returned to Bombay a year ago, and rented a small room in the Shri Ram Guesthouse. I have a hidden talent, Tatyasaheb. I can sew. I found work with a dressmaker in Bombay who makes costumes for theatre companies. I work on golden zari and brightly coloured silken robes, the kind I used to wear myself. Sometimes I pass your beautiful mansion, up on a hill, half-hidden behind so many green trees, and I wonder what you are doing there. I like Bombay. It is a good place to hide in. But it is an expensive city, and a lonely one for someone who has no relations or contacts to fall back on.

I have an old aunt who lives in Poona, and I plan to go and live there. She too has nobody, and is poor. She goes to a few households everyday to wash clothes. I have little to offer her, but I think that she and I could make a comfortable home together. I have identified a small house of two rooms where she and I could live, and where I plan to open a tailoring shop and also give sewing lessons to girls.

Yes, I will have my own small business, Tatyasaheb! You know something of business, and I can see that you are smiling as you read this. But I am unable to do any of this on my present salary. I have no savings. And so I come to you with a request not simply for money, but for a business investment. Don't laugh, I beg you, though I have been known to make you laugh in the past. In short, I am in need of money to buy a sewing

Tejaswini Apte-Rahm

machine and to rent the two rooms for a year. If you would loan me the money, I can start a new life in Poona on my own terms, in my own house, in the company of someone I can call my own.

I feel certain that you will reply to my letter, even if it is in the form of a refusal. I will wait for your letter. Perhaps you will come to see me. I will wait for that too. Nothing would give me more happiness than to rest my eyes on your face again.

I am not in the habit of writing letters. Forgive me, for I do not know how to begin a letter gracefully or end it correctly.

Kamal.

CHAPTER 72

When Tatya came to the end of the letter, he read it again. And then again. How long had Radha kept this letter from him? It was undated; Kamal did not know how to structure a letter. She did not know that one must insert the date in the top right-hand corner. Her writing was patient and precise, a schoolgirl's handwriting in blue ink. This was not so much a letter as the start of a conversation. She was speaking to him, she might as well have been standing in front of him and saying the words while looking him in the eyes. Even while asking him for money she did not humble herself, she did not want charity, she wanted a business loan. He felt something swell inside his chest, an emotion that remained unnamed. She needed him. He must help her, he must go to her. The return address was Shri Ram Guesthouse. He knew the place, had often passed it on his way from Mulji Jetha Market to Rose Mills, a rundown building, meagre washing hanging in each balcony, the name of the guesthouse on an oversized board of cracked and peeling paint. That was where Kamal had lived. But she certainly did not live there anymore, for the place had closed down years ago. The board was still there, but the rooms were dark and derelict, broken glass in the windows. A black knot formed in Tatya's stomach. How long ago had this letter been written? He looked at the envelope again, at the postmark on the stamp. It was mostly a black smudge but when he tilted the envelope to the light, he could see the year written clearly enough. It was 1935. The letter had been written fourteen years ago.

Hands trembling, he clasped the letter to his forehead, and sobbed as if his chest would split into a thousand pieces. He cried because he wanted to explain it all to Radha, and he cried for Kamal's hopeless wait for his reply. Did Radha think he had betrayed her? So certain had she been that the letter was tainted that she had not even bothered to open it, had simply hidden it away. He wanted to hold her face in his hands and take her to his chest and stroke her head till her fears fell away, but it was too late. He would never know how long she had lived with fear and suspicion in her heart. Was Radha justified in keeping the letter from him? Would the letter have pulled him back into Kamal's orbit, so that he encircled her forevermore like a planet? Would it have revived that unnameable relationship, hard to define other than in terms of the simple presence of happiness and longing? But Radha had taken that decision out of his hands; she had chosen his path by hiding this letter. It was a strange thing to hold that letter in his fingers: it was as if he had arrived back at a timeworn crossroad—one he dimly remembered passing by on his journey through life—and the signposts of that crossroad now creaked in the midst of an old landscape, twisting and twirling in the wind so that their arrows all led everywhere and nowhere.

Where was Kamal now? How could he find her? What had she done after waiting endlessly for a reply to her letter? Had she managed to build a life for herself in Poona? There was no way to answer any of these questions. But wait—he would write to Bhalerao. He might possibly have some information about her. He had lived in Poona for years, after all, though he had now retired to Mahabaleshwar.

Later, when he sat down to write to Bhalerao, he felt a sense of foolishness descend on him. What was he doing? He was sixty-seven years old. Kamal had been about twenty-two years old when she had arrived at Rising Sun Films more than two decades ago, and would now be in her mid-forties. She might be married, have children, might be embarrassed at this sudden intrusion of the past into her present. Despite the absurdity of trying to find her—and what would he say to her, after all, if he did find her?—he wanted to tell her: my silence was not intentional.

But no, Bhalerao knew nothing. Tatya was none the wiser after reading the reply that arrived a few days later. Bhalerao had retired years ago; lived a quiet life; expressed a nostalgia for the old days when films were proper films, not the kind you saw nowadays; remembered fondly their days together at Rising Sun Films; but about Kamal, no, he knew nothing.

Tatya tossed Bhalerao's letter towards a table next to the planter's chair where he reclined, his legs stretched out on the leg-rests. But the letter missed its mark and fell to the floor, and Sadaa bent to pick it up. Sadaa constantly hovered around him these days, ever since Durga had returned to Gulwadi. Tatya suspected that Durga had instructed him to do so.

'I don't want you staying up here all alone in your room,' she had told Tatya before leaving. 'Continue your usual schedule. Go to the mills, take a walk in the garden in the evenings, talk to Sharad and Mandar. Visit your friends at Khatryachi Chawl.'

'Don't worry about me,' he had said, making light of her worry that he would be lonely and withdrawn. 'Sharad handles most of the textile business, but I stay up to date. The number of operational looms, the distribution networks, the queries of my wholesale merchants—ask me anything, this old man still knows it all. With help from the new gumastha, of course.'

'You have a new gumastha?' said Durga.

'Shanti Desai,' said Tatya. 'You've met him.'

'But he has been with you for ten years now,' she said.

True, but Tatya still thought of him as new; he jokingly called him the 'third generation' for he had been Kishan Mehta's third assistant before taking over most of Mehta's duties.

Tatya had no intention of stopping work. There was still much to be done. But Durga's prediction had been by and large correct: when he wasn't working, he spent more and more time alone in his room, or reclining on his planter's chair and looking out on to the rolling waves of the sea. At this age, he felt he ought to have some sort of overarching theory about his life. But it seemed like a giant jigsaw of random pieces, some of which fitted, some of which didn't. The boats he had wanted to launch had set sail long ago, making landfall on this shore and that, though not always where he'd intended. On some days the hours stretched out, elastic, as if the long arm of the afternoon sky held back the moon, preventing it from sailing forth and lulling the night to sleep. At other times the sun was a child's yellow marble flung into the sky, travelling in a rapid arc, dragging in the short, sleepless night by its tail.

Days passed. Radha's cabinet was cleared and cleaned. The few letters and books of hers which Tatya wanted to keep were returned to the cabinet in neat sheaves and piles which had very little to do with Radha. She would never have organized her things in this way. Tatya closed the door of the cabinet and did not open it again. He handed the sports cuttings to Sharad one day and gave his son a sudden hug, surprising himself as well as Sharad at this demonstration of affection. Kamal's letter he put in a drawer in his desk. It occurred to him that it was a love letter of sorts, the only one he had received in his life. He ought to destroy it. It must not be read by anybody else after he died, for it would create all kinds of complicated and unnecessary assumptions. But he could not bring himself to tear it up, because he had no intention of dying. There is time for that still, he thought. And so the letter remained with him like a raindrop suspended in the air, an ephemeral thing with no place to go.

Was it fate that Nana's telephone call came shortly after this? Why did it not come before he had discovered Kamal's letter, when it would have meant something else entirely? Why this particular order of events, as if time had decided to speed up, push him forwards, alert him to the possibility that the time for unfinished business had passed, that loose ends needed to be tied up?

The telephone in his bedroom rang. Sadaa went inside to pick it up. The line wasn't long enough to reach the planter's chair in the balcony.

'It's for you, Saheb. Nana kaka,' Sadaa said. Since Durga and Sharad called him Nana kaka, the name had stuck. Everyone in the house called him that now.

Tatya lifted himself off the chair, his muscles stiff, and walked slowly to the telephone. He felt better within a few seconds, but the painful joints and muscle aches were a new development which he resented.

'Nana?' he said. 'What's the matter?' It was not at all usual for Nana to call.

'Nothing is the matter,' came Nana's voice, a bit faint. The line crackled. 'I'll see you on Sunday as usual. But I thought you would be interested to know what I found today.'

'Found?' said Tatya. What could it possibly be, that could not wait till Sunday, he wondered.

'I was at the scrap dealer today,' said Nana, 'to sell him a large pile of old newspapers. While he weighed them, I noticed some flat round cans. Big ones. I wondered what they might be used for. So I go over to have a look, and what do you think I see on them?'

'What?' said Tatya, puzzled.

'The logo of Rising Sun Films!' said Nana, triumphantly. 'You know, the picture of the sun rising behind the hills! I thought, now there's something I haven't seen in years. I asked the raddiwallah, what are you going to do with these? He said that they contained old film reels, and that he was going to flog them. I said to him, I know someone who might be interested, and I'm going to phone him right now. His eyes grew round. No doubt he thought he could earn a good amount from someone who needed to be telephoned about it. And here is the best part. He said, if you want to view them, I have an old projector as well. Your friend is welcome to buy the whole lot, films and projector, I'll give him a good price!'

Tatya listened as if in a dream. Cans of Rising Sun Films—at a junk shop? It had, in fact, never occurred to him that the old films might have survived. Bhalerao and Neelkanth had handled the quick sale of all the equipment. He had assumed that Bhalerao might have kept a couple of the films he was most proud of, but as for the rest he had not enquired after them. He knew that many had already started disintegrating and had been thrown out; some had been sold to small bioscope touring companies, the kind that travelled in bullock carts and pitched show tents in small towns; and others, he remembered, had been stored in tall piles of cans in a room at the studio. Now they were doing the rounds of the junk shops it seemed. He wasn't sure how he felt about that. They were of no use to anyone now, of course. But they had once been a marvellous endeavour of creativity; and all at once the studio of Rising Sun Films appeared in his mind. He saw himself walking under the hefty banyan tree, admiring the still, green waters of the pond. He heard the rhythmic sounds of the muscular handymen spinning the gigantic reels of film through the solution in the developing tank. He saw the queer spectacle of dozens of actors in a procession of pink faces and green clothes; now he was in the special 'outdoors' truck, the name of the film company painted in large colourful letters on its side, as it rumbled towards the cool ghats or the pounding sea or the quivering jungles, carrying its camera and colourful crew crammed in at the back. All of that now sat in a few cans in a junk dealer's shop.

And could it be possible that those cans contained films starring Kamal? After all, she had been the mainstay of Rising Sun Films for half of the company's life span.

'Tatya?' came Nana's voice. 'Hello? Are you still there?'

'Yes, yes, I'm still here,' said Tatya. 'Listen to me. Tell that scrap dealer of yours that I will come tomorrow to see the films. Might as well have a look at them, eh? Is he the one at the corner of your road?'

'The very same,' said Nana. 'Ghanshyam Raddiwallah. I'll tell him. I can't come with you tomorrow but let me know what you find!'

Tatya didn't want Nana coming with him in any case. He wanted to go on his own.

CHAPTER 73

When Tatya arrived at the junk shop the next day he discovered that the owner was out, and had left his son in charge. The son was a sulky young man, clearly not happy about working in the dark old shop. The shop was crammed with old newspapers, dented utensils, broken toys, wooden stools, and piles of unidentifiable iron scrap, all fronted by a large rusty weighing scale and weights of various sizes. It was at the corner of a busy street with a tram line, bicycles ringing their way past the shops, the press of men going about their work and, at the far end of the road, the crowded chawl where Nana lived with his wife. Tatya's car idled nearby with Jagan the driver, now rotund and grey-haired, peering out curiously, bemused at the choice of destination.

The young man had disappeared inside on hearing that Tatya had come about the cans of film. When he came out again, he was empty-handed.

'Where are the films?' asked Tatya in surprise.

'Come with me,' said the man, and slouched off. Tatya frowned at the lack of courtesy, but followed him. They came to a small room adjoining the shop at the back. 'My father has put the films and the projector here. He told me to show them to you.'

The room held a single grubby chair. The window panes were dirty and the floor hadn't been swept in a while. Bits of straw littered the room and it smelled of some kind of overripe fruit. The young man got down to business. Now that he was here, his bored demeanour fell away, and he obviously wanted to get things over with. Tatya watched as he set up the projector in the manner of an expert, and asked Tatya to sit down on the chair. Tatya sat down and looked at the logo on the cans at his feet: an orange sun behind two brown hills under a faded blue sky. Three simple colours in a compact rectangle neatly outlined in black. Like a postcard from an old holiday. There was also the familiar red-bordered label where the film's title would have been inscribed, most of it torn off, obscuring the writing. But as soon as the film flickered to life on the scuffed wall of the room, the projector clattering and gasping, Tatya knew which film it was.

There was the riverbank in Nasik. Its water glistened. Kamal wandering

439

under the trees in the dappled sunlight, dressed as a princess. Kamal boarding her royal boat, festooned with fluttering silks. The good-looking, broad-chested Shinde on horseback waving a ridiculously long sword in the air. A phalanx of dancers with Kamal's graceful form at the forefront. Kamal leaping from a broad-branched tree on to the saddle of a horse. Was it really possible that he had forgotten what a creature of beauty she was? Rosebud lips, flawless cheeks, dark, silken hair, big-eyed emotions dancing across her face: the images pulled him backwards in time to her world of adventure, whimsy, desire. How easy it was to forget that it had all been created by light and lens and cakes of face paint. There were no accompanying musicians, and yet he heard faint echoes of music as she twirled around a pond alive with white swans. He remembered a stray shadow had fallen on Kamal during a scene in this film, when someone off-camera had stood in the wrong place at the wrong time. As if on cue, the scene, with its errant shadow, appeared on the wall in front of him. It was like glimpsing an old friend: it transported him back into Bhalerao's study, the director agonizing over it, for the mistake had been discovered too late, only after the film had been developed.

The reel ended. The young man put in another reel and it began unspooling its images on the wall. The scuff marks on the wall created scars on Kamal's face. Pigeons clacked their beaks against the dirty window pane of the room. Somewhere, a fly buzzed. And now a sense of desolation descended on Tatya. The film had been one of Rising Sun Films' biggest hits. They had made dozens of copies, he remembered, and sent the film to distributors as far as Burma and Singapore, not to mention all over India. But now, in this wretched room, amid the windows soiled with pigeon droppings, the floor littered with straw, the harsh rumbling of the tram outside and the cawing of scavenging crows, in the midst of the hot jumble of life, this film seemed like a hopeless old thing. It was a thing of endings—something that had once, long ago, pulsed with life.

The film snapped and jammed in the machine. A single image remained frozen on the wall for a moment—Kamal galloping her horse out of the shot—she appeared as a faraway blur on a flat horizon of barren land, a strip of sky above her, the forelegs of her horse already beyond the edge of the frame. Then the image vanished. The film began flapping wildly somewhere within the projector like a hissing snake and there was an acrid smell of something burning. The young man jumped up and with a deft

Tejaswini Apte-Rahm

movement turned the projector off.

'It's stuck,' he said. 'There's not much more to see anyway. One more can. Do you want to watch it?'

Tatya suddenly felt that he should not have allowed those reels to play out in this miserable room, on that dirty lime-washed wall, under the gaze of this bored young man. He had sullied the images by forcing them out of their cans into a time and place where they had no relevance, held no meaning.

'No,' he said. 'Enough. I don't need to see any more.'

The man started tinkering with the projector. He glanced curiously at Tatya a couple of times, for Tatya remained seated on his chair without saying a word. Then Tatya cleared his throat and said, 'That was most interesting. I remember some of those scenes well.'

The man nodded, his hands busy with the machine. He is probably wondering, thought Tatya, why this old man wants to see these old, sputtering bioscope reels—useless films without any talking or singing— nothing of note in them but for that archaic, exaggerated style of acting. He couldn't think of anything more to say to the young man. But the time had come to ask a question which had occurred to him as he sat watching the film.

'Do you often find films like these?' he began.

'Sometimes. We have contacts among people who used to work in the bioscope business. They tip us off about old films and equipment for sale.'

Tatya's breath quickened. Where exactly had these film reels come from? A distributor perhaps? Someone who might have heard of what became of Kamal? Distributors in the old days had often approached Rising Sun Films specifically to obtain films starring Kamal.

'Where did you get these cans?' asked Tatya.

'In an old house,' shrugged the young man. 'They were selling off some things.'

'Whose house was it? Where was it?'

The young man looked at him. 'Do you want to go there? Nobody lives there now. That person died. The relatives were clearing out the house.'

'I see,' said Tatya. A dead-end, then. It was not surprising. He felt rather foolish at playing the detective. He got up and turned to go.

'I don't know anything about these old films,' continued the young man, unexpectedly, 'but I know something about the actress, Kamal.'

Tatya turned to look at him, astonished.

'She was a big star in the old days, you know,' the young man said. 'These cans of films were found in her house after she died. My father happened to be in Poona when he heard of the cans, and he went to buy them. There was nothing much in her house. The only other thing of any value was a silver paan box. The relatives sold it to some other dealer because we don't buy that sort of thing.'

Tatya stared at him. Surely the man was mistaken. She couldn't be dead.

'When did she die?' he said. It felt dreamlike that these words were forming in his mouth.

'She died last month,' said the man. He stared at Tatya. 'Did you know her?' he asked.

Tatya shook his head, and leaned into his walking stick. He was suddenly tired, and his throat dry. As if he had not drunk water for days.

The man paused. 'Do you want to buy this film?'

Tatya looked down at the flat, rusting cans of film that lay at his feet. He imagined Kamal's small, luminous face imprinted on frame after frame inside, each rectangle a slight change of register on her lovely features, each frame catching no more than a shifting shape, a wisp of a dream, spooled round and round in a dusty circle.

'No,' he said, softly. 'No, I don't want to buy it. What on earth am I to do with it?'

As he stepped out of the room into the hot glare of the sun, he heard the scraping sound of metal on the rough floor as the man, squatting, dragged the cans towards him to pile them up. There was the grating sound of a rusty lid being jammed down. Tatya turned and looked into the room again. 'What are you going to do with these films?' he asked.

The man spoke without looking up at him, busy in his task, impatient now that there was to be no sale. 'There's silver in there. We use a liquid chemical to extract it from the film.'

'Silver?' repeated Tatya. She was a thing of wonder indeed: this transformation of herself into molten silver and silver dust.

CHAPTER 74

1952

There was a second stroke. A small one. A numbness on one side of his face, and a sudden blurring of vision. He tried to speak, but someone had stuffed his mouth with cotton, his tongue weighed down by a moist bolus of fibres. A sort of poetry took hold of him, and he wanted, as he crumpled, to declaim verse.

It was barely six weeks since his first stroke when he had collapsed in Gulwadi and been rushed to Bombay. He had been visiting Durga and Neelkanth at the time, and they had returned with him to Bombay on that hurried journey. Neelkanth was obliged to return to Gulwadi within a few days, but Durga had stayed on at Greenglades with her children for the past month and a half. Later she told him that during his second stroke his words were mumbled, incomprehensible, like something she had heard herself say once in a dream. She was frightened. He was weak but there was no need, the doctor said, to take him to the hospital. No need to do anything, really; but an oxygen cylinder made an appearance. He didn't need it right away, but it was there, should he require it. It stood in the corner of his large bedroom like an ugly, headless, grey soldier, all rounded shoulders. It was difficult to believe that this hard, inert thing contained life within. Sharad told him that the doctor had shown him how to use it. Tatya nodded weakly. He thought he detected a flaw in the plan, but could not put his finger on it.

'I have no intention of using that thing, you know,' he'd told the doctor. The doctor smiled then, to humour him. Dr Kelkar had retired. This doctor was a young fellow, had been tending him for the past six weeks, since the first stroke in Gulwadi. Sharad, standing next to the doctor, smiled too, but uncertainly. He looks, thought Tatya, the way he did as a boy, when his little brother had died, when he had burrowed his head into Radha's shoulder with great gasping wails. He looked sad and young and bewildered now, and Tatya's heart ached. He wanted to call both his children to his side and confide in them, tell them the story of his life in its entirety, and say, 'take what lessons you can from it, for this is what I have done.' A loneliness enveloped him, for he could not have articulated, even if he had the strength for it, what his life had really been like.

But that night he was a master of oratory. In a dream unfolding as he lay suspended between sleep and the stars, it came to him, the form and the structure needed to elucidate his thoughts: *Listen, my children, you will never know what it was really like, who I really was before the skin on the back of my hand turned into this brittle, papery covering. If you could but see one moment in time with my eyes, you would understand me entirely. But you will never know me, and I will never know you. We talk, we scrape at each other's edges like grains of sand grasping at the sea: the vastness of it all eludes the grains but they think they have understood. I wish you could follow me to those primeval places. Look, that's me, hammering a shoe rack together in the market, ignorant even of what a bale is. That's me, wandering a buzzing beehive, its cells pregnant with honey. That's me, gazing out to a sapphire-blue sea. That's me, crafting the secret of more. I am still there, doing all those things. The sun is still shining on me, on the other side.*

But even as he opened his eyes the next morning, he began forgetting the words. He tried to hold on to the architecture of the sentences he had built overnight, aware that he was losing something vital that he wished to communicate. But no, it was beyond him. By the time Sadaa had sponged his face with a cold towel sprinkled with Eau de Cologne, he could not remember what exactly it was that he had been trying to recollect.

It was a crisp day, a nip in the air, the sun a welcome dispenser of warmth and yellow light. The sun's rays slanted directly on to his bed, where he lay swaddled against the cold in two layers of blankets. A day later he could sit up, and the day after that he ate a rather good breakfast. It hadn't been much of a stroke after all, more like a fainting fit in his opinion. Though he had heard the doctor murmuring something to Durga and Sharad about things being 'in god's hands' and 'wait and watch' and 'a week or two'.

As he lay on his bed, recovering from his stroke, people wafted in and out to see him. At times there was a bustle of bodies and a pattering of feet outside his door. He always hoped for the patter of feet to come in, close to him, for the childish faces to look at him, to feel on his arm their warm breath as they leaned over his bed. The warm breath so peculiar to children—it reminded him of animals. Adult lives were so overshadowed by plans and intentions that the life inside, the warm, beating life, seemed

Tejaswini Apte-Rahm

like just one more facet of a person, like a limb or a liver, assigned to its particular job. But in children—and in animals—life was the very thing, the only thing, expressed in the laughter of limbs, thirst of throat, sun on skin.

But that patter of feet outside his door, which was so joyful to him, would quieten. There would be a shushing, a whisper, a rustle of a woman's padar—and the child would enter, wide-eyed and tip-toeing. It might be Aru, with his trusting eyes, his half-pant neatly pressed, a cricket ball in his hand. It might be Kumi, a little woman, silver anklets chinking in the late afternoon. Or those rascals, Mukund and Dilip, hands washed but knees muddy.

Aru came in. Tatya raised his hand to place his palm on the boy's head, on the neat side parting. That made Aru smile.

'Shall I press your feet?' he asked. Such an earnest boy. How would Aru feel when his Tatya died? It wasn't long now, he supposed. He did not wish to dwell on that, quickly brushed aside the picture of Aru's face as it would appear at Tatya's death—contorted with tears, fear, and incomprehension. He looked away from Aru, as if thinking about it would visit that grief on the boy's head.

'Tatyasaheb?'

He looked again at the boy. Aru's nose was so like his own, it brought a smile to his lips. But it seemed he couldn't smile properly now: he felt his face being pulled into a new shape, and Aru looked alarmed. Good heavens, he was simply showing his teeth when he had meant to smile. He closed his lips and patted the boy's head.

Aru smiled and said, 'I want to press your feet.'

Tatya nodded and Aru slipped out from under the heavy hand on his head, making for the foot of the mattress. Looking around he saw a small wooden stool in the corner of the room. Picking it up, he placed it by the bed. Then he sat down on it and began pressing Tatya's feet. Tatya raised his neck momentarily—it felt very stiff, though—to look at the small boy's gentle, purposeful movements. There was satisfaction in that—he was pleased to see how the boy went about his business silently and with determination. That was the way to get on in the world. You had to do what you needed to do without making too much of a fuss about it. Then he lay his head back down on the pillow, content to feel the little hands massaging and pressing his dry old feet.

A large wave crashed on to the rocks, interrupting the placid, rolling sound of seawater. He wished he could get up and rest his eyes on the sea-green, watch the twinkle of the spray as it caught the afternoon sun. But he felt too tired at the moment. Later he would call for Sadaa to put his planter's chair in the balcony outside his room. He would sit there and look at the sea and watch the children playing cricket and have a smoke. He hadn't done this for a few days, but he would today. All he could see now, out of the window, was the blue sky. Not a cloud in his square of window, not a kite. Well, the kites usually came a bit later, wheeling about on the evening breezes, looking for prey. For now, all was still except for Aru's hands, neatly pressing his feet.

Strains of a film song playing on the radio floated in through the open window, along with the shifting sun. It was a song about love, as all songs seemed to be nowadays. Always some fellow yearning for this or that woman, violins running amok in the background. He thought back to the studio, the extravagant costumes—how long ago it all was—and how glad he was to have left it behind before it influenced any of his family. And now these songs. The children were forbidden to listen. But strange changes were afoot. He had felt it for a long time—perhaps for a decade if he really thought about it, and even more so since Radha had died. With her died many things, but rather than a list of transformations that came to mind, he felt them more as a changing of the weather, a shift in the quality of the sunlight, as if a sunset—or perhaps a sunrise—were hovering above Greenglades. Just that morning Nandu had come bearing news from the city, from the newspapers, from the streets and train stations, from heaven knows where—always the bearer of news was Nandu, and Tatya couldn't decide whether this hectic gathering of information from the four corners of the country would benefit the boy in any way. He had loped in with his long arms dangling at his sides and his anxious lopsided smile on his face.

'Well?' Tatya had said. 'What news from Newspaper Nandu? You should start your own radio station, you know.'

At this there was a titter at the door, well out of sight. No doubt Kumi was hovering about there with Chhabi.

'Tatyasaheb,' said Nandu, settling down on a chair by his bedside, 'people are going crazy, losing their heads.'

'Nothing new about that.'

'I just heard,' said Nandu, 'that the Congress has been using cows as election advertisements. They gathered cows, painted 'Vote Congress' on their flanks, and let them loose on the streets in Calcutta. The government has set up voting booths even in the jungles. In Orissa, tribals came to vote with their bows and arrows. In another voting booth in the jungle, nobody turned up—only an elephant.' Breaking into a guffaw, Nandu had sat back in his chair and laughed at his own stories. Tatya had joined in the laughter, albeit weakly.

That certainly was funny. Well, well, who knew where it was all going. But he wouldn't be around to find out. He looked down again at Aru, busy and earnest in his self-appointed task. If only Aru could look into his life ahead and tell Tatya what he saw there. Tatya felt slightly ashamed, though, of this desire to push himself into the future. It was hardly befitting an old Brahmin. Now was the time for renunciation, for the teaching of the young in the ways of the old. His thoughts stumbled here, however. What could he teach Aru, beyond the common kindnesses and humanity and hard work—those, at least, were things that would not live only in the past. But as for the rest—he felt overtaken by breezes and winds gusting in from the sea, swirling around him, and he closed his eyes, wishing he felt strong enough to pull his blanket up to his chin. That breeze meant it must be getting close to teatime. Sadaa would soon be here with a cup.

As he lay with his eyes closed, his mind returned to the elephant in Nandu's story. An elephant in the jungle plodding and crashing through branches overhead and bushes underfoot. He saw it all in his head, as if he were really witnessing it. There was a high noon sun glimpsed through cracks in the forest canopy here and there, but the old growth pressed around the animal and created a dim, leafy darkness. The elephant continued crashing through the dense greenery till there was a sudden parting of branches and fronds, and he emerged into blinding sunlight and the fresh blue of the open coast. Inexplicably, Tatya was there too, facing the elephant. The elephant stood on the beach looking at Tatya. In the distance, far down the length of the beach, Tatya could see the vague outlines of some huts and houses. One of them, he knew, was where he needed to go. He could hear the soft clanging created by the wind trapped inside a temple bell, and the gushing of the waves as they lapped on to the shore in many watery tongues. A large sailboat lay pulled up on the sand, its sides still glistening with salt water.

The elephant spoke to him. It moved its magnificent head from side to side, flapped its grey ears, twitched its trunk, and stood looking down at Tatya with small, intent eyes. The feet of both man and beast were pooled in wet puddles of sand. Tatya could not hear the elephant's words. But he understood all that the great animal said, and even found himself nodding in agreement, while his mind struggled to decipher the language. This was no ordinary elephant. This was Ganpati himself, come in all his majesty, to tell him things, to take him somewhere.

The great elephant turned and began walking away down the long strip of beach, towards a coconut grove far ahead, and the small houses amid the high, waving tree fronds. Tatya began walking with him, by his side. He heard Aru's voice whipping through the air, shouting out to him; the loud clink of a teacup set down suddenly—*careful Sadaa, it will break*, Tatya wanted to say, but his mind was focused on something else, on something more. The smell of freshly cut mangoes wafted up from the direction of the houses. And sailing on the cool air was the glassy cascading sound of Radha's green bangles.

ACKNOWLEDGEMENTS

First of all, I thank Asha Mahajan for her patience and generosity in answering my many questions, and for the invaluable support she offered during the writing of my novel. Many thanks to Saili Palande-Datar for guiding me towards some fantastic reference material, to Gopalkrishna Nayak for his insights into Mulji Jetha Market, and to Tasneem Doctor, Vasanti Vaidya, Sandeep Apte, Sunita Rajwade, and Anita Bapat, all of whose contributions helped me to build the world of my novel. Thank you to my editors Pujitha Krishnan and Karishma Koshal for their skilled and sensitive editorial support and for backing the story I wanted to tell.

I thank my husband Björn, always my first reader and first fan, for his great suggestions and honest critiques of my early drafts, and for steadfastly cheering me on through my writing journey over the years. And I could not have written this book without my daughter Sukanya's enthusiastic support and cheerful, indomitable belief in her mother's writing abilities; Sukanya, you are my guiding star.

Finally, I thank my father, Arvind Apte, who launched me on a wonderful journey of historical discovery many years ago, which has culminated in this novel. I wish he was here to share this moment with me.

∽

This novel was inspired by my research into the life and times of my great-grandfather. However, the events and characters in this novel are entirely fictitious. The historical background of the novel, particularly information about the social customs and traditions of the time, is based on conversations with numerous family members to whom I am grateful. In addition, some of my key sources are as follows.

For domestic practices, food, and festivals, I relied greatly on the fascinating book *Majhe Avadte Pustak*, written in 1934 by Dr Chintaman Laxman Mule as a go-to guide for housewives. Also useful was a similar guide written in 1914, *Gharatli Kame* by Trimbak Narayan Lele and Vasudev Govind Apte. *Majhi Vrate* by Kusum Apte and *The Fragrance of Mango Blossom: Exploring the Culinary Traditions of the Koknastha Brahmin* by Sunita

Rajwade also gave insights into household customs. The poem in Chapter 15 is a loose translation of a verse in an old publication titled *Sasarchi Paathavni*. Though I did not manage to track down a copy of the book, the verse was recited to me by a cousin who remembered the book and a few lines from it.

Contemporary accounts of women's lives in the late nineteenth and early twentieth century were invaluable, especially *My Story: Autobiography of a Hindu Widow* by Parvati Athavale, *The High Caste Hindu Woman* by Pandita Ramabai Saraswati, *Smritichitre* by Laxmibai Tilak (translated by Shanta Gokhale), and my favourite read among these, Saraswatibai Akloojkar's engaging and moving autobiography, *Aathvani Kaalachya, Maansaanchya*. Also useful was *The History of Doing: An Illustrated Account of Movements for Women's Rights and Feminism in India 1800-1990* by Radha Kumar.

For research on old Bombay, Girgaon, and Bombay's textile industry some of my key references were Rajnarayan Chandavarkar's comprehensive study *The Origins of Industrial Capitalism in India: Business Strategies and the Working Classes in Bombay, 1900-1940*; Sumit Sarkar's *Modern India 1885-1947*; *Bombay: The Cities Within* by Rahul Mehrotra and Sharada Dwivedi for its text as well as its sumptuous photographic history of the city; *Premchand Roychand (1831-1906): His Life and Times* by Sharada Dwivedi; *History of the Cotton Textile Industry* by V. B. Kulkarni; *Indian Cotton Textile Industry Centenary Volume 1851-1950*; and *Govind Narayan's Mumbai: An Urban Biography from 1863*, translated by Murali Ranganathan, which gives a vivid picture of the city in the nineteenth century and which was a helpful basis for my descriptions of the docks, markets, and other sights of Bombay.

The description of the royal visit to India is based on *The Historical Record of the Imperial Visit to India 1911* published by the Government of India in 1914, and *Narrative of the Visit to India of Their Majesties King George V and Queen Mary* by John Fortescue published in 1912. Dada's enthusiastic quotations for Tatya's edification are from *The Student's Manual* by the Reverend John Todd and Lord Chesterfield's *Letters to his Son*.

For information on the silent film era I consulted the *Report of the Indian Cinematograph Committee 1927-1928*; Suresh Chabria's and Virchand Dharamsey's writings in *Light of Asia: Indian Silent Cinema 1912-1934*; Charlie Chaplin's *My Autobiography*; contemporary reviews from October 1928 of the film *Melody of Love* in the *New York Times* and in *Variety*; Govind Nihalani's article 'Through the Viewfinder' in the *Encyclopaedia of Hindi Cinema*; the August 1931 issue of *Cinema* magazine published in

Lahore; and Phalke's biography researched and written in great detail by Bapu Watve titled *Dadasaheb Phalke: Bharatiya Chitrapatsrushtiche Janak*. The autobiography *I, Durga Khote* (translated by Shanta Gokhale) and Hansa Wadkar's autobiography *You Ask, I Tell* (translated by Jasbir Jain and Shobha Shinde), are evocative portraits of the lives of female actors in the early decades of Hindi and Marathi cinema. Khote's autobiography was also a source of information about Bal Gandharva and St. Xavier's College in the 1920s.

The journal *Cinema Vision India: Pioneers of Indian Cinema, the Silent Era (Vol. 1, No. 1, 1980)* was a vital source for information on the technical aspects of the silent era, such as special effects and titling techniques, as well as on cinema theatres, audiences, and actors.

The Phalke Centenary Souvenir published in 1970 was another source of detailed information, including a series of four articles Dadasaheb Phalke wrote in 1917 and 1918 for the periodical *Navyug*, in which he writes about his filmmaking career including fascinating details on costume design and make-up. Also in the centenary souvenir: a talk given by Phalke titled 'Ladies from cultured families for acting in films' and R. Washikar's article 'Shambarik Kharolika'.

For pre-Independence politics in India, the colonial era, and India's first election, I referred to Ramachandra Guha's *India After Gandhi: The History of the World's Largest Democracy*, Lord Birdwood's *India and Pakistan: A Continent Decides*, Shashi Tharoor's *An Era of Darkness*, and *Plain Tales from the Raj: Images of British India in the Twentieth Century* edited by Charles Allen. For the emergence of the sugar industry, Donald W. Attwood's *Raising Cane: The Political Economy of Sugar in Western India* was very informative.

The Oriental Organ, which I very much enjoyed writing about, is based on a real fairground organ made by the company Gebrüder Bruder of Waldkirch, on display at Siegfried's Mechanical Music Cabinet, an intriguing museum in Rüdesheim, Germany. The other musical contraptions referred to are also based on exhibits in this museum.